contents

Prologue 1

Part One: EDYTHE MARRENNER, *Brooklyn, New York, June 30, 1917–June 30, 1935* 5

Part Two: EDYTHE MARRENNER/SUSAN HAYWARD, *Hollywood, December 1937–July 22, 1944* 35

Part Three: MRS. JESS BARKER, *Hollywood, July 24, 1944–April 26, 1955* 83

Part Four: SUSAN HAYWARD, *Hollywood, April 26, 1955–February 8, 1957* 181

Part Five: MRS. FLOYD EATON CHALKLEY, *Carrollton, Georgia–Fort Lauderdale, Florida, February 8, 1957–January 9, 1966* 211

Part Six: THE WIDOW CHALKLEY, *Fort Lauderdale, Florida, January 9, 1966–January 22, 1971* 247

Part Seven: SUSAN HAYWARD, *Beverly Hills, California, September 1971–March 14, 1975* (2:25 P.M.) 273

Epilogue 302

Appendix A: *Last Will and Testament of Edythe Marrenner Chalkley* 308

Appendix B: *Filmography*   311

Index   321

Susan had a very special gift for laying bare the agony of a woman. . . . She had been taught to understand the suffering of others. She learned it the hard way.

ROBERT WISE, Director of *I Want to Live!*

The only thing a woman should ever be afraid of in her life . . . is not having lived it.

SUSAN HAYWARD

❧ a personal note ❧

THE LAST TIME I saw Susan Hayward in person was on April 6, 1959—the night of her greatest professional triumph—at the Thirty-first Annual Academy Awards Presentation.

I desperately wanted her to win, and was almost as nervous as the nominee. As I sat in my twelfth-row-center seat at Hollywood's Pantages Theater and heard her name called out, I jumped up screaming in excitement.

After the awards, my press pass admitted me into the backstage tent erected for the occasion. My attention was focused on Susan. She was like someone before a firing squad. A hundred men and women were waiting to interview her: reporters with notebooks and tape recorders, TV cameramen, press from all over the world. "How did it feel to win an Oscar?" How did it feel, indeed! It was what she had wanted all her life.

Later, at the Governors' Ball at the Beverly Hilton Hotel, I stopped by her table to congratulate her.

A day earlier we *had* talked. I was vacationing at the Beverly Hills Hotel that spring. She had flown in from Georgia and was staying in an outside bungalow. As we were leaving for the dress rehearsal of the Oscar ceremonies Sunday morning, we bumped into each other in the private garden. I felt compelled to tell her how much I was rooting for her and how I had almost kicked in my television set three years earlier when Anna Magnani had cheated her out of the award she had so richly deserved for *I'll Cry Tomorrow*.

"Win it for Brooklyn," I shouted, as we went our separate ways. At the dress rehearsal, we nodded to one another.

On Oscar night, at the festive Governors' Ball, I was seated at the same table as Sonny Tufts, a former Paramount star

whose career had long since faded into oblivion. Sonny had had a great deal of champagne, and he was talking up a storm about "that ambitious little redhead" he knew from the old days. Early in his career Sonny had worked with Susan's former husband Jess Barker but, he told me, "I regret I never had a chance to work with her.

"The big shots didn't care for her. She was about the only starlet they couldn't screw. Now look at her! Someone should do a book about her. Why don't you?"

"Maybe some day I will." I laughed. "But she should really write her own—with Gerold Frank—like Lillian Roth."

From that night on, the idea of a book about Susan never left my thoughts. She had done enough living by that time to have filled a volume. Who could have prophesied what lay ahead?

Susan once said, "Being from Brooklyn is a common denominator among show-business people." Although I was a writer, I always considered myself show biz, and because I was a kid from Brooklyn too, I had followed the career of this local-girl-made-good with intense interest. There was a considerable gap in our ages, and she was a natural beauty—but we had grown up in the same environment. I was eleven when I first saw her in person: she was at the Loews' State, appearing in a vaudeville act with Louella Parsons, and when the show was over I waited outside the stage door to get her autograph. Fourteen years later, as a professional writer, I was a hostess at the *Photoplay* party the night she won their Gold Medal. Living in Hollywood, I frequently visited the sets of the movies she was making: *White Witch Doctor, Demetrius and the Gladiators,* and *I'll Cry Tomorrow* among others. As a writer, I was the first to do stories on many of her leading men, including Don Taylor, Robert Mitchum, Robert Wagner, James Mason, Kirk Douglas, and Charlton Heston, as well as interviews with such men as Jeff Chandler, Stephen Boyd, and John Wayne. Many of them contributed material to this book.

Special heartfelt thanks go to Robert Wagner, who revealed a side of Susan most people did not know—her generosity in helping aspiring young performers.

I am particularly indebted to Jess Barker, Susan's first husband. Jess had refused all requests for interviews concerning Susan for more than twenty years. His warmth and graciousness in speaking to me is deeply appreciated . . . as is the friendliness

and generosity of Jess's and Susan's son Timothy Barker, who phoned me of his own accord, gave me permission to quote him, and assured me that I was the only writer he and his father had spoken to since his mother's death. I hope this book does not disappoint either of them.

Susan's only brother, Wally Marrenner, spent endless hours correcting the myriad errors about Susan's early years that have appeared in print and may continue to do so. He also contributed the only picture in existence of their father. None have ever been seen before. Delightful new material about their childhood, as well as more distressing facts about her final days, came from Wally too.

My acknowledgments to the many others who came to my assistance will be found on page 5.

One final note. The last time I saw Susan Hayward, I was one of millions who watched her present the Oscar to Glenda Jackson on April 2, 1974. I knew the rumors that she was dying were true. That spring I was undergoing a grave personal crisis in my own life. I can truly say that her bravery during her final crisis gave me the will and determination to overcome mine, which was so very small in comparison.

This book does not make Susan Hayward a saint. She wasn't one. I have tried to present her as a human being. And a survivor. And *that* she certainly was.

BEVERLY LINET

New York City

1980

❈ prologue ❈

THE DATE was April 2, 1974; the place, the Dorothy Chandler Pavilion of the Los Angeles Music Center; the event, the Forty-sixth Annual Awards Presentation of the Academy of Motion Picture Arts and Sciences.

That evening, as always, a capacity crowd had endured the preliminaries, awaiting the climax of Oscar night: the winners of the major awards for acting, directing, and Best Picture. Unlike always, however, there was an unusual amount of suspense in the air. Several weeks earlier, the Academy had announced that Susan Hayward would be appearing on stage to present the Best Actress award—but the rumors had been circulating for months that Hayward was gravely ill, even dying, of cancer. Multiple brain tumors, it was said—the words alone were terrifying. She could not possibly appear.

The tension increased as David Niven, who had shared the 1958 acting Oscars with Susan, appeared on stage and announced: "Ladies and gentlemen, Charlton Heston has created many miracles . . . just illusions on the screen. But in presenting our next award, he brings with him, not an illusion, but the real thing—*Miss Susan Hayward*."

And there she was, on Heston's arm. The audience in the Chandler Pavilion exploded in applause, many rising to their feet to pay their respects. What they didn't know, however, was that that night Susan Hayward *was* an illusion.

A blazing red wig covered her head, now bald from cobalt treatments. Her missing eyebrows had been penciled in and her face carefully made up to hide the ravages of the illness. A dazzling, green, form-fitting, sequined gown with a high neck and long sleeves concealed her emaciated body and withered right arm; within her body a massive dose of Dilantin

1

fought to ward off seizures—and, holding it all together was Susan herself: her determination, her refusal to give in, her desire to go out "looking smashing."

And that's exactly how she did look. What the audience saw that night was not a dying woman but a vision of loveliness; a woman who looked only a few years older than she had when she'd stepped on the stage of the Pantages Theater fifteen years earlier to receive her own Oscar for *I Want To Live!*

Only once did Susan waver—the moment before she was about to step on stage. Charlton Heston took her firmly by the arm, murmured, "Easy, girl," and supported her to the microphones. Later she admitted, "He did it at the right moment. I was shaking so bad."

The eyes of fifty million viewers were focused on Susan Hayward that night. Few now recall the award she gave out, to Glenda Jackson for *A Touch of Class*. It was Susan Hayward in the last year of her life who gave the greatest performance of the year. Flushed and wobbly afterward, Susan admitted to her nurse Carmen Perugini, who had been waiting offstage in case Susan needed her help: "Well, that's the last time I pull that off."

In 1974, the Hollywood establishment was behind Susan with prayers and a fervor she could never have anticipated. Hollywood had always considered Susan Hayward a strange one. During the course of a career that had spanned nearly thirty-seven years and five Oscar nominations, she had been called shy, aggressive, fearful, domineering, brilliant, amateurish, impulsive, calculating, ambitious, gracious, inhibited, explosive, parsimonious, and generous beyond words.

Among her directors, producers, and co-stars, she had evoked intense reactions, both pro and con. Richard Denning, a Paramount contractee in the forties, had called her "ambitious, unscrupulous, and selfish," and Bette Davis had said frankly, "It is with sadness that I tell you that Miss Hayward was utterly unkind to me." Yet John Wayne always admired her, Agnes Moorehead would say, "I was her greatest fan," and Robert Wagner, who became prominent overnight after doing *With a Song in My Heart* with Susan, would affirm: "Susan was marvelous. . . . She was a very big star, and I was just a young kid starting out and didn't know much about what I was doing . . . and she must have realized that, because, my God, she was so helpful."

Perhaps the most significant comment came from Fredric
March, who'd worked with her early in her career. "She was
touchy on the set, and it was a rare day she mingled with the
cast," he said. "But somewhere along the line she learned to
act. Every inch of that woman is an actress. She can portray
a lonely, desperate, frustrated woman because she has experienced all those emotions. If you look closely, you'll see they
left scars on her heart."

All through her life, Susan Hayward had to battle for happiness. For over three decades, she dazzled audiences and
critics with portrayals of tragic, stormy women—a gallery of
winners, losers, fighters, and survivors—and she knew them
well, because they were all her.

Born to poverty and bred to insecurity, Susan was left with
a permanent handicap by an automobile accident at the age of
seven that made her the butt of cruel jokes. The defenses she
set up to protect herself caused her to be rejected and unpopular
in her teens; but she found comfort in the fantasies in which
she envisioned herself a great lady, a brilliant actress, a perfect
wife; and with fierce determination she struggled to make those
fantasies realities. She fought the Hollywood casting-couch
system and proved she could make it without cheapening herself. She fought the erosion in her first marriage until it ended
in a headlined donnybrook, then battled her way through a
calamitous divorce and wrenching custody suit.

She endured four losing tries for an Oscar she desperately
wanted before finally grasping the prize; survived a suicide
attempt, scandal headlines over a triangle affair, a devastating
widowhood in her second marriage (to a man she thought she
knew, but didn't), a string of professional disasters, a comeback fiasco in Las Vegas, and a narrow escape from a fire that
destroyed her apartment and almost her life. Finally she succumbed to a cancer of suspicious origin—but not before a
years-long struggle that doctors called "absolutely extraordinary."

These were the external events and most were played out
in the public spotlight. But what was the driving force so deeply
buried in the soul of this complex, volatile woman, the elements
that both brought her to tragedy and gave her the strength to
fight back and triumph—even over death itself?

Tim Barker, one of her twin sons from her first marriage,
says today, "My mother was a very private woman. Very

private. . . . No one can get to the heart of my mother unless one knew my grandmother."

He is partly right. To get to the heart of Susan Hayward— born Edythe Marrenner—one has to know not only her mother, but her father too. And the Brooklyn that shaped all three.

PART ONE

Edythe Marrenner

Brooklyn, New York
June 30, 1917—June 30, 1935

My life is fair game for anybody. I spent an unhappy, penniless childhood in Brooklyn. I had to slug my way up in a town called Hollywood where people love to trample you to death. I don't relax because I don't know how. I don't want to know how. Life is too short to relax.

SUSAN HAYWARD

⊠ *chapter 1* ⊠

EDYTHE MARRENNER'S earliest memories were of fear—and of survival.

She could never pinpoint how old she was when she first learned how it felt to be scared, really scared, but the incident remained vivid throughout her life.

She had been visiting her Grandmother Pearson, when an uncle with a sadistic streak warned her that there was a bogeyman at the top of the stairs waiting to get her if she wasn't a good girl. Edythe was not too sure what a bogeyman was, but she had heard of this terrible creature who lurked in the dark ready to pounce on children who weren't obedient or didn't listen to their elders or who spoke out of turn.

After that she never liked the dark or her uncle, and she avoided both whenever possible. More than a half century later, when she was dying, an acquaintance asked if she was afraid of the dark.

"Let's put it this way," she replied, "I feel more comfortable sleeping in the daytime."

When the sun was shining she was fearless. Although she had been warned repeatedly not to cross the street by herself, she was never afraid that a bogeyman might be hiding behind the automobiles that lined the Church Avenue curbs. Until the accident.

Shortly after Edythe turned seven, she bought a three-penny paper parachute at the local candy store. With the help of a warm summer breeze, she glided it through the air until it floated out onto the avenue and she had to retrieve it. She could hear neighbors warning her to be careful, but she didn't see the car swooping down on her: just a blur. Edythe was very myopic—and she didn't own a pair of glasses.

7

Vaguely she remembered one of the ladies screaming, then felt a terribly sharp pain as she was tossed onto the curb. For a little while, she just lay there, half-conscious, as someone rushed to 3507 Church Avenue and up four flights of stairs to get her mother, Ellen. No one called an ambulance. Edythe never recalled how she was carried there; Ellen never said, but the little girl was taken directly to the office of the neighborhood doctor.

Edythe was lucky. The driver had seen her just in time. Had she been hit a split second sooner, she could have been killed. As it was, no signs of internal injuries were detected: just a broken hip. The physician suggested an ambulance be called and Edythe taken to nearby Kings County Hospital, but her mother was suspicious of hospitals and particularly leery of the city-run Kings County, which had opened a few years earlier. Although it possessed some of the most modern facilities and equipment available at the time, it also carried a reputation among the ill-informed of being a "nut house," and a place where only charity patients went. In fact, the hospital did have a psychiatric wing for the mentally disturbed—one of the most advanced in the country—but mental illness was considered as bad as the plague among the women on Church Avenue. And it did have wards for those unable to pay medical bills, but there were also private and semiprivate rooms for those who could afford it. Ellen Marrenner was aware of none of this. All she knew was that if someone did or said something different in her neighborhood, they were put down with the words, "You should be sent to Kings County." That's how it was in Brooklyn in 1924. Ellen would not have her daughter stigmatized in that way.

Edythe was encased in a plaster-of-Paris cast and carried back to the apartment. Because the doctor insisted she be placed in traction immediately, her father Walter Marrenner set up a makeshift pulley device. Years later, Edythe would relate how Mrs. Robert Emslie, their downstairs neighbor, thinking the contraption barbaric, vainly tried to persuade the family to take the patient to the hospital for proper treatment. Ellen ignored the advice, insisting Edythe would be better cared for and happier at home.

In truth, Edythe *was* happier. She enjoyed being the center of attention and she'd later remember how Deacon Titus of the Baptist church on Nostrand Avenue, where she and her brother

and sister, Wally and Florence, attended Sunday School, would visit and bring her jigsaw puzzles and oranges.

Other neighbors brought her presents too: dog-eared copies of *Photoplay* and *Motion Picture* magazines. Edythe would read about Douglas Fairbanks's exploits in *The Thief of Bagdad* and marvel over the costumes worn by Mary Pickford in *Dorothy Vernon of Haddon Hall*, Lon Chaney, Jr. in *He Who Gets Slapped*, John Barrymore in *Beau Brummell*, and Rudolph Valentino in *Monsieur Beaucaire*.

Edythe was old enough to know it was all make-believe, and young enough to be plunged into fantasies of being part of another world in another time. Her months in bed afforded an escape from the ugly world outside. A child of intense feelings, she hated the effect poverty had had on her mother and on her weary, resigned father. She was repelled by the squalor of the streets and the smell of roach-infested garbage cans. Even before her accident she had detached herself from this world, whenever and however possible.

Decades would pass, however, before she'd admit that "as a child you could say I was the world's biggest liar. I would weave tales like you wouldn't believe. I can still remember walking home from school when I was six, telling the other children about all the beautiful dresses I had at home in the closet—lying through my teeth! I guess that's when I first began acting, or at least getting interested in it—pretending, making believe, using my imagination. This I was born with—an imagination and a natural talent for lying. The perfect ingredients for an actor."

Confined to bed for months, Edythe had ample opportunity to let her imagination go wild. She had an Aunt Lillian, whom she adored, who had escaped from Brooklyn when she'd married a handsome Southern gentleman named Walter Scott Meriwether, editor of the *Mississippi Sun*. Her aunt would often write to the family and send snapshots taken in front of her Mississippi home. Edythe often fancied herself in that setting, dressed in green chiffon or white organdie. These fantasies would later have a profound effect on her vision of the ideal marriage.

Katie Harrigan Marrenner would come by often to look in on Edythe. Grandma Marrenner was shanty Irish down to her fingertips, but Edythe's imagination, helped by the fiction fed her from the fan magazines, transformed her into Katie Har-

rigan, the most talented actress in County Cork, who had given up her career to marry the man she loved. In years to come, Edythe would perpetrate that fiction to such an extent that it would become an accepted "fact" of her background. In truth, neither Katie nor grandfather Joseph Marrenner ever got closer to Ireland than the annual Saint Patrick's Day parade.

But when Edythe looked back on those endless weeks in bed, the happiest moments she'd recall would be the ones she spent alone with her father—when Ellen and Florence were out shopping, and Wally was off somewhere playing with his friends. Her father would read to her, or just talk with her. Sensing her pain and her need for love, fearful of the possibility that she might be lame for life, Walter would tell her, time and again, "You must be like a rubber ball. The harder they hit you, the higher you'll bounce. That is, if you are a good ball to begin with. If not, you might as well give up anyway."

His words were repeated often enough for her to accept them as gospel. For the rest of her life, they would provide Edythe with the impetus to bounce right back and fight.

Sara Little, Edythe's only close childhood friend—the friendship would survive for four decades—would describe Walter Marrenner as the single most important influence in his daughter's early life. "He was an extremely sensitive man, and he had a significant effect on her. There was a beautiful rapport between them."

Edythe had ambivalent feelings toward her mother. She wanted Ellen's approval and love, yet she was unhappy that Ellen was so different from the Aunt Lillian whom she admired so much. Edythe wanted to grow up to be like Aunt Lillian; she didn't want to be like the defeated, careworn Ellen Marrenner. And she wondered how two sisters could turn out so differently.

Edythe was unaware of it at the time, but Ellen herself was consumed with envy when she compared her life to Lillian's. In fact, all her brothers and sisters were living in comfort, while she had to content herself with their children's cast-off clothes for her family. Ellen's father had admonished her, however: "You made your bed. . . ." Had Ellen not met Walter Marrenner, everything would have been different.

Ellen F. Pearson's family had migrated to America from Skåne, Sweden. Most of Theodore Pearson's contemporaries had continued west to settle in Minnesota's rich farm belt, but

Theodore Pearson was attracted to the possibilities of Brooklyn and nearby Queens. He foresaw a need for housing to accommodate the hordes of immigrants wishing to settle in New York City, and set out to fill that need—and his pockets—by building railroad flats on the undeveloped Carroll and President streets, and tenements on the land facing Saint Anne's church on Front Street in Brooklyn.

He was as prolific in bed as in the building business. In addition to Ellen (born October 10, 1888), he sired three sons, Theodore, Jr., Oscar, and Guy; and six more daughters, Lillian, Alice, Jenny, Emma, and twin girls who died in infancy. He built a large house for himself and his family on Hoyt Street in downtown Brooklyn, and made sure his children were well fed, well dressed, and well disciplined. Pearson instilled in his sons the value of the dollar. His wife instilled in her daughters the same attitudes toward sex that had been instilled in her by her mother, who had, in turn, inherited her values from her mother before.

What the Pearsons had in cash, they lacked in class, but, like others of their kind, they had hopes that their wealth would be instrumental in assuring proper marriages for their children. In spite of this, Theodore Pearson wanted his daughters to be self-sufficient and encouraged their working until they were wed.

Ellen was twenty, and working as a stenographer, when she met twenty-nine-year-old Walter Marrenner, a dashing, red-headed Coney Island barker. The details of their meeting and subsequent courtship would never be discussed with their children, but their son Wally is aware that "the old man never cared much for my father." Pearson, in fact, was so opposed to the match that he threatened to disown Ellen if she persisted in seeing Marrenner. He would not have his daughter marry beneath her. He underestimated the extent of Walter's charm and sex appeal, however—and he underestimated his daughter's strong will.

Pearson's antagonism toward the young man was aggravated by the fact that Walter Marrenner was a Catholic. To Pearson, getting involved with a Catholic was doubtless almost as bad as getting involved with a Jew. Ellen's promise to bring her children up in the Protestant faith failed to budge him an inch.

Walter Marrenner's parents were equally distressed by the match. Brooklyn-born Joseph and Katherine Harrigan Marren-

ner were staunch Catholics. To them, a marriage outside the church was the same as no marriage at all—but Walter had always been the rebellious one of their five children, the one who would skip church on summer Sunday mornings in order to beat the crowd to Coney Island. Then, when Walter had been old enough to hold down a job, he'd headed for Coney for a different reason and, being a young man of intense glibness and charm, had been hired as a barker for one of the live attractions—a Brooklyn Billy Bigelow from *Carousel*. During the winter, he worked as an usher at the Brooklyn Academy of Music, to keep himself in spending money until summer rolled around again. Marrenner had no worries, no responsibilities, and a multitude of girl friends until Ellen entered his life. How she was able to land him when so many other prettier, sexier girls had failed was a family mystery, but Ellen had an iron will when it came to getting what she wanted, and she wanted Walter Marrenner.

On August 14, 1909, the two ran off and were married. According to their son Wally, there were no wedding pictures taken of his mother and father; if there had been, he would have seen them. In fact, he remembers today, "My father never posed with any members of the family. Not even for a little snapshot." There had never been an engagement ring, either—a fact that would later trouble the young Edythe.

Two weeks after the wedding, Ellen Marrenner conceived. Their first child, a daughter they named Florence, was born on May 29, 1910. Florence, a captivating baby with red hair, a pert nose and expressive eyes, resembled Walter physically and also inherited many of his personality traits. There would be little of the Pearson heritage in her.

When Florence was nine months old, Ellen became pregnant again. She had fallen in love with Walter because of his gaiety, charm, and dashing, irresponsible nature, but now she demanded he put his Coney Island days behind him and find an honest job. "You have responsibilities," she told him firmly.

Totally lacking in practical experience at the age of thirty-one, Walter found it difficult to get a decently paying position with a chance for advancement. He settled, instead, for blue-collar work as a lineman with the Interboro Rapid Transit Company. His hours were long and erratic. Some months he'd be put on the night shift and not return home until the early hours of the morning; other times he'd be up at the crack of dawn.

Walter Marrenner, Jr.'s birth on December 8, 1911, brought additional problems and expenses. Wally was a frail, sickly child with an undiagnosable stomach ailment that weakened his legs. "It wasn't polio or anything like that," Wally says today. "I don't know what they called it. But I had to wear braces for a long time."

Wally didn't look like Walter Marrenner, nor did he resemble the Pearson side of the family, according to his own evaluation. And his infirmity did little to help the rift between his mother and Theodore Pearson.

"I don't remember the old man very well," says Wally. "He died when I was a kid"—but not before cutting Ellen out of his will entirely and expressing a wish to the rest of the family that he didn't want "that Irishman ever laying a hand on a dime of my money." Grandpa Pearson had convinced himself that Walter's interest in his daughter had been motivated by the Pearson wealth, and his admonishment, "You made your bed, now lie in it," would extend to the grave.

Wally was five when his mother became pregnant for the third and final time. His baby sister, given the name Edythe, was delivered by one W. T. Pink of 160 McDonough Street on June 30, 1917, in the family's Church Avenue apartment. Mrs. Emslie, in keeping with Scottish tradition, put a shiny new dime in the baby's hand a few hours after her birth. It would be symbolic.

Like Florence, Edythe was a perfect, red-headed infant, and Florence would proudly wheel the baby carriage around the block showing off her new sister to the neighbors.

Edythe's crib was placed in the Marrenners' bedroom. When she outgrew it, she shared a room with Florence and Ellen. Wally remembers being moved into his father's room—an arrangement that would last for as long as the family lived on Church Avenue. For years, the Marrenners were unable to accumulate enough money to move to larger quarters, although Walter was moving up in his job and would eventually, according to Wally, "become a wire chief up in the telephone department of the company."

Unlike his sisters, Wally took the family's fortunes philosophically. "Sure we were poor," he confirms, "but so were most people in the neighborhood, so there was nothing different about us. We got along good and had enough to eat...."

Wally resents stories that have portrayed Walter as an alcoholic. "My father was never a drinker. He couldn't take more

than two drinks at any one time. And he never gambled away his money." Almost sheepishly, though, Wally admits that his father had "extra activities" going on. Trapped in a marriage that restricted him, bound to a wife who was increasingly full of gloom and doom, Walter eventually found someone else to escape to.

Wally says he never knew the woman's name, nor is he able to provide definite information as to when and how she entered Walter's life. However, she was definitely a part of it to the very end. The only time Wally saw her was "when my father's lady friend attended his funeral." He doesn't know if his mother ever became aware of her rival, but concedes that Ellen "was suspicious." The chances are she was more than that; certainly her bitterness would affect both her daughters.

Aware that she had been swept away by a physical attraction for Marrenner, Ellen blamed her loveless, poverty-stricken life on her weakness. She was determined to make certain her children would not fall victim to a similar fate—but she never realized how much damage she'd inflict by her harangues against men. In that respect, Ellen was not that much different from other women of her neighborhood and class—women who talked of menstruation in whispers, and considered girls who petted on front porches "fast" and premarital sex the hallmark of whores. Across the bridge in Manhattan, the Jazz Age was in full swing; buildings were getting taller, skirts shorter, and morals looser every day. Ellen's Brooklyn might as well have been located on a different planet; its residents were that far removed from the times.

Florence, fourteen when Edythe had her accident, was painfully aware of what was going on across the bridge and eager to be part of it. A student at Erasmus Hall High School, popular with the boys—and interested in them in return—Florence laughed off Ellen's dramatic warnings that boys were only interested in one thing, and that girls who let boys touch them were ruined for life. Walter's warm blood flowed through her veins, as did his love of show business.

Florence dreamed of being on Broadway. A natural-born dancer, she managed to get together enough money to take tap and ballet lessons at Miss Edna Simmons's local studio. When she came home from dance class, she'd entertain her mother and her bedridden sister by doing the new steps she had learned that day. Ellen did not discourage Florence's ambitions. She

had read of the money paid to show people and perhaps thought that through Florence she'd find a better life. As a result, she tended to favor Florence a bit, without realizing that she was planting the seeds of resentment in Edythe's head. Edythe would grow up always thinking her mother preferred Florence to her.

Florence was possibly unaware of the effect her mother's attentions were having on her baby sister. Florence had always been fussed over as a child. Years later, she'd say, "A lot of people said I was the prettier, but I never agreed with that. When Edythe was run over by the car, I was so scared. I thought I'd die if anything ever happened to her. I guess I always had a protective instinct about her."

Wally was blissfully unaware of the psychological forces at work. Having spent the first nine years of his life in braces, he didn't consider Edythe's temporary cast such a big deal. "I kept outgrowing them," he remembers. "So one day my father just said, 'We can't afford new braces any more. Let the kid go without them.' I was getting a little older and stronger, so out they went. I started running in high school, and when that got too strenuous, I turned to ice-skating. And I haven't had a bit of trouble with my legs since."

Edythe would not be that fortunate.

Ellen Marrenner gave only one magazine interview during her lifetime. Her daughter Edythe had made certain Ellen was off-limits to the press, and the one time she did talk, in March 1957, it was mainly about the automobile accident.

Ellen remembered that "For a year and a half I hauled her three blocks to P.S. 181 in a little wagon, then she hobbled into her room on crutches. In the afternoon, I'd be there waiting with the little wagon. But Edythe never cried. She was full of grit—more so than her brother and sister—and harder to handle. She'd struggle on her legs, making herself walk on pure nerve, stubborn-like. You'd die for her, but you knew she'd do it. She's been like that all her life."

Edythe, however, never told her mother of the humiliations she suffered in her classroom. Young children can be the cruelest of creatures, and Edythe would wince when they'd refer to her as the Gimp. In addition, she was the butt of jokes because of her red hair: redheads were decidedly in the minority

at P.S. 181—they were different, considered freaks. There was also the problem with her eyesight. Young boys and girls who wore glasses were nicknamed Four Eyes and tormented, so, though Edythe could barely see the figures on the blackboard, she never let on.

The situation at school only worsened after her cast was removed. Because of the improper traction, the hip did not heal properly and, according to Wally, Susan was left with "one leg a half inch shorter than the other. That's why she had to wear a lift in her shoe which gave her the strut in her walk. Not a limp—just a different kind of walk, but it was noticeable."

It was a strut that would later be considered "sexy"; at the time, her schoolmates thought it funny. Edythe was determined that no one would know how deeply hurt she was; she merely ignored the other kids at school.

Nor did she partake in the neighborhood's social life.

Wally would remember that whenever he or Edythe or Florence had a birthday, the celebration was strictly a family affair. Their dad would buy a quart of ice cream and a little cake, and that was the extent of it. Edythe once recalled that "We kids never had a birthday party . . . we couldn't afford them. Kids never invited me to their parties, because they knew I couldn't return the invitation. Anyway, I never had a party dress to wear. My Christmas present was hand-me-down clothes from cousins who were living a little higher on the hog. But they didn't fit—always three sizes too big. Our Christmas trees too were castoffs. Wally and I waited until the last minutes on Christmas Eve when the storekeepers threw them out. We'd pick out the least misshapen one and drag it home. How poor was I? When I had a hole in my shoe, I had to slip cardboard into it. I had to pick up second-day bread at the bakery. I had a gray linen dress that meant everything in the world to me because it was a present from my father—not a hand-me-down. When I spilled cocoa on it, there wasn't enough money to have it cleaned."

Eager to have some money of her own, she persuaded Wally to allow her to help him on his paper route on weekends. The two added to their incomes by finding and cashing in milk and soda bottles. Wally remembers going around to the different apartments salvaging old newspapers and selling them to a local junkman by weight. They'd increase their take by cutting

a hole in the middle of the pile and filling it with rocks, until the junk dealer got wise and threw them both out.

Florence detached herself from these kinds of activities. There was always some local boy eager to take her to the picture show and then blow ten cents on an ice cream soda at Mrs. Grossel's candy store. Florence was counting the days until she could quit school and embark on a career as a professional dancer. Wally, by now a whiz on skates, wanted to join an ice show and spent all his extra money going to the Brooklyn Ice Palace.

Edythe, constantly reminded of her slight deformity by her classmates, and abashed by Flo's prettiness, thought all avenues of escape were closed to her. Nonetheless, she'd remember that "Mother believed I could do anything I set my mind to. It was she who always fought our inclinations as youngsters to say, 'I can't do this' or 'I can't do that,' telling us not to say we can't do a thing because, of course, we could do anything anyone else could do."

When Edythe was ten, another world opened up to her. A drama teacher at P.S. 181 named Charlotte Rappaport took an interest in her. Edythe remembered that "Miss Rappaport was tiny and blondish—and she thought it was about time fairy princesses in school plays were brunettes and redheads instead of blondes. She always encouraged me and cast me as the princess in one play after another and took great pride in my performances."

In one such play, *Cinderella in Flowerland*, Ira Grossel, the dark-haired son of the candy-store owner, was cast as Prince Charming. Ira ran into voice trouble during rehearsals, however, and Miss Rappaport reluctantly had to replace him. Edythe was sympathetic, and the two budding performers struck up a friendship that, if not intimate at the time, would be fondly remembered when the two met again in Hollywood a quarter of a century later. He would then be known as Jeff Chandler, and an overromantic press, encouraged by the studio, would conspire to make a big affair of the childhood association and their current dates. Ira and Edythe were not childhood sweethearts. Mrs. Grossel, a religious lady embittered by her husband's desertion, owned a house next door to the local synagogue (at 209 East 37th Street) and would not have her little Ira mixing with any of the *shiksas* in the predominantly Jewish neighborhood.

Edythe was about to enter sixth grade when Florence came home one afternoon and informed Ellen and Walter that she was leaving Erasmus. She had been offered seventy-five dollars a week to tour the East Coast with Ned Wayburn's dance troupe and had been promised a ballet specialty act of her own. This was the chance she had been waiting for, and it meant a lot more to her than a high school diploma. Before Ellen had a chance to become too agitated, Florence promised to send home a generous portion of her salary. Ellen sent her off to Philadelphia with her blessings, and Edythe saw her leave with few misgivings. Edythe was still convinced—perhaps unjustifiably—that she had been playing second fiddle to her sister.

Florence, however, saw things in a different light, remembering that, as Edythe grew up, "We all sort of gave in to her. My mother never ordered her to do any chores around the house, but I was always more of a homebody than Susan, and I used to help with the dishes and cleaning and go to the grocery store. Susan never liked doing things like that, and nobody ever made her do it."

Edythe may have had to help with the dishes now, but she was nonetheless probably at her happiest when Florence was on the road with Ned Wayburn. The bedroom wasn't strewn with Florence's possessions, and when Edythe returned from school she had more privacy in which to indulge in her daydreams.

Meanwhile, the domestic situation was not good. Edythe could hear Ellen berating her husband when Florence's checks came in the mail, "Your daughter is making a better living then you are." There would be many such scenes, not totally understood at the time perhaps, but remembered years later when Edythe would describe her mother as "an intensely emotional, dramatic woman who frequently climaxed emotional arguments with my father by extending her arm and wailing, 'Go on, break it, break it.' With Mom, everything was a three-act play. And she wanted to play all the parts herself. I guess I get some of that quality from her. But Dad would just laugh and leave to join his cronies."

Walter would laugh—and leave. But not always to join his cronies.

Ellen's dramatic flair reached a new high when Florence returned to New York. In the spring of 1929, exhilarated by her success with Ned Wayburn, Florence auditioned for and

won a job as a chorus replacement in the Broadway musical hit *Follow Thru* starring Eleanor Powell, Jack Haley, and Zelma O'Neill. When Florence hinted that she was considering sharing an apartment in the city with another show girl to avoid the long trip back and forth to Brooklyn every night, Ellen put her foot down, as she warned of the fate that could befall a single girl living on her own.

A compromise of sorts was reached. Florence agreed to live at home; Ellen found a larger and better apartment at 2568 Bedford Avenue, which Florence's earnings would now subsidize.

Edythe celebrated her twelfth birthday by attending a matinee performance of *Follow Thru*, and Florence remembered introducing her to Eleanor Powell, who shook Edythe's hand and told her that she was a beautiful girl. Mrs. Rappaport had told her that too. But Edythe didn't feel beautiful. How could she when the kids at school were still teasing her, and when she knew she couldn't see ten feet ahead of herself?

Visiting Florence at the theater, however, left a very deep impression upon her. The dancing girls were all huddled in a large, crowded basement room, where they were forced to strip naked in front of one another. Eleanor Powell, the lead dancer, had a private room to herself on the main floor, and no one could enter without her permission. Being in a show wasn't all that great, Edythe concluded, unless one was the most important thing in the show: the *best* dancer, the *best* singer, the *best* actor. She never allowed herself to forget that. Somehow Florence wouldn't seem very special to her again.

The Wall Street crash the following October, which heralded the Great Depression, had no immediate effect on the Marrenner family. Florence continued on Broadway, going from *Follow Thru* to *New Moon*, and she remained at home with the family.

According to Wally, the two sisters seemed to be getting along well at the time. He can, in fact, remember only one serious fight between them, though the details escape him. "Florence was real mad when I stuck up for Edythe. She thought I was doing it because Edythe was younger. I thought 'Jesus, I'm in the middle now.' But things like that happen in every family and it was soon forgotten." Or so Wally thought.

Early in 1931, the family was shocked when Florence abruptly quit show business. The source for this fact is Wally

Marrenner. "She gave it up," explains Wally, "because she fell in love with some guy, some German. I think she got married. I don't know. I can't say. [Florence never said either.] I guess she threw up whatever her career may have been in the future, and she got a job in a bakery store. Isn't that some comedown?"

Edythe probably felt it and was secretly pleased to be overshadowed by her older sister no longer. Ellen's reaction was probably more of confusion: she had come to depend on Florence's contributions but, more than that, she had hoped that Florence's career would lead her into a marriage with one of the wealthy men who, she read, were drawn to show girls. She wouldn't have known what had gotten into Florence, or considered that her own preaching had likely contributed to Florence's rebellion.

Now Ellen transferred her frustrations to Edythe, pounding into her head the methods men used to lead gullible girls astray—though she never specified exactly what the latter entailed. Mothers couldn't talk openly about sex with their daughters in 1931; they could only hint of the dangers of being "touched." "Advice to the Lovelorn" columns warned: "Boys never marry girls who will tarry."

Ellen did her job well. When Edythe graduated from P.S. 181 in June, she decided against attending Erasmus Hall High School, which most of the kids in her class attended automatically. Edythe had at least three reasons for her decision: She wanted to get away from the schoolmates who had made fun of her. She didn't want to attend a coeducational school. And she felt she could have a whole new life at the school she chose—Girls' Commercial High, located a five-cent trolley ride away on Clausen Avenue in the shadow of the Brooklyn Museum, a few blocks from Prospect Park. It was an exclusive neighborhood, dotted with large private mansions and newly constructed elevator apartment buildings, and Girls' Commercial High was attended by the daughters of professional men— doctors, dentists, and lawyers. Edythe's classmates for the most part were thoroughly upper middle class, majoring in typing and stenography, and hoping to be married before the occasion arose for them to have to use either skill.

In September 1931, Edythe was probably the poorest teenager in her freshman class. Once again, pride drove her into herself. Feeling socially inferior, mistrusting a show of affection that could turn to rejection if her background was revealed,

she pretended disdain and sprouted porcupine quills. Though some of her classmates may have felt she was stuck up, it was a form of defense, her instinctive way of salvaging her ego. And she would never admit that, outside the classroom, her myopia prevented her from recognizing her schoolmates until she was almost on top of them. It was easier to remain aloof. Only Sara Little was able to penetrate her facade. Sara was bright, independent, and, like Edythe, wanted something more out of life than to be a Brooklyn housewife. Years later, Sara would reminisce: "That was the era of the big dream. But there was no question of our ultimate success. We felt we were destined."

At Girls' Commercial High, Edythe's ambition to act was furthered by a teacher named Florence O'Grady: "We once had to write a composition on any subject and I turned in one called 'I Want to Be an Actress.' Miss O'Grady said, 'Well, why don't you do something about it?'"

She did. She appeared in all the school plays, and Mrs. Dorothy Yawger, who ran the dramatic club, recalled, "Edythe always chose the parts no one else would take. Usually it was the unpleasant one, like a toothless old woman—any part with dramatic possibilities. She did them well."

She may have done them well because she identified with them. The toothless hag and the girl with one leg shorter than the other were compatible. Princesses represented perfection—and no matter what her father or Sara Little or her teachers said, Edythe knew she was imperfect.

Nevertheless, she still pursued her dream of becoming an actress. She had her idols. Barbara Stanwyck was high on her list, and not just because Miss Stanwyck was a fine actress. Barbara Stanwyck was a Brooklyn girl named Ruby Stevens who had risen above her background and become both a movie star and a great lady, in Edythe's opinion. Among the Marrenners' neighbors were a couple who had been good to young Ruby when she was struggling. Once a month now, without fail, during these black days of the Depression, the couple would receive a check signed "Barbara Stanwyck," which they would bring to Stokes's butcher shop to cash, after, of course, showing it to the rest of their neighbors. Consequently, whenever a Stanwyck film played the Glenwood Theater or the RKO Kenmore, Edythe would prevail upon her father for a dime so she could go and see it. She studied the way Stanwyck walked

and talked (without a trace of a Brooklyn accent) and dressed. Edythe was forced to wear middy blouses and skirts at Girls' Commercial. That was the way everyone had to dress so that the poorer teen-agers wouldn't feel inferior. However, Edythe vowed that once she got out of school, she would wear the same smart suits Barbara Stanwyck always wore when her pictures appeared in the movie magazines.

Edythe's ambition to become an actress did not go unnoticed by her parents. Ellen, spoiled by the now-lost income she had received from Florence, didn't discourage it, but she reminded Edythe that she would never be able to dance with the same grace and ease as Florence. Ellen equated a theatrical career with dancing. Years later, Edythe would insist: "I can't remember when I didn't want to be an actress, but only my dad and I believed I had any talent."

In her junior year, she found an inspiration to strengthen her belief that she *could* become a great actress in spite of any infirmity she might have. "Edythe," Wally confirms, "could think of nothing except acting. That was her ambition. Not to be a movie star, but to be an actress. Sarah Bernhardt was one of her idols, and she was always carrying around some book about her. She read a lot about Sarah Bernhardt in those days." The reason was simple: here was a woman who had continued to act even after having a leg amputated, who—after countless "farewell tours"—had kept returning to the stage until she died during rehearsals of a new play in Paris . . . at the age of seventy-nine.

Edythe was definitely impressed. She didn't try to emulate Madame Bernhardt's off-stage image, however—the "rouged face and painted lips" that some of Bernhardt's contemporaries had found deplorable. Edythe wore practically no make-up, and her relationships with boys were tenuous at best. Looking back, she'd admit: "In those days boys didn't like me. They thought me too fresh and flip. When a boy asked me to attend a dance, I was sassy, troublesome. I remember once I had a date for a De Molay dance. My friend's date brought her a corsage, but mine didn't. I was burned up and asked him why. He said he had no money. It made me miserable, and I made him miserable. Need I say I never saw him again?"

Nevertheless, during her senior term at Girls' Commercial, she developed a crush on a boy named Eddie Dixon, and she'd remember him fondly for years to come.

"Gosh, he was nice. He was a crackerjack pianist, and he used to encourage me to sing, which he did quite well too." She'd vividly recall going to Oetjens café with him and having a wonderful time, but that relationship also petered out. Perhaps she sensed that, if they became too serious, they could end up with a life like Ellen's and Walter's.

Edythe wanted to be free to pursue her career as an actress. Although she had no intention of leaving school before receiving a diploma, the way Florence had done, she restlessly looked forward to her graduation in June 1935.

In the class yearbook the following credits appear beside her picture: "Dramatic Club—V.O.A., Honors in Math, Science and Art, Arista." Arista was the interscholastic honor society of the time. Seventeen years later, as a promotional gimmick for her movie, *With a Song in My Heart*, Edythe returned to Girls' Commercial High—since renamed Prospect Heights High—to address the class of 1952. "I have a confession to make," she said humbly. "The Yearbook says I was in Arista. I never made Arista. Good marks weren't enough. You had to be voted in, and the girls didn't want me."

In that same yearbook, Edythe was proclaimed, "One of our prize actresses." The following fall, with steely determination, she set out to prove those words true.

❁ chapter 2 ❁

IN MID-AUGUST 1935, Edythe headed for Manhattan to find an acting job.

Despite the depression, there was a remarkable amount of activity on the boards. Producers were auditioning for *Idiot's Delight*, *Porgy and Bess*, *Winterset*, *End of Summer*, *Dead End*, *Victoria Regina*, and *Boy Meets Girl*. The Theater Guild, the Playwrights' Company, the Group Theater, and the Mercury Theater Company all had new productions in the works. The 1935–36 season was about to go into full swing—but no matter where Edythe went, she inevitably heard the same three questions:

"Are you a member of Equity? Do you have any experience? Do you have an agent?"

Her negative replies elicited a chilly, "We're only seeing professionals."

It was the show-business Catch–22: Without an agent or an Actors' Equity card, it was almost impossible to get into a show. Without a show, it was almost impossible to get an Equity card or an agent. There were exceptions, but—in 1935, with jobs at a premium—they were rare.

At the time, actors making the rounds often congregated in Walgreen's drugstore at West 44th Street and Broadway to exchange bits of information, casting tips, anything that might help. Edythe seldom joined them—she didn't really feel comfortable among them—but she was not above learning from others' experiences. One of the things she learned was that aspiring actresses could make ends meet by modeling for "confession" magazines—they were always on the lookout for new and pretty faces to illustrate such "true" stories as "I Was

Branded Back-Seat-of-a-Car Sal" or "I Dared to Love a Boy Above My Class."

The confession-field jobs were at the bottom of the modeling scale financially, but the work was fun, respectable enough, good training, and no agents were required. Besides, the girls could often obtain free professional photographs—a valuable fringe benefit when every cent mattered.

One of Edythe's first jobs, however, was not for a magazine, but for the *New York Daily News*, which was also on the lookout for fresh young faces to pose for its popular feature "The Correct Thing." Edythe was hired for a series of photos illustrating etiquette on a first date. Example: "The girl should not ask the boy to take her to an expensive night spot. The boy must not ask for a goodnight kiss."

The boy posing with Edythe in those pictures was a former child actor named Dick Clayton, who would later become well known as a Hollywood agent, the representative for Jane Fonda, Angie Dickinson, and Burt Reynolds among others. It was about this time, Clayton recalls, that Edythe made a slight change in her identity: "She dropped the double *n* from her last name. She preferred the way it looked in print—Edythe Marrener. Who cared? She was one of the most beautiful girls I had ever met. I was going steady at the time and didn't ask for a date, but I sure wanted to. We met again years later and always had a laugh about 'The Correct Thing.' She could be the warmest woman there was if she didn't think you were a phony."

Edythe Marrener she would remain—for just about two years more. Then a much larger change would come over her identity.

It was about this time too that Edythe learned of the Feagin Drama School. Feagin's was hardly on a par with the American Academy of Dramatic Art, but its tuition and eligibility requirements were lower, and Edythe could just about manage both. By early 1936, Edythe was studying voice, movement, and improvisation. She was also falling in love with one of her fellow students—or so she thought. Years later, refusing to identify the callow youth, she'd recall:

I'd meet him every day after class at a little café. He never worked, but he talked of his well-to-do parents. After dating three months I agreed to marry him . . . that very night. He had

no way of supporting me, but I didn't give it a thought. We were headed for Gretna Green, Maryland, where there were no waiting requirements. The elopement fizzled when we reached Grand Central Station and he wired his father, a Pennsylvania dentist, for money, meanwhile leaving me at the YWCA. The next morning when we returned to the Western Union office, there was no cash. His father was waiting instead.

"Do you love this girl?" he asked his son.

"Well..." My hero hesitated, looking at the ground.

That did it. I took my suitcase and went home to make some explanations to my parents.

Ellen Marrenner did not take the incident lightly. "I told you he was no good when you brought him home," she wept. "What do you want with those actors anyway? All they care about is themselves."

Her father was more sympathetic. "Consider yourself lucky you found out about his character before you made a serious mistake. Divorce is an ugly business." And then, to calm his fears, he asked, "You didn't make *any mistakes* last night, did you, Edie?"

She assured him she hadn't—and *wouldn't*—and he never brought up the subject again. But she never forgot it. It colored her relationship with men for years—perhaps for the rest of her life.

Edythe survived the breakup of her ill-fated romance, more determined than ever not to lose sight of the goals she had set for herself: fame and fortune—with emphasis on the latter. Sara Little, her friend, insists:

> We were the last of the career girls of the Depression. There are no more like us. We were conditioned by hard times and the urgent need to earn a living. It was not a matter of staying around and marrying the grocery boy. You had to be gifted. It was the only way.
>
> That was the era of the big dream. We'd meet every Thursday night in the President Cafeteria on Lexington Avenue. Afterward we'd window shop and talk endlessly about what we were going to do with our lives. One of our dreams was being able to go home to Brooklyn in a taxi

just to avoid the smelly subway.

There was no question of our ultimate success. We felt we were destined.

But destiny needed a push.

Later that year, convinced she had gone as far as possible at Feagin's, and in need of money, Edythe coolly put aside all acting ambitions to concentrate on full-time modeling. By now she was armed with an impressive portfolio, but she still had no agent. And in order to score as a high-priced model, it was not only necessary to have an agent, it was essential to be represented by one of the czars of the field: John Robert Powers or Walter Thornton. Edythe decided to tackle Thornton first.

Through the portals of the Walter Thornton Agency literally passed some of the most beautiful girls in the world. To be chosen by him all but guaranteed a successful career. Thornton dealt only with the top advertising agencies, art directors, and illustrators, and his own taste was impeccable. If a Thornton girl violated the boss's standard, she was quickly and quietly dropped from his "list."

Before an aspiring or even working model could get into the inner sanctum for an interview, however, she had to be carefully screened by Thornton's secretary, who was well schooled in the qualifications necessary to impress her boss. Most applicants never made it past her. When Edythe came in, the woman cast a perfunctory glance at Edythe's portfolio—then a long look at Edythe herself. A few minutes later, the newcomer was being scrutinized by the great man himself.

"A flaming mop of red hair was not to be dismissed without a second or third thought," Thornton would recall later. "Color photography had suddenly produced a loud chorus of calls for redheads and more redheads." He studied her carefully with what he called his "thousand eyes"—his equivalent of a sixth sense. Her dress size wasn't quite right for her height—size 12 to 13 was a bit large for her 5' 3½"—she'd never be a candidate for the high-fashion pages of *Vogue* or *Harper's Bazaar* . . . but there was something about her. Her smile and natural animation, when she let her guard down, were very attractive, and that, with her turned-up nose and expressive

hazel eyes, convinced him she had the quality that could reach out from the printed page to persuade a ten-dollar-a-week shop-girl that all her romantic problems would be solved for the price of a new Tek toothbrush.

"Even then," he recalled, "she revealed a sensitive flair for self-dramatization." In a letter she wrote in answer to a request for early biographical file material, she noted the following, in a discussion of clothes and colors: "In beige I feel like a very good little girl. Butter melts in my mouth. I've worn a great deal of beige lately, and I'm tired of being an angel."

To relieve her of this burden, Thornton sent her out on a call from the advertising company representing Hickory "Lur-alace" foundation garments. Although the one-piece "foun-dation" was more suitable for a middle-aged matron than a twenty-year-old, the agency was anxious to attract younger, more nubile buyers with a campaign that emphasized: "Sweet is the word for you in Luralace *with that artful uplift.*"

Because most of the top models resisted "intimate apparel" assignments, no matter how tasteful, the advertising agencies paid a higher fee to those willing to take them on. Eager for any extra money, Edythe accepted the job. The result showed her from the thigh up, her face in profile, her arms stretched high in the air, and looking sweet indeed in her beige Luralace foundation, a garment far less risqué than the standard one-piece swim suit. She wore her share of those too, in group beach scenes and in one head-and-shoulders ad illustrating how Noxzema brought "Instant Relief" to painful sunburn. In the first photograph, Edythe wears an expression of intense pain, with a balloon spelling out, "Oooh, what an awful sunburn!" In the adjoining picture, her face is lit up in ecstasy as she applies the magical cream, and the balloon farily bursts with the word "AH."

It was in such ads that Edythe's suppressed acting desire came to the surface, and as the months went by she was fre-quently commissioned to appear in these little illustrated dra-mas—all of which promised instant relief or instant romance.

Away from the photo studios, however, there was no ro-mance in Edythe Marrener's life—instant or lingering. Her mother was pleased at her daughter's modeling success, but looked upon it solely as a means to an end—a wealthy husband. After her abortive elopement, however, Edythe regarded the young men she met with disdain bordering on contempt. Most

of the art directors she met were either married or more interested in the male models; and the latter she considered vain and shallow. She had neither the inclination nor the time for casual partying and was appalled when other girls showed up for a job bleary-eyed and listless, or when she overheard gossip telling of how past Thornton girls had burned themselves out by high living before they were twenty-five. She was so distant, in fact, that one of Thornton's most vivid recollections was that of Edythe "stoically enduring the status of wallflower for a party which I gave for all my models. My wife kept saying to me, 'Dance with her. No one's asked her.'

"She was," Thornton continued, "the quietest girl who ever worked for me, a real lone wolf—a girl with no time for friends or a social life. But she was a very fine model."

So fine, in fact, that when Vitaphone decided to do a 1936 short subject about modeling and went looking for girls, Thornton sent her to represent his agency. It was to be Edythe's first experience before the motion picture cameras, and although her "role" of "Edythe Marrener of New York" required little histrionic ability, the experience was enough to convince her that given a real opportunity, she could make it in Hollywood, and that there was where her future lay. But she would have to bide her time and save her money.

Saving was almost an impossibility. It was easy to resist the temptation to find a small place of her own in Manhattan, since a major part of her pay checks was turned over to her family, but clothes were a necessity: the rest of her money went toward building the conservative, tasteful wardrobe essential to making a good impression when she was sent out for a job. By 1937 she was striking an oddly sophisticated note. On East 21st Street where her family, at her insistence, had moved, neighbors remember her as a beautifully dressed, aloof girl, never without a hatbox, the trademark of a model.

She was also beginning to make an impression on many artists and photographers who now specifically demanded her services. Two in particular remembered her.

Jon Whitcomb, the celebrated illustrator and commercial artist, would recall: "She had a kind of self-confidence that made you remember her. The first time I saw her, she swept into the studio as if she owned the place. Long before such catchwords as 'positive thinking' were in vogue, she was using them to propel her way to fame."

Photographer Ivan Dmitri, who remained friendly with Edythe for more than twenty years, remembered the young model as "a nice Brooklyn girl—very, very ambitious. She had that little dynamo going all the time. But she possessed that healthy, unsophisticated look which I felt typified the American beauty at that time."

If Edythe was using positive thinking, she had need of it. She never discussed her personal problems in the studio, but the situation at home was becoming tense and depressing. Walter Marrenner's health was deteriorating. His heart was weak, his kidneys failing, and he was plagued by chronic cystitis. As he was periodically forced to miss work, his morale and his pride were at an all-time low, money was tight, and he and Ellen Marrenner would fight all the time. Edythe learned early how inactivity could affect a man's psyche, behavior, and marriage. It was a lesson she was to remember again much later, to her pain.

Shortly after her twentieth birthday, the break Edythe had been awaiting finally came. She was summoned by Thornton to discuss a very special assignment: the *Saturday Evening Post* had persuaded him to be the "author" of a by-lined piece about the modeling world titled "The Merchant of Venus." Because Thornton's dictum had always been "beauty is not enough," the initial idea of illustrating the piece with a group of Thornton girls had been rejected in favor of a minidrama, "The Day in the Life of a Model." It was essential that a girl with whom the readers could identify be used. Ivan Dmitri had suggested Edythe, arguing that the red hair would be a plus in calling attention to the article.

The script was simple enough:

"A model comes to work. The author [Thornton] looks her over. She's taught to register. Artist [John] LaGotta reads her the script. She poses for him. And another pose—PERFECT! Ready for canvas."

This would not be like any of the clothing ads she was used to: anonymous Edythe in a pretty pose but distinctly secondary to what she was wearing. Not only would her fee be much more substantial, but Thornton would identify her by *name* in the accompanying article. "Edythe Marrener," he would proclaim, "a Brooklyn girl, today is one of the country's most

successful models, and her flaming red hair has contributed largely to making her popular."

The early photographs too looked very promising. Ivan Dmitri would recall: "For the first series of pictures she was a rather demure-looking teen-ager wearing sweater and skirt and dainty white gloves. That fabulous red hair was neatly pinned down. For the photographs with LaGotta, we fluffed out her hair, dressed her in a white satin gown with tulle overskirt. Seated before LaGotta, she looked like a vision from another, more innocent century."

"Merchant of Venus" was scheduled for the *Post*'s October 30 issue. Whatever excitement Edythe felt, however, was tempered by her concern about her father. His once ruddy complexion was now a sickly yellow, and he could barely make it to the bathroom.

On October 17, 1937, according to hospital records, Walter Marrenner collapsed on the job and was rushed to the nearby Metropolitan Hospital on Welfare Island. "He was very, very sick," Wally remembers. "There was no time to bring him back home to Brooklyn."

Possibly not, but anything would have been preferable to Metropolitan, which for the most part contained facilities for what the city termed "destitute incurables." Waves of horror and humiliation engulfed Edythe when she learned of her father's whereabouts. "We could have raised the money to send him elsewhere," says Wally, "but he couldn't be moved."

Less than two weeks later, the *Saturday Evening Post* hit the newsstands.

Across the country, thousands of shopgirls were undoubtedly looking at the redhead in the white satin gown and envying her. Pulp fiction and film had portrayed a model's life as one filled with evenings of dancing at the Stork Club, her closets bursting with exquisite gowns and furs in Fifth Avenue apartments furnished with plush carpets, satin settees, and sleek Art Deco mirrors.

That was the fantasy. For Edythe, reality was seeing her adored father helpless and useless at age fifty-eight. Then she received a call from Kay Brown, David O. Selznick's right-hand woman in New York.

In a work of fiction, what followed would be dismissed as plot contrivance. But as one of those confession magazines Edythe had modeled for proclaimed, "Truth is stranger than fiction."

Throughout 1937, an epidemic of what was to be known as "Scarlett Fever" had been sweeping the country, as David O. Selznick launched his much-publicized search to find an "unknown" to portray Margaret Mitchell's celebrated heroine in *Gone with the Wind*. At Selznick's urging, George Cukor, the director, had agreed to make a tour of Southern colleges on the off-chance that a Scarlett might be hidden among the magnolia trees in some obscure Dixie campus or little-theater group. They were hiding there all right; Cukor was hounded by Scarletts of all sizes, shapes, and ages, but every meeting or audition brought Cukor closer to the conclusion that his Southern trek was a waste of time and money. He headed for New York for a respite.

The story of how Edythe Marrener came to audition for *Gone with the Wind* has undergone many revisions over the years. Some studio biographies have even erroneously credited Selznick himself with the discovery. Those stories insist he saw the redhead's picture on the cover of the *Saturday Evening Post*. However, Edythe wasn't *on* the cover of the *Saturday Evening Post*; her first and only cover for that magazine was on October 7, 1939—nearly two years later. A *Post* piece in 1959 merely deepened the false impression when it reprinted the 1939 cover above a caption that read: ". . . this *Post* cover photograph won a Hollywood screen test for Susan Hayward, who was then an unknown Brooklyn model." Plainly wrong.

Other stories claim that Cukor saw the article and rushed to sign her up; others, that Selznick's wife Irene saw some of her ads and showed them to Selznick. Cukor very firmly says today, "I never saw the story in the *Saturday Evening Post*. Irene never saw the girl modeling hats or anything else. All those stories are pure bull." And Irene Selznick, asked whether she or Cukor brought the star to her former husband's attention, frankly admits: "I honestly can't recall whether I did or he did. I do remember being very impressed with the girl and thinking that she had definite possibilities for movies. It's possible we both became aware of her at the same time and suggested her as a potential candidate for the role."

However it happened, it was in Selznick's New York office that Edythe did meet Cukor, talked with him—and, a few days later, having made an excellent impression, was signed to a "test contract" with Selznick Studios.

Ivan Dmitri remembered that "she came bouncing into my

office with the good news, joyously announcing, 'Dmitri, I'm in the movies,' and when I congratulated her she said archly, 'Well, it's about time.'"

The Selznick office insisted that Edythe, still under twenty-one, be chaperoned to California for the test; sister Florence was elected—her alliance with Wally's mysterious "German" must have ended—and the office booked train space for them both. On the Chicago to Los Angeles leg, it was even on the same crack streamliner, the *Chief*, that David and Irene Selznick would be riding. George Cukor could have done the test right where he was—there were studio facilities in New York—but the director was feverishly preparing to film *Holiday* with Katharine Hepburn and Cary Grant before becoming exclusively involved with *Gone with the Wind*, and had little free time, to say the least.

The office insisted, as well, that Edythe leave New York immediately. Walter Marrenner was disturbed and pleaded with his wife. "Don't let her leave, Ellen. She's not ready. She'll have her heart broken out there." But Edythe's and Florence's bags were already packed. On November 18, 1937, they boarded the train, with Thornton there to see her off, at Edythe's request. Before leaving, she had signed a contract with him granting him an agent's fee of 10 percent of all her future earnings, and, the day before, autographed a picture crediting him with "whatever success I may be fortunate enough to gain."

There was no thought of discord when Thornton and his wife saw Edythe to the train at Grand Central Station.

"In fact," he said, "that day was the only time I ever saw her express any emotion of any kind. She asked my wife if she could kiss me goodbye. I think my wife said 'Yes.' I don't really remember . . ."

And it really didn't matter. Within two years, Edythe would be kissing him off—for good, referring to him coldly as "the nasty man."

And *that* Thornton would never forget.

❈ *PART TWO* ❈

Edythe Marrener/
Susan Hayward

Hollywood
December 1937—July 22, 1944

I worked harder for Susan than I had on any other girl. Her Selznick tests were terrible. She couldn't act. Nobody liked her. . . . Her drama coach at Warners told me, "Benny, this is not a very nice girl." Nobody liked her at Paramount. Henry Ginsberg said, "Benny, what are you wasting your time for? She's got nothing." . . . She was a bitch.

BEN MEDFORD,
Susan's first agent
March 1980

All my life I'd been terribly frightened of people. I thought everyone was so brilliant. I felt so inadequate. The only way I knew how to protect myself was to scare people before they scared me.

SUSAN HAYWARD

⊠ *chapter 3* ⊠

EDYTHE Marrener was a very frightened young woman when she went through the front door of the Selznick studios for the first time in December of 1937. The entire atmosphere of the bustling Washington Boulevard lot in Culver City overwhelmed her. She had bragged to everyone in New York that her time had finally come, but now that she was actually in California, she wasn't nearly so confident. What if they hated her? Everyone around her looked so . . . professional, and here she was with her few months of acting classes. There was nothing for it but to brazen it through.

Her first test, directed by George Cukor, was slated for the morning of December 6, 1937. Contrary to Hollywood history, however, she was *not* being tested for the role of Scarlett O'Hara.

Aware that he is debunking a forty-three-year-old legend, George Cukor says today, with a chuckle, "We never really thought of her for Scarlett. She was very young and not too experienced, in fact, completely inexperienced. It would have been stupid to get a twenty-year-old girl to play a most demanding part. We thought, David thought, 'This girl may have some possibilities. Let's bring her out and use her for tests and put her under contract.'

"She was very pretty, a very sweet, dignified girl. Very correct. Very nice. At least that was her facade. If she was tough underneath, you couldn't tell it, because she was very, very dignified."

Responding to the stories that have circulated for more than four decades that, when Edythe was asked to do a scene a certain way, she replied, freshly, "Who's playing this scene,

you or me?" Cukor protests, "Oh, nonsense. No, no, no. She was a very young girl and very well behaved."

Edythe *did* portray Scarlett, but it was as a vehicle to test other actors for other roles and to see just what she could do. In her first test, she worked opposite Selznick contractee Alan Marshal in what was known as "the Library scene at Twelve Oaks," in which Scarlett declares her love for Ashley Wilkes for the first time, while, unknown to her, Rhett Butler lounges on a couch at the back of the room. For the remainder of her test contract, she was used to assist in the auditioning of potential Melanies, particularly Dorothy Jordan (who would later become the wife of Merian C. Cooper, the director of *King Kong* and one-time vice-president of Selznick International). Seen now, the tests reveal the freshness and intensity that obviously attracted Selznick and Cukor to her in the first place, but they also reveal her great inexperience; her voice clenches, sometimes sinking to barely above a whisper, she seems uncertain of what to do with her body—and she is obviously scared out of her wits. When the director ends the scene, her sigh of relief is audible.

She was painfully aware of her shortcomings. "I looked like a snub-nosed teen-ager," she said later. "What did I know about Southern belles?" The studio executives agreed with her. Though she had potential, they thought, it wasn't enough to keep her on. She was given her release.

In years to come, studio flacks would fabricate a snappy epilogue: "When David O. Selznick broke the sad news to her, he kindly suggested she return home and get some more experience.

"'I like oranges. I'm staying,' was her sassy reply. 'Besides, I've already cashed in my return ticket.'"

That story was repeated often enough to become accepted as fact. David O. Selznick, however, had neither the time nor the inclination to play sympathetic Dutch uncle to any of the hundreds of unknowns he was testing and rejecting. It was one of Selznick's aides who wielded the hatchet, and Edythe's response was not recorded.

There was one element of truth in the flack's story, however. After the test contract with Selznick expired, Edythe did go to the nearest Santa Fe office and cash in her ticket. With that money she rented an inexpensive, furnished bungalow in an unfashionable section of Hollywood and went to look for work.

Her worst fears had been realized: they hadn't liked her—but damned if she was going to give up. There was only one way she was going back to Brooklyn: as a famous movie actress. She blocked out the possibility of failure. She also blocked out the fear that she might never see her father again, and dismissed her mother's pessimistic letters as typical Ellen Marrenner gloom and doom. Mother always had dramatized so. Meanwhile, Edythe scrambled for whatever modeling jobs she could find, with the help of a young agent named Ben Medford, who had been introduced to her by George Cukor.

Life wasn't easy. Florence wasn't contributing much and the little money from Edythe's modeling and the ticket refund went for food and local transportation. Dating was a waste of energy, even though "everyone was on the make for her," Medford remembers. "But Mrs. Marrenner was determined to keep her a virgin." The New Year started miserably, and got worse. She received word from home that her father, still hospitalized on Welfare Island, couldn't risk a transfer. On January 2, Walter Marrenner underwent surgery for drainage of a scrotal abscess. Ellen's letter filled in the depressing details.

Medford, meanwhile, was having problems selling her to the studios. Finally, he recalled, "I got permission to show the *Gone with the Wind* test to Max Arnow," a talent executive for Warner Brothers. Arnow agrees that, although Edythe was no Scarlett, "she had an intangible quality worth developing," and continues: "We signed her to a six-month, one-hundred-fifty dollars a week contract. We then got around to the business of changing that dreadful name. It didn't suit her at all. I was doing business with agent Leland Hayward [Margaret Sullavan's husband, Brooke Hayward's father]. I liked the sound of the name 'Hayward.' But I can't remember where the 'Susan' came from. Maybe Cantor was singing 'If You Knew Susie' on the radio; maybe I saw some black-eyed Susans that morning at a florist. Who knows?"

After sending the newly named Susan Hayward to the gallery for the standard studio portraits, Arnow placed her in the Warner Brothers' drama school. "She worked every day with a great dramatic coach, Frank Beckwith," he recalled, "but this new girl didn't quite have the heart. She had a wonderful mind, but she didn't have the heart."

Arnow was wrong. She had the heart all right, but Susan

was still controlling herself, still keeping her emotions under tight rein. It would be years before she would learn to open herself up on screen—and then the rush of feeling would be stunning.

Peggy Moran (Mrs. Henry) Koster—who married the noted director and gave up her career in 1942—appeared with Susan about then in a thirteen-minute Warner Brothers short subject called *Campus Cinderella*. She also was a student of Beckwith's.

"I remember Susan Hayward well from the days in acting class," she says. "At that time we rehearsed scenes from famous plays and motion picture scripts. She wore no make-up, and sometimes she took pins out of her purse and casually pinned up her flaming red hair without benefit of a mirror. The effect was stunning. It often distracted the rest of us from our work— Diana Lewis [later married to William Powell], Lana Turner, Carole Landis.

"Susan was a great beauty, but she was hard to approach and always seemed aloof [a condition her myopia did not help]. Perhaps she did not want to disclose her private life to others." There Mrs. Koster's impression was right on the mark. There were a great many things Susan didn't want disclosed, her background among them. In a town filled with glamour and exoticism, the poverty of her childhood seemed shameful— and a sure impediment to her success. It also came to represent her greatest dread: "My mother's great fear," Susan's son Timothy Barker reveals today, "was the idea of ever having to return to Brooklyn—the kind of life it represented."

Susan had arrived in Hollywood scared, and she was still scared: scared people would look down on her, scared she wasn't glamorous or talented enough, scared she'd be a total flop. And there was nothing she wanted more than to succeed. Many years later, one of her producers, Walter Wanger, would say, "Susie suffers from one of the strangest and most startling guilt complexes you can imagine. She's embarrassed that she's a beautiful woman. She doesn't think she deserves it. She knows that it is a priceless gift, but she is afraid that on the inside she isn't so beautiful. It causes her to avoid other women on her own level. It's responsible for her fits of temperament. Actually, her beauty makes her miserable. Ironic, isn't it?"

So Susan raised her barricades and arrayed her defenses. She determined never to let anyone get close enough to know

what she was feeling—or to wound her. As a result, she some-times wounded others.

Ben Medford remembers: "George [Cukor] was very helpful to her—and to me. He was a wonderful help to Susan. He got Gertrude Fogler, who was under contract to Metro at the time and was not permitted to teach people off the lot, to work with Susan. It was Gertrude who changed Susan's high-pitched voice to a low-pitched one, and between Gertrude and Frank Beckwith's efforts, she was turned into an actress.

"But after the time Gertrude spent with the girl, do you think Susan ever gave her a little present? Never!

"I got Susan a little automobile so she could get around, taught her how to dress, gave her money. I used to bring her to night clubs with George Montgomery just to have their picture taken, to get her name in the papers. She didn't like him and he didn't like her. . . ."

And just because Susan now had a Warner Brothers contract didn't mean she was getting work. The individual producers and directors on the lot had to be convinced to use her. She was still a hard sell. "Hard to photograph," says Medford. "She had this bulbous nose, and I passed money to the cam-eramen and lighting guys to make sure she got the proper treatment. Their job was to concentrate only on the stars."

Then something happened that would take Susan's mind off her faltering career. On March 16, 1938, at 2:50 P.M. Walter Marrenner gave up. Metropolitan Hospital on Welfare Island noted the official cause of death: "Uremia and complications of arteriosclerosis with narrowing of the coronary arteries."

Susan was not home that afternoon, and by the time she was notified of his death, Walter Marrenner had already been cremated, just another box of ashes to be disposed of by the Fresh Pond Crematory in Meadow Valley, Queens. That night she cried until she was thoroughly exhausted, until there were no tears left to be shed. Future stories about Marrenner's death would undergo assorted variations: the most oft-repeated one that Susan's father had died without ever learning she had failed her test for Selznick. Certainly, though, Ellen Marrenner would have passed the news to her husband, and Susan ob-viously wrote her father during the three months prior to his death. But she was still guilt-ridden that she had been incapable of facing the squalid horrors of Welfare Island the month before she'd left for California.

Publicity stories would also dramatize an emotional death-bed farewell between Marrenner and his daughter beside his hospital bed—this too was a fantasy, as Wally Marrenner confirms: "No, Susan never went to see my father at the hospital before he expired, not that I remember."

With nothing to keep her in Brooklyn, Ellen Marrenner decided to join her daughters in Hollywood. "We came out by bus," says Wally, "and moved in with my sisters in a house near Paramount studios—Irving Boulevard, I think it was called at the time." Susan's reaction to having her mother live with her is not recorded—it must have been a mixed blessing at best—but at least it provided some financial relief. Wally remembers Susan saying to him, "'Oh, Wal, I wish you had come out with me instead of Flo.' I don't think they were getting on too well because Flo made no effort to help out with the expenses. I had a little money I had saved, but that went in a hurry for food and stuff. Ben Medford helped us a bit. I got a job which didn't pay much, but it was a job to keep us going. . . ."

Susan's salary, added to Wally's took care of the rent and their necessities. She was certain that if she was given a chance to prove herself in a halfway decent part, Warner Brothers would increase her salary. Posing for publicity shots and studying with Beckwith for $150 a week was hardly her idea of being a movie actress. Medford had told her she had been assigned a good role in an important new movie called *Brother Rat* and urged her to be patient.

Max Arnow, however, was impatient about the progress she was making. "Beckwith gave her heavy dramatic scenes to see if he couldn't get some emotion out of her and get her to cry. It took quite a while." Susan, aware of her difficulties, described them differently in a letter she wrote her former mentor in late April:

Monday

Dear Mr. Cukor,

I passed the Troc the other noon, and there you were! My first glimpse of you in ages. It was you, wasn't it? You were with a group of about six people and evidently the host. Looking very well and extremely happy. Just as I was about to release a wild scream in greeting, the light changed and a tourist carried me downstream on his bumper.

Life, at present, is not as exciting for your self-appointed protégé as it might be. It will become so tho when "Brother Rat" goes into production. I'm scheduled to play the part of Joyce, the girl who likes boys and a rumpus and not much else. It's going to be a lot of fun! On the other hand "B.R." might not roll for weeks—who knows? In the meantime, the camera and the technical side of motion pictures hold so much of interest. The camera is exceptionally revealing and I've been trying to control my grimacing somewhat. This restraint is causing a studio head no end of anguish. He thinks I'm cold, no feeling. The other day he instructed Frank Beckwith, with whom I've been working, to "Let Hayward overact if she pleases. Let her be a ham— as long as it comes from the heart.". . . Now I ask you . . .

There is so much that must be done. How can I ever thank you for making possible my entry into this world? The only way I can think of is to some day soon win the Academy Award for the finest performance and in return present it to you to whom I owe so much.

I send my love with this and a heart filled with gratitude.

Sincerely,

Edythe Marrener

As things turned out, however, Susan was unceremoniously removed from the cast of *Brother Rat*, and Priscilla Lane installed in the role of Joyce. The explanation: Jack Warner had seen a rough cut of Miss Lane's new movie *Four Daughters*. Astutely aware it would turn her into a major star, he wanted to take immediate advantage of her predictable box-office appeal. He rushed her into *Brother Rat*.

Susan, an unknown quantity, was assigned a tenth-billed role in a sixty-three-minute, soon-forgotten quickie, *Girls on Probation*.

Producer Martin Rackin, one of Susan's close professional friends throughout the years, said, shortly before his death: "Jack Warner used to boast that one actor on his ass was worth two on his feet, and he kept them that way. Susan was very shy and very insecure then. She really got kicked around, and I think it got to her. After the Warner treatment she never let down her guard. It made her a loner, and she never changed."

"Even before her six-month option came due," says Medford, "I heard she was being let go. But I believed in the girl and I didn't want to give up."

The result was an interview with Paramount's head of talent Arthur Jacobson, and there she made a far better impression. Jacobson remembered Susan "entering my office, sedately dressed in a little black suit, wearing sensible medium-heeled shoes and very little make-up." She was a refreshing contrast to the over-made-up glamour girls that had been passing through his offices. He felt she would be an important addition to a group of young players Paramount was trying to build into stars. Medford negotiated a seven-year contract with Paramount at a starting salary of $350 a week with guaranteed yearly raises. "That was a lot of money in those days," he notes.

Marvin Houser, a Paramount press agent assigned to her at the time, observed, "Susan Hayward was a lonely rider tilting at windmills even then. She worked day and night to shed her accent—quaint but unmistakable Brooklynese."

A New Yorker himself, Jacobson was confident Susan would succeed. It was vital for him—and the studio—that she do so.

❧ chapter 4 ❧

In 1939, Paramount was having female trouble. A year earlier, two of its most dazzling leading ladies, Marlene Dietrich and Mae West, had had their reputations tarnished, if not permanently damaged. They, together with Katherine Hepburn, W. C. Fields, and others, had been branded "box-office poison" by a powerful group of movie exhibitors who had, not too subtly, indicated that the fewer films these once-towering stars made, the happier the showmen would be.

In addition to this blow, Paramount was being driven to distraction by the irrational behavior of Frances Farmer, for whom it once had had such high hopes. The studio's two newest imports, Franciska Gaal from Norway and Olympe Bradna from France, had simply failed to catch on with either critics or the public. Of the many young actresses Paramount had signed in the early thirties, when the advent of sound had decimated their contract list, only Claudette Colbert had shown she had staying power. Ruth Chatterton, Sylvia Sidney, and Nancy Carroll had diminished in appeal and returned to Broadway. Carole Lombard and Miriam Hopkins had long since departed for greener pastures.

In addition, although there was still a strong stable of male stars, including Crosby, Hope, Cooper, Fred MacMurray, and Ray Milland, many of these contracts were coming up for renewal, and the studio was in desperate need of "leverage." In an effort to obtain it, Paramount originated what it optimistically called its "Golden Circle," consisting of new young performers who were promised a "star build-up" and paid only about $200 a week. It was a no-lose situation, even if only two or three of these hopefuls turned out to have the golden touch. The others could and would be quietly dropped at option time—and a new Circle begun.

Susan was introduced to the other twelve members of the Circle in 1939 during the shooting of group photographs. Coolly, she sized up the female competition: Louise Campbell, Ellen Drew, Betty Field, Judith Barrett, Patricia Morison, Joyce Mathews, Janice Logan, and Evelyn Keyes. None of them seemed like potential threats. Of the four Circle men, she considered William Holden and Robert Preston, newly recruited from the Pasadena Playhouse, "interesting," and Joseph Allen, Jr., and William Henry "too pretty." The way to the top seemed clear.

Susan's first chance to show what she could do came when Paramount cast her in their remake of the stirring Ronald Colman silent film classic of 1926, *Beau Geste*. This time the three brothers who join the French Foreign Legion would be played by Gary Cooper, Ray Milland, and Robert Preston, with Susan cast in the tiny role of ward Isobel Rivers. Susan would later mock her role by quipping, "I waved goodbye to the boys at the beginning and hello to them at the end," but she was given billing directly behind Brian Donlevy, who played the villainous Sergeant Markoff and probably made the biggest impression in the picture; and her final scene with Ray Milland, as the only surviving Geste brother, John, was appealing enough to inspire Paramount to publicize her as "the personal discovery of producer-director William Wellman." (Even though Wellman privately told the Paramount executives, "She'll never get anywhere with that bump on her nose.")

Beau Geste was booked into the New York Paramount on August 2. Hoping to inject some glamour into an essentially male-oriented film, Paramount sent Susan east a few days before the opening. It was her first trip home since settling in Hollywood, but with the exception of Sara Little, there were few friends or relatives she wanted to see. She had never felt she had much in common with her cousins, and saw no reason to subject herself to a barrage of questions about life in the film capital.

The *Saturday Evening Post* editors, elated by the role their magazine had played—or supposedly played—in her newfound eminence, eagerly asked her to pose bare-shouldered for their October 7, 1939, cover (the same cover later mistakenly credited for her "discovery"), which she did with pleasure. Other than that, Paramount's New York publicity office found themselves hard put to get Susan much coverage other than a few beauty and fashion pieces. Entertainment editors who had

seen a screening of *Beau Geste* were more interested in male angles, and with an abundance of great pictures vying for space that fall, they were indifferent to "just another young starlet." Still, Susan had come home just as she had wanted—as a star (however small)—and nothing could diminish her pleasure at that.

The reviews, when they appeared, were generally good; the critics mostly ignored Susan; but the picture was a rousing adventure yarn, it did well at the box office and, despite the brevity of her role, audiences seemed to respond to her fresh beauty. Her career seemed *finally* to have gotten off the ground.

Paramount, however, dissipated whatever interest there was in their new discovery by carelessly casting her in two "B" clinkers: *Our Leading Citizen*, with former radio comic Bob Burns, and *$1,000 a Touchdown*, an exercise in mindless lunacy starring an also-faltering Martha Raye and Joe E. Brown.

Susan felt enormously frustrated after such a promising start—and then any hopes she may have had for being cast in a major role at Paramount seemed to be shattered for good when the studio signed Paulette Goddard to a long-term contract. As the first runner-up in the Scarlett O'Hara sweepstakes, and now free of a contractual obligation to her "husband" Charlie Chaplin—no one was sure they had actually been married until they were divorced, and even then there was some doubt—Goddard had suddenly become the hottest property in town.

After losing *Gone with the Wind* to Vivien Leigh, Goddard had been borrowed by MGM for strong co-starring roles in *Dramatic School* and *The Women*, but she had been less than enthusiastic about signing with a studio that already had more queens than Henry VIII. Paramount, with its dearth of leading ladies, offered Goddard more money than MGM and better opportunities, and swiftly lived up to its promise by casting her opposite Bob Hope in *The Cat and the Canary*, which became the comedy success of the year.

A fellow New Yorker, Paulette Goddard was six years older than Susan, but there was little difference photographically. Nor was her talent or experience much better: as an actress, Goddard would never walk off with any prizes. She had an appealing screen personality, however, was considered an outspoken, shrewd, and worldly woman, and the Chaplin connection commanded respect.

As Susan watched Goddard being escorted grandly to her

suite in the stars' dressing-room row, she was overcome by feelings of insecurity . . . and hostility. Here was a woman with whom she knew she couldn't compete and one who could influence whatever future there might be at Paramount. Goddard, on the other hand, was barely aware of Susan's existence. Susan could see her career melting away.

It was then, in mid-October, that Louella Parsons decided to play fairy godmother to the neglected Cinderella. She was planning a coast-to-coast personal appearance tour for later that year—four or five live shows at carefully selected movie houses. Paid $7,500 a week for the package, she planned to allot $4,200 of this to be divided among her "supporting cast" of six young contractees. These hopefuls would do the actual performing while Louella sat imperiously behind a desk trying to decide whether the youngsters deserved a plug in her column. The project was self-aggrandizing and blatantly corny, but audiences lapped it up.

Of Parsons' Flying Stars, as they were called, Susan was perhaps the least familiar to Louella's audiences. Of the others, Warner's Ronald Reagan and Jane Wyman had appeared in fifteen films each; redheaded Arleen Whelan, a Zanuck favorite, had co-starred with Warner Baxter in *Kidnapped* and with Henry Fonda in *Young Mr. Lincoln*; blonde, pert June Preisser, under contract to MGM, had won a substantial fan following after appearing in *Babes in Arms* and *Dancing Co-Ed*; and Joy Hodges had made an impression in eight RKO pictures.

Hodges, who returned to the Broadway stage soon after the tour was over, never forgot those eleven weeks on the road— or Susan's behavior during the engagement.

"Frankly I was a little afraid of her—that directness, that lack of humor. I never thought of Susan as a girl I'd want to know well, one to whom I could say, 'Come on, let's go out and have dinner.' Somehow she seemed uneasy and withdrawn with other performers. It wasn't the usual competitive thing. I just think she felt unsure of herself among people in a profession in which she had so little experience. But she was always extremely open and friendly with doormen and elevator operators.

"There was something so alone about Susan. The rest of us each had something going for us. I was a brand-new bride. Jane and Dutch [Ronald Reagan] had each other. Arleen was

very gay, with plenty of beaux. June already had a career on the stage with her sister Cherry. No question, we each had more mileage in show business than Susan, but even then she was special. She'd charge on stage with that bulldog walk, her head bent forward, and plant her feet. The rest of us would sort of float out. Susan—she seemed to have nothing, except talent. And she was so beautiful."

The routines were mainly musical, but Susan had a comedy scene with Reagan that, Hodges remembers, "she played with incredible fervor. I can still see her—the blue velvet dress with that red hair, the spotlight on just the two of them. In the skit, she stabbed Dutch, and every time he'd try to sit up, she'd bop him down again. Susan played it completely straight. The audiences howled, but she never faltered, and not even when Dutch broke up, as he usually did. We all marveled at how she kept her composure."

Jane Wyman, however, found it difficult to keep hers. Then engaged to the actor (they would marry in January 1940) she watched the scene every night from the wings, furious at the "realism" Susan put into her punches.

Susan was equally annoyed by Wyman's presence, and complained to Parsons that it made her very nervous. When Louella passed this on, Wyman exploded: "Too bad about *her!* If I don't stand there and watch, she'll knock Ronnie out. She hits him too hard. She just slaps him that hard because she thinks it makes me mad."

Louella, caught between two warring factions, tried to be conciliatory and, when that failed, took a neutral stand. But despite this infighting, the act played to packed houses throughout the country, and extra shows had to be added when it was booked into the Loews' State in New York for a Christmas week engagement starting December 21. Susan brought the house down when she made her entrance shouting, "Anyone here from Brooklyn?" Even Parsons herself couldn't compete with that show-stopper.

The columnist developed a deep and lifelong fondness for the girl and would later reminisce:

"When I first asked Susan to join the act, she was her completely honest self when she told me right to my face that she thought being associated with me 'will help my career.'

"You come to know people very well when you travel with them, and I was surprised that with all Susan's sexy beauty,

she was at heart a real 'Miss Prim'! She was easily shocked by backstage stories, even when they were mild, and her feelings were so easily hurt she dissolved into tears when anyone even looked at her crossly.

"She seldom went out, even when we hit big towns like Philadelphia and New York. She was an ultra-conventional and moral little thing, a quality that endeared her to me fully as much as her loveliness and sweetness."

When the tour ended on December 27, the other cast members—with the exception of Wyman and Reagan—went their separate ways, relieved to have it over and done with. Susan, however, decided to remain in New York until after the New Year, Louella arranging a special rate for her at the Warwick, where they had all been staying. She told a *Daily News* reporter, happily, that she was up for a leading role in the Group Theater's production of Clifford Odets's *Night Music* with Elia Kazan and Morris Carnovsky, which was about to go into production. Paramount had no new film for her in the immediate future, and she'd never completely abandoned her dream of becoming a Broadway star. Now that the tour had given her the confidence to appear before a live audience, the possibility of doing the play was exciting, and she spent the rest of her time in town going to the theater.

One of the shows she saw was Katharine Hepburn in *The Philadelphia Story*. With Louella's help, she was able to get a ticket for the December 30 Saturday matinee performance. This biographer, not yet in her teens, was seated nearby and, recognizing Susan from the Loews' State show, was as transfixed by her as Susan was by Hepburn.

After the show, Susan was in the crush of matinee women crowding around the Shubert Alley stage entrance. Twice she opened the door, obviously intending to go backstage—and then lost her nerve. Before she tried a third time, Miss Hepburn, in a heavy coat and bandana, dashed by and into a long black limousine. The car sped away, barely missing autograph seekers anxious for a close-up look at the star. The crowds dispersed, leaving just a few stragglers waiting for Van Heflin's and Joseph Cotten's autographs. It had gotten dark, and a freezing wind swept through Shubert Alley as Susan raced across 44th Street and into Sardi's.

She was never signed for *Night Music*. Perhaps Paramount vetoed the idea, blaming the Group Theater for the problems

they had been having with Frances Farmer, who had run out on her contract with them to do *Golden Boy* and *Thunder Rock* with the Group Theater, disdainfully declaring herself a *stage* actress. They may not have wanted another of their players "corrupted" by the theater. More likely, the Group had never seriously been interested in Susan in the first place. She was, after all, hardly up to their standards—not yet—and the whole idea may have been just an agent's dream. Susan never discussed what had to have been a bitter disappointment again.

Nor would she discuss what turned out to be an unpleasant reunion with Walter Thornton. Thornton had heard of her success in Hollywood, such as it was, and wanted both the credit and the money for it. Claiming he was responsible for launching her on her career, he promplty announced plans to sue for $100,000, asserting she had walked out on a personal contract with him.

Flaring up, Susan charged that the whole contract had been illegal in the first place and that she had no intention of paying Thornton one penny. "One hundred thousand dollars is a lot of money," she told reporters succinctly. "He's not going to get it." Thornton made more noises about suing, then changed his mind—"it simply wasn't worth the effort," he declared—and the two never spoke again.

It was in this frame of mind that Susan returned to Hollywood after the holidays, only to be sent packing again. The studio, in a less-than-altruistic goodwill gesture, had arranged to send the remaining members of the Golden Circle on a whistle-stop tour of Paramount exhibitors to hype its spring releases. Betty Field was co-starring in *Seventeen*, Ellen Drew in *Buck Benny Rides Again*, and Robert Preston in *Typhoon*; William Henry had a strong feature role in *The Way of All Flesh*, Judith Barrett was in *Road to Singapore*, and Patricia Morison was Ray Milland's leading lady in *Untamed*. Susan was, in fact, the only member of the group not in a forthcoming Paramount movie. It made her feel a bit odd, but fortunately it made little difference to the exhibitors, who managed to get plenty of local coverage as a result of her appearances.

On tour, Susan was treated like a star. Back home again, however, she was the "invisible" girl once more. When she complained about her lack of work, the studio bluntly told her she should be grateful she was still under salary. Golden Circle hopefuls Janice Logan, Louise Campbell, Joyce Mathews, and

Joseph Allen, Jr., all had had their options dropped, they pointed out, while she had received a $100-a-week raise.

It was little consolation to an ambitious young actress, however, and her impatience with the studio grew. Further, it spilled over into her home life. The Marrenner family was now living in a large, if rather unfashionable, two-bedroom bungalow near Paramount. Wally was still bringing in a small salary, but Florence and Ellen continued to contribute nothing to the upkeep, and not only was Susan paying the rent, she was beginning to find the lack of privacy suffocating. Finally, it all got too much for her.

According to Florence, "One day Susan came home and told my brother and me that she didn't want us to live there any more. She said she just wanted my mother to live with her. We asked why, but she wouldn't say why she wanted us to leave. My brother was working as an usher in a theater and took a bachelor apartment. So I went to live with friends—a man, his wife, and daughter." That seemed to defuse the situation. For a while...

Except for the mandatory twelve-week layoff (a studio contract guaranteed only forty weeks on salary), Susan earned her pay during most of 1940 by doing despised "cheesecake" layouts, either alone or with other young actors on the lot. Richard Webb, who came to Paramount at that time (and was under contract there for nine years) still retains vivid memories of those days:

"For years," says Webb today, "I had an 8 × 10 glossy of Susan and me modeling matching bathing suits around the pool of the Beverly Hills Hotel. In fact, publicity at one time had me engaged to Susan and [actress] Martha O'Driscoll simultaneously. I found Susan very interesting. I dug her.

"Sure, she was disliked by those who didn't have what she had and were jealous of her. They were, in fact, actually afraid of her. She was accused of snubbing people, of being aloof. I noted at times she would get within ten feet of me before saying hello. She would always apologize—but she had bad eyes and didn't want people to know.

"To my knowledge, she never hurt anyone on her climb. If she didn't like someone—or something—she stayed away from them—it. But she had a tremendous will, came on strong. She knew where she was going and wanted it *Now*."

Several years later, after she had left Paramount, Susan

would reflect on her behavior at that time:

"When I arrived at the studio, I had preconceived notions and stubbornly clung to the belief that they were right. I was a green kid, fresh at times, and it was probably that quality that made them see possibilities in me as an actress.

"I was pushed around in those years—so I spoke up. The studio kept referring to me as a promising young actress. What I wanted to know was—just *how* long could a girl be promising? I got the reputation of being, to put it politely, a wave-maker.

"People around the studio had told me that I should change, that my attitude was wrong. So, suddenly, overnight, I stopped being myself and tried to copy everyone else. As a result, I got so mixed up and was more confused than ever. Some people did try to straighten me out, but their approach was all wrong. A word of encouragement produced a glow inside—like good, fine wine. But mostly I was criticized. I guess it never occurred to anyone to find out why I behaved the way I did.

"Other girls were going right to the top while I got the parts no one else wanted. I was getting a good salary by then, but being basically an honest person, I felt like a fraud for accepting it.

"Things went from bad to bedlam."

❂ *chapter 5* ❂

ALTHOUGH her option had been picked up with a substantial pay increase, Susan felt she was languishing at Paramount. Approaching twenty-three, convinced that time was passing her by, she was determined to do something spectacular to make them sit up and take notice.

In mid-1940, as was its annual custom, Paramount invited its exhibitors to the coast for a week of lavish entertainment and screenings of future Paramount products, the whole affair to be climaxed by a gala luncheon attended by top studio brass and spiced by the presence of Paramount's major stars—Hope, Crosby, Goddard, and Colbert—as well as by current hopefuls. Each was to be introduced individually from a stage constructed especially for the occasion. Richard Webb recalls:

"Each speaker had a brief script prepared—the usual bromide thanking exhibitors for their past good work and expressing confidence in their future enthusiasm. Everyone followed the script. Everyone, that is, but Susan Hayward."

Sweetly, Susan made her way to the platform and, after taking a bow, exploded her bomb:

"Most of you gentlemen know me already. When I visited your hometowns you've been good enough to ask why I am not in more pictures. There's somebody here who can answer that question." She turned pointedly to Y. Frank Freeman and demanded:

"Mr. Freeman, will *you* tell these men why I'm not in pictures?"

This display of spunk brought the exhibitors to their feet whooping and hollering for more. Concealing fury and embarrassment with a tone of feigned amusement, Freeman announced, "Don't worry, friends, you'll be seeing Susan Hay-

ward in more movies." But you could tell he was gritting his teeth while he said it.

"That was a stupid thing for Susan to do," Medford insists today. "It only added to the executives' antagonism toward her. However, Paramount was planning some big airplane story, and Susan was perfect for the second female part. I did my best to persuade Freeman to test Susan for the role—she was physically perfect for it—and because there was no one else on the lot the right type, he agreed to the test. I felt sure this would be her big chance."

Unfortunately, according to Medford, "Her work was so amateurish the director suddenly stopped the cameras, snorted in disgust, and stamped off the set, leaving Susan standing there while the crew squirmed in embarrassment. Shortly afterward, Paramount found that other girl—the one with the hair falling all over her face—and she got the part."

The part Medford is referring to was that of Sally Vaughn, the siren of *I Wanted Wings*. It made an overnight star of Veronica Lake, although Lake herself was dismissed by the *New York Times* as a girl who "shows little more than a talent for wearing low-cut dresses." Immediately signed by Paramount, Lake would join Paulette Goddard on Susan's private hate list. She was convinced that both women were the cause of her career impasse. Ben Medford found it difficult to convince her that perhaps she was being her own worst enemy.

Nevertheless, Medford refused to falter in his belief that Susan could be a big star if she could only find the right part and land it. And shortly thereafter, thumbing through the script of *Adam Had Four Sons*, he thought he had found such a part. The story was about a man with—as the title says—four sons, and the beautiful governess who, years later, returns to the household, sure she is in love with the widowed Adam. She runs afoul of Adam's vicious daughter-in-law Hester Stoddard, however, who is married to one son and on the make for another, and it is not until the end that Hester is exposed for the bad lot she is and that Adam and the governess find a new life together. The role of Hester Stoddard seemed to be written with Susan in mind: "a hard-drinking, faithless little baggage who almost destroys the entire family and its governess... malicious and irresponsible. And gorgeous."

"Gregory Ratoff was a client of mine," continues Medford. "I begged him to persuade Harry Cohn to use Susan. I told

Susan, 'This is an important part, regardless of who plays it. The part will take care of you. It will stand out because you're playing a first-class bitch.'

"But first I had to convince Ratoff, who had to convince Cohn."

A few blocks up the street, mogul Harry Cohn was planning Columbia's major "class" production of 1941. Under his dictatorial management, the studio mainly turned out profitable potboilers, but Cohn still came through with one prestigious blockbuster a year. Thus the man who brought America *The Shadow, The Lone Wolf Strikes Back*, and *Blondie Goes Latin* was also responsible for such classics as *It Happened One Night, You Can't Take It with You, Lost Horizon, Mr. Deeds Goes to Town, Mr. Smith Goes to Washington*, and *The Awful Truth*, all but the last under the direction of Frank Capra.

Capra and Cohn had parted company after the completion of *Mr. Smith*, and the latter was now finding himself faced with the task of scoring a bull's-eye without his peerless director. Undaunted, he persuaded David O. Selznick to lend him Ingrid Bergman, who had made a spectacular American debut the previous year in *Intermezzo*, for the leading female role in *Adam Had Four Sons*. As Adam, he cast 1931 Oscar winner Warner Baxter, who'd signed with Columbia after a decade-long association with Twentieth Century-Fox. At forty-eight, Baxter had lost much of his early romantic appeal, but Cohn was convinced that one big hit would revive his faltering career. And as Adam's four sons, Cohn chose Richard Denning, Johnny Downs, Robert Shaw, and Cris Lind.

But what to do about the daughter-in-law, Hester Stoddard? The vixenish role seemed tailor-made for Paulette Goddard, but Cohn's bid for her services came too late. Goddard was committed to a loan-out to United Artists for *Pot of Gold*. So Freeman, not too altruistically, agreed to allow Medford to try to get Susan in the film. For Freeman, the loan-out to Columbia would serve a triple purpose: the studio would get good money for her services; if the picture was a hit and her reviews were satisfactory her price for future loan-outs would increase while her salary at Paramount stayed the same—and, most important, he'd have her out of his hair for a few months.

There was another aspect to the deal too, one that amused Freeman vastly. Once Susan had suffered the trauma of working for Harry Cohn, she was certain to return to her home

studio in a more compliant mood. Susan was looked upon as "untouchable" at Paramount—a real iceberg. For a girl as career-hungry as Susan, this attitude was incomprehensible to many of the people there. And no one cared enough to try to change it. With sex the cheapest commodity in town, many at Paramount felt a good roll in the hay was just what Susan needed.

Harry Cohn, to say the least, was not a man easily put off by any woman. His sexual exploits were legendary. According to the stories, newly signed starlets supposedly had to go through an "initiation" week of unspeakable physical indignities, not to mention liberal doses of his notoriously profane and abusive language. Dubbed White Fang by author Ben Hecht, Harry Cohn, noted Hedda Hopper caustically, "is a man you have to stand in line to hate."

Cohn reckoned without Susan Hayward, however. And Louella Parsons. Inexplicably, Louella Parsons was a rare Cohn supporter and he, in turn, would do nothing to jeopardize that fearsome lady's affection and friendship. When Louella learned her little Susan was set to work at Columbia, she lost no time informing Cohn of her motherly feelings toward the girl. Swallowing his frustration, Cohn promised to behave, and Susan sailed through the picture as virginal as ever.

Selznick was equally as protective of Ingrid Bergman, both personally and professionally. At first when he was approached by Cohn, Selznick had negative feelings about Bergman's doing *Adam Had Four Sons*—he'd rather have paid her salary himself than have her work for that man—but, as Bergman said, "I wanted to work and since it was the best thing available, I chose to do it." Overruled, Selznick made no bones about warning Cohn: Bergman must be accorded the utmost respect—or else!

Too shrewd to antagonize Selznick for what he politely termed "a piece of ass," Cohn kept his hands off her as well.

In a later interview, Susan would call the role of Hester Stoddard "one of my favorites." For Bergman, only ten months her senior, she had nothing but praise. When asked how the two of them were getting on, Susan replied, "She's been wonderful to me and just as concerned about the quality of my close-ups as she is with her own." For years to come Susan would cite Ingrid Bergman as "one of my favorite actresses." Still, although Susan held her in such high esteem and their

professional relationship was always cordial, the two of them never became close. Part of the reason was Susan's natural reserve. Part of it was that Bergman possessed the one quality Susan felt was sorely lacking in herself, no matter how hard she tried to fake it.

Bergman had "class."

Susan was less intimidated, however, by *Adam*'s director Gregory Ratoff, and the association that began with this film would develop into a lasting friendship. ("I don't think," says Ben Medford, "that Susan knew Ratoff wanted to fire her from the picture three times." Medford also scoffs at the legend that Ratoff's actress wife Eugenie Leontovich, who was coaching Susan in the role, threatened, "I will never sleep with you again if you don't use Susan in that part." "If that was true I would have known about it.")

Affectionately dubbed the Mad Russian by his peers, Ratoff's homely, bearlike exterior and heavily accented English was deceptive. Although he is best remembered today as an actor—his portrayal of Bette Davis's producer Max Fabian in *All About Eve*, for instance, is a classic—Ratoff was, in fact, a multi-talented writer, producer, and director as well. After his direction of *Intermezzo*, Bergman trusted him implicitly; within a few days after beginning *Adam*, Susan would too.

Although Ratoff would scream, "Susan, you are the most steenkeengest actress I've ever seen," whenever she muffed a scene, he was equally as emotional in his praise. "You are vunderrr-ful, marvoolooous," he would roar when he obtained the desired results. Susan flourished under his direction and between takes rushed to his side for additional advice and instructions. "She pestered the life out of him," says Medford. Sure she had made enormous strides under Ratoff, she was convinced that, once her bosses at Paramount saw a rough cut of the film, they would follow it up with an important assignment.

She had one particular picture in mind.

Writer Ketti Frings had just completed a beautiful script for Paramount titled *Hold Back the Dawn*, about the plight of European refugees stranded in Mexico while desperately trying to get into the United States. Charles Boyer was scheduled to play the irresistible heel who woos and wins a guileless school teacher for the sole purpose of getting across the border, before reluctantly falling in love with her. Olivia de Havilland was

set for the teacher—an ideal choice that would bring her another Oscar nomination.

There was a second feminine lead, however, the role of Boyer's wisecracking former dancing partner Anita Dixon, who gets them all in a pile of trouble. Three women at Paramount would have been perfect for the part: Paulette Goddard, Veronica Lake, and Susan.

Only Susan was readily available.

Sultry Veronica Lake was scheduled to appear in Preston Sturges's *Sullivan's Travels*, and Goddard was set to star with Bob Hope in *Nothing but the Truth*. As she waited for *Adam Had Four Sons* to open, Susan was free and clear. Besides, even though the role of Anita Dixon was a showy one, it was decidedly not of star caliber, and Susan thought it unlikely, not only that it would be offered to Goddard, but that Goddard would even want it.

Writer Cameron Shipp said: "Susan fought and scrounged for parts, but she never begged. She had a certain angry integrity. She demanded."

But when she demanded the role of Anita Dixon, Buddy De Sylva coldly informed her that Goddard's schedule had been rearranged to do this film as well as Hope's. Instead, he arranged another loan-out for Susan. She would be reporting to Republic studios to play Judy Canova's selfish, snotty cousin in *Sis Hopkins*. After getting third billing to Bergman and Baxter, Susan would be demoted to fifth—following Canova, singer Bob Crosby, character actor Charles Butterworth, and comedian Jerry Colonna.

Just the *threat* of being sent to Republic was enough to terrorize any major studio contract player. An actual loan-out to the studio was considered the proverbial kiss of death. Even a suspension or dropped option was preferable. Republic was a "poverty row" studio that had found gold in the North Hollywood hills with Gene Autry, Roy Rogers, and John Wayne westerns, but to the rest of the industry it was a necessary evil, useful only for feeding the tastes of the least discriminating audiences. If Paramount was hell-bent on punishing Susan for arrogance and temperamant, they couldn't have chosen a better way. But she went. She was miserable, frustrated, and angry, but she went. To her, as to Medford, her agent, "The most important thing was to keep working."

She reported to Republic, played her scenes under the inept

direction of Joseph Santley, remained aloof from the other members of the company, and left the instant the cameras stopped rolling. When her role in the picture was completed, she dismissed the entire episode from her mind.

Adam Had Four Sons was scheduled to open at Radio City Music Hall on March 28, 1941. Cohn was aware that *Adam*, dismissed by preview audiences as dreary domestic drama, needed all the help it could get. (In fact, when Susan finally got a chance to view the completed picture at a sneak preview, she forgot her early estimation of the film and blew up at Medford, "You've ruined my career!") Any excitement engendered by *Adam*'s being Bergman's "eagerly anticipated" second film was also dissipated when MGM rushed Bergman's third film, *Rage in Heaven*, into the New York Capitol exactly one week before the Music Hall opening. Always intimidated by Louis B. Mayer, Cohn could do little more than voice a meek protest.

Bergman, busy completing *Dr. Jekyll and Mr. Hyde*, was unavailable to publicize either film. Media interest in co-star Warner Baxter was nil.

Whatever Cohn's personal feelings toward Susan Hayward, he shrewdly calculated that her combination of Brooklyn background and dazzling looks would prove potent space-grabbers, so, with Paramount's blessings, Cohn made arrangements to fly her, and Florence again as chaperone, to New York. He put them up at the Waldorf, and told the East Coast publicity department to take it from there. In short, she was given star treatment. Susan was elated. Aside from the usual generous distribution of leg art, little had been done for her by Paramount publicity. The fan magazines (which she read secretly) seemed oblivious to her existence. Occasionally a magazine used a pinup shot, but by and large Paramount's fan magazine department made little or no effort to promote her.

The trip to New York for Cohn gave both Susan and *Adam Had Four Sons* some badly needed coverage.

On March 14, 1941, wearing an ill-fitting, rumpled beige suit, she checked into Manhattan's plush Art Deco Waldorf-Astoria. The hotel was just a few blocks from the Lexington Avenue cafeteria where she and Sara Little had once "talked endlessly about what we were going to do with our lives." To spend just one night at the Waldorf—the stopover for millionaires, movie stars, and royalty—had been part of that dream.

In 1937, Edythe Marrener would have been ecstatic with a $7-a-night single there. Now she commanded a suite facing Park Avenue.

Once installed, she obediently glided through the itinerary Columbia had carefully planned: one that ranged from the sublime—a sitting for the coveted cover of the *New York Sunday News* Coloroto section—to the highly ridiculous: a carefully rigged competition for "Presidency of the Perfect Legs Institute." Mostly, however, there were meetings with the press. As both a Brooklynite and a rejected Scarlett, Susan made good copy and a fine impression—"a refreshing relief from the dumb broads" usually foisted on them, one of them said—and so both Susan and the movie got plenty of ink.

When the reviews came out, they were encouraging too. Though the critics agreed with the preview audiences' estimation of the picture, they did like Susan. The *Dallas Morning News* noted that "little Susan Hayward, heretofore an also-ran at Paramount, gives it the works as the mischief-maker," and the *Richmond News-Leader* enthused: "Two unusually talented and charming women walk away with the entire picture. Ingrid Bergman as the gentle, loyal, fiercely devoted governess who would stain even her own name to save the honor of Adam's sons, is contrasted with Susan Hayward as the predatory and treacherous wife of one of them. Miss Hayward is stunning in the latter role, making it quite as outstanding as Miss Bergman's exemplary one." Only Bosley Crowther of the *New York Times*—initiating a love-hate relationship with Susan Hayward that would continue for more than a quarter of a century—was decidedly negative, writing that "Susan Hayward so coyly overacts the romantically unlicensed mischief-maker that often she is plain ridiculous."

Susan didn't care, though; she was riding high. Her first major reviews! Only one thing happened to dull her pleasure in the event—but when that came, it was a blockbuster.

Throughout her press sessions, the newsmen saw plenty of Susan, but never one glimpse of Florence. Whenever an interview was scheduled at the Waldorf, Florence was told to catch a movie or go shopping. Nor, when Susan was invited to an evening on the town, did she ask her host if he could include an extra man for her sister. Susan's resentment of Florence's apparently cavalier attitude toward the expenses had been smouldering for a long time. She felt she was being used,

and she could never jibe Flo's active social life with her own "ultraconventional" sensibilities. Besides, Flo was a living reminder of the Brooklyn past Susan was trying so hard to forget (even while she used it to gain hometown support), and on this trip in particular she wanted desperately to impress the press and movie people who were escorting her about—to have them think of her as Susan Hayward, movie star, not as Edythe Marrenner of the second-day bread and cardboard-soled shoes.

The explosion had been building up for a long time, and on the eve of their departure back to California, it broke. Florence later recalled it this way: she had invited people to the suite—relatives, she said—while Susan was out with some of her movie friends. When Susan got back that evening, however, and saw them, "she got very angry and asked them what they were doing there. And then she got mad at me because I had told them they could come over. I didn't see anything wrong in it. 'How can you *do* this to me?' she screamed. 'How can I entertain my friends when you have company? This is supposed to be a *business* trip for me.' She raved on and said a lot of things. I said a lot of things too. It was a terrible scene. I asked her what made her think her friends were so much more wonderful than her relatives. . . . The next morning she told me she was going to leave me in New York. . . . Looking back on it, I just think she asked me to go to New York because she wanted me to leave Hollywood."

Flo checked out of the Waldorf and went to Brooklyn to stay with friends, hoping her mother might be able to make peace in the family. Mrs. Marrenner was heartsick to learn of her daughters' falling-out and Flo's subsequent decision to remain in the East. After a futile attempt to affect a truce, Ellen Marrenner kept her own counsel. Wally, though working, was unmarried, and eligible for the army. Susan was responsible for her mother's support, and Ellen had no intention of jeopardizing that by becoming involved in a personal squabble. She advised Florence, then thirty-one, to try to find a nice boy and settle down; and a year later, Florence did just that, marrying an old beau named Udo Zaenglin at army headquarters in Spartanburg, South Carolina. As it later turned out, though, Florence's problems were just beginning.

Meanwhile, back in California, Susan was greeted with mild praise for having acquitted herself well on tour, and ordered to report to wardrobe for fittings for *Among the Living*,

an insignificant melodrama. Albert Dekker, the nominal star, was cast in the dual role of an upstanding millionaire and his psychotic twin. Susan had second billing as the daughter of the rooming-house owner—a predatory, money-hungry tramp completely taken in by the murderer during his more lucid moments. Frances Farmer, who a few years earlier had been one of Paramount's most promising young stars, was winding up her contract—billed fourth. The role misused her considerable talents and served as an example of how a major studio could destroy an actress who failed to conform to its standard of behavior.

Surprisingly, *Among the Living* won favor with the majority of the critics. The *New York Herald-Tribune*'s Howard Barnes said, "*Among the Living* is head and shoulders above most of the filler shows which are ground out by Hollywood to perpetuate the double feature system. Susan Hayward is especially good." The *New York Times, Variety*, and the *New York Post* also singled out Susan for special mention. Frances Farmer was generally ignored.

Susan's performance also won the attention of Cecil B. DeMille. After considering almost every sweet young thing on the lot, he cast her as Drucilla Alston, the tragic ingenue of his epic sea drama *Reap the Wild Wind*, starring, as luck would have it, Paulette Goddard. Goddard played the spirited owner of a salvage schooner whose hand is being fought over by a ship's company lawyer (Ray Milland) and an embittered sea captain (John Wayne). Convinced he has been double-crossed by Milland and Goddard, Wayne makes a deal with an evil salvage operator to wreck his own ship; but things go awry when Goddard's cousin (Susan)—who is also the girl of the salvage operator's brother—goes down with the ship. At the end, Wayne and Milland descend to the ocean depths, where the conflict is chillingly resolved.

Although it would be one of Cecil B. DeMille's most popular pictures, the filming left little impression on its huge cast, which also included Robert Preston and Raymond Massey. Even the director's biographer devoted his pages to the giant squid that swam off with most of the reviews. Constructed of bright red sponge rubber, its insides operated by electric motors and its thirty-foot tentacles a complex set of hydraulic, piston-operated cable, the monster deserved the attention it received.

It certainly got a great deal more attention than Susan, who

later said, "On the first day of shooting, I approached Mr. DeMille timidly. 'Excuse me, Mr. DeMille, but do you think that . . .'

"He cut me short, saying. 'I hired you for this film because I want an actress who can think for herself. Do that and you'll take a load of worry off my life and add years to your own.'"

Susan was charming in the picture, her death pivotal to the climax in which Milland and Wayne descend to the wrecked ship and find her shawl . . . just before the giant squid finds them. Seen on television today, it is still a rousing adventure.

Susan's next film encounter with Goddard came when director George Marshall pitted them against one another for the affections of Fred MacMurray in *The Forest Rangers*. Shooting started in March 1942 on location in Santa Cruz, California.

The film, which received mediocre reviews, does not merit description, but one incident does: Susan very nearly drowned during the filming. A log jam on which she was standing broke up, and she was hurled into eight feet of water, among swirling lengths of lumber. Five studio workers plunged in to rescue her and only succeeded in sending her down again, before Roy Mowrer, a thirty-year-old scaler for a lumber company, pulled her out.

She ignored a bad lump on her head and was back on the set the next morning.

In a letter later sent film historian Doug McClelland, Marshall noted how much Susan had impressed him during that hazardous location shooting, and explained why:

> Her courage turned up on *The Forest Rangers* in the part where she and Paulette Goddard had to run through some fire. Paulette was frightened, and in spite of our showing her all the safety factors and how impossible it was for her to be injured or burned, she still backed off and started to cry. I really think that she had a date and wanted to get off early. Susan came up to me and whispered, "Get the cameras going." Then she went over to Paulette, as though to comfort her. When I gave her the signal, she grabbed Paulette by the hand and said, "For God's sake, stop being such a baby!" and pushed her through the scene. Ironically, in the story it was Susan who was supposed to become frightened.
>
> As an actress she was one of the best, because her emotions stemmed from the inside and were not just the

mouthings of an inadequate actress who reads lines without the slightest idea of what they mean. Susan knew her craft. She had sincerity and courage, and at times would be a bit stubborn, but not to the point of being disagreeable.

Susan was obviously beginning to learn her trade. Nevertheless, her career still seemed to be stalling, her next two films doing little for her: Rene Clair's *I Married a Witch* with Fredric March and Veronica Lake, in which Susan unhappily played yet another nasty role—March's fiancée—and an insignificant "B" film called *Young and Willing*, adapted from a moderate Broadway hit called *Out of the Frying Pan*. *Young and Willing* mainly served as a showcase for Paramount's young contract players: Susan had billing in a cast that included William Holden, Eddie Bracken, James Brown, Barbara Britton, and, from the Broadway original, Florence MacMichael.

Both films, curiously enough, though shot on the Paramount lot, with Paramount players, were released through United Artists, in a complicated arrangement that confused many at the time. With the war cutting off a steady flow of European-made films, United Artists was in desperate need of products to fulfill contractual obligations to its exhibitors, so Paramount, with a huge backlog of films awaiting release, agreed to sell them *I Married a Witch* and *Young and Willing*. In the latter case, at least, it was apparently with few regrets.

Paramount had even fewer regrets when they shipped Susan back to Republic for the female lead in what that poverty-row studio considered their musical extravanganza of the year, *Hit Parade of 1943*.

❀ chapter 6 ❀

IT WAS DURING the filming of *Hit Parade of 1943*, in November 1942, that Susan became romantically involved with a leading man for the first—and only—time in her life.

Speaking about her shortly before his death from leukemia in April 1979, John Carroll, at age seventy-two, remembered: "She was something, even back then. I knew a great many lovely ladies in my lifetime, and I can safely say I met my match in that determined little redhead."

For Susan, that was no mean accomplishment. Carroll, born in New Orleans with the poetic name of Julian LaFaye, left home at the age of twelve seeking adventure; and presumably he found it as he became, successively, a steeplejack, barnstorming pilot, range rider, and ship's cook, finally ending up in Italy, where, he claimed, he studied voice with a man named Victor Chesnais. No one was ever sure how much of this was the truth.

In the late twenties he obtained free passage back to America by signing on to conduct a luxury liner's band; migrated first to Florida, then to California; then, after knocking around as an extra for a couple of years, got a role in a 1934 "B" quickie called *Hi Gaucho*. By that time he had fallen in love with a fiery Hungarian dancer-actress, Steffi Duna, married her, and fathered a daughter, Julianna. (The marriage was short-lived, and the first Mrs. Carroll went on to a lasting union with actor Dennis O'Keefe.) Generally disliked in Hollywood social circles, considered a liar, a bounder, and an egomaniac, Carroll still managed to get signed by MGM in 1939. He was convinced he possessed the rugged appeal of Clark Gable, to whom he was frequently compared, plus the strong baritone voice of Nelson Eddy. Eddy's marriage earlier in the year had been

looked upon with disfavor in official circles, and Louis B. Mayer felt it expedient to have another masculine singer-actor waiting in the wings. Despite an inglorious MGM debut in *Congo Maisie*, one reporter commented, "It's practically a natural that John Carroll is going to become Hollywood's next BIG star—that is, if Hollywood and John Carroll can stand each other that long. At the moment neither the town nor Carroll are at all sure at this point."

Carroll's career at MGM was similar to Susan's at Paramount. He was cast in romantic leads in "B's" and supporting roles in major films, and was habitually loaned out to lesser studios in an attempt to deflate his gigantic ego and punish him for his transgressions. Neither Gable nor Eddy considered him much of a threat. Although selected as a male "Star of Tomorrow," together with Van Heflin, Eddie Bracken, and Alan Ladd, in the 1941–42 *Motion Picture Herald* poll of movie exhibitors, whatever charisma he may have had was not given the chance to register on screen. Off-screen, however, he knocked women dead. Much to MGM's distress, he was often linked with some "ladies" of rather dubious repute—among them Virginia Hill, alleged to be the former moll of mobster Bugsy Siegel. Studio pressure put an end to that association in record time. In mid-1942, Carroll, at loose ends and awaiting induction into the air force, was sent back to Republic for what they considered their two most important pictures of the year: *Flying Tigers* (in which he was billed second to John Wayne) and *Hit Parade of 1943* (for which he got top billing).

The story of the latter was all fluff and nonsense: a young songwriter (Susan) has had her song stolen by the owner of a minor music publishing company (Carroll), and within the course of some ninety minutes falls in love with the charming heel. So much for plot. The Ray McKinley, Freddy Martin, and Count Basie bands were dragged in to provide most of the music. Carroll's baritone was heard to moderate advantage, and Susan "mouthed" her songs to the prerecording made by a now-forgotten vocalist.

Wanda Hale in the *New York Daily News* would comment: "In trying so hard to make *Hit Parade of 1943* a gorgeous musical spectacle, the producers have only made a wasteful, trying picture." Second-stringer Tom Pryor of the *New York Times*, though, was less critical, noting, "Republic wisely put forth a modestly backgrounded potpourri of songs, dances, and

romance in a comedy vein—in short, a pleasant and unpretentious entertainment : . . a musical package not too gaudy but all
right." Pryor, however, rather gullibly added: "But it was a bit
surprising to learn that Susan Hayward can include singing
among [her] accomplishments."

During most of the shooting, Susan, as usual, kept her
relationship with Carroll on an exclusively professional basis.
He later reported: "Susan continued to act as if I didn't exist
when we were away from the camera. However, I dismissed
her as one of those super-serious actresses who had to keep
the on-screen emotions going after the director called cut, and
the script called for her to dislike me intensely."

Then, however, something happened. The final days of
shooting centered around a scene early in the script—a rather
intense fight between the two principals, and Carroll remembered: "I was embarrassed to find myself with a perpetual
erection. And Susan suddenly was more communicative between takes. When we wound up the picture, I asked if she'd
celebrate the occasion with me by having dinner. After that
first evening we became what columnists refer to as 'an item.'
Few, however, expressed much interest in us at the time, and
when we dated, we stayed away from photographer-frequented
places, at Susan's insistence. She obviously didn't want anyone
to call us a publicity gimmick."

Although uncertain about the depth of his feelings, Carroll
could not deny that he was totally fascinated with Susan. The
ruthlessly ambitious actress he had worked with on *Hit Parade
of 1943* bore little resemblance to the quaintly old-fashioned
girl he was dating.

"Susan," he'd later tell a friend, "considered a kiss a commitment and anything beyond that a marriage proposal." He
never boasted of going beyond a kiss but, during the Christmas
holidays of 1943, a few days before leaving for active duty in
the air force, he asked Susan to marry him. ("Susan was a
virgin when she was dating Carroll," comments Ben Medford.
"And she was a virgin when she broke their engagement. The
only way he could get her into bed was to marry her!")

Ellen Marrenner was far from pleased by the news. Carroll
was ten years older than Susan, divorced and burdened with
the responsibility of supporting both a young child and a mother
living in his house. A rumor also had it that Carroll was deeply
in debt to Republic's president Herbert Yates. Carroll's mother

Emma LaFaye, an attractive, white-haired Southern lady, took an equally dim view. She felt John could do better for himself than a Yankee starlet.

Although she did not break the news to the press, Susan considered herself engaged. Before Carroll took off, Wally remembers, "He told Susan to pick out a ring and send him the bill." On Valentine's Day they'd notify their respective studios. No wedding date was set, however, and if Carroll had any misgivings about his decision, at least there were no immediate pressures.

Susan spent the next few days on a grand tour of the Beverly Hills jewelry establishments, finally settling on a perfect 4½ carat diamond—the most beautiful ring she had ever seen. "My sister was no dummy," Wally adds. "She picked out the most expensive ring she could find. She told me, 'If he really wants to marry me, he'll buy me that ring.'" (Echoes of the young Edythe Marrenner, troubled over her mother's lack of an engagement ring.)

When Carroll called from his base that night, she excitedly described it to him in detail. His reaction was neither excited nor amused. He was, in fact, furious about the size of the ring, and its price—especially the price. Predictably, a heated argument ensued. By the time the phone conversation had ended, so had the engagement.

The next day, Susan returned to the jewelers and paid for the ring herself. She told everyone it was a Christmas present from her mother.

Louella Parsons happily wrote, "I talked with Susan Hayward the other afternoon, and she is all over her John Carroll infatuation. She is wearing a diamond ring—a gift from her mother. I suspect she received it after she said adieu to John as a reward." Ed Sullivan had his own suspicions when he noted: "Since the Susan Hayward and John Carroll romance is off so quickly, I'm beginning to believe that it was a dream-up by Republic. Susan isn't a bit upset."

In truth, she wasn't.

Ellen Marrenner, convinced that Susan had never been in love with John, told her: "I think you wanted an engagement ring, not an engagement."

Years later when Susan told the "true" story about the ring and the engagement, Carroll would be identified only as "an actor who was in the army." It didn't matter. By that time

Carroll was a forgotten man in films. (His name would later make the papers when a court insisted he return $180,000 to an eighty-year-old woman who claimed he had bilked her out of a considerable fortune.)

Buying that diamond herself may have been the best investment Susan ever made, and she had no trouble erasing Carroll completely from her mind. Wally Marrenner does note, however, that in his possession is a photo of the three of them taken on the set of *Hit Parade*. "Susan had a habit of writing little remarks on photos. On the one I have, she put 'the kid' above me, 'dog meat' above John Carroll's head."

Although Paramount had heard good things about Susan's work in *Hit Parade*, they once again refused to consider her for one of their more important pictures of the year, *So Proudly We Hail*, the story of an army nurse trapped in the South Pacific during the invasion of Bataan and Corregidor. Claudette Colbert was set for the lead, but there were two other major roles for which Susan could have been considered: the sexy, wise-cracking Joan O'Doul and the brooding Olivia D'Arcy, out to avenge the death of her fiancé at Pearl Harbor. Not surprisingly, the roles went to Paulette Goddard and Veronica Lake.

By now Susan was counting the months until her contract finally ran out. She was no longer mystified by Paramount's practice of regularly renewing her options and raising her salary. One loan-out arranged by Medford would cover her salary for a year—the rest was sheer profit for Paramount. It was a no-lose situation for the studio, a no-win deal for Susan. She felt like an indentured slave. If she screamed, she was labeled "bitch" or worse. If she complied docilely, there were no rewards. All she could do was wait and try to build her name as a personality and, hopefully, as an actress. But at twenty-six, she felt she couldn't wait too long.

With no new pictures scheduled, she boarded a train east and arrived in New York on Washington's Birthday to do advance publicity for *Hit Parade of 1943*. The picture was not due to open until April 16, but Republic, grateful to get her, picked up her tab for the first three weeks. On March 19, she garnered an additional thousand dollars by starring on Charlie Martin's "Phillip Morris Playhouse." More importantly, on March 17, she got the opportunity to attend King Features' Banshee luncheon in honor of Barry Faris and Pat Robinson of International News Service, who had recently returned from

the South Pacific fighting fronts.

The invitation from King Features Syndicate was welcome, because leading editors and publishers attended these annual luncheons, and they offered a rich opportunity to get publicity without having to pose in bathing suits labeled "Wild Wind" or endure the indignities of accepting contrived titles such as "Titianette Queen" or, as Susan would later quip, "'Miss Everything' except 'Miss Take.'"

Beyond that, it meant dignified recognition of her success in her hometown—she thought.

Columnist Leonard Lyons, who attended the Banshee luncheon, commented, "Miss Hayward might just as well have remained in Hollywood. For she was introduced at the luncheon as 'Rita Hayward,' and the only news photo she posed for— a photo showing her kissing Sgt. Carl Hickman, one of the Marine Corps' heroes of Guadalcanal—was ordered censored by the Marine Corps as being undignified."

Not quite. One photo managed to make it into the *Daily Mirror* the next day; but, more importantly, the impact Susan made on the attending publishers would serve her in good stead in the years to come.

To Susan's astonishment, she was recognized and fussed over wherever she went, despite the dark prescription glasses she wore to enable her to see farther than a foot ahead. Watching a new building under construction on Sixth Avenue, she was besieged by blowtorch operators who wanted her to autograph everything from a helmet to a scrap of paper that had blown onto the site. To a public oblivious of the power plays at Paramount or the punishing demotions and loans, she was a *star*. Autograph hunters waited en masse outside the Phillip Morris broadcast and oohed and aahed when she left the theater. A friend of Charlie Martin's who was there that night recalls:

"Susan's prettiness in films was always obvious. But she was absolutely breathtaking the night Charlie had her on the show. She wore very little make-up—radio didn't require any, of course—and her skin had an almost translucent quality. Now, Charlie was a charmer in those days. He managed to get all the top glamour girls on the program—Turner, Hayworth, you name it. And they were all crazy about him.

"He could have any girl he wanted for the asking, and he usually dated the stars he had on his show—at least once— even if she had a lover back in Hollywood. Hayward, however,

was all business. She did the show, returned for the rebroadcast
for the West Coast, and went home alone. I guess you can say
she was the one who got away."

(A few years later, Charlie Martin was the one who got
away when Betty Hutton prematurely shouted the news of their
engagement from a stage in Madison Square Garden. Mortified, he never saw her again.)

Since Paramount was in no hurry to have her back, Susan
went on a brief war-bond selling tour before returning to Hollywood in early April. After having been treated like a star for
the nearly two months she'd been away, she bristled at the
indifferent treatment accorded her once she was back on the
lot. De Sylva told her she had been penciled in for both the
female lead in an implausible thriller called *The Man in Half
Moon Street* and the role of Loretta Young's selfish kid sister
in *And Now Tomorrow*. Eventually, she was replaced by Helen
Walker in the former, and the latter was delayed pending Alan
Ladd's return from service. She waited . . . and waited. . . .

Two months later, she was handed the script of *Standing
Room Only*. Once again she'd have to appear as a bitchy society
girl. Once again she'd have to compete with Paulette Goddard
for Fred MacMurray's affections—and come off second best.
It was the same old story—but this time she refused to do it.
Storming into De Sylva's office, ablaze with anger, she told
him what he could do—with his script, Goddard, and the remaining two years of her contract.

As usual, Louella Parsons came to her defense. In her column of August 7, 1943, Louella sympathized: "We don't blame
Susan Hayward for walking out of the cast of Paramount's
Standing Room Only. . . . Her role was much too small for her
talent—much of the footage going to Paulette Goddard, Fred
MacMurray, and Roland Young. Susan claims the studio had
promised her bigger and better roles."

After Parsons's item, bigger but not necessarily better roles
were forthcoming, though not at Paramount. Happy to get "that
ambitious bitch" out of his office, his life, and his now-thinning
hair, De Sylva permitted Medford to make a trio of loan-out
deals for her services: to United Artists for *Jack London* ("I
got her $15,000 under the table for the London film. When
Paramount found out, I was almost barred from the lot"), to
Republic again for *The Fighting Seabees* (opposite John
Wayne), and back to United Artists for a bastardized version

of Eugene O'Neill's *The Hairy Ape*, opposite William Bendix.

Susan breezed through the first two films without either incident or notable display of temperament (or notable reviews, for that matter). For the third, she got some of the best notices of her career. Even though the *New York Daily Mirror* commented cattily during the shooting of *The Hairy Ape* that "Susan Hayward is a darling, but couldn't be more unlike Carlotta Monterey O'Neill, who created the femme lead in *The Hairy Ape* on Broadway," when the picture was released the following July, the critics were united in praise.

Said *Time* magazine: "Susan Hayward, as the girl who drives him [Bendix] crazy, is much tougher—too coarsely so for the size of the girl's penthouse or the height of her social standing—but she is more convincing. She is, in fact, Hollywood's ablest bitch-player."

The *New York Herald-Tribune*'s Otis L. Guernsey, Jr., noted: "Susan Hayward is appropriately hateful as the empty-minded rich girl who is frightened by the animalistic world of the stokehold. She achieves a good deal of villainy in spite of a wealth of corny dialogue that has been included in her scenes." And even the often-sour *New York Times* commented, "Miss Hayward...contributes her full share to the picture."

Susan was understandably delighted—maybe *now* somebody would take notice—but for once, though, she did not have all her attention on her career. Surprising even herself, she found she had far more pressing matters on her mind....

She had just begun work on *The Hairy Ape* in late November when, one Friday night, she decided to drop by the Hollywood Canteen. The canteen was a recreational facility sponsored by Bette Davis to provide a place where lonely servicemen adrift in Los Angeles (usually before embarking for combat in the South Pacific) could spend an evening in the company of lovely, carefully picked hostesses, munch donuts and sandwiches, and be entertained by those top names in Hollywood who felt obliged to do their bit for our fighting men.

Susan was a canteen regular and usually broke up the place with her sure-fire "Anyone here from Brooklyn?" opener. Though she danced with the servicemen, however, she rarely fraternized with her fellow performers and always went home alone.

On this November Friday night, Jess Barker, a twenty-nine-year-old Broadway actor who had just completed two films at

Columbia, was serving as master of ceremonies. Impulsively, he asked Susan to join him for coffee after the canteen had closed for the night—and impulsively, she accepted.

When he tried to kiss her goodnight at her door, she slapped him hard across his face.

Three months later, he asked her to marry him.

❆ chapter 7 ❆

SOMETHING STRONG pulled Susan and Jess together. Something more powerful pulled them apart. From the beginning, they were a mismatched pair, drawn to one another by an overwhelming physical attraction that blinded them to their psychological incompatibility. It would take them nine long years to find that out.

After her experience with John Carroll, Susan had sworn off actors. "I said over and over," she told friends, "I'd never marry an actor. No woman in her right mind would marry an actor. I didn't even want to date one. But after I met Jess..."

That first evening, after playing hard to get, she refused Jess's calls for a week because, she admitted, "I thought he'd be intrigued by such behavior." Susan was nonetheless determined to see him again: "I found out where Jess was likely to be and was there at the same time. Of course, I chased him. Why not? I knew two weeks after I had met Jess that I wanted to marry him."

To her surprise and delight, she learned that her old friend and mentor Gregory Ratoff had been responsible for Jess's return to Hollywood.

Few people were aware that he had even been there before—it was never mentioned in any story or studio biography—but "I came out here in 1935," Barker reveals today. "You know how I got my first screen contract? Leland Hayward, then an agent, signed me, and Walter Wanger brought me to the coast under the name of *Philip* Barker. That's how I got into *The Trail of the Lonesome Pine*, the first outdoor color picture. I played one of the heavies—the youngest son in the Fallin family. Robert Barrett was my father.

"Then I went back to Broadway in *You Can't Take It With*

You. I worked a lot of stock. I worked with . . . well, just go down the line."

In September 1942, Mrs. B. P. Schulberg, the producer's wife, saw a performance of *Magic*, starring Eddie Dowling, but she found her attention riveted on Barker. To Mrs. Schulberg, the handsome young blond looked like movie material. She arranged what was known as "an interview test," cameras rolling as Gregory Ratoff chatted informally with Barker.

"Wait and see," Ratoff shouted to everyone within earshot. "Theese is the only one with talent. If Cohn doesn't sign him, I will." He didn't have to. The test was mailed to Harry Cohn on a Friday. By the following Friday, contracts had been drawn up. When *Magic* proved a misnomer at the box office, Jess left for Hollywood.

Due to Alan Ladd's phenomenal success earlier that spring in *This Gun for Hire*, blond actors were now being sought instead of spurned by filmmakers, and "I was called a tall Alan Ladd," Barker laughs. "I never could work with him because I was six inches taller than he was."

Two months after being signed by Columbia, Barker was given a role in *Good Luck, Mr. Yates*, with Claire Trevor, but after that Harry Cohn, more interested in the careers of his leading ladies than in male contractees, let Barker cool his heels for a while. In August 1943, though, RKO borrowed him for the movie, *Government Girl*, with Olivia de Havilland and Sonny Tufts, and Barker acquitted himself so well that Columbia moved to assure him that he had a future with them. The studio cast him in Rita Hayworth's *Cover Girl*. His role, Otto Kruger as a young man, was limited to flashback sequences and offered little opportunity for Jess to prove himself, but he registered sufficiently to evoke a good amount of fan mail, a promise of the male lead in *Jam Session*, and the interest of other studios whose contract lists had been decimated by the draft.

Barker, exempt from service by an overrapid heartbeat, had three brothers serving as sergeants in the army. Self-conscious about his 4-F classification, he spent almost all his free evenings working at the Hollywood Canteen. "It's old hat to some people," he explained, "but it's little enough for me to do."

A profile released at the time noted: "The Greenville, South Carolinian lives alone in a small Hollywood apartment, has all

his meals out, drives a little blue roadster, enjoys every kind of music, and keeps up with current books, thinking of them in terms of plays and movies."

The sketch went on to reveal that, although Jess was "blessed with a facile tongue and sense of humor, he never keeps letters or is sentimental about anything. He never kills a fly or a moth and reports that consequently he has never been bothered by them."

"That was true," Barker confirms. "It's still true. When a fly comes in and it drives me crazy, I just open the door and out it goes."

During his first year in Hollywood, Jess Barker was linked with so many starlets that when a friend from New York asked whom he was going out with that week, he replied, "That seems to depend on which newspaper you read." In fact, at the time he met Susan, Jess was reported to be engaged to Nina Foch, a twenty-year-old Columbia contract player.

"*Almost* engaged," Jess corrects.

Despite her intellectual European and theatrical background, though, Foch was outclassed by the Brooklyn redhead ("Susan called Nina 'the toothless wonder,'" Ben Medford recalls), and Foch did not take it lightly. "Nina was a great girl," says Barker. "Yet when I went off with Susan she destroyed all my clippings, ripped them to pieces."

Susan did something similar. Once she started dating Jess, she insisted that his little black book be thrown out with the morning trash. He'd see her exclusively or not at all. He saw her exclusively.

Their names began being paired in gossip columns: "Jess Barker and Susan Hayward a newsome-twosome at Perino's," or "Susan Hayward and Jess Barker cheek-to-cheeking at Mocambo." However—remembering the John Carroll fiasco of the previous year, and Susan's bitter disclaimers about actors—few gave the items any significance. After all, Jess was not only an actor, he was a Southerner, like Carroll—one would have supposed Susan would have been turned off by that combination forever.

It was precisely that Southern background, however, that proved so irresistible to Susan. She had never forgotten her dream of the courtly Southern gentleman, the gracious mansion life. If Carroll had fancied himself the second coming of Rhett

Butler and acted accordingly, Barker was in the Ashley Wilkes tradition—passive, gentle, a man with dreams—even if he didn't actually have a mansion.

In fact, the Barkers of Greenville were as poverty-stricken as the Marrenners of Brooklyn had been. Jess's mother Miss Winnie worked as a baby's nurse after the death of his father, a former railroad-yard worker. As with Susan, his genteel poverty was a trap from which Barker was determined to escape. He remembered well being jilted as a youth by a young woman with whom he had fancied himself in love. The girl had told him disdainfully, "Where are you going to get the money to support a wife?"

He had been convinced he'd get it up north. After a few months at the Theodora Irvine School for the Theater and a season in summer stock in New England, he'd made his Broadway debut in *Allure* in 1934. In the next ten years, he'd lost his Southern accent, but not his Southern manner—and, whatever her experiences with Southerners, Susan's affinity with them was almost magnetic.

By the time Susan and Jess started seeing each other on a regular basis, Alan Ladd was out of the army, and Paramount could finally make *And Now Tomorrow*, a pallid film that did neither Ladd nor Hayward any good. By now, Susan's Paramount pact had only a year to go, and she was counting the days until it was over—a feeling that was only intensified by what happened next. The studio informed her that it was loaning her to Benedict Bogeaus, an independent producer working with United Artists, for a highly dramatic role in *Dark Waters*, a chiller-thriller with psychological overtones set in a Louisiana bayou. That seemed promising, until one morning, idly browsing through the Hollywood trade papers, Susan spotted a brief news item in *Variety:* "Merle Oberon was signed yesterday to star in *Dark Waters.*"

By noon, ugly rumors had reached her through the grapevine that Buddy De Sylva wanted to teach her a lesson and consequently would not hold Bogeaus to the loan-out agreement. When she finally got to see De Sylva, he didn't bother refuting the gossip. He told her bluntly that she had been rude and snippy to stars and directors and ungrateful to the studio for the opportunities they had given her to earn while learning how to become an actress.

"In short, Susan," he concluded, "you've been a first-class bitch."

Paradoxically, the studio did not want to release her before her contract ran out. They were privately negotiating with her new agent Charles Feldman to keep her on at a considerable increase.

"This was very ironic," says Medford, "because Susan walked out on me when Feldman promised her that if she signed with his agency he'd personally get her a release from the studio. My personal contract with Susan had another year to go. I could have sued, but what the hell, you get to expect these things in this business." ·

For Susan, her remaining time under the old contract was tantamount to a jail sentence—with no time off for good behavior. The news of Paulette Goddard's supporting Oscar nomination for *So Proudly We Hail* only strengthened Susan's determination to put Paramount and everyone associated with it out of her life . . . for good.

In early February 1944, exhausted by work and the continuing hassles with the studio, Susan fell apart; her doctor ordered four weeks of complete rest. During this period, Jess was a pillar of strength, a comforting shoulder upon which to cry. By the end of the month, he had impulsively proposed marriage.

That was exactly what Susan wanted, though Jess wasn't 100 percent sure it was what *he* wanted. *Cover Girl* was going into release in March, and Columbia was planning a publicity buildup designed around bachelor Barker. Jess was told, not too subtly, that marriage to *anyone* would "damage your popularity with the bobby-soxers." Harry Cohn raged, "Of all the girls in the world, Barker had to get involved with that Hayward bitch."

Still holding a grudge because of his own problems with her during *Adam Had Four Sons*, Cohn's hostilities were aggravated by a paranoid conviction that Hayward was getting a free ride on the Hayworth name. The fact that Barker was coming out in a Hayworth spectacular compounded his annoyance. Unceremoniously, he decided to drop Jess's option and privately cursed Gregory Ratoff, who had now defected to Twentieth Century-Fox, for inflicting Barker upon him.

Only the romantic Russian was genuinely pleased that his

two self-appointed protégés had found one another. He beamed his approval when Susan promised, "We'll name our first son after you."

Ellen Marrenner, relieved when Susan had broken her engagement to Carroll the previous year, had forebodings about Jess. He was an actor. Actors were notorious skirt-chasers, and she feared Susan would endure the same humiliations she had suffered as a young girl with her feckless fellow student at the Feagin Drama School. She was also convinced that Jess was in no financial position for matrimony. With Florence's marriage rocky—Florence was living with her mother again in California with her baby son Larry; Zaenglin's peripatetic army life hadn't agreed with her—Ellen Marrenner was less than ecstatic when Susan told her, "Mom, I'm going to marry Jess Barker."

"I'll believe it when I see the ring," Ellen said. She didn't know Susan had already picked one out—Susan had never been slow with rings—this time in a cocktail-style setting consisting of diamond chips and emeralds.

As it turned out, Ellen Marrenner had some just cause for concern. Within days, the pattern began: the ring was being sized when the engagement was abruptly called off after a quarrel that, Susan claimed, had something to do with Jess's failure to show up for a dinner date. With her mother's warnings echoing in her ears, Susan was convinced that Jess was out with Nina Foch. An explanatory telegram from him placated her, but within a few weeks the fights began again.

The battles were over everything and nothing. One day Susan tossed a gold cigarette lighter—a gift from a former girl friend of his—into the Pacific Ocean. One night he poured all the perfume he had given Susan down the bathroom sink. Another time, the ring went back to the jewelers; by the time the two had made up and Jess had gone to retrieve it, it had been sold. Not being able to find another one either of them liked as much, they decided to forget about a ring. All this time, they continued seeing each other exclusively, but were hesitant about setting a date. Susan came up with a dozen rationalizations for her own temperamental outbursts, but it was Jess's indecisiveness that was at the root of her problems.

In June 1944, uncertain about her professional future and relationship with Jess, Susan was persuaded to attend a mammoth dinner party honoring Clark Gable's return to civilian

life. Actress Jan Clayton, Gable's date for the evening, rec-
ollects that Gable was attentive and affable to her, but "then
Susan Hayward walked in and his attention was gone. Susan
had an intense way of looking at men that was universally
misinterpreted. It wasn't sex; she was terribly myopic. She
was trying to *find* them. When I mentioned after that party that
Clark had stared at her all evening, she said, 'He *was*? Why
didn't somebody *tell* me?' "

Gable, thinking he had been rebuffed, made no attempt to
get Susan's number. If he had, it wouldn't have done him
much good. A few weeks after the Gable party, she and Jess
finally decided to marry.

This time it was no impulse. Jess had finally decided he
was ready, and by now, Susan had endured nine stormy months
of their off-again, on-again affair. If she had stuck with it this
long, she was convinced she really was in love with Jess Barker. Convinced too that her mother was dumping her own
fixations on her, she dismissed Ellen Marrenner's nagging suspicion that Jess couldn't cope with the responsibilities that went
along with marriage. It was time for Susan's dream to come
true.

Of course, there might have been another element involved
in the decision as well. Ben Medford reveals an astonishing
fact: "Ellen Marrenner was violently opposed to the marriage.
In fact, she called me and asked me if I could locate an abortionist."

An abortionist! Prim and proper Susan had finally been
persuaded into bed—and now she was pregnant. If anyone
thought she was going to allow *that* situation to remain without
the sanction of marriage, they were mistaken.

At the same time, Susan refused to abort. Jess was the first
and only man she had had an affair with in her life. She was
sure they could be happy.

Nevertheless, on July 22, Susan did an extraordinary thing
for a bride who was neither princess nor heiress (her yearly
income was now $26,000). She had an attorney draw up an
airtight agreement, attested to by a notary public, irrevocably
separating her income and properties from Jess Barker's.

Susan later claimed she did this to make her marriage safe,
pointing out that it was usually the man who benefited when
the community property clause was waived. Maybe it hadn't
occurred to her, or to Jess, that a legal distinction between

"thine" and "mine"—or an insistence that they both keep possession of their own apartments "until we find a house big enough for the two of us"—was not the most passionate way to warm a wedding bed.

Indeed, Susan at twenty-seven looked far from radiant after she and Jess exchanged marriage vows on July 24, 1944. Publicists Henry Rogers and Jean Pettebone were the only attendants. "Miss Winnie" Barker was unable to make the trip from Atlanta, where she was working as a nurse, to meet her new daughter-in-law; and although Ellen Marrenner attended the ceremony, she was not identified in the wedding pictures released to the press. Sister Florence would later say, bitterly, "I didn't go, because Susan didn't invite me."

Immediately after the wedding, the Barkers left for a brief honeymoon at Rancho Santa Fe, near San Diego.

Theirs may have been one of the briefest honeymoons on record. Within two months, the pregnant bride was seeing her lawyer.

❈ PART THREE ❈

Mrs. Jess Barker

Hollywood
July 24, 1944—April 26, 1955

I married for security and love. I didn't get either. I married a man who wasn't in love with me. I did everything I knew to make the marriage work. Then I had to spill my personal life from coast to coast to keep my sons. I'm a divorcée, and I never wanted to be divorced.

SUSAN HAYWARD, *1955*

After all, I've only been married once. So I must have been in love with somebody.

JESS BARKER, *January 19, 1980*

❈ chapter 8 ❈

As a LOVER, Jess proved gentle and considerate, undoubtedly a decided contrast to John Carroll who, according to impeccable sources, "treated all women as if they were concubines, out-Flynned Errol, and had a decided appetite for the more erotic and exotic aspects of sex."

Nevertheless, during the initial weeks of Susan's marriage, they had troubles sexually—she was "cold as a polar bear," Jess would later say. Susan felt guilty about the premature pregnancy, which only added to her guilt feelings about sex in general—attitudes that had been deeply instilled in her since childhood. Even wedlock could not shake them. They created an emotional turmoil that prevented her from enjoying sex to its fullest. It wasn't Jess's fault, it wasn't hers. Ellen Marrenner had done her job all too well. It was not an auspicious beginning.

Neither was the house situation: the Barkers spent most of August house-hunting, but could find nothing in their price range. Susan was appalled at the cost of even the most modest dwelling. Consequently, they took turns living in one of their two apartments.

Jess had made few friends—other than female—since coming to Hollywood; Susan felt she had none. The Barkers were given no bridal showers, no dinners, no spate of parties. They lived in a vacuum of their own making. Both insisted they hated big parties. Still, when Ann Rutherford and her husband David May invited them to a Saturday night bash at their home on September 17, they were glad enough to go—unfortunately. For, as it turned out, it was a bash that turned into a headlined brawl.

Lana Turner and her current lover Turhan Bey were on the

star-studded guest list, and so was Turner's former husband Steve Crane. Perversely, Turner spent most of the evening dancing with Crane. Noticing that she was wearing the engagement ring he had given her, made from a stone belonging to his mother, Crane demanded that she not wear it while out with someone else. Bey, overhearing this, exchanged insults with Crane, then blows. Crane suffered a bump on the head, Bey several scratches; Turner threw the ring at Crane; the ring fell to the ground, was retrieved by the host and returned to Turner—and she departed, with the ring, Bey, and a badly frayed temper. By that time, everyone's temper, aided by the contents of the well-stocked bar, had reached the breaking point.

In spite of the chaos, Jess Barker was having a marvelous time, but Susan, disgusted with the entire melee, demanded to be taken home immediately. The two left the May house together . . . but Jess returned to his apartment alone.

The following Monday, Susan announced, "I've moved out for good, and I'm planning to see my attorney. My decision is irrevocable."

Jess, unable to reach his bride by phone, tried to explain what had happened. "I wouldn't know about the chances for a reconciliation. The whole thing started as a joke, and the joke turned into something serious. I had a little trouble opening the car door. I thought it was funny—but Susan didn't think so. She tapped her foot for a while and then disappeared. I waited several minutes and then looked for her. I couldn't find her anywhere, so I went home alone. I haven't seen her since."

Susan spent a week alone in her apartment, ignoring the incessant ringing of the telephone. She made calls to her mother; to her attorney, Sidney Justin; to her agent, Charlie Feldman; and naturally, to Louella Parsons who, on September 25, sadly related: "My heart goes out to Susan Hayward . . . who wanted so to make a go of her marriage. I talked to her the day she made up her mind to marry Barker and again when she came back from her honeymoon. But her marriage didn't work out, and Susie has decided on a separation. I don't know Barker, who had a brief fling at the movies at Columbia, but he lost a mighty fine girl."

Parsons's sympathy was wasted. By the time that article had appeared, Susan's temper had cooled, and she was answering her phone again. When Jess got through, she didn't

hang up. Instead, she agreed to meet him for dinner to discuss their problems.

Sitting with Jess in a dim corner of the restaurant, talking quietly with him, she must have realized how ludicrous the incident in the May driveway had been. Had she really been provoked by his delay in opening the car door, or had the whole incident—with an engagement ring as the centerpiece—simply aroused her memories of the disastrous affairs with Carroll and that boy in drama school, and with it the memories of their own stormy courtship? But that was over and done with, wasn't it? She should stop thinking about the past.

In addition, could her mood have had something to do with being with Turner for the first time since they had been kids in Frank Beckwith's class at Warner's? She had been jealous of Turner then, even though they had rarely exchanged more than a couple of words. Now Turner was undisputedly the glamour queen of MGM. She had a beautiful home, a closet filled with furs, gorgeous jewelry—and men making fools of themselves by fighting over her.

In contrast, Susan was the Paramount pest, her career treading water as the years slipped by. She considered herself a better actress than Turner, but Turner had a way with men, a technique Susan couldn't master. Turner had been the star of the May bash—despite the outcome of the evening. And, ironically, Jess had just completed a pallid featured role in Turner's *Keep Your Powder Dry*.

At any rate, when Jess drove Susan home after dinner that night, he stayed. The next morning they prepared a joint statement to the press saying that they realized "our love persisted and we have decided to give our marriage another chance." In the same statement, they announced they "were going house-hunting and were expecting a baby about next April."

Throughout her pregnancy, Susan kept a low profile, avoiding places where photographers and reporters congregated. Although she tried to eat sensibly, she gained an alarming amount of weight and by early winter, X-rays confirmed what her doctor had suspected: she was carrying twins. Financially, things looked grim. She couldn't work, and Jess's agents were trying to find a good deal for him. Finally, after months of agonizing, he signed a term contract at Universal, where he was promised a star build-up. His new salary would enable him to support his family, if not in luxury, then at least in

comfort. The Barkers moved into a small house in Beverly Hills.

On February 17, 1945, Timothy Marrenner Barker and then, seven minutes later, Gregory Marrenner Barker were born. Susan kept her promise to Ratoff by naming one of the twins after him, further complimenting him by giving his name to the boy who bore the stronger resemblance to her. Timothy inherited his father's looks. Susan's choice of her maiden name as both boys' middle name was never explained.

The twins' birth, two months earlier than expected, set the press off on the popular game of finger-counting: July, August, September... yes, it was only seven months. Anticipating this, Susan and Jess provided the standard Hollywood bromide of "premature birth." She made much of the fact that each boy weighed only four and a half pounds. If anyone had bothered to check, this was an acceptable weight for a twin born full-term.

Another fact that set the gossipers buzzing was that, though both parents needed publicity desperately at this point in their careers, Susan and Jess proceeded to antagonize *Time, Life, Look, Newsweek,* and the newspaper syndicates by refusing to pose for photographs with Timmy and Greg. Bigger stars than Susan had posed with their children soon after birth—was she trying to hide something about the babies? Their size, perhaps? Mindful of the talk—"I think people who repeat tales about other people should have their mouths taped," she was later to say privately—Susan quietly left the hospital on March 8, keeping her departure date a secret from the press.

On April 23, 1945, Susan returned to work for the first time, co-starring with Ronald Colman and Lawrence Tierney in the "Lux Radio Theater" broadcast of *The Petrified Forest,* in the role Bette Davis had played in the 1936 film version. The next month, an RKO murder mystery, *Deadline at Dawn,* marked her return to the screen. Susan had no intention of letting motherhood stand in the way of her movies. She was glad to have the boys, but... well, motherhood wasn't quite what she'd pictured it to be.

Later, she admitted to Dutch-aunt Louella about those first months: "When a girl becomes a mother, a whole change is supposed to take place in her. But it hadn't in me. When I came home each night from the studio, things were the same, except we had two babies. There was a nurse who would bring

them to me. I would get a full report on their day. I would
hold them and cuddle them. Then they would be carried back
to the nursery, and I would sit back knowing that there was
something wrong. Something was missing, but I didn't know
what. One night when I was sitting with Jess after dinner—the
babies had been in and were gone again—suddenly, I burst
into tears. 'I'm no good around here.'"

Later, she realized she'd been undergoing a standard attack
of post-partum depression. To overcome it, she tried her hand
at the usual motherly chores before rationalizing, with relief,
that changing dirty diapers was not necessarily proof of ma-
ternal devotion.

Possibly to provide that proof, however—to herself as well
as to the rest of the world—she finally agreed to allow the
Universal still photographers into the nursery in late May after
the completion of *Deadline at Dawn*. Tim and Gregory were
a robust fourteen weeks old by then, and the differences in
their looks and personalities made for a very attractive set of
pictures. Much to Universal's—and the Barkers'—satisfaction,
these were picked up and printed by *Time* magazine, a majority
of the country's newspapers, and—of equal importance in
1945—by all the leading fan magazines. The exposure would
be welcome since sixteen months were to elapse between Susan's last screen appearance in *And Now Tomorrow* and *Deadline at Dawn*'s release in April 1946.

Of more immediate importance to Universal was the plug
for Jess's first film with the studio, *This Love of Ours*. The
Merle Oberon–Charles Korvin starrer was their class production in a year that included such schlock as *Frisco Sal, Shady
Lady*, and *Jungle Captive*. No question, the studio was in
serious trouble—barely avoiding bankruptcy only by the grace
of now-fading Deanna Durbin, repetitive Abbott and Costello
comedies, and periodic returns from the grave by their *Frankenstein* monster. In desperate need of new blood, the company
decided to allow independent producers on the lot for the first
time, and to package and release their films. Walter Wanger
was one of them. It would turn out—at last—to be the break
Susan had been waiting for.

Wanger, married to Joan Bennett, was fifty-one when he
moved onto the Universal lot. By then he had produced some
three dozen pictures, among them: *Queen Christina* (with
Garbo), *Stage Coach, Foreign Correspondent*, and *Algiers* (for

the last he had discovered and made a star of Hedy Lamarr).
He was a man of impeccable taste, manners, and sophistication,
a refreshing contrast to the grittier De Sylva, and from 1939
to 1944 had even served as president of the Motion Picture
Academy of Arts and Sciences.

Now Wanger had a script ready to film called *Canyon Passage*, and he thought Jess Barker might be a possibility for a
leading role. Susan and Jess were vacationing in Palm Springs
when, Barker confirms, "Walter Wanger sent me the script of
Canyon Passage. I was up for an important part [that of the
second male lead] and I spent five hours coaxing Susan to read
it."

Ironically, Jess never got his part, losing it to Brian Donlevy, but Susan got one instead—Wanger not only liked the
idea of using her in his picture, he promptly signed her to a
long-term contract. Later, the story would go around that Susan
signed with Wanger because she was "furious Selznick kept
me waiting to see him about a contract," but that had about
as much truth in it as the fairy tale about Katie Harrigan and
County Cork.

While the studio papers were being drawn up, Susan and
Jess quietly celebrated their first wedding anniversary. She
looked radiant, and for the first time in years was filled with
optimism about the future. A week later, she called Parsons
about the Wanger deal: "Life is beautiful," she bubbled. "My
career is moving along, and you should see my babies! Jess
has been such a good boy, and we believe we are making a
success of our marriage."

Louella didn't think it odd that Susan should refer to her
husband as "a good boy." In passing along the conversation
to her readers, she added, in her most motherly manner: "Susie
and Jess are working hard to plan for their babies' future, and
the little ones have brought them closer together. Right now,
they are getting on but wonderfully."

Susan was also getting along wonderfully with her new
boss. Wanger's gentlemanly ways and astute taste were a breath
of fresh air to her after the people she'd been dealing with at
Paramount, and, reminiscing about Wanger nearly three decades later, Susan said, "I owe *everything* to Walter. He was
the guy who had faith in me. We both agreed about the sort
of roles I should play on screen and went after them." *Canyon
Passage* didn't turn out to be the ideal professional debut for

the new relationship—a middling adventure yarn with gorgeous scenery about a girl traveling to Oregon to join her fiancé, and the escort with whom she falls in love, Dana Andrews—but soon better, much better, things were to come.

Meanwhile, however—call it coincidence or bad timing— after Susan's arrival on the Universal lot, Barker's career went into a tailspin. The studio gave him seventh billing in a dismal Abbott and Costello comedy called *The Time of Their Lives* and then unceremoniously let his option drop. Susan would later rationalize that "it was best in a way that Jess wasn't cast in *Canyon Passage* because both of us couldn't have been away from home and leave the twins."

The awkwardness of the Barkers' role reversal, three decades before it would become trendy, did not escape notice by Universal employees.

One of Susan's wardrobe women, Mollie Briggs, reminisces: "Shortly after I married, my husband, who worked for a studio, went on layoff. When I arrived home and discovered he hadn't started dinner, I was a bit peeved. The next day I asked Susan, 'Don't you get a little upset when you come home and find Jess has been sitting around all day?'

"Well, this was the only time Susan ever got mad at me. She really flared up. 'Jess works very hard,' she protested. 'You have no idea of all he does.' She was very loyal and protective of him.

"I thought Susan was wonderful. So did most of the other people who worked with her on a one-to-one basis. Though she was very down-to-earth, she was a private person. And she was a lady. She never swore, never allowed anyone in her dressing room when she was taking her clothes off, like some stars who would perform that act before the mail boys, or whomever!

"I was in her dressing room—she was fully clothed—when Walter Wanger came in. She addressed him as 'Mr. Wanger.' He told her to call him Walter, but she wouldn't. 'As long as your name is on my pay checks, you are Mr. Wanger,' she replied.

"She was extremely conservative with money. She usually didn't discuss money; once, however, she let slip that she was putting $2,000 a month away for the boys because she never wanted them to be poor like she was as a child. I never met her mother, but when she talked family (other than Jess and

the twins), it was about her late father. It seemed to me that Susan worshipped him.

"Then, one day—I'll never forget this—Susan was finishing a take when she was given the message that someone was at the gate who kept insisting she was her sister. Susan asked one of the girls to get her and take her directly to her dressing room. 'Tell her to stay there until I'm finished on the set.' Everyone was so surprised! Susan had never mentioned having a sister, though we knew about her brother Wally.

"I was more surprised when I saw the sister. The woman . . . she looked just like a . . . well, a hooker! I'm not saying she was . . . she just looked like one. Susan didn't talk about the visit and I never again saw the sister on the lot." Before long, Mollie Briggs found herself subjected to several more surprises. . . . "One time, Susan called at two o'clock in the morning. Jess was out of town, I think. She told me she was alone in the house and was afraid to be alone. She wanted somebody to talk to. I never thought Susan was afraid of anything."

Even more astonishing to the young wardrobe woman was what she termed "the diamond ring incident."

"We were on location and staying in a motel. I stopped by Susan's room to say goodnight. She was getting ready for bed, and she had a large diamond on her nightstand. I told her that it should be put in a safe; it was dangerous to have it in her room. She interrupted my warning by saying:

" 'What would you do with this ring, if I gave it to you?'

" 'Pay off the loan on my house.'

" 'Then I won't give it to you!'

"Of course, I wouldn't have accepted the ring. And I'm still not sure she was seriously considering giving it to me. But when I got back to my room, I remembered she was always scolding me for spending money on my new home and not saving it.

"As I have said, she was *very* conservative about money. Jess was too. I once heard him bawling her out for spending $7.50 for four director chairs to place around the pool."

As early as March 1946, there were subtle indications that Jess's involuntary idleness was having an effect on Susan. Even her would-be upbeat anecdotes sounded slightly off. Susan told newspaper woman Virginia Tomlinson of Jess's fury as he talked her out of buying a fur coat, adding, "Then he

turned around and gave me a *down payment* on a more expensive one."

If that reporter thought it strange that Susan should emphasize "down payment," she didn't pursue the subject, nor did she ask why Susan needed a mink coat during a balmy spring season. The truth was, for Susan, the mink was a tangible symbol of success—of stardom—that had always figured in her fantasies. It was the only fur she had ever wanted—she was contemptuous of the typical starlet's white fox. She felt she was at the plateau in her career where she belonged in mink. And she was too impatient to wait until her husband could afford to make the final payments.

Soon she would be able to afford the payments herself. Sometime earlier in 1946, Wanger had sent her the script of her next picture. Originally titled *Angelica*, it was alleged to be a *film à clef* of the Bing Crosby–Dixie Lee marriage, in which Susan would play a neglected young wife turned alcoholic because her husband's spectacular singing career has left him little time for their marriage. As the story goes, lonely and depressed, unable to compete with the predatory women in her husband's life, Angelica turns to liquor for comfort and eventually loses complete control of herself. After her husband Ken sues for divorce and custody of their daughter, Angelica kidnaps the little girl and almost destroys both of them when she falls into a drunken stupor while smoking. Badly burned rescuing the child, Angelica is given another chance at happiness when her husband, suddenly aware of the problems that led to Angelica's alcoholism, decides to give the marriage another try—a blatant Hollywood "happy ending."

There was no question that it was the strongest role Susan had yet received, and Wanger cast the other parts carefully to show her off, passing over Jess Barker to put the weaker Lee Bowman in the role of the singer husband. Wanger was taking no chances of Susan's being outshone by anyone. With his wife Joan's box-office potential declining, Wanger had a desperate need for a strong female star, and was confident he could turn the girl he had been calling "a Brooklyn Bette Davis" into just that.

With this in mind, he gave Susan top-star billing, retitled the film *Smash-Up, The Story of a Woman*, and issued an ironclad edict to everyone concerned with the production, from director Stuart Heisler to film editor Milton Carruth: "Favor

Susan Hayward in every possible way."

For Susan, the film marked a turning point in her career and in her life. Before filming began, Wanger told Heisler with remarkable insight the lines that have been quoted earlier: "Susie suffers from one of the most startling guilt complexes you can imagine. She's embarrassed that she is a beautiful woman. She doesn't think she deserves it. She knows it's a priceless gift, but she's afraid that on the inside she isn't beautiful."

Then added: "If we can get her to bring that complex to the surface in this role, we'll get a performance worthy of an Oscar from her."

❀ chapter 9 ❀

SUSAN HAYWARD, an expert at hiding almost everything, never attempted to conceal her fondness for Scotch. She freely admitted that she enjoyed a stiff drink with Jess when she arrived home from the studio exhausted. When they went to Mocambo or Ciro's, she thought it ridiculous that coffee cups were substituted for liquor glasses whenever a photographer wanted to grab a quick shot. Everyone in Hollywood drank, and everyone knew it—but the edict came from the studios, and heaven help the photographer who violated it.

Strictly a social drinker, however, Susan didn't know what it was like to get drunk. She had gotten giddy at times but never smashed, therefore when filming of *Smash-Up* began, she found it difficult to reach inside herself for the necessary effects. Director Stuart Heisler tried everything he could think of. One afternoon, in desperation, he even sent out for a couple of bottles of booze and persuaded Susan to try to get drunk, but it didn't work. She did manage to get fairly tipsy, but drunk actors can't play drunk scenes—that's an accepted show-business axiom. Finally, Heisler enlisted the aid of Yale University's authority on alcoholism, Dr. Elvin M. Jellinek. Susan spent hours with him and, somehow, whether it was through his help or her own inner resources, between the three of them, Susan's performance began to take shape.

It was different with Lee Bowman, however. Bowman—who would appear in seventy-five movies during his film career, from 1937's *I Met Him in Paris* to 1964's *Youngblood Hawke*—was one of those competent, noncharismatic actors who just never caught on with the public.* Orginally signed

---

*He would retire in 1968 to take up teaching camera techniques to GOP politicians and the art of public speaking to corporate executives at Bethlehem Steel. He died in December 1979, at the age of sixty-five.

by Paramount, Bowman had his option dropped in 1939, the same year that studio had put Susan under contract. After two years at RKO, he had again met the same fate.

Bowman was perpetually cast as the guy who lost the girl to the male lead. In fact, coincidentally, he had played the modern socialite who lost Rita Hayworth to dancer Gene Kelly in *Cover Girl*—Jess Barker had played his turn-of-the-century counterpart ditched by "grandma" Rita for "piano player" Johnny Mitchell. Further in the coincidence department, Bowman's wife Helene was the daughter of Victor Fleming, the man who had replaced Susan's first mentor George Cukor as director of *Gone with the Wind*—and the Bowmans were close friends of Steffi Duna, John Carroll's first wife.

One might assume that Susan and Bowman shared enough background for hours of small talk, but between takes they barely exchanged a word. Bowman made no effort to conceal his hostility toward Susan from the day *Smash-Up* started production. "Of the many stars I've worked with," he later said, "she was the only one with whom I ever had any difficulty." A great deal of the difficulty, actually, came from the fact that he was seething with resentment. When he had signed for the film, he had been certain it would make him a major star after ten years as an also-ran. After ten days of shooting, however, he no longer had any such illusions; he felt he was being shafted by Susan, by Heisler, and by Walter Wanger.

Susan, however, was exhilarated. Bowman had been hoping for recognition as a star; Susan wanted to be accepted as a serious *actress*. Grateful for Heisler's professionalism, she responded to his direction with an uncharacteristic obedience, and had little doubt that this time she would reach her goal. Yet when Wanger, after seeing the rushes of some of the more dramatic sequences, suggested that she might just possibly snare an Oscar nomination, she refused to allow her hopes to be built up. That would be *too* much to expect.

By the time she had completed *Smash-Up*, however, she felt secure enough to start looking at houses. Since her marriage, she and Jess had been virtual gypsies. They had already been evicted from two homes because the owners had objected to pets and then to children, a commonplace occurrence in southern California. They had felt they would be secure for another year or two in the three-bedroom house they had been leasing in Bel Air, but then in May the owner had returned

from Canada and wanted possession as soon as possible. The postwar housing shortage hadn't peaked, and it was a seller's market.

Jess complained bitterly, in an interview, "Sure, we can buy a lot of those Spanish-type houses built in 1925 for $30,000 and up. They're worth maybe $8,000 and most of them are broken-down wrecks. The real estate people all give us the same line: 'You can do wonderful things with this house.' Sure we can do wonderful things with another $10,000.

"We heard of a house near us in Bel Air. The price was $35,000. We went to see it. The real estate people recognized Susan. The price suddenly shot up to $55,000."

"And we can't afford $55,000," Susan chimed in. "Sure, *I* saved a little money. I've been saving it for a rainy day. I can't see putting it all into a house. Especially now when taxes are so high. Sure I make good money, but you should see those checks I write to the Treasury Department."

The Barkers' only alternative was to forget about Bel Air and Beverly Hills, and start house-hunting in the San Fernando Valley. At that time, the suburbs west of Universal City still had a country atmosphere, and homes there were comparatively new, well built, and reasonably priced. After a long search, Susan and Jess found a charming place complete with swimming pool at 3737 Longridge Avenue in Sherman Oaks, well worth the $47,000 asking price. Its value, she was assured, could only increase. Unlike most married women, however, Susan went to the real estate broker alone, wrote the check, and put the house in her name—alone. The family moved in on Christmas Eve, 1946.

Smash-Up was released in April of 1947. The film received mixed reviews, due mostly to the inevitable comparisons with *The Lost Weekend*, but Susan's performance was a revelation to most of the critics.

Variety commented in its inimitable style: "Just as Ray Milland achieved his greatest prominence because of *Weekend*, Susan Hayward gets her biggest break to date in this one. . . . Miss Hayward handles a difficult thesping job with ease and assurance, faltering only where the story bogs down. Pixie quality and her beauteous looks enhance greatly her characterization of a gal who becomes a dipso to overcome an inferiority complex. . . . Cast, though overshadowed by Miss Hayward, does well."

Howard Barnes of the *New York Herald-Tribune* particularly applauded the film's writing, "A female alcoholic takes her place in the gallery of psychiatric cases. *Smash-Up* is a somewhat savage account of dipsomania. . . . John Howard Lawson, Dorothy Parker, and Frank Cavett have written sequences which are literate and terrifying, while Stuart Heisler has staged them with ominous underlining. . . . Since Susan Hayward plays the heroine with considerable power, the production is definitely disturbing."

Of Lee Bowman, *Life* magazine said he played his part "with all the enthusiasm of a stuffed moose." *Variety* simply noted: "Bowman is miscast as the husband."

Susan, encouraged by her exceptional reviews, began taking Wanger's Oscar nomination predictions seriously, and was beginning to regret he had released the film in April, prolonging the suspense for another ten months. However, she had little time to ponder about the future. She was busy enough in the present.

First there was a film called *The Lost Moment*, which had begun shooting on March 12, a bastardized version of Henry James's *Aspern Papers*, which, Susan later admitted, "was a disastrous film. As miserable a failure as you've ever seen. Their name for it may have been *The Lost Moment*, but after I saw it I called it 'The Lost Hour and a Half.'" (The critics later agreed.) Then, in June, she began preparations for *Tap Roots*, from a book that Jess Barker, in fact, had persuaded Wanger to read and buy. Being idle, Barker had immersed himself in Susan's career, though few people were aware of it at the time.

"Yes, I brought that to Mr. Wanger myself," he points out today. "A certain Italian producer on the lot said, 'Jess, did you ever read *Tap Roots* by James Street?' and I said, 'No.'

"'Well,' he said, 'it's in the library. You should go get it. I think Susan would be great in it, because it's just like from *Gone with the Wind.*'"

In *Tap Roots*, Susan played Morna Dabney, the spitfire daughter of the leader of an independent group in Lebanon County, Mississippi, which decides to secede from the state when Mississippi secedes from the Union. With the Confederate army closing in, Morna has her own problems when she becomes paralyzed after a fall from a horse; loses her fiancé to her selfish sister, and finds herself attracted to a "notorious

newspaper publisher and duellist," Keith Alexander. In the end, Lebanon County is lost, Keith Alexander is won, and all ends happily.

Wanger was forced to give Van Heflin top billing in order to borrow him from MGM for the Rhett Butlerish character of Alexander—but, as with *Smash-Up*, Susan was favored in every sequence in which she appeared. Aware of this, she occasionally stepped out of bounds. George Marshall was the director on *Tap Roots*, and he later remembered:

"In one scene her reputed stubbornness came to life. The scene, I admit, was rather clichéd, but it played an important part in the plot. Susan was in a wheelchair, since she was not supposed to be able to walk. The character played by Van Heflin thought that she could, and was intent upon proving it. He felt that if he could make her mad enough, she would get up.

"The first take was a real dud. She played it almost to the point of apathy, and here is where our wills clashed for the first time. She felt she should play the scene in this deadened form, while I knew it had to be explosive, to be in contrast to everything she had done before. I told this to her and insisted she loosen up. The director has to be boss or an agreement must be reached. The next take was even worse. She got up from the chair, ran to her dressing room, and slammed the door. I thought, 'Well, that screws up our schedule for the day.'

"But she returned in a little while, after she had fixed her face, to give me a big kiss, and say, 'I'm sorry. I knew in my heart what you wanted. I just didn't want to give in. But I still think you are a miserable so-and-so.'

"I didn't believe those cuss words for a minute. Susan always remained one of my favorite people."

She had another slight problem during the shooting too, a rather curious one. Yvonne Wood, who designed the costumes for *Tap Roots*, remembers, "I had a little trouble with Susan and bust pads. After the censor had passed on all the wardrobe tests, Walter Wanger called me frantically to say, 'Susan is showing a lot more cleavage in the dailies, and we're going to have to reshoot some scenes.' I went straight to the set, reached into Susan's dress, and pulled out bust pads and other assorted things she had stuck in there. After that, Susan behaved herself." Miss Wood isn't the only one who recalls

Susan's concern about her breasts. Jane Greer, who had worked with her the previous year in *They Won't Believe Me*, laughs. "Even back then, Susan hated to wear bras. She used to tape herself under the arms so her breasts would flow freely. Every night she'd yank off the tape, to the horror of the wardrobe lady."

No bras but bust pads? Extra cleavage from a woman legendary for her modesty? Perhaps it was one more way for her to compensate for her fear, as Wanger said, "that on the inside she isn't beautiful." Or maybe she had simply become more determined than ever to make an impact on the screen—even if it meant showing more skin.

As it turned out, she needn't have worried. After her rejection for *Gone with the Wind*, she had said, "What did I know about playing Southern belles?" But in the decade since, she had learned quite a lot. As a movie, *Tap Roots* left much to be desired, but the critics generally admired Susan—"the film owes its effectiveness mostly to the expert performances...especially Miss Hayward's," wrote *Newsweek*—Susan liked the Scarlett-type role, and working and living on location in Asheville, North Carolina, had been very pleasurable.

While there, she had had the opportunity to visit the famed Vanderbilt estate, a fifty-eight-bedroom mansion on five hundred acres of land situated nearby. A member of the clan in residence had invited the cast to a cocktail party in honor of the movie. Susan had been overwhelmed.

"I'd never seen anything like it. It was all I could do," she grinned, "to keep from standing in the middle of that baronial hall and shouting, 'Anyone here from Brooklyn?'" That's what she said. In reality, the last thing she had wanted to be reminded of that day was Brooklyn. For a few hours, she had been in the kind of home she had always fantasized about—as her own.

Returning to Longridge Avenue, to a house partially furnished with studio rejects and a living room used for storage space, only heightened her sense of the gap between what she longed for and what she had. She loved Jess. There was no question about that. Yet that love was almost overshadowed by his inability to fill her psychological needs—to make the fantasy come true.

Jess Barker's career was "on hold." He didn't want to leave his family, so he made no effort to get jobs in summer stock

or to return to Broadway. Maritally, that may have been a fatal mistake. Had he left Susan and gone east, he might have regained his self-respect and put the marriage back on an even keel. He might also have regained the respect of the rumormongers in Hollywood who said he simply did not want to work. Not want to work? He was dying for a role—any role. When Susan suggested he take classes in agriculture and operate a ranch, or go into the jewelry business, he stuck to his guns. "I'm an actor."

The arguments multiplied: About his career. About her career. About money. About everything and nothing. Finally, the conflict proved more than the marriage could endure.

For the second time in three years, Susan walked out on her husband. On October 1, 1947, she had her attorneys draw up divorce papers and brought suit against Jess on the ground of "cruelty and grievous mental anguish." Again, however, the matter went no further than that. Before any definite action was taken, both agreed to consult with Dr. Paul Popenoe of the Institute of Family Relations and, later, with Dr. Maurice Karp, a professional marriage counselor. Soon Susan dropped the divorce proceedings, explaining:

"I've come to the conclusion, as has Jess, that marriage is a contract that should be lived up to. There really isn't very much in life for you when you reach sixty, say, unless you have lived up to it. . . . Now I know that, when I went to see a lawyer, my faith had wavered and that somehow I'd gotten off the track. Working out my marriage problems has made me realize that I am growing up and maturing.

"I've said some things I have regretted, and Jess has done the same thing. But doesn't that apply to *every* married couple? I mean *every* married couple—not just movie people."

Other than an item or two in the gossip columns, little attention was paid to the split and hasty reconciliation. The two top fan magazines of the time didn't even consider it newsworthy.

Through the wartime years, *Modern Screen* and *Photoplay*, with the exception of an occasional candid shot, had ignored Susan with a regularity bordering on insult. Even now, neither her Oscar nomination for *Smash-Up*, nor the short-lived separation and reconciliation with Jess, nor Susan's luminous beauty had inspired either magazine to assign stories about the couple. Nor were Susan and Jess invited to the lavish star-

studded parties held annually by each magazine to present awards to the stars whom the public had chosen as their favorites of the year. Susan Hayward fans could read about her in the lesser publications, *Motion Picture, Silver Screen*, and *Movieland*, but never in the two giants of the field.

Asked about this today, Albert Delacorte, then *Modern Screen*'s young editor and later the Dell publisher, replies: "You know the answer! Susan Hayward was always a personal favorite of mine, but my opinion didn't count. We followed our readers' poll to the letter—or should I say to the number! And in 1945, even after the kids were born, Susan Hayward wasn't even able to register in the top fifty. I admired her work on the screen, my staff shared this feeling. We are all amazed that our readers didn't ask for her. I was just the guy who ran the magazine, but the public told me who to run. That policy was too successful to tamper with; we had an estimated readership of anywhere from thirteen million to damn near fifteen million every month."

In June 1948, Delacorte turned over the editorship of *Modern Screen*, and made plans to start another kind of publication (which ultimately never got off the ground), "a *Parents* type magazine," inspired by his own fascination on the subject. "I wanted a monthly feature on the way movie stars raise their kids. With this in mind, I asked my West Coast rep to visit the Barker house and send back some intimate information on the Barker boys. Nothing like starting with twins." This was the wire he received back:

Timothy much more sensitive than Greg. Needs more affection. Some people think Susan spoils Tim. Susan always aware of this need in him. (STOP) Tim has exceptionally deep voice for small youngster. Likes to sing. Knows tunes and lyrics. Usually croons when sitting on Susan's lap. (STOP) Timothy stomach-happy. Asks nurse, "Dinner ready, Annie?" Looks immediately for meat when he sits at table. Will eat everything, but meat's got to be there. Inherited this from Susan. (STOP) She and Jess extra careful not to show favoritism. No jealousy between boys. If one is patted on the head, the other gets same treatment. When one is spanked, the other becomes quiet. Then protests punishment for his brother. (STOP) Twins love water, don't object to baths, splash around in swimming pool. Will learn to swim next summer, according to Susan. . . . Love of water extends

to sailing toy boats in the john. (STOP) Both are helpful around house. Never miss a trick. If Susan asks where baby oil or red shirt, etc., is, one or both can tell her. (STOP) Susan doesn't dress them alike. Exception coats, boots and sailor suits. She says they're different people, besides being fraternal twins, so why try to make them identical. STOP Barkers got them through the don't-touch stage with little difficulty, except for wall sockets. These fascinated them, and they were forever crawling to one to try and find out what makes lamps light. Used to give Susan strokes. (STOP) Kids love to be read to. Timothy has crush on gingerbread man. Has three different versions of book on subject, plus albums and a toy G.B. man. For Christmas cook baking him one, with gumdrops for buttons. (STOP) Twins will be four February 17. Barkers seldom have guests numbering over four. . . . Don't like more because of kids. Incidentally Susan impresses me as being an exceptionally good mother. (STOP)

Nevertheless, despite this picture of domestic bliss and even after four years of motherhood, Susan still had *some* doubts about that. Although she said, "It seems obvious to me what children require is not necessarily the constant presence of their mother, but the constant knowledge that they are loved and cherished," there were subtle indications that she might be wrong.

Later she admitted, "At first when friends visited us and the babies were brought in, I was sometimes hurt because Greg and Timothy would turn away from me when I held them and want to go back to their nurse. Now that we have a new family deal working, things are different."

It was wishful thinking. Anyway, the boys didn't need to run to their nurse: their father was constantly with them.

In February 1948, it was official: Susan had been nominated for her performance in *Smash-Up*. Although she was competing against such heavyweights as odds-on favorite Rosalind Russell (*Mourning Becomes Electra*); Joan Crawford (*Possessed*); Dorothy McGuire (*Gentleman's Agreement*) and Loretta Young (*The Farmer's Daughter*), Wanger was optimistic about a last-minute upset. As it turned out, Wanger was absolutely correct. There was, indeed, an upset. The award went to the least likely

of all of them—Loretta Young—and Hollywood and Miss Russell didn't come out of shock for months. A wag suggested RKO change the name of her movie to "Mourning Becomes Roz Russell."

Susan took the defeat with good humor, although she had splurged on the most expensive gown she had ever bought. "I can always wear the dress again. And I'll be nominated for an Oscar again. Maybe not next year. Maybe I'll have to wait until the fifties. But I intend to win some day. That's my goal."

In 1948, it was also Walter Wanger's goal. He may have been president of the Academy, but he had never produced an Oscar-winning film, a failing he intended to correct with his multi-million dollar production of *Joan of Arc*, starring Ingrid Bergman. He poured all his time and money into it—the film was running way over on both—and as a result, there was little time for Susan. With his permission, Universal used her in the Robert Montgomery starrer *The Saxon Charm*. It was hardly the best follow-up to her Oscar nomination: As John Payne's wife, her part was secondary to the story, and the second female lead, Audrey Totter, stole the film.

Then, after *Joan of Arc* was completed—he thought—Wanger brought Susan and director Stuart Heisler to Eagle-Lion, for which company he was producing the less-than-epic *Tulsa*. Robert Preston and Susan were reunited for the third time in a story about the "black gold" industry, but Wanger came up with a dry well. *Time* magazine commented: "*Tulsa*, like a damp fuse, provides a loud bang at the end of a long sputter. Its plot is so rambling and logy with clichés that its climax— a big fire scene—seems wonderfully good."

Joan of Arc's final fire scene too was spectacular, but much of the rest of the film was disastrous. Desperate for money for additional sequences and for an expensive ad campaign that he thought—erroneously—might save the picture, Wanger sold Susan's contract to Darryl Zanuck for a reported two hundred thousand dollars.

Susan's feelings about the sale were mixed. She regretted losing Wanger, whom she trusted and respected as a mentor— but the deal he and the Feldman office had negotiated with Zanuck was overwhelmingly in her favor.

"We'll work together again," Wanger predicted sentimentally.

"I know. I'll work for you any time, in anything," she replied.

That would come to pass nearly a decade later. For now, however, her future was tied to that of the lengendary Zanuck himself—and it would be a bumpy ride.

⊗ chapter 10 ⊗

*I cannot remember when I first saw her or under what circum-
stances I engaged her and put her in her first Fox film. This
calls for a great deal of thinking. . . . All I can recall is when
I last saw her [in 1963] it was not a very pleasant encounter.*

DARRYL F. ZANUCK, *shortly before his death*

WHAT HAPPENED during that final encounter will never be
known, for Zanuck died in December 1979. What is certain,
however, is that, for all Susan's anticipation, the relationship
began inauspiciously.

Zanuck could be wildly extravagant in some ways, but notoriously tight-fisted in others. Susan's salary, prorated on the
usual forty-week year, came to $5,000 a week. Zanuck wanted
maximum value for his studio's money, so he put her to work
immediately (on December 22, 1948) in Joseph L. Mankiewicz's production of *House of Strangers*. There was nothing
wrong with *House of Strangers*, but it was basically a male-
oriented melodrama about a family vendetta, starring Edward
G. Robinson and Richard Conte; and Susan's brief role, as
Conte's girl friend, was not the kind of studio debut an Oscar-
nominated actress might have expected.

Zanuck knew, however, that Susan was next due to report
to Samuel Goldwyn on June 19 for *My Foolish Heart*, and he
scented a winner in that one. It was easy to project the effect
that *Heart* would have on the career of his newest property:
he merely had to sit back and let Goldwyn turn her into a
potential superstar, while he lined up properties pending her
return to Twentieth.

There was nothing male-oriented about *My Foolish Heart*. It was a woman's picture right down to the last haunting strains of its theme song, which would be (and still is) requested nightly in every piano bar in the country:

> The night is like a lovely tune,
> Beware, my foolish heart.
> How white the ever constant moon,
> Take care, my foolish heart.

Adapted from J. D. Salinger's *New Yorker* story, "Uncle Wiggily in Connecticut," Julius J. and Philip G. Epstein's screenplay put alcoholic, unhappy Eloise Winters at the tail end of a disastrous marriage to a man she had married out of expediency. The sight of an old gown arouses memories and takes her back to 1941—when as a nice girl from Boise, Idaho, she had met a charming Greenwich Village wolf (Dana Andrews) at a party and soon found herself madly in love. At first resisting his sexual advances, she'd finally given in right before his leaving for the army, but then kept her subsequent pregnancy a secret, unwilling to trap him into marriage. On his own, he scribbles a proposal—just before his plane crashes in an army training accident. Desperate, she seduces her best friend's fiancé into a marriage that has made them both miserable. . . . Back in the present (1949), Eloise decides to give up her child rather than to tell her husband the truth, but he too has a change of heart and realizes that the child's place is with her mother.

Yes, in 1949, *My Foolish Heart* was *definitely* a woman's picture.

Dana Andrews in the male lead acquitted himself admirably, but pitted against Susan's portrayal of Eloise and the song title, he came off third best.

Here, as in *Canyon Passage*, the intimacy between Susan and Andrews came to a halt the minute the cameras stopped rolling. Commenting today upon their offscreen relationship, Andrews echoes the words of most Hayward leading men. "I could say Susan was self-centered, but almost everyone in our profession is. She was a very strong young woman with a steel will. She was most attractive and always pleasant to me; we worked extremely well together. But we almost never saw each other socially." (There would be one time worth commenting on, but not until a few years later. . . .)

Director Mark Robson observed: "You know, there are times when it is advantageous to a love story if the two leading players are not too close; they save their emotions for the cameras. I've seen enough instances when co-stars were making it in the dressing room. When they were called on the set a few minutes later, the effect on their performances, particularly in a romantic scene, was disastrous. They were so afraid something would come across, especially when one or the other (or both) were married. They subconsciously froze. Take Elizabeth Taylor and Richard Burton. They were madly in love when they did *The V.I.P.'s*, yet their chemistry in the film was nonexistent."

Returning to Susan, Robson continued, "I think she didn't trust actors or actresses. She had a few directors at the beginning of her career who were out-and-out bastards and gave her no help at all, but once she felt she could trust a director, she'd work her ass to the bones for him. She trusted me and the part of Eloise Winters—ranging from sweet innocent to alcoholic young matron—was an actress's dream.

"It had 'Oscar' written all over it, and I can remember the exact moment when I started placing bets that she would cinch a nomination. It was during the scene—just leading to the flashback—when she sobs: 'I was a nice girl, wasn't I?'

"By the time *Foolish Heart* wrapped, we were convinced we'd sweep the Oscar field."

Oozing with optimism, still preening over his *Best Years of Our Lives* triumph the year before, Sam Goldwyn rushed *My Foolish Heart* into Los Angeles theaters early to qualify for the 1949 awards. The reviews only reinforced everyone's optimism. *Look* magazine's review was typical:

"*My Foolish Heart* tells of a simple wartime love story that ended in heartbreak. These are ingredients for a typical soap opera. But *My Foolish Heart* rises above its material every step of the way ... proves that freshness can be given a much-worn story if it is approached with a light touch, an adult point of view and a warm understanding for the weaknesses of recognizable human beings. It merges a rich, delicious movie that every grown-up moviegoer should cherish. ... In her best screen job to date, Miss Hayward makes the tragedy of a girl in love in wartime very real indeed."

My Foolish Heart opened in New York at the Radio City Music Hall on January 20, 1950. A few weeks later, although

the anticipated sweep failed to materialize, Academy Award nominations went to the title song—and to Susan Hayward.

"And the winner is . . ."

On March 23, 1950, for the second time in three years, Susan had to sit and watch with a frozen smile as another actress rushed to the stage of the Pantages to accept the coveted Oscar. This time, it was Olivia de Havilland for her portrayal of Catherine Sloper in *The Heiress*. The award was not entirely a surprise. Earlier in the year de Havilland had been chosen Best Actress by the New York Film Critics' Society, and most of the Academy felt that she had deserved an Oscar for her role in the previous year's *The Snake Pit*, as well.

Nevertheless, de Havilland now had two of the statues (the other one for *To Each His Own*), and Susan had none. With her eyes blazing and just a trace of a smile on her lips, Susan repeated the prediction she had made two years earlier. "There will be other chances. Don't worry, I intend to win one of those things someday." Now, no one scoffed.

Inexplicably, though, Zanuck continued to cast her in less than star-caliber roles. After stifling her resentment at being cast in *House of Strangers*, she finally rebelled when the studio announced its intention to cast her in a foolish comedy called *Stella* about a family of crazy crooks: despite top star billing, her part would have been entirely secondary to the development of the story. Play, or be suspended, the studio warned. Susan opted for suspension. Her replacement was Ann Sheridan, another redhead and one whose star was waning.

Susan was confident Zanuck would not permit her to remain idle for long, and sat back to wait. Jess Barker, however, had no reason to be that optimistic about his own career.

In 1949, he had worked in two minor films—*The Black Book* and *Take One False Step*—but now at the start of the decade, there were no new offers and none on the horizon. He tried to be philosophical.

"I admit frankly," he told a friend, "that when a man isn't working, especially an actor, it can get on his nerves. He begins to brood, becomes jumpy and irritable. It's happened to me. But you've got to snap out of it. It's not fair to you, not fair to your wife, and certainly not fair to your children.

"Susan and I regard our marriage as a partnership. Whatever

each of us earns goes into the family bankroll. The very nature of the entertainment business is cyclical. Right now Susan is having a great run. Next year or maybe the year after, it will be my turn. There's no point in becoming neurotic just because your wife is having a big success."

That's what he said. He tried hard to convince outsiders he meant it and tried even harder to convince himself.

To Jess fell the responsibility of running interference between Susan and outsiders making demands on her time. He took all calls—she hated telephone conversations—screened scripts, and talked to fan-magazine reporters clamoring for stories about the idyllic Barkers. To these persistent intruders, Jess always put on a happy face—though the resemblance to Fredric March in the 1937 *A Star Is Born* was not missed by everyone.

In one story for *Motion Picture*, under his by-line and approved by him, Jess wrote, "When Susan is working and I'm not, I take charge of things around the house. I do the shopping, discipline the twins, just take over. She's too busy, naturally, to have time to run a house on top of everything else. Sometimes we disagree about how to bring up the children. Susan feels I am too stern. And I feel the boys would never learn if I didn't show them I meant what I said."

Barker was determined to present a strong masculine image to his five-year-old sons, and so emphasized order and discipline. It was obvious, though, that there was little order in the household. Jess noted:

"Susan spent two years looking for the drapes for the bedroom. In the meantime, we had no drapes—no nothing. Just old shades we pulled down. Our living room also looks very peculiar. We never furnished it. No sofas, no rugs. In it we have a 16-millimeter projector, a television set, a player piano, and two tables. It is, in a word, empty."

Jess also admitted that "Neither of us is very neat either. We have one of those desert lamps which I generally throw my trousers over. Nobody touches them. And Susan's clothes are hung over the door. Not on the hook—on the door. No one touches anything Susan or I put in a certain place.

"We put our mail down where we open it—on top of the table, under plates, all over the place. Sometimes I go through it to find the bills. I have a little place where I hide them—in back of the philodendron plants. Then when Susan says,

'Whatever happened to such and such a bill?' I just reach behind the plants.

"Whenever we expect company, we both go tearing around putting stuff away."

In this article, and elsewhere, Barker also tried to make light of "silly domestic problems," hoping to convince everyone that the problems the two of them had had in the early years of their marriage were a thing of the past. As it would turn out, though, they were very much a thing of the present.

Meanwhile, Susan had been successful in her war of nerves with Zanuck. Loath to see his high-priced star idle, he had broken down and offered her the co-starring role opposite Tyrone Power in *Rawhide*. The plot: entertainer Vinnie Holt, taking her niece east by stagecoach, is held hostage in a station by a small group of bandits and falls in love with stationmaster Tyrone Power. Susan didn't like the script particularly, despite a fondness for westerns—she would say, many years later, "I enjoy watching westerns more than any other type of film I can think of. I always know how everything is going to turn out—the bad guys are always going to get knocked off, the good guys are always going to win." This time, however, Zanuck was persistent rather than threatening, and finally Susan agreed, telling Zanuck, "I still don't trust this script, but I trust you."

Actually, her trust was not misplaced. Although *Rawhide* was played more for suspense than for action, Thomas Pryor of the *New York Times* conceded: "Director Henry Hathaway has turned out a surprisingly good entertainment," and added that "Miss Hayward, who has more opportunity to express her indignation and gnawing terror . . . does well by her role." Pryor concluded that, although "*Rawhide* may not be a prize addition to the screen's vast western library, it is sufficiently different to warrant attention"—a view that was generally shared by audiences and critics alike.

Much of *Rawhide* was filmed in a chilly location site (shooting started on January 9) at Lone Pine, California, a four-hour drive from Los Angeles, and there was little social contact between Susan and Tyrone Power. The latter, recently back from Europe with his new bride Linda Christian, was less than happy in a kind of role he could—and did—play better ten years earlier; wanted to get the picture over with as quickly as possible, and made no secret about it. There was little

camaraderie between him and the other members of the cast. Susan, for her part, spent much of her free time with forty-nine-year-old character actor George Tobias, an old acquaintance of the Barkers who had originally met Jess when both had been featured in *You Can't Take It with You*. A wise, unpretentious bachelor, Tobias was among the select few Susan would invite to dinner, then or later.

Susan, however, would see little of Tobias—or anyone else—during most of the remaining months of 1950. She had barely finished *Rawhide* when she had to travel to Georgia on May 18 for *I'd Climb the Highest Mountain*, then to New York on October 2 for *I Can Get It for You Wholesale*, a biting, behind-the-scenes look at Manhattan's garment center.

Based loosely on Jerome Weidman's 1937 best seller, *I Can Get It for You Wholesale* presented Susan as Harriet Boyd, a cold, calculating, model-turned-designer-turned-dress-manufacturer who ruthlessly claws her way to the top of the rag heap. Although saddled with a conventional Hollywood happy ending—the ruthless career woman is redeemed by "the love of a good man"—the movie was generally well received, the *New York Herald-Tribune*'s James S. Barstow commenting that "Miss Hayward is just right . . . fast and sassy on her double-crossing climb from $10.95 models to Paris creations; she's nasty-nice enough almost to carry the contrived good-girl-after-all conversion of the climax." "To say that Susan was a highly talented and able actress would be merely to state the obvious," director Michael Gordon notes today. "In a word, she was thoroughly professional in the best sense of the word."

The *New York Times*'s Thomas Pryor had some reservations about the metamorphosis the original novel had undergone, but agreed: "Give Susan Hayward some quick recognition for bringing to life a hard-shelled dame who travels as fast and as loose as the screenplay permits her to. . . . Stories about such chameleon-like characters as Miss Hayward plays . . . are difficult to put over with complete success, and that is why this film falters as a character study, though Miss Hayward does nobly." He was carried away, though, by the "freshness the picture has to offer [in] the scenes which reflect the pulse-beat of the dress-industry—the crowds scurrying along Seventh Avenue amidst the traffic of dress carts and the frenetic atmosphere of the showrooms. . . . The cameras rove excitingly through this fabulous hurly-burly. . . ."

To achieve this realistic effect, the studio had sent Susan, co-star Dan Dailey, and other key personnel to New York, and photographed them in Seventh Avenue dress establishments. Some of the street scenes had even been shot with hidden cameras.

Susan found the experience exhilarating. As in the past, a return to New York had an electrifying effect on her, renewing her energies and elevating her spirits. She was the hometown girl who had made good, the queen returning to her subjects, and she was treated accordingly. Although her eyes were usually hidden by large tinted glasses with prescription lenses, her long flaming hair made her easily identifiable. Yet she wasn't mobbed in public places—just admired from a discreet distance—and she loved every minute of it. To a *New York Post* reporter who visited a location site one afternoon, she freely admitted: "It's *wonderful* being a movie star, being able to go to the best Fifth Avenue shops and buy the toys for your children you never could have."

But the movie star still couldn't shake some of the "little girl from Brooklyn" ways.

After her scenes for *Wholesale* were completed, Susan stayed on at the Hampshire House with Jess for a few additional days to catch a few shows and do some shopping. A young movie-buff photographer, with whom she had become acquainted during the Parsons's tour, was invited to her suite to say goodbye, and recalls that afternoon as being "absolutely chaotic, frantic. Susan wanted to take some of the hotel's soap back to California with her and asked the maid to get her some additional bars. The maid came back with about a dozen of the guest-size packages. Susan looked at them and told the girl, 'No, this isn't the right kind.' Obviously, the hotel had two different brands covered by their own wrapper, and Susan favored a particular one. The maid disappeared and returned with the proper brand. It was all very strange, since the large economy size could have been picked up at any grocery or drugstore in California at the time for about a dime. I could have understood her doing this if she was traveling about Europe, where good soap was still hard to come by in 1950, or if the Hampshire House soap was made from some special formula. But this was plain Lux or Ivory or Cashmere Bouquet.

"The madness continued when she went downstairs to check out. Jess was busy seeing to the luggage, as I recall. The hotel

had charged her for certain meals which Susan insisted the studio should be absorbing. There was quite a to-do about it, and finally the hotel agreed to make an adjustment. I teasingly told Susan that she should consider herself lucky she wasn't charged for all that soap. She was not amused."

By this time, thanks to *My Foolish Heart, Rawhide*, and *I Can Get It for You Wholesale*, Susan's career was accelerating rapidly. Shortly after her return from New York, she was selected as "Queen of Glamour" by the Motion Picture Photographers' Association, and with that lofty though somewhat gaudy title, a siege of calls and letters began, from portrait painters asking her to sit for them, and cosmetic firms wanting endorsement of their products. Dress manufacturers wanted to produce a Hayward gown for the following fall, and a florist announced that he had created a Susan Hayward–Queen of Glamour Rose.

Susan would have none of these projects, but there was no doubt that the glamour build-up had finally begun in earnest. Even as she was stocking up on free soap, Zanuck was mulling over her next project, a rather elaborate rewrite of the Bible that would, as the good book says, "come to pass" and usher in Susan's reign as the queen of Twentieth Century-Fox.

Back on March 26, 1947, James Mason and his wife, Pamela Mason, had made their American stage debuts in *Bathsheba*, "a comedy-drama based on the Old Testament" written by Jacques Deval. Despite Mason's overwhelming personal appeal, the play had lasted a limp twenty-nine performances. Zanuck, who owned the film rights, blamed this in part on the writing, in part on the casting—Mrs. Mason lacked the sexuality to make the steamy affair convincing, he thought—and in 1950, set out to right both wrongs.

First, he threw out the Deval play, and hired prolific writer Philip Dunne to flesh out a two-hour screenplay on the bare bones of the Book of Samuel. The story in the Bible begins, "And it came to pass that David arose from his bed and . . . from the roof he saw a woman washing herself," and ends tersely, "But the thing David had done displeased the Lord." That was about as much of the Bible as could be found in the finished screenplay too. Dunne's final product owed considerably more

to Hollywood than to the Old Testament and, to top it off, it was largely written in blank verse.

"Bathsheba has sinned," Raymond Massey would proclaim sonorously as the prophet Nathan. "She has brought adultery and murder. She has brought the drought and the famine. She has brought the wrath of God upon Israel." And so on.

For the casting, Zanuck was convinced that Gregory Peck, who had so admirably "passed for Jewish" in the Oscar-winning *Gentleman's Agreement*, would be the perfect choice as the Lion of Judea. And Susan Hayward, in spite of her flaming red hair and less-then-Semitic features, was just the one to generate the fire that would justify David's defiance of his God.

Susan didn't exactly fall over with gratitude. She let it be known that she'd be happier if the stage title was retained or if it were called "Bathsheba and David." Then, told that Zanuck was toying with the possibility of filming in Europe or Palestine, she had her agent insist upon a clause in her contract guaranteeing transportation for her twins to either place.

As it turned out, Zanuck had a change of heart about a journey to Jerusalem, and built the holy city on his spacious back lot. And in November, Susan took her famous Biblical bath on a "closed set" behind an opaque screen.

Zanuck called upon Henry King to serve as Susan's director. King had guided Susan through *I'd Climb the Highest Mountain*, a leisurely, presumably inspirational little story about a rural Methodist parson and his perky, city-bred wife, just a few months before, but Susan had not cared for it or him. Known as a "man's director" who had previously helped Tyrone Power achieve stardom, King had directed Peck in such powerhouses as *Twelve O'Clock High* and *The Gunfighter*, and obviously favored his male star. There is no other explanation for his allowing Susan to come across like a 1950 lovesick cheerleader admiring the college football hero. After a suggestive romp on a knoll, she breathlessly inquires:

"David, did you *really* kill Goliath? *Was he as big as they say?*"

To which Peck modestly replies, "*I admit he grows a little bigger every year.*"

For all his idotic lines, Peck's portrayal of King David was unanimously applauded. Susan's Bathsheba and the film itself

drew mixed notices. *Time* magazine's review was possibly the most definitive.

> It comes dangerously close to serving as a sleeping potion.... Peck's performance carried surprising authority. But the script is more notable for words than action, and its pretensions toward serious drama are undermined by a plot that never quite overcomes its resemblance to boudoir farce.... Disappointing as a spectacle, *David and Bathsheba* is no more successful in its frank tale of adultery. Even the most sensational episodes are weighed down with portentous airs and long-winded prattle. And while the picture gathers an ever-loftier mood of religiosity, David and Bathsheba spend nearly as much time suffering and repenting their sins as committing them.

Despite its objections to the film, though, *Time* conceded that Susan's performance was thorough. The *New York Times*'s A. H. Weiler, however, while blessing the epic for its "reverential and sometimes majestic treatment," found the cast "entirely overshadowed" by Peck's performance and damned Susan's Bathsheba as "a Titian-tressed charmer who seems closer to Hollywood than to the Bible." Perhaps the most appropriate middle ground was found by *Newsweek*, which allowed that "under the trying circumstances in which they find themselves, both Peck and Miss Hayward bring considerable dignity and conviction to their roles."

The reviews would not appear until the following August, but when the picture wound up its shooting in early February, Susan, still smarting at what she called her "starlet treatment" by King, flippantly told Zanuck, "Well, I'm not counting on any Oscar nominations this year."

"Maybe not," replied Zanuck, "but you'll feel differently after completing your next one." Beaming, he handed her a script tentatively titled *The Jane Froman Story*.

❈ *chapter 11* ❈

She's my twelve-million-dollar baby.

DARRYL F. ZANUCK

SUSAN'S LOOKING GLASS confirmed what Darryl F. Zanuck had benevolently proclaimed: that among his leading ladies, she was unequivocably the fairest of them all. Approaching her thirty-fourth birthday, she still photographed like a woman in her midtwenties. Furthermore, prompting Zanuck's comment, she was now the star of twelve million dollars' worth of Twentieth Century-Fox's films. In the first four months of 1951, three of them would be released.

With a Song in My Heart was not scheduled to go into production until late spring of that year, but in the interval the movie-going public was deluged with Susan Hayward pictures. Susan had hoped to take a prolonged vacation trip to Ireland with Jess during that time, but the studio wasn't about to let her go away, with so much at stake. Among other duties, it insisted that she (together with Henry King) attend the gala premiere of *I'd Climb the Highest Mountain*, set to take place at Atlanta's Paramount Theater on February 17. Georgia's Governor Herman Talmadge agreed to be on hand to accept an engraved copy of the script. Despite a driving rain, several thousand fans jammed the theater. The picture received some needed publicity, and spurred on by the Twentieth Century-Fox publicity department, the state senate passed a resolution officially naming Susan "an adopted daughter of Georgia." It was an honor that would prove prophetic.

I'd Climb the Highest Mountain did not reach New York until May. However, with *Rawhide* opening at the Rivoli in late March and *I Can Get It for You Wholesale* set for the Roxy

..., Susan was, without exception, the screen's most
... that spring.

...egan work on *The Jane Froman Story*, now retitled
Wit. Song in My Heart, on June 15, 1951.

As produced and written by Lamar Trotti, *With a Song in
My Heart* follows the life and career of Jane Froman, beginning
with her rise from young radio singer in 1936 to nationally
popular radio, recording, and nightclub star. Her career
triumphs, however, are counterpointed by domestic discord,
as her songwriter husband (David Wayne) fails to become
successful. With the advent of World War II, Froman volun-
teers to entertain the troops in Europe—when tragedy inter-
venes. The plane crashes, many aboard are killed, but Jane
and pilot John Burn (Rory Calhoun), who later falls in love
with her, are among the survivors. Not without cost, however:
Froman's left knee is shattered, her right leg almost severed,
and there is doubt she'll ever walk again—but after a long
series of operations, she returns to the stage, to nightclubs, and
eventually to her interrupted USO tour: still on crutches, and
a shining example of courage both to the wounded GIs and the
general public. Her romantic crisis is resolved when her husband gives her up, enabling her to find happiness with John
Burn.*

It was a strong script, possibly strong enough to stand alone
without benefit of songs, but Twentieth was taking no chances
and stuffed the film full of such popular standards as "Blue
Moon," "Tea for Two," "That Old Feeling," "I'll Walk Alone,"
"Get Happy," and the title song. That song, the especially
written "Montparnasse," and "Jim's Toasted Peanuts" provided
three dazzling production numbers, as did the rousing "American Medley," comprised of songs with state titles: "Deep in
the Heart of Texas," and so forth.

Susan was working on her strenuous dance routines with
choreographer Billy Daniel when Jane Froman arrived in Los
Angeles in May to act as technical advisor and record the songs
for the movie. Later, she would remember her time on the set
as "one of the greatest emotional experiences of my life."

Susan had been Froman's personal choice for the role, not
because of any physical resemblance—there was none between

---

*Burn and Froman were later divorced, and in 1962, Froman married
Roland H. Smith, a childhood friend. Froman died on April 22, 1980.

her and the olive-skinned, dark-haired singer—but because "her heart and spirit were right."

"All the time Susan was doing the picture," Froman would recall in a *Photoplay* article, "off the set as well as on, she lived me and breathed me. And so similar to mine was the quality of her speaking voice that it seemed perfectly natural when my songs seemingly came from her lips.

"When I recorded my songs for the picture, Susan was always around. She sat on the set day after day, three and four hours at a time, watching every move I made as I sang, watching, always watching. Susan struck me as being a strange girl, so sensational in appearance, so quiet of voice and manner.

"Then ten days before we went before the cameras, she came up to me in the commissary and said, 'I'd like to have a long talk with you.'

"Half an hour later we met in Susan's dressing room and spent the whole afternoon and far into the night discussing my life. She asked about my childhood, my mother, my father, my grandmother. She wanted to know what my drives were, my tastes, interests, and hobbies.

"We went over the script scene for scene. I can't, of course, recall our conversation word for word.

"But in essence she wanted to know my exact feelings when I was in the water after the clipper went down, what I talked to the pilot about as he held me up in the water, the exact nature of my injuries, and my exact emotional condition before and after my many operations.

"Susan would, in fact, go to director Walter Lang and demand, 'Look, make me ugly—a girl can't go through all this and come out looking beautiful.' And so in this sequence she looked and sounded as I used to—gray, grim, hair messy, tongue thick."

One of the scenes in the picture portrayed a deeply moving true experience: the time when Froman, on crutches and back again with the USO in May 1945, managed to bring a "hopelessly" shell-shocked young soldier out of his trance for the first time. "It was so stirring," Froman remembered, "to be able to make a shell-shocked boy walk and talk when the doctors couldn't, when the nurses couldn't. Oh, brother!"

In recreating the incident, Walter Lang and Zanuck agreed that the proper casting of the boy's role was crucial. Both wanted a comparative unknown, to lend reality to one of the

picture's most touching episodes. Zanuck was also shrewd enough to realize that the role could turn that unknown into a valuable property for the studio if, of course, the boy was able to deliver.

After a search, twenty-one-year-old Robert (R. J.) Wagner was the unanimous choice to play the boy, a role listed in the cast sheets as simply "GI Paratrooper." Wagner—who had come to Los Angeles from Detroit and caddied for the stars at the Bel Air Country Club—had had no formal acting training when Twentieth had signed him to a "stock" contract. Up to now, his main achievement had been a fourth-billed role in the Richard Widmark starrer *The Halls of Montezuma*. Now the stunning impact he'd make in *With a Song in My Heart* would set him on the road to stardom.

Bob credits Susan for his success. "When Zanuck put me in that picture," he recalls, "he said it would be the greatest thing I'd ever do, because people would walk out of the theater and ask, 'Who is that guy?' That's true, you know, but when I did it, I had no idea of how it all worked or what was going to happen. And Susan was marvelous to me.

"Before I did the picture, I used to see Susan Hayward on the lot all the time. She was a very big star, and I was just a young kid starting out, but even before we worked together I remember her being so very nice to me—so very, very gracious.

"The Jane Froman role was a very difficult and demanding role for her—to have to 'sing' with all those playbacks, and act a living person. Because Walter Lang, the director, liked me, I was permitted to watch the recordings and be around the music department and all, to get the feeling of things.

"Everything I did in the picture was with Susan. Our first scene together was at the theater where she is appearing in *Artists and Models*, and she calls me to the stage and sings 'Embraceable You.' Then, later on, she recognizes me, a shell-shocked victim in one of the hospitals at which she's performing. It was a very moving thing, because the guy was real and the scene a real incident.

"The thing about that moment was, I didn't know very much what I was doing. You know, they say that young actors or child stars who don't know much about what they're doing are sometimes better. Well, Walter Lang said to me, 'Just watch her. . . .' There's an old saying in our business—one I've often

used—that goes, 'It's like working with Rin Tin Tin... you just pull the cat out of the bag and the ears will go up.' That's what they used to do with Rin Tin Tin. When they wanted his ears to go up, they'd have a guy standing offstage with a cat in a bag... and then let the cat out at the crucial moment. For me, Susan was the best 'cat' I could possibly have had, because when she started to work, I automatically responded. I didn't know how to put the proper emotions across. What she did was produce a whole reaction in me.

"I didn't go home and start to rehearse the part and say to myself, 'Now I have to get tears in my eyes,' because I didn't know how to do that. She must have realized that because, my God, she was so helpful, and it was such a marvelous real moment. When she sang 'I'll Walk Alone' to me in the hospital scene, I got so caught up in the moment that the tears just came. It got to her too—because after it was over, she ran to her dressing room and just came apart.

"Whenever I saw her after that—at the premiere of *The Robe*, for example—she couldn't have been nicer. She was terrific to me always. A few years later, a couple of gossip columnists decided to link our names—but that's a lot of bull. I had a lot of respect for her—always—but it was a totally professional relationship."

Robert Wagner also remembers meeting Ellen Marrenner during the filming—one of the few times Susan ever invited her mother to the lot. And Jane Froman recalls the twins being brought to the set during the big production number featuring the title song: "Susan's attitude toward them was so adult. She treated them like little men... with courtesy, charm, and humor."

Over the years, many of the directors who had worked with Susan had admired her ability to lose herself in a role, to actually become the character she was portraying in the film. On the testimony of Wagner, Froman, and others, it is apparent that for the first time in her career, Susan was projecting a *behind-the-scenes* warmth that endeared her to everyone connected with the picture.

She was a model of cooperation. Although she had a clause in her contract forbidding the studio to cut her hair for any role, she herself suggested it be done for this film.

Director Walter Lang would say, shortly before his death in 1972, "I found Susan to be a most dedicated actress, one

with great talent—wonderful to work with—one of the screen's greatest stars."

Rory Calhoun, cast as airline pilot John Burn, the man who became Froman's second husband, had admired Susan when he co-starred with her in *I'd Climb the Highest Mountain*. By *With a Song in My Heart*, admiration had turned to adoration. When asked by Merv Griffin in 1972 if there were any players he remembered with special fondness, Rory quickly replied: "Yes, Susan Hayward." As with Wagner, however, the relationship did not extend beyond the studio walls. Only one member of the cast would become a close friend and dinner guest: Brooklyn-born Thelma Ritter, who played her nurse.

On August 10, coinciding with the national release of *David and Bathsheba*, Susan left the set early to get to Hollywood in time to place her footprints in cement in the forecourt of Grauman's Chinese Theater. For the first and only time, the cement was sprinkled with gold dust, in anticipation of the profits the studio expected to make on Hayward pictures.

When *With a Song in My Heart* was released in April of 1952, the accolades Susan received were as lavish as the film itself.

Look magazine praised: "In *With a Song in My Heart*, Susan Hayward steps into the character of singer-World War II heroine Jane Froman and makes her so alive that from now on the two women will be one in the public's mind. . . . All in all, Susan Hayward, with the warmth and range of the artist she has become, makes the Froman story a convincing experience."

David Hanna of the *Hollywood Reporter* applauded: "*With a Song in My Heart* is a picture with everything—great stories, great songs, and great performances. Susan Hayward is warm and lovely as Jane Froman." And *Variety* echoed: "Susan Hayward responds to the [Walter] Lang direction in first-rate fashion. She punches over the vocal simulation and deftly handles the dramatic phases." In all, in critic Helen Bower's words, the role was "far and away the best role Miss Hayward has ever done—and she had plenty to challenge her talents."

Only Bosley Crowther of the *New York Times* struck a discordant note: "We have to report that Lamar Trotti, who wrote and produced the film, Walter Lang, who directed, and Susan Hayward, who plays the leading role—have combined to do a job that is just about as grandiose and mawkish as Hollywood homage can be. . . . Miss Hayward makes it un-

mistakably clear that chin-up and eyes-on-the-horizon are the attitudes she wants to get across. One would not call her performance either subtle or restrained. And in her pantomiming of the heroine's delivery of songs, she does it as though she was conscious of performing for posterity."

Mr. Crowther was definitely a minority of one. Had his eyes been as sharp as his tongue, however, he would have really had something to write about.

Bob Wagner laughs as he recalls: "One of the theater owners wrote in, terribly shocked, saying that one of Susan's breasts fell out of her dress in one of the numbers. Now, in 1952, that was pretty heady stuff. I went with Walter Lang and Lamar Trotti to the projection room, and we looked at it over and over and over again—and couldn't find it.

"Finally, in the Movieola, you could see it in just a couple of frames—in a number in which she was dancing with Dick Allen."

With hundreds of prints in distribution and the film breaking house records throughout the country, the studio was faced with a dilemma. Apart from the expense of recalling and re-editing the film, the attendant publicity would not have been the kind Zanuck wanted associated with an inspirational family film. So the eagle-eyed exhibitor got a new print, and the studio gambled on no one else's being able to spot the offending frame. No one did—not even the Hays office, that notorious protector of movie-goers' morality.

In April of 1952, Susan was riding high. Between the shooting and the screening of the film, however, a great many things had occurred—not all of them pleasant.

chapter 12

I introduced Susan to Howard Hughes in 1938. She cooked him a chicken dinner. He disliked her intensely. She disliked him. That was that.

BEN MEDFORD

HOWARD HUGHES had been aware of Susan Hayward's development for years, but it wasn't until she had signed with Zanuck and starred as the sensuous Bathsheba that his interest became truly aroused. Maybe it was time for another chicken dinner.

In addition, Hughes, and producer Jerry Wald—who would later become the head of Twentieth Century-Fox—had seen a rough cut of *With a Song in My Heart*. Both were acutely aware of Hayward's box-office lure, particularly with women, and that's exactly what an upcoming production of theirs, *This Man Is Mine*, sorely needed. So, mixing business with pleasure, Hughes resolved to "borrow" Susan.

This involved a little horse trading. Hughes owned Jane Russell's contract, and Zanuck wanted *her* for a projected musical of *Gentlemen Prefer Blondes*, which would co-star Marilyn Monroe, whom Zanuck was building toward stardom. If I can have Russell, Zanuck told Hughes, you can have your pick of the Twentieth Century-Fox ladies. Done, said Hughes. In point of fact, he had had his pick of Twentieth's women for some time. He had already made a minicareer of romancing such Zanuck stars as Gene Tierney, Jean Peters, and Linda Darnell, among others. There was, in fact, an industrywide joke that Hughes didn't need a little black book, he merely had to check the obliging Zanuck's contract list.

In any case, Hughes promptly selected Susan, and Susan found herself perplexed as to why she was being exiled to RKO

for *This Man Is Mine*. Any one of a dozen starlets could have played the part of Arthur Kennedy's wife in what was essentially a man's picture. In fact, its rodeo sequences would so far outshine the picture's rather tame domestic triangle that, when the film was released in late October, it would be more suitably titled *The Lusty Men*. Susan felt misused, even though guaranteed top billing.

She also did not get along at all with her chief co-star, Robert Mitchum. The script called for a great deal of antagonism between her character, Louise, and Mitchum's Jeff, and the emotion required no great acting ability on either part. Although respectful of his professionalism, Susan was turned off by Bob's boisterous behavior and off-color language. She was not amused when, seeing her walk by on the way to the set, he'd bellow, "There goes the old gray mare." She was even less amused when Mitchum tried to liven up their working hours by eating garlic before their intimate scenes. Soon her complaints reached to the top.

Hughes was sorry. He couldn't control Mitchum's mischievous behavior—nobody could at that time—but he could and did make certain that both on the lot and on location Susan was otherwise accorded a treatment usually reserved for visiting royalty. The courtesies mollified Susan—and piqued her curiosity.

The details of Susan's first private meeting with Howard Hughes are unrecorded, and it is highly unlikely that their affair began during the filming of *The Lusty Men*. For all his bizarre behavior and varied sexual exploits, Hughes had an almost prudish morality in some ways, which included a self-imposed proviso against bedding another man's wife. However, he was well aware of the problems in her marriage, and he probably concluded it was only a matter of time until she was free. Meanwhile, he made himself agreeable, exercising his not inconsiderable charm in her presence, and let matters take their course.

Before long, word of Hughes's interest in Susan leaked out, and came to the attention of the formidable Hedda Hopper, who requested (demanded) that Susan come to tea at her house. Susan resisted. Although there was no open hostility between her and Hopper, Susan was still extremely loyal to her friend Louella Parsons—anything important was said to Louella first—and, besides, she resented being summoned to Hopper's

house as if she were still a schoolgirl or struggling starlet. She agreed to meet Hopper for lunch at the studio if it was absolutely necessary, but she had no intention of making house calls. Hopper, for her part, was equally adamant that the interview be conducted in the privacy of her own den—without publicity people or interruptions. And she knew how to get her way.

Hopper promptly called Harry Brand at Twentieth Century-Fox publicity and promised him a spread on Susan in the kingsize *Graphic* magazine of the *Chicago Tribune*, with subsequent syndication by the Chicago Tribune Syndicate, if he would get Susan to her house. They'd talk at length about *With a Song in My Heart*, she indicated. Aware this could mean a million dollars' worth of free publicity for the forthcoming film, Brand guaranteed Susan would be at Hopper's door at the appointed time even if Zanuck himself had to carry her over his shoulder. Fortunately, such drastic measures were not necessary.

Susan appeared at Hopper's manse looking and acting every inch the star. True to her word, Hopper did talk to Susan at length about Jane Froman, *With a Song in My Heart*, and other career matters (all of which were dutifully recorded in print), but with that out of the way she was free to zero in on more personal topics. Hopper would write:

> Susan Hayward is one of the most gorgeous girls in the star line-up. And when high frequency sex is needed in a starring role, Hayward is the girl who can deliver it. This redhead, whose perfect profile runs clear to the ankles, epitomizes everything a man looks for in a woman.... Susan's the perfect location for a mink coat. If you toss in a sky-blue scarf, four diamond wedding rings, a huge mirror-cut solitaire ... she looked like wolf bait, and we promptly got into the subject.

Miss Hopper, of course, had one particular wolf on her mind. Too shrewd to name names, however, she hoped that Susan could be led unwarily into the trap. But Hopper, it seems, had met her match.

"Wolves," countered Susan. "Do we have any wolves in this town? I wouldn't know! I'm a happily married woman and the mother of large and active twins who manage to keep very

much in evidence. What wolf wouldn't be very much discouraged with such a setup!

"A woman gets back what she invites, largely. Remember, the woman is always the aggressor, although it is her wily way to make the man believe he has thought of the whole thing. That is part of nature's plan. I happen to be a very happy woman, and I'm not naturally the flirtatious type."

Susan was letting Hopper have it with both barrels.

"My husband is one of the most interesting men I've ever met. That's why he and I are seen so seldom in nightclubs. We find we have better Scotch at home, and if we feel like talking we don't like to be interrupted. It's not unusual for us to sit in our own living room and discuss books, plays, pictures, and life in general all night long if I don't happen to be working the following day. Jess is not only a good actor. He's one of the best. He has humor along with intelligence, and I'm in love with him."

And when Hopper tactlessly referred to the slump in Jess's career and the huge gap in their earnings (Susan had reported $374,000 that year; Jess $665), Susan rushed to his defense, calling it just one of those arid spots that come to all Hollywood actors.

"I could have been one who had to ride it out," she explained. "That would have been more serious as I have less to offer than he. It will be over one of these days when the right part comes up, the part he just has to do. The important thing is not to take a lot of little unimportant things in the interim just to say you're busy. This is harder by far for the one who isn't working than for the one who is; if my turn ever comes, I am certain of Jess's backing and loyalty. Marriage is so many things—it's decency and honor and love and respect. It's hanging onto the solid thing."

So there! Any more questions, Hedda? No? Then I must be leaving. But Susan couldn't quite resist going a little too far. "Money doesn't mean too terribly much to me," she concluded. "Perhaps that's because we have everything we want." But then she made a revealing slip, when she added, regarding a new, jeweled wedding ring Jess was getting for her: "An actress should pick larger stones; you get more for them in a pawn shop if you get into trouble."

Hopper didn't catch it, though, having been snowed under by the rest of Susan's performance. Hedda Hopper was neither

sentimental nor gullible nor prone to show partiality to one of Parsons's pets, but by the time Susan had finished, the columnist had become convinced that all was rosy with the Barkers and that the gossip about Hughes was just a rumor. It may have been one of the greatest performances in Susan's life. And there the matter lay—for a while . . .

Actually, Hopper didn't realize what it took to get Susan to come to her house. Susan rarely went *to* anyone, usually they came to *her*. And where they came to was the Twentieth lot. Although her living room was finally livable, she refused to permit reporters, photographers, or press agents into the house. Family photographs, when she allowed them, could be taken only in the garden or at poolside.

Other than that, Fox publicity woman Sonia Wolfson remembers, "Susan Hayward was one of the most cooperative stars I've worked with," and Miss Wolfson, now in retirement, has worked with a great many of them. She has other things to add too about that period in the star's life.

"I was assigned to her when she did *David and Bathsheba* and *With a Song in My Heart* and a couple of other films. I never had any fault to find with her. Susan was very warm to me; she never tried to postpone an interview. I met Jess Barker just once, but I was never in her home. However, she told me that she was a silk sleeper. She only slept on satin sheets and pillowcases. But once a week she'd cream herself all over and put old cotton sheets on her bed. Funny, the odd things you remember . . .

"I don't think Susan ever told me an untruth. When she was in the mood she could be sharp—I mean with a quip, not with a fib. She was very quick on the uptake."

Miss Wolfson would usually ask the stars in her charge to expound about kissing. "Susan had a good sense of humor, and when you got her in the right mood, she would love to be provocative." The essence of Susan's dissertation on kissing was hardly one to endear her to any of her leading men. She insisted that the men who had kissed her for the magazine ads when she was a Thornton model had performed their assignments with more mastery than Gregory Peck, Dana Andrews, Rory Calhoun, Robert Mitchum, or any of the others with whom she had worked.

"I had a new man in every ad," she told Sonia Wolfson. "And we kissed harder and longer for those stills than was ever permitted for a movie. That was my education. I kissed more guys and never saw them again. I remember some of those poses got my back out of whack a couple of times—once so severely that the doctor bill was bigger than my modeling fee. It's interesting, but none of those male models I worked with made it to Hollywood. I guess I must have ruined them."

Susan made sure to add that none of the male models ever "made it" with *her*, either.

Sonia Wolfson had no idea of what caused the friction between Susan Hayward and Darryl Zanuck. She does speculate, though, from her many years at Twentieth Century-Fox:

"Maybe she kept turning him down. He was the one who tried to get every girl on the lot to sleep with him. Some of the gals told me things they wouldn't tell anyone else. And what they said and what he said—well, they're totally different stories.

"Maybe Zanuck kept trying to make passes at Susan, and she wouldn't respond to his advances. That would certainly leave him with an unpleasant feeling about her...

"But the wardrobe girls, the make-up men, the crew—they all seemed to like her very much. I never heard any of them say an unkind thing about her."

Something else stands out in Sonia Wolfson's mind: Shortly after Susan checked back at Fox after her loan-out to RKO for *The Lusty Men*, Susan said ambiguously: "You know, Sonia, there are times when the grass looks greener...."

And there was one other portent of the future: about that time, Dana Andrews's business manager, who was also Susan's, came to him and said, according to Andrews, "I don't know what I'm going to do about that girl. She insists on filing an income tax return separate from Jess Barker's and, even though I've yelled until I'm sick that she could save a *lot* of money by filing a joint return, she's too damn stubborn to do it.... Dana, she always liked you, and she'll listen to you even if she won't listen to me. *Try* to persuade her to file joint returns from now on."

Andrews said he'd try. He called the studio and made a date to see her for lunch. He then launched into every argument he could think of to get her to file jointly with Jess Barker. She finally stopped him and said something like: "But Jess and

I are having problems, and if I file jointly and then subsequently divorce him, he can lay claim to half of everything I've got—which he doesn't deserve."

"Then," Andrews said, "I gave what may be the worst advice I ever gave to anyone. I took her hand and kindly but firmly told her: 'Susie . . . you and Jess have had problems for years, but you've always weathered them, and there's *no* reason to believe you won't again. It's wrong for you to waste so much money on a separate return when it's so unnecessary. You know I'm thinking of what's best for you. Won't you do as I ask?'

"She hesitated, then smiled and said: 'Of course, Dana. You're right, I know.'"

Andrews laughed. "It wasn't long after that that the Barkers were telling it to the judge. . . ."

chapter 13

BY THE START of 1953, Susan was on the verge of a nervous collapse, although she wouldn't face up to it. Since signing with Zanuck, she had made nine films nonstop. Irritable and exhausted—"Whatever it is you want, the answer is *no!*" a studio aide remembers her snapping—she now found falling asleep impossible without the aid of pills, and was smoking up to four packs of cigarettes a day to relieve the tension.

Yet on the surface everything seemed to be going her way. Joseph Schenck, controlling the fortunes of Twentieth Century-Fox from New York, boasted, "On the basis of our investment alone, Susan Hayward is our most valuable player. We've tied up nearly one quarter of our studio budget on her." And the investment was earning out. In 1952 alone, Susan's films returned a then-outstanding eleven million dollars. The reports on *The Snows of Kilimanjaro*, released in September, were still coming in, and *The President's Lady* (with Charlton Heston) and *White Witch Doctor* (with Robert Mitchum) were being readied for distribution. Zanuck was a happy man.

Throughout January and February of 1953, Susan was showered with honors.

The magnetic power of Hayward's box-office appeal had carried her from nineteenth place in the 1951 *Motion Picture Herald* Poll of American Theater Owners to ninth in 1952; Doris Day, in seventh position, was the only other woman on the list. *Box Office* magazine chose Susan as the most popular star of 1952.

At Twentieth Century-Fox, she soared ahead of Betty Grable as the Number One fan-mail draw, although Susan rarely looked at her fan mail and almost never answered it. She let studio secretaries take care of paid requests for photographs.

The idea of paying a private secretary out of her own salary appalled her.

Her public took no offense.

With a Song in My Heart and her performance as Jane Froman were overwhelmingly voted *Photoplay*'s Gold Medal winners, coveted awards in the film community. Gary Cooper, with whom she had worked as an obscure ingenue in *Beau Geste*, won the award for most popular male star for *High Noon*. Only one thing spoiled her enjoyment. *Photoplay* always featured its winners on the cover of its announcement issue, but this year, its editors inexplicably chose to use Jane Powell instead. For fifteen years Susan had wanted to appear on the covers of *Photoplay*, *Modern Screen*, and *Life* magazine. All ran and would run articles on her, and she would appear on the front of other magazines, yet she was consistently passed over as "cover material" by these three giants. Not even her box-office appeal could alter the situation. And now, when she should have had the cover of *Photoplay* guaranteed, she had been passed over. What she considered a deliberate slight understandably diminished her appreciation of the award.

Nevertheless, when *Photoplay* held its awards party in the Crystal Room of the Beverly Hills Hotel on February 9, she was there. Sylvia (Mrs. Irving) Wallace, West Coast editor of the magazine, buzzed about, making sure everything was running smoothly. This biographer, covering the story, was recruited as an official hostess; greeting the guests and assigning them to their table, in Susan's case the dais.

Magnificently gowned in an egg-shell lace gown with tight bodice and bouffant skirt, wearing elbow-length white gloves and large diamond clips, Susan was breathtakingly beautiful. Zanuck escorted her into the reception room, where the photographers were waiting. Jess hovered uncomfortably in the background.

The photographers' attention, however, was abruptly diverted by the late arrival of Marilyn Monroe (who had been voted the most popular newcomer of the year), escorted by the diminutive gossip columnist Sidney Skolsky. Marilyn was shrewdly attired in a skin-tight gold lamé gown—which, to everyone's amusement and delight, fell apart at the seams before she even got to the table. The proceedings were delayed and flash bulbs popped as Marilyn was sewn back into her dress in full view of everyone: producers, stars, and the press.

Susan never got their attention back. Monroe, whose first starring picture *Niagara* had opened a few weeks earlier, was the evening's sensation, all the while innocently protesting embarrassment about the dress. Furious, Susan was overheard voicing her conviction that Zanuck had been a co-conspirator in the stunt. Indeed, had he wished, Zanuck could have insisted that Marilyn be decently dressed for the occasion—but he was wise to the ways of building a new sex symbol. Susan received her gold medal, then left the party as quickly and quietly as possible.

A week later, on February 15, she gracefully accepted another award, this time with no disruption: the gold "Henrietta" given by the Foreign Press Association as the World's Favorite Screen Star of 1952. Appropriately, she took the occasion happily to tell the assembled journalists that she soon would be realizing a lifelong dream—her first trip abroad.

In 1951, she and Jess had made plans for a European holiday, but then had had them cancelled when Zanuck wouldn't allow her sufficient time away from the studio. Now she felt secure enough to turn a deaf ear to his pleas to stay home and represent the studio at the Academy Awards.

For the first time in their history, on March 19, 1953, the awards were going to be seen on nationwide television, and to Zanuck's chagrin no Twentieth Century-Fox production was in competition for Best Picture. Only three times before during his reign—1936, 1939, and 1945—had there been such an oversight. He had been certain that one of his three blockbusters that year—*Viva Zapata, My Cousin Rachel,* and *With a Song in My Heart*—would be one of the top five, and to be passed over in favor of *The Greatest Show on Earth* (the ultimate winner), *High Noon, Ivanhoe, Moulin Rouge,* and Republic's *The Quiet Man* was galling. He concluded (probably accurately) that his three films had split the Twentieth vote and thereby cancelled one another out.

If Zanuck couldn't be a factor in the Best Picture category, however, he could at least be represented at the ceremonies by his stars. The problem was that he couldn't depend on Brando, still steaming over the injustice of being the only member of *A Streetcar Named Desire* cast snubbed the previous year. Newcomer Burton and old-timer Quinn had promised to be there, but neither could be relied on, and the studio needed coverage. Susan was his best hope.

All his efforts to persuade her to change her mind, however, failed.

"Look," she said adamantly, "I attended twice, and lost twice. And had to explain to some of those vultures who had been dying for me to lose, how 'there'll always be a next day.' Well, I'm not going to make a television spectacle of myself in front of a few million viewers, and that's that!"

Susan's attitude was based, not only on a need for a vacation, but on some cold calculation. The previous December, Shirley Booth had won the New York Film Critics' Award on the first ballot, and none of the other Oscar nominees had received a single vote, herself included. For all Zanuck's optimism, and the other awards Susan had won that year, she knew that that vote would influence the Academy. "Uncommercial," Booth might be, but she was the one with the edge for the Oscar. So she might as well go ahead with the trip as planned, Susan figured.

On February 23, Zanuck grumpily wished Susan bon voyage, though he couldn't help adding that she still would have had three weeks abroad if she should change her mind and return for the Oscars. Susan smiled.

In New York, the Barkers boarded separate planes for Paris. To a perplexed reporter, she said, matter-of-factly, "We always travel on separate planes as protection for the boys. After all, if one plane crashes, there would still be someone to look after Tim and Greg." (While they were away, they planned to have Ellen Marrenner look after the boys.)

The flight to Paris in those pre-jet days took twelve hours, and Susan had much to think about—most particularly her marriage. In five months she and Jess would be celebrating their ninth wedding anniversary, practically a record according to Hollywood standards—Lana Turner had already gone through four husbands and God knew how many lovers. No matter how angry Susan had become at Jess over the years, it had never led her to seek vengeance by being unfaithful. And, unlike her father, Jess had never sought outside feminine companionship as balm for his bruised ego. Had he done so, word would have reached Louella—and "well-meaning" Louella would certainly have passed the information to Susan. There were times, to her own amazement, when Susan almost did wish that Jess were seeing someone else. Then she could at least justify a divorce—even if she still wasn't totally sure that was what she wanted.

What she did want, undeniably, was a working husband. And Jess hadn't had a job in over thirty months. In November he had been up for a lead on television—it had seemed like such a certainty that she had told Louella about it, prompting Parsons to comment in her destructive motherly way: "Susan Hayward may find things a lot less strained around her house now that hubby Jess Barker has been lined up to star in a new TV series." The series, however, had gone down the drain.

A great many jobs Jess was up for had done likewise. Susan wanted a working husband, but her relationship to Jess Barker often was the reason for his *not* working. Later an unattributed friend of his would say in a *Motion Picture* article, "Producers looked at him oddly when he tried to get work. 'So he wants a job and his wife makes $400,000 a year?' They'd give the part to someone else who needed the work to pay the rent.

"Or he'd be sent a script that someone wanted Susie for and tell him if he could interest her in it, there might be a part in the picture for him. It was like throwing a bone to a hungry dog. And Jess wasn't interested in getting a job that way."

Prior to their leaving for Europe, Jess had told a writer friend of his, "I'd give my life for Susan." The friend had used that line in another *Motion Picture* story and added a tag line: "In a way he has."

"Susan was burned up about that story," Jess remembers. "My friend denied writing it, and it didn't have his by-line, but I know who did it."

Jess doesn't elaborate as to why Susan was so angry. Perhaps she hated to face that realization on a printed page: "*In a way he has.*" Or perhaps she was guilt-ridden about her own ambivalent feelings at the time—guilt feelings that were intensified by an indirect pitch from Howard Hughes.

It was about then that one of Hughes's "aides," by-passing Susan's agent Ned Marin, as well as the mighty Zanuck, had let Susan know that Hughes had been so impressed with her work in *The Lusty Men* that he was considering her for the lead in an upcoming multimillion-dollar epic. The aide, notorious for being one of Hughes's prolific procurers, had also hinted that his boss's interest went beyond her talent, adding, not too subtly, "Too bad you're tied up."

It was a great temptation. Both Hughes's charm and wealth held a powerful fascination for Susan and, of all the opportunities she had had since marrying Jess, this was the only one that gave her pause. She was well aware of his reputation as

a ladies' man—his well-reported liaisons with Billie Dove, Katherine Hepburn, Ida Lupino, Olivia de Havilland, Lana Turner, Ava Gardner, and the current Jean Peters, among many others, had provided ample evidence of that. But still . . . what if she were to accept?

It was in that state of mind that Susan approached Orly Airport. Still, it could not have occupied all of her attention. This was, after all, a vacation she had dreamed about all her life. A war, then motherhood, then a career had made it an impossibility. Perhaps that was a blessing. She was coming to Paris not as a green kid or a wide-eyed tourist to be shoved around, but as a glamorous star, newly chosen the world's favorite actress.

Exhausted from the long trip, and concerned as always about her appearance, Susan spent a long time in the ladies' room upon arrival, repairing her make-up and hair, in order to make a dazzling entrance into Paris. Jess's flight had set down an hour earlier, and he was there to meet her. They were pleased to learn that Twentieth Century-Fox's Paris branch had assigned affable, twenty-three-year-old Jean Papote to serve as a combination guide, chauffeur, translator, and press secretary for their stay abroad; also that a low-slung Jaguar had been placed at their disposal. Although Zanuck was annoyed at Susan for not remaining in Hollywood for the Oscar presentations, he was not vindictive.

He was also aware that a good impression abroad would add to the European grosses of her movies, and he had some plans for Europe himself. Studio assets abroad were still being frozen by many countries in desperate need of postwar funds— all monies had to be spent in their countries of origin—but Darryl Zanuck had definite ideas about their eventual use. Because of his passion for his new CinemaScope process, he was planning to produce many films in their actual locales— a sure-fire way of luring viewers away from their tiny black and white television screens.

The Barkers remained at the Lancaster Hotel three days. Paris in February offered little enjoyment. Planning to return in April, they headed for Spain with Papote. "He was a funny little man," Jess recalls today. "Whenever we approached a town, he increased our speed so we'd get through it as quickly as possible. He was in Paris during the Nazi occupation and that had something to do with it." Equipped with Rollei and

Stereo cameras, they toured the château country and southern France, photographing all the historic sights enroute, then crossed the border into Spain.

Susan's postcard to her mother read: "Cased every castle in the country. Looking forward to the bullfights."

In mid-March, Susan and Jess arrived in Valencia, where they were the honored guests of the mayor and were escorted by a protective if rather sinister-looking man named Señor La Fuente—"an eighteen-dollars-a-month branch manager for Twentieth," says Jess—to the *corrida*. The weather in Valencia was as chilly and penetrating as it had been in Paris, and Susan had wrapped herself in her full-length mink, with wrist-length white gloves and dark glasses—highly noticeable, to say the least. Toreador Julio Aparicio dedicated his first bull to her as she watched the fights from her front-row seat, and La Fuente explained the finer points of the action as Jess, ignored, and nauseated by the slaughter, regretted not remaining at the hotel. After the fights, Susan was photographed between La Fuente and toreador Antonete. Jess Barker was unceremoniously shoved into the background. Totally unknown in Spain, Jess was inevitably addressed as "Señor Hayward" and treated with even more indifference than Jean Papote.

A few days later, the Barkers ran into Betsy Blair and Gene Kelly touring the peninsula with their little girl Kerry, which stimulated thoughts of their own two boys. That night they put in a call to Tim and Greg in California and were reassured both were happy and in good health.

Leaving Spain soon after, the Barkers, still with Papote in tow, toured the Mediterranean before heading for Italy. Checking into the Grand Hotel in Rome, Susan was handed a wire informing her that Shirley Booth had, as anticipated, won the best-actress Oscar.

"So much for that," she commented, shrugging. "Thank God I didn't listen to Zanuck."

Rome was chaotic. Susan couldn't leave her suite without being besieged by reporters. Photographers dogged her every move, rudely pushing Jess aside, shouting, screaming, and generally behaving in a manner unique to the Italian press. Their American counterparts weren't much better. Those who couldn't get interviews let their imaginations go wild inventing such fantasies as:

There were moonlight nights with Jess, near the Colosseum;

*love-filled nights on the banks of the Arno, that picturesque
river which snakes its winding paths from the Apennines in
Central Italy west to Pisa. The Barkers are truly one of Hollywood's few happily married young couples. When two people
are as ecstatically happy as Susan and Jess are here in Italy,
they've reached the perfect pattern for life!*

The night before this idyllic portrait appeared, Susan, according to testimony given two years later by Jess, had taken
an overdose of sleeping pills. News of the incident was miraculously kept from the press, however, and an Italian doctor
bribed to maintain his silence and attribute his visit to an upset
stomach due to exotic food.

It is not known why Susan took the overdose. It might well
have been an accident, though it ominously foreshadowed future events, and certainly her insistence on staying in Rome
for a full ten days indicates a quick recovery. The next day
she was up and about. But it was evident that she was becoming
overly dependent on the dangerous yellow capsules.

By now Susan had become enervated by the tedium of
motoring, Papote's incessant conversation—he was invaluable
for arranging hotel accommodations and negotiating purchases,
but his presence could get wearing—and the variables of spring
weather. Instructing Papote to drive the Jaguar back to France,
they took a flight to Paris, where they again checked into the
Lancaster.

April in Paris was not quite the way the song had described
it. The hotel provided all the luxurious little touches befitting
a movie queen, but Jess was still frequently addressed as
"Monsieur Hayward," which nettled. Susan, for her part, found
her spirits in a state of fluctuation. She became totally enraged,
for instance, by the hotel's telephone system, which turned her
attempts to contact the twins in North Hollywood into the
Battle of Waterloo. Used to her behavior by now, Jess explained to a reporter: "She seldom keeps any of her problems
to herself. When she gets into a mood, I don't barge in and
break the spell because I know within a short time she would
bring up the subject herself. Not that I cater to the moods. I
just consider them."

One of the moods he had to consider was her reluctance to
spend money, a hangover from Brooklyn. ("Susan always
seemed to have a fixation about money," her sister Florence

later said. "She said to me once that she was going to keep working and working and making money because maybe something would happen some day . . . she would lose some of it or she wouldn't be able to make as much as she has now.") One afternoon she ard Jess went shopping on the Rue de Rivoli. She had planned to buy a dozen pairs of gloves all in different lengths, but the prices appalled her. When the saleswoman translated the francs into dollars, she stomped out of the salon muttering, "I can get them for half the price at Robinson's [a Beverly Hills department store]."

Since Susan also felt children's clothing and toys were selling at ridiculous prices, she decided to pick up the boys' gifts in New York. Explaining her thriftiness, she frankly admitted: "When you're traveling on studio expense, it's one thing. When you're vacationing on your own, it's blood money." "Spends it like molasses," Jess wisecracked. She did find a couple of antique fans in an out-of-the-way shop, but other than those, and a singing bird in a miniature gold-plated cage, she bought nothing.

Because she was not required to be back in Hollywood for several weeks, she toyed with the possibility of flying to London and then on to Ireland for a few days, but rejected that idea. She also rejected an invitation from the Cannes Film Festival, explaining how anxious she was to get back to her boys. That was probably true. What was even more true, however, was that being with Jess day and night was beginning to get on her nerves. The trip abroad had solved nothing. As far as she was concerned, she was just going through the motions. She didn't know how or when things would finally come to an end, but her emotions now told her that the end would not be long in coming.

❁ chapter 14 ❁

ON APRIL 18, Susan boarded a Pan Am Clipper for her flight back to the States, with Jess following a few hours behind on a TWA Constellation. Instead of flying straight to California, however, she stayed in New York to promote *The President's Lady*, a film about the romance between Andrew Jackson and his wife Rachel Donelsen Jackson made from the Irving Stone best seller, and due to open at the Astor Theater in May.

Charlton Heston, who played Jackson, today recalls their relationship as being "very easy" and "a cordial working ambiance." "Cordial" was about the best that many of the critics could say about their performances as well, the *New York Times*'s Crowther noting that "the stars make sincere and energetic but hardly memorable protagonists," and *Time* magazine finding that "in its writing, direction and acting, it comes out as a too-slick biography film."

Fortunately for Susan, the West Coast trade papers were kinder—the *Hollywood Reporter* gushing, "Miss Hayward is nothing less than wonderful as Rachel. She draws out all the tragedy of a woman who gallantly showed forbearance under the most unbelievable of insults and skillfully she imbues the role with a gaiety and fire that is captivating"—and the grosses looked promising. By and large, audiences ignored the criticisms and flocked to the box office.

Susan was in no mood to look at the grosses, however. Not only were her marital problems weighing on her mind, but she'd just heard some very disturbing news. Whenever she came to New York, she spent time with Sara Little, who'd remained her very close friend throughout all those years. On this trip, Sara confided that her sister Martha had contracted cancer and the doctors had given her just a few more months to live.

Susan, who'd known Martha since their teens, was devastated by the news and by Martha's appearance. "The doctors here aren't gods," she insisted. "I've heard of doctors in California who have had remarkable results with your kind of malignancy. Get packed. I'm taking you back to the coast."

When Martha protested that she was able to afford neither the trip nor the high-priced specialists, Susan cut her off with, "Let me worry about that."

Martha finally agreed to be a houseguest in Sherman Oaks; she was desperate for any chance of survival. In the following months, Susan spent a minimum of five thousand dollars on medical expenses for her, but whenever Martha protested about being a bother, Susan told her, "Believe me, Martha, you're the least of my burdens." And even though she had been informed by the specialists that Martha's chances were exceedingly slim, she continued to radiate optimism about Martha's recovery in her presence, doing everything in her power to make her feel better.

Susan, in fact, was so preoccupied with her friend that she was oblivious to the changes that had taken place at Twentieth Century-Fox.

No longer was she queen of the lot. Despite her film successes, the meteoric rise of Marilyn Monroe under the careful on- and off-screen grooming of Darryl Zanuck, had put her in the shade, and now, in a stunningly short period of time, she had been dethroned. It was but another example of the mercurialness of Hollywood. Zanuck still valued her, but he had found a new toy, and Susan's remaining movies under contract to him were, to put it politely, second-rate.

In early May, Susan reported to the studio to portray the wicked Messalina, wife of the Roman senator Claudius in *The Story of Demetrius*. In 1953, Zanuck had announced, with much fanfare, the introduction of wide-screen CinemaScope projection, and with it the first-ever CinemaScope production, an epic called *The Robe* about the aftermath of the Crucifixion. Imperiously, Zanuck had proclaimed, "Hollywood will rise and fall on the success of *The Robe*" and, as an incentive to theater owners to undergo the expensive conversion process, promised a steady flow of CinemaScope films.

As it turned out, though *The Robe* did not actually shake Hollywood to its foundations, it was promising enough to encourage Zanuck to immediately begin making a sequel, even

before the first movie was released—and *The Story of Demetrius* was it. Actually, it was a no-lose situation for Zanuck. Since *Demetrius* picked up exactly where *The Robe* left off—the last few minutes of the film were even replayed in *Demetrius*'s pre-credit sequence—producer Frank Ross was able to keep his budget down by utilizing many of the expensive sets of *The Robe* and the costumes that had been created for the proverbial cast of thousands were simply recycled: when you've seen one toga or Roman breastplate, you've seen them all.

Casting Susan as the sadistic, sinful Messalina, however, was hardly the right move to endear the film to a public who had adored her as the courageous Jane Froman and the gentle, loving Rachel Jackson. In an abortive attempt to soften audience reaction, scriptwriter Philip Dunne hoked up a climax where, after the assassination of Caligula, Messalina emerges a reformed woman and devoted wife to the newly crowned Emperor Claudius. It is all supposedly very heart-warming, and hardly authentic—as best as we can tell today, Messalina was a trollop who lived and died without a twinge of guilt—and the audience, when the film was released in September, would not buy it.

During the filming itself, Susan was, even for her, abnormally quiet and withdrawn. Before the cameras, her scenes with Victor Mature were as torrid as the censor would allow, but, Mature recalls, "After director Delmar Daves yelled 'cut,' she just wandered forlornly back to her dressing room.

"Susan acted like someone a hundred years old. I didn't know what the trouble was. We were practically on a 'Mr. Mature' and 'Miss Hayward' basis, but it was obvious something was worrying her. We all wished we could help her, but we didn't know how to go about trying."

Costume designer Charles LeMaire agrees: "There was a haunting sadness in her eyes," he says. Not even her sexy wardrobe excited her, all "richly embroidered and jeweled . . . and hand-woven of the most clinging, gossamer fabric," says LeMaire.

At the party on the last day of shooting, Susan sat alone, surrounded with her own little coterie—hairdresser, wardrobe woman, make-up man. She was so withdrawn that Johnny Cook, head of the studio's photo-publicity division, instructed his photographers not to bother her. "I couldn't get near her.

I sensed it would be better to keep my distance."

There was indeed a great deal disturbing Susan throughout May and June. She was offended by Zanuck's indifference and his apparent disinterest in her performance in the film. Everyone from Zanuck down to the boys in the mailroom were falling all over themselves to get into Marilyn Monroe's good graces. It was a generally accepted perception, true or not, that Marilyn's explosive rise at Twentieth was the result more of her sexual than her screen performance.

One former employee insisted, "Every afternoon Zanuck had to have his virility assured. It was a compulsive thing." And a director who preferred to remain nameless said, "The single most important thing in Zanuck's life, bigger than movies or success, is sex."

Zanuck, of course, flatly and angrily denied all this, adding, many years later, to his biographer Mel Gussow, "Not even Marilyn Monroe. I hated her. I wouldn't have slept with her if she paid me." Nevertheless, he was hardly blind to her appeal and to her potential for dynamite at the box office. Therefore, while Susan brooded through *Demetrius* (released as *Demetrius and the Gladiators*), Zanuck devoted a lion's share of his attention to the promotion and production of *Gentlemen Prefer Blondes* and *How to Marry a Millionaire*. Whatever free time Zanuck had was spent with a Polish adventuress renamed Bella Darvi, whom he was obstinately determined to turn into the new Garbo. So inept was her acting talent, however, that studio wags referred to her as the "new Garbage."

Generally ignored by Zanuck, Susan's confidence was further eroded with the release of *White Witch Doctor* on July 1, 1953. Edited to a meager ninety-five minutes, this story of a dedicated missionary nurse, circa 1907, and a cynical white hunter, played by Robert Mitchum, was generally labeled a "jungle soap opera." Acerbic Bosley Crowther of the *New York Times*, though intrigued by the Equatorial African atmosphere provided by the second unit, dismissed it as "an amazingly unsurprising romantic adventure moving methodically along well beaten film paths."

The script of her next projected film, Charles Brackett's production of *Garden of Evil*, seemed equally trite. An aging Gary Cooper was cast as the leader of three men hired by Hayward to ride with her through dangerous Indian country to rescue her husband buried in a gold mine cave-in. Shooting

was scheduled to begin on location in Uruapan, Mexico, at the end of November, with the wrap planned for early February. Already, the studio, more infatuated with the CinemaScope process they were using than with story credibility, was pouring much of its budget into the shooting site.

The only thing that looked good about the film was the enormous luxury of having all summer and most of the fall off. For the first time since signing with Twentieth Century-Fox, Susan would be able to spend the entire summer with Tim and Gregory. She promised to take them on a long fishing trip. She had been hooked on fishing from the day she had caught her first trout and often remarked that, apart from acting, nothing gave her more pleasure "than spending a day on a stream or river and going after a big one." She had even toyed with the possibility of investing in a cabin cruiser—she certainly could afford one now—but the cost of the upkeep went against her grain. It was a great deal more economical to rent a boat for the day or fish from a public pier.

She planned to do a great deal of fishing that summer. It was the one thing that could help her unwind, and she needed to unwind desperately. Her sleeplessness was leaving her irascible and lethargic. The pressures kept building.

The climax came on July 16, 1953, six days short of her ninth wedding anniversary.

At 11 P.M. all hell broke loose.

After that night there was no turning back.

⊠ chapter 15 ⊠

UNTIL the following February 25, the unsavory details of that nightmarish evening of July 16 would not become public knowledge. During those seven months, gossip, innuendo, and half-truths would keep the local columnists feverishly grinding out copy about the forthcoming Hayward-Barker divorce. Susan would receive the lion's share of sympathy, but several members of the press, led by Sheilah Graham, whom Susan detested, would be on Jess's side.

The morning of July 17, Susan packed a couple of bags and, together with Martha Little and the twins, temporarily moved in with friends. The phone at the Barker house rang incessantly. It remained unanswered.

On July 23, Susan celebrated her ninth wedding anniversary by issuing a terse announcement to the press: "I plan to file for a divorce as soon as possible. I'll leave shortly for a Nevada ranch to establish residence. My brother Walter will accompany me and so will my sons. Reconciliation *seems highly unlikely*. I'm only worried about the pain this will inflict on our two boys, Gregory and Timothy."

From Jess, there was total silence; columnist Erskine Johnson reported that, "Jess Barker is still refusing to make any statements on Susan Hayward's decision to divorce him and refers all question-askers to her."

Susan, however, was unavailable to answer any questions. With her twins in tow, she took off to parts unknown, and on August 10 Sheilah Graham mysteriously noted, "Not even Twentieth Century-Fox knows where Susan Hayward is."

Two days later, Susan and her sons were back at 3737 Longridge Avenue, surprised there'd been any mystery regarding her whereabouts. "Everybody in Bishop [Nevada] knew we were there. We went fishing every day and to the movies every night." She phoned Darryl Zanuck, assuring him she had changed her mind about setting up residence in Nevada and would file for divorce in Burbank, California, on September 9 instead. This would give them enough time to get proceedings started before she had to leave for Mexico to shoot *Garden of Evil*.

The press still clamored for interviews. Anxious to get Hopper and Graham off her back, Susan paid a private visit to Louella Parsons. As always, Louella proved to be a warm and sympathetic friend. The article she wrote was a four-hankie tear-jerker:

> When she came in [wrote Louella], I noticed she was trying to keep one side of her face away from me. "Susie darling, don't do that," I said. "I already know about that black eye Jess gave you. Don't you know by now that I am your friend?"
>
> Suddenly she was in my arms, not crying or sobbing, but holding me tight, just as she used to do when she was one of my little starlets on our stage tour and someone had hurt her feelings. No, she was not crying. The tears had dried up a long time before this or else they were dropping back inside instead of spilling down her face.
>
> That poor eye. So discolored and swollen. The whole side of her face was puffed, distorting one of the loveliest faces in the world.
>
> In a voice so low I had to lean close to hear her, she told me how he [Jess] had beaten her unmercifully, blacking both eyes and bruising her body.
>
> "We had been quarreling," Susan whispered, "and I saw that he was going to slap me. He had slapped me many times, but this time I knew it was going to be worse. His face was distorted with rage. I knew he had lost control of himself. I knew I was in great physical danger." Her lovely red hair was moist against her forehead as she sat talking

with me across a table in my playroom. I had ordered coffee, and she sipped it gratefully. This girl, I realized, was exhausted, not only physically, after the beating she'd taken, but *emotionally* and *spiritually as well*.

Her voice was calmer as she said, "I don't have to tell you that Jess has never contributed any money to my support or to the support of Timothy and Gregory. You know all about that.

"And I know you realize that I was deeply sympathetic with him, at first. I believed him when he said he was an actor and couldn't do anything else. But there must come an end to the unnatural way of living in which the woman is the wage earner and the man sits home with the children. The little boys couldn't understand why I got up early every morning and went to work and Daddy stayed home. It was not that way in the homes of the children they played with. Children can be cruel. I'm sure their playmates often taunted Greg and Timmy about their father's going to the market and driving them to school, when in their homes it was the mother who did these tasks.

"A mother can give her children love and tenderness, but she cannot set the example of a father, a leader—a man who is head of his home. Boys need to respect their fathers, and Jess was letting things ride to the point where he didn't even try to get work—as an actor or anything.

"I was not only terrified when I saw Jess's fury—but I realized he was trying to ruin my face, the very means of which I earn my living." Susan paused, then sadly added, "My reputation is highly valuable to me, or I would not be telling these things against the man I have loved for so many years.

"But I am shocked about some of the terrible stories being circulated about why we separated. What I have told you is the truth.

"Since I first met Jess, there has never been any other man for me, and I really believe there has never been any other woman in his life."

A little sigh escaped Susan; she leaned back against the wall and closed her eyes, as though she were consciously remembering Jess as he was when they first met and fell in love.

"Jess can be so charming. He is handsome and young, and no one has insisted louder than I that he has real ability as an actor.

"Recently, he has been getting some offers. I hope they keep coming for him. If so, I'm sure Jess will be himself again. He is easily discouraged and he had only three days work in his new picture."*

"If Jess does change, is there any chance of your taking him back, Susan?" I asked. "Perhaps he has learned his lesson."

"No, no," she cried. "Never. It's too late. There have been too many 'lessons,' too many 'new' starts, too many times to forgive. When I could keep things to *myself and no one else knew* about it, I could take it. But this time, no.

"Now that the end has come, I want it over as soon as possible." She picked up her bag and prepared to leave.

She had talked as fully and as much as she could. The wounds were literally so fresh that she could go no further.

But as she rose, she said, "There's just one thing, Louella. Despite the sad memory of what brought on our final break, don't be too bitter against Jess in the future. In every marriage breakup, there are two sides, and I'm not pretending to paint myself as an angel and Jess as a devil.

"I have a temper and a hot tongue, and I work so hard I'm frequently tired and almost sick with nerves. Movie stars are never easy to live with, and no one knows that better than I."

I said, "I suppose a psychiatrist might say that Jess's sudden violence was a defense mechanism against living in a set of circumstances intolerable to a man's pride, or perhaps a guilt complex from doing nothing about the situation.

"Perhaps, Susie," I added as I walked with her to the door, "Jess's violence was not really directed so much against you as it was against himself."

"Maybe," she replied softly. "I don't know. I just know that my marriage is finished and done with—a sorry, shabby ending to many moments of happiness. My heart aches very much, but it is closed forever on the past."

Louella was so unraveled by Susan's story that she was unable to make it to her typewriter without the help of a double Scotch. No matter how ruthless she could be to those she felt

---

* Unidentified. Perhaps *Marry Me Again* or *Dragonfly Squadron*, both released in 1954.

had cheated her out of a scoop or had done her any real or imagined wrong, Miss Parsons was enormously gullible when it came to her special pets.

Therefore, it is quite possible that she neither asked—nor was told—about Susan's then-current dinner companion. By then, a thin, dark-headed gentleman was making frequent visits to the little house on Longridge Avenue.

⚘ chapter 16 ⚘

AT FIRST, Susan introduced the "stranger" to Timothy and Gregory as "Mr. Magic."*

Eventually he'd be properly referred to as Mr. Hughes.

Every day, a profusion of fresh-cut flowers would arrive at her doorstep. No card was necessary. Howard Hughes had an extravagant romantic compulsion for smothering his ladies with expensive floral arrangements. These would often be followed by trifles of more tangible value: a diamond ring, an emerald bracelet, an automobile. In some instances, after a romance had run its course, Hughes would even bestow an apartment building or small house on the broken-hearted woman.

Just as eccentric was his alleged habit of bedding only once a beauty he admired, even though their dates might continue for weeks or even months more. Perhaps, for Hughes, it was the pursuit that was all-important, the knowledge that he could go after what he wanted—and get it. Certainly, by all accounts, the women pursued did not mind. Paradoxically, no lady linked with Hughes has ever had an unkind word to say about him—not even after his death.

It would be impossible to try to pinpoint the exact moment Howard Hughes and Susan Hayward became intimate. Throughout his courtship of Susan, Hughes was still being linked publicly with his long-time interest Jean Peters, and starlet Debra Paget was coyly flashing a large diamond ring that Walter Winchell, among other columnists, insisted was a trinket from the billionaire. However, knowing Hughes's predilections and Susan's vulnerability at the time—particu-

*According to later court testimony.

larly for a man like Hughes—it seems certain that intimate they were, and it was probably during the latter part of 1953.

Certainly Susan's mood improved considerably. That August, less than a few weeks after the dramatic recitation that had so destroyed Louella, Susan was back on the phone to Parsons feeling full of fire and newly returned from an Hawaiian vacation with the boys. "You needn't worry about me," she said. "I'm not running from anything, and I'm not going to cry on anyone's shoulder. All that is over. There have been so many false stories, and I'm not even taking the trouble to deny them. Why should I? I'm going ahead with my career, and I'm going to see that my boys are brought up right. I don't even see Jess anymore."

"There's not a chance in the whole wide world" that she and Jess would get together again, she said. "I know that I should have left Jess a long time ago. He'll be better off without me to depend upon, and I'll be better off not having to worry about him."

Although Louella was too tactful or too fearful to bring up Howard Hughes's name, the tycoon was on her mind when she asked: "Will you marry again?"

Susan kept her cool, replying, "Well, that depends on whether I meet the right person. I think it is silly for any person to say he won't remarry. In the first bitterness of a separation, many people say that they will never remarry, but I don't think that's right. If you'll pardon my being bromidic, time heals everything, and I don't see any reason not to marry again."

Louella, in the mother-hen mood that seemed to overcome her whenever Susan was involved, concluded: "I personally hope that Susan will find happiness. She is an unusual girl—sensitive, high strung, and very proud. She says she is not easily hurt, but that I don't believe. I know how deeply hurt she was when the storm of her broken marriage broke over her head."

Another storm was about to break over Susan's head as well. Just back from her vacation, she was entertaining a few friends on Labor Day weekend when Jess stopped by to spend some time with his sons. It started mildly enough, but the events that followed were of hurricane proportions. As with the night of July 16, the details miraculously remained a private affair until February 25, when it all came out in court.

In the meantime, because of the pending divorce and be-

cause the Howard Hughes rumors were too loud to ignore,
Zanuck demanded that Susan get out and around with a variety
of men to provide a more conventional romantic life, on the
surface at least. For instance, she was escorted to the star-
studded premiere of *The Robe* at Grauman's Chinese Theater
by her agent Ned Marin, a white-haired bear of a bachelor.
Marin was often used as a decoy to divert attention from an
actress's closet lover.

No one was deceived.

Throughout October, Susan had what columnists alternately
referred to as "a strong shoulder to cry on," "a constant companion," "a new romantic interest," or simply, "a new beau."
Then on October 19, Sidney Skolsky revealed that "Jeff Chandler and Susie Hayward don't even go to the hideaway spots,
but he does drop in and visit Susie at her valley house." Hedda
Hopper observed, "Susan Hayward and Jeff Chandler are a
mighty handsome couple." The same day, Erskine Johnson
wrote that Susan Hayward and Jeff Chandler "no longer keep
it a secret that they are in a romantic whirl"; then, forgetting
himself, said in his October 24 column: "Susan Hayward and
Jeff Chandler are having secret dates."

Sheilah Graham added her two bits as well, noting in her
syndicated bulletin on November 11, "Jeff Chandler's dates
with Susan Hayward are getting numerous enough to be serious."

Only Louella Parsons failed to jump on the bandwagon.
Unable to dismiss the gossip, she allotted it only two brief
lines: "Again Susan Hayward and Jeff Chandler were at the
Bandbox. They say they are old friends from Brooklyn and it's
nothing serious."

She was right. It wasn't.

Chandler had recently separated from his wife Marjorie, but
no divorce was imminent; he still had hopes of saving his
marriage: "We have a great rapport still in so many things."
The friendship with Susan—started when they were children
at P.S. 181—had casually resumed when both were under
contract at Universal. Chandler had also worked at Twentieth
Century-Fox in *Broken Arrow* (as Cochise), *Two Flags West*
and *Bird of Paradise*, after Susan had moved to that lot. Although the Chandlers and the Barkers had never become close
friends, a good feeling had always existed between the "two
kids from Brooklyn." Their brief reunion in early February at

the *Photoplay* Gold Medal Awards had been warm and cordial.

While tactfully advising his wife not to be disturbed by the publicity linking him with Susan, Chandler was, at the same time, astutely aware of the value of this manufactured romance. Until now, his "private" image had been painfully mundane. Susan, in turn, was genuinely fond of Chandler, whom she considered a very understanding friend—and their dates did divert the press from her association with Hughes and even, temporarily, from the fireworks that were about to explode.

Because of complicated California divorce laws (since changed), Susan and Jess were required to appear in Children's Court of Conciliation on November 17. A week earlier, reporter Harrison Carroll had written: "Jess Barker won't file a cross complaint for divorce, but he will fight. All he wants is a reconciliation. He won't even talk about a property settlement. His attorney insists that Susan is worth $400,000 in real estate and investments. All in her name."

When November 17 came, the Barkers spent two agonizing hours with Court Conciliator Margaret C. Harpbrite. Unyielding, Susan insisted she "didn't believe continuance of the marriage would be best for our twin sons, since I no longer love Mr. Barker. You can't revive what's dead."

The following day, Jess denied Susan's allegations of cruelty. His lawyer asked the Superior Court to deny her a divorce and requested a legal ruling that would prohibit her from taking the twins out of the country on a movie-making trip. The latter request was granted, and the divorce hearing was put on the court's calendar for January 19, 1954, pending Susan's return from Mexico. Furious that she had been prevented from taking Timothy and Gregory along on location, especially with the Christmas holidays approaching, Susan retaliated by obtaining a court order preventing Jess, who had been living in a motel in nearby Encino, from staying with the twins on Longridge Avenue while she was out of the country.

After spending Thanksgiving with her sons, Susan, together with Gary Cooper, Richard Widmark, Cameron Mitchell, and Hugh Marlowe, boarded a plane for Uruapan to begin *Garden of Evil*.

On Monday, December 7, Jess, anxious to spend as much time as possible with his sons, moved back to his former home. Two days later, Susan started a long-distance contempt action against him, charging that "he not only kept the twins up past

their bedtime, but had moved back into the home in violation of the court order." Even from hundreds of miles away, the bitterness raged.

Meanwhile, life for the cast and the crew of *Garden of Evil* was fairly unpleasant itself. Director Henry Hathaway was more concerned with catching the exquisite vistas of Uruapan in CinemaScope and Technicolor than with the creature comforts of his high-priced company. The cast was dragged through banana tree jungles, ancient deserted villages, and the black volcanic sands surrounding Paricutin Mountain. When shooting was completed for the day, everyone just wanted to take a bath and fall into bed. Studio hopés that a minor romance between Susan and Gary Cooper would provide provocative copy were quickly dashed. Cooper, soon to reconcile with his wife Rocky after his abortive romance with Patricia Neal, chose instead to have a brief fling with a local girl.

The company even had its share of disaster, or at least potential disaster, in which Susan was personally involved. On December 10, in a driving rainstorm, a seven-year-old Indian boy slipped from a lava ledge on Paricutin Mountain during filming and fell five feet to another ledge. He was about to tumble another fifteen feet when Susan jumped down and caught him, risking the same fall herself. The boy was unhurt, but Susan required medical treatment for a sprained ankle.

To top it all off, due to political red tape involving work permits for foreigners, the cast was prohibited from leaving Mexico until the filming there was finished—which meant nobody could go home for Christmas. On December 21, however, Louella proudly proclaimed, "All by herself, Susan Hayward managed to get a waiver on her work permit from the Mexican government, and she is the only person in the *Garden of Evil* company who will be allowed to return to Hollywood for the holidays. She'll make the seven-hour flight Christmas Eve."

All by herself? Doubtful. If Gary Cooper, who had tremendous clout, couldn't get the precious waiver, then the request had to have come from someone far more powerful than a movie star, or a congressman, for that matter. It was not difficult to surmise who had pulled the strings. Howard Hughes had a date with Susan on New Year's Eve.

Actually, if the story in Richard Matheson's 1977 book *His Weird and Wanton Ways: The Secret Life of Howard Hughes*

is true, Hughes actually had *three* dates that evening—simultaneously. With the maître d' of the Beverly Hills Hotel in collusion, Hughes supposedly had Susan, Jean Peters, and an unnamed starlet, each in a different dining room in the hotel, each unaware of the others. Hughes bobbed back and forth among the three of them, making excuses, until finally Susan, suspicious, cornered him in the same room as Jean Peters. Denouncing him for his duplicity (actually, triplicity), Susan left the hotel in a huff, while Peters, only vaguely aware of what was going on, made her exit. There is no report of what happened to the third girl.

Whether that story—which sounds too much like a situation comedy to be real—is true or not, one thing is certain. Shortly thereafter Jean Peters walked out on Howard Hughes. On May 29, 1954, she suddenly married Stuart W. Cramer III, a native of Charlottesville, North Carolina, described by her studio as a "civilian in Army Intelligence in Washington, D.C."

As for Susan, she enjoyed her holidays with Tim and Gregory, if not with Hughes. However, she had a contract to do a movie for Hughes that summer—the multimillion-dollar epic had finally gotten off the drawing board and been given a name, *The Conqueror*—and she had no intention of damaging the relationship.

On January 2, she flew back to Mexico in a pensive mood. In spite of its professional honors and financial rewards, 1953 had been a nightmarish year, and she was glad to see it end.

Nonetheless, she was apprehensive about 1954.

Her apprehensions were well founded.

☸ *chapter 17* ☸

Garden of Evil, plagued by foul weather, ran overtime and over budget, requiring another delay in the divorce hearing. Because Susan could not leave Mexico before the weekend of February 4, she was frantic over the possibility that the judge might refuse a continuance. Twentieth Century-Fox and Susan's attorneys struggled through the maze of legal maneuvers and, to everyone's relief, the court hearing was pushed back to February 25.

In the meantime, the columnists were having a field day. Dorothy Kilgallen commented on February 1, "When the Susan Hayward–Jess Barker divorce comes to trial, the big rhubarb will be over their children. Barker will claim he's closer to the boys than Susan is because he was home with them while she was making movies." Louella Parsons countered on February 15: "Susan Hayward was escorted to Jack Warner's party by Jeff Chandler. I've never seen her look as pretty or as happy. She says she feels free as a bird . . . for the first time in years she's able to spend her money just as she pleases."

Ten days later, court proceedings finally began. Demurely attired in a simple dress, flowing beige jersey coat ("In beige I feel like a very good little girl," she had told Walter Thornton) and dainty gloves, Susan obligingly posed for photographers before the hearing officially opened. The first few minutes of testimony dealt with the Barkers' premarital financial agreement. This was followed by a morning of startling revelations.

Milton Rudin and Martin Gang represented Hayward. S. S. (Sammy) Hahn represented Barker. Judge Herbert Y. Walker presided. The testimony here is taken directly from the transcript of the Superior Court. Susan was on the stand.

Q What time of the day or night was it?

A Well, it was late at night, because my husband had gone out to get the late editions of the newspapers; it was on his return.

Q Who was at home on that night, July 16, 1953?

A My husband and myself and my house guest.

Q Where were the boys?

A And my children were upstairs.

Q All right. And it was after dinner then, late at night, about eleven or twelve at night?

A Yes. We had been talking before this.

Q What were you doing on that occasion?

A I had been studying and Mr. Barker had been watching television.

Q Studying what?

A My script, or a script. I can't remember right now whether I was working on something at the time or preparing.

Q When Mr. Barker went out for the late editions of the newspapers, where were you at the time he came back?

A In the living room.

Q Can you describe what happened on that occasion?

A Yes. As I said before, we started to argue. We argued about most of things we've argued about in the past. I remember one thing, that I asked Mr. Barker for a divorce, because I said to him, under the circumstances, that I felt a divorce might be the only solution to these problems. He said I would never get a divorce.

Q Did you discuss the question of employment or his not working?

A Yes, this was part of our argument.

Q And the effect on the children?

A Yes.

Q Give the conversation, please.

A As well as I can remember, it wound up in the fact that he said to me I'd never get a divorce. And I said, "If you don't love me, and don't want to do what I consider right, why do you want to hang on?" And he said, "Well, you're a good meal ticket."

Well, when he said that, I didn't understand, and I looked at him, and I said, "I don't understand you. I think you're very queer."

Q What did he do?

A   And he walked over to where I was sitting and he slapped me.

Q   In the face, Mrs. Barker?

A   Yes.

Q   Go ahead; proceed.

A   He slapped me again. I tried for him not to hit me. He threw me on the floor, and pulled off my robe, and proceeded to beat me. . . .

Well, when my husband was beating me, I tried to get loose from him, first of all, because it hurt; secondly, because there were children in the house, and Martha Little, who is not well. I didn't want to disturb them. But when he beat me, it hurt, and I was crying.

So finally I got loose and ran out of the house into the back garden. I just wanted to get away. Mr. Barker caught up with me; he forced me back into the house. I was struggling with him, and he hit me again.

Q   Where did he hit you, do you remember? I know it's tough, but we've got to do it.

A   I don't remember where he hit me; he hit me wherever he could.

Q   What were you wearing, by the way, Mrs. Barker?

A   I was wearing a terry-cloth bathrobe.

Q   And what underneath that?

A   Nothing. I sleep in the raw.

Q   All right. Then he was dragging you back in the house. Continue the story.

A   When he continued to beat me, I had to get help. I ran to the telephone. I was going to dial the operator, call the police, or anything I could.

Q   What happened?

A   He came after me and knocked the telephone out of my hand, and he said, "I'll cool you off," whereupon he yanked me by the arm, and dragged me out again, back through the garden and up the steps to the swimming pool.

Q   And what did he do then?

A   He threw me in.

Q   And will you relate what happened after he threw you in?

A   Well, as I said, I was wearing this terry-cloth robe, and it's pretty full. It's a big, pink, voluminous thing, and when I hit the water, the water soaked it up, and I went down. It's

hard to get up because there are many folds in a garment. I got up to the top, and I started screaming again, because I was afraid, whereupon he pushed my head under the water.

Q Were you in fear of your life?

A Of course I was.

Q And what did you do after he held your head under the water—pushed it under?

A I suddenly realized that I was not dealing with a person who was quite himself. I knew that he was so highly enraged that he wasn't responsible for his actions that night.

Q So what did you do?

A So when I came up the second time, I kept my mouth shut, and didn't make any noise. He said, "Now get back into the house." So I went quietly.

Q What happened to the terry-cloth bathrobe?

A That was soaking wet; and as I said, it was very heavy. It was left by the pool side.

Q And you therefore had to go into the house without any clothes at all?

A Yes.

Q What happened then? Proceed. You walked in with Mr. Barker behind you?

A Yes. I walked into the house with Mr. Barker. He pushed me into the bedroom, and he said, "Now stay there." Naturally, by this time I was pretty scared, and I knew I had to get out and get help somehow, because I didn't want to stay in the same house with him. So I went to the closet and threw on whatever clothes I could find. . . . There's a little door that leads out of the bedroom, a side door, so I didn't have to go out around again through the den where I thought he might be. I opened the door quietly and walked through the garden, and then, as I remember it, around by the kitchen door, because that leads out into the driveway, and freedom. I got as far as the kitchen door, and it was suddenly—I hate to tell these things.

MR. GANG: I don't know what else we can do. . . .

A It was suddenly opened by Mr. Barker. He said, "Where do you think you're going? Get back in there." At least I think that's what he said; it's hard to remember.

THE COURT: You can't remember exactly. The Court wouldn't believe you if you gave me the exact wording. Give it as near as you can recollect.

THE WITNESS: He grabbed me and threw me into the kitchen ahead of him, and that was lucky, because he threw me with such momentum that I could race to the front door. You go through the kitchen and the dining room and the hallway to the front door. And I opened it, and I ran out, and I ran down the driveway, and he caught up with me and started to hit me again. He said, "You're not going anywhere." . . .

At this point, of course, again I was screaming for help. I was screaming the man's name next door. It was dark outside, and I was screaming for help from the man across the street, anybody.

The next thing I remember, he tried to get me into the house, and I refused to go, and I was struggling with him, and he threw me over the hedge and I was down on the ground, and he still kept beating me. And that's all I can remember until Martha came out the front door, and she yelled, "What's going on?" because—

Q "Martha" was Martha Little, your house guest?

A That's right. She came out the front door, and she ran over and said, "Stop it; stop it." Well, when she said that to him, he stopped momentarily, and I ran back into the house and grabbed the telephone, because I was going to call the police. He ran back in after me, and again knocked it out of my hand. And then suddenly, I don't know, there was a commotion outside, and I ran out, and the police were there. I said, "Would you please call me a taxi?" I told the policeman—

Q By the way, do you know who called the police?

A No, I don't; I never reached them.

Q Proceed. What happened?

A So, when I asked the policeman to call me a taxi, I must have looked a mess. I said I wanted to go to my mother's house. So they called me a taxi. They offered to drive me in their squad car, but I said that wasn't necessary. So they called a cab, and I got in it, and Miss Little came with me, and we went over to my mother's house . . .

Q You spent the night at your mother's house?

A Yes. And then I tried to reach your office in the morning but I wasn't successful, so I called Mr. Wood, my business manager, at his home, and asked him would he go back to the house with me, and ask Mr. Barker please to leave. Also, my brother came with me.

Q And you went back to the house the next morning?

A Yes.

Q With Mr. Wood and your brother?

A Yes, and Miss Little.

Q And Mr. Barker left the house that day?

A Yes, he left the house that day.

Q It was after that you filed your complaint for divorce, and asked for a restraining order?

A As soon as I could reach your office, one of your attorneys came to my home; I explained to him what happened. . . .

Q And did you secure medical treatment for your injuries?

A Yes. I was X-rayed, and taken care of.

Q And can you describe what your injuries consisted of as a result of what had happened the night before?

A You want a description of how I looked?

Q Yes. What were your bruises, contusions?

A Well, I had a black eye, I guess you call it; bruises on the left side of my face, on the temple, the jaw, the nose. I thought my jaw was broken. The eyeball was injured—it was all bloody. My body was covered with bruises, mostly on my "fanny" [indicating], and my feet and legs were scratched and bleeding.

Q What was that from?

A From being dragged up the steps and down the steps and being knocked against things.

Q And how long a period of time did it take before the visible evidences of your injuries cleared up?

A Well, that black eye lasted quite a while . . .

Q About a week, or two weeks?

A Two weeks.

Q Now, Mr. Barker did not live at the home from that time on, did he?

A He did not.

Q Did he come to take the children with him on occasion?

A Yes, he did.

Q Would you, on those occasions, see him?

A Yes, sometimes I would.

Q And he could not stay at the house, however?

A No.

Q Just come and get the children, and bring them back?

A   That's right. Or if he wanted to pick up any of his clothes, or things like that.

That's most of what Susan Hayward remembered in court about the fight on July 16. But this is the way Jess Barker remembered the same evening.

After dinner I was sitting in front of the television set for a while, and the programs were dull, and I left it. Mrs. Barker wasn't studying a script, because she wasn't working at the time, and there were no scripts, to my knowledge, that had been sent to her. . . .

Q   You know about scripts?

A   I should know; I have worked with them enough.

Q   You studied the scripts with her?

A   Always.

Q   And you advised her?

A   Yes, I did.

Q   And what else do you do helping prepare for the work as a star?

A   To give her every bit of knowledge I have had in the years in the theater, and what I have had in the motion picture business.

Q   Did you attend interviews with her?

A   I was frequently present in interviews with magazines and newspaper people. Quite frequently Mrs. Barker would ask me to join, as she termed it, for the "light touch."

Q   Did you have to advise her about costumes at the studios?

A   I was with Mrs. Barker on practically every picture she started on the costumes and I saw the tests made, suggested camera angles, anything connected with her work.

Q   In addition to that, you bought the groceries for the house?

A   I bought the groceries for the house.

Q   And you bought the supplies, and maintenance for the house?

A   I did to the best of my ability.

Q   And raise the children?

A   That I did to the best of my ability.

Q   All right. Now, tell us what happened from there on. You say she was not working?

A Mrs. Barker was sitting in front of the television set when I went to get the newspapers. . . . Mrs. Barker . . . started reading . . . I had a newspaper. . . .

Q What happened? What was done by you or her?

A There was a discussion about families in general in Hollywood—not gossip—just in general, about this person, which is the way many of our conversations started out. During the course of our conversation something was said where a remark about my mother was brought into the conversation. Why it was there, I don't know.

Q What remark did she make about your mother?

A Well, it isn't very pleasant. It was about an incident I told her about when I was a child. "Possibly," she said, "that's what's wrong with you . . ." . . . after the mention of my mother, I sat in complete stunned silence; Mrs. Barker gave me all of the bad things that she could think about me . . .

Q What did you do then?

A I sat on the couch. I stayed right there wondering why a woman that I had all the respect for in the world should say that to me, the father of her children. Mrs. Barker leaned across to me to get a cigarette, and said right in my face, "Besides, I think you're queer." And with that, I think I said, "You're not going to get away with that." And I slapped her, and the struggle was on from then on. . . . She struggled back. I tried to quiet her down, and by this time Mrs. Barker got hold of me, and bit me very hard in the left arm, in the muscle. . . .

Q Then what happened? How did you get to the swimming pool?

A Mrs. Barker ran outside; I brought her back inside. I let her back inside; and I gave Mrs. Barker a spanking. . . . I asked her to please keep quiet, the children were upstairs, and I picked her up, carried her and put her into bed, and covered her. . . . And Mrs. Barker got up again, and ran outside, and I said, "If you don't keep quiet, I'm going to cool you off."

Q What did you do to cool her off?

A I picked Mrs. Barker up, carried her to the pool, and dropped her in.

Q Which side of the pool did you drop her in, the nine feet deep or the three feet deep?

A It's approximately four feet deep. . . . The robe, by the way, that she was wearing, slipped right off. . . . And I said, "Now are you cooled off?" And Mrs. Barker was still scream-

ing, and I helped her out of the pool, and took her back in the house. Mrs. Barker never entered the parkway area gate in the nude—never...

Q Did you ever drag her?

A I never dragged Mrs. Barker. Mrs. Barker fell a couple of occasions pulling away from me, yes...

Q You did not try to drown her as she says?

A No, Mr. Hahn. I helped Mrs. Barker out of the pool...

Q Then you went back in the house, and what happened then?

A Mrs. Barker was in the room for quite some time, and I was in the den, and in the state I was in, I decided to take a walk in front of the home....I was sitting outside by the driveway which has the drain, and Mrs. Barker came out fully dressed with a coat on; I mean fully dressed apparently to the eye, with a scarf over her head. She had the dog in her arm, and she was going down the street in the dark....I tried to get her back, and there was a struggle....I took her to the front door, and asked Mrs. Little to please put Mrs. Barker to bed, and she said, "I will."

Q That's the first time you saw Mrs. Little that night?

A That's the first and only time I saw Mrs. Little until she left shortly after that with Mrs. Barker....Mrs. Little opened the door and was waiting.

Q And then the police arrived?

A ...I sat on the front doorstep, or stoop, and sat there until a gentleman walked up to me in uniform and said, "What's the trouble here?" And the only word I spoke to the gentleman was, "Domestic."...

Q Did you at any time throw her over a fence of some sort?

A I did not.

Q Did you at any time hear her scream loud and long, "Don't kill me, don't kill me?"...

A I don't remember that.

Q Did you try to kill her?

A No, sir, I did not.

Q Did you try to do her any physical harm other than what you say you considered she deserved, a spanking?

A I did nothing else, Mr. Hahn....I left the home in the hopes that the home would be reunited and perpetuated....I

was back on a Tuesday with flowers. This is the first occasion. . . .

Q You brought her flowers for your and her anniversary.

A I did.

Q She accepted them?

A Yes.

Q She appreciated them?

A She thought they were lovely. . . .

A third witness was called to describe the same incident. Her testimony came between Susan Hayward's and Jess Barker's. Her name was Dodee Hazel Swain, and she had been a maid at the house next door to the Barkers. And she had a room with a view.

Q . . . you could see from your bedroom into the area in which the pool is located?

A Yes.

Q All right. Now, on the night of July 16–17 of 1953, did anything occur which you remember at this time?. . .

A In the early morning of July 17, I was awakened with a loud scream—a lady's voice. . . . And then I got up out of bed with the loud scream still on. Then I went back to my bathroom and I went straight to the back kitchen door, and I stood in the doorway looking and listening.

Q At this time of the morning were there lights on in the yard of the Barker home?

A There was two lights, big headlights, in the back way.

Q And did you see anything at the time?

A I saw a lady run by out of the gateway, the back of the house, and she didn't have on anything. If she did, it was very sheer to me. . . . A few minutes after she was in the house, I heard a loud scream, then they ran outside in the backway, direction of the pool, and I heard screaming real loudly, and she was screaming, "Don't kill me; don't kill me," and "Somebody help me; somebody help me; please don't kill me." I heard a man mumbling, said, "You're going to sign that deal." She said, "No, no." And I heard a big splash as if something bumped in the water, and she was screaming and struggling. And then, I heard conversation out near the pool, but I couldn't

see, so I just heard mumbling. I couldn't understand what they were saying otherwise...

Q And did you go back to bed?

A I stood there for a little while, and then I laid back down. And later, in the early morning, I heard a man in the back way, two men, talking. I didn't even get up to see who it was.

Q Now, did you recognize any distinctive part of the person you saw running—the lady; was her hair noticeable to you in the light?

A It was kind of reddish-like...

Q Was the person you saw Mrs. Barker?

A I would say she was.

MR. GANG: Thank you very much. You may cross-examine....

MR. HAHN: Did you notice the naked lady again?...

A I saw her twice.

Q All right. Now, after you saw her run into the door, when did you see her again?

A When she ran out the back door next to where I am....

Q Did you notice her for just about a second again?

A It was running so fast I guess it was a second.

Q And that lady was still naked?

A Yes....

Q Where did the naked lady run after she got to the driveway?

A In the direction of the pool. I don't know where she ran after that.

Q That's the last you saw of the naked lady?

A That's right....

Q When did you hear somebody yell, "Don't kill me, don't kill me," after she ran to the swimming pool, or when the naked lady ran through the door the first time?

A When she ran back to the swimming pool.

Q That's the first time you heard a lady say, "Don't kill me?"

A No. She was just hollering when I was awake. I was awakened with a scream; that's what I told you.

Q Yes, and with screams, "Don't kill me?"

A Yes, when she ran back to the pool, and there was some slaps like that.... Then I heard her hollering, "Don't kill me...somebody help me...." Then I heard a man's voice

say, "You're going to sign that deal," and she said no, and splash, he throwed her in the pool, and there was a screaming, and scrambling, and that's the way it was. . . .

Q   A scrambling over a deal?

A   In the water.

Q   Did you go over there and look?

A   No, I didn't go over, because I didn't want to interfere.

Q   Did you call the police?

A   I didn't call the police, because I didn't want to inter-fere . . .

Q   . . . When you saw the naked lady run in the house, and when you saw the naked lady run out of the house in the swimming pool, you didn't see a man follow her?

A   Yes, there was a man following her, but I didn't look at that second. He was sure following. . . .

Q   Now, when the man's voice said, "Sign the deal," where was that?

A   That was outside.

Q   Outside, when she ran out the first time or second time?

A   The second time.

Q   Well, how soon after she ran out towards the swimming pool did you hear a man say, "You'll have to sign this deal"?

A   It wasn't long afterwards, because that's when the most screaming was.

Q   About how long?

A   About a few seconds. I don't know just how long it was, but it wasn't very long.

Q   How long did this yelling, "Save me, don't let him kill me," go on?

A   It went on quite a while, because I don't see why some-body in the neighborhood didn't hear beside me. . . .

Q   How long did they talk quietly in the swimming pool, in that direction, after the screaming stopped?

A   Quite a while, I guess, because I went and laid down.

The Barkers were the only witnesses who appeared to de-scribe their next struggle. Their disagreement about what hap-pened on Labor Day was even greater than their disagreement on the other night. Susan was examined first.

Q   What occurred on the Labor Day weekend of 1953? . . .

A   I had taken the children and gone to Hawaii, and we had

a sort of vacation, and I hadn't seen Mr. Barker, and he called and asked if he might take them out on Labor Day. And I said, "Of course." And they came back, and they were happy together. They were all, you know, laughing—stuff like that. I had guests, Mr. and Mrs. Dorsen.

We were up by the pool. I guess Jess brought the children back about around six o'clock, and as is the custom in our home, we dine early, usually six-thirty, latest a quarter of seven, because of the children. The children always eat with me.

As Mr. Barker came in, he knew Mr. and Mrs. Dorsen, and I felt it would be embarrassing for me not to ask him up at least to say hello, because the children would wonder why I didn't ask him. So I asked him would he come up and join us in cocktails. We had just started. He said he'd like to, and he came up by the pool side, and he poured himself a drink.

We discussed this and that, social conversation, and then he said he'd like to talk to me. I said, "All right." Mr. and Mrs. Dorsen left, and went down into the house. I said, "Please, Jess, will you please be sort of quick about it, because dinner is almost ready and I don't want any delay." He started to talk about reconciliation. . . .

Q What did you say?

A I said it was impossible, and I didn't want a reconciliation. I felt it would be better for both of us to be apart. He is sort of insistent, and, well, to make a long story short, he didn't want to leave. This caused delays in the kitchen, in my guests, and the children wondering why dinner wasn't there, and why their mother wasn't ready to sit down.

I asked him again and again to please leave—"Let's talk about it some other time, not tonight." It was a holiday; I had guests; it was time for dinner.

Mr. Barker said he would leave when he was good and ready to leave.

Q Did the guests come in at any time?

A Yes, they did. They came in to see what was wrong, and tried to persuade him to leave. They were unsuccessful.

Q Then what happened?

A Well, I was furious, because I tried to get him to leave peaceably, because I didn't want there to be any disturbance. . . . The children were there, and I had guests, and besides, it's not good. I was quite furious. He was sort of standing

near me, and I had a cigarette in my hand; it was lit; and I have a temper, and I said, "I would like to push this cigarette right in your eye."

Q   What did he say?

A   He said, "You haven't got the guts."

Q   What did he do?

A   He put up his hand [indicating] and then smacked me.

Q   You did not succeed in getting the cigarette in his face?

A   This I can't remember.

Q   But you remember—

A   I aimed.

Q   And did you get smacked?

A   Yes, I got smacked.

Q   What happened then?

A   Well, I yelled, and Thelma came running.

Q   Who is Thelma?

A   She's Mrs. Dorsen.

Q   All right; continue.

A   Oh, I forgot when they came in before they tried to calm down the argument, and said, "Well, have another drink, and then leave." So Thelma went out into the kitchen to make this drink, and as she ran back into the room, when I screamed, she had the drink in her hand, and I grabbed the drink and threw the contents of the glass in Mr. Barker's face.

Q   And where were the children?

A   They were in the dining room. Mr. Dorsen, as I understand it, was talking with them about various things trying not to let them hear the commotion going on in the house; but it was pretty loud. Mr. Barker said that he didn't hit me, and that I was a liar.

Q   In whose presence did he make that statement?

A   Mrs. Dorsen, although other people could hear him because he said it pretty loud. I just wanted him to get out of there; and I ran into the kitchen, and he ran after me; and I ran into the den, and he ran after me, and insisting I didn't tell the truth, and that I was a liar.

Q   Did the children hear this?

A   Yes, of course; they must have heard it, although they didn't say anything to me about it.

Q   All right; proceed.

A   Well, finally he was prevailed upon to leave. He left. That's all.

Q What happened after that?

A I called you the next day. I said it was impossible, that I want a divorce, and I want it fast . . .

But Jess's report is quite different.

Q Let's go to . . . the Labor Day incident. Tell us exactly what happened there, briefly, when you came over . . .

A . . . I said, "Do you mind if I take the boys down to Studio City and see your picture, *White Witch Doctor?*" because they had been promised to see it. And I said, "Would you join us?" Naturally, I was refused; however, I did take the boys to see their mother. . . . We returned home afterward in a very happy frame of mind. The boys talked about the picture, and I felt that they liked it very much, which I was very proud that they had seen their mother and enjoyed her performance.

I was invited up to the pool, and Mr. and Mrs. Dorsen were present. . . . I asked Mrs. Barker if I could speak to her, and Mrs. Dorsen left the pool and we chatted quite a while; and Mrs. Barker informed me that: "How did it feel to know I'd be the recipient of $100,000 at the end of the week?" I thought it was rather a large amount. My remark was, "Is that all?" I didn't know what she was talking about.

She told me—she informed me she was going ahead and get a divorce.

At this point Barker testified that he had been going to the marriage counselor under the impression that he was a psychiatrist and that their visits to him were for the purpose of working out a reconciliation.

We were going for a reconciliation, but Mrs. Barker told me since then that she was going merely for the children, which she said, about how the children should be handled.

Q Go ahead and tell us the rest of it.

A Well, we went into the home. I sat on a chair and Mrs. Barker sat on a small love-seat, and we discussed at length about. various things. And Mrs. Barker wanted a quick divorce—go to Nevada right away—give a settlement.

So I continued talking about the home, and about the children, and our obligations to the children. Mrs. Barker walked away from me to the table, lit a cigarette, came back and during the course of the conversation (I was standing beside her),

looked at the end of the cigarette and said, "I ought to push this right in your eye."

I said, "Well, I don't think you've got the guts to do it." I thought she was joking. With that, Mrs. Barker reached up and pushed the cigarette towards my face, and with my left hand I knocked the cigarette out of her hand, put my foot on it, and what turned me around was Mrs. Barker yelling and screaming that she had been hit.

I grabbed Mrs. Barker by the shoulder, sat her on the couch and said, "What is the matter with you?" With this, Mr. and Mrs. Dorsen came in, and I said, "This girl claims she's been hit. Would you please take a look and see if she has a mark on her? She's got very sensitive skin; it would show." Mr. and Mrs. Dorsen answered me.

Q Did you hit her?

A I did not.

Q Proceed. What happened next?

A The next thing I know, I was getting a drink in my face.

Q A drink of what, water or whiskey?

A Well, the part that came down my face tasted very much like whiskey.

Q All right. What happened next?

A I said to Mrs. Barker, "Will you please tell the truth?" Mrs. Barker kept yelling that, "You hit me, you hit me," and started moving around, and I moved with her, and I said, "Please tell the truth. I'll not leave the house until you tell the truth."

By this time I knew the children had heard it, and I wanted the children to know the truth too. And after several minutes of this I decided to leave, because I wasn't getting any place, and might have made matters worse. And I left, and the divorce was filed the following day.

In spite of their concern for the welfare of the children, the testimony of both the Barkers implied that their only worry, besides protecting them from the knowledge of their parents' disagreements, was protecting themselves from each other in the eyes of their sons.

Susan told about the questioning of their children about the separation.

THE WITNESS: They didn't quite understand why their mother and father didn't live together anymore.

Q What did they say, and what did you say?

A Why don't their daddy live here any more? And I said, "Sometimes when people grow up, and they can't get along together in happiness, it's better for them to live apart."

Q You started to say something about putting Gregory to bed one night. What did he say?

A He said, "Wouldn't you like it if daddy lived here?"

Q All right. Did you answer him?

A Well—

Q Or did you evade the answering?

A I answered him.

Q What did you say?

A I said, "It's too bad, but sometimes grown-ups can't get along together." ...

Q With reference to visitation rights, Mrs. Barker, will you relate to the Court the observations on the children when they leave for weekends, and when they come back?

A Yes. During the week they're pretty much relaxed, except for, well, boys will be boys, and once in a while they'll get out of line. But they're nice kids, normal, happy, and they have, well the best way I can describe it is a rather relaxed and free relationship with me. I do notice when they come back over the weekend with me, they're tense, and it takes a day or two, for the tenseness to leave. I don't know why. I'd like to be able to talk with Mr. Barker and discuss with him how we can work this thing out so that we can work together and not against each other. . . . I told him it was wrong for two people to be in conflict, and try to outdo each other.

Q What did Mr. Barker say?

A May I give an incident that's just come to my mind?

Q Yes. Go ahead.

A Mr. Barker came to the home after we came back from Hawaii . . . I said, "Tell Daddy how you were surfboard riding, and deep sea fishing, and so forth, and so on." And Mr. Barker said, "Were they very good boys?" I said, "Yes, they were very good boys, but once in a while I'd have to give them a little crack on the behind." So he looked at the children, and he said, "Oh, you've got a very bad mommy."

Well, it wasn't the kind of thing that you say in front of kids, because then, you know, they get confused.

And Jess Barker told the Court why he wanted to keep his wife from permitting her mother to live in the home with the children.

Q   You don't want your mother-in-law to be in the house with you, your wife and your children?

A   I do not.

Q   Tell the Court why.

A   The children told me, during the time I had them at Christmas, that they couldn't understand something. I said, "What are you talking about?" They said, "Something that Grandma said right after you left home." I said, "What do you mean?" The child said, "Grandma said she would kill you." And the child said, "Grandma said to Mommy, 'Get rid of Daddy.'"

It wasn't until that afternoon that Howard Hughes's name and his visit to the house on Longridge Avenue came up in Jess's testimony. Susan admitted that Hughes had been in her home and met her sons, but she insisted he had been there for the sole purpose of picking them up before going out to dinner; they had had business to discuss; she was doing a movie for him in June. Outside the courtroom, cornered by a local reporter, she added that she was "also trying to get work from Hughes for her jobless husband."

On March 15, 1954, relief finally came for Susan. Pending the divorce, the Court awarded her custody of the twins, with Jess receiving permission to take them on Wednesdays and alternate weekends. She was also ordered to pay his legal fees of three thousand dollars, which stung a bit. What stung more was Judge Walker's stern admonitions that both parents watch their language when talking about each other in front of the boys.

For Tim and Greg, not having their father home every day was bewildering. "Wouldn't you like it if Daddy lived here?" Greg had asked, and all Susan could say was, "Sometimes when people grow up, and they can't get along together in happiness, it's better for them to live apart." But the boys were only nine at the time, and they loved their father very much. Now, more than twenty-six years later, Tim says tenderly of Jess Barker, "He's a good guy."

❧ *chapter 18* ❧

SUSAN WAS ANXIOUS as the month of June approached. Her suit for divorce coincided with the starting date of *The Conqueror*, and neither could be put off any longer. Hughes, however, promised she'd be given a few days off for the trial, and made arrangements for Susan to film a couple of her scenes in Hollywood, so she'd be close by.

On June 14 Susan was back in the Burbank court. The testimony over the next few days was a prolonged replay of the February hearing. There were no startling new revelations: Susan stuck to her story, Jess to his. Jess even contested the trial, insisting that he still wanted a reconciliation with his wife.

For reasons never fully explained, the court adjourned to the house on Longridge Avenue for a closer look at "the scene of the crime." Susan avoided Jess's gaze as, wearing a curiously inappropriate large picture hat and black taffeta cocktail dress, she showed the judge around the house. Soon after, the divorce was granted; Jess's lawyers said they'd appeal.

On August 18, the court ruled that Susan could keep the more than a quarter-million dollars she owned in nine savings accounts, her house, her future earnings, and her car. Jess Barker was given their 1952 Ford station wagon and was awarded visitation rights to the boys on alternate weekends. And with that, the case was over. Once and for all, the Barkers were dissolved.

Meanwhile, Susan had received court permission to take the twins on location with her, and on June 30, a photograph was released from the set of *The Conqueror* showing the boys in Saint George, Utah, together with John Wayne, Dick Powell, and the rest of the cast and crew, watching their mother

Susan Hayward

Portrait of a Survivor

Edythe Marrenner (the spelling would change later) with mother, Ellen Pearson Marrenner, in 1917, just a few weeks after the baby's birth. Inset: The only picture ever published of Walter Marrenner, snapped in 1936, two years before his death. (Wally Marrenner)

Sister Florence, fourteen, with seven-year-old Edythe in 1924. Susan never discussed Flo, as their relationship ended bitterly in 1941. She later disinherited Flo and her children. (Author's collection)

Walter Thornton model Edythe Marrener (new spelling) in a 1937 millinery ad. Shortly after, she went to Hollywood for her screen test for *Gone With the Wind*. (Doug McClelland Collection)

Rejected by Selznick, Edythe was signed by Warners, and renamed Susan Hayward. This is the second studio portrait she ever posed for. (Saul Goodman Collection)

This deceptively romantic poolside idyll between the starlet and future President was arranged by Warner Brothers to create interest in a 1938 Reagan flick, *Girls on Probation*, in which Susan received her first screen billing. Jane Wyman, co-featured with Ronnie in *Brother Rat*, was furious when the studio chose Susan for this layout, and the feud continued for a year. Both the movie and the relationship were flops. Susan was dropped by the studio—and by Ronnie—and the photo remained in the "dead file" for 42 years. (Warner Brothers)

In the fall of 1939 Susan, now with Paramount where she had made *Beau Geste,* went on Louella Parsons' "Flying Stars" vaudeville tour, with hopefuls Jane Wyman, Wyman's husband-to-be Ronald Reagan, Joy Hodges, Arleen Whalen and June Preisser. (Author's collection)

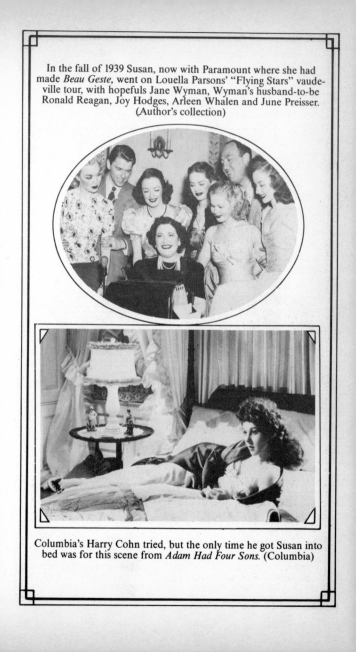

Columbia's Harry Cohn tried, but the only time he got Susan into bed was for this scene from *Adam Had Four Sons.* (Columbia)

Although the public and critics were beginning to take notice, "home studio" Paramount kept lending Susan to "poverty row" producers. Here, with brother Wally in 1942, on the set of Republic Pictures' *Hit Parade of 1943*. (Author's collection)

Susan met Jess Barker in November, 1943. After a stormy courtship, they were married at St. Thomas Episcopal Church on July 23, 1944. (UPI)

Susan left Paramount to sign with Walter Wanger, and received the first of five Oscar nominations for her portrayal of Angelica Evans, the neglected alcoholic wife of a singer in 1947's *Smash-Up—The Story of a Woman.* (McClelland)

David and Bathsheba, Susan's fifth movie for Twentieth Century-Fox, was a story of lust, God's wrath, and repentance; it took liberties with the Bible and made millions. Gregory Peck was the covetous King David. (Twentieth Century-Fox)

At six and a half, Gregory and Timothy, Susan's twins, with Susan and Robert Mitchum on the set of *The Lusty Men*. (Author's collection)

In February 1953 Susan was reunited with old Brooklyn buddy Jeff Chandler at a Photoplay Magazine Party. Susan was the winner of Photoplay's Gold Medal award for her portrayal of Jane Froman in *With a Song in My Heart*. It was her third Oscar nomination—and she was passed over again! (Moreno)

In 1952 Susan was the undisputed queen of Twentieth Century-Fox, named by the foreign press "The World's Favorite Screen Star of 1952." Within two years her studio crown would be usurped—by Marilyn Monroe.

On July 16, 1953, following their European vacation, the Barker marriage ended. On June 14, 1954, Susan was fighting for her divorce. The court adjourned to the "scene of the crime" to see the pool in which Jess (background) allegedly tossed his naked wife after physically abusing her. (AP)

Susan's 37th birthday on the set of *The Conqueror,* filmed near a former atomic testing site, which some say caused the cancer that eventually killed Susan, co-star John Wayne (center), director Dick Powell (center left) and others. Susan's son Tim is concerned both for his twin Greg (center) and himself; he recently suffered a benign tumor of the mouth. (Author's collection)

On April 26, 1955, Susan took a near-fatal overdose of sleeping pills. Alerted by Ellen Marrenner, police broke down the door and rushed her to the hospital. (Author's collection)

Taken just before Susan was named Best Actress for *I'll Cry Tomorrow* at the Cannes Film Festival, 1956. Old acquaintance Ingrid Bergman was about to film *Anastasia,* the film that would bring her back into public favor. (UPI)

Above, the confrontation between alcoholic Lillian Roth and her mother, played by Jo Van Fleet, was among the scenes in 1955's *I'll Cry Tomorrow* that won Susan her fourth Oscar nomination. Below, the jaunty "I'm Sittin' On Top of the World" number was cut from the final version, but can be heard on the movie soundtrack. (McClelland)

In 1958, Walter Wanger interested Susan in *I Want to Live!*, the story of Barbara Graham, the fast-living "party girl" executed for murder. (United Artists)

Pressure caused this dramatic scene of "police brutality" to be cut from the movie. Nonetheless, Governor Pat Brown of California called the Graham execution "one of the most distasteful episodes in California history." (United Artists)

Oscar night, April 9, 1959. Said Wanger, "Thank heavens! Now we can all relax. Susie's got what she's been chasing for twenty years." But Susie told the press that her second husband (she wed Floyd Eaton Chalkley in February 1957) was more important to her than Oscar; she planned to limit her screen appearances in favor of domestic bliss. (Author's collection)

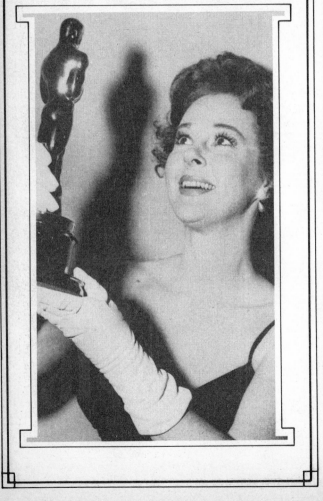

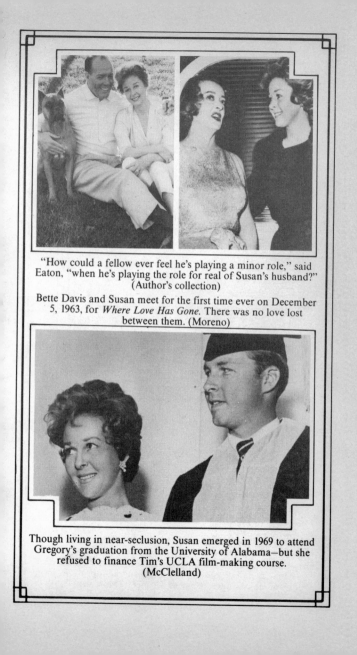

"How could a fellow ever feel he's playing a minor role," said
Eaton, "when he's playing the role for real of Susan's husband?"
(Author's collection)

Bette Davis and Susan meet for the first time ever on December
5, 1963, for *Where Love Has Gone.* There was no love lost
between them. (Moreno)

Though living in near-seclusion, Susan emerged in 1969 to attend
Gregory's graduation from the University of Alabama—but she
refused to finance Tim's UCLA film-making course.
(McClelland)

Refusing to accept death, Susan appeared as a presenter at the 1974 Oscars in a glowing green sequined gown. Frank Westmore provided the wig and make-up job which led viewers to believe reports of the tragedy were exaggerated. They weren't. This is the last photo taken of her. (UPI)

Susan *Hayward*

Aug. 10. 51.

Susan was buried in Carrollton, Georgia, on March 16, 1975. Her professional memorial: Susan's footprints and handprints in front of Hollywood's "Chinese Theater." (Moreno)

cut a giant birthday cake, a present from the cast. Susan was thirty-seven that year.

The Conqueror was a rather silly Wild East show about Genghis Khan, played by John Wayne, of all people, and a beautiful Tartar princess, played by Susan. She would later say, "I had hysterics all through that one. Every time we did a scene I dissolved in laughter. . . . Me, a red-haired Tartar princess. It looked like some wild Irishman had stopped off on the road to old Cathay."

During the course of the film, she would develop a lasting affection for Wayne, perhaps the only leading man for whom she would feel that way. "He was tough and strong, just like his screen image, but there was tremendous gentleness about him. Of all my leading men, he was my favorite."

Although Wayne was too tactful ever to name his own favorite leading lady, he was always complimentary about Susan as well. Not long before his death he reminisced: "I have had the good fortune to work with Susan in several pictures, in a variety of backgrounds from the sea to war to world conquest. At no time does her magnetism ever let you forget that she is a woman."

Studio efforts to fabricate a romance between Susan and Wayne during the filming of *The Conqueror* came to nothing, however. Wayne had just gone through a divorce that was in most respects even messier than Susan's, and needed time for a breather. More importantly, despite their liking for each other, the two simply weren't each other's romantic type. Wayne had a passion for fiery Latin ladies, and Susan couldn't shake her obsession with Southerners. Besides, there was always the shadowy figure of bossman Howard Hughes lurking in the background—though he seemed to be getting even shadowier than usual these days, at least when it came to Susan. She put it down as his reluctance to be seen while the divorce action was still pending.

Besides Wayne, though, her relationship with most of the rest of the cast was about the same as usual: reserved and private. Actor Thomas Gomez, who played the sybaritic Chinese prince Wang Khan, recalled: "Susan had a house and a cook. One night she invited several of us, including John Wayne and the Dick Powells, for dinner. Once she greeted us, she disappeared into the kitchen, and despite the fact that she had a cook, we scarcely saw her again until dinner was served.

In an evening after work, she may be so cordial that you think you've finally broken through the barriers and made a friend of her, but that wasn't usually the case!"

Susan did, however, stay close to Agnes Moorehead, with whom she had worked twice in the past. Miss Moorehead had been one of Susan's few supporters when both had been making *The Lost Moment* in 1947, and would remain so until the end of her life, telling everyone, "I was one of her greatest fans." Later, Miss Moorehead would remember the day during the filming of *The Conqueror* when Susan showed quite another side of her personality altogether. Saint George, the town in which the film company stayed, was trying to raise money to pay off the debt on a local playground, and the RKO movie-makers had obligingly agreed to play the local chapter of Elks in a benefit softball game. Susan took her sons to the affair, but had no intention of participating, until hecklers got the best of her. She then kicked off her shoes, went to bat, got a hit, and stole two bases in her stocking feet, to the delight of the twins as well as the onlookers.

Another aspect of *The Conqueror* was less amusing. Occasionally wind storms would halt production, giving both cast and crew a breather. It was an ill wind that blew into their lungs, however. Though they did not know it, working in Utah was hazardous to their health. In fact, it might have been fatal.

On May 19, 1953, an atom bomb had been exploded in Nevada, and a freak wind had swept the radioactive fallout across the Utah desert, leaving in its wake an atomic cloud that would later become known as "Dirty Harry."

No one thought much about it then, nor did they in the summer of 1954 on the set of *The Conqueror*. It was not until 1979 that the effect of "Dirty Harry" would finally be known, and become nationwide news, to the accompaniment of lawsuits and banner headlines. But that would not be until twenty-five years later . . . and by then it would be too late.

With *The Conqueror* completed, Susan reported back to Twentieth Century-Fox in early September to appear with Tyrone Power in a movie called *Untamed*. The studio was touting it as a South African *Gone with the Wind*, and, if the columnists are to be believed, the production certainly had as many mishaps. On September 16, Sheilah Graham reported: "During a fire on the *Untamed* set, Susan Hayward rushed in to extinguish

the flames while all the men ran to a safe distance. And when hornets invaded the set, Tyrone Power and Richard Egan fled while Susan fought them off with a prop corset."

Susan wouldn't have minded if the whole set burned down, but at least there was one bright spot. She and Richard Egan had first met casually during *Demetrius and the Gladiators*, in which he had had a featured role. An emotional wreck then, she had not talked to him much, but now, to their studio's delight, they began to see each other. In early October, they attended the premiere of Judy Garland's *A Star Is Born* together; and Susan started crying so violently during the film they had to leave before it was over. Obviously it had hit home—reminding her again of her situation with Jess. She later admitted that she returned to see it again—alone. Egan also escorted her to a large party at the Beverly Hills Hotel, and they had several dinner dates, which, needless to say, excited the columnists' imaginations.

The two made a handsome couple, but no one was foolhardy enough to predict marriage. Egan's brother was a priest, and Egan himself a devout Catholic: under no circumstances would he have considered taking a divorced woman as his wife. Still the two had fun together, their dates helped hype *Untamed*, and he diverted Susan's mind from her problems.

The rest of the making of *Untamed* was unmemorable, and with it not due to open until the next March, Susan had time to make another quickie called *Soldier of Fortune*.

On October 13, Susan was back in court asking Superior Court Judge Herbert Walker's permission to take Timothy and Gregory to Hong Kong, where she was scheduled to start work on the film. "I don't think a mother should be away from her children for long, and the trip would help broaden the boys' education."

Studio officials testified the twins would be given first-class accommodations if allowed to go. Judge Walker, however, sustained Jess Barker's contention that Hong Kong was not a safe place for children.

The studio had two choices: replace Susan in the role or film her exterior scenes before a process screen. Co-star Clark Gable had no objection to a replacement: he had originally requested Grace Kelly as his leading lady anyway. It was only when Miss Kelly had wisely turned the role down that Susan

was cast. Informed of this, Gable, who had stared at Susan throughout that party a decade earlier, couldn't remember who Susan Hayward was.

In the end, Twentieth Century-Fox decided to send Gable and several other members of the cast to the Orient to shoot what they could, keep Susan in the part, rewrite the script to require very few of the glaring, obvious process shots, and shoot her scenes at home. Once again the studio tried to spread rumors of a real-life romance between the co-stars. Some columnists picked up on such fictional items as: "Clark Gable has started driving Susan Hayward home from work"; "Kay Spreckels and Clark Gable have had some sort of misunderstanding and lately Clark is finding comfort with Susan Hayward"; "On February 2, Clark Gable celebrated his 54th birthday with Susan Hayward." The photograph of the two of them cutting a cake with one candle on the occasion of that birthday was reprinted in newspapers across the country, to the delight of the publicity department. It meant nothing, however, and the reviews this dull little melodrama received are not worth repeating. Gable and Hayward together for the first and last time received about as much enthusiasm as the Hong Kong flu.

Susan had been aware that *Soldier of Fortune* was a bomb from the beginning. The only reason she'd agreed to do it was for the free trip to the Orient for herself and family. When that fell through, she considered her assignment nothing more than marking time.

In late February, Susan agreed to help publicize *Untamed* by attending its multiple premieres in the Miami area, on the condition she'd be permitted to go on to the Bahamas for a few days' rest. The studio's motivation for choosing Miami as the site of a premiere of a movie about South Africa and Zulu uprisings was never clear. It was a typical media event, long before that expression had been coined. Twentieth's Miami office hired the 110-piece Greater Miami Boys Drum and Bugle Corps to serenade her, and on premiere night, March 1, the corps picked up Susan at the Algiers Hotel, where she was staying, escorted her first to the Lincoln Theater, then down Lincoln Road to the Capri. Miami's mayor Harold Shapiro met Susan on a specially constructed podium and presented her with the key to the city. The whole affair was filmed by Fox-Movietone News for replay in theaters across the country.

It was a smashing success—which didn't help the reviews much, unfortunately.

Mocking the studio's attempt to come up with another *Gone with the Wind*, the *Philadelphia Inquirer*'s Mildred Martin wrote: "Compared with Katie O'Neill, Scarlett O'Hara was a little sit-by-the-fire. For Katie, to whom the film's title refers, is just as conniving and several times as active as Scarlett ever dreamed of being. She is, as played by fiery Susan Hayward . . . quite a collector of masculine scalps, acquiring a couple of husbands, a lover, and two sons before screen time and the authentic South African backgrounds run out.

"While Scarlett only had the Civil War to worry her on a grand scale, poor Katie meets hoards of howling spear-throwing Zulus face to face on the South African veldt. . . . But the result unfortunately is just a combination of *Gone with the Wind*, parody style, with South African-flavored horse opera."

Variety also observed that, "Miss Hayward struggles somewhat grimly with a part that would defy any actress. However, she's easy on the eye, wears some attractive period dresses and is emotional when the occasion demands."

And *Time* magazine, calling the entire cast "*Gone with the Wind* machines," dealt the final blow when it quoted Tyrone Power's immortal line when he is reunited with his lost love: "You . . . here in Africa fighting Zulus . . . I can hardly believe it." Neither could anyone else.

Back in Miami, Susan had stayed around to do a little fishing, she said. "I hear Miami has the most magnificent fishing facilities anywhere," she told reporters. What she *didn't* say was that Howard Hughes was floating around in the area and that he was the fish she was interested in catching.

Hughes, however, was the one that got away. Ever since the divorce action, when his name had been dragged through the court, he had been noticeably cool toward Susan and, in fact, Susan had hardly seen him at all. She was ready to make another stab at it, but it was too late. The only reason he was in Miami now was to be with Jean Peters; she had established residence there to obtain a divorce from Stuart Cramer. By now Hughes had decided he cared enough for Peters to marry her, and didn't even bother to return Susan's frequent phone calls. With a deflated ego, Susan left Miami for the Bahamas.

Back home, things were even more depressing. She received a wire informing her that Martha Little had succumbed to

cancer, and, tearfully, she booked the next flight east to attend Miss Little's funeral. While she was in New York, columnists, unaware of her affection for the Little family, blamed Susan's melancholy on Hughes's reconciliation with Jean Peters, but it was much more than that. She had been jilted, true, but also a good friend had died. She had just been through several emotionally exhausting months of personal turmoil, and her career, once so bright, seemed to be on the downswing. The final straw came on the weekend of April 23.

That weekend, Susan agreed to meet Jess in a bungalow at the Ambassador Hotel. Jess later called it "a peace meeting to stop this tug-of-war over the twins. Susan never talks to me when I call to see the boys. She won't even let the servants talk to me. The children see this, and it is bad for them.

"I admit I blew up at the finish of this meeting. We got absolutely nowhere. I said some unpleasant things, but they had been on my chest for two years."

On Monday afternoon, Susan issued a reply: "I have my reasons for not seeing him alone. . . . Moreover, I have an interlocutory degree, and I don't want to jeopardize it. I'm a good mother. I don't believe the boys have ever been so well."

During her eighteen years on the Hollywood scene, there had been many who had compared Susan to a machine—a piece of steel without a heart.

At three o'clock Tuesday morning, the machine broke down.

❁ *PART FOUR* ❁

Susan Hayward

Hollywood
April 26, 1955—February 8, 1957

*You aim for all the things you have been told stardom means—
the rich life, the applause, the parties cluttered with celebrities,
the awards. Then it is nothing, really nothing. It is like a drug
that lasts just a few hours, a sleeping pill. When it wears off
you have to live without its help.*

SUSAN HAYWARD

❋ chapter 19 ❋

THERE WAS SOMETHING she had forgotten to do...

What was it?

The pills were beginning to take effect, and her thoughts and memory were confused.

Oh, yes. She had forgotten to call her mother. She didn't want Ellen Marrenner to feel she was being left destitute. Losing her sole means of support would disturb Ellen more than a loss of a child. There were other children. Susan had always felt the least loved; in fact, sometimes she had felt Ellen would have been happier if Florence had become the star. Ellen wouldn't grieve long for Edythe. It was the money that mattered. It was always the money that mattered. Throughout Susan's girlhood, Ellen had made that quite clear: reminding Walter Marrenner that Florence made more money than he did; fawning over Florence because of her earnings.

Susan dialed Ellen's number by rote. It was unlikely she could see the letters on the dial or the time on the living-room clock. It was 3:15 A.M., and Susan had taken far too many pills.

Mrs. Marrenner was awakened by the phone. There were seconds of silence. Then she heard a slurred voice mumble, *"Don't worry, Mother, you'll be taken care of."* And a click.

Aware of her daughter's depression, Ellen Marrenner phoned the North Hollywood police. She was hysterical as she told them: "I think there is something wrong with my daughter, my daughter is Susan Hayward. I'm afraid she's going to commit suicide."

Police detective G. W. Wilkerson and another officer sped to Longridge Avenue in nearby Sherman Oaks. Unable to get in the front door, the detective yelled repeatedly, "Susan, this

is Wilkerson of the detective bureau. Let us in."

The two officers went around to the patio, kicked in a door, and found Susan sprawled unconscious on the living-room floor in a white quilted housecoat and pajamas.

After speaking to the police, Ellen Marrenner had called Wally, who rushed to Sherman Oaks. By the time he arrived, photographers were already on the scene. Remarkably, the chaos hadn't disturbed Tim and Gregory, peacefully asleep in their upstairs bedroom.

The police couldn't prevent cameras clicking as they carried the unconscious woman from the house to the police car: Wilkerson couldn't risk waiting for an ambulance. They sped Susan to North Hollywood Receiving Hospital to have her stomach pumped. After the emergency treatment, her condition was described as fair, and the attending doctor said, "It's just a matter of sleeping it off. It was a close one. We acted on the premise that it was an overdose of sleeping pills."

Executives at Twentieth Century-Fox and MGM (to whom Susan was about to be loaned for Lillian Roth's *I'll Cry Tomorrow*), as concerned about the adverse publicity upon their upcoming movies as about Susan, made arrangements to have her removed to Cedars of Lebanon Hospital where, fooling no one, she was registered under the name of Mary Brennen.

Dr. Stanley Imerman, whose name was on one of the two bottles of sleeping pills found in the house, took charge. Someone had to talk to the reporters gathered in the hospital's vast lobby.

Imerman, protective of his patient, had his statement carefully prepared. "Miss Hayward has been despondent for some time because of marital problems. She has also been working very hard in film productions. She took some sedatives to enable her to sleep and find relief from tension, and I am sure the overdose was mainly accidental.

"Her condition is satisfactory and she should be home in a couple of days."

Lillian Roth, questioned at the same time and protective of *I'll Cry Tomorrow*, echoed Dr. Imerman's sentiments, adding, "Susan is too vital, too eager and ambitious a girl to want to end her life. No, I think she was highly nervous about the filming of the picture and might have had a few cocktails. The alcohol and the sleeping pills fought each other, slowing her pulse, making her respiration very shallow, lowering her skin

temperature. When your nerves are a little off-the-beam, this can happen to you. It happened to me." Neither Miss Roth nor Dr. Imerman made any reference to Susan's phone call to her mother.

Susan had barely emerged from her coma when Jess Barker, in New Orleans on a personal appearance tour for his movie *Kentucky Rifles*—since the divorce, he had found some work—boarded a plane to Los Angeles. Just before take-off, he wired: COMING HOME AS FAST AS I CAN. LOVE, DADDY. At first he had signed the wire "Jess," then changed it to "Daddy," remembering her pet name for him during their marriage. Chill Wills, also in New Orleans for the picture, told reporters who hadn't been able to get to Jess before he'd left town, "It's a shame that people in love have to have this happen to them. He's been carrying the torch for her for so long, and she's still in love with him."

She loved him. She hated him. She loved him.

But she would not give in to him. The money had been a weapon. The children had been weapons. Perhaps the suicide attempt had been one too: another manifestation of the tremendous need she still had to punish him. And herself.

More obvious was the No Visitors sign she had posted outside her hospital room after receiving Jess's wire.

On the evening of April 26, Jess drove to Cedars of Lebanon, and was told by night supervisor Jane Allen that Susan was "resting well," but that Dr. Imerman had left instructions that no one was to see her. After a ten-minute phone conversation with Dr. Imerman, Jess told reporters waiting for him:

"Dr. Imerman said that Mrs. Barker is not to see anyone—not even her mother—until she is fully recovered. He said that my visiting her would bring emotional stress. I took Stanley's advice in this matter. He's always been a good friend of mine."

Jess had nothing more to say that night but, frustrated by evasive studio comments, suspicious of Imerman's statements, the Hollywood press wouldn't give up. Besieged for interviews, Jess Barker relented and agreed to a press conference on April 27 at the home of close friends in Reseda.

Discussing the blaring headlines of the previous afternoon, Jess denied that he had collapsed in New Orleans when informed of his estranged wife's suicide attempt or that he had said, "My God, I love her," as had been attributed to him. So when reporters asked why, then, he was so eager to see her

at all, he replied quietly: "Ten years together and two children mean something. Or maybe it should be the other way around—two children and ten years."

When he had not been able to gain admittance to the hospital, Jess had driven to the house on Longridge Avenue to spend some time with his sons. "The boys asked if I had been to see their mother, and they wanted to know if we had made up. I told them I had been to the hospital and she was asleep. The boys know there is something wrong with their mother without knowing the full details. I plan to see them after school today and play basketball or baseball with them. We usually go to a public park or to the home of friends."

As to using the incident as grounds for regaining custody of his sons, he said, "That's a bridge to be crossed later. The important thing now is her recovery and that the children are properly supervised." Jess concluded that he "had no idea" why Susan had taken the pills.

"I know of no other romance in her life. Her family may have an explanation of this, not me. She's the type to let emotions stir up over a period of years. I've said numerous times that it might build up to a sort of breakdown. But in moments of depression she never dwelt on suicide. But remember, I've hardly seen the lady in a year and eight or nine months." He did not mention the meeting the two of them had had the weekend before. Two days later, Jess returned to New Orleans, the orders to bar him from the hospital unrescinded.

While Susan was recovering from the effects of her ordeal, the Hollywood press was having a field day, and the local TV stations built up huge ratings replaying all her old films. Newspapers dug into their files and reprinted whatever pictures they had, supplemented by the grotesque candids taken on the night of the attempt; and, horrified by the pictures that were appearing, Susan finally granted photographers the privilege she had denied Jess Barker. They were allowed into her hospital room.

On April 28, the public was relieved to see a radiant Susan, beautifully coiffured and attired, smiling at them from the front page of their afternoon dailies. The following morning, wearing a white linen strawberry print, and the inevitable white gloves, Susan departed Cedars of Lebanon Hospital looking as if she had never heard of sleeping pills. Hospital rules required that all departing patients be taken out in wheelchairs, but the min-

ute she hit the door she jumped to her feet.

Surrounded by studio press agents and greeted by an army of photographers and reporters, Susan submitted to a few minutes of questioning. She firmly stated that there wasn't a chance in the world of a reconciliation with Jess. She was joyfully looking forward to a reunion with the twins. "They're at school now, but I'll be there waiting for them when they return home." She refuted the rumors that she wanted to get out of her MGM commitment. "Nonsense, I'm starting rehearsals for *I'll Cry Tomorrow* next week!"

She wanted the press on her side—completely. But when one reporter as:.ed the question on everyone's mind—"Why did you take the pills?"—she just shook her head and replied, "That's something that's between me and God." Then, reaching for the young man's hand, she added, "And don't let anyone ever tell you that there is no God. There is."

That was her exit line. She got into the limousine the studio had had waiting and drove home. There Susan called Louella, her protectress, who cheerfully told her readers: "Susan sounded so wonderful—so happy and full of pep—when she told me she was home and rarin' to go. She'll be back at MGM on Monday, and she's having lunch tomorrow with Danny Mann to discuss the script."

On May 2, as scheduled, Susan checked into MGM to begin dancing and voice lessons. She was not expected to sing in *I'll Cry Tomorrow*, merely to record her pronunciation and range for dubbing, but to her astonishment, when she got there, MGM musical supervisor Johnny Green said her voice might be good enough to sing the Lillian Roth songs herself. It required weeks of persuasion and a number of tape-recording sessions with Charles Henderson, the movie's musical arranger and conductor, before Susan was convinced she could do it; but when she was, she threw herself into the sessions with enthusiasm. Soon, all the songs were on tape, recorded in her own deep, resonant contralto.

Everyone, from producer Larry Weingarten to Danny Mann to Johnny Green, was excited. Green immediately called a show-wise group of the Hollywood press to the studio and played them two reels of Susan's songs: "Sing You Sinners," "When the Red, Red Robin Comes Bob, Bob, Bobbin' Along," "Happiness Is a Thing Called Joe," "I'm Sittin' on Top of the World," and the waltz from *Vagabond King*.

The Hollywood press heard a new, fresh voice and liked what they heard.

Johnny Green's eyes lit up. "She's a female bass, isn't she, boys?" he said. "Did you ever hear such timbre?"

Susan herself admitted, "It was a big surprise gift, a new career to be explored."

Donald Pippin, then a young musician, now a leading Broadway musical director, insists, "Green got all of the publicity and credit for Susan's singing, but it was Chuck Henderson who did all the work. I know, I was there. I met Susan at a vocal session at Chuck's for the first time. If it weren't for him, she could never have come through as well as she did."

There is no argument, however, as to who was responsible for Susan's dazzling performance in *I'll Cry Tomorrow*. For the balance of her life, she credited Danny Mann for that achievement.

"Danny checked every detail. He wouldn't let me cheat with lipstick or even a curl. If he thought my hair wasn't mussed up enough, he put water on his hands and mashed it down. Danny and I went to A.A. meetings, hospitals and even jails because I had to know that woman's life and what it had become."

The best source Susan could go to, of course, was Lillian Roth, herself, and Miss Roth served as "technical adviser" on the film.

I'll Cry Tomorrow, based on Roth's autobiographical best seller, was the story of a beautiful and talented young girl, deprived of a normal childhood by an ambitious mother, who first achieves Broadway and Hollywood stardom before she is twenty and then endures sixteen years of alcoholic degradation before she is able to overcome her illness and start a new life. In the film, Roth takes her first drink to help her recover from the death of the first man she loved. From then on, it is a one-way downhill slide: drinking to help her to forget; then drinking to enable her to face her fast-dwindling audiences; finally drinking in remorse and self-pity.

In an alcoholic haze, she finds herself married to an immature aviation officer and, when that fails, to a physically attractive but brutal sadist (Richard Conte). Kept a virtual prisoner and tormented by the man, Roth hits bottom and attempts suicide. Finally, with the help of Alcoholics Anonymous and

a former alcoholic (Eddie Albert), she makes the climb back to sobriety and happiness. In the final scene, she tells her story on television, in the hope it will help others who feel beaten by the bottle.

After meeting Lillian Roth for the first time, Susan told International News Service reporter Emily Belser: "It's a man's world, and women must make their way in it the best way they can. Miss Roth went into alcoholism and despair, but her spirit never completely flickered out, and she found a way to restore it. I think this is something worth saying to women, and I think women will understand what it means. . . . This is not fiction. . . . It is the story of a life—a real life. It should have a tremendous impact on people, especially women who have experienced or are experiencing the damnation of alcoholism. It should prove to them once and for all that a person can return to normal with sufficient courage and with the help of God. For me, this film will be a work of love."

Although Miss Roth was thrilled that MGM was able to get Susan to portray her life, she admitted later,* "I was very shocked when I was told that I wasn't going to do my own singing, but she had made her mind up that *she* was going to sing. And that's one thing you find out about Susie—that when she makes her mind up to do something, that's it. I thought she did a good job, but I was so disappointed. . . . I was heart-broken they didn't use my *voice*. Eventually there were two record albums on the film. I did one for Coral, and then there was the sound-track recording which got all the publicity.

"I never found out an awful lot about Susie except that she was a very *forceful* person. We had talked for hours and hours, days, but she never allowed me to get to know *her*. But she wanted to know everything about me. Everything!

"There was so much in my life that was left out of that movie because they were so nervous about the subject of alcoholism! And they were afraid to touch the subject of the nut house I was in. But even if it wasn't in the script, Susie wanted to know about it. . . .

"And whenever I came to the set she'd keep staring at me and staring. Things eventually got to the stage where I didn't know if I was me or Susie was me, and vice versa.

---

*In an interview with this writer just two months before Miss Roth's death on May 12, 1980.

"But I thought she was wonderful in the part—real wonderful! Later, when it was all over, they had us attend a lot of the premieres together, but, as I said, I never really got to know her, and she didn't keep in touch. Then maybe fifteen years later I get this beautiful Christmas card from her.

"But I don't think Susie remained close or got close to anyone on the picture except Danny Mann and that Barry guy."

More about "that Barry guy" presently.

A relative newcomer to the Hollywood scene at that time, Mann had a quiet but forceful way of handling the most difficult personalities. Susan, however, presented a different kind of problem. Mann knew that if the picture was to be a success, Susan had to trust him completely—at no time could he seem to be a threat or a problem to her. To convince her that he sincerely wanted to be a friend, he avoided the usual Dutch-uncle talks, and instead invited her to his home to meet his wife and children, to show her how he lived. They discussed the picture very little. They talked about their kids.

"Susan's ability," says Mann, "was matched only by her courage. She reached for the ultimate, and had an enormous capacity for digging into herself emotionally while playing a role. Her ability to concentrate in areas where it is required was remarkable. When an actress goes through the emotional wringer as Susan did in *I'll Cry Tomorrow*, it can't help but be a great strain. The director must be indulgent. But Susan neither required nor wanted indulgence while making the picture. She gave her utmost to the scenes, but when they were over, she stepped out with no bleeding."

When a reporter visiting the set remarked that it took guts to play in that story, Susan, with her usual directness, shot back, "It took guts to live it."

An example of her coolness under fire was demonstrated in a particularly harrowing scene during which Susan had to writhe in bed in the grip of violent delirium tremors, while several members of Alcoholics Anonymous tried to sober her up. The acting was so real that it caused hardened drinkers in the crew to shake in their boots. Yet when the scene was cut, Susan crawled out of the bed and calmly retired to her dressing room to run through the lines for her next scene. Between takes, she cheerfully posed for poster art. If there were any aftereffects of the suicide attempt, she did not show them.

Throughout the filming of *I'll Cry Tomorrow*, Susan and

Danny Mann continued to grow closer. On Susan's thirty-eighth birthday, he held a surprise party for her on the set. In turn, when Mann celebrated his forty-third birthday on August 8, Susan, aware that Danny considered nine his lucky number, had ninety-nine roses delivered to him. No one suggested the relationship was anything deeper, however. By now, Susan was extremely interested in someone else.

It was yet another gentleman from the South, from Houston, Texas, this time, whom she had met when he had played a small part in an Alcoholics Anonymous sequence early in *I'll Cry Tomorrow*. He had been born Donald Barry de Acosta. He was better known in Hollywood circles as Don "Red" Barry. And he had already built up quite a reputation for himself as a cowboy star—and as a great lover. Later, one of his former lady friends would say: "I can't define what Don Barry *has*, but whatever it is, he should bottle it."

Susan probably would have been better off if he had.

❈ *chapter 20* ❈

"SUSAN HAYWARD," Don Barry reflected a few weeks before the 70-year old ex-loverboy blew his brains out following a fight with his estranged wife in July 1980. "Every man alive should experience one Susan Hayward in his lifetime. I wrote that in a poem about her called 'Portrait of a Lady.' That's what I think. She was to me one of the most wonderful and exciting experiences of my life."

It was an experience that started almost casually, rapidly developed into an affair, then exploded into violent headlines across the country. In the end, it would cause Susan humiliation, contribute to her losing an Oscar—and come close to costing her custody of her sons.

From the beginning, however, the two made no secret of their interest in each other. In August, prior to her leaving for New York for special location shooting on *I'll Cry Tomorrow*, Susan and Don were seen having dinner together at the Captain's Table, a popular seafood spot. Later, after the movie was wrapped, the two resumed dating. Their frequent meetings caused Louella Parsons to report reluctantly in early September, "Just before Susan took off for Honolulu with her twins, she had dinner with Don "Red" Barry at Holiday House. She's been seen quite a lot with him lately, but Susie has had so much trouble with the opposite sex that I don't look to see her getting involved again."

Miss Parsons's crystal ball was decidedly muddy. Barry was at the airport to see Susan off to Hawaii. He would be there when she returned.

In Honolulu, Susan checked in at the Royal Hawaiian Hotel and looked up old acquaintances and beach boys who had been particularly helpful in the past—Chick Daniels of the Outrigger Canoe Club, Philip at the Princess Kaiulani. The latter promised to keep an eye on the twins when they went surfing.

On rare days when the weather failed to live up to expectations, Susan went on shopping expeditions. The afternoon before leaving Honolulu for Hana-Maui, she took her sons to some native boutiques. Although she never believed in dressing them identically for school or for parties, she bought them swim trunks with matching beach coats, and found several swim suits with paké coats for herself.

It was on this expedition that Timothy spotted an antique hand-carved ivory chess set in a window, which he dearly wanted. Susan was pleased by her son's good taste, but not by the price tag, which read $395. She explained her resistance to the purchase by rationalizing, "This is the sort of set that a person owns after he has become a very great chess player. It is a sort of reward. I'd like to have you own it, but it will have to be earned. When you become a champion, I'll buy this one or one like it for you."

The next morning Susan, Timothy, and Gregory flew over to Hana-Maui. It was then a quiet, elegant, native resort. There was little to do except eat, sleep, rest, and swim. Some nights, the three of them attended the hula shows. These were the sights Susan wanted to share with her sons. More importantly, the ten days away from Hollywood afforded her the privacy to more completely win their affection. Jess was as anxious as ever to obtain full custody of the boys; Susan was determined to fight it with every ounce of her energy.

Back on the mainland, she resumed her relationship with Don Barry. When she was invited to attend a rough cut of *I'll Cry Tomorrow* on September 28, she asked Don to share it with her—but frustrated photographers by leaving through a private door.

Column items appeared regularly:

Parsons, 10/2/55: "Hollywood is talking about Susan Hayward's frequent appearances with Don "Red" Barry, who had practically disappeared from the public scene since he once escorted Joan Crawford about town."

Skolsky, 10/5/55: "Don "Red" Barry and Susan Hayward are solid regardless of what you might have read elsewhere."

Kilgallen, 10/10/55: "Susan Hayward, whose marriage to Jess Barker caused her such bitter unhappiness, is feeling optimistic enough to consider trying matrimony again. The chap who looks like Mr. Right is Don "Red" Barry, the actor."

Nonetheless, Hollywood's army of press photographers were still unable to catch the two together anywhere. When the two of them *were* "caught," it was in his bedroom one Friday morning, and it wasn't by a photographer.

Later, Susan would say: "Why do these things happen? The answer is a question. Have you ever been lonely?" And it was loneliness rather than love which led Susan to spend the night at Don Barry's apartment. She trusted his discretion. What she couldn't have anticipated was Jil Jarmyn's jealousy.

Before he had met Susan, Barry had been going steady with a sexy starlet whom he had met the previous June, when both had been working in a film called *A Twinkle in God's Eye*. As late as October 14, Army Archard, the columnist for *Variety*, reported, "Don Barry, who'd been dating Susan Hayward, now calling Jil Jarmyn from the Lone Pine location of *Seven Men from Now*."

He had been calling Susan too. As a footloose bachelor, that was his prerogative. It seemed obvious that he preferred Susan's company, but Jarmyn wasn't about to admit defeat that easily. In fact, she may have been encouraged by an item in Hedda Hopper's October 31 column: "Hal Hayes sure gets around. This time with Susan Hayward at L'Escoffier at the Beverly Hilton." Maybe Hayward was finally about to ditch Barry in favor of the handsome builder columnists had described as a "zillionaire."

Unable to reach Barry on the phone early in the morning of November 4, 1955, Jill Jarmyn drove to his home in North Hollywood. Finding the door open, she entered the house and headed for Barry's bedroom. What happened next depends on whose version one wants to believe—Hayward's or Jarmyn's. Jarmyn's version was the juicier one:

"I had barely gotten into the room when—pow! Susan pushed Don out of the way and yelled, 'Who is this girl?' Before Don could say anything, she socked me in the jaw.

"Don tried to tell her who I was, she wouldn't listen. She picked up a wooden clothes brush and hit me over the head. I kept saying, 'If you'll get out of my way, I'll leave.' Don

kept saying, 'Susan, will you let her by?'

"Susan calmed down, but then she lunged at me again and the furniture went all over the place. She quieted down and wanted some coffee. Then she came back at me with a lighted cigarette. She threw me down...ripped the buttons off my blouse and socked me.

"I finally got out of there!"

Displaying a sore left jaw, a badly bruised arm and a bitten thumb, Miss Jarmyn told reporters, "Twentieth Century-Fox studios was on the phone all day pleading with me to hush up the story."

Miss Jarmyn, in turn, was on the phone with Jess Barker's attorney Sammy Hahn and the Van Nuys police department. Contacted, Hahn coolly said: "This incident will help Jess's appeal to get back his children."

That's what terrified Susan. Rather than antagonize the press clamoring for more of her side of the story, Susan revised her original statement, which claimed that she and Barry had been having "a casual cup of coffee" when Miss Jarmyn came bursting in.

"I could say I was in the dining room at the time, but I wasn't. I was in the bedroom in my pajamas. Miss Jarmyn walked into the bedroom and made an insulting remark. It was nasty.

"Being Irish, this infuriated me, and I went toward her and a wrestling match ensued.... I don't know who swung the first blow. I struck her.... It wasn't over Don Barry. My anger was at this woman whom I never saw before daring to use such language—so insulting that I cannot even repeat it. I don't take that kind of talk from anyone."

Whoever story was true, the next sequence of events must have been slightly confusing to the outside world. Jil Jarmyn entered a signed complaint with Deputy City Attorney Stephen R. Powers, Jr., of Van Nuys. Then, just as abruptly, on November 7, she announced she was dropping all charges against Susan Hayward because "Susan's children might suffer." Plainly, Susan's attorneys had done a bit of talking with the starlet.

Don Barry too broke his silence by asking, "What's the fuss? I just happened to invite both girls to drop in for coffee some time."

After that, it was left to Marlene Dietrich to make the definitive comment on the whole mess: "That Red Barry must make *some* cup of coffee!"

Despite the embarrassment, Susan continued to see Barry. Early in December, she moved to a new house on Longridge Avenue, just two doors away from her former residence, and Sidney Skolsky noted, "Her first guest was Don Barry, who came over to see the place and have a cup of coffee with Susan." (Apparently Susan's coffee too was pretty good.) Mike Connolly of the *Hollywood Reporter* spotted the twosome "strolling on Longridge Avenue at 1:30 A.M., arm in arm."

Shortly before Christmas, Jess Barker filed a special appeal with the California State District Court, still fighting to have the divorce, which had become final in August, nullified. Susan was advised he didn't stand a chance of having the appeal granted, and gave the matter no more thought. She was in a wonderful mood and refused to allow anything to interfere with the upcoming holidays.

Only Louella knew who really had Susan smiling again: "Now it's Hal Hayes who has been taking Susan Hayward out to dinner. . . ." One needed a score card to keep up with the action.

❈ chapter 21 ❈

SUSAN JUBILANTLY waltzed into the New Year in the arms of charming, wealthy businessman Hal Hayes, her date at socialite Cobina Wright's elegant holiday soirée. Noted character actress Lurene Tuttle (mother-in-law of composer-conductor John Williams) recalls: "It was kept quite a secret, but Susan was madly in love with Hal. So were a number of other Hollywood women. He was considered the most eligible bachelor in Hollywood."

A week later Susan left for New York, Philadelphia, and Washington for ten days' publicity on *I'll Cry Tomorrow*, due to open on January 12, 1956, at Radio City Music Hall. Hayes followed her east to—as Dorothy Kilgallen cattily noted—"bask in the stardust," but the stardust must have faded suddenly. On January 13, Susan provoked a mystery by leaving New York in the middle of the night to return to California. "It was too cold," said Susan. "Too hot," said Earl Wilson, chuckling. "Hal Hayes is wearing some scratches on his nose given to him by Susan Hayward during a little disagreement they had. . . ." Wilson didn't go into specifics. Hayes, always the gentleman, refused to discuss his injuries.

Susan's depression following the quarrel with Hayes, however, must have disappeared when she read the reviews accorded her performance as Lillian Roth.

Look magazine devoted a cover story to her: "She gives a performance that does the industry great credit—a many-sided and poignant dissolution of a human being and her right to be rehabilitated. . . . The story's emotional power is vividly communicated by Susan Hayward in a shattering, intense performance that may win her the Academy Award." (It would win her the *Look* award for the Best Actress of the Year in 1955.)

Edward Schallert of the *Los Angeles Times* let out all stops: "Susan Hayward becomes an indisputable candidate for the Academy of Arts and Sciences because of her performance. Her acting effect is likely even to be more appreciated than the film. . . . The story is basically repellent, but . . . Miss Hayward deserves all the praise that can and will be bestowed for this, her major screen effort. She had one prior alcoholic role to play in *Smash-Up*, which gained her Academy recognition. But that was pygmy-like by comparison to this fearfully demanding assignment which seemed to require the utmost, both mentally and physically, from the star."

With less verbosity, Kate Cameron of the *New York Daily News*, giving the picture four stars, wrote: "Susan Hayward tears the heart out of you."

Even the usually critical *Time* magazine conceded that "Susan Hayward plays her part right up to the cork: she can make the audience see not only the horror of the heroine's life but the wry humor of it." And *Life*, devoting a three-page spread to the film, summarized: "Susan Hayward does a superb portrayal of Lillian Roth from the spotlight to blackout—including some fine, unexpected throaty singing."

Only the hard-hearted Bosley Crowther of the *New York Times* had some reservations: "The vaudeville singer that Miss Hayward puts on the screen . . . gives little signs of being neurotic, unstable, or perverse. However, once her baleful lady gets into her cups, she is thoroughly authentic and convincing, shattering and sad. . . . The strong part is when Miss Hayward indicates the actual agonies of Miss Roth."

Heady stuff, indeed. In spite of these raves, though, the New York Film Critics failed to give Susan a single nod when they cast their ballots for Best Actress of 1955. Instead, Anna Magnani scored a first-ballot victory with thirteen votes for her performance in *The Rose Tattoo*. Susan concealed her disappointment and prayed that, come Oscar time, the often-chauvinistic Academy would ignore a foreign actress.

Meanwhile, her social life was showing a marked improvement. Early in February 1956, columnists dismissed Hal Hayes and Red Barry and began linking Susan to men anonymously identified as "an F.B.I. agent," "a tall, balding fellow," "a Virginia attorney," "a handsome Washington lawyer," and "an Atlanta used-car dealer." It wasn't until Susan introduced Floyd Eaton Chalkley to the press at a *Redbook* party that the

news hawks (and the public) became aware that her flurry of dates were all the same man. She didn't let him out of her sight all evening.

But who and what exactly was Floyd Eaton Chalkley? Where did he come from? And what did he have that Susan found so fascinating?

First of all, it was his Southern background. Chalkley was a native Virginian now living in Georgia, and he was quiet, charming, gentlemanly. He had been an FBI agent before and during the war, he said, then allegedly made a fortune as a used-car dealer. Now he dabbled in projects that interested him. He had a hint of mystery, flashed a pile of money, and seemed ready-made for Susan.

If she had wanted to check a little deeper, however, she would have found more than just a hint of mystery. FBI records checked on March 3, 1980, reveal that he was born on June 19, 1909, but give no place of birth. He started working for their offices in Washington, D.C., as a file clerk-typist on June 29, 1934; on October 11, 1937, he was promoted to a position listed as "Special Agent," and he resigned from the bureau on February 16, 1940—six years before he later claimed J. Edgar Hoover dismissed him for budgetary reasons. His salary at the time was $3,200 a year. The reason for his resignation is not recorded in the FBI's files.

The FBI also has no statistics about Eaton Chalkley's personal life, education, army record (if any), or marital life. Regarding the latter, shortly after Eaton became interested in Susan, his sister, Mrs. Peggy Irwin of Carrollton, Georgia, where Eaton still had a car dealership and forty acres of choice property, let slip that Eaton had been divorced twice and had three teen-age children then living with their mother nearby. This was later changed to one divorce.

Curious discrepancies. There would be more later.

Right now, however, it was December 1955, and Chalkley, together with his buddy, restaurateur Harvey Hestor, had arrived in Los Angeles, where they contacted another mutual friend, Vincent X. Flaherty, the author of *Jim Thorpe—All American.* Flaherty invited both men to his gala Christmas bash. Hestor invited Susan, whom he had known for some time, to be his date. Since Hal Hayes had other plans that evening, Susan thought it would be fun to spend some time with—as she called him—Uncle Harvey.

Early in the evening, Hestor introduced Chalkley, who had brought his own date, to Susan, and the two made small talk for a while, but there was little opportunity for private conversation. When the crowd thinned out, Flaherty remembered, "I suggested a small group of us continue the party at the Mocambo." Noticing that Chalkley, a shy man, did not seem to be enjoying the festivities, Flaherty said, "Hey, Eaton, why don't you dance with Susan? Mix in, pal. Mix in."

"That did it," Flaherty boasted. "For the first time I saw my cool and collected pal beset with shakes."

He must have calmed them, however, because Eaton Chalkley invited Susan out before he returned to Georgia, and they agreed to keep in touch. When business brought him back to Hollywood a little later, they had a pleasant dinner at the Sportsman's Lodge. They began seeing each other regularly.

Asked if it was a serious romance, Susan laughed it off. Imitating Scarlett O'Hara, she drawled, "Oh fiddle-de-dee, Mr. Chalkley and I have fun going out together, but that's all there is to it."

Meantime, in the midst of what appeared to be a pleasant social life, Susan was still embroiled in legal controversies, as Jess's lawyer filed yet another divorce appeal. In addition, a series of nasty little items began appearing in the columns, attributed not to Jess, but to rival studios attempting to sabotage Susan's Oscar chances: items about Hughes, Don Barry, the suicide attempt. Preview scuttlebutt about *The Conqueror*, scheduled for release ten days after the awards, was also devastating.

Although she had originally planned to have only the twins as her date for the Academy Awards evening, Susan got a fourth ticket for Chalkley, stirring up further speculation. Uncharacteristically, the woman who never gave parties made arrangements for a "win or lose" bash immediately following the presentations.

When the five nominees were announced that evening in alphabetical order, they were: Susan Hayward for *I'll Cry Tomorrow*, Katharine Hepburn for *Summertime*, Jennifer Jones for *Love Is a Many Splendored Thing*, Anna Magnani for *The Rose Tattoo*, and Eleanor Parker for *Interrupted Melody*. Susan Hayward's name was greeted by sustained applause.

A hush filled the Pantages Theatre as the celebrated envelope was opened.

"And the winner is . . . Anna Magnani for *The Rose Tattoo*." The presenter visibly found it difficult to conceal his disappointment, and the groans from the audience were clearly audible.

Nevertheless, Susan's party went on as scheduled. Louella, who left the party for the winning picture, *Marty,* early, so as not to disappoint her pet, wrote: "Susan Hayward would never give a better performance in her life than she did when the Oscar went to Anna Magnani. Sitting in front of me at the Academy Awards with her twin sons when the announcement was made, she turned to me and said, 'We'll have to try harder next year.' At her party, Susan sang song after song and was the gayest of the few friends who gathered at her home. Her two boys looked more downcast than Susan. I hear it was very close between her and Magnani."

Commenting on that night, Susan confided, "I managed not to shed any tears until everything was over. Then I sat down and had a good cry and decided that losing was just part of the game." Her real feelings were probably unprintable.

Eaton, who remained after the other guests had gone home, provided a strong shoulder for Susan to cry on . . . until the wee hours of the morning. It is possible he provided a great deal more. Harvey Hestor remembered his returning to Georgia behaving like a love-sick kid. For her part, although she admitted to being very fond of him, Susan remained uncommitted. She didn't want to mess up things with Chalkley—but she didn't want to be tied down, either.

Shortly afterward, she was due in Cannes for the film festival, where *I'll Cry Tomorrow* was in competition. Although she still wasn't friendly with Sheilah Graham, she agreed to have dinner with the columnist and was surprisingly talkative under the circumstances.

"The monkey's off my back," she said cryptically, a remark Graham attributed to the divorce from Jess. "My seven-year contract with Twentieth Century-Fox ends in August, and I'll be a free woman not only in my private life but with my career.

"I believe my troubles have been beneficial. You must have problems to be able to understand others. Now that it's almost over, and I pray it is, I realize it is better for the children to have a home that is peaceful, and I aim to keep it that way. I can't take the boys with me to the film festival—they're in school, and besides there's always such a bother with Jess

when I want to take them out of the country. But one thing I promised them, and this they will get. They love to travel, and when they're 14 years old we're going on a tramp steamer around the world. I have put this money away already for them. The three of us are very close, the twins are different shapes and sizes, but we all love the same things. When I took them to Sun Valley, we all had a great time."

To Graham's surprise, Susan talked frankly of remarriage. "You can be sure I'll be very careful before I marry again, but I'd hate to think I'd live alone for the rest of my life. I'm not the type who can live alone and like it." Reiterating that her marital problems had not soured her on the subject, she added wistfully, "I'd like to marry again. But for now I'm feeling free and wonderful, thank you, and I aim to have a great time at the festival."

Throughout the evening she never mentioned Eaton Chalkley's name.

On April 27 Susan arrived in Cannes. Surrounded by hundreds of reporters and photographers, she yelled out: "Where are the men around here? I don't mean actors, I mean men!"

They'd find her quickly enough.

✣ chapter 22 ✣

SUSAN ALWAYS CLAIMED redheads had to be the center of attention. At Cannes, she was just that.

During the film festival, the sleepy Côte d'Azur town turns into Babylon—crowded, noisy, every event a mélange of foreign tongues, men and women shouting, pushing, and generally causing chaos. Everyone wants to be number one—and, in 1956, the competition for the position was particularly formidable.

Kim Novak, then rivaling Marilyn Monroe on the top of the American popularity polls, was undoubtedly the photographers' favorite subject. Ginger Rogers and Ingrid Bergman, the latter still *persona non grata* in America because of her open affair with Roberto Rossellini, were treated respectfully, like grand dames.

On April 29, 1956, however, columnist Bernard Valery cabled New York: "There's murder in the air, and the objects of the looks that can kill are Susan Hayward and Kim Novak. The conspirators: Many other stars of both sexes gathered for the annual film festival. Motive: The other stars have just about been abandoned by the 600 reporters and photographers who have eyes, ears, and lenses only for the two Americans. When Susan Hayward hit the Carlton Hotel, British actor Richard Todd left Cannes and Martine Carol cancelled her reservations. Susan is expected to get the award for the best female acting for her role in *I'll Cry Tomorrow*, which got rave reviews."

Valery called the shot correctly. At the gala held on May 10, with Ingrid Bergman seated at the same table, Susan was awarded the prize for the year's best performance. *Adam Had Four Sons* seemed light years away for both of them, and theirs was a warm and genuinely happy reunion. Soon, Bergman

would make the film that would put her too back in America's good graces: *Anastasia*. As for Kim Novak, she was nowhere to be seen.

Susan had planned to be gone two weeks, but she remained in Europe two months. She wrote Tim and Gregory and phoned home to find out how the twins were getting along; scribbled a few post cards to Louella, to her agent, to Eaton Chalkley, and to her mother, frivolously signing them, "Susie Magnani."

Chalkley phoned several times when she was in Cannes. She promised to have dinner with him when she returned, but it was quite obvious that she was in no rush to get back—she was having the time of her life. Besides, abroad, free of her mother, away from her family, relieved of the Hollywood pressures, it was inevitable that she'd become involved with someone, and she did: an attractive, attentive British publisher named Gordon White, whom she met at the festival. White, who had previously been linked with Grace Kelly, knew how to treat a lady, and their romance was the talk of Cannes. As an intimate gift, White presented Susan with a Yorkshire terrier. She adored Sukeh, but British airline officials prevented her from taking him on the plane en route to the Cork Film Festival in Ireland. A scene at the airport ensued, with Susan screaming, "The dog needs me," but the airline won the argument. White promised to take care of the dog. He also promised to see her again in Hollywood that June.

On May 25, to no one's surprise, Susan's performance in *I'll Cry Tomorrow* took the Cork Film Festival's best-acting award. A couple of days later, Susan flew into Idlewild Airport and left immediately on the next plane to Hollywood. When she arrived home, the studio announced her for the starring role in *Three Faces of Eve*, but for some reason, the casting fell through, and Joanne Woodward eventually played the part.

Gordon White's trip in June fell through too. He called Susan to say he couldn't get to California that month, but would try for July. Sorry. Deeply hurt by White's casual attitude, Susan was particularly vulnerable when the persistent Chalkley phoned from Georgia: he would like to fly to Hollywood and help celebrate her upcoming birthday. She was just a year short of forty, though Chalkley didn't know it then, nor did most other people. For years, her birth date had been listed as 1918 on the studio biographies, instead of the actual 1917, but even that statistic depressed her. She ordered the

studio to remove her birthdate entirely from all further handouts, with the result that, over the next two decades, her birth
would be cited anywhere from 1919 to 1922. In Hollywood,
this was standard operational procedure, but in Susan's case,
it distorted chronology to such a degree that in future stories
she'd be referred to as a child model and a teen-age Scarlett
contender.

Eaton Chalkley couldn't have cared less about Susan's age.
As the father of three—two girls and a boy—he was indifferent
to the possibility of starting a new family. When Susan was
in Europe, he had read up on her past and asked a great many
questions about her personality. The *Barker v. Barker* divorce
testimony was on public record; anyone could obtain a copy.
By this time, Chalkley was well-schooled on Susan's background and temperament. His friends had warned him that she
would never give up her career and that Barker would never
allow Susan to take their sons out of California permanently,
so it was up to Chalkley to convince Susan that, as his wife,
not only could she have the best of both worlds, but that, with
his legal background, he could find a way for her to have total
custody of Timothy and Gregory.

He was patient and persuasive; Susan was evasive. Eaton
remained in California until mid-July, telling pals he was there
on business. No one could pinpoint its exact nature, however.

At the end of the month, Susan signed an unusual six-picture
deal with Twentieth Century-Fox, guaranteeing her $300,000
a year over a twenty-year period, and allowing her to work for
other studios. That certainly didn't seem the act of a woman
preparing to throw away her career in favor of domesticity in
Georgia—or anywhere else. Chalkley was in no mood to admit
defeat, however; he wanted Susan and he was a man who
always got what he wanted.

On August 1, Susan took off from Idlewild Airport in New
York for a holiday in Brazil, as the guest of the Jockey Club
of Rio de Janeiro. The club's chairman Jorge Guinele met her
at the airport and escorted her to the club's annual Sweepstakes
Ball. She was back in New York on August 10, and spent a
few days on the town before returning home to begin work on
her next film.

In Burbank, a chauffeur drove her to Warner Brothers for
pre-production meetings on *Melville Goodwin, U.S.A.* The
appearance of the studio had not changed too much from the

way she remembered it in her starlet-student days. The old New York street was still standing; the sound stages were humming, though for the most part, it was with pilots for future television productions.

Warner made certain his former one-fifty-dollar-a-week contractee was treated like a queen. The man hadn't softened— but he needed Susan a great deal more than she needed him or his films. The John Marquand novel had been slated originally for Humphrey Bogart and Lauren Bacall. With Bogart stricken with cancer, though, Bacall had backed out. Susan and Kirk Douglas were the only suitable substitutes available, and Warners had already sunk a considerable amount of money into the project, so, retitled *Top Secret Affair,* the script was retailored and pruned to suit the Hayward and Douglas personalities; and even when Susan insisted that Charles LeMaire design her wardrobe, Warner quietly acquiesced. As it turned out, he should have shelved the project completely. The story of an aggressive lady publisher out to discredit a distinguished war hero was a box-office bust.

Susan was winding up *Top Secret Affair* when Gordon White finally found time to visit her in Hollywood. The man, who had seemed so romantic under a Riviera moon, now left her cold. They dined together a couple of times, but it was plain Susan was merely returning the hospitality he had shown her when she was in Europe. Not that she was committed to Chalkley. In fact, Susan continued to play the field, and on November 17, 1956, we have this surprising scoop from surrogate-mother Louella:

"The friendship of Susan Hayward and brilliant Dr. Frederick Meyer, a young professor of philosophy at the University of Redlands, has been a great thing for Susan. She's reading books on philosophy and her whole outlook on life is different. . . . He may be the man she's been looking for all these years. He is certainly in love with her and they are together practically every night." The mysterious Dr. Meyer, however, was never mentioned again.

Jorge Guinele too popped up again, flying in from Rio to spend the Thanksgiving holidays with Susan, but apparently, as with Gordon White, the reunion was a letdown.

In November too, according to Sidney Skolsky, Susan and Jess Barker had a private and friendly meeting and "agreed on new and equal visitation rights concerning their sons, who have

just been enrolled in an out-of-town private school."

Throughout all this, Floyd Eaton Chalkley had been hanging in there. Like a Southern summer cold, he simply wouldn't go away. If Susan wanted to date ten, a hundred, or a thousand different men, that was fine with him. He'd give her enough time, wait for the right moment, and then step in.

On November 28, Susan entered a hospital to "undergo surgery." Her physician reported her in good condition, but would not reveal the nature of the operation, saying only "it was to correct a minor ailment." Such vague announcements were commonplace in Hollywood in the 1950s, and they usually meant only one thing—an abortion. The whispers began immediately, the most vicious being that she had done it because she had no idea as to the father's identity. It was ironic, because, a month later, a court declared that, in spite of his denials, Jess had fathered a daughter, Morgana Ruth, by a twenty-five-year-old actress named Yvonne Dougherty. The two had had a casual affair after his divorce from Susan.

It was time to take stock of the life Susan had led in the nineteen months since her suicide attempt. Always contemptuous of girls who "slept around," she realized she had been guilty of promiscuous behavior. She had never stooped to between-take "quickies" in her dressing room, or to sleeping with men just to advance her career, but though she had romanticized the affairs to make them respectable, they were still basically sex-without-love relationships. After the Don Barry scandal, she had tried to be more discreet, but there was no such thing as being discreet enough in a town filled with gossipers. She was running the risk of being branded an unfit mother.

With the New Year approaching, Susan promised herself her future life would be different. She decided to end the old year with a blast. Although she wasn't much of a hostess, she made plans to hold what she tagged a "Point of No Return" party at her home on December 29. Floyd Eaton Chalkley received the first invitation. He didn't have to be asked twice. A few days later he arrived in Los Angeles carrying Susan's Christmas presents.

Mike Connolly, unaware of the turmoil Susan had been going through, romanticized: "It was a wonderful party. Looking back, I believe this was the time when the actual marriage plans were made by the happy couple. Why do I think so? Because immediately after Christmas, Eaton went back to

Georgia, and Susan stopped reading the scripts submitted to her. And the two began acting very mysteriously."

Nevertheless, on January 3, Susan resumed song coaching, with Bobby Tucker, hoping to persuade Fox to cast her as Nellie Forbush in the film version of *South Pacific*. Her hopes were dashed, though, when twenty-six-year-old Mitzi Gaynor got the nod. Susan looked young, but not young enough to make the May-September romance between the French planter and hick nurse credible.

On January 11, Mike Connolly noted that Susan had quietly slipped out of town. For a week, no one knew her whereabouts. Then, on January 18, in a mishmash of misinformation, Sheilah Graham noted: "I'm assured that wedding bells for Susan Hayward and Eaton Chalkley, handsome Washington D.C. attorney, are unlikely. Though he is legally divorced, his religion prevents a second marriage."

Four days later, Connolly let slip that Susan's mystery trip had been to Carrollton, Georgia, to see Eaton's home and meet his family. Mike Connolly's earlier romantic theory had been slightly off. Eaton may have proposed to Susan during the Christmas holidays and invited her to visit his home in Georgia, but she hadn't consented to become his wife—until that final week down South. By the time the two flew back to Hollywood on February 1, Susan had called Charles LeMaire and asked him to whip up a pretty blue dress and matching stole for an afternoon wedding she was planning to attend. She avoided mentioning whose wedding it was going to be.

When Susan and Eaton Chalkley eloped to Phoenix, Arizona, on Friday, February 8, 1957, almost everyone was caught off guard. Neither Ellen Marrenner, the twins (attending school outside Los Angeles), brother Wally, Twentieth Century-Fox nor the doting Louella Parsons suspected that the wedding was to be so imminent.

Even during Chalkley's FBI days, it's doubtful that he had ever pulled off an operation with such secrecy and efficiency. Chalkley had arrived in Hollywood the week before, the houseguest of Vincent X. Flaherty and his wife, and it was during that week that Chalkley and Susan had made their plans. In order to marry as quickly as possible, though, Chalkley realized he would need help. Two days before the wedding, he returned

to the Flaherty home after an evening with Susan and took his friends into his confidence.

"Don't tell anybody," he cautioned Flaherty, "but Susan and I are getting married—right away. Do you know anybody in Phoenix who can help us have a quiet wedding?"

Flaherty called Neil McCarthy, an attorney friend in Phoenix, only to find him en route to his ranch. Nervous and impatient, Chalkley wanted faster action. Flaherty next called Frank Brophy, a banker in Phoenix and friend of McCarthy's. After being sworn to secrecy, Brophy agreed to arrange everything for a Saturday ceremony.

The plan was for Susan and Chalkley to leave Friday, with Flaherty following on Saturday to act as best man. On Friday morning, however, Chalkley suddenly made an alarming discovery: he had forgotten the ring! He rushed nervously into Beverly Hills and bought a diamond wedding band, came back and packed his bags, then took off to collect Susan.

"Please be there," he urged Flaherty at the door. "I'll call you as soon as we arrive."

Meanwhile, Susan had risen early and packed two bags, confiding in no one where she was going. Even when Chalkley arrived to take her to the airport, the servants were told only that she wouldn't be back until around Easter. Wearing dark glasses, Susan walked unrecognized through the busy air terminal, and soon they were flying to Arizona.

When they reached Phoenix, their well-laid plans ran into a hitch, though. Applying for the license at city hall, Susan managed to escape recognition with her dark glasses and by using her real legal name, but there they were reminded of a detail that everyone had apparently overlooked in the excitement: Arizona law required a forty-eight hour wait before the license could be used. That meant a Sunday marriage instead of Saturday, as planned. Chalkley called Flaherty to tell him to cancel his flight and make later reservations.

There the matter rested uncertainly for several hours. Susan and Chalkley were disappointed over the delay but resigned to it, when something unusual occurred. That same afternoon, the governor of Arizona provided them with a special writ waiving the usual waiting period. The incident is still unexplained. Rather than wait for the revised arrival date of their best man, Susan and Chalkley decided to be married on the spot, unattended.

Susan had been a divorcee for exactly two years, five months, and twenty-two days when she became Mrs. Eaton Chalkley in a civil ceremony performed by Justice of the Peace Stanley Kimball. Even Kimball had been kept in the dark. He had received a phone call at 4 P.M. asking if he would be available to perform a wedding at 5 P.M., but not until Susan and Chalkley appeared at his door had he learned the identity of the couple.

The newlyweds left immediately for a New Orleans honeymoon. They were still honeymooning there when the Appellate Court in California ruled that she didn't have to pay Barker's attorney's fee ($7,500), and once again affirmed her divorce and her rights of property.

Curiously enough, New Orleans was also the city where Scarlett O'Hara and Rhett Butler had gone after they were married. Maybe it was more than just a coincidence. Timothy remembers teasing his mother after the family had settled down in Georgia: "Well, Mom, you finally got what you wanted. You are playing Scarlett O'Hara in real life."

Susan's fantasy life had begun to take shape.

PART FIVE

Mrs. Floyd Eaton Chalkley

Carrollton, Georgia—Fort Lauderdale, Florida
February 8, 1957—January 9, 1966

Eaton was the first man I had ever met that I felt I could lean on completely. He was the strongest male I ever knew. He had the greatest amount of gentleness and a totally even temperament. I wanted to be with him all the time for the rest of our lives.

SUSAN HAYWARD CHALKLEY

⊗ *chapter 23* ⊗

Her marriage to Chalkley turned her into a totally happy
woman. She deserved all the happiness she could get. . . .
ROBERT WAGNER, 1980

WITH ALL HER HEART, Susan planned to be the perfect wife to
Chalkley, to devote herself totally to the new life she envisioned—that of a gracious lady, one who'd entertain her husband's friends in the true tradition of Southern hospitality. She
had always called her first husband Jess. Chalkley, she would
refer to as *my husband* or, in the more Southern tradition, *Mr.
Chalkley*. Scarlett would never go hungry again.

The house they returned to from New Orleans was a seventy-
five-year-old red and white farmhouse in Carrollton, Georgia.
Susan fell so much in love with the house and its surroundings
that, though the two of them pored over blueprints for a new
and larger home, they finally decided to add on to the original
building instead.

"Until now," Susan confided to Harvey Hestor, "I've always
lived in places meant for other people. This is the first that
will be built for me. Fixing it up has been a tremendous joy
to us."

The house occupied her days throughout most of 1957. At
night, for the first time in years, she could fall asleep without
the aid of sleeping pills. Perhaps, at some point, she thought
of the lines she had spoken in *Smash-Up:*

> To Lie in Bed and Sleep Not
> To Wait for One Who Comes Not
> To Try to Please and Please Not . . .

They no longer applied to her; she was certain they never would again.

Over the Christmas holidays, she invited Sara Little to Carrollton and proudly showed her every inch of her home.

Roofed with crushed marble and nestled in a pine grove overlooking a fifteen-acre lake, facing Stone Mountain, the house could be reached by a long driveway that stretched from the entrance gate. The wide entrance hall was a miniature art gallery of original oils—no longer would she settle for reproductions, as she had in Sherman Oaks. The kitchen, located next to the glass-enclosed breakfast room, contained ultra-modern appliances, but her greatest pride there was the double-duty fireplace, which served the master bedroom on the other side of the wall as well. The bedroom, decorated in yellow and white, faced the lake. Susan's adjoining dressing room was pink, with matching marble-top counters. "Finally I have enough closets for all my clothes," she said.

Susan took pleasure too in her spacious living room, a startling contrast to the mess in Sherman Oaks. The interior was built of tongue-and-groove logs painted white, with a floor of black slate. Susan did most of her entertaining in this immaculately kept, comfortably furnished room.

Outside was a small glass-walled playhouse for informal entertaining, which also faced the lake. One of its two rooms was a dressing room for swimming parties, the other contained all of Susan's awards, trophies, a player piano, and an indoor barbecue. A pile of scripts, unopened and neglected, was stacked in a corner—a reminder that producers were still clamoring for her services.

Harvey Hestor was considered a member of the family. "The other guests at intimate dinner parties were old friends of Eaton's whom she hoped to make her friends as well. For the most part, they were professional people: Dr. Hadley Allen, the Chalkleys' family physician, and his wife Betty; pharmacist T. R. Griffin, Jr., and his wife; attorney A. B. Parker; Mr. and Mrs. Joseph Kane, Sr., residents of Atlanta.

Mrs. Kane later recalled, "When we got together, the conversation was always interesting and stimulating, and covered practically everything from current events to plumbing. Susan's career seldom entered into our conversation."

In fact, it seldom entered into anyone's conversation. Once the initial excitement of having a movie star in their midst

abated, the townspeople took Mrs. Chalkley's presence in stride, though they did ask for her autograph every once in a while when she shopped in town. She graciously agreed.

She tactfully rejected most invitations to join local civic groups, explaining, ingenuously, "I want to do my share, but if I answer all requests, I wouldn't have a chance to be a good wife and mother and that comes first." She did participate in enough activities, however, to inspire goodwill. She served as chairman of the Muscular Dystrophy campaign; attended a performance of *Ondine* at West Georgia College and visited the budding young actors backstage; christened a boat, opening a private lake in nearby Jonesboro; and threw out the first ball on opening day for the local Georgia Crackers baseball team.

The girl who had identified with Scarlett now cast herself as a genteel Melanie Wilkes, a shadow presence beside her husband. Eaton's children lived with their mother, and Susan made no effort to usurp their affections. She described her mother-in-law, Mrs. Alma Chalkley, as "a wonderful person with a terrific sense of humor and an amazing amount of energy that must be put to use," then paused and added: "But I don't want to make her responsible for my decisions. I'm a naturally moody person and always have been. My nerves are very close to the surface. My husband realized how moody I am before we were married. He's so calm and patient and understanding that I'm on a more even keel now than ever before. I love my husband, and I want to be a full-time wife."

One night when Eaton was occupied with some business affairs, Susan sat outside with Harvey Hestor. He said softly, "Tell me, Susan, don't you ever miss Hollywood even a smidgen?"

"Not even a smidgen," she echoed. "All I can ever want is here. I used to make pictures for Academy Awards—but no more."

That state of affairs lasted for exactly nine months, until October of 1957. Then her old friend Walter Wanger made her an offer that, as they say, she couldn't refuse.

⊗ *chapter 24* ⊗

IN LATE 1957, Walter Wanger's career looked to be a gigantic question mark. He had trouble putting deals together; people he had valued as friends turned away. The reason for it: the once-distinguished producer was now an ex-convict.

On December 13, 1951, suspecting his wife Joan Bennett of adultery and, in a jealous rage, Wanger had shot Bennett's agent Jennings Lang. Lang had survived the bloody assault; Wanger, mortified, had waived trial; and on April 22, 1952, he was sentenced to four months at the Wayside Honor Farm in Castiac, California.

While at Wayside, Wanger became fascinated by the injustices of the California penal system. Working in the prison library, he read everything he could on the subject and, in 1953, after his release, he managed to get backing for a low-budget film made at Folsom Prison called *Riot in Cell Block II*. Released in New York the following February, it prompted the *Times* to comment: ". . . [It] is a sincere and adult plea for a captive male society revolting against penal injustices. . . . [It] attains an almost documentary quality . . . in short punches, and preaches with authority."

Riot in Cell Block II was only a warm-up, however, to the major project Wanger had in mind—the picture he was gambling on to restore his fortunes.

On March 3, 1953, an eighty-year-old, crippled woman named Mabel Monahan was found murdered—pistol-whipped—in her Burbank home; the motivation, robbery—the widow had reputedly hidden $100,000 somewhere in her house. One month later, a "B-girl" named Barbara Graham was apprehended by the police in Inwood, a suburb of Los Angeles, together with three male accomplices, Emmett Perkins, Jack

Santo, and Bruce King, and charged with the murder.

"Bloody Babs," as the press immediately tagged her, had been in and out of reform school and prisons since the age of thirteen for prostitution, narcotics possession, forgery—and now murder. Despite her protestations that she had been at home with her husband Henry on the night of the murder (he had disappeared in the meantime—police never did find him), she was put on trial in California State Superior Court in Los Angeles in the fall of 1953. Persecuted in the press more for her sordid past than on the basis of any tangible evidence, unable to discredit the men's story that she had been with them, not her husband—their trial was tied to hers and they were certain the Court would not send a woman to the gas chamber— Graham was found guilty and sentenced to death.

Curious discrepancies had come out in the trial, however: testimony showed that Mabel Monahan had been murdered by a right-handed person—and Graham was left-handed. Psychiatrists testified that she was temperamentally opposed to violence. A "confession" she had supposedly made was found to have been tricked out of her by a hired alibi—actually a police officer. Buoyed by a wave of sympathy for Graham and a growing national furor over capital punishment, her lawyers launched a two-year-long campaign of appeals to overturn the verdict, but in the end the appeals and the temporary reprieves only prolonged the agony. On August 3, 1955, Bloody Babs was put to death in San Quentin's gas chamber.

It was a highly dramatic story, and one particularly meaningful to a man who had just gotten out of prison himself for assault, and on March 22, 1957, after three years of research and planning, Wanger set the wheels in motion for the picture that would become *I Want to Live!*

Based on public accounts, letters written by Barbara Graham prior to her execution, and articles written for the *San Francisco Examiner* by Pulitzer Prize–winning journalist Ed Montgomery—who had been one of the first to attack Graham, then changed his mind and helped lead the fight for her acquittal— *I Want to Live!* was not an objective movie. In fact, the script by Nelson Gidding and Don Mankiewicz was designed to show, not only her innocence, but the impossible dilemma into which people with a less than impeccable past could be plunged by newspaper and legal pressures. That it was stacked in favor of Graham's innocence could be discerned when, near the

beginning of the film, Babs was, indeed, shown to be at home with her husband on the night she was supposed to be bludgeoning Mrs. Monahan to death.

Susan's attitude toward the verdict was more ambivalent. Before accepting the part, she read all the available material on the trial, talked to some of the people involved, and even visited women's prisons. "I was fascinated by the contradictory traits of personality in this strangely controversial woman who had had an extraordinary effect on everyone she met," she said. "She was first a juvenile, then an adult, delinquent, arrested on bad check charges, perjury, soliciting, and a flood of misdemeanors. But somewhere along the line she was a good wife and mother. I read her letters, sometimes literate, often profound. She loved poetry and music, both jazz and classical. None of this seemed to square with the picture drawn of her at the time of the trial. I studied the final transcript. I became so fascinated by the woman I simply had to play her."

After all her research, Susan finally decided for herself that Graham had been innocent of the murder—but that she also had been present when the widow was killed by one of the men. It made no difference to her portrayal, however—the Graham role was just the kind of part to take her back up to the top, and she plunged into it with all the intensity at her command.

She had other incentives as well. Wanger judged Susan so important to the success of his movie that he had also agreed to give her 37 percent of the profits, sole star billing—and casting approval. The cast would eventually include Simon Oakland, Theodore Bikel, and Alice Backes. The director would be Robert Wise, who had made a name for himself with *Somebody Up There Likes Me* and *Executive Suite*, and would go on to direct *The Sound of Music* and *West Side Story*.

The only other female role of any importance was that of Barbara Graham's girlhood friend Peg—third-billed in the film. A sensitive young character actress named Virginia Vincent remembers being tested and personally chosen by Susan. "She was so beautiful. Oh, that nose, that sweet chin, those eyes, and yet she had a lot of strength though there was something fragile. She was small-boned, everything was in the right place . . . a sweetness and yet such strength."

Later, they met at the old Sam Goldwyn studios, where both were being fitted for wardrobes. "I went over to Goldwyn

for my costume calls and my fittings, and we took publicity pictures. Susan and I had to put on these short dresses. They came above our knees, and I felt naked.

"Susan's body was adorable, everything was perfect. She was about 5' 3", very feminine-looking . . . soft and trim. Her body was in great shape, not an ounce of fat on her, but not scrawny. She felt her legs were 'terrible,' but they were adorable, and I thought if she's complaining, what am I doing here?

"In the party scene, my dresses were a little too skimpy. Robert Wise said, 'Oh, we ought to put a little more material around it because I don't think Susan would okay it as it is.' I was surprised when I saw the dress she wore, because it seemed very modest for a girl who was a hooker. She was sedate, but you know a lot of people once tore her over the coals. She was very nice to everybody. She was working on scenes in the party, doing all those crazy drills with the sailors and soldiers. She was right there with us, having a good time and enjoying it. She was very professional and just very involved in her work. From what I could see the important thing was the work. She gave it 100 percent.

"Susan was basically very private. She didn't joke, but she laughed a lot when we were doing that rowdy scene. And she just seemed to be enjoying that very much, just as I was and everybody else. You know when you're working on a good movie, it's incredible, it's a real high. Everybody's in a great mood. . . . I saw no temperament from Susan, and I was there when she was talking to Bob Wise and others.

"She was a lady. I never heard her curse, not even an 'Oh damn!' In fact, the only time I ever heard her complain about anything was when she returned to the studio on March 31st, after an awful bout with the measles that she had probably picked up from the twins in Georgia." [Her illness had delayed the start of the shooting.]

" 'My room was kept dark for a week,' she said. 'I couldn't read or watch television or do anything. It was driving me up the wall. And I kept worrying about the cost mounting up till I was well enough to return. How could I have predicted that? A woman of my age getting the measles!' "

Her illness had also prevented her from attending the Academy Awards on March 26th. She hadn't been nominated for anything, but she had still looked forward to the evening. "After her return," Virginia Vincent continues, "we worked

on a few scenes, when suddenly in mid-April, Susan's mother died. A couple of days later, Susan told me, 'My mother seemed tired and the doctor put her in the hospital for a little rest—so we wouldn't have anything to think about. It was just for a little rest, that was about it. I visited her at the hospital. Then without warning she had a coronary thrombosis attack and passed away.

"'It was so unexpected!' Susan said. She was so broken up, and was crying at home. Wanger insisted, 'She's got to come to work.' They all talked it out, and she agreed it was the best thing for her. Next time I saw her was when Bob Wise called me. He said, 'Susan would like you to go over the lines of the prison scene.'

"I told her I'd recently lost my mother too, of a heart attack, and we established a rapport. I have something about me that makes people want to open up. Maybe she felt that with me. We went over the lines—it was the scene where I'd come to visit Babs in the prison after they'd laid the murder rap on her. We hadn't seen each other for many years, and Peg, my character, had gone straight, but she'd still come to visit Barbara. Peg was plain and sweet now. She wasn't the B-girl anymore. At first, Barbara doesn't recognize me, and then she tells me I shouldn't be there because of our past association. I say, 'No, my husband knows all about me, I told him everything about my life.' It's a very touching episode. I think it made the audience feel that Barbara was totally innocent, that she couldn't have committed murder. During this crucial scene, Susan had to say, 'If only I could have seen the handwriting on the wall.' And that's when she broke into tears. The scene was filmed when she was so affected by her mother's death. She was using that, you see. *'If only I had seen the handwriting on the wall.'* She just broke up."

Regarding Barbara Graham's guilt, Virginia said, "I remember when Walter Wanger invited the lady I played to visit the set. She was living in San Pedro, married, and had four children. She had a sweet face, but very fat. She had been brought to Hollywood to see Susan. Then she talked to me afterwards. She said, 'I'm telling you the same thing I told Miss Hayward. I knew Barbara, and we did a lot of crazy things, but she could never do a thing like that. She never could hurt anybody. Couldn't! I know her like I know myself. Barbara Graham was innocent. We could tell each other every-

thing.' She said, *'No way.'* This woman convinced me."

Virginia Vincent also met Eaton Chalkley:

"Susan introduced him to me on the set of *I Want to Live!* He was, oh God, he was lovely! Good looking, charming, a gentleman, you know? He was very warm, very sweet. And they were so, so happy. I guess she figured she was pretty lucky having a guy like that. He wasn't hanging around, but he was in and out. I think he was aware she needed time to be alone, to work on the part. There was a lot of work, long, long days and nights. You shoot all those scenes from every angle; it can be very, very tedious."

For all Susan's involvement with the part of Barbara Graham and her breakdown in the scene with Virginia Vincent, she was still, however, the same cool, detached actress she'd always been. As in *I'll Cry Tomorrow,* her ability to shake herself out of the mood of the scene was remarkable. Roman Freulich, a still photographer assigned to shoot action shots of Susan on the set, recalls weeping during the scene in which Barbara Graham goes to her death in the gas chamber. He expected Susan too to be shattered by the sequence. Still wiping away his tears, Freulich went to Susan's dressing room and "found her dry-eyed and humming a little tune!"

I Want to Live! finally concluded shooting in early June, with Robert Wise letting out all the stops: "In motion pictures Susan Hayward is as important a figure as Sarah Bernhardt was on the stage. [How Susan must have delighted in that comparison!] Somewhere within her is a chemical combination that can excite and hold audiences as surely as could Garbo and very few other greats of the screen. Susan is one of two or three actresses who can hold up a picture all by herself.... As a performer, so far as I know, she is the only one who completely dominates female audiences. Why? Except for the fact that she is a natural actress, a powerful and honest actress, I don't know. Certainly she has debunked every theory on the necessity of coming to the movies from some outside activity, such as the stage, television, or the serious and dedicated 'method' schools of acting.

"Susan never had a drama lesson in her life. But she can give a few."

Walter Wanger was just as excited. To his good friend Ben Hecht, he proclaimed: "If Susan were a European actress, she'd sweep the world."

They were not alone in their estimation. The reviews, when the film was released in November, made even their enthusiasm sound like understatement.

Bosley Crowther of the *New York Times*, who had never been particularly partial to Susan in the past, was overwhelmed by her performance:

> Susan Hayward has done some vivid acting in a number of sordid roles that have called for professional simulation of personal ordeals of the most upsetting sort. But she's never done anything so vivid or so shattering to an audience's nerves as she does in Walter Wanger's sensational new drama, *I Want to Live!* Based on the actual experience of a West Coast woman named Barbara Graham, Hayward plays it superbly. From a loose and wise-cracking B-girl she moves onto levels of cold disdain and then plunges down to the depths of terror and bleak surrender as she reaches the end. Except that the role does not present us a precisely pretty character, its performance merits for Miss Hayward our most respectful applause.

Paul V. Beckley's Sunday feature in the *New York Herald-Tribune* was a solid gold valentine:

> Susan Hayward's performance in *I Want to Live!* is probably her finest. She was excellent in *I'll Cry Tomorrow* a couple of years ago, setting a pace for honest portrayal of hard roles, but I feel she has inched up above the peak in this current hard-bitten dramatization of the trial and execution of the late Barbara Graham.
>
> The performance has balance. One has only to consider how easily it would have been to slip off into the raptures of hysteria or tear-drenched self-pity or melodramatic heroics of defiance to realize how sensitively she has walked the knife-edge story line. Her style here is naturalistic, but it is a naturalism with depths that indicate how perceptive an insight she has brought to the role. Although it is by no means a one-woman picture, it is focused so intimately and so continuously on her life that its success is largely hers.
>
> Miss Hayward's Barbara has courage, humility and an affectionate nature, qualities which could have led her into a satisfactory life had they not been oriented by an unpleasant childhood toward entirely antisocial habits. So oriented, they helped to bring her to her dread finish, for most of her

mistakes were the result of a distrust of society and an unreasonable trust in the criminals with whom she early cast her lot.

Although no footage in this film is given over to her early life, it is there implicitly and unmistakably in Miss Hayward's performance, which has the strength and sharpness of a master drawing—one might say that she exhibits a talent for the incisive dramatic line. Not even at the end, when the details of preparation for her execution become a kind of throb in our nerve ends as we watch, does her performance crack to let the emotions spread out in indefinite pools of misery. Watching it we may feel a misery, but she holds things together in such a way that our vicarious suffering takes on a kind of intellectual focus, almost abstract and certainly aimed at capital punishment itself rather than the guilt or innocence of this particular woman.

There was no question about her receiving an Oscar nomination, but Susan was far from convinced that the Academy, which had already rebuffed her four times, would finally let her have the prize she had wanted for so long. Eaton, however, told her to buy the most gorgeous new dress she could find. Not only were they going to nominate her, he said, this time she was going to win.

❈ chapter 25 ❈

MR. AND MRS. EATON CHALKLEY, together with their friend Vincent Flaherty, were driving home from the Santa Anita race track on February 24, 1959, when the nominations for the 1958 Academy Awards were announced.

After what seemed like an eternity, the newscaster got to the Best Actress nominees. As expected, Susan's name was among them, but Susan remained calm. She had been through this before. And the competition was formidable: Deborah Kerr for *Separate Tables,* Shirley MacLaine for *Some Came Running,* Rosalind Russell for *Auntie Mame,* and Elizabeth Taylor for *Cat on a Hot Tin Roof.* It was Kerr's fifth nomination, Russell's fourth and Taylor's second. MacLaine was considered the dark horse.

Flaherty recalled Susan turning to him and saying, "Oh, I don't give a darn about that thing. But I'd like to get it, just once, for this guy sitting here."

Winning the Oscar would put a perfect cap on a new year that was already award-filled. Exactly one month earlier Susan had flown into New York to receive a plaque from the New York Film Critics for *I Want to Live!* Although nine women had been in competition, Susan had won on the fourth ballot—her counterpart David Niven had not been chosen Best Actor, for *Separate Tables,* until the sixth time around. Years later, she would say of her awards, "The big treat was winning the New York Film Critics Award. That's a tough one to win, not because they know so much, but because they're such rats and they don't like to give anyone a prize, especially anybody from Hollywood."

At the party following the presentation at Sardi's, Susan's cup flowed over with gratitude, even for the "rats." "To think

that this could happen to a girl from Brooklyn!" she kept saying throughout the evening. Not only was the award itself an honor, but she was acutely aware that Academy members were influenced by the New York Film Critics' choices—no matter how vehemently they denied it. More and more in recent years, the Oscars had been playing follow-the-leader.

Then, on February 13, the Foreign Press Association announced that Susan and David Niven would be the recipients of their Golden Globe Awards as well. Everything was falling into place. The awards were presented at a banquet, on March 5, two days before Susan was due to complete a picture called *A Woman Obsessed* at Twentieth. Then Susan returned to Georgia on March 9 for a few weeks of rest before the festivities. She promised that she'd be on hand April 5 for the Sunday afternoon Oscar dress rehearsal. But not before.

Her timing was carefully calculated. Ingrid Bergman had won an Oscar in absentia the previous year for *Anastasia* (Cary Grant had accepted for her), and for this year's ceremonies was setting foot in Hollywood for the first time in more than a decade. To prove her sins had been forgiven and forgotten, the industry had laid out a red carpet welcome for her. Bergman would present the Best Actor award on Oscar night, serve as an honored guest at the Governors' Ball, and, most prominently of all, receive a gala dinner in her honor to be held in the Crystal Room of the Beverly Hills Hotel on Saturday night, April 4. Stars who had turned down requests to appear at the Oscar ceremonies themselves scrambled for invitations to the Bergman party, to be hosted by Twentieth Century-Fox, the producers of *Anastasia*. Sir Laurence Olivier, Cary Grant, Lucille Ball, Louis Jourdan, and hundreds of others crowded into the room to greet Bergman and her husband Lars Schmidt.

It was the party of the year, but Susan Hayward Chalkley avoided it. She still needed to be the center of attention, and this was Ingrid Bergman's night. Susan felt she could wait.

At the Oscar rehearsal there were rumors of a surprise upset: Susan Hayward was considered a sure thing, but Rosalind Russell might just steal the award. Twenty-four hours to go . . .

Early on Monday, Walter Wanger gave Susan a gold medal, roughly the size of a quarter. On one side was the figure and message: "St. Genesius—Please Guide My Destiny." On the other, "To Susan—Best Friend. W.W."

For this Oscar night, Susan chose a simple black satin gown

with a tight bodice setting off a full skirt. The only jewelry noticeable were diamond-and-pearl drop earrings. Her usual white gloves hid her wedding band.

Ingrid Bergman appeared as a presenter wearing an elaborately jeweled gown and looking like a crown princess.

Susan Hayward looked like a lady.

". . . and the winner is . . ."

"The winner is Susan Hayward in I Want to Live!" There was a roar of approval as Susan rushed to the stage. She kept her speech short and simple, first expressing her gratitude to Wanger, then thanking the members of the Academy "for making me so happy." Later she admitted, "I'm in shock. After being up for it so many times, I didn't expect to win. . . . This industry has been so good to me I don't know what to do in return." But when photographers asked her to kiss the statue just presented to her, she demurred: "I only kiss my husband." It was a great line, but Walter Wanger delivered an even better one, one that would be quoted often in the following weeks: "Thank heavens, now we can all relax. Susie got what she's been chasing for twenty years."

The most relaxed person in Beverly Hills the morning after was Susan Hayward. She had danced and drunk champagne until the wee hours, yet she was still fresh and bursting with energy. The chase was over; she had emerged victorious. Enthusiastically she greeted the press for the post-Oscar interview ritual. As always, Susan managed to steer the conversation to subjects she wanted to talk about. She refused to rehash the past, choosing instead to speculate about her future, as she sat curled up on a couch in her Beverly Hills bungalow.

She startled James Bacon by declaring: "I'd like to quit now when I am ahead. . . . I don't want this bit where I have to have my face lifted and have the wrinkles painted out in order to play leading ladies. I'd prefer to quit now. Then, if I felt like it, come back after a time and play character roles. You know me. I love to act. The heavier the better. . . . I used to be the girl who could play all night and work all the next day, but I wasn't happy. My sleepless nights and nervous days are all behind me."

Susan's other interviews that morning were all variations on the same theme: A gold-plated Oscar would make a lovely sight in her trophy room back on the ranch, but it came in a

poor second to the heart-of-gold guy she had at her side.

Syndicated columnist Joe Hyams was told, "I love my husband. I want to be a full-time wife. I want to be with him all the time. My husband would be happier if his wife was there when he came home. That's my job and I want to be with him all the time."

Eaton's buddy, Vincent Flaherty, speaking for the couple, said: "Susan's marriage to Eaton is a great one. He's a wonderful guy. A little swept over now, perhaps by being a kind of prince consort, which he dislikes, and when he's here he can't get out of town fast enough. But the same goes for Susan. Their lives are wrapped up in their new home. Eaton wanted Susan to get out of films. Perhaps she will make two or three more, then quit."

But was that true? Eaton appeared to be dancing to the sound of a different drummer. He told columnist Paul Denis, "Susan was an actress when I married her, and I accepted that. So why would I want to change her now?"

At the Governor's Ball, a *New York Daily News* reporter asked Chalkley how he felt being married to a celebrity. Did he feel he was playing a minor role?

"How can a fellow ever feel he's playing a minor role when he's playing the role for real of Susan's husband? I love to stand around and watch people rave over her."

He certainly did. By all indications, Eaton was basking in the reflected glory—and the fuss made over Susan by his associates in Atlanta and Carrollton wasn't hurting business either. The money she was bringing in helped too—a later remark by Susan would show just how much. Contrary to Flaherty's view, he seemed in no hurry to get back—who could blame him?

And when they did return to Carrollton, there was a surprise waiting for them. A delegation met the Chalkleys at the Atlanta airport and escorted them home for a ticker-tape parade. Susan had described her new-found Southern friends as people who "didn't eat, drink, and sleep pictures. They have a lot of other things to think about and to talk about." For the next few days, however, all they were thinking and talking about was Susan, and by her side always, beaming, accepting congratulations, was Eaton.

One of the things their friends probably avoided mentioning, though, was the reception being accorded the two films Susan

had made immediately upon completion of *I Want to Live!*

Paramount and Twentieth Century-Fox, aware they had two bombs in the can, had held up the release of *Thunder in the Sun* and *A Woman Obsessed* until after the ceremonies, anticipating that, after an Oscar win, the public would flock to see Susan Hayward in anything. They were wrong, however; the box-office takes were bad, and the critics were appalled by Susan's lack of discrimination. Of *Thunder in the Sun*, an eighty-one-minute-long western co-starring Jeff Chandler, the *New York Herald-Tribune*'s Paul V. Beckley moaned on April 9: "Miss Hayward's performance last year in *I Want to Live!* makes the waste here more than usually obvious."

A Woman Obsessed, showcased in May, caused equal distress. The perplexed Bosley Crowther complained, "It's hard to say what goes with Miss Hayward when she gets into these rugged outdoor films. Her good sense and concern as a dramatic actress appear to go by the boards. . . . Fresh air seems to unhinge her. She behaves more reasonably in jail."

Susan seemed indifferent to the pans. "I already have far more offers than I can fulfill," she said with a shrug.

Having sold her property in the valley a few months earlier for $2 million (according to Louella Parsons), Susan also seemed to have more money than she could spend. Paradoxically, she said: "I'm not concerned about winning Oscars any more. Too many disappointments. I'm not retiring, but now I'll act for the joy of it and for the money!" Always the money.

She spent the rest of the spring in Georgia with Eaton and her sons. On July 20 she and Eaton arrived at Idlewild Airport in New York; that evening they left for a three-week vacation in Europe that included stops in Paris, Athens, and Italy. In Taormina, Susan added the David di Donatello Award, the prestigious Italian movie industry prize, to the others received for *I Want to Live!*

The walls and tables in the playroom were running out of space. "I don't think there's an inch left for another award," Susan said, laughing.

As it turned out, her concern was unwarranted. There would be no others.

The 1950s had been a decade filled with traumas and transitions for her, but she was sure she'd never have to look back. Susan welcomed the new decade with a deceptive sense of well-being, convinced that she now had everything she had

ever wanted in life. She ignored the warning signs—and they were there.

By the time the 1960s had ended, she'd never be sure of anything again.

⌘ *chapter 26* ⌘

On May 16, 1960, Susan returned to Twentieth Century-Fox for a spin on a movie called *The Marriage-Go-Round*. She had had an offer to return under more glittering circumstances, but later she'd thank God she hadn't accepted.

After his triumph with *I Want to Live!*, Walter Wanger had opened discussions with Twentieth Century-Fox about the possibility of producing several pictures for them. Susan was delighted, until he told her what he had in mind for the first movie: an epic based on *The Life and Times of Cleopatra* by the Italian historian Carlo Maria Franzero. Enthusiastically, Wanger painted Susan as the new Queen of the Nile. Affectionately, she told him to buy new glasses.

At the age of seventeen, Susan had seen Claudette Colbert in the role in Cecil B. DeMille's spectacular, and in 1945 had been enchanted by Vivien Leigh's portrayal of the Egyptian queen in George Bernard Shaw's *Caesar and Cleopatra*. Nevertheless, she was aware of what had happened to one of Broadway's most respected talents who'd tackled the part in 1937. John Mason Brown had reported: "Tallulah Bankhead sailed down the Nile in a barge last night and sank." Susan shuddered to think what the critics would have to say about her in the role. "They'll probably change *sank* to *stank*." She laughed. She persuaded Wanger to find someone more appropriate. So it was that Elizabeth Taylor sailed down the Nile in a multimillion-dollar extravaganza that almost sank that studio in a river of red ink.

Not that *The Marriage-Go-Round* was all that much better—just less spectacular in its shortcomings. As her final role under contract to Fox, Susan chose a part that had been created on Broadway in 1958 by Claudette Colbert, co-starring with

Charles Boyer. At fifty-five, Colbert was considered too old for the movie version, as was Boyer, and so Susan was cast in the part of a professor's wife determined to protect her husband from the wiles of a predatory younger woman. James Mason was the professor of cultural anthropology. Julie Newmar, the Bo Derek of her day, was recruited from the Broadway cast, as the Swedish siren who wants to mate with the professor because she insists that, with his mind and her body, "they could produce the ideal child."

Due to censorship restrictions, the film adaptation had to sacrifice much of the bawdier humor, and *Time* magazine complained about the casting of Mason, "an actor who could not crack a joke if it was a lichee nut, and Susan Hayward, a bargain basement Bette Davis, whose lightest touch as a comedienne would stun a horse." The *New York Times,* however, disagreed. "Mr. Mason is excellent. Susan Hayward is likewise excellent. Being a dandy with poison-tipped sarcasm and plenty of a looker herself, she easily holds her own against the menace and makes the standard moral ending bearable."

Though Susan was glad to be wrapping up her relationship with Fox, and anxious to part company with them as fast as she could, Sonia Wolfson remembers that during the filming, "She was as obliging as she had been a decade earlier. She was delighted that Charles LeMaire had designed her wardrobe, and she told me how pleased she was to have all her old crew assigned her for a final reunion—Emmy Eckhardt, her hair stylist; Tommy Tuttle, her make-up man; Margie Fletcher, her wardrobe gal. 'It's like old home stuff!'

"She talked about her trip to Ireland the previous year and confided that she and Mr. Chalkley had loved it so much they were thinking of buying one of those inland islands near Galway Bay and building another home there.

"Susan had brought the boys to California with her while she was making the picture; Mr. Chalkley kept commuting back and forth on business. I did meet him on the set one day. He was very friendly, an awfully nice man. I think that was the day I asked Susan what she would do if she and Eaton were ever faced with the situation that was the basis of the plot of her movie. She blurted out, 'In this situation, the girl wouldn't have lasted in my house two seconds.'" The production under Walter Lang's direction went smoothly; the general consensus was that domestic bliss had turned the tiger into a pussy-cat.

Hedda Hopper wasn't buying, however. Hedda confided in her old friend Adele Fletcher that she found "something highly suspicious about Chalkley. Everyone says he's such a nice guy, but that's all you ever hear, such a nice guy. You don't go from a minor F.B.I. man to millionaire in a few years by being a nice guy. And he seems to wear more hats than I own—automobile dealer, rancher, attorney, baseball stadium promoter. Now I hear he's planning to get into movie production with Susan! What in carnation does that guy know about movie making? And just where is all his money suddenly coming from?" It was the first public rumbling that perhaps the famous "ideal marriage" had something less than ideal about it, after all.

As it turned out, Hedda's suspicions that the money was coming from Susan were dead on target. Wally Marrenner confides today, "Susan did tell me that her money went into a lot of her husband's promotion deals. My mother was still alive when she married Chalkley, and she said to me, 'All of a sudden she's investing a lot of her money in Georgia. Building this and that and building a beautiful lake. Why is she doing this?'

"Later, Susan admitted to me that it was most of her money that was going into these estates. Like my mother I often wondered, 'Why would she go back to Carrollton where Chalkley had a family and buy property?' It didn't make sense to me." If Chalkley was the much-bruited "Georgia millionaire," why wasn't his own money going into these projects?

Wally also remembers one afternoon when the Chalkleys came to the race track where he was working as an usher—Hollywood Park—and "Eaton only played at the hundred-dollar window. I asked Susan where she was betting, and she replied, 'On paper.' Then she handed me twenty dollars and said, 'Pick a horse for us, Wal, and if it comes in, I'll split it with you.' That was the extent of her gambling. But Chalkley—he never bet under a hundred dollars and he didn't win all that much."

Timothy Barker also confirms that Chalkley's personal financial situation was far from what it seemed. "If anyone knew what their incomes were . . . the comparison of their incomes over the years . . . they simply wouldn't have believed it."

Nevertheless, Susan held fast to her faith in Eaton. Only once, when she had had a few stiff drinks, did she discuss her husband's financial wheeling and dealing with an outsider and, even then, she maintained the illusion that all was well. "My

husband was a shrewd businessman, a horse trader, as they might say in the South, and he took charge of the finances and advised me wisely and I paid attention."

Not so wisely, as it turned out. Chalkley's grandiose $15-million sports stadium and hotel-complex project never reached fruition, and by then, a substantial amount of money had already gone into the planning. According to Chalkley, "There was an impasse as to whether the city of Atlanta, the state of Georgia, or private monies [Susan's?] would finance it." Susan may have been paying attention, but not to the right signals.

Old friend Louella Parsons hustled in to dispel any notion of difficulties. On August 12, 1960, she noted that with *The Marriage-Go-Round* completed, "Susan Hayward takes off today for Georgia. She says she's eager to get home to see the new mare her colt dropped and . . . has to get the twins, who are now fifteen, ready for Georgia Military Academy. She'll be back in September and has rented a house in Beverly Hills where she and her husband will live while she's making *Back Street*." Of more interest to Louella was the fact that "Susan is wearing a new diamond ring and baguette diamond earrings—not her birthday or anything like it, just that her husband loves her. . . ." By now, one has to wonder who paid for the trinkets.

A month later, after losing fifteen pounds on a strict liquid diet, Susan checked in with producer Ross Hunter for wardrobe fittings on *Back Street*. Hunter, a glamour buff, provided Susan with a $112,000 Jean Louis wardrobe, thirty-nine gowns in all, and magnificent sets by Jacques Mapes but, unfortunately, what he failed to provide was an intelligent script. Hunter's version of *Back Street* marked the third time around for the classic Fannie Hurst tearjerker about a married man and the woman who sacrifices all for him, and for all its opulence, it was distinctly the worst of the three. Both the Irene Dunne–John Boles 1932 original and the Margaret Sullavan–Charles Boyer 1941 remake held more conviction. In addition, the Ross Hunter–Carrollton Production was updated in period, and the locale switched to Paris, and the modernization proved to be ineffective.

Upon its release in 1961, Bosley Crowther of the *New York Times* blasted Susan's portrayal of Rae:

> Behind her make-up and her burlesque stripteaser's dragfoot strut, this little woman of Miss Hayward's is just the figment

of someone's cheap and tacky dreams. The square-jawed gentleman of Mr. Gavin's is right out of the Sears, Roebuck catalogue, the other characters are flabby fictions and the film itself is a moral and emotional fraud.

Fortunately for Susan, the Fannie Hurst story worked its usual magic anyway, and *Back Street* became one of 1961's top grossers, but she could not have been comforted by the reviews. Nor could she have been pleased by the reception accorded *Ada*, an implausibility directed by Danny Mann about a celebrated former whore appointed governor of an unspecified Southern state, which had actually been shot after *Back Street* but was released six weeks before it. Dean Martin, who had co-starred as a guitar-playing politician, had been heard muttering that "the experience was enough to drive a man to drink."

It hadn't helped Susan, either. Because of her work in *Ada* and *Back Street,* the Harvard *Lampoon* voted Susan its annual award of "the worst actress of the year." It was quite a turn-around from 1959.

While Susan had been working in *Ada,* Eaton had commuted regularly between Beverly Hills and Georgia. On their fourth wedding anniversary, he had sent six dozen roses to the set. Susan certainly deserved them. Just a short time earlier, she and her husband had invested in a six-hundred-acre ranch near Heflin, Alabama, a short drive from Carrollton, and called it Chalkmar.

The Chalkleys' publicized spending did not escape the attention of Susan's former Beverly Hills lawyers—Gang, Tyre, Rudin, and Brown. On April 25, 1961, they filed suit for $240,000 for unpaid legal fees against Edythe Chalkley and Carrollton Productions.

The lawsuit did little to enhance Susan's public image, which had already been damaged by a couple of magazine articles that month. A few weeks earlier the slipping but still sensation-seeking *Confidential* magazine had come out with a cover headlined: "My Sister Susan Hayward Has Millions—BUT I'M ON RELIEF," written under Florence Marrenner's by-line by a professional writer.

Confidential paid well for these kinds of "confessions," and from the story's content it was evident that Florence was badly in need of money. She claimed that Susan had allowed her mother's ashes to remain in a cardboard box at the Chapel of the Pines instead of buying an urn and sending it back to New

York, accused Susan of being selfish and a thief as a child and ungrateful to her mother as an adult, and ended by hinting that Susan's suicide attempt had been over Howard Hughes. The story mixed some truths with many more half-truths and enough misinformation to make the piece suspect.

Florence also revealed some facts about herself in *Confidential*. Apparently, she had finally obtained a divorce from Udo Zaenglin (or, as she put it, "Udo got his divorce from me") shortly after Ellen Marrenner's death. Then, only a little while later, she had met a mining engineer named John Dietrich. "He seemed like a fine man and all his friends were nice people. He asked me to marry him . . . so I agreed. I thought how nice it would be to have a home for Larry, and I thought John would make Larry a good father. But things didn't work out that way. He went off and left me right after I became pregnant." It seemed Florence wasn't destined for marital happiness.

That same month, *Modern Screen* also came out with a Susan-Florence story entitled, more modestly, "The Sisters." It too used inaccurate information about Susan mixed with quotes from Florence, but it did provide some interesting sidelights on what had happened to Florence after being abandoned by Dietrich.

> I happened to have an exercycle. I sold it for $175 and came back to Hollywood with my son, Larry. When we arrived I didn't have a dime. And I discovered I was going to have a baby. I was desperate. I took the only job I could . . . working in somebody else's home. When I was in my seventh month, I could no longer do the heavy work. I went to the Bureau of Public Assistance for help. I took charity. . . . It was either that or seeing my boy go hungry. I was given $40 a month for rent money and $8 food check every week. I was able to get a one-room place in downtown Los Angeles, and I could manage with a hot plate. It was terrible, but at least we weren't starving. . . . They took me to the City Hospital to have my baby. They put Larry in Juvenile Hall while I was in the hospital.

This took place in late December 1960. Florence had a daughter, Moira. She concluded the interview by saying:

> She was such a beautiful baby. . . . She had such a beautiful face with a turned-up nose and red hair like Susan

when she was a baby. I don't know if they'll let me keep
my baby. I've got to give my baby a home and provide for
her... otherwise they'll give her out for adoption. I'm at
the end of my rope. When Susan and I used to talk in our
bedroom about what we wanted to be when we grew up,
whoever dreamed that Susan would go so high and I would
end up as I have....

Susan Hayward never made a comment on the stories, but
it is unlikely she forgave or forgot.

She had other things to worry about, as well. Her dear
friend Ira Grossel—Jeff Chandler—had been operated on for
a ruptured spinal disc in May and suffered severe abdominal
bleeding. Susan sent a large arrangement of yellow roses, but
the hospital informed her that only the immediate family would
be allowed to visit. She phoned almost daily for news of his
condition. Another seven-and-a-half-hour operation followed,
during which fifty-five pints of blood were administered, and
then another operation on May 27, when the bleeding started
again. On June 17 Susan learned that Ira, who was just forty-
two, had passed away.

His friends started a petition to investigate, and court permission was granted to Chandler's family for a damage suit
against the hospital where he had died. Although hospital officials denied any negligence, Chandler's pal Clint Walker
insisted, "Nobody is satisfied about the explanations given
about Jeff's death."

Susan certainly wasn't; her lifelong distrust of hospitals was
only intensified.

In July, her own lawsuit over unpaid legal fees was still
pending when the Chalkleys flew to London. The opportunity
to work there and in Ireland may have been the only motivation
for Susan's involvement in *I Thank a Fool,* a murky melodrama. Director Robert Stevens and Susan were at odds from
the start, the on-screen chemistry between her and Peter Finch
was tepid, the Karl Tunberg screenplay turgid, the reviews
dreadful, and the box-office receipts nonexistent.

Susan pretended indifference, but she was hurting inside.
She could have accepted bad notices ("I don't like critics very
much," she said at one point. "I have much more respect for
my own opinions."), but now the critics and public were actually laughing at her. Her own opinion couldn't have been too
high, either. Susan had a strong streak of vanity. ("If we all

weren't vain about certain things, we'd just let ourselves go,"
she said), and it was beginning to rebel against all the knocks
she was receiving.

It was time to take a breather.

She lost herself in the operations at the Chalkmar ranch in
Heflin. She and Eaton remodeled the main farmhouse, making
it airy and comfortable, and designed a new $25,000 air-con-
ditioned barn with special loading doors that protected the feed
from the weather. Eaton modernized a small studio house on
the property for Susan to indulge in her current hobby—mo-
saics. The money continued to flow.

In the spring of 1962, there were 225 head of cattle roaming
the ranch, under the experienced eye of a manager named Guy
Carrington. Susan told friends, "We plan to turn out a hundred
head every hundred days when we get into high gear." Shortly
thereafter she casually spent $30,000 on a whiteface bull with
the official handle of CMR Perfectionrol. His son, a four-
month-old bull calf dubbed Susan's Pride, and a thoroughbred
palomino named Texas Sunset, were Susan's personal pets.

In June, Timothy and Gregory, seventeen, graduated from
Georgia Military Academy and joined the Chalkleys in Heflin.

"It's wonderful for them in Heflin," Susan told *Atlanta
Constitution* reporter William Hammack. "There are horses to
ride, woods to explore, streams and lakes to fish." Gregory,
though, seemed more taken with the life than Tim. The former
told his mother he was seriously considering going to veterinary
college, which pleased her—it was such a suitable thing for
a rancher's son to be doing. Timothy, however, was interested
in movie-making. When he asked his mother for a loan to pay
tuition for a film course at UCLA, she turned him down, telling
him to go out and earn the money himself. The reason was
never made clear.

Life at Chalkmar never particularly suited Tim. While Susan
went on for paragraphs to the press about the number of good
friends the twins had made and how much they enjoyed the
country life, she never allowed the press to talk to the twins
themselves, nor, interestingly enough, did she ever mention
their relationship with Chalkley or with their stepsisters and
stepbrother. Maybe she didn't dare.

Today, Timothy says rather ominously: "Nobody can talk
about those years in Georgia. Even my father doesn't know
about them—because he wasn't there. Other than my brother

and I, there was only one person who was physically there [the Chalkley maid, Curlie Crowder] and that woman won't talk!"

Of Chalkley, Timothy says: "There was a public image, and there was a private image. I *know* what his background was. I'd rather not discuss that now. My stepbrother, Joseph, and I became great friends when I was living in Georgia, and we were in concert about the man.

"To be honest about it, I didn't get along well with Eaton Chalkley. I didn't like him. He was a pontificating... well, he was a jerk!"

Bitterness over some slight? Jealousy of the man who had replaced Jess Barker? (The twins had remained in contact with Barker all through this time and once even hitchhiked north to visit him in Chicago, where, Barker says today, he had become "a disc jockey and TV personality for a while—from 1957 to 1961.") Or was it something more? Only Timothy and Gregory know—and they don't care to tell. One thing is sure, though—there was trouble in paradise.

Susan divided her time between Heflin and Carrollton until the late spring of 1962. Asked if she ever got bored, she told Hammack, "I like to sit quietly in all this solitude and peace and look at the trees and the little creatures." In truth, she was getting restless again.

Unwilling to risk another dud like *Ada* or *I Thank a Fool*, she accepted the Mirisch Films, Ltd., offer to star in *Stolen Hours,* an updated and relocated version (from Long Island to England) of the 1939 Bette Davis classic *Dark Victory,* about a woman slowly dying of a brain tumor. As with *Back Street,* however, the remake failed to live up to the original. Reviewing the film on October 17, 1963, Bosley Crowther, with mixed emotions, said:

> What's wrong, you may ask, with Miss Hayward? Why isn't she able to give as strong a performance as Miss Davis memorably gave?
>
> Well, for one thing, she postures. She strikes dramatic attitudes. She acts like an old opera singer delivering a thundering aria. When she gets the first word from a physician that she may have this trouble in her head, she flashes a rush of resentment that might suffuse a Miss America rudely scorned. And when she finally gets the terrible knowledge that nothing can be done to save her life, she

reels and snarls like a drunkard. Miss Hayward overacts.

But for all that there comes a marked and respectable turning point when the heroine and her new husband—the physician who has tended her, of course—go off to the west of England to spend the last few months of her life.

Suddenly, Miss Hayward is surrounded with sense and sincerity, with humanity and humility.

And so her heroine is able to die simply and decently, and even the most hard-hearted skeptic is able to shed a genuine tear.

Genuine tears, perhaps, but not genuine dollars. *Stolen Hours* did not overwhelm the box office, and the scripts kept getting worse. "I read a script," Susan wrote friend and producer Martin Rackin, "it bores me and I send it back."

So Rackin himself tried. By return mail, he sent a script he hoped Susan would not find boring; trashy perhaps, but not boring. For whatever reason—continued restlessness, Rackin's persuasiveness, the need to earn some income—Susan accepted it . . . but it would prove to be yet another disaster; in fact, according to many, the worst so far.

The prospects for *Where Love Has Gone* didn't *seem* all that bad at first. The film was based on a hot Harold Robbins novel and Joseph E. Levine, who had just released Robbins's *The Carpetbaggers* to rock-bottom reviews and soaring box-office receipts, was prepared to score another financial coup with this new *roman à clef,* allegedly based on the Lana Turner–Cheryl Crane–Johnny Stompanato scandal of five years earlier.

In 1958, Lana Turner's lover, Johnny Stompanato had been found stabbed to death in her home, and Turner's fifteen-year-old daughter Cheryl Crane had been charged with the crime. Crane claimed she had done it because Stompanato had been beating her mother; others thought it was jealousy; still others wondered if maybe Turner hadn't done it herself, and Crane was covering up for her. Whatever the true story, Cheryl Crane was convicted and sent to a girl's correction home. In the Robbins version, the Turner character, Valerie Hayden, was played by Susan; and the daughter, Dani, by Joey Heatherton. His denouement: it *was* Dani who had wielded the knife—but she had been aiming for Val, and the two-timing lover had gotten in the way.

Pretty hot stuff for 1963. Further portents of success, Levine hoped, lay in the hiring of director Edward Dmytryk and scripter John Michael Hayes to repeat their *Carpetbaggers* chores. And to top it off, the studio expected an avalanche of publicity from casting Bette Davis and Susan Hayward in their first picture ever together—with Davis playing Hayward's mother.

That Susan had signed for the film after completing *Stolen Hours,* a remake of Davis's all-time favorite *Dark Victory* was reason enough to start sparks flying between the stars. The fact that Davis, just nine years Susan's senior, would be made up in platinum silver hair and inky eye make-up to look more like her grandmother added fuel to the impending fireworks.

At their first meeting, however—at a gala press luncheon held on December 5, 1963, by Paramount and Joseph E. Levine—the ladies acted extremely warm and cordial to one another. And if, as some members of the press suspected, Davis was outraged when Susan appeared in a simple black suit, making her seem overdressed in a satin brocade cocktail dress, she concealed her feelings—then.

In 1970, though, when film historian Doug McClelland asked Davis about Susan, she replied: "It is with sadness I tell you Miss Hayward was utterly unkind to me on *Where Love Has Gone.* The title was prophetic. There was no one whose performance I admired more *up* to working with Miss Hayward. . . ."

Edward Dmytryk was caught in the middle.

In his book *It's a Hell of a Life but Not a Bad Living,* Dmytryk recalls:

> The first mistake was Susan. She had serious misgivings about playing a promiscuous woman. Yet Marty Rackin felt she was the only actress for the part, and he made a number of character concessions to win her agreement. The concessions improved the moral tone of the script, but diminished its dramatic possibilities. . . .
>
> Most female stars come on pretty strong—it comes with the territory—but Bette was undoubtedly the champ. . . . A diplomat she is not. It began when I had been shooting for some days, rewriting as I went along. Early one morning, I came on the set with a handful of new pages and found Miss Davis in her dressing room, ready for work. . . . I sat down with her and went over the proposed changes, with which she heartily concurred. Then, since Susan was still

being made up, I went back to my office. Bette walked out on the set, where the crew was preparing our first setup, with her usual cheery greeting.

"Hold everything, boys," she said. "We've just made a few changes in the scene."

The "boys" were used to Bette, and didn't miss a beat, but the scuttlebutt factory went to work, and in a few minutes Susan heard that Bette Davis was rewriting her scenes. Unlike her opponent, Susan was an insecure actress, and suspicions immediately flooded her mind. Her agent was soon at the studio, and the three of us were in Rackin's office. We discovered that Susan's contract specified that she was bound only to the script she had originally read, and, good or bad—and even [John] Hayes admitted it lacked quality—that's all she was going to do. And that's all she did.

That's how Dmytryk saw it. When a reporter told Susan she "looked to have died for no special reason at the movie's end," she responded: "I agree with you. It wasn't written that way. Bette Davis was supposed to die until she suddenly insisted that she couldn't suicide in less than two pages of dialogue. So we flipped a coin. I lost, and won the death scene."

Miss Davis saw the dispute in yet another way, explaining that there had been a "dispute about my interpretation. So I said to them: 'If the mother has to be shown as a monster, at least give me one scene being really monstrous to the daughter. So people will really believe it.' Unfortunately, Miss What's-her-name didn't see it that way and she did get top billing. So . . ."

It was a miserable experience for all concerned and no happier for the critics who were forced to sit through it. Bosley Crowther wrote indignantly: "Everything harsh and unflattering ever said about Hollywood films as vulgar entertainment might be said about the one that has been made from Harold Robbins's dexterously salacious and highly popular novel, *Where Love Has Gone*. It is cheap, gaudy, mawkish and artificial—offensive to intelligence and taste."

Newsweek was equally appalled: "One watches . . . in disbelief, wondering how in a movie from a major studio there could be such universal and serene ineptitude. Even the sets are ridiculous. . . . One must credit Hayward at least for slashing a terrible portrait of Bette to shreds."

Susan's career continued to slide. Stricken, she began to retire from the movie community, seeing fewer of her friends, rejecting all the scripts that came her way. Of course, the scripts that came her way these days were easy to reject. As things turned out, however, that winter she had things far more important to think about than bad reviews and bad scripts.

⚘ *chapter 27* ⚘

SUSAN'S FRIENDS in Hollywood and Eaton's associates in Georgia had continued to consider their marriage perfect. "That lucky bastard," Harvey Hestor would say, "that guy can't lose!" In 1964, his luck ran out.

His only son by his first marriage, Joseph, was killed. According to Timothy, "Joe's plane rammed into a mountainside in West Virginia." Timothy, then nineteen, was left devastated by the tragedy.

Outwardly at least, Eaton stoically accepted the loss. "It was God's will," he said. Inwardly he was guilt-ridden for failing to be the friend and father he should have been—he and Joe hadn't really gotten along all that well, and now it was too late to do anything about it. He was determined, however, not to show it.

His years as a file clerk at the FBI had taught Eaton Chalkley everything he had to know about hiding things. His previous wife—or wives, remembering Peggy Irwin's "twice-divorced" slip—was never referred to (and he was supposed to be a devout Catholic). He was able to shroud his business affairs in secrecy; he never revealed the name of the law school he had attended or his wartime activities. No one ever knew—not even the FBI—which town in Virginia he had been born in. He merely presented himself as a wealthy, healthy man.

He was neither.

The first indication that Eaton's health was not up to par had come during 1958, when he had been stricken with a liver infection. Susan had rushed to Georgia from the *Thunder in the Sun* location to be with him, but he had made a swift recovery and refused to harp on the illness, rumored to be hepatitis.

After Joseph's accident in 1964, however, there was a decided change in Eaton's appearance. He lost an alarming amount of weight, his jaundiced face became drawn, his eyes dead. He was in fact almost unrecognizable as the man Susan had married.

Throughout the early part of 1965, Eaton continued to have what his neighbors described as "sick spells." He seemed less interested in the estates in Carrollton and Heflin, preferring to spend his time at their home at 220 Nurmi Drive in Fort Lauderdale. The Chalkleys' three boats, the *Oh Susannah*, the *Old Susannah*, and the *Young Susannah*, were moored behind the property. Only when the two took off for a day's fishing did Eaton seem his old self again.

That spring, Joseph Mankiewicz sent Susan the script of *Anyone for Venice*, a modern comedy based loosely on the classic Ben Jonson play *Volpone*. She thought it funny, liked her part, and agreed to come out of semiretirement to work with him for the first time since the long-forgotten *House of Strangers*. Shooting was due to start in Italy in September. By then, however, she was seriously concerned about Eaton's physical condition. He seemed debilitated, lacking in enthusiasm—yet he insisted they make the trip to Rome. It would provide a much-needed lift, he said.

They checked into the new Hilton Hotel, and Eaton remained by the poolside, baking in the warm Roman sun, while Susan went to the Cinecittà Studio. Soon he came down with a bad cold, then a definite hepatitis attack. Susan's nerves went completely on edge. The strain of nursing Eaton in the early mornings and evenings while working all day at Cinecittà began to show on her face and affect her relationships with other members of the cast, though she did her best to be professional and cooperative.

Susan was working on a dream sequence, later eliminated from the film, when she consented to an interview with an American film-magazine reporter on a busman's holiday in Rome. The two were chatting in her dressing room during the lunch break, when Susan's private phone rang. The reporter recalled:

"Susan's youthful face suddenly aged with worry, and she turned ashen.

"'My God, Eaton. I'll be right there. Don't worry.'

"She banged the phone down and mumbled with controlled

anxiety, 'My husband has been taken seriously ill. I must get to the hotel immediately.'"

With her role in the film partially completed, she persuaded Mankiewicz to shoot around her for a couple of weeks so she could accompany Eaton back to Florida. Chalkley wanted his personal physician, feeling the treatment he had been receiving from the Italian doctors had only aggravated his condition. With Susan's help, he was able to descend the stairs and cross the Fort Lauderdale airfield, where a car was waiting to rush them to Holy Cross Hospital.

At the end of the week, Dr. Leonard Erdman told Susan she could return to Italy and finish the picture, but she had only just made it back there when she received a cable notifying her that Chalkley had become comatose. She was on the next plane back to the States.

Eaton emerged from the coma, but by now he had a premonition that death was imminent. After two weeks at Holy Cross, he asked to be taken home to die.

On January 9, 1966, at 7:55 A.M., Floyd Eaton Chalkley was gone. According to a later report by a friend of hers, Susan ran into the bathroom and let out a chilling series of screams. Finally pulling herself together, she emerged to call the physician and ask: "What do we do now?"

Dr. Erdman signed the official certificate of death. Eaton had died from hepatitis, an illness he had originally contracted in 1955, but which had flared up again in 1963 and stayed with him all this time. A contributing factor was cirrhosis of the liver—Eaton had been a heavy drinker.

Susan, seemingly composed, accompanied the body back to Carrollton the next day for a quiet burial, attended by some of Eaton's friends. The gravestone faced the home they shared.

Immediately afterward, Susan boarded a plane to return to Rome to finish work on *Anyone for Venice,* which was released in 1967 as *The Honey Pot.* The cast and director Joe Mankiewicz offered quiet condolences and watched with admiration as Susan calmly completed her remaining scenes. "I came back because that's what my husband would have wanted me to do," she explained.

And then she collapsed.

Twenty-six months earlier, Jacqueline Kennedy had been eyewitness to her husband's assassination, and the public had expected her to play a black-clad, grieving martyr for the rest

of her life. It wasn't her natural role, however, and, after an interval, she had resumed her social life, confounding their expectations.

After Eaton died, Hollywood too knew what it expected Susan to do. Her history of resiliency was so well known, her ability to overcome setbacks and emerge, smiling, on top again, that it predicted she would go through a decent period of mourning, then bounce back again, stronger than ever. But this time it was Susan's turn to confound. She did not bounce back. She entered a mourning that, to those around her, seemed extraordinary in its depth of feeling, and from which she did not emerge for years. It was almost as if she had set forth on a deliberate course of self-punishment.

Why? Did she see in Eaton's death an echo of the devastating death of her father—an event that she had learned about too late to even see his body—and from which Ellen Marrenner had so speedily recovered? Was she mourning the loss of the fantasy she had yearned for all her life—the gracious, easy marriage to the courtly Southern gentleman? Was she grieving over the sudden end of the one element of stability she thought she had had in a life increasingly filled with professional setbacks?

One thing is certain—she had buried the man in the red earth of Georgia, and there was one part she could yet play. Approaching forty-eight years of age, the perfect Southern wife became the perfect ante-bellum widow. Chalkley's faults had all faded with his death, and only his virtues remained. She mourned.

Only once did she let slip that there had been a flaw in the fantasy.

In an unguarded moment, she admitted to Wally, "If Eaton had lived a couple of years longer, I'd have gone bankrupt."

✖ *PART SIX* ✖

The Widow Chalkley

Fort Lauderdale, Florida
January 9, 1966—January 22, 1971

When you say ten years, it sounds like a long time. When you live it and are truly happy, it's only a moment.

MRS. SUSAN CHALKLEY

After her husband's death, she grieved like a Spanish widow. For years she couldn't look at anything she and Eaton had become involved in.

MARTIN RACKIN

⊗ chapter 28 ⊗

HAVING NO ONE ELSE to turn to, Susan turned to God.

"I look to God for strength," she later told Martin Rackin. "I won't say when or how I found Him, but when I'm under pressure I rely on God."

On his deathbed, Chalkley had expressed concern for Susan's spirit. Many times during their years together she had considered embracing the Catholic faith—the faith her father had taken so lightly, and which, during his last days, her husband had clung to tenaciously. Now that she was alone and floundering, religion became an obsession with her.

Discussing it only with an old friend, Father Daniel J. McGuire, she quietly began taking instructions for conversion. Father McGuire had first met Eaton in 1952, then Susan in 1958, in Rome, where he had been serving as an American secretary at the Jesuit headquarters. They'd stayed in touch over the years, establishing a warm friendship. Eventually, Father McGuire had become the pastor of St. Peter and Paul Roman Catholic Church in East Liberty, a suburb of Pittsburgh, Pennsylvania (he is now associated with Loyola College in Baltimore, Maryland).

He vividly remembers the furor that accompanied Susan Hayward's conversion to Catholicism and says sadly: "God bless her. I baptized her into the Church. Susan and I were good friends. I got calls from Hollywood and all over the place, and I said, 'I have nothing to say.'

"All this is sacred to me. I know at the time of the conversion, I called Susan and I mentioned to her I was getting all these calls. She just said to me, 'Do me one favor. Don't say a word. Please don't say a word.' That's what she said, and that's what I do.

"The girl is dead now, thank God—thank God in the sense that it is all over."

Father McGuire's reticence is understandable. Susan had taken great pains that her conversion not be turned into a Roman circus. On Wednesday, June 29, the day before her forty-ninth birthday, she left Fort Lauderdale incognito for East Liberty, Pennsylvania. She was baptized a Catholic the following morning and received her first Holy Communion at the mass. Contrary to written reports, though, the bishop of Pittsburgh was not present at that Holy Communion—Father McGuire did consent to correct that error, as well as the reports that it had been he who had given her the crucifix that she would keep with her for the rest of her life. The crucifix came from another.

Unfortunately, several persons at the services recognized Susan Hayward. Fans crowded around her, desecrating the beauty of the moment. One anonymous parishioner rushed to a nearby telephone to alert the press. Within a few hours, a bulletin about Susan Hayward's conversion had been teletyped to newspapers throughout the world.

Susan fled back to Fort Lauderdale and remained there in seclusion. She refused all interviews for several months, then, yielding to one persistent reporter, she broke down and discussed her reclusiveness. "There are times in your life when you jump into the stream and swim," she said. "There are other times when you jump out of the stream and watch it go by—until it comes time to jump in again."

Locked tight in her grief, she sold the ranch in Heflin, Alabama, "because a woman can't manage a cattle ranch alone—at least not this woman." She sold the Carrollton home as well.

She lost track of time. One day slipped into the next. With the help of prayer and Scotch, she endured her nights.

On fair afternoons, she'd wander down to the Fort Lauderdale dock and sail off for an afternoon of fishing, now her favorite occupation. Occasionally, she'd take in a movie, horrified at the prices being asked, though of course without admitting that salaries being paid to "bankable" stars were partially responsible.

"My idea of relaxing is just—doing nothing," she'd later say. "Stretching out and looking at the sky. I can do that for hours." And that's what she did. She visited almost no one. She discouraged people from coming to see her. Occasionally,

she saw her sons. Greg was at Auburn University now, and Tim was studying cinematography at the University of Southern California prior to leaving for the army. Wally made it to Florida when he could.

Finally, sixteen months later, she decided to dip her toe into the stream again. Her dear friend, director Mark Robson, (*My Foolish Heart*) persuaded her to return to Twentieth Century-Fox to replace Judy Garland in the film adaptation of Jacqueline Susann's *Valley of the Dolls,* a tale of the rise and fall of three female stars and their drug problems. *Dolls* was already in production, but Garland's own pill problem had become so acute that, even after a week of shooting, Robson had not been able to obtain any usable film footage of Garland's scenes. Producer David Weisbart finally had to let her go before she jeopardized the whole picture. Although sympathetic to Garland's dismissal, Susan accepted Robson's offer:

"I'm doing it for you, Mark. The terms are secondary."

Her agent, however, did arrange a spectacular deal: fifty thousand dollars for two weeks' work, and a special framed billing at the end of the cast list: SUSAN HAYWARD AS HELEN LAWSON. The role consisted of only four scenes, but they were pivotal. She reported to work at her old "home studio" early on Monday, May 15.

Jack Bradford, then the "Rambling Reporter" columnist for a Hollywood trade paper, remembers catching up with Susan as she stepped down from her limousine onto the Twentieth lot to meet with David Weisbart, Mark Robson, and the cast. "'It's great to be here again.' She smiled. 'As long as I know I can go home again.'"

And that's what she intended to do. *Valley of the Dolls* was not meant to be a comeback film, merely a tentative few steps into the world again. While there, she would do what was expected of her; when it was over, she would leave. She would not rule out the possibility of doing another film—"An actress should never say, 'never,'" she told Bradford; "she never knows when she'll get the urge"—but there were no plans for resuming her career in a more permanent way.

Though *Valley of the Dolls* was plagued by discord—each of the stars (Patty Duke, Sharon Tate, and Barbara Parkins) felt *she* should be the star of the film—Susan stayed above it all. Instinctively, she knew what Robson wanted from her and, in the process, her acting put the rest of them to shame. A

prime example is in the movie's climactic scene, the ladies-room brawl between Lawson, an aging singer, loosely based, some said, on Ethel Merman, and the ambitious Neely O'Hara, portrayed by a badly miscast Patty Duke. Duke had won an Oscar as the young Helen Keller in 1962's *The Miracle Worker*, yet it is plain from the screen that she is simply unable to hold her own against Susan Hayward. The tussle ends with Neely pulling off Lawson's red wig, exposing the singer's white hair, then, laughing hysterically, throwing the wig into the toilet. When a sympathetic attendant asks Lawson if she'd like to leave from the back entrance, the latter, covering her disheveled hair with a scarf, replies, "I'll leave the way I came in—through the front door!" It is the film's most memorable moment.

During the shooting, Susan stayed at the Beverly Hills Hotel, where a bellman remembers she had few visitors and did little socializing. The studio picked up the bill. Upon completing her final take, Susan returned to Florida. She would not come back to Hollywood for a year.

Valley of the Dolls was released in December 1967 and received unanimous pans. The loudest came from Bosley Crowther, in the final month of his long career: "As bad as *Valley of the Dolls* is as a book, the movie Mark Robson has made from it is worse. It's an unbelievable, hackneyed and mawkish mish-mash. . . ."

Only Susan escaped his barbs:

"Amid the cheap, shrill and maudlin histrionics of Patty Duke, Sharon Tate as a no-talent show-girl who gives up when she has to have a breast removed and Barbara Parkins as a little lump of New England maple sugar who goes astray in the wilds of Broadway, our old friend Susan Hayward stands out as if she were Katharine Cornell. Her aging musical comedy celebrity is the one remotely plausible character in the film."

Anticipating a box-office blockbuster regardless of the critical opinion, Twentieth arranged for an extravagant world premiere of *Valley of the Dolls* to be held aboard an empty 12,000-ton cruise ship called the *M.V. Princess*, anchored just off the Dodge Island seaport near Miami. Three hundred Dade County notables accepted invitations to "dine on sumptuous buffet, while being treated to a fashion show of $175,000 worth of dresses created for the film," plus the presence of Jacqueline Susann, Patty Duke, Sharon Tate, and Susan Hayward.

Ian Glass, covering the gaudy event for the *Miami News,* observed: "Considering how trying the evening was—with TV cameramen, bright lights, interviews and congratulations—it is remarkable the way the girls got through the whole thing without the aid of . . . a tranquilizer . . . or an amphetamine . . . . Miss Hayward who usually leaves her Fort Lauderdale home to fish . . . would obviously have preferred to be at sea."

Susan would have preferred to be *anywhere* else—after posing for a few photographs with Patty Duke, to show that the ladies harbored no hard feeling for one another in their private lives, she left early. Most of the others stayed to the end, however. After the screening, when a studio executive was cornered by a disgusted viewer who wondered why *Valley of the Dolls* had been given such an expensive launching, he smugly replied: "It just happens to be the biggest thing to hit the screen since *Peyton Place,* that's all. . . ."

Actually, he was wrong; it turned out to be much bigger: the highest-grossing movie Twentieth Century-Fox had produced in its history to that date.

The success of the film, and her own decent reviews, were not enough to draw Susan back to Hollywood, however. She returned to seclusion, and found excuses to turn down all the movie scripts sent her. "I crave anonymity," she insisted and did her best to attain it. Her dip in the stream had been just that—she was not yet ready to jump all the way in. That would come in a most surprising way nearly a year later.

In the interim, Susan made only one public appearance, in the spring of 1968, oddly enough, for the benefit of a man named Jack Frost, a nonprofessional organist who had been giving her private lessons. She had liked Frost so much that she had airmailed one of his demo records to her agent with firm instructions: "Tell Joey Bishop Jack would be wonderful on his show." The late-night host had agreed to the booking, but with one catch: Susan had to introduce him to the audience. Other than an appearance on *Person to Person* in 1958, Susan had avoided talk shows, but she boarded a plane with Frost and his wife, showed up at the ABC studios and introduced her protégé cheerfully, saying: "You know he has to be great if I give up three days of fishing." But she was anxious to get back to Florida.

"I love Fort Lauderdale," she told local writer Bob Freund. "I haven't lived in Hollywood for any length of time for over

ten years. I can never live there again. No, I couldn't . . . I say that with absolute conviction. I always fished on vacation, now it's a daily way of life.

"I just live like an ordinary human being."

In the interim too, Susan underwent an operation. In 1967, her gynecologist detected a small tumor and recommended she undergo a hysterectomy, which she did. Small uterine cancers were removed and her recovery was rapid . . . She tried not to think about it and did not talk about it.

Then, in the summer of 1968, something happened that would throw her back into the stream with a vengeance. She got a call from her friend of nearly twenty-five years, Marty Rackin. An idea had been fermenting in Rackin's head. . . .

He remembered:

"I was one of the owners of Caesar's Palace then, and I phoned her in Florida. I didn't know how she would react, so I tried the old buddy approach. I'd always called her 'Hooligan'—with affection, of course, because of her early days in Brooklyn. I said, 'Hey, Hooligan, how long are you going to stay with the old folks in Sun City? How about coming to Vegas to do *Mame* for me?' I wasn't sure she wouldn't tell me to go jump in the river, but she said she'd think it over."

Mame? A musical? The only time Susan had ever appeared on stage was with Louella Parsons's Flying Stars, thirty years ago, and her sole professional singing experience had been in *I'll Cry Tomorrow*. How could she expect to survive the grueling demands of two performances a night with that background, and after the almost completely reclusive life she had led for over two years? Yet something was itching inside Susan. She'd been away for a long time, and even in her own eyes she had been the grieving widow for too long. It was time to get back to work. And, besides, here was something *new*—what a fabulous way to recapture her audience.

Before signing, Susan told Rackin, "I'm doing this with my eyes wide open. There is a certain part of me that is nutty—I can't resist a challenge. And that's what it's all about, isn't it—how you meet the challenges."

❀ chapter 29 ❀

In early September 1968, outwardly bursting with optimism, inwardly apprehensive, Susan flew to New York for a week of conferences with the producers of *Mame*, during which they decided to present the show almost in its entirety rather than in the usual "tab" version of a Broadway musical popular in Vegas. The production, Susan was assured, would duplicate the high artistic standards of the original. In mid-October, Susan returned to New York, sublet Cyril Ritchard's Central Park West apartment, and went into training.

The company assembled around her included many excellent professionals: John Vivyan, TV's Mr. Lucky, as Beauregard Burnside; a talented off-Broadway actress named Loretta Swit (later famous as Hotlips Houlihan in *M*A*S*H*) as Agnes Gooch; Broadway veteran Betty McGuire as Sally Cato and Susan's understudy. Onna White, a celebrated choreographer, came in to stage the musical numbers and supervise the direction, following the Gene Saks original. Donald Pippin, who had met Susan briefly when she'd worked with his friend Charles Henderson on her songs for *I'll Cry Tomorrow,* and since become one of Broadway's leading musical directors and arrangers, was signed on to supervise the Caesar's Palace version. He'd also served in that capacity for the original Broadway production starring Angela Lansbury.

Pippin was reunited briefly with Susan in September. When she returned in October for rehearsals, he invited her out to dinner, hoping to establish a rapport for the weeks of grueling work that lay ahead of them.

"I've worked with many big lady stars, but Susan was more radiant, more beautiful even than she'd been on screen. Her personality and warmth and charm were infectious—and I'd

been afraid that she might come on like the big movie star, the kind who won't give you the time of day when you're not working with her. Other than that, I can't remember anyone I'd looked forward to having dinner with as much," says Pippin.

During cocktails, he mentioned that he was from Georgia. "Well, I remember her face just lit up when I told her that. . . . She wanted to know how much time I'd spent in the South and eventually she began talking about her husband. I had known she had been widowed recently, but not much more, and I really didn't want to intrude upon her privacy. But I gathered she was finding it very difficult without him. . . . I got the impression, though, that she didn't want to lay her woes on anyone else. She wanted to fill her life with constructive things—getting busy and working. This was part of her reason for doing *Mame*.

"Maybe the timing was right, maybe the environment, possibly my background, but that evening she was completely open. I know only one thing, my heart went out to this woman. I was so taken with her."

After that evening at dinner, Pippin and Susan developed a totally relaxed working relationship.

"We rehearsed in my apartment," he remembers. "I worked with her on the dramatics and taught her the score. She was very nervous about making her theatrical debut. She told me, 'Oh my goodness, I'm so used to working with cameras, I don't know anything about stage values.'

"But she was so eager to learn. She was the most conscientious, hard-working professional . . . so intelligent . . . so at home. . . .

"When we worked on the score, she'd stand and lean over the piano and sing right to me; she had this wonderful, intimate way of working. We'd usually work late mornings—late mornings to me, in theater terms, usually means between noon and 3 P.M.—and there were some later afternoon sessions, because she had costume fittings. But she was always on time, always. One day I came flying back home—I'm kind of a fanatic about being on time myself—and I was about one minute late; she was sitting in the lobby waiting for me. Many of the star ladies don't have that virtue . . . being on time is something they seem to ignore. Susan Hayward was not only punctual, but always ready to work.

"I find I don't usually like to drive a performer too much, and sometimes I would actually have to say, 'Look, Susan, let's just stop a minute and relax—let's not cover too much at one time.'

"But she was a workaholic. If she was having trouble with the modulation of the key, I would just get her to relax a minute. 'Look, let's get off it for a minute, then come back to it.' When we'd come back to it—she'd have it. It just seemed to sink in. So my memories of working with her were really of great, great pleasure."

In order for her to get through two shows a night, Don Pippin felt Susan needed vocal exercises to give her stamina. He suggested she work with Lehmann Byck, who had been Lily Pons's mentor when the soprano was the toast of the Metropolitan Opera.

Maestro Byck too remembers: "Susan Hayward was the most studious student I ever had. That's what I respected so much about her. Though a big star, she never acted like one. I never knew anyone who worked as hard. And if things were correctly done, she was the easiest person in the world to get along with. She wanted people to know their job and not be afraid to execute it. But if they didn't...

"I remember her calling me one Saturday morning. She had hurt her toe and asked me to come up to her apartment for her lesson. I said, 'Susan, I don't like to teach outside my studio, but if this is an exception, I'll do so...'

"We worked alone for about forty-five minutes; then the accompanist joined us and we went over the songs for about another hour. Then I said, 'That's that.' She knew I was en route to the country and kept insisting the maid get me something to eat before I left the apartment. I told her that wasn't necessary, that I was behind schedule and had to get going. She threw her arms around me, kissed me and said, 'Thank you so much, darling, for coming up here. I appreciate it so.'

"Then... and this was the only time I ever saw her act The Star. She turned to the accompanist and in a spine-chilling tone of voice demanded: 'Now *you* get back here by three o'clock sharp.'

"She could be the most adorable person in the world one minute and then turn into a shrew the next. Anyone she respected, she cooperated with a thousand percent. But with an underling, someone who felt intimidated by her name, she

turned tough. I've never seen such a divided personality and it shocked me—completely."

It was at this time that Susan met Larry Ellis, a buoyant Broadway actor and singer who was also a student of Byck's. Her abrupt about-faces neither surprised nor shocked him.

"My lesson was at 11 A.M. after hers. It was arranged that way at my request so I could see her every day. That's how I got to know her.

"When Susan met someone for the first time, she was on her guard. She was polite enough, but she couldn't have cared less if you walked out the window after that. But once she liked you—she was a totally different person.

"You had to be on her level, though; you couldn't baby her. The minute someone seemed overly conscious of the fact that she was Susan Hayward and treated her like Susan Hayward, Movie Star, she played *that* role to the hilt. There's the answer to her personality changes.

"I remember the day we really became friends. She hadn't been absorbing a certain vocal exercise. I had been waiting outside for my session when Mr. Byck asked me to come in: 'Larry, come over here. Do this exercise.' Then, turning to Susan, he instructed, 'Now, Susan, I want you to walk around Larry and put your hand on his back and see how he's doing it.'

"Well, to tell you the truth, I was pretty thrilled, having her hand very low on my back, but I kept vocalizing, and suddenly she said, 'Oh my God, he's singing through his ass!' Mr. Byck laughed, 'Not quite, but you're getting the point. Now you do the exercise.'

"When she did it, I walked around her and put my hand low on her back, too, and she yelled, *'Hey, what are you doing???'*

"'What do you mean, what am I doing?'

"'What did you do to me?'

"'I'm just trying to find out if you're doing it the right way. Isn't that how you found out I was doing it the right way?'

"She became thoughtful for a moment, then smiled. 'Oh, that's right. O.K., go ahead,' she said.

"That's how quickly she was able to change. As I said, though, you had to be on her level, and treat her like someone you liked for herself. Then she was wonderful."

On October 31, Lehmann Byck held a surprise birthday

party for Skip Redwine, a musical director and mutual friend of his and Ellis's. Among the guests were many of his students who were friends of Redwine's. A couple of days earlier, Byck had casually mentioned that he'd be very pleased to have Susan at the party.

"I'll be there," she promised.

"And she was," Maestro Byck says. "It was the first time I had ever seen her dressed up. She was always en route to rehearsals when she studied with me, looking neat and clean, of course, but very casual. The night she came to the party she had on a magnificent dress and was all decked out in her furs and jewelry, and she was breathtakingly beautiful.

"Now at my parties, I don't usually ask my students to sing. But that night, for some unknown reason I just felt like it. I asked Larry Ellis to start things going. In those days all you had to do was say, 'Larry, would you get up and...,' and before you got the word 'sing' out, he'd be up there.... He sang and so did four or five of the other kids.

"Then I turned to Susan. 'Now you get up and sing some numbers from *Mame*.'

"'Oh no, Maestro.'

"Well, she stalled. '*Susan, get up and sing,*' I ordered.

"And she got up there and sang every one of the numbers she had been rehearsing for Las Vegas.

"The next day, when she came for her lesson, she said: 'You know, I simply adore you, because no one would have done that except you.'"

"That's another thing we learned about Susan," observes Larry Ellis. "Her whole basic thing was that she didn't like weak or subservient men. She wanted men to grab her by the hair and tell her what to do. Professionally, anyway.

"Thanksgiving dinner was her own idea. When she learned that we had no specific plans for Thanksgiving Day, she invited the Maestro, Skip, and myself to her house. It was just the four of us. She fixed the dinner herself—the whole works—and it was just like a family affair. She didn't talk about her family, her children or late husband, though. [She didn't talk about Walter Wanger either, although he had died just a few days before.]

"We stayed away from shop talk too. She'd been working so hard on the show during rehearsals she just wanted to forget about it for a few hours. If she was tired, she didn't let on; but

rehearsals can be more grueling than actual performances, and I knew from the rest of the cast that she never let up a moment."

In early December, a charity group announced that Susan would do a benefit performance of *Mame* at the Winter Garden, and engraved tickets were printed with Susan's name on them.* The performance never came off, however. A columnist later noted that Susan had begged off, claiming a bad cold, then added acidly, "It probably settled in her feet." Maestro Byck, however, is not so sure Susan had ever agreed to do the performance in the first place. "I know that woman and she would never have agreed to do a single performance in New York under any circumstances. If she had contemplated it, I would have known."

He continues: "Just before she left for Vegas, I said to her, 'Susan, I know Las Vegas. Let me go out there with you for the first week to get you started.' If I had gone out there with her, I would have insisted to the producers that 'Miss Hayward is going to do certain rehearsals once to get balance and then that's it!' I could have foreseen warning of strain on her voice.

"'Oh, Maestro, I've been in this business a long time. I know how to handle people,' she said.

"Her mind was made up. Fine. I didn't argue with her. Susan had the same lovely quality in her singing as she had in her acting—but frankly four weeks here wasn't enough to prepare her for two performances a night."

In Las Vegas, William S. Weinberger, president of Caesar's Palace, arranged for two previews prior to the gaudy premiere. He recalled: "Six hundred men from nearby Ellis Air Force Base were brought in for the first run-through with an audience at 11 A.M. in the morning. That evening was a $25-a-head social event—strictly local. I watched *both* rehearsals, the only two shows I ever sat through, and Miss Hayward was fantastic. The boys stood and shouted. The evening crowd was one of those 'show me' audiences, and she certainly *showed* 'em. But she was one frightened girl."

Susan Hayward as *Mame* opened in the valley of the dice on December 27, 1968.

C. Robert Jennings flew in from Florida to interview Susan

---

*The invitations read: "You are invited to attend the run-through of Susan Hayward in *Mame*, Sunday, December 15—3 P.M., Winter Garden Theater. Contributions requested for Ben Irving Memorial." It is unclear who Ben Irving was.

and review her performance for *Tropic*, a Sunday magazine supplement. "She lacked stage authority and her timing was terrible . . . but she was a curiously affecting Mame . . . danced passably and handled the vocals with an effective, low-key mezzo soprano. . . . Best of all, she was never boring. This *Mame* moved like Haley's Comet."

Jennings beat the crowd heading backstage to offer congratulations. When he asked if she was nervous, Susan replied, "*Oy gevalt!* You mean it didn't show? I was scared stiff the first fifteen minutes on that stage. . . . My hands may not have been shaking, but [indicating her stomach] I was shaking in here. I figured the worst they could do is fire me. Yet, it's fun. It's not exactly *easy* twice a night, but is anything worthwhile easy? After thirty years, I'm finally in the theater!"

When Onna White came into the dressing room, Susan happily credited her with her accomplishments that night, but Miss White insisted all the glory belonged to Susan: "I was really rooting for her with every nerve in my body. With no tryouts, it's quite amazing. She's a fantastic lady, a lady with a lot of guts, a very calm woman even when things are falling apart. A very *top* lady."

As for the critical reaction, a caustic San Francisco reviewer who had hated the show couldn't stay away from the dressing room—"I've always wanted to meet you," he told Susan—then went home to say patronizingly, "I'm glad it's Vegas and not New York, or even Los Angeles. It's like a charity turnout for Princess Margaret—they even applauded the costumes."

A piece in the January 11 issue of *Cash Box*, however, though hardly a rave, was fairer and more representative of the general critical view:

> Susan Hayward opened a new window, traveled a new highway, and danced to a new rhythm. She made her stage debut in Vegas in the over-forty flapper in the Jerome Lawrence–Robert E. Lee musical *Mame*. Having never sung nor danced, nor appeared on any stage before, there were, accountably, some thorny moments on opening night. Miss Hayward seemed unnerved and awed by the 1,000-seat Circus Maximus. Wooden at first—then overmannered. Thankfully the audience neither minded nor noticed. They applauded her every entrance, each new gown. By the time she had warbled her way into "We Need a Little Xmas,"

she was beginning to capture the audacious, unpredictable, last typhoon spirit of Mame Dennis. It didn't matter to most that she strayed from the melody and occasionally mangled the meter.

It's possible—even probable—that given a week or two to tame butterflies, she'll be charming the husk right off of everyone's corn. To us she's as endearing as ever—as enchanting as when she first lost Robert Young in *They Won't Believe Me*. The production is incidentally an occasion for lighting sparklers, crashing cymbals, and blowing bugles. It's all happening at Caesar's Palace, by the way. An open-end affair that could last into next June.

But it didn't last until June. By February, Susan was in serious trouble. First she was out with the flu, then with a twisted ankle, then her voice started giving out.

Maestro Byck remembers, "She woke me about 3 A.M. New York time. Her voice was barely more than a whisper. 'Maestro, I'm having a little voice trouble. Could you come out here and help me?'

"I replied, 'Let me see what I can do.'

"The next day, I sent her a wire. *'Find out I can leave immediately. My fee will be $2,500 a week, first class round trip transportation.'* I wasn't asking an outrageous amount. She was making ten times that much. I also specified that I wanted to stay at her home so that we could work in total privacy. That was essential. When anybody has trouble like this, you work with them, say, five or ten minutes at a time, then rest fifteen or twenty minutes. You can't work for any long periods of time without stopping.

"I didn't receive a reply. I waited three days and telephoned her.

"She was very friendly, but quite definite: 'Oh, Maestro. Forget about it. I'm better, and I don't think it's necessary for you to come here.'

"So a few weeks later she had a chronic case of laryngitis, and that's when Celeste Holm was called in."

Don Pippin was fully aware of Susan's difficulties. "I had planned to go out for the opening night," he says—prior commitments had prevented him from going on to Vegas with the company—"but at the last minute I couldn't get anyone to cover me on Broadway. I spoke to her the next night, though,

and she admitted, 'Oh God, this is hard. It's so very tiring and I get so dry.'

"That terrible dry air in the desert is the most horrendous thing. So I said: 'Now, Susan, you get a humidifier. Don't you dare go to sleep without one on, and get one for your dressing room too, and be sure to keep it on all the time. If you don't, you'll get "desert throat"—all the good singers do.'

"We spoke almost every other night when she was in Las Vegas. She told me the humidifier was a tremendous help, but she was still having problems. Part of that could have been fatigue and strain, but a great deal was emotional stress. With a singer using a voice, it becomes a treadmill of tension. She becomes worried that the voice is going, and that makes her even more tense.

"There was no way I could have been released from my Broadway commitment, but I wanted to get out there so badly when she told me she was having trouble. I wanted to be with her and take care of her. She brought that out of me. That woman had something . . .

"God, how I wished I could have been with her, maybe I could have prevented it from happening. I have a feeling she was beginning to push too hard, getting overtired and a little frantic. It becomes a squirrel cage.

"I was heartbroken when I heard they were planning to replace her with Celeste Holm. I know she was. I think that having to leave that show was much more important to her than just performing. It was an emotional thing. She was so sad inside because this was the one thing that had given her a feeling of identity. It was so important to her to be able to hold on to something. . . ."

And Susan fought to hold on. In a desperate attempt to squelch the rumors, she protested, "I don't pretend to be a Barbra Streisand, but I think I'm a very good Mame. Nobody is replacing me. I don't cop out. I never have."

On February 17, 1969, however, Susan appeared at a hastily summoned press conference, where it was announced that, on the advise of three doctors, she was leaving the show. The strain on her vocal cords could cause severe damage, they said. Then, breaking down in tears, Susan whispered: "I've never copped out on anything in my life. That's why it is so hard to do this. . . ."

She didn't put the blame on the show or the producers or the desert air or anything.

Except herself.

She had one last gesture to perform, however. Before leaving she held a party for the cast and crew, complete with orchestras and plenty of food and drink. In the middle of it, according to one report, she called over Celeste Holm, with whom some of the cast had worked before, and had apparently found trying, and said, "I want you to know that these are great people you're working with."

Miss Holm's response must have been less than whole-hearted, because Susan's next words were:

"I don't think you heard me right. They're great people and if I ever hear of your abusing them, so help me, I'll come here and kick your ass back to Toledo, Ohio!"

❧ *chapter 30* ❧

DESPITE THAT LAST ACT, however, Susan Hayward had copped out, and she could not forgive the transgression. She had let down her dear Marty, her audiences, and perhaps, most importantly, she had let down herself.

The rubber ball of her father's optimistic saying, worn out by too many years of use and misuse, had failed to bounce back. Reluctantly, she faced up to the truth. The Vegas fiasco had been her own fault—brought on by a combination of avarice and pride.

Maestro Byck remembers: "When Susan refused my offer to go to Vegas, Larry said, 'That's the end of you and Susan.' Well, shortly after she left *Mame*, she sent me a two-page typewritten letter, saying in essence that one of the biggest mistakes she had ever made in her life was not letting me come out there. She wondered why she had been so frugal when she hadn't had to be and I could have been such help. And if I had come out, she was convinced she would still have been in the show. Would I please forgive her and try to love her as she loved me?

"That letter is an indication of what a big person she was—to write and tell me what a mistake she had made. Not many people would do that."

Susan licked her wounds quietly and retreated into herself again. On a sudden impulse, she sold the Nurmi Drive house, and in April bought a lovely ninth-floor, two-bedroom condominium, with balcony, at 333 Sunset Drive in Fort Lauderdale. Interestingly, it was an address very similar to the one she'd had in Carrollton, a fact that intrigued her.

At the same time, she gave away to a neighbor a collection of her films that Eaton had gathered together years ago as a

265

gift. "I never showed them," she said. "They just took up space. You see, things like that, holding onto the past, would just bog me down. Not everyone, perhaps, but me, yes."

The condominium building, named The Four Seasons, included daily maid service in the maintenance charge, and the rooms were large and cheerful, but as with most apartments built in the 1960s and 1970s, they were not totally soundproof.

Susan lived directly above Dr. and Mrs. Russell Carson. Eleanor Carson vividly remembers the two years Susan was her neighbor. "She played her organ often—but it didn't bother us, because she didn't play it at an hour that would disturb us. My husband, who's a physician, is never here. He's always working.

"When she first moved into the building, she remained aloof from the tenants. You never saw her without big dark glasses, or a hood or a kerchief around her head. And she seemed terribly, terribly lonely. With that magnificent worldwide popularity, to be so lonely! Yet I think her loneliness stemmed from the fact that people were always after her for something other than just friendship.

"She was like a little teddy bear in life, not at all like in her movies—but who is, I guess. Just like a little teddy bear, she gave me the feeling of wanting to put my arms around her. And protect her.

"I'd often see her shopping, and we'd exchange hellos. In time, we established a rather neighborly relationship, but we were not close friends. She never discussed her late husband or any personal matters except her boys."

Tim was in the army then, serving with the Green Berets in Greece, Turkey, and Cambodia (but not Vietnam, as has been reported). Greg was finishing up his studies at Auburn University in Alabama, from which he graduated in June of 1969. Susan flew to Alabama to be on hand when he received his degree in veterinary medicine, and the next day returned home.

Eleanor Carson's nephew Ty French, a Manhattan artist and designer, recalls: "I saw Susan Hayward for the first time in our elevator [in Florida]. I recognized her instantly, in spite of the large fedora hat and dark glasses. She was frequently at the pool. There was always a great deal of socializing going on there—The Four Seasons had a fun ambiance—but Susan never joined in. Her neighbors discuss that. She was *always*

by herself. I never saw her with a guest, never. After a while we struck up a casual acquaintance, just small talk. When she asked me to join her, we often sat in silent communication."

Eleanor Carson observes: "She was really not a very friendly person—except on a one-to-one basis. But I think she had a spiritual nature, and she seemed to be searching for this deeper thing within her.... I know that she was very active in the Broward County Heart Association, and there was a young man involved in it who squired her around. He was an escort for her for the affairs she chose to attend...."

The young man was Ron Nelson, a dark-haired, bespectacled bachelor who would become head of the Broward County Heart Association. According to Tim Barker, Nelson began coming to the condominium on Sunset Drive in 1969, and eventually became a regular there.

Wally Marrenner, however, remembers that the relationship didn't take at first. When the two of them first met, sometime after Chalkley's death, "she used to tell me she didn't like him all that much. Then she had this lovely white dog that fell into the canal, and he went down and rescued the dog. From then on, Susan was friends with him." He paused. "I never cared too much for that association...."

Neither, apparently, did Tim Barker. According to Barker today, in his own words, "The man moved himself into my mother's life because he needed something from her. She, in turn, needed something from him. My mother was vulnerable ... what I'm trying to say is that he had his own ax to grind.

"When I met him, I said to my mother, 'What is *this?*'

"'Oh, he's very big in the Heart Association. He takes me out socially.'

"'Are you kidding? All these people you're seeing are from the Midwest. And you have nothing in common with them.' And after I'd met Nelson, I said to her, 'You have even less in common with him.' I used to kid my mother when she'd say, 'Hey, he's making advances at me.'

"I'd say, 'Come on, you know better than to believe *that!*'"

"My mother knew exactly where he was coming from. And she was cautious up to a point.... But I almost threw that man physically out of my house."

Exactly why Tim Barker is so angry at Ron Nelson is something he prefers not to spell out. Whatever Nelson may or may not have wanted from Susan, however, it is obvious what she

wanted from him—companionship. She had made few friends, Tim was in the army, Greg—who was living in Jacksonville then—she saw only sporadically. She was a lonely woman.

On Christmas Day 1969, for instance, Eleanor Carson had a mild surprise: "We had an open house, and a few days earlier I'd timidly invited Susan to come down. I didn't think she would, but all the neighbors were invited, and I felt it would have been rude to exclude her.

"It really surprised me when she came through the door. Naturally I asked her if she would like a drink. And in that deep, throaty voice she said, 'I'll have a Bloody Mary.'

"At our Christmas parties it was a tradition to serve only eggnog . . . but we finally found the ingredients, and she went and sat right down in the middle of the living room floor. There were about twenty people in the apartment at that point. She just sat down on the floor and visited with everyone very casually . . . just in a very offish kind of way . . . not a close way. But she did sit on the floor, and I'll never forget it."

On Christmas Day, Susan had nothing else to turn to but a neighbor's casual invitation.

And it continued. The 1970s started badly for Susan. Early in the year, she broke an arm while trying to pull in a big one fishing in the Bahamas. It had just about healed when, restless and bored, she went on safari in Africa. Her vacation was ruined when she was felled by a mild case of pneumonia. She returned to Fort Lauderdale in April and suffered a broken ankle when her motorbike fell on her leg.

On May 11, 1970, she slipped quietly into Los Angeles to see what was going on. She wanted no part of the horror movies that aging glamour girls were now being misused in, nor was she interested in a guest-star shot in any of the current television series. She had too much pride to lower her sights and too much money to have to be forced to. Susan saw a few friends, then flew back to Florida, more depressed and as lonely as ever.

Eleanor Carson remembers: "Every so often during 1970 Susan was in our apartment with small groups. I never saw her drink a lot, but she seemed depressed to me; she wasn't alive. She was just sort of a recluse."

Although Eleanor Carson was unaware of it, Susan was drinking—heavily. Some time later, Susan would say to interviewer Robert Osborne, when asked if she had tried mari-

juana, "No. Evidently a lot of people do [smoke it], but knowing myself . . . well, I'm afraid I could become addicted because whatever I do, I always do intensely." And now she was beginning to drink intensely, not to the point of alcoholism—she could still *not* take a drink if she wanted to—but the Scotches and Beefeater martinis and Bloody Marys served as potent cures for her chronic attacks of insomnia.

On Friday night, January 21, 1971, they proved all too potent.

Alone and lonely, she had a few drinks and snuggled into an armchair. She was chain-smoking as usual while she read a news-magazine account of the sensational Charles Manson trial. Although she had had no scenes with Sharon Tate in *Valley of the Dolls* and had scarcely said more than a few words to the girl at the premiere, she had taken the brutal killings on August 9, 1969, almost personally. There was no mercy in her heart for Manson or his followers. She had told friends, "If somebody hurt anyone who was close to me or whom I loved and they weren't put to death for it, I'd kill them myself."

She lit a cigarette, unaware that the one she had been smoking had dropped into a crevice of her chair. Then, groggy, she went into the bedroom, put on a pair of blinkers, and fell into a deep sleep.

The next hours are etched into Eleanor Carson's memory: "We were getting up at six-thirty when we heard screams. We ran out on our balcony and saw smoke billowing from Susan's apartment. There she stood at the edge of the balcony screaming 'Fire, fire!'

"You wouldn't believe the smoke that was coming out of that apartment! We thought we had to do something to help that lady, so we pulled the sheets off our beds and began to tie them together into knots—but before we could throw them up to her, the firemen arrived. They had a terrible time getting through her door, because it was double-locked. You know, I'd always had visions that the fire department knocked down the door in situations like this—but they didn't. They just cut the lock out, and went in and rescued her through the smoke. At that point, my husband had gone up there too. I kept talking to her on the balcony to keep her calm, because we had the feeling she was going to jump. It was kind of frightening— she was so frightened. When the firemen opened the door, my

husband brought her down here. She hadn't taken anything with her other than her crucifix and a picture of her first husband."

Did Mrs. Carson mean Susan's second husband Eaton Chalkley?

"No. No. I mean her first husband, the actor."

Reminded of the unpleasant divorce Susan went through twenty-three years before, Eleanor Carson impatiently exclaimed, "I know all about that. It was in all the newspapers, and the fan magazines I read in the beauty parlor were filled with it. I know what Jess Barker looked like. I've seen his movies on TV. The man in the *photograph* Susan rescued was *Jess Barker*. Take my word for it."

Jess Barker. It's an accepted phenomenon that, panicked by unexpected disasters—earthquakes, floods, or fires—people have a tendency to rescue strange possessions. What is remarkable here is not that Susan salvaged Barker's photograph—a secret Jess and their sons never found out, by the way—but *that she kept the photograph at all.*

Plainly, for all the bitterness and the blood and the intervening years, there was still something about Barker that she could not let go. He was the first man with whom she had been intimate, the father of her sons. She had invested an awful lot in the man—both love and hate. Perhaps, after all, she could not bring herself to throw away her memories.

Susan remained with the Carsons for the rest of the day and well into the evening. Meanwhile, a Fort Lauderdale staff writer, Patty Allen, got a tip that The Four Seasons fire had been in Susan Hayward's apartment. She managed to get a brief statement from Susan before the press descended en masse: "I'm fine, but the apartment is a wreck. Nothing valuable was lost, but it's a complete wreck. When I saw flames, the first thing I did was pick up the phone and call the fire department." Susan expressed her gratitude to the department.

Lt. Kenneth Nation of the department returned the compliment. "She went to the balcony, which was real good. She got outside the smoke and heat. She could have suffocated."

"I think," says Eleanor Carson, "that Susan was more in shock than frightened by this time. She told us when she had been awakened by the smell of smoke, she had had her blinders on her eyes and blackout curtains on her window, and she couldn't find her way out of anywhere.

"When my husband brought her downstairs, she was still in her night clothes, covered from head to toe with soot. It took about an hour to remove all that soot Later, she sent my husband upstairs to look in the files for a dividend check for $45,000. Then she remembered her long mink coat and thought maybe that ought to come out too."

Dr. Carson suggested Susan have her lungs examined to be certain there was no smoke damage. Since Susan had her own physician in town, Carson drove her there. "By evening, Susan was very calm, amazingly so."

Eleanor Carson concludes: "People were terribly unkind. They practically knocked down my door after the fire. The phone was ringing right off the hook from fans and press who wanted her phone number or demanded to talk to her. I kept a record of how many calls we received, just for the fun of it.

"One photographer phoned and asked if he could come up to my apartment and take a picture. Susan refused. So he went across the canal and waited in somebody's backyard for I don't know how long. Susan and I went out on my balcony for a bit of fresh air—she was wearing a kerchief over her head—and in some flukey way that man got his picture.

"It was amazing to me. I didn't know that Susan still had that much of a press following. I wasn't aware of her magnificent popularity, I guess. But friends from all over the country and Europe sent me clippings."

That evening, Susan went to Jacksonville to stay with Greg and his new wife Susan.

"I was in Jacksonville a couple of weeks after the fire. Susan wasn't there, but I talked to Gregory about her and he assured me she was fine.

"That was that. I didn't hear anything from her after she left here. Not a word, not even a Christmas card. I guess I felt a bit hurt at the time, but that's how it goes."

Susan had survived trial by fire and then blocked it from her mind. The fire did have one beneficial effect, however. Perceiving the disaster as an omen, she was shaken out of her lethargy.

At fifty-four, she wanted to live again—as an actress.

She had no doubts that she could. The "angel on her shoulder" was still there.

Or so she thought.

❈ *PART SEVEN* ❈

Susan Hayward

Beverly Hills, California
September 1971—March 14, 1975
(2:25 P.M.)

I felt like a pianist who hadn't touched the piano for years. You wonder if you can still play, and you are terrified. Then you hit the first note, and it all comes back to you. The only thing I worried about was whether I had lost the ability to remember lines. Fortunately, my brain is in good shape.

SUSAN HAYWARD

❈ *chapter 31* ❈

WHILE SEEKING the stamina required for a comeback, Susan sold the condominium and spent the next several months idly traveling about. For brief periods, she stayed with her sons. In 1971, Tim, discharged from the army the year before, married a woman named Ilse Schenke and settled down in California, where he went to work for Susan's public relations agent Jay Bernstein. That year, too, Gregory made Susan a grandmother, which proved a somewhat difficult milestone for her. When asked later if she spent much time in Jacksonville with Gregory and her new grandson, she skirted the question with a curt:

"I see my grandson every few months. After all, he's not my son, he's my son's son, and I try not to be a smotherer. Anyway, with telephones and airplanes, we are never far apart. I can get on a plane and within hours get to wherever Greg and his family are."

Finally, Susan leased a house behind the Beverly Hills Hotel, and concentrated on reactivating her career. In early fall, she approached Norman Brokaw, a vice-president of the William Morris Agency.

"Look, I want to go back to work," she said. "And Norman, I still want to play the same rough, tough roles I did before. I want to play Tugboat Annie or somebody like that."

Brokaw recalls, "She had mellowed over the years. She was still very attractive, youthful-looking, and a pro. We didn't anticipate any problems getting her going again—not as Tugboat Annie, of course, but in a strong female role."

Before Brokaw could do anything specific, Marty Rackin called and asked, almost apologetically, if she'd care to do a cameo for him in the male-oriented *The Revengers*, starring

William Holden and Ernest Borgnine. (The role was of an Irish woman Elizabeth Reilly, who nurses Holden back to health after he's been shot in a quarrel.) It was as good an opportunity as any to see if her technique was still there, and for her friend Marty, she was glad to do it. Perhaps too she felt guilty about *Mame*. She even refused to take more than the Screen Actors Guild minimum for the role, $487. She wasn't doing this for the money.

After a short location shoot in Mexico, her part in the film was done (it would be released in the fall of 1972), and she was relieved to find she still knew what to do. Meanwhile, Norman Brokaw had been reading scripts. Susan had turned down dozens of offers to make her TV debut, but now she conceded, "That's where the action is for women my age who aren't about to undress on the screen. I like these *Movies of the Week*, as they call them."

She got her first one through a twist of fate. *Fitzgerald and Pride*, the pilot for a projected series about a liberated woman lawyer (Barbara Stanwyck) and her young law partner (James Stacey), was in production when Stanwyck suddenly had to be rushed to the hospital for a kidney operation. "Ron Roth and Dick Berg were trying to figure out who could step into the role, and I suggested Susan Hayward," says Norman Brokaw. "But a name star like Susan Hayward would have wanted to have been offered the role first—correct? So in mid-November, I flew to Mexico City and met with her, with the script. I said, 'Susan, I'll tell you why I came down here to see you. Barbara Stanwyck took very ill, and she was in production for a TV movie that I think is a fabulous role. I'm sure that if Barbara had a choice of who she would want to replace her, it would be you. And from your standpoint, I felt that if you liked the role, you'd consider doing it.'

"She then ordered Brandy Alexanders for us, and she said, 'Norman, you sit down and relax. I'll start reading the script.' By the time I left the next day, she had agreed to do it . . . and did a helluva job."

Fitzgerald and Pride resumed shooting on December 6. While Susan was before the cameras, Brokaw feverishly worked to keep the momentum going—and was almost immediately successful. Aaron Spelling–Len Goldberg Productions liked the idea of Susan on television, and after negotiations, Brokaw secured a firm contract guaranteeing three

Movies of the Week—each of which would serve as a pilot for a forthcoming series. It would be left to the American Broadcasting Company to decide which.

"If these TV movies are good enough for Helen Hayes, they're good enough for me," she laughed.

Don Taylor, who had played Lillian Roth's first husband in *I'll Cry Tomorrow,* and turned to directing in the midfifties, was behind the cameras on *Fitzgerald and Pride.* He recalls "working well with Susan during the filming, but no long-lost buddies type of thing." What remains foremost in his mind is the fate of its three stars. "Jim Stacey lost an arm and leg in a motorcycle accident, Lee J. Cobb had a heart attack a couple of years ago, and Susan ... well, Fritz Weaver and I seem to be the only survivors."

Susan intended to be a survivor too. Having hired an aggressive press agent, Jay Bernstein, she made herself available for any important interviews he could get. She could no longer make the selection herself. The old guards were all gone now. Hedda Hopper was dead, others were in semiretirement writing books about the golden days, or, as in the case of Louella Parsons, vegetating in nursing homes. Rona Barrett was Number One now. Susan knew Barrett, but the other names and faces drew a blank. It was a totally new ball game with an entirely new team.

But she was in control. In a *TV Guide* interview, she said, "I came back to work because the grief finally was all wrung out of me. . . . I looked around Fort Lauderdale and realized I was a freak in that society. I suddenly had an overwhelming desire to get back to Hollywood, where I could be just another freak among freaks."

When a woman reporter who had checked the files carefully reminded her she had once said she could never live in Hollywood again, she smiled and resorted to her trick of answering a question with a question: "Did I say that?" Then, remembering that new rules applied to the new game, she brought the woman up to date, sending her home with enough copy about her TV movie (and *The Revengers*) to almost assure additional audiences.

Jack Zink, entertainment editor of the *Fort Lauderdale News,* did a telephone interview with her in Hollywood. Sensing a juicy local story, he asked her about her remarks in the *TV Guide* piece.

"There's a lot of 'la-de-da' about life in Florida," she replied, "and while I can take some of it, I couldn't take it forever. The ocean and trips to the Bahamas kept me busy for a few years. But I had to start doing something again. I feel much more at home here in Hollywood. But," she added quickly, "if you print the story, I'd like you to send my love to all my dear friends in Fort Lauderdale."

Due primarily to Susan's presence, *Fitzgerald and Pride*, now more provocatively titled *Heat of Anger*, garnered a 23.2 rating and a respectable 37 percent audience share when it was telecast by CBS on Friday night, March 3, 1972. Kay Gardella's review in the *New York Daily News* summed up the attitude of critics and public alike. "Miss Hayward, still shapely and attractive, gave a very solid performance. It wasn't an easy story to move along and sustain viewer's interest, though, since there wasn't very much to it."

Her next movie—and, as it would turn out, her last—was *Say Goodbye, Maggie Cole,* the first of the three pilots she had contracted to do for Aaron Spelling. Directed by Jud Taylor, co-starring Darren McGavin, it was the story of a research doctor who breaks with her past after her husband dies of a heart attack, and takes a job with a Chicago slum clinic. Various plot turns had to do with a man with a brain tumor and a girl dying of leukemia, and, finally, Maggie's own realization that one can't run away from sorrow and heartbreak. Scheduled for September 1972, the critical reaction pretty much echoed the *Heat of Anger* verdicts: Hayward, yes; movie, no—though it too did decently in the ratings.

Maggie Cole had been filmed at Twentieth Century-Fox. Although Susan was reluctant to discuss the past, she had to admit that she "found it strange seeing all the new tall buildings where the old back lot used to be." The acreage that had once been the Africa of *Snows of Kilimanjaro* and *White Witch Doctor,* where Demetrius had fought the gladiators and David had slain Goliath, was now the mammoth Century City complex. Like Goliath, it was growing a little bigger every day. "But that's progress." She shrugged. "Either you move forward or backward. You can't stand still."

Willing to do anything to advance her reborn career, Susan did more than her share of prerelease publicity. "I love the pace of television," she exclaimed to the *Boston Sunday Herald-Tribune.* "It's a new challenge because it reaches to many

millions of people. I'm excited and thrilled at the prospect of being seen by a whole new generation of young people."

When reminded that this whole new generation had been seeing her old films on television, and that *I Want to Live!* had practically been turned into a cult movie by then, she protested, "But they've chopped it up so badly. No one really gets to see the movie as it was made. I wish they would." Smiling, Susan added, "I still get one third of the profits."

Caught off guard by a more intimate question, she didn't hedge. "Marry again? It's a possibility, but not a probability. I have been a widow for nearly seven years. Of course, I have opportunities, but I think it's unfair to marry anyone unless I can completely love him and be willing to spend the rest of my life with him. So far, the gentlemen who have offered themselves and their fortunes—or misfortunes—to me have not been ones I could love deeply or live with the rest of my life.

"I have lived alone a long time now. I have accepted it; I'm used to it; and I've become more independent than I ever was. If God wants it, the right man will come along again. If not, so be it."

It was at this time, on August 18, 1972, that she agreed to see freelance writer Robert Osborne for yet one more interview on *Maggie Cole*. There was something different about this one, however. Susan was in a more somber mood, her answers more thoughtful, less flip than those she had been giving to others. It was almost as if she knew what would only become apparent much later: that this was the last interview she would ever do in her life.

Osborne remembers:

"It was done at 1301 Belfast, off Sunset Plaza Drive, in the Sunset Strip area, in her living room. Jay Bernstein was there, and I felt there was a great friendship-rapport between them of long standing. On the coffee table was a toy train and tracks, and a copy of *Hedda and Louella*. The house was nice, but cold ['I've no interest in homemaking, as you can see']; her body trim, face good but blotchy (the result of skin cancer Susan refused to admit to); she wore tinted glasses and answered the questions *to the point*, with conviction, and could only be described as being friendly in a cool way. She sat the whole time, gave total focus, and concentrated. At this vantage point, I can only say I have a strong suspicion she had no idea whatsoever of the affection with which the public held her. . . ."

Osborne recalls her sighing: "Everything that's worth telling about me has been said a thousand times. For that reason we decided to do something different. I tossed her a variety of words, asking her to say anything at all on the subject as it came up. My tape recorder was running; naturally I never erased that tape."

These are some of the highlights:

On ambition: "I feel sorry for anyone who doesn't have some drive and ambition. If you don't have it, you're nowhere—and going nowhere. You have to have a purpose in life, a reason for being. Otherwise, why be here?"

On her career: "If I were starting out in this day and age, I don't think I would choose an acting career. The motion picture industry has all changed so tremendously. I think I'd be much more attracted to a career in something like archaeology or geology. Acting, no."

On fans: "I don't think there are as many fans around now as there used to be; maybe for rock musicians, but not for actors, and that's good. People today are more sophisticated; they can accept a performer for what he does and not idolize him. I could never understand youngsters putting actors on a pedestal; it should be men and women who really contribute something to humanity. The man who makes a really fine law or does something in medicine—they're the ones who should have fans. Not actors."

On the star treatment: "I couldn't care less—and I never did care—about the A-Number One treatment. It's nice if you can have it, but it was never important to me. Some performers wouldn't work if their dressing room wasn't as posh as someone else's. Just externals, it means nothing. The only thing that's important is what you put on the film and what it does to your audience. Of course, now that I've said that, the next time I work they'll probably make me dress in a broom closet."

On her technique: "I had to learn to channel my energy very early in my career. In the old days of movie-making, when a director said, 'Action' and he meant for tears or laughter or whatever mood was needed, you had to be ready—or they'd get someone else to do the job. You couldn't take time to get 'in the mood'; you were paid to be in the mood. You have to have your emotions right on tap, to turn it on—snap! Like that. I got my early training with some very good directors—Gregory Ratoff, DeMille, William Wellman—and they weren't about

to sit around and wait for me or anyone to get 'in the mood.' I didn't spend time between scenes joking with the crew or playing poker with the wardrobe women. I saved my energy so that when they said, 'Action,' I was ready. I learned it because it was part of my trade. And by the same token, I learned to turn the emotions off just as quickly."

On her sense of humor: "There's room for improvement. But I can laugh at myself, and that keeps it all straight; as long as you can laugh at your mistakes, you'll be all right."

On loneliness: "I know it well."

"I've been told," says Osborne, "that this was the last interview Susan Hayward did before she got word of her illness, after which she didn't grant any interviews. I remember her reply to my penultimate subject—Utopia. She said:

"The word should be struck from the dictionary. Do you know anybody who's ever found it? Anyone who's even visited or been there? I don't. The politicians all guarantee it, but I don't think there is any such thing; if there were, we'd probably all get very tired of it very fast. Life seems to be a constant battle with a few moments out now and then for relaxation. If there is a Utopia, you probably find it only when you're dead."

Four months later, Susan Hayward would discover that she herself was a dying woman.

❈ chapter 32 ❈

How could she have failed to recognize the symptoms: the headaches, the dizziness, the blisters on her fingers from cigarette burns she didn't feel? She had had them all nine years earlier in the movie *Stolen Hours*. But that had been a *movie*. In real life, things like that simply didn't happen—at least not to you. So she chose to ignore them. She discussed the headaches with no one. She wore gloves to cover the suspicious burns, she refused to see a doctor and continued to talk optimistically about her plans for the future.

In December 1972, she was visiting friends in Georgetown in Washington, D.C., when she suffered a convulsive seizure. She was persuaded to check into Georgetown University Hospital for an extensive physical examination. Several brain specialists examined her and suggested she remain hospitalized for further tests and examinations over a period of time, but she was "feeling fine" and anxious to return to Hollywood. She blamed the headaches on nervous tension, the burns to carelessness.

Tim remembers, "She procrastinated a long time and by the time she found out what it was, it was too late."

She found out—when, early in March, she suffered another seizure at a party in Los Angeles. She left, pleading dizziness, but it was obvious that it was more than dizziness that evening.

Norman Brokaw recalls that he was in the process of negotiations for a series for Susan when he received a confidential call from Dr. Lee Siegel, who had been Susan's and Marilyn Monroe's physician when they were under contract to Twentieth. Both had retained his services after leaving the studio.

"Siegel," says Brokaw, "advised me not to accept any further offers for Susan's services. After giving a brief explanation

of her illness and extracting a promise of secrecy, Lee sadly added, 'She is a dying woman.'"

Mr. Brokaw did not betray the confidence. When he spoke to Susan, he was his usual cheerful self. She, in turn, gave no indication that there was anything out of the ordinary happening in her life. She continued to be optimistic about her career. It was not possible that she was dying.

But a secret of this nature had to come out in time.

Later that month, Hollywood became aware that there was something terribly wrong with Susan Hayward's health.

Her entrance into Cedars of Lebanon Hospital, under the name of Margaret Redding, and a terse "no comment" announcement concerning her condition set off a buzz of wild rumors. The corridor outside her room became crowded with reporters bent on finding out the mystery of her illness, and Susan had to be moved in the middle of the night to the quieter Century City Hospital.

It was Timothy who, under pressure, finally broke the story: Susan was suffering from multiple inoperable brain tumors. The doctors said she had only months to live. Tim added, "When I last saw my mother she was alert—but her condition fluctuates. She is a strong-willed woman, and she willed herself to accept her condition philosophically. However, I think she would like us to believe that the miracle will occur and that she will beat death as she has defeated so many things in her life. She is a fighter. She has a great conquering spirit, and everything that can be done is being done for her. Still her faith gives her the strength to face death without flinching. Don't forget, she's a Catholic. It's in the hands of God."

Susan, however, was determined to give God all the help she could. She would not die. *Would* not.

She was furious at Timothy for giving that interview; and even further upset when Tim was granted legal permission to take over her estate. "I hope people understand that I am doing this in my mother's interest. I hope they realize that her welfare is my concern—not greed or opportunism. It just had to be done," he explained.

And it did have to be done. "About $40,000 in unpaid bills had piled up because my mother was incapable of signing checks," he adds today. "Important bills such as insurance payments, things that couldn't be put off any longer."

Tim tried to explain that the courts had final jurisdiction

over every check he signed, but it failed to pacify Susan. It wasn't the money so much as the *helplessness* she felt.

Susan returned home on the third weekend in June. "Mother looks absolutely marvelous," Tim said. "She's never been more beautiful. Naturally, she has a lot of continued rest and care ahead, but she'll be in familiar and comfortable surroundings and that means a lot to her and to us."

Tim told no one the greatest secret of Susan's confinement. Wally found out about it later: "When they transferred her to Century City Hospital, she was in the psycho ward. She went a little off her rocker. You can't blame her, because she was getting so much medicine and chemotherapy."

At that time, Wally was having his own problems. A bachelor until his mother had died, he'd finally married and settled down, but in 1973, his wife of fourteen years died. Then he was stricken by a heart attack—the first of two—and hospitalized.

Susan came to see him. "That's when I noticed Susan was sick. She had her nurse with her. After I got out of the hospital, we used to go to the Brown Derby for dinner and again we had the nurse with us. Susan had lost the strength in her fingers for cutting meat or lifting up a fork. The nurse—Carmen—had to cut the steak or whatever Susan ordered. Susan didn't talk about being sick. But I could see it was getting worse and worse."

Susan continued extensive chemotherapy treatments under the care of Dr. Siegel's nurse Opal Fauss, who came to the house to administer the injections. She continued to lose weight; she refused to lose hope, however. She was particularly happy when reading the cards and letters that poured in daily, filled with prayers, optimism, and good wishes.

One such letter came from a man with problems of his own. When President Richard Nixon, himself immersed in Watergate, learned about Susan's condition, he personally wrote a letter, very cheerful and upbeat, about how he and Mrs. Nixon were "delighted to learn her condition was so improved that she had been able to leave the hospital and return home to recuperate," reported columnist Dorothy Manners. "He saluted the gallant fight she had put up and expressed the wish she would soon be well enough that he and his family could welcome her to San Clemente. It was a warm and heartfelt letter, and it did wonders for Susan's spirits."

It was about this time that Larry Ellis reentered Susan's life. "I had just made the move to California," says Larry. "I had heard Susan had been ill, and I hesitated for a while before calling her. But Mr. Byck insisted upon it. He was worried about her and wanted me to tell him how she really was. He had given me a letter she had written him *after* the news first came out, and this will give you an idea of her frame of mind. The letter was typed on that script typewriter she had:

June 25, 1973

Dearest Maestro,

It was so lovely to hear from you. As you know, I'm too stubborn to let anything happen to me. We're in there punching and ready to practice our la-la-la's. Outside of that, what else is new? With love and kisses and all good wishes. I hope Larry is hard at summer stock work. Say a prayer for me when you pass St. Patrick's.

Love, love, love—

"And then she wrote in her red pen—*Susan*—and drew in that little face with a smile that was such a fad in 1973."

After receiving Mr. Byck's letter, Larry called Susan and their friendship resumed as if it had never been interrupted, as if she were still well.

Larry Ellis says: "I remember one time when Susan said, 'Let's go to San Diego and make a day and night of it.' I offered to drive, but she protested, 'No, let's go in the big car and we'll have lots of leg room.'

"We were planning to be together from 10 A.M. until maybe two or three o'clock in the morning.... You know, I've read stories that said Susan hoarded her money. One said that she kept $400,000 in a paper bag in her safe-deposit box in Florida and would make trips to the bank to look at it and touch it. Who comes up with these things? That wasn't the Susan Hayward I knew.

"She was aware that I was a struggling actor and while we were sitting in the living room waiting for the chauffeur, she put five $20 bills in my hand. 'Here, take this.'

"'What's this?'

"'Well, that's for the day. If you need more, let me know.'

"I said, 'Wait a minute, Susan, you're not paying for the day.'

"'Then I'm not going. Look, don't act with me. You're not a big star actor; you don't make a lot of money.'

"'That's true, but I have enough to take Susan Hayward out. Don't worry about it. I'll put it on my credit cards.'

"'You're not going to pay interest charges on a hundred credit cards.'

"That was a nice thought, but I said, 'Oh, come on, Susan.'

"'Now, Larry . . .' I could see the Irish flaring up. I kept throwing the money back at her and she kept throwing it back at me, and finally she said, 'If you throw that back at me one more time—go home!'

"Well, would you believe, after all that, we both decided all we wanted for lunch was a hamburger at Hamburger Hamlet!"

Ellis continues: "When we went visiting friends in San Diego and they asked, 'How do you feel?' she'd reply, 'I feel great. How do I look?'

"'You look fabulous.'

"'Well, that's how I feel.'

"'How's the operation healing?'

"'What operation?'

"And all the time I'd be looking at the hole in her head. The only way I'd spotted it in the first place was that I'd been behind her when we'd come out of the house, and the sun had been blazing right at the back of her head . . . She had on a wig, a gorgeous red Susan Hayward wig, and the hair was very thin back there to let the air circulate around the bandages. . . .

"She always wore a wig or a turban; kerchiefs really. I remember how shocked I was when one fell off. She looked the way Bette Davis had in *The Virgin Queen,* except Bette had had a little hair left. Susan was almost completely bald. It was heartbreaking. She had always been so proud of her beautiful hair. . . .

"But whatever misery she was feeling about that loss, she kept to herself. Only once do I remember her asking, 'How do I look, Larry?' It wasn't one of her good days, but I knew she didn't want any bull. 'Well, let's say I've seen you look better.' I think—I know—she appreciated the honesty.

"Whenever I came to the house, I always kissed her on both her cheeks. Once she said, 'Larry—what's with you? Why do you have to kiss me on both sides?' And I said, 'Well, it's double value.' She broke up laughing. She got such a kick out

of the fact that someone would talk to her that way. That was my philosophy. The only way I could let her know I was not pitying her was to be flippant and stay away from gloom and doom.

"Susan would say I was the funniest guy she had ever met. That was an act, but I wouldn't let her know it was an act. Except for one time, I never saw her sad or feeling sorry for herself. There was an anger, of course—the kind of anger that made her fight back so hard, to say, in effect, 'I'm not going to let this happen to me'—but no self-pity."

There was that one time, however:

"We had a date for Sunday brunch. Carmen was off that day, the door had been left slightly ajar, and when I rang the bell she called, 'Come on in.'

"She was standing in the center of the room dressed in a white slack suit, no make-up: she looked absolutely beautiful. The stereo or radio was playing, and she went to turn it off. I would have done it for her, but she insisted upon doing certain things by herself; she hated even being helped into the car.

"She went over to the console, and squatted slightly, her legs in a 'V' position. Then suddenly she froze there.

"'Larry, come here quick and help me. You're going to have to help me.'"

Larry hurried across the room to assist her. She was holding tightly to the set, trying not to fall. He put his arm around her waist and helped her to a chair in front of the fireplace.

"I was shaken. Now I was face to face with her illness. She started to cry. That was the first time she had ever given an indication of how deeply she was affected by it. 'Larry, what am I going to do? What am I going to do?' Then she added—as if it was important to me—'I can't go out to lunch today, I can't make it today.'

"I told her I would carry her to the car and we could go to a drive-in, but she replied, 'No, I can't.'

"I wanted to do something, anything, but she said, 'I think I want to be by myself now. If you would just help me to my bedroom and leave, I'll be fine.' I did as she asked. There were still tears in her eyes when I left."

In October 1973, Susan entered Massachusetts General Hospital for tests. The news was not good. And although she still refused to give in to the inevitable, she thought it wise to have a new will drawn up, and did so on December 6.

Declaring it to be her last will and testament,* and with "the support and welfare of my brother, Walter Marrenner . . . one of my primary considerations," her sons being "gainfully employed," Susan set up two trusts: One was for $200,000 and was for Wally, "the said trustee [United California Bank] to pay the net income therefrom to my said brother, in monthly installments during his lifetime," with provisions for allowing Wally to dip into the principal should he come down with an illness requiring funds in excess of the income. Florence was nowhere mentioned.

The other trust was for the boys, consisting of the rest of her property, to be held for them "until they attain the age of 35," the two of them to share equally in the net income of that trust until they reached that age. With her usual sense of frugality, she added, "While both of my sons are self-supporting and successful, I request them to refrain from extravagance and from any substantial donations from the bequests I have made to each of them. It is my hope that each will save a very substantial part of the principal and use the income conservatively. The bequests to my sons will not be in a trust after they reach the age of 35, as both will be then more able to make their own judgments, but it will be helpful to them throughout their lives to have a reserve in event of need."

It was just such a reserve that Susan had always made sure she kept for herself—particularly when it came to the last person mentioned in her will: "My late husband, Floyd Eaton Chalkley, and I had no children. My former husband, Jess Barker, is not an heir at law and I bequeath him nothing. I request my two sons likewise to give him none of the funds that they receive from me. I do not believe that he has any claim upon me or my estate; we were divorced many years ago."

"I request my two sons likewise to give him none of the funds that they receive from me." Not even a cup of coffee! That was the line that shocked both Gregory and Timothy. Says Tim: "My mother and father had had several rendezvous after she returned to Hollywood. This was an emotional decision on her part. I don't question her action, but as far as I was concerned, she could have taken it [the money] and lit a match to it. And I expressed that to her: 'Hey, don't hang this over my head. Take it out in the street and burn it.' My mother

* The text is quoted in full in Appendix A.

had very strong opinions . . . but I was floored by this."

When it was suggested to Tim that perhaps it had been his mother's way of controlling Jess Barker's destiny from the grave, he murmured quietly: *"That's it."*

It wasn't a cheerful Christmas. A large tumor growing on the left side of her brain had left the right side of her body paralyzed except for her arm. According to her doctor, the tumor would eventually spread to the right side of her brain as well, and leave her totally paralyzed. But still she refused to give in.

Early in 1974, she received an invitation to be a presenter at the forty-sixth annual presentation of the Academy Awards. The Academy was aware of her illness, but since it was customary to invite prior winners, they'd wanted to extend the courtesy anyway. Nobody expected her to accept—but there they were wrong. With her condition again in a state of temporary remission, Susan had every intention of going.

Oh, she hesitated for a while. First, she thought of accepting, then she changed her mind—but finally screwing up her determination, she decided she had to make one final spectacular appearance before her public. She owed herself that much.

Early the following week, she phoned designer Nolan Miller, and asked to see him about creating a gown for her appearance. Mr. Miller remembers: "I told her I'd do some sketches and she could pick the one she thought she'd look the most fabulous in. It was a labor of love.

"After I'd done about six sketches, Susan, accompanied by her nurse Carmen, came down to the shop. I showed her all of them. At first she liked a brown gown, but when I showed her the green, she really went mad for it. The gown was of chiffon completely covered with bottle-green piettes; high in front, with a dolman sleeve. I took her measurements—she couldn't have weighed more than eighty-five pounds by then, and I promised I'd have it completed well before Oscar night on April 2."

As Oscar night approached, however, she began having second thoughts about attending. By now, her brain seizures had become longer and more frequent. "What if I can't go through with it?" she asked Larry.

"Of course you can go through with it," he replied, and Nolan Miller echoed the sentiments when Susan came to him

for a final fitting, even though more problems seemed to be presenting themselves. The dress was dazzling, but she needed more than a dress to complete the illusion.

"What should I do about covering my head?" she asked Miller.

"We're going out and getting you the goddamndest red Susan Hayward wig that anyone has ever seen," he said, and we got the wig and had it set in her old style and it looked fabulous.

"Suddenly it occurred to her that something was missing. 'Oh,' she moaned, 'I have no jewelry. It's all in the vault down south. What are we going to do about that?'

"I said, 'Well, let me see what I can do.' I picked up the phone and called Van Cleef on Wilshire Boulevard. Susan had been a very good customer there. I explained the situation, and Bill Rouser said, 'Bring her over and let her pick out anything she wants to wear.' So I went into the fitting room and said, 'Susan, forget about the dress for a few minutes. We're going over to Van Cleef and pick you up some jewelry.' By the time we got there, Bill had about six trays of necklaces, bracelets, and earrings out, and he said, 'Take whatever you want—and we'll have a messenger pick it up when you no longer need it.' It was fabulous!

"She picked out a diamond necklace and bracelet and ear-rings, then we returned to the shop and got her all together—just as a trial run, to see the way she looked. She was very pleased. Then she decided she would ask Frank Westmore if he'd come to her house and do her make-up before she had to leave for the Music Center telecast the following Monday."

Had she requested it, she could have been excused from attending the dress rehearsals on Sunday morning—but she didn't want to start any rumors about the possibility of her not making the show. Right now, it was the most important thing in her life.

Bob Osborne recalls: "I saw Susan at the rehearsals and she was a dynamo. She was dressed casually in a slacks outfit and wore no make-up, but that was par for the course at Oscar rehearsals, and one of the reasons the Academy kept the photographers away. I noticed she was limping slightly and seemed thinner than when I saw her last, but she was in a very 'up' mood, and to be truthful, I was beginning to wonder if all the

gossip making the rounds had any basis in fact."

That's exactly what she wanted people to think . . . although she would confide in Nolan Miller, "This is the last time the public will ever see me."

The night after the rehearsals, Susan had dinner with Larry Ellis at an Italian restaurant on Santa Monica Boulevard. "It was her favorite place; they all knew her there, and they didn't treat her as if she were an invalid. She hated that kind of treatment.

"She talked about the way the dress rehearsal had gone and about how much she looked forward to the next evening and what a knockout her dress was. It was an early evening, because she wanted to get a good night's sleep. She didn't say it, but I sensed she knew that people were going to study her, to decide on their own if those death-watch stories were true. She really wanted to look gorgeous. I knew she would, though, because that face, even without make-up, was still lovely. And she could still walk on her own if she was on a level floor—if she had to go from a bare floor onto a rug or the reverse, she'd lose her equilibrium, but otherwise she was able to walk around without any noticeable trouble."

On the day of the ceremonies, Susan impulsively decided to add her magnificent sable coat to the gorgeous sequin gown and the jewelry she would be wearing that evening. She told Miller that she had worn the coat just once before, when she was in New York, and wanted to be photographed in it while she had the chance. It wasn't an admission that she was dying, just an acknowledgment that she was retiring from public life. She still wouldn't admit to anyone she was dying. She never mentioned the word—not even to her son Gregory, who came to visit periodically.

Miraculously, the illness, as Ellis said, had done little damage to her face. She was still remarkably pretty, even without make-up—but that wasn't enough, she told Miller: she wanted to look spectacular.

Frank Westmore remembers: "On the afternoon of the Oscar ceremony, Susan Hayward called and told me she was going to be a presenter and wanted only a Westmore to do her make-up." He went, of course. When he saw her, however, he was distressed at her appearance: the rays of the cobalt treatment had destroyed not only her hair, but her eyelashes and eyebrows

as well. "I had to reconstruct her as she had been thirty years before. I worked feverishly for hours.... I was never more proud of my craftsmanship."

Nolan Miller shared that sentiment. He prayed that nothing would go wrong. Nothing did.

Immediately before she walked on stage, Dr. Siegel gave her a massive dose of Dilantin, a drug used to ward off seizures. Moments later, she heard David Niven announce her name— "Miss Susan Hayward"—and, shaking badly, she wavered a bit. Charlton Heston took her by the arm, murmured, "Easy, girl," and together they walked out to the podium to a thunderous ovation—and amazement: she looked so *good*. Surely she couldn't be dying, as everyone had heard. Susan barely remembered what happened next: the reading of the nominees for Best Actress, the announcement of the winner, Glenda Jackson. All she knew was that when she made it backstage again, exhausted, she said to Carmen, "Well, that's the last time I pull that off." Heston himself remembers: "That was the last time I saw her."

Leaving the Music Center afterward, Susan was drained; still she insisted upon going on to a small party, promising to stay "just a few minutes." She collapsed in a seizure later that evening.

As she had so many other times in the past year, though, she recovered. "Susan phoned me the next morning," Nolan Miller says. "She told me about Heston's supportive gesture and mentioned that she had caught a glimpse of me with Missy [Barbara] Stanwyck at the awards. She said she'd spent the rest of the evening trying to find us so she could be introduced to Missy. Isn't that funny how one big star wants to meet another one? However, there's a story behind this. When Susan was filming on *Heat of Anger,* she was very concerned about Missy's health. The minute I'd walk on the set, she'd ask, 'How is she? Have you checked on her today?' She really kept tabs. Then Susan started sending Missy little notes and flowers. Susan called me and asked what Missy's favorite flower was and I said, 'Red or pink roses.' Then she called Flower Fashions and ordered roses. When Harry Finlay, the owner, asked how many she wanted to send—one dozen, two—she said, 'No, I want to send *roses*, that means at least twelve dozen.' The doctors wouldn't allow Missy to keep flowers in her room—

she'd been getting so many—but when she saw Susan's arrangement she insisted on keeping it for awhile to really look at; they had to set up a table in the corner. It looked like a bush, it was so huge. And they hadn't even met. Then Susan got sick.

"Anyway, right after the Academy Awards, I mentioned to Susan that I was taking Missy to the Getty Museum—it hadn't opened yet and a friend of mine had arranged for me to take her on a private tour. As soon as I said it, Susan said she'd love to see it also, so she and Carmen joined us.

"It was so funny. When I introduced Missy and Susan, they were very formal about it. 'Hello, how are you,' in very elegant tones of voice. At the end of the afternoon, when we walked Susan and Carmen back to Susan's limousine, they were both hugging and kissing, with tears and the whole thing.

"Then the earlier situation reversed itself. Missy was calling me to ask, 'Did you speak to Susan? How is she?' She would write Susan little notes. But they never saw each other again. They'd talk about having dinner. A couple of times we'd be getting ready to pick Susan up when Carmen would call and say, 'I think you better not come, she's having a bad day.' "

Isn't it funny how one big movie star wants to meet another one?

Burt Reynolds too had wanted to meet Susan, as much as she had wanted to meet Stanwyck—"She had always been— no, still *is*—one of my favorite movie ladies"—but their careers had always crisscrossed. Reynolds's home, Jupiter, was only a short distance from Susan's Fort Lauderdale home, "but I just couldn't have rung her doorbell and said, 'Hi, I'm Burt Reynolds and I've always wanted to meet you,' could I?"

He could have if he had mentioned that he was a client of Dick Clayton—that same Dick Clayton with whom Susan had done "The Correct Thing" and who had come to the Charles Feldman Agency when Susan was a client there. Clayton had been a close friend of Ned Marin's, and there had been many encounters over the years.

Clayton promised Reynolds, "The next time I see her, I'll mention you want to meet her, and we'll get together for lunch. That was just before Susan was hospitalized." The next time Clayton saw her, Reynolds happened to be with him.

Reynolds remembers: "Dick and I were lunching at Scandia.

I saw her first. I nudged my pal and said, 'Look, Susan Hayward's heading in our direction. O.K., buddy, keep your promise.'

"Dick rose, and when she got a little closer she recognized him and stopped at our table. Dick introduced us, and we said a few words. There was such a tremendous warmth and graciousness about her. I couldn't take my eyes off that lovely face. She had tinted glasses on, a scarf about her head, and she looked like a young girl. I never forgot that face. I'll lay it on you straight, I was thrilled."

"Burt was thrilled, all right," Clayton confirms. "He couldn't get his mind back on business. Burt has a tendency to be shy when he meets somebody he admires; he was like a schoolboy. The conversation was 'fan stuff' on both their parts. Susan, as honest as ever, admitted she hadn't seen any of Burt's films, but added he broke her up on the talk shows, Merv, Carson, whatever. Looking at them together, I thought, 'What an explosive team those two would have made if they had been of the same era. Though she usually steered clear of entanglements with leading men, I have a hunch she'd have gone for him personally.'" Of course, Reynolds is a Southerner too.

"It was just that one brief meeting," Clayton concludes, "but what an impression it left on him—particularly in light of what came afterward. . . ."

Stanwyck and Reynolds were not the only stars to want to meet Susan.

When she was feeling well enough to see visitors again after her Oscar-night collapse, Susan invited Larry Ellis to the house.

"She was so excited," Ellis remembers. "'Oh Larry, Larry,' she said, 'you should have arrived a few minutes earlier. You'll never guess who was here. Katharine Hepburn. She just dropped by unexpectedly. Someone had told her I wasn't feeling well, and she told me that she was concerned about my eating correctly, so she brought a basket of food. Can you imagine that? Oh, I wish you were here so you could have met her!'"

Ironically, for all the years they had worked together in Hollywood, Hepburn and Hayward had met for the first time at the Oscar ceremonies that night. In fact, for all the emotional

impact of Susan's appearance, Hepburn had unintentionally stolen some of her thunder when, earlier in the evening, she had appeared to present an honorary award to Lawrence Weingarten, a dear friend who had produced her films *Without Love*, *Adam's Rib*, and *Pat and Mike* as well as the Hayward starrers, *I'll Cry Tomorrow* and *Ada*.

Though a three-time Oscar winner, Hepburn had never before (and has never since) appeared at the ceremonies, but she had done so this time because, as George Cukor notes, "Kate was one of the few people who knew that Weingarten was dying. It was her way of paying a final tribute to him—but the Academy had to promise that her appearance would be kept secret until she walked on stage."

The same spirit and admiration for courage that had moved her to pay tribute to Lawrence Weingarten now brought her to see Susan. In fact, all Hollywood, once so divided in its emotions toward Susan, was divided no longer. As one, they watched with empathy as she battled death.

Though Susan still refused to accept the fact that death was imminent, by July she did know she needed further treatment. Finally willing to undergo exploratory surgery, she made arrangements to fly east to Emory University in Atlanta. Larry Ellis stopped by for a visit the afternoon before she left. Carmen was packing Susan's things.

"Susan put on an awfully brave front for me," he remembers. "She told me she was returning south to get in some fishing and how much she was looking forward to getting back on the ocean again.

"Carmen was standing directly behind her and as Susan kept talking, Carmen just kept shaking her head, silently telling me that things were far more serious than Susan wanted me to know. I didn't let on that I thought there was anything unusual about the trip. I had read somewhere that Susan had always wanted to bag a black marlin, so I kidded her about that and told her to catch two and I'd stuff one and mount it above my fireplace. That day I may have given the best acting performance of my life."

In Atlanta, the doctor gave her his verdict. Ron Nelson later told Frank Greve of the *Miami Herald* that he had been with Susan when the doctor came in to deliver the report from pathology. According to Nelson, Susan said, "If he's gonna

tell me what I think he's gonna tell me, you better leave."

Greve wrote: "He [Nelson] heard screams of disbelief, then silence, and went back in."

"Do you want to talk about it?" asked Nelson.

"Nothing to talk about, is there? I'm going home to Fort Lauderdale, and I'm going to act as if nothing happened."

Reverend Thomas Brew, a friend of Eaton Chalkley's from Carrollton, visited Susan in Fort Lauderdale, and at her request delivered communion. She made one more trip to Emory for a brain scan. On October 17, Dr. George Tindall informed the press that "Miss Hayward is quite ill." Shortly thereafter Susan went into a coma.

Four days later, she came out of it. A nurse admitted that her survival was nothing short of a miracle. "The woman simply refused to die."

✿ chapter 33 ✿

*Her two-and-a-half-year struggle to keep herself alive was ab-
solutely extraordinary. It's amazing to stay alive that long with
this kind of illness. There is no other case like it in medical
literature.*

DR. LEE SIEGEL, BEVERLY HILLS

BY LATE OCTOBER, Susan was back in Los Angeles. The doctor
at Emory had warned her what to expect: she would lose the
power of speech, then her memory, then her swallowing reflexes. At that point, unless she was fed intravenously, she
would die.

Her will to live was stronger than the medical reality, however. Her mind was as active as ever. She'd been home less
than a week when, going through her papers, she realized she
had made a glaring omission in her last testament. On November 7, she asked her lawyers to draw up a codicil that would
leave no doubt about her intentions to disinherit Florence.
Under no circumstances did she want Florence or Florence's
children to be beneficiary of a single dollar.

With each day, her condition worsened, but she knew if she
gave in she would die. She did not wish to die, nor did she
wish to vegetate. She insisted on keeping in touch with those
close to her, but would allow only a handful of people to visit.
She told Marty Rackin, "If you come up here I'll never speak
to you again." However, she called Larry Ellis and invited him
to lunch. Later, Carmen Perugini called Larry: "I'm going to
have to prepare you for a shock. . . ."

"When Susan left here for Florida," Larry remembers, "she
was still walking, still doing things for herself. When I saw
her again, she was completely paralyzed. She could move

297

nothing but her left arm. She could barely put a cigarette in her mouth. She tried, but Carmen would have to catch it and put it in her mouth for her.

"She was in a wheelchair—a special chair that converted to a type of cot. She was conscious of the fact that she wasn't looking very well. When she mentioned her appearance, I knew she wasn't fishing for phony compliments.

"'Look, Susan, the last time I saw you, you looked better. Who knows, maybe the next time I come to see you you'll look better than you do now.'

"She laughed. 'Oh boy, you sure have a way with words.'

"She didn't look too well that afternoon. Her body had shriveled so. I think her weight was down to about eighty pounds. But even toward the very end she was still gorgeous. From her hairline to under the chin she was still the Susan Hayward who had won the Academy Award. That face never changed. There were no lines on it—just freckles and she never wore make-up. And the eyes—they were never half-closed. She still had those wonderful eyes.

"I used to tease her a lot, and she loved it. She couldn't help feeling everyone was pitying her so, and she hated *that*. When she said something incorrect, I'd just say, 'Oh come on, Susan, don't be so stupid.' She felt I was talking to her as if she had the energy to fight back, which pleased her."

Early in her illness Susan had gone to an astrologist to whom she had given her correct date and hour of birth—she'd been a lifelong believer in astrology. He'd assured her she would be alive in January 1975, and she was. "But," says Larry Ellis, "I knew by then she was going to die. One afternoon Carmen, who was usually very close-mouthed, confided, 'She is two years overdue dead.'"

Heartsick, Larry watched Susan slowly lose inches of ground. "And yet she never stopped fighting, never gave in, never gave up. It was unbelievable. She no longer dressed for the street, but the robes she wore could have been worn to a party—pink satin, pink lace, even the kerchief covering her hair was pink. But by now she had given up the wheelchair. She was totally bedridden."

Susan wasn't afraid to look at what lay ahead. And she no longer rejected the past. "Susan kept personal scrapbooks when she was a kid and a model, and Carmen would read all those things to her," Larry remembers. "Carmen was the only one there now. She was living with Susan morning, noon, and

night. I'd come by; after I said goodnight to Susan, I'd sit down at the kitchen table with Carmen and look through those books with her. Everything was there—Susan's Holy Communion picture, her confirmation picture, things I'd never seen before."

Katharine Hepburn was a frequent visitor to the hilltop house, bringing baskets of food or freshly cut flowers. "She comes here," Susan told Larry Ellis, "and DEMANDS I get well. Not hopes. DEMANDS." Larry remembers what a big kick Susan got out of that.

"She rented a piano," Larry continues, "and Skip Redwine, my accompanist, would play and I'd sing all the songs she particularly liked. Her favorite, oddly enough, was *Happiness Is a Thing Called Joe*. Ethel Waters sang it originally, in *Cabin in the Sky* and it was one of Susan's numbers in *I'll Cry Tomorrow*. She couldn't get enough of it.

"She wanted to see some of her old movies again and hated the way they were edited for television out here. I had a movie projector and told her I was sure I could rent or get hold of some of her films. The one she particularly wanted to see was *Ada*, which made my mouth fall open. *Ada* was the last one I would have chosen. 'Why *Ada*?'

"'Because that's the one I want to see.'

"Actually it was her second choice for the evening. The one she really wanted to see that night was *Rooster Cogburn*, with John Wayne and Katharine Hepburn. It hadn't been scored yet, but she wanted to see it anyway, and somebody had promised to send a print—not Hepburn: if she had told Hepburn to get it, it would have been gotten. Anyway, that movie didn't come, but she arranged for a giant screen, nine feet wide, to be placed in her bedroom, in front of her bed . . . and she watched *Ada*."

Ada was the story of a reformed prostitute who becomes acting governor of a Southern state. It didn't inspire her to talk about the South or her life there, though.

"Come to think of it," says Ellis, "she never talked about Chalkley or Jess Barker either. Just about her sons. She'd affectionately call them 'my angel' and 'my devil.'

"She mentioned that man she knew from Florida—Ron Nelson—but I don't think he got out here until the last week or two of her life. If he was here, I would have met him. I was at the house every day."

As Ellis watched in pain, he became aware that Susan was gradually losing control of her speech. "Yet, when she could

hardly talk, she still tried to sing along with me. . . .

"I was singing the same old songs to her over and over again. Then I fell in love with a new song from *Mack and Mabel*. I told Susan, 'Hey, I learned a new song this week,' and I started to sing "Time Heals Everything." The first line in the song is the title—'Time heals everything'—and as I sang it, I suddenly realized that there she was, sitting there, six inches from me—and the song, which refers to a broken heart, suddenly took on a completely different meaning. I kept on singing in order not to let her know what I was thinking, and when it was over she said, 'Larry, you know what my favorite song is?'

"'Yes, *Happiness Is Just a Thing Called Joe*.'

"'Well, now *this* is my favorite song.'

"I had to sing it three more times for her. From then on, whenever I came over to see her, she said, 'I don't care how many songs you sing, Larry. Unless you sing "Time Heals Everything," I want you to leave.'"

Oddly enough, *Mame*'s Donald Pippin had been musical director of *Mack and Mabel*, and the man about whom the song was sung had been Robert Preston. Bob Preston—one of Paramount's Golden Circle in 1939—back when it had all begun for Susan Hayward. "Time Heals Everything" would be her last "favorite song." The circle was almost completed.

"Time Heals Everything." There was, of course, another meaning to the title. And time was closing in.

By the end of February, a new slate of Oscar nominees had been announced, and plans were being made for a new Oscar-night show. Unaware of the severity of Susan Hayward's condition, and remembering how spectacular her appearance in 1974 had been, the Academy wrote to say it wanted to present a special tribute in her honor: would Susan be able to come? She sent her regrets and requested they forget about the tribute.

By now, Dr. Lee Siegel was becoming alarmed. Susan was having trouble swallowing, and she had to be turned in bed, yet she refused to be hospitalized again. Siegel ordered an intravenous machine sent over.

On March 12, Susan asked Timothy to come to the house. She had spoken to Gregory a few days earlier. Now she had some private things to say to her other twin. At the conclusion of their conversation, Tim remembers, "She said she loved me, then whimpered and collapsed."

Her condition worsened. Her lungs were beginning to fill

with fluids, yet she kept struggling to stay alive with every ounce of strength left in her. Wally remembers seeing his sister for the last time on March 13. He recalls seeing a suction device on her chest and attached to a pump, meant to drain the fluid from her lungs. There had been a one-week accumulation.

"She was conscious at the time," Wally says. He stayed with her as long as he could. After he left, she had another seizure and went into comma. Even in coma, she put up a fight to cling to life. Tim was with his mother constantly during these last dreadful days. It would take years before he would admit:

"My mother was pathetic at the end. She was in a fetal position . . . she had lost her swallowing reflexes, she had pneumonia."

At the end, it wasn't the cancer that caused her death. It was bronchial pneumonia, brought on by her weakened condition.

On Friday, March 14, 1975, Susan Hayward's eye flew open in a sightless stare. At that moment, Timothy knew his mother had gone.

At Dr. Siegel's request, an ambulance was called and Susan's body was transferred to Century City Hospital, where an autopsy was performed before she was sent on to the airport for the trip to Carrollton, Georgia.

No one knows who leaked the news to the press. The phone kept ringing, but Timothy wouldn't answer it. He was a publicity man by profession, but at that moment he deeply resented the invasion of his privacy. Later in the afternoon, he met with the reporters who had gathered outside the door of the house on the hill. He knew most of them, but his announcement was brief:

"My mother died at 2:25 this afternoon. I have nothing more to say."

That evening TV stations throughout the country broke the news of Susan Hayward's death. A great many showed film clips highlighting her career.

The clip usually screened last was from *I Want to Live!*

The majority of the newspapers began their stories: "Oscar-winner Susan Hayward. . . ."

Susan Hayward would have liked that. Edythe Marrenner would have too.

❈ *epilogue* ❈

EDYTHE MARRENNER CHALKLEY had expressed a dying wish to her son Timothy that she be buried with simple dignity. The hoopla that a movie star's funeral attracted had always appalled her.

Tim did his best. He gave the Hollywood press an incorrect day of burial, so reporters would not descend on the small cemetery in Carrollton, and he tried to keep the news from Carrollton too, but he underestimated the fervor of the quiet people of that town. In a replay of the triumphal march they had given Susan and her Oscar sixteen years earlier, people lined the seven miles of highway from the Alton Funeral Home to the cemetery on Sunday, March 16, and watched as her body was driven by. Larry Ellis saw snapshots taken in Carrollton that weekend: "There were signs hanging on the windows of the stores shouting. *Welcome Home Susan*. When I saw those pictures, it almost destroyed me. *Welcome Home Susan*—God, how she would have hated that!"

She would have liked the eulogy, though. "She was a good woman who loved her family, her home, and her country, and I was proud to know her," the Reverend Thomas Brew told the five hundred mourners who had gathered in the tiny Our Lady of Perpetual Help Catholic Church. Three priests and a monsignor said the Requiem Mass.

Then, in a chilly drizzle, Timothy and Gregory helped carry their mother's rose-and-orchid covered coffin to the grave site, and, like her husband, Mrs. Eaton Chalkley was buried in the red clay of Georgia. The grave, located on the east side of the church, faced her home at 320 Sunset Boulevard.

It was exactly thirty-seven years to the day since her father had died.

Larry Ellis remembers how he first heard of Susan's death. He had not seen her for two weeks, and had made a tentative appointment to come to the house on Friday, March 14. On Wednesday, he called Carmen to find out if the date was still on. No one answered. For two days, no one answered. "On Friday, I decided to go up the hill to see if anything was wrong. I had to make a quick stop at a friend's house first. His television set faced the door, and, as he opened it, a still of Susan Hayward flashed on the television set. The sound was off. But I didn't need sound to tell me what had happened. I cried, 'My God, she's dead. She's dead.'

"This was a strong, lovely woman who loved life and was cheated out of many years—but when she was here, she gave it all she had. She was the most basically honest person Hollywood had to offer. Ambitious? *Yes*. Drive? *Yes*. But she was no con artist. If you were in her way, she wouldn't try to hurt you to get ahead; but if someone tried to hurt her, she was like a locomotive—and you'd better get out of her way.

"Susan wasn't scared of anyone. Nothing scared her. Nothing frightened her. Not even dying."

After the funeral, Wally and Timothy went back to California, Gregory to Florida. At sixty-eight, Wally lives in retirement now, playing golf and taking it easy. He had another heart attack a few years ago, but "I'm doing fine now," and has no plans to remarry. "I'm too old—who wants an old man?" He finds no fault in the way Susan set up his monthly payments in her will. "When Susan was getting very sick, she said, 'I took care of you, Wal, I took care of you.'" And she has.

Although he won't reveal her whereabouts, he admits he still sees Florence occasionally, the last time during the Christmas holidays of 1979. Her financial condition is still not good.

Florence Marrenner Dietrich is seventy now; her son Larry, thirty-six; her daughter Moira, twenty. A year after Susan's death, on March 19, 1976, Florence protested the codicil in her sister's will disinheriting her, and filed a claim against the estate for twenty thousand dollars. The court rejected the petition. At the time, she gave her address as 4555 North Figueroa, a seedy area of downtown Los Angeles.

Shortly after Susan's death, Dick Clayton remembers Florence's coming up to his office with Moira and asking if he could get her into pictures. "She was a beautiful kid," says

Clayton. "Reminded me a little of Susan when I did that first modeling job with her. There was nothing I could do at that time and I didn't hear from them again." Soon thereafter, though, Moira was spotted by a Susan Hayward admirer on the location set of Peter Bogdanovich's movie *Nickelodeon*. The young man, startled by her resemblance to Susan, started a conversation with the pretty young red-haired teen-ager. "She told me that Susan Hayward was her aunt and that she wanted to be an actress as soon as she completed Catholic school. Then she wandered away. I wasn't sure whether she was an extra on the film or had just been watching the filming." As of this writing, there is no listing for Moira with the Screen Actors' Guild or the Screen Extras' Guild. Of Florence's other child, Larry, little is known.

According to the records of the County Clerk of Los Angeles, the last person to request the file on Edythe Marrenner Chalkley was named *Dietrich*.

Gregory Barker still makes his home in Jacksonville, Florida, with his wife Susan and their two children, and his veterinary hospital thrives. ("Oh God, is he successful!" exclaims Jess Barker proudly.)

Tim, associated with the Garrett Simes office as a publicist and personal manager, plans to break away on his own soon and concentrate on management of rock musicians. Asked about the Chalkley siblings—unmentioned in Susan's will—he says tersely, "I'm not in contact with any of the relatives except my brother and my father."

Jess Barker had never considered the possibility of being mentioned in Susan's will in any way, "but," says Tim, "he was floored by that paragraph about him. *I* was floored." *"I request my two sons likewise to give him none of the funds that they receive from me."* Barker accepted the edict "philosophically," yet says quietly, "That's why I couldn't get any presents from the boys."

He talks of his sons with great affection. Tim lives a few minutes away, and they have dinner together frequently. Tim and Ilse Barker have been divorced for several years, but Tim often takes his daughter Nadja to see her granddad. Jess goes to Jacksonville to visit Gregory and his two grandsons whenever possible.

The years have not been generous to Jess Barker. After returning to Hollywood in 1961, he worked for a while on television, and made his last film, *The Night Walker*, with

Barbara Stanwyck and Robert Taylor, at Universal in 1968. After that, acting jobs were hard to come by. "I haven't worked in . . ." He'd rather not be reminded. But when he moved in 1977, he didn't bother to notify the Screen Actors' Guild of his change of address. Ironically, what may have contributed to Jess's inactivity in the 1970s was that a great many people thought Jess Barker was dead. In the 1950s, he was often confused with Lex "Tarzan" Barker, Lana Turner's former husband. In Shelly Winters' autobiography, Shelly mentions living next door to Susan and Lex Barker right after they got married. Lex Barker died of a sudden heart attack in 1973. In fact, one of Susan's Los Angeles obituaries noted "she had been divorced from the late Lex Barker."

Jess didn't come forth to correct it. Reporters who knew the difference and asked for interviews after Susan's death were all turned down. "I don't want a hatchet job on Susan." About restoring his own battered ego: "That's not important. All I want is to keep her in the same light she has always been." At age sixty-six, Jess has exorcised past demons. There's no rancor in his voice when he talks about Susan.

The twins claimed their inheritance in March of 1980, shortly after their thirty-fifth birthday. It is their money to do with as they choose. They love their father—they always have—and whether they will follow the terms of their mother's will remains to be seen. It will be a very private decision. They remain terribly loyal to their mother too. They loved her as well: "My mother was super," says Tim. "She taught us decency and honesty and gave us a true sense of morality."

There is one final postscript to the story of Susan Hayward. In June and July of 1979, the death of John Wayne from cancer released an ocean of eulogies and tributes to the star. In August, however, a different story appeared on the wires and in newspapers across the country. A journalist named Peter Brennan had become aware of some macabre facts: John Wayne had died of cancer. As had Susan Hayward. As had Agnes Moorehead in 1974 and Dick Powell in 1963. The one thing all four of them had had in common, besides the cause of their death . . . had been a film called *The Conqueror,* a movie made in the summer of 1954 in Saint George, Utah, a town fanned by radiation from eighty-seven above-ground atomic blasts in the adjacent Nevada desert during that period. One of the largest of those blasts had spawned a wind dubbed "Dirty Harry,"

which had swept across the desert in 1953, dropping radiation everywhere. In addition, according to Lee Van Cleef, the last surviving principal member of the cast, tons of contaminated earth had been shipped back to Hollywood for further shooting, thereby prolonging the actors' exposure.

And it did not end there. Ted de Corsia of *The Conqueror* cast had also died of cancer. Pedro Armendariz, had committed suicide in 1963 after learning that he had contracted lymph gland cancer. An unbilled actress, Barbara Gerson, was suffering from cancer of the skin, and many other members of the cast and crew had been similarly affected.

Featured actress Barbara Gerson suffered from cancer of the skin, and recently admitted she had undergone a mastectomy. In all, 91 of the 220 cast and crew members of "The Conqueror" had contracted cancer, and 40 (in addition to the stars of the film) have died from it.

In February of 1969, a study was released showing that children born in southern Utah in the 1950s died of leukemia at a rate two-and-a-half times greater than that of those born before the test. As a result, some seven hundred residents of Saint George have filed suit against the federal government, claiming exposure to large doses of radiation without warning. The suits could run into the hundreds of millions of dollars if a connection between the tests and the cancer deaths is ever firmly established. With the furor of Three Mile Island and other nuclear "accidents," the government shudders at the publicity a proven "Conqueror" connection could set off.

At first, the Wayne family shrugged off the story as "coincidence." They were reluctant to admit that Patrick was operated on for a breast tumor (benign) when he was thirty and that his brother, Michael Wayne, developed skin cancer at age forty in 1975.

In the fall of 1980, Dr. Robert Pendleton, a former Atomic Energy Commission researcher and now director of radiological health at the University of Utah, said that "this case could qualify as an epidemic. The connection between fallout radiation and cancer in individual cases has been practically impossible to prove conclusively, but in a group this size you'd expect only 30-some cancers to develop. With 91, I think the tie-in to their exposure on the set of "The Conqueror" would hold up even in a court of law."

And what of Susan Hayward's twin sons, Gregory and Timothy?

Tim admits that he had a benign tumor removed from his mouth in 1968. "I still smoke a pack a day," admits Tim. "So who knows just what might have caused it? Smoking doesn't help. But I'll tell you, radiation doesn't help either."

Tim cannot offer proof that his mother's fatal brain tumor was caused by exposure to the radiation, but he is furious at the possibility. "I can tell you this was not a lot of fun. If the government knew there was a possibility of exposure, why didn't it warn us?"

In my final conversation with Tim Barker, I mentioned that he would understand his mother's behavior when she was fifty, when he turns fifty.

"If I get to be fifty," Tim said grimly.

Because Tim had just mentioned the death of his good friend, top model Wilhemena from cancer at age 41, this remark was attributed to his depression about that loss.

Then suddenly one remembered . . . The twins were in Utah with their mother that summer of 1954. Today Tim says, "What do I have to look forward to?" "Will I have to go through what my mother did?"

It is the final irony: it may have taken an atomic explosion to kill Susan . . . the woman who had survived so much throughout her lifetime.

A sign on Susan's resting place, put there probably by some Carrollton townsperson, reads, "Grave of Susan Hayward Chalkley," but the tombstone itself reads simply, "F. Eaton Chalkley, 1909–1966" and "Mrs. F. E. Chalkley, 1917–1975," with the inscription, "I am the resurrection and the life." No other epitaph than that.

Yet Susan herself may have voiced an appropriate one for herself in the course of her final conversation with Robert Osborne:

"When you're dead, you're dead. Nobody is going to remember me when I'm dead. Oh, maybe a few friends will remember me affectionately. Being remembered isn't the most important thing anyhow. It's what you do when you are here that's important."

"It's what you do when you are here that's important."

And it is for exactly that reason—for what she was and what she did—that she *is* remembered.

As a star. As a woman. And as a survivor.

❀ *appendix a* ❀

LAST WILL AND TESTAMENT
OF
EDYTHE MARRENNER CHALKLEY

I, EDYTHE MARRENNER CHALKLEY, declare this to be my Last Will and Testament and I hereby revoke all prior wills and codicils to wills.

FIRST: I am presently a resident of the State of California but I intend to move to the State of Florida within a short time, and I intend to maintain my domicile there.

SECOND: I am not married. My husband, Floyd Eaton Chalkley, is deceased. My sons are Gregory Barker and Timothy Barker. I have a brother, Walter Marrenner.

THIRD: The support and welfare of my brother, Walter Marrenner, is one of my primary considerations. Both of my sons, Gregory Marrenner Barker, a resident of Florida, and Timothy Marrenner Barker, a resident of Los Angeles, are gainfully employed.

FOURTH: I give, devise and bequeath my furs to my friend, Carmen Perugini of Los Angeles.

FIFTH: All my other real and personal property (other than cash, bank accounts and stocks and bonds) I authorize my executor to sell, except such keepsakes my sons may wish to have.

SIXTH: I give, devise and bequeath to United California Bank, as trustee, for the benefit of my brother, Walter Marrenner, the sum of $200,000 and direct the said trustee to pay the net income therefrom to my said brother, in monthly installments during his lifetime. This trust shall be created when a preliminary or final distribution of my estate is made. Until the said trust for his benefit is established and provides a source from which to pay my brother Walter the monthly sum herein provided, the executor shall pay to him monthly $835 for his support. I believe that the annual income from said trust will produce a sufficient income for my brother's support who also has

Social Security benefits for his further support. Should he have an illness requiring funds in excess of his income from the trust, such funds shall be paid from the $200,000 herein provided. The principal of the trust shall not otherwise be invaded. Upon my brother's demise, then the said principal sum of $200,000, together with any unexpended income remaining in said fund at the date of my brother's demise, I give, devise and bequeath to my trustee to be included in the trust referred to in Paragraph EIGHTH hereof if said trust is still in existence; otherwise, I give, devise and bequeath said sum to my two sons equally. Either the trustee or my sons shall make provisions for the reasonable funeral expenses of my brother.

SEVENTH: (a) I have invested in an annuity. Should any further payments therefrom become due and payable after my demise, I give, devise and bequeath such payments to my two sons equally.

(b) My jewelry has substantial value. I bequeath it to my sons to be divided, as equally as possible in value. An appraisal in my possession was made in 1967 and is a sufficient basis for the division of the jewelry.

EIGHTH: All the rest and remainder of my property, I give, devise and bequeath to my trustee above named, in trust for the benefit of my two sons, Gregory Marrenner Barker and Timothy Marrenner Barker, until they attain the age of 35. Until they attain that age, the trustee shall pay to them equally the net income of said trust. When my sons reach the age of 35, the assets of the trust shall be distributed to them equally and they shall receive the remainder of my property not otherwise disposed of herein, in equal shares.

NINTH: My late husband, Floyd Eaton Chalkley, and I had no children. My former husband, Jess Barker, is not an heir at law and I bequeath him nothing. I request my two sons likewise to give him none of the funds that they receive from me. I do not believe that he has any claims upon me or my estate; we were divorced many years ago.

TENTH: While both of my sons are self-supporting and successful, I request them to refrain from extravagance and from any substantial donations from the bequests I have made to each of them. It is my hope that each will save a very substantial part of the principal and use the income conservatively. The bequests to my sons will not be in a trust after they reach the age of 35, as both will be then more able to make their own judgments, but it will be helpful to them throughout their lives to have a reserve in event of need.

ELEVENTH: No interest in the principal or income of any trust created under this Will shall be anticipated, assigned, or encumbered, or subject to any creditor's claim or to legal process, prior to its actual receipt by the beneficiary.

TWELFTH: If either of my sons dies before the final distribution of my estate, and the trust herein created, then the remaining share of any such deceased son I give, devise and bequeath to my remaining

son then living. If both of my sons shall die prior to such distribution, then I give, devise and bequeath the estate which my sons would have received had both or either survived, to the children of each son, one half to go to the children of Timothy and the other one half to the children of Gregory.

THIRTEENTH: If I am a resident of California at the date of my demise, I appoint my sons Gregory Barker and Timothy Barker as joint executors, and they shall serve without bond. If for any reason only one of them shall serve, he shall not be required to file a bond as such executor. If neither son survives or qualifies as an executor, I appoint United California Bank as executor, if I then reside in California. If I am a resident of Florida at the time of my demise, then I hereby appoint the Everglades Bank of Fort Lauderdale, Florida, as my executor.

FOURTEENTH: I desire to be buried at Carrollton, Georgia. I shall leave funeral instructions with my sons or with others, as they need not be set forth in this will.

Executed at Beverly Hills, California, this 6 day of December, 1973.

EDYTHE MARRENNER CHALKLEY

On the date written below, EDYTHE MARRENNER CHALKLEY declared to us, the undersigned, that this instrument, consisting of four (4) pages, including this page on which this attestation clause is concluded, was her Last Will and Testament and requested us to act as witnesses to it. She thereupon signed this will in our presence, all of us being present at the same time. We now, at her request, in her presence and in the presence of each other, subscribe our names as witnesses.

We declare under penalty of perjury that the foregoing is true and correct.

Executed on December 6th, 1973, at Beverly Hills, California.

JOHN E. HOFFMAN
*Residing at Los Angeles
California*

L. MCLAUGHLIN
*Residing at Hermosa Beach
California*

❀ *appendix* ♭ ❀

FILMOGRAPHY

NOTE: *All dates are based on the New York openings. The director's name appears in italics after these dates. Susan made several short subjects. These are indicated by an asterisk before the title.*

* CAMPUS CINDERELLA. Warner Brothers, 1938. *Noel Smith.* Johnnie Davis, Penny Singleton, Anthony Averill, Peggy Moran, Oscar O'Shea, Wright Kramer, Janet Shaw, Rosella Towne, Dorothy Comingore. 13 minutes.

GIRLS ON PROBATION. Warner Brothers, October 27, 1938. *William McGann.* Jane Bryan, Ronald Reagan, Henry O'Neill, Elizabeth Risdon, Esther Dale, Sig Rumann, Sheila Bromley, Joseph Crehan, Anthony Averill, Dorothy Peterson, Emory Parnell, Ed Stanley, Vera Lewis. 63 minutes.

BEAU GESTE. Paramount, August 2, 1939. *William A. Wellman.* Gary Cooper, Ray Milland, Robert Preston, Brian Donlevy, J. Carrol Nash, Broderick Crawford, Albert Dekker, James Stephenson, Donald O'Connor, Harold Huber, Ann Gillis, Heather Thatcher, Billy Cook, David Holt, Martin Spellman, Charles Barton, George P. Huntley, Harry Woods, James Burke, Henry Brandon, George Chandler. 120 minutes.

OUR LEADING CITIZEN. Paramount, August 23, 1939. *Alfred Santell*. Bob Burns, Joseph Allen, Jr., Elizabeth Patterson, Gene Lockhart, Kathleen Lockhart, Charles Bickford, Clarence Kolb, Paul Guilfoyle, Fay Helm, Otto Hoffman. 87 minutes.

$1,000 A TOUCHDOWN. Paramount, October 4, 1939. *James Hogan*. Martha Raye, Joe E. Brown, Eric Blore, John Hartley, Syd Saylor, Don Wilson, Joyce Mathews, Tom Dugan. 71 minutes.

ADAM HAD FOUR SONS. Columbia, March 27, 1941. *Gregory Ratoff*. Ingrid Bergman, Warner Baxter, Richard Denning, Fay Wray, Johnny Downs, Helen Westley, June Lockhart. 80 minutes.

SIS HOPKINS. Republic, April 30, 1941. *Joseph Santley*. Judy Canova, Charles Butterworth, Bob Crosby and Orchestra with the Bobcats, Katherine Alexander, Jerry Colonna, Elvia Allman. 97 minutes.

AMONG THE LIVING. Paramount, December 12, 1941. *Stuart Heisler*. Albert Dekker, Harry Carey, Frances Farmer, Maude Eburne, Jean Phillips, Gordon Jones, Archie Twitchell, Dorothy Sebastian, Harlan Briggs, Ernest Whitman, Frank M. Thomas, Rod Cameron, Catherine Craig, Richard Webb. 68 minutes.

REAP THE WILD WIND. Paramount, March 26, 1942. *Cecil B. DeMille*. Paulette Goddard, Ray Milland, John Wayne, Robert Preston, Raymond Massey, Lynne Overman, Charles Bickford, Louise Beavers, Martha O'Driscoll, Janet Beecher, Elizabeth Risdon, Barbara Britton, Hedda Hopper, Victor Kilian, Walter Hampden, Milburn Stone, Byron Foulger, James Flavin, Julia Faye, Maurice Costello, narrated by Cecil B. DeMille. 124 minutes.

THE FOREST RANGERS. Paramount, October 21, 1942. *George Marshall*. Fred MacMurray, Paulette Goddard, Albert Dekker, Lynne Overman, Eugene Pallette, Regis Toomey, James Brown, Clem Bevans, Rod Cameron, Chester Clute. 87 minutes.

I MARRIED A WITCH. United Artists, November 19, 1942. *Rene Clair*. Fredric March, Veronica Lake, Robert Benchley, Cecil Kellaway, Elizabeth Patterson, Robert Warwick, Mary Field, Eily Malyon, Emma Dunn, Monte Blue, Robert Homans, Reed Hadley. 82 minutes.

* A LETTER FROM BATAAN. Paramount, 1942. *William H. Pine*. Richard Arlen, Janet Beecher, Jimmy Lydon, Joe Sawyer, Keith Richards, Esther Dale, Will Wright. 15 minutes.

STAR SPANGLED RHYTHM. Paramount, December 30, 1942. *George Marshall*. Walter Abel, Eddie (Rochester) Anderson, William Bendix, Karin Booth, Eddie Bracken, Virginia Brissac, Rod Cameron, Macdonald Carey, Jerry Colonna, Bing Crosby, Gary Crosby, Cass Daley, Albert Dekker, Cecil B. DeMille, Dona Drake, Ellen Drew, Tom Dugan, Katherine Dunham, Frank Faylen, Susanna Foster, Eva Gabor, Frances Gifford, Paulette Goddard, William Haade, Sterling Holloway, Bob Hope, Jack Hope, Betty Hutton, Johnnie Johnston, Cecil Kellaway, Alan Ladd, Veronica Lake, Gil Lamb, Dorothy Lamour, Arthur Loft, Richard Loo, Jimmy Lydon, Diana Lynn, Fred MacMurray, Marion Martin, Mary Martin, Ray Milland, Victor Moore, Lynne Overman, Mabel Paige, Barbara Pepper, Dick Powell, Robert Preston, Anne Revere, Marjorie Reynolds, Betty Jane Rhodes, Preston Sturges, Franchot Tone, Arthur Treacher, Ernest Truex, Vera Zorina. 99 minutes.

YOUNG AND WILLING. United Artists, February 5, 1943. *Edward H. Griffith*. William Holden, Eddie Bracken, Barbara Britton, Robert Benchley, Martha O'Driscoll, Mabel Paige, Florence MacMichael, James Brown, Jay Fassett, Paul Hurst, Olin Howland, Billy Bevan, Cheryl Walker. 82 minutes.

HIT PARADE OF 1943. Republic, April 15, 1943. *Albert S. Rogell*. John Carroll, Eve Arden, Gail Patrick, Walter Catlett, Melville Cooper, Mary Treen, Astrid Allwyn, Tim Ryan, Tom Kennedy, Grandon Rhodes, Dorothy Dandridge, Wally Vernon, Count Basie and Orchestra, Ray McKinley and Orchestra. 90 minutes.

JACK LONDON. United Artists, March 2, 1944. *Alfred Santell*. Michael O'Shea, Osa Massen, Virginia Mayo, Harry Davenport, Frank Craven, Ralph Morgan, Louise Beavers, Regis Toomey, Hobard Cavanaugh, Morgan Conway, Jonathan Hale, Olin Howland, Paul Hurst, Pierre Watkin, Richard Loo, Sarah Padden, Leonard Strong, Dick Curtis. 92 minutes.

* SKIRMISH ON THE HOME FRONT. Paramount, for U.S. Government Office of War Information, 1944. Alan Ladd, Betty Hutton, William Bendix. 13 minutes.

THE FIGHTING SEABEES. Republic, March 19, 1944. *Howard Lydecker and Edward Ludwig*. John Wayne, Dennis O'Keefe, William Frawley, Leonid Kinskey, Grant Withers, J. M. Kerrigan, Paul Fix, Addison Richards, Duncan Renaldo, Ben Welden, William Forrest, Jay Norris, Ernest Golm, Adele Mara. 100 minutes.

THE HAIRY APE. United Artists, July 2, 1944. *Alfred Santell*. William Bendix, John Loder, Dorothy Comingore, Roman Bohnen, Alan Napier, Tom Fadden, Raphael Storm. 92 minutes.

AND NOW TOMORROW. Paramount, November 22, 1944. *Irving Pichel*. Alan Ladd, Loretta Young, Barry Sullivan, Beulah Bondi, Cecil Kellaway, Grant Mitchell, Helen Mack, Darryl Hickman, Anthony Caruso, Jonathan Hale. 84 minutes.

DEADLINE AT DAWN. RKO, April 3. 1946. *Harold Clurman*. Bill Williams, Paul Lukas, Joseph Calleia, Osa Massen, Lola Lane, Jerome Cowan, Marvin Miller, Roman Bohnen, Joe Sawyer, Constance Worth, Steven Geray, Joseph Crehan, William Challee, Jason Robards, Sr. 83 minutes.

CANYON PASSAGE. Universal, August 7, 1946. *Jacques Tourneur*. Dana Andrews, Brian Donlevy, Hoagy Carmichael, Patricia Roc, Ward Bond, Rose Hobart, Lloyd Bridges, Andy Devine, Tad and Denny Devine, Stanley Ridges, Fay Holden, Victor Cutler, Dorothy Peterson, Onslow Stevens, Halliwell Hobbes, James Cardwell, Peter Whitney. 90 minutes.

SMASH-UP, THE STORY OF A WOMAN. Universal-International, April 10, 1947, *Stuart Heisler*. Lee Bowman, Eddie Albert, Marsha Hunt, Carl Esmond, Carleton Young, Charles D. Brown, Sharyn Payne, Robert Shayne, Janet Murdoch, Tom Chatterton, George Meeker, Larry Blake, Bess Flowers. 113 minutes.

THEY WON'T BELIEVE ME. RKO, July 16, 1947. *Irving Pichel*. Robert Young, Jane Greer, Rita Johnson, Tom Powers, George Tyne, Don Beddoe, Frank Ferguson, Harry Harvey, Janet Shaw, Anthony Caruso, Milton Parsons. 95 minutes.

THE LOST MOMENT. Universal-International, November 21, 1947. *Martin Gabel*. Robert Cummings, Agnes Moorehead, Joan Lorring, John Archer, Minerva Urecal, Eduardo Ciannelli, Frank Puglia. 89 minutes.

TAP ROOTS. Universal-International, August 25, 1948. *George Marshall*. Van Heflin, Ward Bond, Boris Karloff, Julie London, Whitfield Connor, Richard Long, Arthur Shields, Griff Barnett, Sondra Rogers, Ruby Dandridge. 109 minutes.

THE SAXON CHARM. Universal-International, September 29, 1948. *Claude Binyon*. Robert Montgomery, John Payne, Audrey Totter, Henry (Harry) Morgan, Harry Von Zell, Heather Angel, Cara Williams, Chill Wills, John Baragrey, Addison Richards. 88 minutes.

TULSA. Eagle-Lion, May 26. 1949. *Stuart Heisler*. Robert Preston, Pedro Armendariz, Chill Wills, Lloyd Gough, Paul E. Burns, Ed Begley, Lola Albright, Harry Shannon, Jimmy Conlin, Roland Jack, Pierre Watkin, Dick Wessel, Tom Dugan, John Dehner, Charles D. Brown, Selmer Jackson. 88 minutes.

HOUSE OF STRANGERS. Twentieth Century-Fox, July 1, 1949. *Joseph L. Mankiewicz*. Edward G. Robinson, Richard Conte, Luther Adler, Efrem Zimbalist, Jr., Esther Minciotti, Debra Paget, Hope Emerson, Paul Valentine, Diana Douglas. 101 minutes.

MY FOOLISH HEART. Goldwyn-RKO, January 19, 1950. *Mark Robson*. Dana Andrews, Kent Smith, Robert Keith, Jessie Royce Landis, Lois Wheeler, Gigi Perreau, Karin Booth, Martha Mears, Edna Holland, Philip Pine, Barbara Woodell. 98 minutes.

RAWHIDE. Twentieth Century-Fox, March 25, 1951. *Henry Hathaway*. Tyrone Power, Hugh Marlowe, Dean Jagger, Jack Elam, Edgar Buchanan, George Tobias, Jeff Corey, James Millican, Louis Jean Heydt, Ken Tobey. 86 minutes.

I CAN GET IT FOR YOU WHOLESALE. Twentieth Century-Fox, April 4, 1951. *Michael Gordon*. Dan Dailey, George Sanders, Sam Jaffe, Vicki Cummings, Barbara Whiting, Randy Stuart, Mary Phillips, Marvin Kaplan, Harry Von Zell, Richard Lane, Steven Geray, Charles Lane, Marion Marshall, Marjorie Hoshelle. 91 minutes.

I'D CLIMB THE HIGEST MOUNTAIN. Twentieth Century-Fox, May 10, 1951. *Henry King*. William Lundigan, Rory Calhoun, Barbara Bates, Alexander Knox, Lynn Bari, Gene Lockhart, Ruth Donnelly, Jean Inness, Kathleen Lockhart. 88 minutes.

DAVID AND BATHSHEBA. Twentieth Century-Fox, August 14, 1951. *Henry King*. Gregory Peck, Raymond Massey, Jayne Meadows, Kieron Moore, James Robertson Justice, John Sutton, Francis X. Bushman, Paula Morgan, Teddy Infuhr, Gwyneth (Gwen) Verdon. 153 minutes.

WITH A SONG IN MY HEART. Twentieth Century-Fox, April 5, 1952. *Walter Lang*. David Wayne, Rory Calhoun, Thelma Ritter, Robert Wagner, Helen Wescott, Una Merkel, Lyle Talbot, Max Showalter, Robert Easton, Leif Erickson, Richard Allan, Carlos Molina, Nestor Paiva; the singing voice of Jane Froman. 117 minutes.

THE SNOWS OF KILIMANJARO. Twentieth Century-Fox, September 18, 1952. *Henry King*. Gregory Peck, Ava Gardner, Hildegarde Neff, Leo G. Carroll, Torin Thatcher, Ava Norring, Helene Stanley, Marcel Dalio, Richard Allan, Lisa Ferraday, Ivan Lebedeff. 114 minutes.

THE LUSTY MEN. RKO, October 24, 1952. *Nicholas Ray*. Robert Mitchum, Arthur Kennedy, Arthur Hunnicutt, Frank Faylen, Walter Coy, Carol Nugent, Lorna Thayer, Maria Hart, Karen King, Eleanor Todd, Jimmy Dodd, Burt Mustin, Sam Flint, Riley Hill, Robert Bray, Sheb Wooley. 112 minutes.

THE PRESIDENT'S LADY. Twentieth Century-Fox, May 21, 1953. *Henry Levin*. Charlton Heston, Fay Bainter, John McIntire, Margaret Wycherly, Carl Betz, Whitfield Connor, Trudy Marshall, Gladys Hurlbut, Nina Varela, Charles Dingle, James Best, Willis Bouchey, Jim Davis. 96 minutes.

WHITE WITCH DOCTOR. Twentieth Century-Fox, July 1, 1953. *Henry Hathaway*. Robert Mitchum, Walter Slezak, Mashood Ajala, Joseph C. Narcisse, Michael Ansara, Timothy Carey. 95 minutes.

DEMETRIUS AND THE GLADIATORS. Twentieth Century-Fox, June 18, 1954. *Delmer Daves*. Victor Mature, Michael Rennie, Debra Paget, Anne Bancroft, Jay Robinson, Richard Egan, Ernest Borgnine, Barry Jones, William Marshall, Charles Evans, Jeff York, Carmen de Lavallade, Selmer Jackson, Dayton Lummis, Woody Strode, Paul Richards. 101 minutes.

GARDEN OF EVIL. Twentieth Century-Fox, July 9, 1954. *Henry Hathaway*. Gary Cooper, Richard Widmark, Hugh Marlowe, Cameron Mitchell, Rita Moreno. 100 minutes.

UNTAMED. Twentieth Century-Fox, March 11, 1955. *Henry King*. Tyrone Power, Richard Egan, Agnes Moorehead, Rita Moreno, John Justin, Hope Emerson, Brad Dexter, Henry O'Neill, Kevin and Brian Corcoran, Philip Van Zandt. 111 minutes.

SOLDIER OF FORTUNE. Twentieth Century-Fox, May 27, 1955. *Edward Dmytryk*. Clark Gable, Gene Barry, Michael Rennie, Anna Sten, Tom Tully, Jack Kruschen, Alex D'Arcy, Russell Collins, Richard Loo. 96 minutes.

I'LL CRY TOMORROW. MGM, January 12, 1956. *Daniel Mann*. Jo Van Fleet, Richard Conte, Eddie Albert, Don Taylor, Margo, Virginia Gregg, Don Barry, Carole Ann Campbell, Ruth Storey (Conte), Peter Leeds, David Kasday, Veda Ann Borg, Tol Avery, Nora Marlowe. 117 minutes.

THE CONQUEROR. RKO, March 30, 1956. *Dick Powell*. John Wayne, Agnes Moorehead, Pedro Armendariz, Thomas Gomez, John Hoyt, William Conrad, Ted de Corsia, Richard Loo, Lee Van Cleef, Peter Mamakos, Leslie Bradley, Sylvia Lewis, Jarma Lewis, Fred Graham, George E. Stone, Jeanne Gerson, Leo Gordon. 111 minutes.

TOP SECRET AFFAIR. Warner Brothers, January 30, 1957. *H. C. Potter*. Kirk Douglas, Paul Stewart, Jim Backus, Roland Winters, John Cromwell, Charles Lane. 100 minutes.

I WANT TO LIVE! United Artists, November 18, 1958. *Robert Wise*. Simon Oakland, Virginia Vincent, Theodore Bikel, Alice Backes, Wesley Lau, Dabbs Greer, Philip Coolidge, Gage Clark, Russell Thorson, James Philbrook, Lou Krugman, Joe DeSantis, Raymond Bailey, Marion Marshall, Peter Breck, Brett Halsey, Jack Weston. 120 minutes.

THUNDER IN THE SUN. Paramount, April 8, 1959. *Russell Rouse*. Jeff Chandler, Jacques Bergerac, Blanche Yurka, Carl Esmond, Fortunio Bonanova, Bertrand Castelli, Felix Locher, Veda Ann Borg, Pedro De Cordoba, Jr. 81 minutes.

WOMAN OBSESSED. Twentieth Century-Fox, May 27, 1959. *Henry Hathaway*. Stephen Boyd, Theodore Bikel, Dennis Holmes, Barbara Nichols, Florence MacMichael, Ken Scott, James Philbrook, Arthur Franz. 103 minutes.

THE MARRIAGE-GO-ROUND. Twentieth Century-Fox, January 6, 1961. *Walter Lang*. James Mason, Julie Newmar, Robert Paige, June Clayworth, Joe Kirkwood, Jr. 98 minutes.

ADA. MGM, August 25, 1961. *Daniel Mann*. Dean Martin, Wilfrid Hyde-White, Ralph Meeker, Martin Balsam, Frank Maxwell, Connie Sawyer, Larry Gates, Ford Rainey, Charles Watts, Robert F. Simon, William Zuckert, Richard

Benedict, Kathryn Card, Robert Burton, Helen Beverly. 109 minutes.

BACK STREET. Universal-International, October 12, 1961. *David Miller*. John Gavin, Vera Miles, Virginia Grey, Reginald Gardiner, Charles Drake, Natalie Schafer, Tammy Marihugh, Robert Eyer, Dick Kallman, Joyce Meadows, Alex Gerry, Hayden Rourke. 107 minutes.

I THANK A FOOL. MGM, September 14, 1962. *Robert Stevens*. Peter Finch, Diane Cilento, Cyril Cusack, Kieron Moore, Athene Seyler, Richard Wattis, Laurence Naismith, Brenda de Banzie. 100 minutes.

STOLEN HOURS. United Artists, October 16, 1963. *Daniel Petrie*. Michael Craig, Edward Judd, Diane Baker, Paul Rogers, Robert Bacon, Joan Newell, Peter Madden, Gwen Nelson. 97 minutes.

WHERE LOVE HAS GONE. Embassy-Paramount, November 2, 1964. *Edward Dmytryk*. Bette Davis, Michael Connors, Joey Heatherton, Jane Greer, Anne Seymour, DeForest Kelley, George Macready, Ann Doran, Willis Bouchey, Anthony Caruso, Whit Bissell. 114 minutes.

THE HONEY POT. United Artists, May 22, 1967. *Joseph L. Mankiewicz*. Rex Harrison, Maggie Smith, Cliff Robertson, Edie Adams, Capucine, Adolfo Celi, Luigi Scavran. 131 minutes.

VALLEY OF THE DOLLS. Twentieth Century-Fox, December 15, 1967. *Mark Robson*. Barbara Parkins, Patty Duke, Sharon Tate, Paul Burke, Tony Scotti, Lee Grant, Martin Milner, Charles Drake, Alex Davion, Naomi Stevens, Robert H. Harris, Robert Viharo, Richard Angarola, Jeanne Gerson. 123 minutes.

HEAT OF ANGER. New CBS Friday Night Movies/Stonehenge Productions-Metromedia Producers Corp., 1972. *Don Taylor*. James Stacey, Lee J. Cobb, Fritz Weaver, Bettye Ackerman, Jennifer Penny, Mills Watson, Ray Simms. Tyne Daly. 75 minutes.

THE REVENGERS. National General Pictures, 1972. *Daniel Mann*. William Holden, Ernest Borgnine, Woody Strode, Arthur Hunnicutt, Roger Hanin, Scott Holden. 110 minutes.

SAY GOODBYE, MAGGIE COLE. ABC Wednesday Movie of the Week/Spelling-Goldberg Production, 1972. *Jud Taylor*. Daren McGavin, Beverly Garland, Dane Clark, Michael Constantine, Jeanette Nolan, Michele Nichols, Maidie Norman, Richard Anderson. 75 minutes.

NOTE

Susan Hayward also appeared in seven "Lux Radio Theater" broadcasts: *Hold Back the Dawn*, Nov. 10, 1941 (with Paulette Goddard); *Petrified Forest*, Apr. 23, 1945 (with Ronald Colman); and recreations of her original roles with her film co-stars in *Tap Roots* (Sept. 1948); *My Foolish Heart* (Aug. 28, 1950); *I'd Climb the Highest Mountain* (Oct. 29, 1951); *I Can Get It for You Wholesale* (Mar. 31, 1952); *With a Song in My Heart* (Feb. 9, 1953).

She was also seen on television in a cameo role in Louella Parsons's 1956 *The Gay Illiterate* telecast; *Person to Person* with Edward R. Murrow in 1958; and the *Joey Bishop Show* in 1968.

⌀ index ⌀

Academy of Motion Picture Arts and Sciences, 90
Academy Awards, xv, 1, 103–04, 109, 133, 134, 200–01, 224–27, 289–92
Acosta, Donald Barry de, 191–96, 198
Ada, 234, 299, 318
Adam Had Four Sons, 55–60, 79, 312
Albert, Eddie, 189
Allen, Dick, 123
Allen, Joseph, Jr., 46
American Academy of Dramatic Art, 25
American Broadcasting Company (ABC), 277
Among the Living, 62–63, 312
Anastasia, 204, 225
And Now Tomorrow, 72, 78, 89, 314
Andrews, Dana, 107, 128–30
Angelica, 93
Anyone for Venice, 244, 245 See *Honey Pot, The*
Archerd, Army, 194
Armendariz, Pedro, 306
Arnow, Max, 39
Aspern Papers, The (James), 98
Atlanta Constitution, 237
Atom bomb tests, Nevada (1953), 176, 305–06

Auburn University, 251
Auntie Mame, 224

Babes in Arms, 48
Bacall, Lauren, 206
Back Street, 233, 234, 319
Backes, Alice, 218
Bacon, James, 226
Ball, Lucille, 225
Bankhead, Tallulah, 230
Barker, Gregory Marrenner, 238, 268, 291, 300, 302–05
  birth of, 88
  childhood of, 88–89, 102–03, 121, 134, 144, 150, 155, 170, 172, 173, 184, 193, 200–02
  education of, 208, 233, 237, 266
  and last will of S. H., 288, 308–10
  marriage of, 271
Barker, Ilse Schenke, 275, 304
Barker, Jess, 185–86, 200, 238, 270
  acting career of, 73–77, 109–10, 127, 135
  divorce trial testimony, 156–73
  and last will of S. H., 288–89, 304, 309
  marriage to S. H., 75, 91–93, 96–97, 100–01, 109–11,

126–29, 134–39, 144–49,
    151–54
Barker, Lex, 305
Barker, Nadja, 304
Barker, Susan (Gregory's wife),
    271
Barker, Timothy Marrenner, xvii,
    3, 40, 210, 232, 237–38,
    266–68, 282–84, 300, 301,
    302–04
  birth of, 88
  childhood of, 102–03, 121,
    134, 144, 150, 155, 170,
    172, 173, 184, 193, 200–02
  education of, 208, 233, 237
  and last will of S. H., 288,
    308–10
  marriage of, 275
Barker, Winnie, 78, 82
Barnes, Howard, 63, 98
Barrett, Judith, 46, 51
Barrett, Rona, 277
Barry, Don. *See* Acosta, Donald
    Barry de
Bathsheba, 114
Baxter, Warner, 48, 56, 59, 60
Beau Geste, 46, 47, 132, 311
Beckley, Paul V., 222, 228
Beckwith, Frank, 39, 41, 42, 43,
    87
Belser, Emily, 189
Bendix, William, 73
Bennett, Joan, 89, 93, 216
Berg, Dick, 276
Bergman, Ingrid, 56–60, 104,
    203, 225, 226
Bernhardt, Sarah, 22
Bernstein, Jay, 275, 277, 279
Best Years of Our Lives, The, 108
Beverly Hills Hotel, xv
Beverly Hilton Hotel, xv
Bey, Turhan, 85–86
Bikel, Theodore, 218
Bishop, Joey, 253
Black Book, The, 109
Blair, Betsy, 137
Bogart, Humphrey, 206

Bogeaus, Benedict, 78
Booth, Shirley, 134, 137
Borgnine, Ernest, 276
Boston Sunday Herald-Tribune,
    278
Bowman, Helene, 96
Bowman, Lee, 93, 95, 95n., 96,
    98
Box Office magazine, 131
Boyd, Stephen, xvi
Boyer, Charles, 58–59, 231, 233
Bracken, Eddie, 65, 67
Brackett, Charles, 143
Bradford, Jack, 251
Brand, Harry, 126
Brando, Marlon, 133
Brew, Reverend Thomas, 296,
    302
Briggs, Mollie, vii, 91, 92
Britton, Barbara, 65
Brokaw, Norman, 275–76,
    282–83
Broken Arrow, 152
Brother Rat, 42, 43
Brown, James, 65
Brown, Joe E., 47
Brown, John Mason, 230
Brown, Kay, 31
Burn, John, 118, 118n., 122
Burns, Bob, 47
Burton, Richard, 108, 133
Butterworth, Charles, 59
Byck, Lehmann, 257–62, 265,
    285

Cabin in the Sky, 299
Caesar's Palace, 254, 255, 260
Calhoun, Rory, 118, 122, 128
Cameron, Kate, 198
Campbell, Louise, 46
Campus Cinderella, 40, 311
Cannes film festival, 201, 202
Canova, Judy, 59
Canyon Passage, 90, 91, 107,
    314
Carpetbaggers, The, 239
Carroll, Harrison, 153

Carroll, John, 66–70, 77, 96
Carrollton, Georgia, 213–14, 302
Carson, Eleanor, 266–71
Carson, Johnny, 294
Carson, Russell, 266, 269–70, 271
Cash Box, 261
Cavett, Frank, 98
Century City Hospital, 283, 284, 301
Chalkley, Alma, 215
Chalkley, Floyd Eaton, 198–207, 221, 223, 224, 243
  death of, 245–46
  finances of, 232–33, 243
  health of, 243–45
  marriage to S. H., 208–15, 227, 231, 232–34, 238
Chalkley, Joseph, 238, 243, 244
Chalkmar (ranch), 234, 237
Chandler (Dorothy) Pavilion, 1
Chandler, Jeff, xvi, 17, 152, 153, 156, 228
  death of, 236
Chandler, Marjorie, 152
Chaplin, Charlie, 47
Chicago Tribune Syndicate, 126
Cinecitta Studios, 244
CinemaScope, 136, 141, 144, 154
Clair, Rene, 65
Clayton, Dick, 25, 293, 294, 303–04
Clayton, Jan, 81
Cobb, Lee J., 277
Cohn, Harry, 55–56, 57, 60, 76, 79
Colbert, Claudette, 45, 54, 70, 230, 231
Colman, Ronald, 46, 88
Colonna, Jerry, 59
Columbia Pictures, 56, 74, 76, 79
Confidential magazine, 234–35
Connolly, Mike, 196, 207, 208
Conqueror, The, 155, 174, 176, 200, 305–06, 318
Conte, Richard, 106, 188
Cook, Johnny, 142

Cooper, Gary, 45, 46, 132, 143, 153, 154
Cooper, Rocky, 154
Cork Film Festival, 204
Corsiia, Ted de, 306
Cotten, Joseph, 50
Cover Girl, 76, 79
Cramer, Stuart W., III, 155, 179
Crane, Cheryl, 239
Crane, Steve, 86
Crawford, Joan, 103, 193
Crosby, Bing, 45, 54, 93
Crosby, Bob, 59
Crowther, Bosley, 61, 122–23, 140, 143, 198, 222, 228, 233, 238, 241, 252
Cukor, George, 32, 33, 37, 38, 39, 41, 42, 96, 295

Dailey, Dan, 113
Dallas Morning News, 61
Daniel, Billy, 118
Daniels, Chick, 193
Dark Victory, 238
Dark Waters, 78
Darnell, Linda, 124
Darvi, Bella, 143
Daves, Delmar, 142
David and Bathsheba, 115–16, 122, 316
David di Donatello Award, 228
Davis, Bette, 2, 58, 73, 88, 231, 238, 240, 241, 286
Deadline at Dawn, 88, 89, 314
de Havilland, Olivia, 58–59, 76, 109, 136
Dekker, Albert, 63
Delacorte, Albert, 102
Demetrius and the Gladiators, xvi, 143, 177, 317
DeMille, Cecil B., 63, 230, 280
Denning, Richard, 2, 56
DeSylva, Buddy, 59, 72, 78, 90
Deval, Jacques, 114
Dickinson, Angie, 25
Dietrich, John, 235
Dietrich, Marlene, 45, 195

Dietrich, Moira, 235–36, 303–04

Dmitri, Ivan, 30, 31, 32–33

Dmytryk, Edward, 240–41

Donlevy, Brian, 46

Dougherty, Yvonne, 207

Douglas, Kirk, xvi, 206

Dowling, Eddie, 76

Downs, Johnny, 56

Dragonfly Squadron, 148n.

Drew, Ellen, 46, 51

Duke, Patty, 251–52, 253

Duna, Steffi, 66, 96

Dunne, Philip, 114, 142

Egan, Richard, 177

Ellis, Larry, 258, 259, 265, 285–303

Emory University, 295, 296, 297

Emslie, Mrs. Robert, 8, 13

Epstein, Julius J., 107

Epstein, Philip G., 107

Erdman, Leonard, 245

Farmer, Frances, 45, 51, 63

Farmer's Daughter, The, 103

Fauss, Opal, 284

Feagin Drama School, 25, 80

Feldman, Charles, 79, 86

Feldman (Charles) Agency, 293

Field, Betty, 46, 51

Fighting Seabees, The, 72

Finch, Peter, 236

Fitzgerald and Pride, 276, 277, 278. See *Heat of Anger*

Flaherty, Vincent X., 199–200, 208–09, 224, 227

Fleming, Victor, 96

Fletcher, Adele, 232

Fletcher, Margie, 231

Flying Tigers, 67

Foch, Nina, 77, 80

Fogler, Gertrude, 41

Follow Thru, 19

Fonda, Henry, 48

Fonda, Jane, 25

Foreign Press Association, 133, 225

Forest Rangers, The, 64, 312

Fort Lauderdale News, 277

Fox-Movietone News, 178

Frank, Gerold, xvi

Freeman, Y. Frank, 54–55

French, Ty, 266–67

Freulich, Roman, 221

Freund, Bob, 253

Frings, Ketti, 58

Froman, Jane, 118, 118n, 119–22

Frost, Jack, 253

Gable, Clark, 66, 67, 80–81, 177–78

Gang, Martin, 156, 234

Gardella, Kay, 278

Garden of Evil, 146, 154, 156, 317

Gardner, Ava, 136

Garland, Judy, 177, 251

Gaynor, Mitzi, 208

Gentlemen Prefer Blondes, 124, 143

Gentleman's Agreement, 103, 115

Georgia Military Academy, 233

Gerson, Barbara, 306

Gidding, Nelson, 217

Ginsberg, Henry, 35

Girls on Probation, 43, 311

Goddard, Paulette, 47–48, 54, 56, 59, 63, 64, 70, 72, 79

Goldberg, Len, 276

Golden Globe Awards (Foreign Press Association), 225

Goldwyn, Samuel, 106, 108

Gomez, Thomas, 175

Gone With the Wind (film), 32, 33, 47, 96, 179

Gone With the Wind (Mitchell), 32

Good Luck Mr. Yates, 76

Gordon, Michael, 112

Government Girl, 76

Governor's Ball, xv, 225, 227

Grable, Betty, 131

Graham, Barbara (Bloody Babs), 217–18, 220–21, 222

Graham, Sheilah, 145, 146, 152, 176, 201, 202, 208
Grant, Cary, 33, 225
Grauman's Chinese Theater, 122, 152
Green, Johnny, 187, 188
Greer, Jane, 100
Greve, Frank, 295
Griffin, Merv, 122, 294
Grossel, Ira, 17. *See also* Chandler, Jeff
Group Theater, 24, 50, 51
Guernsey, Otis L., Jr., 73
Guinele, Jorge, 205, 206
Gussow, Mel, 143

Hahn, S. S. (Sammy), 156, 195
Hairy Ape, The, 73, 314
Hale, Wanda, 67
Halls of Montezuma, The, 120
Hanna, David, 122
"Happiness Is a Thing Called Joe," 187, 299, 300
Harvard *Lampoon*, 234
Hathaway, Henry, 111, 154
Hayes, Hal, 194, 196–99
Hayes, John Michael, 240, 241
Hayward, Leland, 39, 75
Hayward, Susan:
    Academy Award nominations, 103–04, 109, 200–01, 224–27
    awards given to, 114, 132, 133, 204, 224, 225, 228, 234
    birth of, 13
    and cancer, 1, 282–301
    in car accident, 7–8, 14, 15, 16
    childhood of, 7–20
    conversion to Catholicism, 249, 250
    death of, 301–04
    divorce trial testimony, 157–74
    education of, 20–23
    home in Carrollton, Georgia, 213–14
    last will and testament of,
        287–88, 297, 308–10
    marriage to Barker, 3, 75, 91–93, 96–97, 100–01, 109–11, 126–29, 134–39, 144–49, 151–54
    marriage to Chalkley, 3, 208–15, 227, 231, 232–34, 238
    modeling career of, 28–31, 128–29
    named Susan Hayward, 39
    singing of, 187–88, 257–62
    sleeping pill overdose, 183–87
Hayworth, Rita, 71, 76, 96
Heat of Anger, 278, 319. See *Fitzgerald and Pride*
Heatherton, Joey, 239
Hecht, Ben, 57, 221
Hedda and Louella, 279
Heflin, Van, 50, 67, 99
Heiress, The, 109
Heisler, Stuart, 93–94, 95, 96, 98, 104
Henderson, Charles, 187, 188, 255
"Henrietta" award, 133
Henry, William, 46
Hepburn, Katharine, 33, 45, 50, 136, 294, 299
Heston, Charlton, xvi, 1, 2, 131, 140, 292
Hestor, Harvey, 199, 200, 201, 213, 214, 215
High Noon, 132, 133
His Weird and Wanton Ways: The Secret Life of Howard Hughes, 154
Hit Parade of 1943, 65–70, 313
Hodges, Joy, 48
Hold Back the Dawn, 58
Holden, William, 46, 65, 276
Hollywood Canteen, 76
Hollywood Reporter, 122, 140, 196
Holm, Celeste, 262, 263, 264
Honey Pot, The, 245, 319. See *Anyone for Venice*

Hope, Bob, 45, 47, 54, 59
Hopper, Hedda, 57, 125–28, 146, 152, 193, 232, 277
House of Strangers, 106, 315
Houser, Marvin, 44
Hughes, Howard, 124, 125, 135, 150–55, 173, 174, 175, 179, 180, 235
Hunter, Ross, 233
Hurst, Fannie, 233
Hutton, Betty, 72
Hyams, Joe, 227

I Can Get It for You Wholesale, 112, 113, 114, 117, 316
I Married a Witch, 65, 313
I Thank a Fool, 236, 319
I Want to Live!, 2, 217, 221, 301, 318
I Wanted Wings, 55
I'd Climb the Highest Mountain, 112, 115, 117, 316
I'll Cry Tomorrow, xv, 184, 187–93, 197–204, 318
"I'm Sittin' on Top of the World," 187
Immerman, Stanley, 184, 185
Intermezzo, 56, 58
International News Service, 70, 189
Irwin, Peggy, 199, 243
It's a Hell of a Life but Not a Bad Living (Dmytryk), 240

Jack London, 72, 314
Jackson, Glenda, xvii, 2, 292
Jackson, Rachel Donelson, 140
Jacobson, Arthur, 44
Jam Session, 76
James, Henry, 98
Jane Froman Story, The. See With a Song in My Heart
Jarmyn, Jil, 194, 195
Joan of Arc, 104
Johnson, Erskine, 145, 152
Jones, Jennifer, 200

Jordan, Dorothy, 38
Jourdan, Louis, 225

Kazan, Elia, 50
Keep Your Powder Dry, 87
Kelly, Kerry, 137
Kelly, Gene, 96, 137
Kelly, Grace, 177, 204
Kennedy, Arthur, 125
Kennedy, Jacqueline, 245
Kentucky Rifles, 185
Kerr, Deborah, 224
Keyes, Evelyn, 46
Kilgallen, Dorothy, 156, 193, 197
King, Henry, 115, 116, 117
King Features Syndicate, 70–71
Korvin, Charles, 89
Koster, Henry, 40
Koster, Peggy Moran, 40

Ladd, Alan, 67, 76, 78
LaFaye, Emma, 69
LaFaye, Julian, 66
LaGotta, John, 30–31
Lake, Veronica, 55, 59, 65, 70
Landis, Carole, 40
Lane, Priscilla, 43
Lang, Jennings, 216
Lang, Walter, 119–23, 231
Lansbury, Angela, 255
Lawrence, Jerome, 261
Lawson, John Howard, 98
Lee, Dixie, 93
Leigh, Vivien, 47, 230
LeMaire, Charles, 142, 206, 208, 231
Leontovich, Eugenie, 58
Letter from Bataan, A, 313
Levine, Joseph E., 239, 240
Lewis, Diana, 40
Life magazine, 88, 98, 132, 198
Little, Martha, 140–41, 145, 158, 160, 161, 164, 179–80
Little, Sara, 10, 21, 26, 140, 214
Logan, Janice, 46
Look magazine, 88, 122, 197
Los Angeles Times, 198

Los Angeles Music Center, 1
Lost Moment, The, 98, 176, 315
Lost Weekend, The, 97
Louis, Jean, 233
Lusty Men, The, 125, 135, 317
Lyons, Leonard, 71

Mack and Mabel, 300
MacLaine, Shirley, 224
MacMichael, Florence, 65
MacMurray, Fred, 45, 64, 72
McCarthy, Neil, 209
McClelland, Doug, 64, 240
McGavin, Darren, 278
McGuire, Betty, 255
McGuire, Father Daniel J., 249,
    250
McGuire, Dorothy, 103
McKinley, Ray, band of, 67
Magic, 76
Magnani, Anna, xv, 198, 200,
    201
Mame, 254–64
Mankiewicz, Don, 217
Mankiewicz, Joseph L., 106,
    244, 245
Mann, Danny, 187–91, 234
Manners, Dorothy, 284
Mapes, Jacques, 233
March, Frederic, 3, 65, 110
Marin, Ned, 135, 152, 293
Marlowe, Hugh, 153
Marquand, John, 206
Marrenner, Edythe. *See* Hayward,
    Susan
Marrenner, Ellen, 8–23, 39, 41,
    42, 62, 69, 80–82, 121,
    173, 183, 184, 208, 232
  death of, 220
  marriage of, 11–12
Marrenner, Florence, 9–10,
    14–22, 33, 42, 60, 61–62,
    80, 82, 92, 138–39, 183,
    234–36, 303–04
  birth of, 12
  dancing career of, 18–19
  and last will of S. H., 297, 303

Marrenner, Joseph, 10, 11
Marrenner, Kate Harrigan, 9–10,
    11–12
Marrenner, Wally (Walter, Jr.),
    xvii, 10–22, 62, 69, 70,
    145, 160, 184, 208, 232,
    246, 251, 267, 284
  birth of, 13
  marriage of, 284
  and last will of S. H., 288,
    303, 308–09
Marrenner, Walter, xvii, 8–26,
    183
  death of, 41, 42
  illness of, 31, 33, 39
  marriage of, 11–12
Marriage-Go-Round, The, 230,
    233, 318
Marshal, Alan, 38
Marshall, George, 64, 99
Martin, Charlie, 70, 71, 72
Martin, Dean, 234
Martin, Freddy, band of, 67
Marty, 201
"M*A*S*H," 255
Mason, James, xvi, 114, 231
Mason, Pamela, 114
Massachusetts General Hospital,
    287
Massey, Raymond, 63, 115
Matheson, Richard, 154
Mathews, Joyce, 46
Mature, Victor, 142
May, David, 85
Mayer, Louis B., 60, 67
Medford, Ben, 35, 39, 41, 42,
    44, 55, 56, 58, 59, 68, 70,
    72, 77, 79, 81
Mercury Theater Company, 24
Meriwether, Lillian, 9
Meriwether, Walter Scott, 9
Merman, Ethel, 252
Metro-Goldwyn-Mayer (MGM),
    41, 47, 99, 187
Meyer, Dr. Frederick, 206
Miami Herald, 295
Miami News, 253

Milland, Ray, 45, 46, 63, 64, 97
Miller, Nolan, 289, 291, 292
Miracle Worker, The, 252
Mirisch Films, Ltd., 238
Mitchell, Cameron, 153
Mitchum, Robert, xvi, 125, 128,
    131, 143
Modern Screen, 101, 102, 132,
    235
Monroe, Marilyn, 124, 132–33,
    141, 143, 203, 282
Montgomery, Ed, 217
Montgomery, George, 41
Montgomery, Robert, 104
"Montparnasse," 118
Moorehead, Agnes, 2, 176
    death of, 305
Morris (William) Agency, 275
Morison, Patricia, 46
Motion Picture Herald's, 67, 131
Motion Picture magazine, 9, 102,
    110, 135
My Foolish Heart, 106, 107, 108,
    316

Neal, Patricia, 154
Nelson, Ron, 267, 295–96, 299
New York Capitol, 60
New York Daily News, 25, 50,
    67, 198, 227, 278
New York Daily Mirror, 71, 73
New York Film Critics' Society,
    109
    awards, 134, 198, 224
New York Herald Tribune, 63,
    73, 98, 112, 222, 228
New York Post, 63, 113
New York Sunday News, 61
New York Times, The, 61, 63, 67,
    73, 111, 112, 116, 122, 140,
    143, 198, 216, 222, 231,
    233
New Yorker, The, 107
Newmar, Julie, 231
Newsweek, 88, 100, 116, 241
Night Walker, The, 305
Niven, David, 1, 224, 225, 292

Nixon, Richard M., 284
Novak, Kim, 203, 204

Oakland, Simon, 218
Oberon, Merle, 78, 89
O'Keefe, Dennis, 66
Olivier, Sir Laurence, 225
$1,000 a Touchdown, 47, 312
O'Neill, Eugene, 73
O'Neill, Zelma, 19
Osborne, Robert, 268, 279, 280,
    281, 290, 306
Our Leading Citizen, 47, 312
Out of the Frying Pan, 65

Paget, Debra, 150
Pantages Theater, Hollywood, xv,
    2, 109, 200
Papote, Jean, 136, 137, 138
Paramount Pictures, 44, 45, 65,
    70, 228
    Golden Circle, 45–46, 51
Parker, Dorothy, 98
Parker, Eleanor, 200
Parkins, Barbara, 251
Parsons, Louella, xvi, 48, 49, 50,
    57, 69, 72, 86, 90, 134,
    146–49, 151, 152, 154, 156,
    187, 193, 196, 201, 204,
    206, 208, 228, 233, 277
Pearson, Ellen F. *See* Marrenner,
    Ellen
Peck, Gregory, 115, 116, 128
Person to Person, 253
Perugini, Carmen, 2, 289, 295,
    297, 298, 299, 303
    mentioned in last will, 308
Peters, Jean, 124, 136, 150, 155,
    179, 180
Petrified Forest, The, 88
Pettebone, Jean, 82
Peyton Place, 253
Philadelphia Inquirer, 179
Philadelphia Story, The, 50
Photoplay magazine, xvi, 9, 101,
    119, 132, 153
Pickford, Mary, 9

Pippin, Donald, 188, 255, 256, 257, 262–63, 300
Powell, William (Dick), 174, 175
    death of, 305
Powell, Eleanor, 19
Powell, Jane, 132
Power, Tyrone, 111, 115, 176–77, 179
Preisser, June, 48, 49
President's Lady, The, 131, 140, 317
Preston, Robert, 46, 63, 104, 300
Pryor, Thomas, 67–68, 111, 112

Quinn, Anthony, 133

Rackin, Martin, 43, 239, 240, 247, 249, 254, 275–76, 297
Radio City Music Hall, 60, 108, 197
Rappaport, Charlotte, 17
Ratoff, Gregory, 55–56, 58, 75, 76, 79, 280
Rawhide, 111, 112, 114, 117, 316
Raye, Martha, 47
Reagan, Ronald, 48, 49, 50
Reap the Wild Wind, 53, 312
Redwine, Skip, 259, 299
Republic Studios, 59, 67, 70, 72
Revengers, The, 275, 277, 320
Reynolds, Burt, 25, 293–94
Richmond News-Leader, 61
Riot in Cell Block 11, 216
Ritter, Thelma, 122
RKO, 48, 76, 88, 104, 124, 176
Robbins, Harold, 239
Robe, The, 121, 141, 142, 152
Robinson, Edward G., 106
Robinson, Pat, 70
Robson, Mark, 108, 251
Rogers, Ginger, 203
Rogers, Henry, 82
Rooster Cogburn, 299
Rose Tattoo, The, 198, 200–01
Ross, Frank, 142
Roth, Lillian, xvi, 184, 188, 189, 190, 197
Roth, Ron, 276
Rudin, Milton, 156, 234
Russell, Jane, 124
Russell, Rosalind, 103, 104, 224, 225
Ruth, Morgana, 207
Rutherford, Ann, 85

Saks, Gene, 255
Salinger, J. D., 107
San Francisco Examiner, 217
Santley, Joseph, 60
Saturday Evening Post, 30, 31, 32, 46
Saxon Charm, The, 104, 315
Say Goodbye, Maggie Cole, 278, 279, 320
Schallert, Edward, 198
Schenck, Joseph, 131
Schenke, Ilse, 275
Schmidt, Lars, 225
Schulberg, Mrs. B. P., 76
Screen Actors Guild (SAG), 276
Selznick, David O., 31, 32, 38, 56, 57, 90
Selznick, Irene, 32, 33
Selznick International Studios, 33, 37, 38
Separate Tables, 224
Seven Men from Now, 194
Shaw, George Bernard, 230
Shaw, Robert, 56
Sheridan, Ann, 109
Shipp, Cameron, 59
Siegel, Dr. Lee, 282, 283, 284, 292, 297, 300, 301
Silver Screen, 102
"Sing You Sinners," 187
Sis Hopkins, 59, 312
Skirmish on the Home Front, 314
Skolsky, Sidney, 132, 152, 193, 196, 206
Smash-Up, The Story of a Woman, 93, 95, 96, 97, 98, 99, 101, 198, 213, 315
Smith, Roland H., 118n

Snake Pit, The, 109

Snows of Kilimanjaro, 131, 316

So Proudly We Hail, 70, 79

Soldier of Fortune, 177, 178, 317

Some Came Running, 224

Somebody Up There Likes Me, 218

Sound of Music, The, 218

South Pacific, 208

Spreckels, Kay, 178

Spelling, Aaron, 276, 278

Stacey, James, 276

Standing Room Only, 72

Stanwyck, Barbara, 21–22, 276, 292–93, 305

Star Is Born, A, 110, 177

Star Spangled Rhythm, 313

Stella, 109

Stevens, Robert, 236

Stevens, Ruby. *See* Stanwyck, Barbara

Stolen Hours, 238, 239, 319

Stone, Irving, 140

Story of Demetrius, The, 141, 142, 143

Street, James, 98

Streetcar Named Desire, A, 133

Sturges, Preston, 59

Sullavan, Margaret, 39, 233

Sullivan, Ed, 69

Sullivan's Travels, 59

Summertime, 200

Susann Jacqueline, 251, 252

Swit, Loretta, 255

Take One False Step, 109

Talmadge, Herman, 117

Tap Roots, 98, 99, 315

Tate, Sharon, 251, 252, 269

Taylor, Don, xvi, 277

Taylor, Elizabeth, 108, 224, 230

Taylor, Jud, 278

Taylor, Robert, 305

They Won't Believe Me, 100, 262, 315

This Gun for Hire, 76

This Love of Ours, 89

This Man Is Mine, 124, 125. See *Lusty Men*

Thornton, Walter, 27, 29, 30, 33, 51, 156

Three Faces of Eve, 204

Thunder in the Sun, 228, 318

Tierney, Gene, 124

Tierney, Lawrence, 88

Time magazine, 73, 88, 89, 104, 116, 140, 179, 198, 231

Time of Their Lives, The, 91

Tindall, Dr. George, 296

To Each His Own, 109

Tobias, George, 112

Todd, Richard, 203

Tomlinson, Virginia, 92

Top Secret Affair, 206, 318

Totter, Audrey, 104

Touch of Class, A, 2

Trail of the Lonesome Pine, The, 75

Trevor, Claire, 76

Trotti, Lamar, 118, 123

Tucker, Bobby, 208

Tufts, Sonny, xv–xvi, 76

Tulsa, 104, 315

Tunberg, Karl, 236

Turner, Lana, 39, 71, 85–86, 87, 134, 136, 239, 305

Tuttle, Lurene, 197

TV Guide, 277

Twentieth Century-Fox, 56, 79, 114, 117, 124, 131, 141, 205, 225, 228, 230, 251, 252, 253, 278

Twinkle in God's Eye, A, 194

Typhoon, 51

"Uncle Wiggily in Connecticut," 107

United Artists, 56, 65, 72, 78

Universal, 87, 89, 104

Untamed, 178, 317

Valery, Bernard, 203

Valley of the Dolls, 251, 252, 253, 269, 319

Van Cleef, Lee, 306
Variety, 63, 97, 98, 122, 179,
   194
Vincent, Virginia, 218, 219, 220,
   221
Vitaphone, 29
Viva Zapata!, 133
Vivyan, John, 255
Volpone, 244

Wagner, Robert, xvi, 2, 120,
   121, 123, 213
Wald, Jerry, 124
Walker, Clint, 236
Walker, Helen, 72
Walker, Judge Herbert Y., 156,
   177
Wallace, Sylvia, 132
Wanger, Walter, 40, 75, 90, 91,
   93, 96, 98, 99, 100, 103,
   104, 215, 216, 220–22, 225,
   226, 230
  death of, 259
Warner, Jack, 43, 156, 206
Warner Brothers, 35, 39, 41, 43,
   87, 205
Wayne, David, 118
Wayne, John, xvi, 59, 63, 64,
   67, 72, 175
  death of, 305, 306
Weaver, Fritz, 277
Webb, Richard, 52, 54
Weidman, Jerome, 112
Weiler, A. H., 116
Weinberger, William S., 260
Weingarten, Lawrence, 187, 260,
   295
Weisbart, David, 251
Wellman, William, 46, 280
West Side Story, 218
Westmore, Frank, 290, 291
Whelan, Arleen, 48

Where Love Has Gone, 239, 240,
   241, 319
Whitcomb, Jon, 29
White, Gordon, 204, 206
White Onna, 255, 261
White Witch Doctor, xvi, 143,
   170, 317
Widmark, Richard, 120, 153
Wilkerson, G. W., 183–84
Williams, John, 197
Wills, Chill, 185
Wilson, Earl, 197
Winchell, Walter, 150
Wise, Robert, 218, 219, 220, 221
With a Song in My Heart, 2,
   117–24, 132, 133, 316
Wolfson, Sonia, 128, 129, 231
Woman Obsessed, A, 225, 228,
   318
Wood, Yvonne, 99
Woodward, Joanne, 204
World's Favorite Screen Star of
   1952, 133
Wyman, Jane, 48, 49, 50

Yates, Herbert, 68
You Can't Take It With You, 56,
   112
Young, Loretta, 72, 103–04
Young, Robert, 262
Young and Willing, 65, 313

Zaenglin, Lorence. *See*
   Marrenner, Florence
Zaenglin, Larry, 80, 235, 303,
   304
Zaenglin, Udo, 62, 80, 235
Zanuck, Darryl, 48, 104, 105,
   106, 109, 111, 114–17,
   119–20, 129, 132, 133, 135,
   136, 141, 142, 143, 146,
   152
Zink, Jack, 277

Glittering lives of famous people!
Bestsellers from Berkley

★ ★ ★ ★ ★ ★ ★ ★ ★ ★ ★ ★ ★ ★ ★ ★ ★ ★ ★ ★

By Gillian Roberts
Published by Ballantine Books:

CAUGHT DEAD IN PHILADELPHIA
PHILLY STAKES
I'D RATHER BE IN PHILADELPHIA
WITH FRIENDS LIKE THESE. . .
HOW I SPENT MY SUMMER VACATION

Praise for Gillian Roberts and her Amanda Pepper mysteries

With Friends Like These . . .
"A pleasurable whodunit with real motives, enough clues to allow a skillful reader of mysteries to make some intelligent guesses, and a plethora of suspects."

—*Chicago Tribune*

Caught Dead in Philadelphia
"Roberts provides a story that quickly engages the reader. . . .Her writing sparkles with warmth and humor."

—*The Virginian-Pilot & The Ledger-Star*

Philly Stakes
"Entertaining . . . Amanda never loses her sense of humor, and her upbeat narration gives the story its breezy verve."

—*San Francisco Chronicle*

I'd Rather Be in Philadelphia
"Literate, amusing, and surprising, while at the same time spinning a crack whodunit puzzle."

—*Chicago Sun-Times*

HOW I SPENT MY SUMMER VACATION is an Alternate Selection of the Mystery Guild®

I'd be remiss to ignore the contribution made by Eleanor Carson, Susan's neighbor in Fort Lauderdale. Dr. and Mrs. Russell Carson were eyewitnesses to the 1971 fire that almost cost Susan her life. Eleanor Carson related the story in its entirety, as well as other anecdotes about Susan's lonely life in Fort Lauderdale. Thanks too to Mrs. Carson's nephew Ty French.

I am particularly indebted to three highly respected physicians, Dr. Morton Marks of New York University Medical Center, Dr. Jerome J. Hoffman of Fort Lauderdale, and Dr. Donald Rubell of Beth Israel and Lenox Hill hospitals in New York City, for the assistance they gave me with my very difficult medical research. These experts in their diversified fields would not accept a fee for their help. Donations will be made to Cancer Care in their names.

Reverend Daniel McGuire, the priest who converted Susan Hayward to Catholicism, and Carmen Perugini, Susan's nurse and companion during the final years of her life, were both contacted. Although each adamantly refused to violate Susan's confidences in any way, they generously corrected glaring errors that had previously been printed and accepted as gospel. For this, I both thank and respect them.

Rebecca Boyd Stern was as always my "lucky charm"; Harry Kroft was another. My appreciation extends to Allan Maybee, who did my Southern research, and the indomitable Joan O'Brien who, as before, did most of my California legwork. Barbara Grether interviewed Susan's former make-up woman, Molly Briggs. Requesting anonymity are the various men and women at the Court of Records in New York and Los Angeles, and the FBI, OSS, and CIA headquarters in Washington who searched for and found legal and public documents that supplied accurate information contradicting a myriad of previously published fallacies.

But I could never have made deadlines without the help and push of my cousin Arlene Bobker. I am in her debt for her assistance in every way.

B. L.

agent, Mr. Medford supplied information I couldn't have gotten elsewhere—and did not pull his punches.

Donald Pippin, today executive musical director of the new Radio City Music Hall Entertainment Center and one of Broadway's most respected musical figures, spent three months preparing Susan for *Mame*. He spent precious free time rehearsal breaks in order to supply details of a period in Susan's life never before fully documented.

Maestro Lehmann Byck, Susan's vocal coach during *Mame* rehearsals, provided additional details, as did Larry Ellis, a Broadway singer-actor, who met Susan at this time, and then reentered her life as it was slowly ebbing away. It was as painful for him to talk about those final days as it was for me to record them. But Larry's recollections, as shattering as they may be, inspired my title—*Portrait of a Survivor*—as did Nolan Miller's heartbreaking experience: designing the dazzling green sequin dress Susan wore for what she knew would be her last public appearance. Larry and Nolan told their stories exclusively to me. How do I find the words with which to thank them?

I am equally beholden to my dear friend Robert Osborne, who taped the last interview Susan gave and generously donated his valuable material for me to use in whatever way I felt fit. Jack Bradford, who often interviewed Susan Hayward, also put his exclusive material at my disposal.

Another good friend, editor-reporter Douglas McClelland, presented me with his extensive Hayward archives, personal correspondence, and rare photographs. His encouragement was also invaluable. Eduardo Moreno, the owner of the most extensive photograph collection of Susan Hayward in existence, was equally generous as were Vicki Pagliaro and Loraine Burdict. Publicists, John Campbell, and Sonia Wolfson, whom Susan adored, were able to provide insights on the star. New York ace publicist Sy Presten and Henry Malgreen, were also wonderful, as were Richard Webb and Saul Goodman, who were there when...

The recollections of Darryl F. Zanuck, Walter Wanger, Martin Rackin, Mark Robson, George Marshall, Lee Bowman, Jane Froman, Hedda Hopper, Adele Fletcher, and Stuart Heisler; and of the very alive, well, and active Danny Mann, Bob Wise, Maxwell Arnow, Frank Westmore, and Edward Dmytryk, were essential to my efforts to create a definitive portrait of this private woman.

❀acknowledgments❀

AFTER the immediate family and co-stars, who does one thank first for the time, effort, and other contributions that go into creating a biography? So many helped. . . .

My appreciation goes to Norman Brokaw, vice-president of the William Morris Agency, Susan's final Hollywood agent, and my current one, both for his remembrances of Susan and the encouragement he gave me with this project; to Helen Barrett, also of William Morris, my New York literary agent whose practical and emotional assistance got me through some very difficult moments. And of course my gratitude to my editor Neil Nyren, who was always available above and beyond the call of duty and who turned what could have been an ordeal into a challenging pleasure.

I am beholden to director George Cukor for finally setting the record straight as to the *exact* circumstances that led to Susan's initial trip to Hollywood and for telling me for the *first time* the true story that invalidates every other myth printed about Susan's Scarlett O'Hara screen tests.

I spoke with Lillian Roth, whose life Susan portrayed. Miss Roth, Dick Clayton, Burt Reynolds, Peggy Moran Koster, actress Lurene Tuttle, *I Want to Live!* co-star Virginia Vincent, Irene Selznick, and Jane Greer unhesitatingly answered my persistent questions. Don (Red) Barry, involved in that unfortunate, headlined episode with Susan, shared his happier memories of her before he made shocking new headlines by committing suicide after a quarrel with his estranged wife. I also caught up with John Carroll just prior to his less violent demise. His recollections added a bit of spice—since few remember his short-lived engagement to Susan. Ben Medford remembers it and much more about early Susan Hayward. As her first

This Berkley book contains the complete
text of the original hardcover edition.
It has been completely reset in a typeface
designed for easy reading, and was printed
from new film.

SUSAN HAYWARD:
PORTRAIT OF A SURVIVOR

A Berkley Book / published by arrangement with
Atheneum Publishers

PRINTING HISTORY
Atheneum edition published 1980
Berkley edition / December 1981
Second printing / March 1983

ISBN: 0-425-06425-5

A BERKLEY BOOK ® 757,375
Berkley Books are published by Berkley Publishing Corporation,
200 Madison Avenue, New York, New York 10016.
PRINTED IN THE UNITED STATES OF AMERICA

Portrait of
a Survivor
Susan
Hayward

BEVERLY LINET

BERKLEY BOOKS, NEW YORK

Beverly Linet

Hollywood's Foremost Biographer

At age fifteen, Beverly Linet wrote the star-making PHOTOPLAY column that helped launch the careers of Robert Mitchum, Grace Kelly and Charlton Heston. She knew Hollywood's "Golden Age" firsthand as a writer with SILVER SCREEN and WHO'S WHO IN HOLLYWOOD. Today she is best-known as the author of the bestselling *LADD: The Life, The Legend, The Legacy of Alan Ladd*.

Of her latest work, she says: "I was honestly there. I saw Susan at Loew's in 1939. When Susan saw 'The Philadelphia Story' in New York, I was in the audience, too. I was there when she won her Oscar in 1959. I identify with the redhead from Brooklyn— that's me, I'm one myself."

secrets. She used to worry about my sex life—mostly she worried that I managed to have one. Now, the euphemism for unmarried was *financial security*. She mailed clippings about long-term investments and, much more depressingly, about trophy wives. Nothing subtle about her message. My mission was to snag a doddering millionaire and live securely ever after.

The horrible truth was that every so often—as today, lost in my unattainable beach fantasies and not at all entranced with the teacherly lifestyle of making do—the idea didn't sound half bad. Well, maybe not quarter bad. Although where in my daily rounds I was supposed to meet the tycoon instead of his adolescent great-grandson, I didn't know.

"So maybe you don't really want a beach," Sasha said.

"Not enough to put up with my mother's nagging. I'm thinking of installing voice mail to save her breath and long-distance charges. You know, 'Press one to nag about my economic security. Press two to remind me that I haven't yet produced grandchildren.' You're lucky your parents let you lead your own life."

"They're afraid I *will* get married. Again. That I'll be like them." Sasha's parents had been in the divorce avant-garde. Long before it was commonplace, they split, reassembled, remarried, and redivorced unto the point of utter confusion—theirs and everyone who knew them. An inability to choose wisely or maintain relationships seemed a genetic inheritance. Sasha herself had already had two kamikaze hitchings, and her quality control, when it came to men, hadn't improved appreciably since. "Every time I mention a man, they shudder. I told my mother about this fellow I'm going to see tomorrow—" She stopped short. "That's it! Cinderella Pepper, you're looking at your fairy godmother!"

I would have thought fairy godmothers were more petite. Six feet tall, with wild black hair, wearing multicolored layers of gauze and high-topped sneakers, Sasha didn't fit the storybook image, but I listened.

"You have just won yourself an almost all-expenses-paid trip to the edge of an authentic, genuine ocean! Sand included free of charge."

"How?"

"I have a seaside shoot complete with room and meals. What's the diff if I share my room with you? All you'll have to spring for is what you eat, and you'd have to do that here, too."

"Are you serious?" A genuine getaway, a beach vacation for free? The seabirds struck up the chorus in my head again.

"What are friends for?"

Sasha might bemoan the lack of a regular salary or a predictable income, but she did get to take her photographs in exotic locales now and then. I thought about shoots on the Mediterranean, or the Caribbean, or even the cold waters off Maine. Anywhere would be splendid. I'd pay for the plane tickets somehow.

The boy in the earflaps had snagged a bag of chips, and his mother, face red and puffed, shouted, "Not more *snacks*! What did I tell you? They're *bad* for you!" She grabbed the bag from the boy and pushed a handful of chips into her own mouth. Talk about mixed messages, no wonder the kid covered his ears. By the time he'd wind up in my classroom in a few years, those leather sound barriers would have become internalized and unremovable. And I'd be expected to teach him something.

Sasha ate the last of the biscotti. I couldn't protest or complain, given that she was offering a vacation in exchange.

An imagined sun warmed my head—but I willingly accepted a bleak beach as well. Deserted and overcast, heavy with clouds or fog—it sounded wonderful. The silence, the waves, the chance to think and breathe deeply ... bliss. "Thank you," I said. "I gratefully accept."

"Thank the saltwater taffy consortium."

"Saltwater taffy? Where is this job?"

"Where else?"

Atlantic City. Of all the beaches in all the world. My good fairy had arrived with a whole lot of small print. Sand and water, yes, but Atlantic City! Casinos and slums and junk food and all-night lights and noise. More high rollers than breakers. More pigeons than sea gulls. Not the point at all.

"Atlantic City is America's Number One Vacation Destination," Sasha said. "Pure adventure, one hour away. Would you honestly rather clean closets? And by the way, my car's acting weird. I don't need it—I hired an assistant in A.C. and she's renting all the equipment there. So could you drive?"

AND THAT'S WHY ON MONDAY MORNING, WHILE IN SEARCH of the soothing touch of nature, I instead wound up parking my Mustang in a labyrinth below several stories of steel, concrete, and glitz.

Sasha and I walked through a lobby done in Eclectic Excess, a potpourri of design history. Greek columns separated Renaissance-style murals beside equatorial waterfalls near an Ozlike yellow-brick walkway. Everything was highlighted with tiny white lights. Our bellman's outfit was Mittel European Operetta. A neo-something marble statue in a toga pointed the way to the registration area. I tried in vain to find a theme, a connecting thread—aside from blatant expensiveness.

Outside, the sky had been tight and sallow, but now we were hermetically sealed in eternal, nuclear day lit by a thousand suns. The eye-tearing indoor season had nothing to do with the existence of the clock or the solar system.

"Why a casino, Sash? Atlantic City has normal hotels. Why'd the saltwater people put you here?"

"I asked them to. I thought I'd be alone, and a place like this is more alive. No matter what hour. I was here once. . . ." We passed the entrance to a cavelike side room called the Hideaway. Sasha dropped her suitcase, said, "Just a sec," and ducked in.

I was close to the casino entrance. I waited for Sasha, listening to the siren sounds of silvery music and money.

"He's still working here," she said when she returned a minute or so later. "The bartender, Frankie. One of the good guys."

Which probably meant she had no interest in him. It's women like Sasha who—unintentionally but just as lethally—make men think they have to be rotten with the rest of us. Nice guys do not finish last with me—unless you're being semantically sloppy and equating *nice* with bland or dull. But Sasha's different. Her dials are set for challenge, which often translates into danger or misery.

However, at this point in our long friendship, I was trying not to editorialize about Sasha's fondness for losers. As she was overly fond of pointing out, my own off-again, on-again relationship with the detective was no shining example of brilliant selection.

"I was here before," she now said. "Couple of years ago."

"With Frankie the bartender?"

"No, no. This other guy. Dimples. A genuine louse. Frankie the bartender saved the day, and maybe me—from jail. I didn't think he'd still be here."

"From jail? Why? Or do I want to know?"

"Because Dimples was a little bit of a criminal, and the police thought I was his accomplice." She laughed at the thought. I found it less humorous.

We had reached our destination, the registration desk, decorated in the style of medieval French palaces. I wondered which era, theme, and climatological zone our room would feature. Art Deco Romanesque? Tropical French? Greek Chalet?

It turned out to be Basic Brothel. The room was small, its walls covered with silver foil. The bedspread, drapes, and carpeting were as silvery as fabric can get, shot through with metallic threads. Where there wasn't foil or silver cloth, there were mirrors. Including the ceiling. Cigarettes still sealed in their foil-lined boxes must feel the way I did.

"A money motif, do you think?" Sasha asked.

"I'd prefer the greenbacks room, then."

"The room I had with Dimples was nothing like this. But then, we had an ocean view."

We viewed neither ocean nor bay. Instead, we faced the rooftops and fire escapes of yellow-brick buildings that clashed with our color scheme. I closed the drapes. "I'll take the right-hand drawers, right side of the closet."

Sasha nodded, but before either of us began to unpack, our phone rang and she picked it up. "Sasha *Berg*," she said midway through the conversation. "The photographer. Are you talking to the right person?" And: "The saltwater taffy association isn't going to pay for any—" Then she just listened.

She hung up. "They're moving us to a suite." She sounded bemused. "No extra charge. I thought they only did that for really high rollers."

"It isn't possible that this upgrade is in honor of the guy you were here with, is it? The criminal? That maybe they think you're still involved with him?"

"They didn't comp him a suite then, so why now, when he's dead? And it's not like they don't know. It was in all the papers."

"Tell me the man died of natural causes. Please."

"The man died of natural causes."

I sighed with relief.

"After all," Sasha continued, "it's pretty natural to die when there's a bullet in the back of your skull."

I've often wondered why Sasha's incredible bad luck with men doesn't deter or sour her—or leave her with the slightest trace of post-traumatic shock. She's no dummy or masochist. Maybe it's because she has so much fun until each adventure sours. Maybe she's the world's last great optimist.

"We're not supposed to look a gift horse in the mouth," she now said.

I hoped that neither the horse nor his teeth nor the walls were capped in silver. One ounce more and I'd start mining it.

THE SUITE WAS EXQUISITE, LEAVING ME WONDERING. WERE nickel-and-dime gamblers mirrored-ceiling types, while the major players—a group I wouldn't expect to be particularly elegant—connoisseurs of all that was fine?

The living and bedrooms were decorated with Asian tansu chests, porcelain, jade carvings, Chinese rugs in soft pastels, and cushiony contemporary furniture. Shoji screens covered the windows. A six-paneled gilded screen filled the wall behind two oversized beds.

"A Jacuzzi!" Sasha called from the bathroom. "What a shame to be here with *you!*"

Understated and quiet, the rooms were the antithesis of the world downstairs. Things were definitely looking up. This in itself could be my retreat. I unpacked in record time, like a creature nervously establishing her turf.

Sasha dawdled. She arranged her cameras and equipment. She switched to another pocketbook and slowly decided what she'd need. She emptied half her suitcase onto the bed, then worried over the condition of her travel kit. She decided her nails needed polishing and wondered whether she could include a manicure on her expense account. "Did I tell you I'm going out tonight?" she asked.

I didn't mind. This was a place in which to vacate, to luxuriate. This was a style to which I wanted to become accustomed.

I had a four-day vacation and a choice of three books. *War and Peace*, which has been on every summer reading list of my life, because every autumn has arrived without my having read it. *Gift from the Sea*, one of my all-time favorites. And a threadbare paperback with negative literary value and a title like *Lust and Sleaze*. A student had left it behind when she galloped off to summer vacation. Of course, I was reading it purely as research into adolescent interests. But all the same, it might go well with a Jacuzzi.

"I met this guy three weeks ago, when I was down here. At Trump's, the bar in Trump Plaza. We made a date for when I'd be back on this job. If he remembers, and I hope so. He reminds me of Cary Grant."

In what way, I didn't dare ask. More dimpled chins? An English accent? A face to die for? A gift for comedy—or, more likely, a lot of wives?

"He's elegant. Continental. A gentleman." She examined her hand, first with fingers curled toward her, then held straight, nails up. "But not stuffy, the way that might sound." She stood and tossed the nail file back onto the bed.

She pushed back the shoji screens for a view of a chilly—but inviting-looking—beach and ocean, sighed, and looked likely to stay awhile.

I suddenly found the room and the situation less comforting. It was too peaceful, too deliberately serene, too incomprehensible and overrich a setting for the facts of my life.

What am I doing? I don't belong here. This is wrong.

This Asian palace was no place to figure things out. Which I felt incapable of doing, anyway.

What am I doing? What am I going to do?

The angst itch began between my shoulder blades and rose through my spinal column into my brain. At such times, it's hard to sit still and impossible to endure Sasha's glacially slow progress. "How about I meet you

somewhere later?" I asked. "Downstairs. Maybe in that
bar we passed? I have to . . . I have to move around."

"Going up to the health club?"

"No. The beach, I think. See you." I pulled on a
sweater and headed out.

In the living room of the suite there was an odd
woodcut. A mythical beast, mostly equine, but rearing
on thick bird legs. It had thick-lashed almond eyes that
seemed to ask me directly, *Do you have any idea what
you're doing?* and its mouth was open wide, revealing
not horse teeth, but long and lethal fangs.

I looked at that mouth, those fangs. "Tell me you're
not the gift horse," I whispered.

Two

MAYBE I SHOULDN'T HAVE COME AT ALL. THIS WAS MOST definitely not the beachscape I'd had in mind.

For starters, there wasn't a hint of salt and sea in the air. When I was a child, sitting in the backseat of the family car, a unique scent gave advance notice that the separate universe of the ocean was close. A mix of salt, fish, seaweed, and something indefinable, it was my favorite perfume.

Nowadays, from far off, the seashore doesn't smell of anything unless it's massively polluted. I don't know what's happened to that aroma. Either it's been overwhelmed by concrete and competing scents, or my nose has grown old and insensitive, or, according to my most Pollyannaish hypothesis, the childhood fragrance I miss was pollutants that have been removed. Unfortunately, that is also my least plausible theory.

Despite the homogenized smell of the wind, and its chill, and even this early in the season, when only private schools like Philly Prep had disbanded for summer, the boardwalk was well-populated. People eating pretzels, cotton candy, fudge, and saltwater taffy. People wearing floppy hats and bare tattooed potbellies and faded T-shirts advertising last year's action adventure movie. Muumuus over flip-flops, and baggy pants over

13

unlaced high-tops. Instead of an ocean flavor in the air, there was the pungency of peanuts, pizza, and hot dogs. Instead of the rhythmic crashing of waves, there were the pop-pops of an electronic arcade, the solicitations of tarot and palm readers, and the repeated warning "Make way, comin' through" from the Atlantic City coolies— men pushing canopied wicker chairs, oversized porch furniture on wheels. The occupants of the rolling chairs looked mildly embarrassed, but happy to be off their feet.

Nonetheless, there was an ocean a few yards off. I hurried across the boards and down the steps onto the beach, imagining the time when this stretch of marsh-land belonged to the Lenni Lenape Indians and wild ducks.

If I'd been the first outsider to discover the long, windswept sand-edged marsh, would I too have said, "Hey, this is *great*! Let's build a resort here and spoil it!"

"Ocean, emotion, promotion." Somebody's choice of motto for the city built on hucksterism.

Philadelphia was settled by people looking for a new life, new freedom, greater dignity. Atlantic City was set-tled by people looking for a buck. History shows.

The marsh was gone, but the beach was still there, slowly eroding, slowly choking on pollutants—but still there. And on this chilly day, I shared it with only one man, who made his stooped way across the horizon with a metal detecting rod. He, too, was still there, a fa-miliar piece of my childhood landscape, the beach-comber searching for lost rings and left-behind coins.

A haze of wind-agitated sand gave the tan ground a gauzy edge. Nonetheless, I pulled off my shoes and socks, rolled up my jeans, and headed for the ocean. The sand stung my ankles and was chilly under my feet, and the surf was pure ice.

On the plus side, the beach was relatively clean. No red-bag medical waste floating down from New York's hospitals, no untreated sewage visibly pouring out of storm drains, and none of the heartrending dead dolphins of a few years back. I took a deep breath and, with some relief, watched minuscule crabs diligently wait for the foamy surf to recede, then pock the wet sand with their burrows. Years ago, along with every other child, I had dug up the tiny crabs by the bucketful, and I was comforted that they had survived all of us, that a beach was still a beach, and, even slightly compromised, still good medicine.

I made my way back to the boardwalk stairs and paused to watch a silhouetted seabird dip and swoop.

Something hissed. Loudly, distinctly. The bird was too far up in the sky, and I couldn't see anything else to account for the sound—no cat, snake, leaky steampipe, or deflating balloon.

The sibilant exhale repeated. The metal-detector man had long since moved on to the next section of beach, and there was no one left except a man in a warm-up suit and a golden retriever in a kerchief, both jogging by the water's edge.

Hsssss.

Was this the fabled singing sand? Another example of poetic hyperbole?

The late-day shadows under and around the boardwalk suddenly shifted and fragmented, one piece moving forward and translating into a figure in layers of sweaters, socks, and skirts. Her hair, uncovered, was pale brown, fuzzy and thin, reminding me of a doll I had once overloved into baldness.

Still crouched, as she must have been under the boardwalk, she looked up at me from dark eyes set in a rumpled face, and, having found her balance, slowly drew herself up straight. "*Steps,*" she hissed. "*My steps.* Below for a while because it's nippy, that's all. I'm still alive, you know, even if money thinks I'm dead." Her voice darkened. "My place. Find your own."

"But—"

"One part of the beach as good as another." She waved her hands toward *elsewhere*. She wore one red and one blue glove. "People are slobs. Cans and bottles all over come summer. You'll make a buck anywhere. Wherever you are, they try to round you up, roust you out, every night. Here, too."

"But I ... I'm not ... I'm just visiting for a few days. At the casino." I wanted to think it was funny that my worn jeans and threadbare turtleneck had made her decide I was poaching her turf. But I couldn't. She was a face for my worst fears, for, I suspect, almost every underpaid, underinsured single woman's worst fears. To become the bag lady, street person—or, in this case, sand person—alone, homeless, destitute, and perhaps slightly mad. "I didn't mean to intrude."

"You get the winners." She made a throwing motion with both hands. "Pennies from heaven. Losers, too. What the hell, they say. Understand how it feels. Turn their pockets inside out."

"I'm sorry I bothered you." And I turned.

"Got a buck, then?"

At home I carry a bill or coins in my pocket for just this purpose, but I hadn't thought the situation would arise on the beach. "I only brought my room key," I said lamely. "I'll be back."

"Sure," she muttered.

"No, honestly. Will you be—are you always here?" What's a nice former girl like you doing on a desolate beach like this? I wanted to know her story—every street person's story—every step of the way down. If I knew how and why this happened, would I also know ways to keep it from happening to me? Unfortunately, the more stories I heard, the less defined and more easy the slide appeared to be.

She squinted at me intently, and, as if she'd read my mind and worst fears, she said in a matter-of-fact tone, "I was once like you. You don't think so, but I was." She chuckled softly.

Her words had a rehearsed or at least overpracticed sound, and probably were both, and she sounded slightly cracked and probably was. And that should have made her and whatever she had to say less ominous, but it didn't.

"Yes!" She flung mismatched hands toward the heavens. "Ruined!" she shouted. Then she dropped her arms and looked at me, her brow furrowed. "Men, you know?"

Just exactly how much like me had she been?

"I watch all day long." She pointed the red-gloved index finger in my direction.

"Me?"

"Everybody. The visitors. Saw The Donald last week. You know who he is? Had a good talk with him about high finance." She cackled again. Her right incisor was missing.

Of course that hadn't happened at all, but nonetheless, I had to ask. "Was he generous?"

"Generous?" She laughed so hard, she collapsed down in the sand. "Not a penny. Said he never carries small bills!" She flopped onto her back and looked up to me, and then in a world-weary voice said, "Rich men are the worst, aren't they?"

I went down the staircase and helped her up, brushing sand off her clothing, which was purely symbolic, given her residence. "Are you all right?" I asked.

"I'm Georgette."

I wondered if that was supposed to be an answer to my question. "And I'm Mandy," I said. "Pleased to meet you."

Suddenly serious, she looked me directly in the eye. "Yes," she said. "I was once like you. I had curtains at my windows, too."

SASHA WAS NOT YET IN THE BAR, BUT BEFORE I WENT UP TO retrieve her and money for the sandwoman, I detoured to the ladies' room to, among other things, wash the grit off my hands.

I couldn't stop thinking about Georgette, which is probably why I almost plowed into a nervous-looking, fussily dressed senior citizen blocking my exit. I hesitated, expecting her to move in one direction or the other, as in the normal order of business. She didn't. "Are you leaving?" I finally asked.

"What?"

"Leaving." I amplified my voice. "The door's behind you. May I use it?" I sounded stupid and she looked fuddled. "Are you all right?"

"All right. Am I all right?" She tilted her head, the better to consider the issue. Her hair was baby-chick yellow, sculpted into curls that didn't budge as she moved. "Don't trouble yourself on my account, dearie. You young people have lives of your own. I'll be fine."

Definitely off kilter and none of my business. I reached around her for the door handle.

"That is," she said, "I *hope* I'll be fine."

I took a deep breath. I had already had my peculiar-old-lady fix for the day. I had people to see, vacations to create. "What do you mean, you *hope*?" I asked, my big mouth once again working independently of my brain.

"If you insist." She folded her arms across her commodious bosom and launched into her spiel with so much gusto, I knew that I was the unfortunate fly this spider lady had been awaiting. "I'm being harassed." She leaned closer and whispered, "Sexually, like that sweet girl with the judge on the TV."

"Anita Hill? What are you talking about?"

"Why? You think she lied?"

"No—I just don't see what any of this has to do with blocking the door. Or with me."

"Honey," she said, "my *boundaries* are being *violated*. Just like they say on Sally Jessy Raphael."

"Sounds painful, but I'm supposed to meet my friend, so—"

"You have a heart of stone or you don't believe me? Which one? You think I'm too old? *He's* too old? You ever hear the expression 'dirty old man'? Or do you think men improve with age, like wine?"

I took a deep breath. "If you have a problem, report it to one of the guards, or the management, or the police."

"Nobody can touch him. He's beyond the law."

"I'm sure that's not so, miss."

"Mrs. Rudy . . ." The last name sounded like *Smirtz*. She wiped her eyes and moved on. "My late husband, may he rest in peace, was a good man. Lala. Call me Lala."

"That's quite an unusual name."

"A family nickname. My grandmother's and aunt's, too. We're all really named Henrietta. Lala is short for lallapalooza." She leaned closer to me again. "Tommy is beyond the law. Nobody would dare touch him. He nuzzles my neck and says I have heroic bosoms like a Valkyrie. He says my ankles make him weep with pleasure. But me? I'm finished with men since my Rudy passed. Tommy says he loves my spirit, that he's a romantic and he'll never give up. He comes down on the bus with me and goes back with me, too. Tries dirty things as we ride."

"Why don't you flat out tell him to get lost?"

"I'm afraid. He's connected, you know what I mean? I can't enjoy my life. I can't enjoy the casino. What kind of woman does he think I am?"

"Look, I have to leave. My advice is: take a different bus."

She curtly shook her immobile curls. "I'm not made of money, dearie. I'm an old woman, and every nickel—the bus is a charter. We pay eight dollars, they drive us here. A bargain, already, right? But then they give us five dollars for the day and a five-dollar voucher toward the next bus. How could I take another bus?"

"Don't come at all."

"I'm not entitled to a little fun? A little pleasure?"

"Well, that's quite a problem you've got." I hated to be rude to my elders, but I was going to knock her down, if necessary, to get out of here. "Be a modern woman. Risk it. Tell him you're not interested. Bring a lady friend. Bring a different man friend. Get a restraining order against him. Learn self-defense. Use your common sense!"

"Actually." She put her veiny hand on top of mine. Her nails were polished the color of bubble gum. "There *is* something you could do."

"Excuse me?" It is possible that I am actually one of those noisy ghosts who try in vain to be recognized because they don't know that people can't hear or see them. "I'm sorry," ghostly me said. "I can't."

"Such an easy thing."

I shook my head.

"Pretend to know me. Please." She stepped back and looked up at me. "Save me." At five-eight, I was a good seven inches taller, and, I assumed, forty years younger.

"I'm sorry, but—" I'm working on this other case, the lady who lives under the boardwalk, you see. The guilt office has met its daily quota and is closed.

"Five minutes, that's all. It's for a good cause. You'll do it, won't you, darling? Play along with me. In the name of sisterhood!" She raised a clenched fist.

Shameless manipulation. Impersonating a feminist. But what the hell? She really seemed afraid of this man. "Five minutes," I said, and arm in arm, we entered the darkened bar. I scanned for someone dark and broody, visibly *connected*.

Lala delivered me to a frail, freeze-dried male.

This villainous lecher who'd struck terror in Lala's heart pushed back his chair and leaped to attention. In thrall to the calendar rather than outdoor temperatures, he wore a seersucker suit and white shoes. All he lacked was a straw skimmer hat to be a perfect turn-of-the-century dandy. "Lala! Dear heart!" he said as she approached. "I was worried."

"Tommy, I want you to meet the granddaughter of an old, dear friend. . . ." Self-absorbed Lala had never asked my name. She merrily skipped on. "You remember I told you about Sherwin? The man who's infatuated with me? Can you believe that his granddaughter just showed up, and says that Sherwin is searching for me." She spoke at about twice the tempo she'd used in the ladies' room, and things moved so quickly that as angry as I was becoming, when Tommy put out a hand that looked like a pterodactyl's, I shook it.

"I'm Amanda," I said.

"Oh, no," he answered. "*I'm* a-man-da. You're a-girl-da. Sit, sit, sit." He waved at the table he'd been at. We all continued to stand.

"Pleasure to meet you," Tommy said, covering his wretched joke's flat wake. "Any friend of Lala's . . ." His attention returned, adoringly, to Ms. Smirtz. "I don't seem to remember any Sherwin," he said.

"Really?" Her laugh was an incredulous tinkled scale, like spoons on crystal. "He's the one who took me to Rome that time I had an urge for pasta."

I exhaled loudly, angrily. "It's been great, but—"

"I think maybe I won't go back to the city with you tonight, Tommy. Sweetie here says Sherwin's desperate to see me." Lala sighed extravagantly.

"Whatever happened to subtlety?" I muttered. "Or honesty?" They both ignored me.

"Please, Lala!" Tommy said. "Come back with me."

Lala shook her head like a wild young thing, although the glued-together curls refused to toss and she looked like she had a crenelated skull.

"Don't make any rash decisions. Let's talk this through." Tommy interrupted his pleas to wave at a beefy bald man. The man's companion, a creature with straight black hair and a red dress laminated to her flesh, flicked a glance our way. The man did not. "I was just telling Big Julius there about you, Lala," Tommy said.

"That's Big Julius? Isn't he . . . oh, my, I've heard about him. The garbage business, isn't it?" She looked at me and hissed, "See what I mean? *Big Julius!* And what did you tell Big Julius about me?" she asked in her normal voice.

"That I was crazy about you, of course." He elbowed me. "I'm crazy about this lady," he said. Then he looked back at his love object. "Big Julius is a nice man, despite his reputation."

"It's been a treat, but I have to run now," I said.

"She's leaving you stranded, Lala," Tommy said. "All mine again. That means you're not running off with this Sherwin person. I'll wine and dine you and we will ride off into the sunset together at the back of the bus. Look, over there. It's McDog. The one whose business partner blew himself up, or so the official story goes. And over there . . ."

Watching them was mildly fascinating, a game of ego Ping-Pong. Tommy served hyped inside dope on mobsters he pretended to have known, and Lala returned the serve with ever-escalating tales of the imaginary Sherwin's generosity and lust.

"They all love me," Tommy said with some desperation. "Every single one of them. They tell me everything. They call me the Safe Deposit, get it? I keep their secrets. See him?" he said of a respectable gray-haired business type in conversation with the bartender. "He has three days left to pay off his loan or die. He's not lucky at the tables the way I am."

"You didn't seem so lucky today," Lala said.

"Not yet, maybe," Tommy answered. "But I was out of the game for a while, after all."

"He was hit by a roulette ball that jumped," Lala explained.

Tommy rubbed the back of his hand. I could see a dark bruise on the leathery skin. "My luck's changing," he said. "I feel it in my bones—long as you're with me, Lala."

"But Sherwin—"

"See her?" Tommy pointed at a woman with yellow-white big hair. "Sinatra used to be very fond of her. You catch my drift? *Very*. But she is reputed to have killed her husband and eaten the corpse so there was no evidence."

"Sherwin says every woman deserves a—"

"See him?" Tommy said of a redhead who had just entered the cocktail lounge. "Supposedly an antique dealer, but really Jersey's number one hit man."

Lala shuddered with delight.

"Aren't drinks free in the casinos?" I asked. "Why are all these men coming into the bar?"

"A change of scene," Tommy said.

"A little socializing," Lala added. "A little schmoozing."

"A little business," Tommy said, sotto voce.

I thought about the vacation plans I had abandoned. At this point, cleaning closets sounded like keen fun.

"I broke her grandfather's heart when I turned him down," Lala said.

"Turned him down for what?" Tommy asked.

Closets sounded irresistible.

"Turned him down for *marriage*," Lala said. "Despite his money."

Tommy is not one of my responsibilities, I told myself. I do not have to warn him. If he'd reached this age without realizing when a scam was being pulled on him—and a shaggy, preposterous, clichéd scam at that—then he deserved Lala.

Tommy was nearly hyperventilating. "You see that woman? A Mafia princess raised in total seclusion, they were so afraid somebody would take her hostage, but she and Ralph the Scar . . ."

I obediently swiveled once again. It seemed the polite thing to do. And I did a double take. The Mafia princess was none other than Sasha, who now stood resplendently at the bar in peacock silk and high-button boots. Gee, and I'd always thought that her father was simply a much-married orthodontist. What a unique front for his criminous ways. "Good luck to both of you," I said.

"Darling," Lala began. "Don't run away because you're so upset that I might not wind up with Grandpop."

I went to join Sasha, who was in a clump of casino escapees. A few were on stools—including the gray-haired man Tommy said had three days to pay or die. He didn't look particularly worried about it, and in fact seemed tilted toward Sasha, a smile on his face. She smiled back. And that's how it was—a pending date with Mr. Wonderful didn't mean you couldn't meanwhile line up his successors.

I tapped her on the shoulder.

"Where've you been?" she asked. "Frankie," she said to the bartender, "this is my friend Mandy, the one I was talking about." Frankie nodded at me without much interest. "You had a call from your detective," Sasha said.

"Mackenzie? Why?"

"He must have detected you."

Which didn't take much skill. My answering machine message said where I was.

"He's here in River City, too," Sasha said. "You can run but you can't hide." She handed me a hotel postcard with a phone number scrawled on its back.

The elusive cop was here. I shook my head in wonderment. "I thought it was only hype, but it's obviously true. This really *must* be America's most popular vacation destination."

Three

ANY OBJECTIVE REEVALUATION OF MY RELATIONSHIP WITH
Mackenzie required distance, so I gave up on both objectivity and reevaluation for a while.

Mackenzie mysteriously manages to seem writ in capital letters, despite his easy Southern style. He doesn't strut, he doesn't shout, he doesn't push, and I honestly don't know what it is he does do. It can't all be his smile and drawl, can it? That's some of what I'd meant to work out while I was here.

"I came down because Nicky B. grew up here," he explained. Nicky B. was the prime suspect in a missing and presumed murdered child case. The police were so positive that Mr. B. had done it that they had turned the press on him, but they could find nothing except an abiding and unwholesome strangeness in the man's interests, and that was not enough to make a case or an arrest. "Thought maybe there was somethin' we'd missed, somethin' relevant. Turns out, the house he grew up in at the Inlet's gone. Whole street is pretty much gone. In fact, the entire neighborhood looks like Beirut. Nothing but rubble except for a lone, half-boarded-up house here and there an' people who look like they barely survived the destruction."

I knew, so he definitely knew, that he could have

found out about Nicky B.'s former neighborhood by
telephone and fax and computer database. Or even
through common knowledge. The Inlet, never prime
real estate, had been bulldozed a decade and a half ago
in anticipation of a casino-supported renaissance that is
due to appear along about the same time as Godot.

When the casino referendum was pending, the pro-
moters' ads showed $100 bills falling from the sky, and
when the referendum passed, people danced in the
streets. But money has not yet descended from the
stratosphere, certainly not in the direction of the Inlet,
and anybody who knew anything about the gilt-edged
poverty-stricken city knew about the ruins at the end of
the boardwalk. That probably even included Mackenzie's good old boys back home in the Louisiana bayou.

"Guess I'm not the best detective in the whole entire
universe. Guess I goofed and I'm forced to take an actual day or so off," he drawled. "Thought maybe we
could spend it together."

Actual time together, without murderous interruptions. My defenses against the man wobbled precariously.

"Thought we might watch the sunset, find a really
good restaurant, maybe gamble a little bit, hear
music . . ."

His voice was as soothing, his accent as balmy as I'd
hoped the beach would be. I shelved all decisions of
what to do about him until some less enjoyable moment
in our relationship.

THAT MOMENT CAME—AND IT WASN'T EVEN MACKENZIE'S
fault—via a telephone call to his hotel room at approximately one A.M. I could barely remember where I was,
let alone where the telephone might be. Mackenzie
reoriented himself more quickly, finding both a lamp
switch and the receiver.

I heard a deafening squawk from the other end. Yet

another crank or drunk or pervert. "Hang up," I said. "Just hang up. Don't listen. Shouldn't have turned on the light." I replumped my pillow.

"She's right here." Mackenzie handed me the receiver. "Sasha," he said.

"Mandy!" she shouted. "Thank God! I was going crazy! At first, I couldn't remember where you'd be. Couldn't remember—"

Shades of my mother when I stayed out too late on a date. But this was Sasha and this was ridiculous. "What's wrong with you? Stop shouting!"

"—what hotel he'd said he was at, so how was I going to find you and—"

Frankly, I had barely thought she'd notice my absence. "Calm down," I said. "What's the big deal?"

She spluttered through every word I said. "Big deal? Mandy, you don't—"

"Calm—"

"*Don't tell me to calm down!* I've been arrested for murder!"

How do you respond to a statement like that? The replies that charged into my mind seemed clumsy and primitive, not to mention disloyal. Questions such as: who? why you? did you? Instead of asking any of them, I mouthed her words to Mackenzie, who glared at the phone. I held the receiver slightly out, between the two of us, so he also could hear.

I took a deep breath. "Tell me about it," I said.

"I came back to the room an hour or so ago."

"Alone?" You couldn't get into trouble if you came home alone. Wasn't that what Mama always said?

"Yes! If you'd just *listen*! Alone. I thought you might be in there, remember? I wasn't going to bring anybody in. But instead of you, there was a dead man in the bed, in my bed! And blood all over the place. And all over my clothing. That lamp—that gorgeous marble lamp, remember? The police think its base was what killed—oh, God—my clothing—my *slip* covered with blood on the floor!"

Maybe my mind wasn't willing to compute everything she was saying, so it fixated on the slip. I hadn't known she wore such garments. They seemed too prissy and middle class for Sasha, wrong for her loose-flowing style. Whole or half? What color? What fabric? I had to literally shake my head to dislodge the issue of the slip.

"My bra. *My own things!* Scattered around, as if I'd dropped them one by one. You know I didn't. You were there when I left."

"Yes." She left her room neat, Ma.

"The beds had been turned down and all. There was still a chocolate on yours, Mandy!" Snuffling and nose-blowing.

"Listen, calm— I'm sorry, didn't mean to say that, but—"

"There's more. Worse. An open bottle of champagne and two glasses. A bloody washcloth, wet towels, as if I took a shower and washed off. I feel like I'm going crazy, and these cops, they act like it's an open-and-shut case. I don't think I even know the man!"

"It's obviously some horrible mistake." I was on autobabble, putting out noise because I wished she hadn't said *think*. "You mean there's a chance you do— did know him?" I whispered.

"I can't tell. If you'd seen him—he was bloody, crushed—I couldn't even *look*, let alone—" She inhaled and exhaled loudly. When she spoke again, her voice was firmer, more resolute. "I didn't recognize him and I certainly didn't kill him. But they found his card in a pair of my slacks in the closet. With a private phone number penciled on it. How did they find his card there?"

I shook my head and made sympathetic noises. I didn't have any answers. Surely not at 1:09 A.M. after forty-two minutes of sleep. I did have a question, however. "Who is—who was he?"

"Somebody named Jesse Reese, they said."

I looked at Mackenzie. "What happens next?" I whispered.

He was shaking his head and blinking hard, trying to wake up fully. He mumbled a catalogue of procedures, all the while getting out of bed. Preliminary examination. Middle of the night. Probable delays. Arraignment. Bail. He left the room.

Obviously, a lot had to happen, and all of it would take time. "So let me get this straight. They think you came in and murdered this guy? What time?" I heard the shower run in the bathroom.

"Around nine or ten." Sasha's voice was dull, mechanical. "They say I cleaned myself up and left, then came back again around eleven and pretended to be shocked by what I found." She sounded exhausted.

"But you have an alibi, Sasha! Did you tell them?"

"What is it?"

She was really not herself. Her brain had frozen. "Your date—Cary Grant!" I tried not to sound impatient.

"Dunstan?"

"If that was his name. You were with him, weren't you?"

Only silence on the line.

Having completed the world's shortest shower, Mackenzie reentered the bedroom during this frustrating exchange. He looked at me quizzically. I looked back at him, but not quizzically. I looked at the man's long and lovely body, wrapped in a towel, and I mourned the minivacation we were now not going to have. Worst of all, I couldn't even blame the ruin of this one on him.

"Not exactly," Sasha finally said. "The evening didn't go all that terrifically. He turned out to be pretty boring."

"Listen, I don't care about your romantic life. I care about your *neck*. He can get you out of this mess."

"Don't bother."

"What is he, another one hiding out from the cops like your dead Dimples? Another big- or small-time hoodlum?"

"No. He's a photographer. Like me. But he wasn't with me the whole time. After dinner, we walked awhile, then we split. I went back to our hotel, and he said he was going back to Trump's."

"When exactly did you separate? How long was he with you?"

"Mandy, was I ever the kind to watch the clock? I don't know. That's the problem. Maybe nine o'clock, maybe later. I walked, then I stopped in the bar and kind of made a date with Frankie the bartender."

"God, Sasha, your frenetic social life is literally killing you!" I hadn't meant to be that loud or sharp, but I must say it felt good to be openly angry about her stupidities and excesses. "Okay, then, did *Frankie* go upstairs with you?"

Mackenzie raised an eyebrow at the name switch.

"I told you," Sasha said. "Nobody did. We were going to meet later on. He was working two shifts."

"Even so, if Dunstan was with you till near nine—and maybe it was actually later—and Frankie a while later, maybe between them we could establish that you were not in the room. Where can I find Dunstan? What's his whole name? Is he in the book?"

Mackenzie was almost dressed, and flashing me looks that said I should do the same.

"I don't know his last name or address," Sasha said, "and don't you dare say a word. You don't know the first name of somebody you've been seeing for a year!"

I held my tongue—an extremely painful activity. I didn't say that it was not the same thing at all. I did hope, however, that it was not the same thing at all.

"When I met him three weeks ago, he was at the next table. We were both with groups of other people. It was all very flirty. A fifties movies thing. No data, just patter. Fun, you know?"

I grudgingly admitted that I did know. It could happen. Last names would have weighted down the bubble.

"I was coming back down for this job," Sasha said, "so we planned to meet again, same place, which is what we did. He either remembered, or he's always there. We ate in the casino, at Ivana's—you'd think he'd have changed that name to Marla's, wouldn't you?"

"Dunstan?"

"Donald."

"Maybe somebody at Ivana's will recognize you."

"Yeah." She sounded doubtful.

"Did he charge the dinner?" How many Dunstans could there be? Last name or not, we'd find his charge slip. And while we're visiting fantasyland, let's add that the charge slip wouldn't be the preprinted form, but one of those vertical printouts that list the time of sale. And, of course, that would turn out to be precisely the same moment as Jesse Reese's time of death. Alibi by Visa.

Sasha was silent while she thought about this, and when she spoke, her voice was dull. "Cash. Said he'd just won a bundle. I think maybe he gambles a lot."

"Did you tell the police?"

"About his bets?"

"No, about—"

"That I was on a sort of date with a man whose last name and address I don't know at about the time when they think this man was murdered? Yes. They weren't too impressed." She sighed, and I could feel more bad news coming. "They have a witness," she said.

"How is that possible? To what?"

"To my going into the room with Jesse Reese and another man, right before it happened."

"Another man? Who?"

"How would I know? *I wasn't there!* The witness is crazy. None of it's true!"

This seemed a good time to reassure her that help was on the way, in the form of the Pepper-Mackenzie posse, and to more privately cross fingers and hope that was the truth.

I SET OUT WITH MACKENZIE FOR SASHA'S JAIL, BUT EN route I realized that I had to go to Trump's instead. Mackenzie was not pleased by the idea.

"Even if just for moral support, shouldn't you be with Sasha?" he asked. "Ah'm certainly not a real welcome sight to her." He was *ahm*ing, a sure sign he was agitated, really didn't approve of my detour. Or he just didn't want to be alone with Sasha, his longtime antagonist. But the *ahm*ier he got, the more resolute I became.

"Explain it to her," I said. "I'll be there as soon as I can, but meantime, somebody's done a good job of making Sasha look guilty as hell, and this Dunstan is her only alibi."

"True," Mackenzie said. "But even so—"

"He told her he was coming back here after their date. We don't have a last name or an address, so the first hurdle is finding him, and I have a better chance of, um, discovering him than you or the police."

"You playin' bar girl or detective?" he grumbled.

He didn't particularly like my playing either role, so I stayed with my thesis. "You have a much better chance of speeding up the process with the local force than I do," I said. "This is an appropriate division of labor. Find out what they know. About that witness, particularly. About what's going to happen to Sasha."

"Still an' all—"

"What if Dunstan bolts and disappears when he picks up his morning paper and sees his date in a mug shot? I have to find him tonight, before he knows what's going on."

"Maybe he's left. Gone to bed."

"Easy enough to find out. If so, I'll nurse a pot of decaf and wait for you. I'll be safe, indoors, and I'll feel like I at least tried to do something useful."

When he let me out of the car, he leaned over and gave me a brotherly kiss on the forehead. "Can't tell you how much I didn't want this kind of adventure," he said. "Can't begin to."

I took that inarticulate pronouncement to be the best news in a long time on the subject of us.

I TRIED TO BECOME SASHA, TO ADD FOUR INCHES TO MY height and geometric increments to my self-confidence. Otherwise, I would have had to admit how creepy I felt about sashaying into a bar in the wee hours of the morning. Particularly this bar, with columns that looked sequined and a loud combo playing "Feelings." What else, but "Feelings"? How would Sasha do it? *Why* would Sasha do it?

I tried a round of Intuitively Spot the Dunstan, and failed. Cary Grant's image fell between me and the bar like a glowing scrim. Nobody came close. Why hadn't I asked for a description of her date?

I sat down. The bar was copper-topped with red leather trim. Above it two TVs played, their sound off. On the right screen a game of tennis silently proceeded. The left featured men in togas. *Quo Vadis,* I thought, but it was hard to tell, as they appeared to be lip-synching to the band's inimitable and interminable rendition of "Feelings."

"Help you?" The bartender had bright red hair and an air of competent no-nonsense. I ordered a Virgin Mary. She nodded brusquely. It was too early in my truncated day for alcohol. Anyway, at long last, I was high on life. Or at least high on the small thrill of being awake and in a bar at this hour, an experience completely off my bell-shaped curve. I had inverted time and entered a night world I generally missed.

The bartender put down my spicy tomato concoction. "Delicious," I said after sipping. I wondered what she was doing here, past midnight, what kind of a job this

was and how it worked for her life. My speculations
must have shown.

She chuckled. "Husband can be home with the kids
this way," she said. "Until he finishes grad school.
That's what brings me here. How about you?"

"I'm . . . my friend . . . I'm looking for a guy named
Dunstan."

She raised her eyebrows. "Wouldn't have expected
that," she said, with a quick, sad shake of her head.
"He's a fixture around these parts. Stays, off and on, till
three or four A.M. most nights." She turned around and
busied herself polishing the pour spout of a scotch bottle. Then she turned back. "Look, whether you want it
or not, here's some unsolicited advice. In the spirit of
sisterhood, right? Forget Dunstan. He's all packaging.
There's no future there. Not much of a present, either."

"I'm not planning to be involved with him," I said,
but of course, that's female code for just the opposite,
which is how the bartender took it. "But what are you
trying to say? Is he married?"

She looked amused. "I doubt it, although he says so
to stay clear of entanglements. Saw it in an old Cary
Grant movie."

"Were you here all evening? Did you see him tonight? Was he with a woman?"

She shrugged. "I didn't come on until midnight, and
when I saw him, he was alone. I hope that doesn't encourage you." Then she did a minor double take, and
cocked her head to the right. "But speak of the devil."

So there he was, the devil or Cary Grant. Take your
pick. He wasn't nearly as handsome as I'd expected,
and much shorter than anticipated. Not a midget, but
average. Sasha must have towered over him in her high-
button boots. She might be accused of homicide, but of
heightism, never. I took a deep breath, lifted my glass in
a toast, and smiled.

If this didn't work, I was going to be profoundly hu-
miliated and my best friend was going to spend the rest

of her life in a dungeon. I sidled off my bar stool. "You must be Dunstan," I murmured.

I felt like a fool. Going on two A.M., running on adrenaline and anxiety and borrowing lines from a B movie. But that was all I could think of except for the infinitely tackier "Hi, stranger."

Dunstan didn't faint with joy at my approach, but neither did he hold up a cross and say *begone*. He waited for more data. I hadn't expected him to be this cautious. "Sasha wanted me to look you up," I said.

He moved his head to the left and looked at me from a side view, eyes narrowed, judgment suspended.

How bad of a date had they had? "Sasha Berg," I said. "You remember her, don't you?"

He laughed, showing teeth that did, indeed, rival Cary's. "You mean do I have short-term memory loss?" he asked. "Remember her after what, a few hours?" He waved me to a booth. "Join me," he said. "But what is this? Some sort of tag team? A relay?"

His accent was semi-Cary, like someone from a mid-Atlantic island, if only there were such a place. But unidentifiable didn't mean uncharming.

In his engaging voice he asked standard opening questions. The how-long-are-you-down-for and where-are-you-from and what-do-you-do preliminaries.

Then I remembered that I was the one who was supposed to be doing the interviewing. "What about you?" I asked when there was a lull. "Your accent isn't quite English or American."

He laughed. "Doesn't it sound like Trueheart, Wisconsin?"

"Not really."

"Thought I'd pass for a native by now. We moved there when I was fairly young." He smiled with the ease of someone who takes it for granted that his audience is smitten.

And in truth, it wouldn't be difficult to be smit. There was something elegant, continental about him. I suddenly remembered a personals ad I'd seen. I window-shop that section. In case of emergencies. This particular ad promised "great looks and manors, too." I, of course, never found out whether the ad-placer had country mansions or simply bad spelling. But Dunstan had that "great looks and manors, too" attitude.

"I'm a Trueheart boy. 'Trueheart, Trueheart,' " he sang. " 'Through all our days, we who love you sing your praise.' Brilliant lyrics, don't you think?"

"Listen," I said. "I need your help. So does Sasha. Not in any big way, just by establishing that she was with you." I told the incredible story of her arrest, skipping the more tawdry details, such as her bloody slip. "Obviously, somebody's done a very good job of framing her, but they couldn't have known that she was with somebody, out in public. Probably other people saw you both, too. Waiters. The bartender on that shift. Other people in the restaurant. Sasha's kind of . . . she's generally noticeable."

"Murder?" He sounded stuck on that, horrified in a refined sort of way.

I nodded. "Isn't it awful? How about we take a cab to the station and you make your statement and clear this up now?"

He looked at me for a long while before speaking. His eyes were pale brown, almost caramel. For the first time, I noticed how little light there was in them. "I'm afraid you've misunderstood," he said. "I have nothing to tell the police. I barely know your friend." Each word was clipped with precision. Trueheart's English teachers must be great.

"But you were with her. You said so yourself, didn't you? Didn't you just say that to me? That's all I'm asking you to tell the police. You two had a date. You're her *alibi.*"

"You misheard. I *saw* her. Right here, at some point in the evening. Briefly, and I can't say when. I remember her. That's all I was agreeing to."

Is that what he'd really said? Meant? Why? Unless Sasha was lying. All the deferred exhaustion flooded me. "You're saying you were not with her tonight?"

"Yes," he answered quite calmly. "That is precisely what I am saying."

"But that isn't true, and it would be *easy* to help her out."

He shrugged, and then he bolted. He stood and walked away double time, out of the bar, across a small open space, and into the casino.

He had left me—and the bill—without a backward glance. Once I realized he had gone AWOL, I leaped up and followed after him, but I couldn't see over the tops of the one-armed bandits. I searched each avenue peopled by solemn folk who pulled levers as if it were an obligation to be completed as quickly as possible. Even when their efforts were rewarded by a cascade of coins, they seemed only dimly interested.

I felt like a lost child. The heavy chandeliers and the gilded mirror ceiling that refracted and reflected the scene below further disoriented me. There was light everywhere, its source nowhere, and obscure music as well, a barely audible up-tempo like a subliminal racing pulse.

"Dunstan?" I called, even though I knew it was both futile and annoying. Everyone's eyes stayed glued on the machines. I ran toward where I thought I'd seen him. "Dunstan?" The craps players nodded, pointed, pushed chips across the table, watched with rapt attention as a woman threw the dice. Not a one of them reacted to my voice. I moved aside to make way for a cocktail waitress in a tiny gold-thread tutu. She handed a man a drink, and he plunked a tip of chips onto her tray.

"Dunstan," I said, no longer bothering to call it out. I just barely controlled the urge to have either a tantrum or a crying fit.

What the devil was going on?

Four

I WENT BACK TO THE BAR, HOPING FOR INSPIRATION. IT never arrived, but Mackenzie did. He looked as weary as I felt. He also looked grim as I told him my bad news and he told me his. Sasha was still being held. She'd be arraigned in the morning, if we were all lucky. And bail would be set if we were luckier still.

"They're reluctant to let a killer awaiting trial loose," he said.

"Sasha? A killer? That's the most ridiculous . . ." I shook my head. "She can't hold a grudge more than five minutes, particularly against a man. That's part of her problem. And this man—she didn't even know him."

I brushed away the memory of her hesitation on that point. "Can I see her?"

"Now? At nearly three A.M.?" He sighed and changed the topic. "I saw the witness. He was there, makin' his statement."

"Who is he?"

"Feeble old guy. Looks caved-in, curled up. But he can see pretty well with his glasses on. Came up to his room to take his pill at nine o'clock, he says. Waitin' for the elevator to go back down when he saw them at the door of the room. Thought some hanky-panky—

38

that's what he called it—was goin' on. Somethin' kinky with one big woman and two men. I'm not sure if he wanted to be the morality Nazi—or the third man in the hanky-pank. Anyway, he ID'd a picture of Jesse Reese. That's who he saw. Then he ID'd Sasha in a lineup, too. Says the other guy had dark hair and was shorter than Sasha, but that's all he remembers. Unfortunately, it was 'the big woman'—actually, he said girl, the 'big girl with all the hair' who caught his eye."

"He probably didn't have his glasses on, or he was confused. Maybe he was watching an entirely different room. Did they think of that?"

"They tried to find other witnesses to corroborate his story. Woke up the couple in the next room. They knew nothing. Hearing aids were off. The woman on the other side was down at the tables all night."

"Or so she says. She picks up two guys and frames—"

He shook his head as if it were heavy. "She's maybe three hundred pounds and short. Not easily mistaken for Sasha or either of those men."

"Who? Who is—was—the dead man?"

"Jesse Reese."

"I know that part, but who *was* he?" I wanted to hear that he was scum and that the world was well rid of him.

"Your basic man-of-the-year type. Had a multimillion-dollar investment firm plus did a lot of teachin', 'specially for senior citizens. Courses in Financial Survival. No charge. His way of paying back society, he said. Called it his *pro bono* work. Safeguardin' little old ladies' purses."

I hated it. He sounded like the hero of a Frank Capra movie, which made the whole situation worse for Sasha. "What was he doing in a casino hotel?" I demanded, as if being in such a room—my room, in fact—constituted guilt.

Mackenzie raised one eyebrow. "He was dyin', although I suspect he had other hopes for the evenin'. He was a familiar face there, a regular. Generally given that very suite, in fact. Wasn't expected last night, however."

"So he's a gambler." I folded my hands. "The mob did it, then. I rest my case."

Mackenzie sighed. "It is really not their style to buy champagne first. Or to sprinkle undies around. This is— forgive me, but this verges on the baroque. It's overorganized crime, almost *cute*, an' that is not the mob's style. Assumin' there's a reason for them to be miffed with him in the first place."

"That's the only thing that makes sense."

"Mandy, I think you'll have to accept the idea that nothin' makes sense to you right now. An' worse, it may *never* make sense. But to the police, it makes sense already, and what makes sense to them is that Sasha killed him."

"Simply because somebody chose her hotel room to break into." *Our* hotel room, a solemn voice in me corrected. Ours. What if Mackenzie hadn't shown up? I had planned on room service, an evening of luxurious solo vacationing. Did the real killer know I was also checked in there? Care? Would I have been a second corpse?

Mackenzie tilted back on his chair. I think men feel compelled to balance chairs on their rear legs just so women can warn them that they'll topple over—and be proved wrong. What macho test is it, anyway? I managed not to say a word and almost to pay attention to what he was saying—although, of course, the whole time, I waited for him to fall over backward.

He had the ability to balance on two chair legs and read my mind at the same time. " 'Course," he said, "th'other most likely suspect would be you, darlin'. You are also tall—"

"Not as tall as—"

"—an' dark-haired."

"Sasha has black hair. Mine's brown, a lot of red and no curls."

"The thing is, you need not worry. You have the perfect alibi. Me. An officer of the law. Who could doubt me? Hope you're properly grateful." He brought his chair back to normal position. "Or, when the time is more appropriate, improperly grateful."

"Everything," I said, "is so obviously a setup. Every bit of what they think is evidence could have been planted and arranged—and in a matter of minutes. His business card in her slacks. The slip and the underwear. The champagne. I mean it adds up to *nothing* when you think about it."

"Had a reputation as a ladies' man. Married, but been there before with various and sundry."

"So he *was* a scumbag."

"What's your point? That it's okay to kill people who are morally deficient?" he asked mildly.

"No, but—"

"If we base character evaluations on whether or not somebody's sexually adventuresome, then your friend Sasha is likely to be put in the same cubbyhole as the late Mr. Reese. An' aside from that failure of the flesh, Jesse Reese was considered a paragon of virtue."

I snorted my disdain, something I wouldn't dream of doing at normal hours when I am more in control.

"A real Mr. Do-good," Mackenzie said.

"Well, I'm sorry. I just don't think somebody who is *infamous* for gambling and whoring around is Mr. Wonderful." Nonetheless, I felt a growing chill inside, something like having a prison bar slipped down my esophagus. Innocent though she was, Sasha was in deep and profound trouble.

"Okay," Mackenzie said, "let's look at a different issue." His tone was obnoxiously patient, almost pedantic. I didn't want reasoning or evidence—I wanted magical solutions. "Aside from havin' a witness *see* her enter, there's the question of how an imposter would get

the key. There wasn't any break-in. It's real hard to duplicate those computerized cards, and it's not like the
last tenant could pass it on, 'cause they change it every
time."

I waved away that objection. "I heard that's not true,
that they lie and reuse keys. Besides, I'm sure it's possible to get a duplicate."

"How? Go to the desk and say 'Hi, make me a room
key'?"

"Don't be facetious. This is life and death."

"What would you say? 'I'm so busy holding this
drugged man—' "

"Drugged? They think somebody drugged the dead
man?"

He nodded. "Staggerin', the old man witness said. He
didn't drink enough to be drunk." He looked at me and
shook his head. "Nobody at the desk got a request for
a duplicate."

"Maybe she lost her key, dropped it somewhere, and
the killer found it."

"And knew the room number, right?" Mackenzie
said. " 'Cause it's never on those keys."

"Well, maybe—"

"Sasha didn't lose her key, Mandy. She used it to let
herself into the room, remember?"

I sat in silence, fiddling with the wedge of lime on
my Virgin Mary. Was it possible that Sasha had become
involved in somebody else's bad dream? That she *was*
involved, and the second man, the accomplice, was one
of her evening's two men? Dunstan, or even Frankie the
good guy?

The red-haired bartender eyed me and my second-
shift male companion either enviously or suspiciously.

Mackenzie ordered orange juice.

"This is very strange." My voice sounded hollow,
foreign, as if coming in on a poorly engineered sound
track. I had the dissociated sensation that this wasn't really happening. Soon I'd wake up and chuckle over

how *real* it had felt. "Every detail makes it stranger," I said. "And there are so many details."

I squeezed the lime over my ice cubes. "She wasn't there!" I bleated, lamely, because how was she going to prove that, or anything? Even I was beginning to find her denial boggy and suspect. I couldn't think my way past the bloody slip or the business card in her slacks, or the witness or the door key. The only possible route around that seemed with Dunstan, who, I hoped, wouldn't turn out to be part of the crime, the second man the witness saw. I stood up. "We have to find that lousy date of hers."

Mackenzie's expression was blank, as if he'd turned off his mind. "Not now, surely," he murmured. "I was plannin' on maybe a little rest. It's nearly tomorrow. My eyes feel corrugated."

"Aren't you the one who always says the first forty-eight hours are the most important?"

"Yes, but . . . but . . ."

I went over to the bartender. Business was slack, even here, at three-thirty Tuesday morning. The combo played "Sunrise, Sunset," in a whine of violins, but softly. "Hate to bother you again," I said, "but I need Dunstan's last name."

She put down a glass she'd been polishing and looked at me with open disgust. "Why?" she asked. "Your new one's cuter. And he's not a lounge lizard. In fact, I've never seen him in here before. Isn't it time to end the stereotype of women only wanting rats? The Dunstans of this world have had a free ride for too long!" She seemed on the verge of climbing onto the bar and declaiming.

"Halt," I said. "This has nothing to do with me. I agree with you completely, but I'm asking on behalf of a friend."

"Hah! The old *friend* business! You tell your *friend* that I don't want anything to do with Dunstan and neither should she!"

"Do you know his last name?"

"He's just Dunstan. Like Svengali. Or Zippy, in the comics."

"Do you know anybody who knows his last name?"

"He gave me his card. Slick piece of work, just like him. Looks like a camera. Clear plastic in the middle, for the lens. That's where his name and phone number were. But why give it to me, a bartender? Unless I was supposed to pimp for him—pass it along to likely conquests."

"Could I see it?" I knew the answer, but I had to ask anyway.

The red spikes of hair looked lethal. "Think I'd keep it? Tossed it right out!"

I sighed. "Can you remember what it said?"

"I'm not procuring for an arrogant lounge lizard with an accent!" For emphasis, she pounded her fist on the copper-topped bar. "I'm not one of those traitors who swoons at the sound of the King's English. I don't care what Princess Di wears. I don't even think they should keep that parasitical royal family!"

"All I want is Dunstan's last name."

"I swear, if my daughter shows tendencies in this self-destructive direction, I will personally take her out and—"

Bartenders were supposed to be listeners, not impassioned orators. Another myth shattered, and I had so few of them left. "Please," I said. "I am not interested in Dunstan, except for his last name. Maybe even where he works. My friend is—"

She shook her head in irritation. "Take responsibility for your life! Stop playing games, hiding behind the cloak of a friend. If women would only own their own lives, if—"

What the hell? It was going to be all over the papers in two hours or so. "My friend's accused of murder."

Amazing what that word will do. "Murder?" she whispered.

"She's only accused," I said. "She didn't do it. She was with Dunstan at the time. I came to find him, to get him to go to the police. Only he heard the word 'murder' and ran away. I never found out his last name. My friend doesn't know it, either."

She wiped the bar top, vigorously. "So who is this Dunstan-loving murderous friend of yours, then?"

"Her name is Sasha Berg. She's a photographer. She doesn't love Dunstan at all and she isn't a murderer. And what I need is *his* name."

She tilted her head back, let her jaw drop and rolled her eyes up in a great show of concentration. Even the spikes of hair seemed to stand on tippytoe, the better to strain for memory. "Dunstan, Dunstan," she murmured. "Dunstan—something-wrong-for-him-last-name. Something wholesome. With an S . . . no, an F . . . F-R . . . Frrr . . . Fllll . . . Nothing's coming."

There were other ways, I reminded myself. Even if nothing pulled up from her data bank, I didn't have to despair. There'd been another bartender on duty earlier who might remember Sasha. There was the restaurant, with waiters, hostesses, and fellow diners. Together, they might be able to put together a good accounting of Sasha's time.

If, of course, anyone had been paying attention. If, of course, the tourists who ate in the restaurant tonight were staying over until such time as we found them or they read a notice in the paper about the crime. If, of course, they hadn't gone home, been too drunk to notice, been on some illicit assignation which they wouldn't want to discuss with the police. If, of course, there were enough of those lucky, available rare types who know what they saw at what hour so that together, we could piece together a patchwork accounting of Sasha's evening.

Which meant we were never going to find nonstop Sasha monitors. Even if every improbable witness contingency worked out, there was always the lapse, the

unaccounted-for period while the observers got on with
their own lives or simply went to the bathroom. Only
Dunstan could establish that Sasha had been far from
the murder scene for that long block of time.

The bartender was still making sounds, but more feebly. "Foooo . . . Hold on, it's getting close. I can almost
hear it now. Fill . . . Fit . . . Fis . . ." She shook her head.
"Hell, I give up."

"Keep going—her life is at stake."

"Faaa . . . Famm . . . Farr . . . *Farmer*!" She was so
loud that Mackenzie popped up from his chair.

"I thought he was a photographer." Cary Grant tend-
ing New Jersey chickens and pigs?

"That's his name. Dunstan Farmer."

"And where does he live?"

"Someplace nearby, must be. He's here almost every
night, after all. In the casino, then in here for finding
women. Doesn't seem to have steady male pals. Or
steady female pals, at that."

His skewed social life didn't bother me. I had his
name now, and a light-headed giddy conviction that I'd
find him and settle this—a hope that was so unfounded,
it couldn't have happened except at four A.M. to a
woman worn down by a year of teaching, a dubious relationship, serious sleep deprivation, and a best friend
accused of murder.

THE POLICE WOULDN'T LET ME HAVE MY CLOTHING. NOT
even my toothbrush. "Crime scene. They're still working on it," the guard at the door said. And then he questioned me on my whereabouts at the time of the crime
and brought in a buddy with the same questions all over
again, just in a higher-pitched voice. They bullied me in
the name of the law until Mackenzie intervened and I
was freed.

But I still couldn't have my toothbrush. From now
on, just in case of murder or other emergencies, I'd
carry one with me at all times. But right now I couldn't

understand why I couldn't have the one inside the suite. What need did the cops have of it or of my dental floss? In fact, what were they still doing there? They were supposed to come in, sprinkle, measure, photograph, dust, speculate, and leave. I knew from personal experience that it wasn't as if they cleaned up the messes they created. But these fellows had a real dog-in-the-manger attitude toward the suite, and particularly toward my innocent belongings.

I was pretty sure my insurance wasn't going to reimburse me for the toiletries, let alone for a wardrobe perk-me-up. This was, perhaps, how bag ladies got their start. All of a sudden, through one agency or another, their worldly goods were gone. It wouldn't matter for what rationale or in what way—a fire, a robbery, a murder in their bedroom. Lost is lost. Gone is gone.

I trudged back to the elevator in the same sweater, rumpled linen slacks, and mildly too-tight loafers that I'd put on, taken off, and put on again since the evening before. I felt dirty, exhausted, miserably unhappy, and a victim of police harassment.

The policeman I'd been leasing for a year yawned extravagantly as he punched the elevator's *down* button. "Told you so," he said. "*Told* you we shouldn't bother to come up here. Told you you wouldn't get your things back yet."

And as I stood there without a toothbrush or a bedroom of my own, with my best friend in jail for murder, my already pathetic vacation gone and my sanity definitely questionable—I looked sideways at C. K. Mackenzie and his I-told-you-so's and decided to skip the heavy-duty thinking I'd planned for this getaway. What was the point? He and I did not have a future. The end was near, the hands of the doomsday clock nanoseconds from midnight.

Told you so.

Five

NEXT MORNING, I WAS STILL SUFFUSED BY A SENSE OF doom, and putting on my shoes added to it. My best friend was in serious jeopardy, my semilove relationship felt like a wobbly tooth waiting to be yanked, and it was possible that I might wind up with nothing in the world except these shoes.

It was easier agonizing over stuff than over people. What if I never got my belongings back? No matter that I had clothing enough at home and at least enough funds to buy a new toothbrush.

Anything could happen. Anything did. You could be suddenly and unfairly arrested. You could have your possessions impounded. You could have very few possessions to start with because you lived on a private school teacher's pathetic salary.

I knew the stats on women and poverty. I knew the odds. Mostly, I knew self-pity.

My dark mood was not helped by the fact that my butter-soft, elegantly cut loafers were too tight. They'd been on sale, reduced so drastically I refused to acknowledge their poor fit. Besides, I had been with Sasha, to whom the only sin was paying retail. She wasn't guilty of murder, but she was surely guilty of coercive encouragement to buy bargains.

To add to my misery, my freshly washed panty hose hadn't quite dried, so the shoes were pinching toes encased in damp nylon.

At some point the night before, my cream cotton sweater had acquired a bloodred Virgin Mary stain. I borrowed one of Mackenzie's summer sweaters, a maroon crew neck that was too large for me but had the advantage of being all one color. Besides, it hid some of my rumply slacks and made me feel vaguely like Doris Day borrowing Rock Hudson's oversized jammies in some schmaltzy old comedy. Maybe we really were a couple if I wore his clothing.

Mackenzie had treated me to a toothbrush at an all-night pharmacy. The hotel provided a hair blower. I did not yet look like one of the homeless, which provided some comfort.

I really missed my eyeliner, though. I felt naked, exposed, something like a cave creature forced into the light.

I'll say this, the *Atlantic City Press* is quick. I'd gone downstairs to buy a paper, and then I was sorry I had. Jesse Reese's untimely death was headlined in type just slightly smaller than might announce the end of life as we have known it.

It was obvious that Reese had been a respected somebody, and that Sasha was on her way to becoming a notorious somebody. FINANCIAL ADVISOR BLUDGEONED TO DEATH: WOMAN HELD. There was a great deal about the esteemed Mr. Reese, advisor and teacher, protector of what he'd called the "potentially dispossessed." There was mention of the first Mrs. R. and of the present wife, Poppy Summerfield Reese, a former Miss America contestant.

There was also an unfortunate overabundance of information about Sasha Berg. This included, much to my horror, mention that she had once been the companion of a reputed gangland figure, the late Peter "Dimples" Bosco, who had, by coincidence, also been murdered.

"Why don't they just hang her and be done with it?"
I said. "Guilty by prior associations and insufficient
sexual scruples, is that what they're implying? Why
isn't anybody saying it's just a matter of unfortunate
room assignment—somebody else's assignment, I might
add. Who, in fact, arranged to have us in that room,
anyway? Isn't it a tad suspicious?"

Mackenzie half nodded, a gesture that meant "I didn't
hear a word you said, but I don't want you to be aware
of that." He sat on the edge of the bed, thumbing
through the phone directories in the night table.

I concentrated on the newspaper. I had to read almost
the entire article before I spotted the name of my hotel.
It was interesting how scrupulously its reputation was
being protected compared with that of the innocent suspect, the former girlfriend of.

Jesse Reese had slightly receding light hair, gray or
pale blond. He was a graciously aging clean-cut man
complete with the requisite square jaw and earnest expression. He looked like he exercised and ate sensibly.
It was a trust-me-with-your-money face, unfrivolous
and well-meaning, perfect for an annual report or pro-
spectus. I resented his features—as if he'd shopped for
them deliberately, just to make things worse for Sasha.
Then I wondered why I was so angry with a dead
stranger, why I was having trouble remembering that he
was the victim.

And why did he look somewhat familiar? "Do you
know this man?" I asked Mackenzie, hoping for a lead.
He put his finger on a column to hold his place in a
phone book, peered at the photo, and shook his head before returning to his odd reading.

"You think it's a common face, and that's why I feel
as if I've seen it before?" I asked.

He continued to read off names, but shook his head.
"Not so common. Head's almost square. Mouth pulls a
little to one side. Eyebrows are heavy. Big earlobes."

Now that he mentioned it ... "I finally know what they mean by trained observer," I said.

He turned his trained eyes in my direction and observed me like a pro. I awaited his pronouncement, hoping it wasn't of the nose-slightly-off-center sort. I wanted muzzy generalizations along the lines of *dazzling*.

"No Dunstan Farmer listed in any of the nearby towns." He leaned over and picked up the phone receiver, punched a few numbers and asked for new listings in each of the small surrounding towns, oblivious to having just shattered another romantic delusion.

Dunstan Farmer was neither a new nor an old listing anywhere.

"Maybe his phone's under the name of his company, whatever that is. Photo-Quik, Dunstan Farmer, Prop., or what have you."

"I looked. His name isn't visibly attached to any of them." Mackenzie drummed his fingers on the night table. "We'll have to interest the police in findin' him. See if they have somethin' on him, maybe. I have a gut feelin' about the man. Bet he won't be easy to find, and I bet he isn't at that bar tonight. Or tomorrow, or ever again, for that matter."

I didn't accept the bet. The odds were all on Mackenzie's side.

The arraignment felt like something out of Kafka. We sat in a small but intimidating courtroom. Sasha, up in front of a dark wood barrier, looked as stained as the mahogany, like a sepia print of herself, a browned-out reproduction of what had formerly been living color. I waved at her, smiled, but she looked too frightened to respond.

The judge listened impassively to a full account of the violence of the crime and its damning circumstances. I wished I knew more about the mechanics of raising bail. Did you have to put something up as collateral? Were there good and bad bail bondsmen? Was there some expertise we lacked that would lead to further complications? Did Mackenzie know about this side of it, or did his interest flag after he'd caught someone?

What *did* those trained eyes see when he looked at me?

My reveries came to a sharp end. So did a lot of hope. The judge did not grant bail. Sasha would stay behind bars. She was a real and present menace to society.

I couldn't believe it and neither could the lawyer. "I protest, Your Honor!" he said. "This woman has no prior record, and is innocent of this crime as well."

"File a motion," the judge mumbled.

The lawyer nodded curtly.

They apparently were comfy with the pas de deux of law, the dance of power, but meanwhile, Sasha, wide-eyed with fear, was taken back to jail. I thought I had seen this movie already on the late show, starring Susan Hayward. They were going to fry my friend for a crime she never committed, and worse, everyone was behaving as if this were proof positive that the system worked.

I WAS ALLOWED TO SEE THE REAL AND PRESENT MENACE TO society—but only after Mackenzie had a series of good-old-boy consultations with his peers on the Atlantic City force, and only for five minutes, they warned me.

It was like watching somebody emotionally drown. Sasha would bob up to the surface, her old, buoyant self, then be pulled under, over and over again. I reassured her that all would be well, but her IQ wasn't sinking, only her spirits, so I stopped making nice or treating her like a child and cut to the chase. We had problems.

"The old man saw somebody who looks like you, or who was pretending to be you," I said. "Somebody who knew how to set you up—somebody who knew you had that room. Who?"

She shrugged. She was being dragged under the waves again. "Didn't find Dunstan, did you?" she asked in a lifeless voice.

"No. You remember anything more about him that might help?"

"Not much, except one stupid thing that probably doesn't mean anything. The night I met him, three weeks ago, before I'd really even spoken to him much, a person—a very drunk Brit—came up and called him Edgar."

"Called Dunstan Edgar?"

She nodded. "Insisted he was Edgar, and in fact, was somebody named Jeannie's husband, too, from some little town in Yorkshire. Said how glad he was that Edgar wasn't dead after all. Always thought Edgar was too good a sailor to fall overboard, like they said. And he really did seem pleased, as if he'd found a long-lost friend. I thought it was funny, everybody did. One of those drunk things that you have to be there for. Except Dunstan just got more and more annoyed, and finally said something like, 'Whoever Edgar is—or was—he's still dead, so get lost.' The Brit finally said he was sorry and backed off. That was all there was to it, completely forgettable, except that Dunstan was unduly pissed for a long while after. I mean, people are always mistaking me for somebody they knew back in high school. That's all it was. Not much, I guess, except maybe to show he has a temper or a poor sense of humor and tolerance. And other than that, all I know about the man is that he drinks vodka, knows how to do the two-step, is an only child and allergic to shrimp."

Okay, then we'd drop back five yards and try again. "About the room," I prompted. "Who knew what room you were in?"

She sighed. "I appreciate your efforts, Mandy, but re-

ally, who cares? The police think the case is closed.
They aren't interested. Won't do a thing."

"I care. I'll do something. Mackenzie, too. So who
knew what room you were in?"

"Frankie," she said in a dull voice. "He's the one
who got it for us. Well, really for me. He thought I was
alone."

"The bartender?" Was he, then, the second man the
witness had seen? I tried to remember whether Frankie
was shorter than Sasha, then realized she'd been seated
last evening, and he'd been behind the bar. I'd have to
check it out myself.

She smiled with a hint of the real Sasha's personality.
"Frankie always had the hots for me, way back to Dimples, can you blame him? He knew the suite was vacant, and a guy at the front desk owed him a favor, so
he—wait a minute!" She sat up straighter. "Last night,
at the bar. He made some kind of joke about the room.
Anybody could have heard, at least anybody nearby."

Finally. The field had opened, the possibilities of a
setup had become real. "Who was there? What was
said? Think. Whatever you remember might help."

She took a deep breath and ticked items off on her
fingers. "First of all, this guy in a pin-striped suit. Gray
hair, nice-enough looking, must be a high roller because
he was usually comped the suite we were in. That's
what Frankie's joke was about, that I was in the guy's
room, and did anybody object. He made it sound like I
was in there with the guy, of course."

"Did anybody object?" I wanted her to say that yes,
indeed, somebody had leaped up—his furious six-foot-
tall wife with curly black hair and her short but loyal
man friend—and had publicly vowed to destroy both
Sasha and the man in the suit. I wasn't asking for much,
just a clear, speedy, and unambiguous finale to all of
this.

But Sasha shook her head. "The suit made some really stupid joke back about what a thrill it was to share

it with me, how much I had improved its decor. You know the riff. Very stale stuff."

I tried to think quickly, to get something to hold on to before the matron's stopwatch reached home. "Backtrack, then. Who else was there besides Frankie and the suit?"

"Who knows? A bunch of people. An Indian couple—Hindus. She was in a green and gold sari, and he had eyes to die for."

"Control the libido until you're free again, okay?"

"They were amazing eyes, Mandy. And another great-looking man. I thought he was Harry Belafonte at first. He went off with some girl in a black straw picture hat, like nobody except maybe Princess Di wears when she's off to a garden party. Looked great, though." She squinted her eyes. "I'm going to get a hat like that if—when—I get out of this mess."

"Good, that gives you some motivation."

She rolled her eyes. "And there was a young guy—soft, flabby fellow with acne. Wearing a bowling shirt and a baseball hat. He was with a pregnant girl with straw-colored hair in a ponytail. She had to be his wife, and that was about it, except for a couple of other women."

"What about those women?" Sasha had a genetic eye affliction that made her blind to humans with double-X chromosomes. She didn't fully perceive members of her own sex. Sometimes she noticed their accessories, but seldom their personalities, features, words, or actions. "Think hard. What do you remember?"

She tilted her head. "Okay. There was a flashy one who looked bolted together."

"Like Frankenstein?"

"Not her head. Her clothing. Brads down the side of the slacks and the sleeves. Gold chains, gold rings."

"Gold hair?"

"No, dark. And big. You know the type, all teased up

and out. And a loud voice that sounded like it had rivets in it, too."

"Age? Looks?"

Sasha shrugged. "Thirty-something, probably? And okay looks, except for the metalworks."

"And that's it? Nobody else? You said *a couple* of women."

"Oh . . ." she said. She shook her head. "No, okay—there was a drab one in there, too. That's what I remember about her. Drabness."

"Come on, Sasha. That's not at all helpful."

She shrugged. "What's to notice about drabness?"

"How old? How big? No rivets?"

The matron cleared her throat. I interpreted the sound as a warning bell and leaned forward, literally pressing for information.

"Not so young," Sasha said. "Not a kid and not ancient, you know? But she had a great bag."

"Her *pocketbook*?"

"Uh-huh. Blue and purple leather."

"For God's sake, Sasha, isn't there anything more relevant?"

"I noticed because I've been eyeing one like it forever. It's Italian and way too expensive and they never mark it down, not anywhere."

"Okay, then, forget her. Nobody would confuse you with a drab woman, anyway. Can you remember anything or anybody else?"

She shook her head just as the matron tapped her watch with great, pursed-lipped solemnity. I stood up and gave up. "I'll be back tomorrow. Is there anything you need?"

"I need to believe I'll be out of here before tomorrow," Sasha said. "My cousin Herb the lawyer's coming down this afternoon. We aren't telling my parents until we have to, okay?"

I nodded. Her parents were far away, one in Canada

and one in Arizona at last check. Maybe, just maybe, they'd never have to know.

Sasha suddenly looked panic-stricken. "Oh, God— it's Tuesday, isn't it?"

I nodded. What was wrong with her?

"What time is it?"

"A little after nine."

"My *shoot*! It's supposed to be now! I hired an assistant and a stylist down here, and the assistant rented everything and she's probably *there*. You have to call her, lie, make up some reason I'm delayed. A day, tell them. Say I'll be in tomorrow and . . ." She lowered her eyelids and shook her head. "I'll pay them for the lost time." She sighed. "There go any profits."

She told me how and where to call, and I agreed.

"Tell them I can't be reached," she said. I agreed to that, too. But I had great reservations, because I suspected that to fill the waiting time, the assistant might have already looked at the front page of the newspaper and figured out what was delaying Sasha.

When I finally did call the assistant, I told her that Sasha had been called away. That part seemed true, although *hauled away* would have been more accurate. I said she'd be gone three days, to give Sasha and the legal system some slack.

And that was that for the jailhouse visit, except that as she was being escorted away, Sasha half turned. "I forgot. The woman in the sari?" she said. "She had on sandals and a gold toe ring. Is that the kind of thing you want?"

If ever an accessory committed a crime, Sasha would be a perfect witness.

I RELAYED THE BITS AND PIECES SASHA HAD OFFERED UP TO Mackenzie, then told him I wanted to go back to the casino. I wanted my earthly possessions back and that room of my own that Virginia Woolf said all women needed. She had also mentioned a small annuity, which

wouldn't be bad, but I doubted that the hotel would provide it.

The situation was stupid, perverse. What was I doing
in a lavish Atlantic City hotel now that Sasha was bedding down in a cell? But how could I leave town while
she was imprisoned—or afford to stay, once the saltwater taffy people noticed that their photographer was
missing in action?

"No problem," Mackenzie said in his off-in-space
voice. "Gonna find me that Farmer boy, meantime. It's
too easy for them to think she made him up."

"How?" I asked. "Can the police find the addresses
of unlisted phones?"

He raised one eyebrow.

"Forgive me for questioning your powers. And
thanks," I added grudgingly. "This is really decent of
you."

He grinned, quite pleased with himself. "This whole
business is an elaborate ruse to get your attention. I had
a fear it was wanin' back in the city, so I set all of this
up."

I put my arm on his sleeve. The feel of worn-soft
broadcloth over worked-hard muscle was tempting.
There were better ways to spend the day than what
faced both of us, much better ways to perk up the waning attention. Although, of course, I had come here to
decide whether or not perking was advisable, and just
about decided last night that it was not. "C.K.," I said
before I thought it through, "we really do have to talk."

His exhales contained an entire vocabulary that could
have been translated into comic book cursing—little
stars and question marks and exclamation points
whooshing out of him. His accent became acute. Verbal
farina. "Ah trust you're referrin' to a need for conversation 'bout Sasha and the business at hand," I thought he
said. "Your friend's in deep trouble."

I glared. Obviously my eyes did not speak the vol-
umes that his exhalations did, or he would have been

horrified. Instead, he went on figuring out what Sasha needed to get herself out of this mess. I couldn't fault him for that—she was my friend and that was generous of him, particularly since he'd never approved of her.

I faulted him anyway.

THE HOTEL MANAGEMENT WAS NOT GLAD TO SEE ME. Somehow, they blamed me for what had happened in the suite. Who was I, anyway? Ms. Berg's reservation had been made by her employer. Why was I there? Why did I exist? What was the meaning of life?

If they gave me—the person who shouldn't have been there in the first place—a room, did I honestly think the saltwater people would pay for it?

"Listen," I reminded them, "I've been grossly inconvenienced—and possibly endangered. What if I had been in that room? What kind of security do you have here that lets strangers break into somebody's room?"

They huffed and they puffed. They took every precaution, they insisted. Not their fault, certainly. Never happened before. Spotless reputation.

What were my alternatives? Moving in with Mackenzie, even short-term, didn't seem like a great idea when what I most needed was space and time away from him.

Home sounded lovely, but dangerously disloyal to Sasha. After all, I could have easily been the one to come back to the room first. I could have been the one in jail. Or another one dead.

I finally handed over my credit card as collateral for their least expensive room. If management didn't relent, or Sasha didn't return to snap photos and get a free room, I would check out tomorrow and commute from the city to Sasha's rescue.

I tried not to remember that this was supposed to be my vacation. While the officious desk clerk grappled with finding me a lousy room, I tapped my too-tight loafers, readying myself for the next battle, the repossession of my wardrobe.

"Well, young sweetie! Look, it's Sherwin's granddaughter."

Tommy and Lala seemed characters out of another, more comic, life. "Hi," I said. "But weren't you supposed to go back on that bus yesterday?"

"Well, if you recall, when you left us, we were having a drink and talking about Sherwin," Tommy said. "One thing led to another, I guess, and we never did make our bus."

Lala tittered. There was no other word for the sound that came from between her clenched lips. She batted her heavily mascaraed eyelashes at Tommy, her tormentor, her sexual harasser.

Tommy, dressed in his white shoes and seersucker, shorter than I remembered, bowed at me and grinned. "Tell Granddad that it's too bad, but he lost out. Sweet Lala has honored me by promising to become my life companion." He enunciated with great solemnity.

"His *wife*." Lala eyed me intensely. "I'm marrying Tommy." Did I get it? His sexual advances were going to be legitimized and therefore no longer offensive or unwelcome. She held out her hand, on which glimmered a knuckle-sized diamond ring. "Bought it on the boardwalk last night, the impetuous man!" she simpered. "This big softie had a big win, and spent it all on me!" She winked at me.

"Told you my luck was changing," Tommy said.

It would serve her right if the headlight on her ring finger turned out to be as fake as Tommy's organized crime stories or his imaginary rival, Sherwin. This betrothed couple should skip the blood test and have a premarital lie detector test instead.

"Grandpa's heart will be broken," I murmured.

"What a day," Tommy said. "Good news and bad. You heard, didn't you?"

"About you? No, actually, not until you just said."

"No, no. I mean the other news. Jesse Reese. It's all over the papers."

"Oh. Yes, I . . . I heard."

"Remember who told you first," Tommy said.

I must have shown my confusion.

"In the lounge," he said. "I told you he was in deep trouble with you-know-who. Only I was wrong on one point, I admit. I thought he had three days to live. I was two off the mark."

Yesterday. In the bar. That man Tommy had used as one of his stories? I remembered a man in a suit—*the* man in the suit? The one that Sasha had mentioned? It had to be the same person; he was the only man in a business suit I'd seen in the hotel. That must be why the photo in the paper had looked vaguely familiar. Jesse Reese had been in the bar last night. Jesse Reese had been the man who'd joked about what was normally "his" suite. I took a deep breath and exhaled loudly.

I was disproportionately relieved, the doubts and nagging questions I'd had about Sasha now gone. Sasha had not known Jesse Reese, had no prior relationship—but she'd been honest enough to acknowledge a sense that she'd met him, had known him in some way.

And then I was disproportionately upset. What had happened in the bar after I left? Had Sasha really gone out with Dunstan? I remembered Jesse Reese tilting toward her, my sense that low-level flirting was under way.

Had Sasha perhaps switched from Dunstan to Jesse, in which case anything was possible? Had she gone back to the bar to make plans with Frankie—or with Jesse Reese? I hated thinking in these terms, but it would be foolish not to consider the possibility.

The desk clerk rang a bell—as if I had luggage.

"You and Granddad will come to the wedding," Tommy said.

"If he can bear the heartache of the loss," I said. With Sasha in jail and Mackenzie in limbo, it was good to

have an imaginary friend as company for the ride upstairs. Just me, Granddad Sherwin, the dead Jesse, and
a hundred million questions.

———————

Six

MY NEW DIGS WERE NEITHER GILDED NOR SOPHISTICATED. They were grudgingly designed in serviceable style for those who worried about money and weren't likely to be real gamblers. A no-frills room. No hair dryer or complimentary bathrobe. A small clock-radio, and no premium channels or in-house movies on the TV. In their place, a VCR—bolted down—and a notice that nearby video rental stores would be glad to deliver one's tape of choice.

I pulled the bedspread off one pillow, just to make a personal statement. Otherwise, I had nothing to unpack, nothing to mark the place mine, and no sense of what to do next.

I had detoured to the scene of the crime en route to this room. The men hanging around the place were unaware of how crucial, how central, a woman's makeup is to her mental health. They insisted on continuing to hoard every bit of it, including my hairbrush. Either they were doing make-overs on one another or they were as sluggish and inept as I suspected.

Or maybe they'd cut an overnight deal for yet another instant crime-of-the-week movie and were already using the room as a set. I wondered who was playing Sasha.

Cher had the right spirit, but was too short. Sigourney Weaver was the right size, but insufficiently wacky. . . .

There had to be something more profitable to do with my time than casting the film of my friend's worst moments. I thought about Dunstan—or was it Edgar—and I checked the clock. It was early morning in Trueheart, Wisconsin, and most public schools, unlike their private cousins, were still in session.

After several conversations with robots who knew phone numbers, I reached an actual human being, who identified herself, rather merrily, as "School office, Jean speaking."

I was immediately suspicious. Not only did she not sound computerized, she also did not sound angry, grudging, or particularly wary. My experience with the guardians of attendance records and supply cabinets had not prepared me for civility. Maybe it was true what they said about the Midwest's friendliness.

The unexpected cordiality made me stumble and stammer. "This is—I'm— This is so embarrassing!" I squealed. "I'm with Photos R Us here in New York. We're a clearinghouse, you know, and—"

"*Just one moment!* With whom am I speaking?" So much for geographical differences. All school secretaries are sisters under the skin. They don't burn out the way teachers do; they calcify.

"My name?" I decided to tell the truth. "Mandy Pep—" But why tell the truth about that when I was lying about the rest of the call? "—salt." I never claimed to have much imagination.

"Mandy Pepsalt?"

"Right. So this man sent us photographs of Trueheart. Absolutely *brilliant*, and we want to hire him and use them for syndication, you know? Except—this is the humiliating part. Someone who shall remain nameless spilled her coffee all over the cover page, and the man had written in ink, and his address just floated off in a mess of coffee. We are *beside* ourselves here."

"I'm quite busy, Miss Pepsalt, and I can't really follow why you're calling me from New York."

"Because he's one of your graduates. Grew up out there. His pictures are a photo essay called 'Hometown,' and I'm hoping against hope that you keep up-to-date alumni records and that you'll know how we can contact him. Unfortunately, I can't tell you what year he graduated because the, ah—"

"Coffee?" Her tone was disdainful. She would never spill her coffee on an important document. She would never ingest anything spillable around an important document.

Dunstan had looked in his forties. "I think I see a six in that blur," I said. "So he graduated mid- to late sixties, I suspect. I must assure you this has never, *ever* happened before. I don't want you thinking we are anything less than meticulous in our care for our clients' portfolios."

"Miss Pepsalt! This is a small high school. I'm the entire clerical staff. If students contact me, fine. If they come in and visit me, fine. But this isn't like a college that has a regular alumni news. If you knew his exact year—"

"Oh, if I had only taken proper precautions with my coffee! There! Now you know who the clumsy culprit is. Can't you help me?"

"—and if that class had a reunion lately, the chairman of the event might have traced the man. That's who does that kind of thing, calling parents and last known addresses and asking other people for information. I certainly can't. I'm too busy with the current crop of students to bother with somebody who was here a quarter of a century ago!"

Now she sounded like a school secretary. It simply took longer to get up to speed in the Midwest.

"I know the ones who come say hello," she said, "bring in their children and, a few times now, their grandchildren. But the others, no, so if that's all you—"

"It sounds as if you've been there awhile. Perhaps you'd remember this man."

"Only if he was exceptional. Good or bad. If I had to order engraved awards or trophies for him—or put him on the detention roster a lot of times. Otherwise, the hairdos change, the music gets worse, but all the same, they blur, Miss Pepsalt."

"Does the name Dunstan Farmer strike a chord?"

She gasped. The chord had been struck. Would it be trophies or detentions she recalled?

"So you do remember him? The boy who moved there from England when he was young?"

"Is this a prank call? Because I don't find it funny at all."

"I'm sorry. I don't understand."

"Of course I remember Dunstan Farmer. Everybody in these parts would. We knew his parents, too, since they were born. They didn't move here from any foreign country. They've lived here forever, for generations, except for when the family moved South and the tragedy happened. Atlanta, or Mobile—one of those places. They came back after. And stayed." She sighed, twice. "Broke the town's heart, how bad we felt for them."

"How . . . what happened?" I whispered.

"Broke his neck in one of those freak accidents during a practice scrimmage down in Atlanta—or Mobile. I never can remember. He was a junior in high school. He was a good young man and it was a hard loss when he died. Family never got over it, either. Whoever you met, whoever sent you those photographs, was most certainly not our Dunstan Farmer."

When I hung up, I was dizzy, light-headed. The man who'd borrowed the identity of a dead teenager could be anybody—Edgar from Yorkshire, that married man who'd made himself seem dead. Or he could be a murderer. And where did Sasha fit into all this?

I felt as if I were in that Poe story where the walls

contract and crush their inhabitant. Something dreadful had happened and was continuing to happen, and I wanted desperately to do something about it, but I had no idea what that something could be. In lieu of action, I accepted motion.

I left my room and walked down the hall toward the elevator bank, pondering the past twenty-four hours spent in the Twilight Zone. Nothing whatsoever made sense, yet it had all happened, starting with the mysterious motives, methods, and identities of the people who'd used Sasha's and my room as their killing ground. And how the devil had they gotten in?

And then I stopped in my tracks. At the other side of the elevator bay, a chambermaid's cart piled high with towels and cleaning apparatus propped open a door. The most ordinary of hotel sights—but now it looked like one of the puzzle pieces.

I tested my hypothesis by rushing through the open door. "Oh!" I said to the startled woman making up the bed. "I'm interrupting, sorry! I had wanted to use my bathroom, take a shower, but I'll come back later."

"No, no. Is fine." She waved me toward the bathroom. "Has clean towels already."

I went into the bathroom, closed the door, ran the taps and flushed. I went back into the room, sat down, picked up a book on the desk, flipped through it, then smiled at the chambermaid, who was nearly finished. "I'll come back later," I said. "No problem. Thanks for making the room look so great."

And that was how it could be done. Nobody had needed a key to our room. Chambermaids couldn't be expected to know the ever-changing guest faces. So anyone could enter, look as if she belonged, and wait out the maid. And then later, after propping the door to make sure it didn't lock, reenter along with an accomplice and a future victim.

And the entry technique was possible twice every day. The same open-door policy held in the evenings,

when towels were replaced and bedspreads removed.
Sasha had mentioned that throughout the carnage, my
bed had remained pristine, turned down, a chocolate on
its pillow.

A good thing to know if I ever wanted to murder or
even simply ambush somebody. A bad thing to know if
I ever again wanted to feel entirely comfortable or safe
when entering a hotel room.

It was only after I was downstairs and out on the
boardwalk that I inventoried what I'd seen at the site of
my room experiment. A pair of men's shoes near the
bed. A technothriller as leisure reading. A man's leather
toiletry kit in the bathroom. Not a sign of a female inhabitant. I tried to imagine what the chambermaid had
made of my intrusion.

I walked briskly past a woman standing by her storefront fortune-telling parlor under a sign reading KNOW
THE FUTURE. I might have been tempted—the future was
certainly something for which I needed a clue—but she
was talking on a cellular phone. It seemed to me that
people with extra powers should not need to rely on Ma
Bell in order to find something out. I walked on.

I paused at the wide-open front of a raucous arcade.
I could see a Skee-ball game that I remembered from
years past, although that was the only manual,
nonelectronic game in sight, almost a fossil. The aisles
were packed with loud machines. A talking tic-tac-toe
was nearest to me. This, then, was casino prep school,
or the really poor man's casino, where a quarter would
buy a chance. More likely, this was where the people
who had my room and a losing streak came to get rid
of their spare change.

I wandered inside and saw that if you took chance after chance and won, you were eligible for the world's
sorriest collection of prizes. A life-sized moose head
made of polyester plush. Almost life-sized plastic figures of the Brady Bunch. Garishly painted plaster carousel horses.

I was on my way out when I saw a machine that promised to tell my romantic future. It wasn't quite as valuable as finding out who the real killer was, but neither could I pass it by.

I put in my four quarters and punched in my name and birthdate. And was almost immediately stymied, because next I had to enter Mackenzie's name. Feeling vaguely ashamed, I pushed a C and a K. Let the machine figure out how to pronounce it.

After a lot of whirring and flashing, a computer printout emerged. I took it onto the sunny boardwalk and read it en route. It wasn't a real mood lifter. *You're a dreamy-eyed idealist,* it said under ROMANCE. *You become enslaved by negative situations.*

Mackenzie, on the other hand, seemed straightforward and to be envied. *It's sheer romance,* it said. *You love love.*

What did a machine know, anyway? *You love school, or the learning process in general,* it said for me. Okay, so it guessed well now and then. *You are a workhorse,* it said of Mackenzie. *You can drive souls past their point of sanity.* I cut to the quick and looked at our overall compatibility. It appeared that I needed distance, while Mackenzie needed partnership. Ridiculous.

I tossed the printout in the next wastepaper basket I passed and focused on my fellow board-strollers, but that didn't provide relief. The look of the place had certainly changed since its glory days. My mother sometimes reminisces about the times she paraded her new spring suits and hats on the boards. Today, white gloves and a flowered bonnet—except on the stunning woman Sasha had seen with the almost–Harry Belafonte—would be hooted off the place, and an elegant suit would be a shocker.

When my mother talks about long-ago stays at the shore, the place sounds regal. Hail Britannia and all that. Her hotels had names like Marlborough, Blenheim, and Claridge. Now, in the cause of progress, or all-

Americanism, it was de-anglicized. Bally, Caesar's, and Trump this and that. A potpourri of nowhere.

But that train of thought chugged into the station called Dunstan, the de-anglicized man. The thought of Dunstan still made me nervous, and nerves made me hungry. Besides, it was close to lunchtime, and breakfast had been a shared bagel en route to the arraignment.

However, the boardwalk had never been an epicurean haven, and now it was a junk-food smorgasbord. Peanuts, saltwater taffy, pizza, hamburgers, assorted candies, and my secret favorite, a garlicky hot dog dipped in cornmeal batter and fried—just in case its innate fat content wasn't sufficiently astronomical.

I zipped over to the yellow and green stand. "A lemonade and a . . . a Dip Stick," I said in the voice of a spy passing on information.

"Miss Pepper!"

A Philly Prep student. Eric Stotsle. He of the amazing Adam's apple. He'd been in my homeroom, but not my class yet, and had seemed one of those ordinary people with a mildly annoying tic—his was an unblinking stare—who never receive attention until they take down an entire village from its bell tower. "He was a good kid," neighbors and classmates tell the press. "Never would have suspected this. Stared a lot, sure, but otherwise . . ."

You just didn't notice Eric Stotsle, except for that bobbing apparatus in his throat. But Eric Stotsle noticed you.

I looked plaintively heavenward, but saw, instead of a compassionate deity, the inflated Dip Stix lemon. I therefore asked a plastic citrus fruit whether this, too, was necessary. I already had a murder and a jailed friend. Did I also need to be observed by a Philly Prep student? The lemon did not choose to answer. Never ask a sign for a sign.

"What are *you* doing here?" Eric stood, mouth slightly open, a lemonade cup in his hand.

"You mean at a Dip Stix stand?" Wasn't a teacher allowed to clog her veins?

"I mean in Atlantic City!"

Ah, yes. He, too, had the common student delusion that when school wasn't in sessions, teachers were deflated and stored in trunks along with the basketballs. "Vacationing." I took the lemonade out of his hand. "And you? Aren't you a little young to have this kind of job?"

"Look, I—don't say anything, all right? It's legal. Really."

He had fudged some form somewhere, I was sure. But given that the purpose was to get himself an honest job, not to deal crack or run guns, who was I to squawk?

It was Eric who squawked, actually. "Hey," he said, flicking his wrist dismissively. "Get lost. Do I have to tell you again?"

"Excuse me?"

"Not you, Miss Pepper!" Various portions of his face flushed. He looked down and to his side. "You, out! I'm gonna get in trouble! You can't stay here."

"I could pour lemonade," the voice said. "Put in ice."

"You can't even reach the spout. Besides, you're too young to work." Eric heard his own words and looked at me guiltily, then back down again. "*Really illegal* for you to work, understand, man?"

A door in the counter swung open and a small child—I estimated five or six—walked out. Like Eric, he wore a baseball cap backward and attempted a serious swagger as he made his way to a three-legged stool, high enough to give him difficulty perching on it. "Then do you have, like, leftovers?"

Urchin was the only word for him, with all its Dickensian overtones. "Are you lost?" I asked softly.

He stared at me as if I were one of the deinstitutionalized his mother had warned him about, then seemed to decide I wasn't dangerous. "I know where I am," he said.

"Your mom waiting for you?"

He shrugged.

I turned and tried to see if I could spot his mother, but I couldn't find a woman watching the boardwalk stand.

"You sure you don't have food?" the little boy asked Eric. "Something that didn't come out looking too good?"

"Ask your mother for money, like I told you," Eric said.

"I can't," the boy said. "I'm not allowed in."

Barred from his home? What was going on here? It was lunchtime, and the child was hungry. "Here." I handed him the sizzling hot dog Eric had given me. A cardiologist of the future would thank me for this. I ordered a second one, so my future cardiologist could also pay his mortgage. "What's your name?"

He took an enormous bite and answered unintelligibly, muffled by corn-battered hot dog.

"Lucky," Eric translated. "That's his name, he says. You really shouldn't encourage him."

Encourage him to do what? Eat? "Let me take you home to your mom," I said. That was a definite action I could perform. It wouldn't help Sasha's mess or my pending romantic incompatibility, but I'd be doing *something*.

Lucky shook his head and chewed away. "Plin." He sounded like somebody talking through flannel.

Eric translated. "She's playing. He's not allowed."

He wasn't making sense. I imagined Lucky's mother turning a jump rope, covering her eyes for hide and seek, tossing a ball.

"Have to be twenty-one," Eric said, "to get in."

"She's in the casino?"

The little boy nodded and finished off his hot dog. "I'm dyin' of thirst," he said.

I wondered how long he'd been on his own while his mother gambled. I wondered if she'd understand if I tracked her down and gave her whatever piece of my mind I could spare. I wondered if she'd remember her kid if I reported her to Family Services.

Oh, God, but I didn't want to have further doings with the police just now. I handed Lucky a lemonade.

"She said she'd only be a while," Lucky said.

"He was here last night, too," Eric said. "I made him go back inside the casino. It was like *dark*."

The hot dog smelled delicious, but suddenly my stomach didn't feel up to it. I offered it to the boy, but he declared himself full, so I held it like a small pennant. "Come on, Lucky." It felt indescribably sad calling him that, and even sadder that he was so willing to go with me, to trust me, to be taken care of. "Let's find your mom."

I wished I had never come to this city.

Seven

"Hey!" It was the homeless woman who lived under the boardwalk. Georgette. She raised her fingers in an almost military salute. "Who you got there?" She lounged on a bench by the stairs that led to the beach, her thin hair ruffling in the breeze. She wore a knee-length denim skirt with a ragged hemline over a long plaid skirt that touched the tops of her orange socks. A small and rumpled stack of newspapers was next to her, but she wasn't reading them. I was glad of that, because the topmost page featured the portrait of Jesse Reese.

There was no escaping the murder. There was no trying not to think about it.

Georgette was reading a thick paperback that looked bloated, as if it had done time in a tub.

"This is Lucky," I said. The little boy stared at her gravely.

"Yours?"

"Borrowing him for a while." I could see the faded but still legible title of her book. *War and Peace.* Her thumb held her place far into its depths. She followed the track of my eyes. "Saw this goin' out to sea one day."

So that's what other people did with their overly ambitious biodegradable summer reading lists.

74

"Nearly done now," she said. "It's good, except those Russians have so many names it hurts the eyes. So hello, Lucky. Makes sense I'd meet you today. This is a lucky one for me, all right." She leaned closer to the little boy. "I've been at war, but now I'm at peace," she said in a stage whisper. "Get it?"

Lucky shook his head.

"Don't have to." She flashed her gap-toothed smile. Then almost immediately, her expression darkened. "I had my own kid, once." She looked up at the clear blue sky, blinking hard.

I watched her mood dip and wobble and was reminded of Sasha earlier today. I knew what had hit Sasha and sent her reeling, and I hoped it was short-term, and that she'd regain her equilibrium soon. I wondered what had slammed into Georgette with such hurricane force that it had permanently destabilized her emotions.

She regained composure and sniffed deeply. "Good air here, ozone, they call it. Nice people, too." She nodded in the direction of the hotels. "The chambermaids over there, they let me wash up in the rooms. Before they make it over for the next people. Who does it hurt? Nobody did that for me anywhere else. Better money than Philly, too. People are on vacation, in good moods, they share."

Speaking of which. "Want this?" I asked. She accepted the hot dog, for which I still had no appetite.

I retrieved Lucky from using the boardwalk railing as a tightrope. "Dangerous," I said softly.

"'Ahhh . . .'" He sneered at my old lady timidity and shook me away with five-year-old daredevil disgust.

"Worked after Kurt was gone," Georgette said when she'd finished eating. "But then we were robbed." Her voice had no emotion. "And I got sick. Since then, money thinks I'm dead."

I needed to know how a woman who read *War and Peace* had come to this.

"Sister . . . my sister, she . . ." Georgette twisted the denim skirt fabric with both hands. Lucky fidgeted, darted forward, then back, nearly tripping half a dozen slow walkers. I looked across the boardwalk at a store that said PEANUTS on a hand-lettered sign. I missed their fresh-roasted smell along with Mr. Peanut, a seven-foot legume who used to nod and greet strollers, but he'd fallen victim to newer advertising concepts, or to his flashier kin at Disneyland. A sophisticate like Lucky might have sneered, anyway.

"Over there, you see the store that sells peanuts? Here, look, I'll show you." I lifted Lucky and my lower back twinged, or perhaps that is too mild a word. What I felt was more like the muscular equivalent of a warning gong. I put Lucky down, took a deep breath, convinced myself that my back no longer hurt as much, pulled out my wallet and gave him a bill. "Buy nuts for the pigeons." I wondered if his mother had ever ventured out into the fresh air and shared such a moment with him. "And come right back." He scampered off, again heedless of approaching pedestrians or rolling chairs. I sat down next to Georgette, so that I could watch Lucky's whereabouts. Near to her, the salt air took on a hint of recently ingested alcohol.

Georgette snuffled. "My sister should have lived." She nodded, almost rhythmically, as if the motion were also a part of her fixed story.

I nodded, too. Why not? Meanwhile, my mind had become a multiplex theater. On one screen, I monitored Lucky. On the next, Georgette told her fragmented tale. And in the main theater, Sasha's saga endlessly replayed, word by word, except when interrupted by short features about Dunstan and Jesse Reese.

"If she'd lived, this would be her lucky day, too."

"Why is that?" I murmured. "Because it's so beautiful?" I tried to calculate exactly how long it would take a peanut seller to notice and serve a small boy whose head was counter height, exactly how long before I checked up on him.

"What does weather have to do with it? Today is lucky because our enemy perished!"

"Good." Lucky reemerged with a small paper bag. A dollar was at least worth peanuts. Center screen I once again watched the scene with Sasha in the bar last night. It seemed central, pivotal, but I couldn't yet see it clearly enough.

Georgette sighed. It was a contented sound. "I wrote President Reagan about it, and he listened. Took time, but look." She picked up the stack of newspapers to make room for Lucky. He gave each of us a nut.

I replayed the scene in my head again, and suddenly saw the other eyes that were watching. Frankie. The bartender. I really had to talk to him.

Georgette snapped apart her shell. "Look what that President Reagan did for me—even when he's retired." She tossed the peanuts to a nearby bird. Within seconds his extended flock received an extrasensory nut alert. Lucky giggled and tossed peanuts to a chorus of ruffled grabbing sounds.

"You see?" Georgette's hands didn't seem to belong to her. They were gnarled and arthritic, the hands of a very old woman. One slightly twisted index finger pointed at the uppermost newspaper, the one featuring the recently perished Jesse Reese. Her ragged nail tapped his nose. "You see?"

I could see the dead man's photograph and her finger, but not her point. Because, of course, even disregarding the theory that the ex-President had executed Jesse Reese on Georgette's behalf, the woman was missing a few connector wires and had been drinking. The picture must be serving as a generic enemy. I could even understand it if she considered the entire world her enemy.

In any case, her need to share her story seemed abruptly over. We fed pigeons in silence, and when the bag was empty, I gave Georgette a few dollars and made my way into the hotel to find Lucky's mother and talk to the bartender.

Two real things to do. I was on a streak.

"WHERE WERE YOU SUPPOSED TO WAIT?" I ASKED LUCKY. "On the stairs." He pointed to the carpeted flight that led to a balcony lounge. "But it's boring, except when you slide down the rail."

The brass rail was periodically ornamented with spiky protuberances, and at one point it rose a good thirty feet above the lobby.

I expected to find a terrified woman racing up and down the staircase, calling his name, or perhaps the police, or the hotel staff or a posse engaged in an all-points search. But no one was looking for him.

Of course, he wasn't allowed inside the casino. If he were, there would, presumably, have been no problem in the first place. I wasn't eager to leave him unattended again. I corraled a security guard. "Is there any way to page somebody in there?" I asked.

"Well . . ." He looked reluctant to tell me, then he noticed my companion. "Hey, Lucky boy," he said. "Found yourself a friend, did you?" He winked at me. He was in his sixties, with florid good looks, a snow-white crew cut, and a trustworthy, experienced sense about him. "Hope you won't take this as an insult, ma'am, because it's meant as a compliment—he always finds attractive friends."

"Always? His mother has left him before?"

"It's not my habit to keep tabs on them," he said. "But she's a not unfamiliar face."

"But—he's just a baby!"

"I am not!" Lucky insisted. "I'm five and a half!"

"I didn't mean it that way," I said. "He was out on the boardwalk, panhandling. That's neglect. That's abuse!"

"It's just that nobody likes to report them—"

"Them? Who? Lucky and his mother?"

He shook his head. "Them," he said very gently. "The ones who leave the kids. His mother, she's at least here mostly in the daytime. It's the ones left all night long, tired and hungry, that are the real problem. Or the little ones still in their carriages. They're left out here for hours, with all that goes on in this world." He shook his head wearily. "I try to keep an eye on our own casino kids, but it's not right."

Casino kids. There was even a term for it. I was furious.

"Just between us, we need child care here," the guard said. "They have health clubs for the grown-ups, so why not a place to park kids?" He waved away his words. "Ah, but they say there's no problem, so they aren't likely to fix it, now, are they?"

I was itching to fix it single-handedly, to create the episode that made them admit there was a problem, to haul Lucky's mother out of the casino by her follicles and make her an example for all the fools who gambled their children's welfare along with their money.

The guard read my face. "Listen," he said in his soothing voice. "I'll find her, and I'll keep an eye on Lucky meantime. You've been a good Samaritan, but he's safe now, and if it's all the same, I'm nearing retirement and I'd like the management to stay fond of me, know what I mean? She intends no harm, you have to understand."

I climbed off my high steed and became a mere mortal again. I pictured the boy's mother, probably very young, already semidefeated, raising him without help, coming here when possible for entertainment, escape from her routine, hoping to make a quick killing, to be a winner, to find the round of luck that could make a difference. Look what she called her baby boy. "You'll try to make her understand what could happen to him?" I asked.

He nodded. "I've got five grandkids myself," he said softly. "I'll give it my best. And I'll explain about hav-

ing to report it next time, except that might make her
switch casinos, not habits."

I hugged Lucky, suggested that next time he bring
along books and crayons and something electronic for
entertainment. Maybe if he made enough little-boy mess
and noise, and I made some very real grown-up noise,
our combined impact would stun the management into
noticing that they had both children and a problem on
their hands.

I checked the desk for messages, but Mackenzie had
obviously not yet located Dunstan Farmer, a situation I
found both frustrating and oddly satisfying. I left a message as to my whereabouts and set off for Frankie.

There were very few patrons in the bar. My back hurt
and my head was dizzy with competing problems. I
wanted wine along with information, but I hadn't eaten
all day and was afraid of making alcohol my midday
meal. I sat down at the curved teak bar and ordered a
glass of mineral water. "I'm Amanda Pepper," I said, to
jog his memory.

"Hey, no problem." I found that response distinctly
confusing. "I'm permitted to serve alcohol to strangers," he added. Obviously, I had not made much of an
impression on him.

He didn't ask for my ID, either. I have not, alas, been
carded in the past three years, since two days after my
twenty-eighth birthday, not that I'm counting.

"I'm Sasha Berg's friend. I met you last night."

He sucked in his breath and nodded. "Big mess, all
right," he said. "I can't believe it, just can't believe it.
You're the roomie, okay. But where were you? I mean
when it . . . it happened in your room."

"Out. On a date. All night." I felt a recidivist flash of
embarrassed fear, as if Frankie might phone my mother.
"Mandy didn't come home *all night*," he'd tattle.

He did some more deep breathing. "You know, she
came in here yesterday to say hello when you were
checking in, and I thought maybe I'd impress her. Al-

ways had a soft spot for Sasha. So I called on a favor
and got her that suite. Didn't know you were along, by
the way. Then Reese shows up dead in that very room.
Some way to impress a girl, right? She was going to
meet me here when my shift ended. Finally going to get
the girl, like in a movie, only my luck . . ." He shook
his head and sighed.

"Do you remember what time she came in here last
night?"

He shrugged. "Tenish? I dunno. I been stuck with
two shifts, covering for a sick pal, like today again, and
it gets blurry." He was tall, with wide shoulders, around
Sasha's height, but quite slender. He didn't fit the witness's description of a small man—unless the man was
referring to girth, not height, but even so, and despite
his candid style, I couldn't bring myself to trust him
completely. Frankie was still in the best position to have
set Sasha up.

"If we can get her out, maybe you can still get the
girl," I said. "You know her date? This Dunstan
Farmer?"

"Never heard of him."

"How about Jesse Reese?"

Frankie shrugged. He was probably a good and classic bartender, best at responding quietly to others' stories, but not too good at telling his own. This was the
time for the other night's—impossible to believe it was
only last night's—aggressive and verbal bartender, but
life doesn't work out that way. "Knew him like I'd
know you if you came here on a regular basis and
talked a little."

"Is—was—he a drinker?"

Frankie shook his head. "Not particularly, although
last night he seemed tanked by the time he left. Probably would have flagged him if he'd asked for more.
Started celebrating somewhere else, I guess."

Not tanked. Drugged, Mackenzie had said. Very possibly and logically in here. By Frankie? Was his wide-

eyed speculation all an act? "What time was that?" I
asked, inwardly begging him not to say *with Sasha* or
when Sasha left.

Frankie shook his head again. "Like I say, it blurs,
but it wasn't till . . . he stayed awhile. He wasn't gambling last night, just stopping by."

Odd. The paper said he lived in Haddonfield, almost
all the way back to Philly. Why would a gambler come
down here, if not to play?

"Maybe he left around the same time that Sasha left
for her date," Frankie finally said. "Or a little after? I
can't remember."

One more unanswered prayer. Or maybe Frankie was
trying to frame Sasha. I surely wasn't suddenly accepting Sasha's judgment as to whether a man was or
wasn't someone to have faith in. "Do you know if he's
in debt?" I asked. "In trouble?"

Frankie laughed. "You mean was like the Godfather
after him?" He laughed again. "The man was clean.
Gambled a lot, but he had the money. Always paid up.
I got the feeling he'd never mess with his image, you
know? They called him Professor Money. He taught in
the junior colleges and retirement centers and he was
even going to have his own show on TV."

"What do you mean?"

Frankie put his finger up, signaling me to wait while
he poured a draft for a young man whose belly testified
to a precocious and continuing affection for the brew.
And then he was back. "An infomercial. He'd be selling
his business, but it'd look like a seminar on investing.
A first seminar—there were also going to be tapes to
buy. He's—he *was*—pretty good at what he did, I hear.
And successful. Costs a lot to produce those things,
don't you think, and it came from his own pockets. And
he was ready to roll. Already taped the whole first
show."

"I wish I could see it."

"Won't air now," Frankie said. "Besides, it'd be boring. Or maybe that's just my point of view. Financial management is not my strong point." He laughed softly, a little bitterly.

"But it'd give me a handle on the man."

Frankie shrugged. "Like I said, the man was doing fine. Only trouble he was likely to get into would be with his wife, because half the time he's up in that suite with somebody else. As a matter of fact, his wife used to be one of those somebody else's, and she can't forget how she got her current position, so she's always looking over her shoulder to see who's gaining on her, especially since the accident."

I must have looked puzzled, because he offered further explanation. "Car crash a year or so after they married. Something doesn't work in one of her hips anymore. Uses a cane and has to drive a special car. Damn shame. She was a gymnast when she ran for Miss America." He wiped at the counter. "But the thing is, this one time, he was here on business, he said. No hanky-pank. Not even gambling."

The good news was that there was a perpetually jealous wife as suspect. The bad news was that she was lame.

"And she didn't seem angry last night, anyway. She smiled at some dumb joke I made about Sasha sleeping in Jesse's room."

"She was here?"

Frankie nodded.

"What's she look like?" I asked.

He shrugged. "You know," he said. This, then, was the definition of a not-trained observer. "Nice-looking."

Which one had been Mrs. Jesse Reese? Not the sari, not the pregnant ponytail, so if I remembered correctly, that didn't leave a wide field, and as she'd once been a pageant contestant, she wasn't the drab one, I'd bet. "Does she wear a lot of metal on her clothing?"

His eyebrows rose. "So you've seen her. Sure. Mrs. R. designs the stuff. Once, she's sitting in here and I comment on the brass trim, and she says, 'Frankie, this is not trim. This is a fashion statement.' "

Good. The wife, the often deceived wife, had been here last night and had known who was occupying the suite. And she had big, teased dark hair, Sasha had said. "She's tall, isn't she?" I asked, allowing myself a flare of hope.

Frankie shook his head. "You're thinking of somebody else, then, maybe. Mrs. R.'s an itty-bitty one."

A small, lame woman. We were back to zero. "Who else was here?" I asked. "Who else heard the joke about the suite?"

"Anybody who was around, I guess." Frankie worked at an imaginary stain on the bar top and I drummed my fingers. Finally, he looked up with an expression that suggested that he was tired of the conversation and of me. "There were people all over the place. I don't pay much notice. They're faces and orders."

People were haircuts and bad music to the secretary in Wisconsin, faces and orders to Frankie. I couldn't decide whether I'd stumbled on a great unifying truth or a trivial sadness.

"Was anybody else here, aside from his wife, who knew Jesse Reese?"

"How'd I know something like that?" Frankie asked, with some justification. "He had his briefcase. I guess he was doing business down here, so whoever that was with might have been around."

"Do you have any idea with whom?" Why did I ask? He shook his head.

"Do you remember anybody else? How about a woman in a sari?"

"Probably. There often is, even though they're not drinkers, you know."

"Somebody pregnant with a ponytail?"

Frankie shrugged. "Why would I remember? And what are you trying to say? That somebody who heard my joke about the room framed Sasha?" He sounded nervous, overly incredulous, like a bad actor. "That doesn't make any sense." He wasn't doing a convincing job of making the idea preposterous.

Neither of us mentioned that there was one person who didn't have to overhear a thing in order to know about the room because he'd arranged for the switch.

"Who'd have done such a thing?" Frankie asked.

"Somebody who wanted to get away with murder, that's who." I left him a generous tip, to stay on his good side.

Eight

I CHECKED THE DESK. HALF AN HOUR AGO MACKENZIE had called in a message that he'd be back "soon." Exactly how long from now constituted soon? An advanced degree in semantics would come in handy around that man.

Explication would also be helpful with Frankie the bartender. I mentally poked through everything he'd said, and came up with precious little. The papers had already made clear Reese's solid financial status and prestige, but they hadn't mentioned the angry wife. Or the pending TV show—could it be relevant? Or the business he had in Atlantic City. What had it been?

The paper had said that Jesse Reese's office was in Cherry Hill, New Jersey, about an hour away, just across the bridge from Philly. What better place than a man's home away from home to dig for information about appointments, angry wives, and pending TV shows? I knew I was throwing out a net over nothingness, but maybe something would come up. Something that would get Sasha out of prison before sundown.

I WISHED I WERE WEARING MORE BUSINESSLIKE GARB THAN Mackenzie's oversized maroon sweater over linen slacks which were even more intensely wrinkled after the hour-long drive to Cherry Hill. And my convertible-whipped hair was the most rumpled of all. I smoothed myself down, futilely, and hoped my creased aura made me look authentically a member of the working press. Whether I could behave like one was another question. I had only old movies and the six o'clock news upon which to base my performance, but I felt in need of an alias here. I didn't want anybody associated with Jesse Reese to know that I was associated with his accused murderer.

I was surprised by the modesty of the investment counselor's offices. I always thought the handling of money required vaulting spaces and the hush of expensive carpeting, but Jesse Reese's reception area looked a lot like a dentist's waiting room. Three chairs covered in a blurred orange and brown stripe sat on colorless flat carpeting across from a desk occupied by a middle-aged woman in taupe hair and suit. A small name plaque said NORMA EVANS.

"Yes?" She stood up. She was about my size, but managed to make me feel unequal, intimidated. "Can I help you?"

"Hildy Johnson here," I said, hand outstretched. Would she recognize the reporter in *His Girl Friday*? It was the only journalistic name my mind summoned. "Hilda," I added. "Glad to meet you, Ms. Evans."

She looked at my hand as if it were a puzzling offering. "What is it you want, Ms. Johnson?" She sat back down, but did not invite me to do the same.

"Well, a good interview, of course. Or did you mean that metaphysically?"

She blinked, her mouth set in a tight, straight line. "I'm afraid I don't do interviews."

"I meant Mr. Reese. I'm his three-thirty appointment." I looked down at her desk, pointing my index finger, pretending to be aiming for a date book, pretending to believe that Hildy Johnson would be written on it.

Miss Evans, who, after all, had just lost an employer and probably a job, looked at my pointed finger as if it were a gun, and seemed ready to call the cops. "If this is a joke," she said, her bottom lip just this side of a tremble, "it's in poor taste."

It was in poor taste, and I knew it, but Sasha's being in jail was in worse taste. "A *joke*?" I said. "I sent him tear sheets and my résumé, and drove all the way from McKeesport. I specialize in geriatric issues, for *Modern Maturity* and *Senior* and oh, geez, you wouldn't believe how many publications there are for our older citizens. I'm calling my story 'More Gold for Your Golden Years,' and I have an editor really excited about it."

She looked so unhappy and uncomfortable, I felt like the predatory press, the people who jam microphones into the faces of the newly bereaved and demand to know whether they are really, really upset or not.

Norma Evans seemed unable to compose herself. She aligned the edges of papers, tapping them this way and that, her full attention on the job. As soon as they were uncovered, I tried to read the top one, a list of names or words and numbers, but it was upside down and she kept the papers in motion. Finally, she lifted the stack and slid it somewhere out of sight, and only then did she look up at me. She cleared her throat. "I'm sorry, Miss—Jackson, was it? I'm not quite myself today."

"Um . . ." Was it Jackson? What was it? "Johnson!" I finally said, rather too urgently.

"Johnson, yes. I've been with Mr. Reese for seventeen years." She paused, closed her eyes and took a deep breath. "He always praised my command of details. I never forgot things. I took care of every aspect of his personal and professional life and work, and certainly of his calendar, and I don't remember any . . . But in any case, there's been a tragedy, you see. Mr. Reese . . ." This time she groped for a handkerchief, but her suit skirt had no pockets. I pushed the box of tissues that was on the side of her desk in front of her, and she nodded, took one and dabbed at the corners of her eyes. "Mr. Reese died last night," she whispered.

"Died?" I sat down in the chair next to her desk. "Ohmigod! That's *horrible.* I didn't even know he was sick. It must have been so *sudden."*

"It was."

"Heart attacks are scary," I whispered. "I did an article on ten warning signs that your heart might—"

She sniffed loudly and put the tissue to her nose, shaking her head all the while. "It's worse than that. He was murdered. Killed by a young woman, a, um, brand-new acquaintance. Such a good man." She glanced at me. "But human. That little . . . weakness for women. Still, it's terrible. Terrible. I'm sorry about your story," Norma Evans said, "but of course, as you can see . . ."

"I'm sorry for you. You seem to have been quite fond of Mr. Reese."

"Seventeen years," she murmured. "Longer than either of his marriages, he always said. You know they call a man's secretary his office wife, don't you? Not, of course, to imply that we had anything except a professional relationship, but when you take care of every detail of a man's life for all those years . . ."

"Then who—what should I—what's to become of all this—are you running the office now?"

"The office is closing. Is already closed."

"You mean for the day?"

"I mean forever. Without Mr. Reese . . ." She shook her head. "If he still had a partner, maybe, but on his own, who's to replace him? But I'm sure you can find another counselor to interview."

"But Mr. Reese's focus on senior citizens was the whole point, and how many financial advisors specialize in that? Especially to the kind of small investors he cared about. Could you recommend somebody else?" It was hard to whine, seem sympathetic, and simultaneously snoop. "That former partner you just mentioned, maybe?"

"Ray Palford?" She looked doubtful, troubled. "I wouldn't bother. I don't even know if he still handles the elderly. As you said, not many people are interested in the ordinary retiree, the modest portfolio. Mr. Reese was a rarity. Besides, Ray Palford moved his office all the way down to Margate. I don't think it would be worth your while." She waved off the suggestion, but I definitely did not. Margate was a hop, a jitney ride, or a brisk boardwalk trot away from my hotel. What a happy geographic relocation.

Margate was also a close enough home base from which to zip down and murder someone in Atlantic City. "Was the partnership dissolved recently?" I asked. "Because maybe Mr. Palford would remember—"

"Three years ago."

Not exactly the kind of new and painful rupture that could lead to murder. I was disappointed. The image of a tall ex-partner in a wig had a lot of appeal.

"I'm sorry I can't be more helpful."

"Looks like I'm back at Go," I said. "Could I bother you for my tear sheets?"

She was going to have neck problems if she didn't stop punctuating her sentences with head shakes. "I'm sorry, but I don't understand what sheets you're talking about. I'm sure I would have noticed if something of yours came in, and we wouldn't have torn it, anyway. Now if you'll excuse me, as you can see, I'm packing things up and there's so much to do. . . ."

I wanted to see the inner office, to get to know Jesse Reese by his artifacts, if through no other way. "Tear sheets are pages from magazines with my stories on them," I said. "I know it's crass to ask for them when you have so many more important things on your mind, but I don't really have all that many—I sent him originals, not copies, and if I have to start all over again . . ."

"There are no magazine pages in the office. I would have noticed."

"There must be! He *thanked* me for them. *Complimented* me on them—and said he'd return them."

She had a sturdy middle-aged body, but the suit enclosing it behaved as if there was nothing inside it at all. There wasn't a wrinkle anywhere, not even at the lap or inner arms. Some other time I'd love to ask her the secret of her imperviousness. "Please," I said, really into my role as professional pest, "maybe you're not recognizing them. *Senior*'s on newsprint. It doesn't look like a magazine." My parents always picked it up at the deli. It was a free paper.

Miss Evans raked her fingers through her gray-brown hair. "If I let you peek in his office, do you promise not to touch anything? We have to get things ready for the estate and the clients."

"We? Are there other employees here?"

"A figure of speech. I'm so used to referring to us as . . ." This produced another round of head-shaking and nose-blowing.

"Normally, I wouldn't intrude," I said, "but free-lancing's so hard, and a good set of tear sheets is pretty valuable."

The phone rang just as she touched the doorknob to his office. "The machine will pick up," she said. "The message says everything anybody needs to know. I wouldn't get a single thing done if I answered every call. Besides, I can hear the caller, in case of an emergency."

I was glad I hadn't phoned ahead. I would have been told that the office was closed, which was the message I now heard beginning, in Norma Evans's patient but tired-sounding voice. She didn't say what had happened, but you could tell by her melancholy timbre that something dire had occurred.

Jesse Reese's office was a larger, slightly more opulent space. Still, there was something slick and surface about it, a sense that the woods were veneers, the velvet sofa a rental item, the liquors in the cabinet inferior brands poured into expensive bottles.

It was obvious that most of Reese's business must have been carried on elsewhere, at those junior colleges and retirement homes Frankie had mentioned, with elderly people reluctant to travel.

There were few personal touches, although some things had either already been put in cartons or were never unpacked. Two boxes, flaps open, sat near the bookcase. The books on the shelves looked fake, or chosen for their binding colors, the furnishings safe and predictable. The only individualized items hung on the wall behind his desk: a plaque from the Chamber of Commerce, a framed photograph of Mr. Reese and a hearty-looking man, and a soft-edged portrait of a woman, painted, apparently, by a brush full of marzipan. "His wife?" I murmured.

"Yes."

The portrait must have been commissioned in Mrs. Reese's pregrommet phase. She was wearing something translucent and dreamy.

Half Norma Evans's attention was still in the outer office, listening to a droning male voice on the answering machine. I could make out his inflection—questioning—but not the words.

"Poor Mrs. Reese. She must be devastated," I murmured. Jesse Reese's desk was bare except for a clock and a narrow dish in which lay a pen, so I looked back at the wall, at the photograph of Reese in this very room, at this very desk below a wall that then held only the saccharine portrait of his wife. He was half out of his chair, en route to a handshake, one hand extended, the other flat on the desk, giving him balance. His little finger touched a photograph of a woman in a swimsuit and high heels. Miss Wannabe America. A smiling man who looked like a gone-to-seed athlete offered up the Cherry Hill Citizen of the Year plaque that now hung on the wall next to this picture.

Those tear sheets in which I had come almost to believe were, not surprisingly, nowhere to be found. "I don't know what I'm going to do," I said in my Hildy whine.

She shook her head. "Sorry. I can't imagine what became of them."

"Did his wife take her photograph?" I asked. "The one on the desk in this photo?"

Miss Evans looked startled, checking me, then the desk, then the photo on the wall, then me again. "No," she said. Miss Evans wasn't in a mood to chatter.

The phone rang again, and again was followed by the patient, tired sounds of Norma Evans explaining the changed status of the office. It was a very changed status and a very long message.

"Maybe my tear sheets are inside one of the cabinets," I suggested.

"I'm sorry, but those cabinets are false fronts," she said in her near whisper. "They contain stereo equipment and a TV. There are no tear sheets here, Miss Johnson."

In the outer office a querulous voice spoke—shouted, actually. *"Norma,"* it said, "don't give *me* that crap about being closed. I know you're there, so . . ."

The voice sounded mixed in a cement truck.

Norma Evans bolted and raced from the office, diving for her desk. She got to the receiver with amazing, middle-age-defying speed. For a second longer I heard the voice utter expletives, but then Miss Evans pressed a button and the sound stopped. "I'm *here*," she said. "Somebody was—is—in the office and I'm *busy*."

I couldn't hear anything more, except for excited squawks from the caller. I crossed the room and looked into those two cartons.

Videotapes. Prerecorded. "An Afternoon with Jesse Reese," it was. "Seminars on Savings." My pocketbook was too small, but I shoved a tape under the baggy excess of Mackenzie's sweater, my heart racing. Then, taking a deep breath, I went out to the reception area where Norma Evans was still on the phone. As I walked in, I faced the back of the woman's desk, and I saw that the papers she'd been straightening so obsessively had been shoved, corners helter-skelter, into a large violet and navy bag, not into a desk drawer. Norma Evans, receiver still to her ear, followed the arc of my eyes and looked ashamed. I'd caught her being less than efficient. Downright slovenly, in fact.

When she hung up, I thought it was time for Hildy Johnson to be concerned about something besides her own prematurely terminated story. "The people who had accounts with Mr. Reese, what happens to them?" I asked.

"But surely," she said, "since you won't be interviewing—"

"I was thinking that if we're protecting financial futures, we have to know what happens when your financial counselor dies." Well, actually, it wasn't John Q. Public as much as I who needed to know if there was any percentage in killing off your financial advisor. "Is it possible to get a list of his customers? Or do you call them clients?"

"I'm sorry," she said once again. "That's privileged information, not something I could share with you. But I can assure you that Mr. Reese's clients are being duly notified." She took a moment to compose herself. "It will be up to each of them to determine how and with whom to manage their funds from now on."

"Given"—I gestured at the unoccupied office— "what's happened, I'm thinking of a whole different spin for the article. 'The Death of Professor Money.' That's what they called him, wasn't it?"

"That sounds ghoulish," she whispered, her hands to her chest.

I agreed, but there were still things I wanted to know. How did real journalists ferret out information, aside from those who arrived with big bucks as bribes? "It wouldn't be," I assured her. "I promise you that. It would be . . . moving. A *tribute* to him. You said . . . it . . . happened in Atlantic City. Was he there to see a client? Maybe that's my angle."

She looked startled again. She had a very small repertoire of visible emotions—timidity, unsettledness, shock, sorriness.

"Oh, maybe you're worried about that . . . that woman. I wouldn't mention any of that in print. I promise. That's just between the two of us."

"And the entire world. There will be a trial, of course, and it's already in all the papers."

"I meant, was he on business before then? Could I interview his last client? Follow her through what she does now, something like that?"

She shook her head. "The fact is, I don't know who his appointment was with last night." She looked as if that failure burned inside her with an angry flame. "It wasn't on his calendar. Just the way you weren't."

"So, then, you can't help me?" I forgot myself— Hildy Johnson forgot herself—and gesticulated, thereby almost dislodging the pilfered tape. I gasped and clutched my side, holding the tape in place.

Miss Evans blanched. Her eyes widened. A tiny spot of rust appeared on each cheek. She shook her head. "Are you all right?" she asked.

I nodded. "Just . . . disappointed," I stammered.

I knew what was coming next.

"I'm sorry," she said.

Me, too.

I got into the car a bit shakily. It must take a while to get used to stealing, lying about who you are, and preying on and pestering the newly bereaved. I was really tired, and the recent tension had upped my back pain a few notches.

I thought longingly of my house, my bathtub, my

bed, and my cat, but I didn't feel brave enough to visit the last of these love objects, Macavity.

Leaving home without Macavity is more dangerous than without an American Express card because of the unique attention he receives at Old Mrs. Russell's Cat Camp.

Nancy Russell, a lovely dealer in tribal jewelry, is my friend and neighbor who lives, when not shopping in obscure slivers of the world, with her mother, who is deaf, dictatorial, and convinced that most people and all "strange" animals are verminous disease carriers. Except for Macavity, who's been granted special exemption from disgustingness. When I leave town, he goes to Old Mrs. Russell's Cat Camp, where he does not exactly pine for me.

Old Mrs. Russell poaches him fresh salmon and bluefish fillets. She lights a fire on even the muggiest days and has a special Macavity pillow that she places in front of the flames. She tells him stories of delectable mice and exotic alleys, and makes sure that a dozen new catnip-laden play toys are on hand per visit. She provides a constant on-demand lap and petting hand and a special litter pan that's got a little house built around it.

And then, to my and her daughter's amazement, one day Old Mrs. Russell produced—proudly—her secret weapon, a vibrator with which she massages old Macavity's stomach. "A nonsexual massage, you understand," she said in her prim and haughty voice as I stood gape-mouthed. "But quite satisfying, as you can see."

Neither I nor her daughter dared cross the haughtiness barrier to ask where and how the elderly woman had procured her instrument of delight.

But the bottom line is that a cat's loyalty—make that *my* cat's loyalty—is not the stuff of heroic ballads. Cats are pragmatists, not romantics. They know a good thing when they find it, and are not big on altruism. Macavity doesn't speculate about whether he can go home again—he just knows he doesn't want to.

So if I did visit, he'd ignore me, hoping I'd go away, and I wasn't sure I could handle the additional stress right now.

I mentally wished my kitty a gloriously hedonistic holiday, looked up at the sky, which had turned thick, ominous, and lifeless, and reluctantly put the convertible top up, pointed the car east, and heard the first smack of rain as I pulled away. A summer storm without a summer. Or perhaps the half day of blue skies this morning had been it. I hoped I had enjoyed it sufficiently.

Nine

SOON OBVIOUSLY DIDN'T MEAN QUITE THIS SOON, EVEN though nearly three hours had passed since I first read Mackenzie's message. Well, it was commuter time now, so I gave him further slack on getting back from wherever he'd gone in his search for Dunstan.

I wanted to believe he was taking his time because in the interim he'd found, arrested, and booked Dunstan Farmer.

I pushed Jesse Reese's tape into the VCR and looked for the *play* button. And then I laughed out loud. All alone, laughing at nothing like a crazy person, but all the same it struck me as nearly hysterial that here I was, on the world's most pathetic vacation, doing exactly what I had left home to avoid: sitting alone, watching a tape, and waiting for Mackenzie.

The musical introduction to Jesse Reese's seminar sounded prefab, as if someone had pushed the soothingly-nondescript-background-tune button on a computer.

But the man himself was definitely not nondescript. Properly lit and photographed, he was better-looking than his portrait in the paper had suggested. His voice was deep, soothing and convincing. A man to be trusted with your life's earnings.

98

After a short introduction the screen was filled with a shifting montage of senior citizens enjoying what he called, in his voice-over, the dividend years. There were golfers and sailors and mall-walkers and grandchildren-cuddlers and travelers and gardeners and ballroom dancers and hammock swingers. The images almost made me want to fast-forward the next thirty or forty years of my life and get to this plane of pure pleasure.

Then Reese's voice faded and we heard from the seniors themselves. "My whole life I dreamed of getting a college degree, and at age seventy-six, I . . ." "I always loved dollhouses, and now, with the time to collect and design them, I . . ."

I, of course, was Jesse Reese's nightmare. A pension plan that wouldn't kick in for years, and then only feebly. No savings. No safety net. Where would I be when I was their ages? On a soup line along with Frankie the bartender and other merry souls who thought financial planning was a boring topic? In a rocker at the Indigent Old Teachers' Home? Or—worst of all, the nightmare—under the boardwalk along with Georgette?

Jesse Reese infomercialized me into slavish attention. How could I save myself before it was too late?

He sat, elegantly tailored, in a living room that had an edge of forced fakery, like a homey talk-show set. Two women and a man faced him, smiling nervously. One of the women looked like Norma Evans might if she invested in makeup and time.

Everybody's awkwardness was endearing. They were marvelous actors who imitated nervous amateurs brilliantly.

"I've been a homemaker all my life," a blond marshmallow puff said. "When my husband died, I realized I didn't know the first thing about how to take care of myself financially."

"My investment goals are pretty simple," the man said. "I want to be able to stay independent. Don't want to rely on the kids or anybody else, ever. Don't want anybody's handouts, but I don't have enough money to interest one of those professional money managers, so what do I do?"

"I've worked all my life," the second woman said. I squinted at her. She was handsome, in a large-boned, strong way. Clearly defined, and not all muzzy, the way Norma Evans had been. Her eyes were lined and lashes mascaraed, her lips were a bright crimson, her cheeks rosy. I was certain, almost, that she was, indeed, Jesse Reese's secretary, testifying for her boss, being the serious ant contrast to the chubby blond homemaker's grasshopper. "I couldn't save much until recently." She sounded like somebody who hadn't quite fully memorized her script. "For a long time, I had a lot of family expenses because of illness and things like that. So now I'm really concerned about protecting myself."

And to each, Jesse Reese extended sympathetic sounds, a pat on the hand, a smile, and then advice. He stood and made lists on an easel that happened to be part of his living room decor. He explained, he charted, he offered suggestions. And through it all, like a subliminal message, was the clear idea that if you wanted more guidance than a thirty-minute tape could provide, and no matter how large or small your net worth, Jesse Reese, a man who cared, a man with years of experience, would be more than happy to become your personal financial advisor.

"You convinced me, Jess," I said. Talking to one's TV is one of the ten warning signs of Needing to Get a Life. There was a message in all this, and it wasn't about investments.

The rooms here had doorbells. Mine made an unpleasant noise between a honk and a howl. I wonder what designer having a bad day decided that all the irritants of home should be built into the hotel's wiring. The bell sounded again, like an agitated goose.

And here we were, together again at day's end, Ma

working over a hot TV and Pa bringing news of the larger world.

"Find him?" I asked when he'd settled into the second upholstered chair.

"Him?" He pointed at the television.

"No," I said. "That's Jesse Reese. We know where he is."

Mackenzie looked at the screen. "What's that you're watching, the news?"

"A tape," I said. "An infomercial that was going to run, probably on a local cable channel. Seminar number one for senior citizens on what to do to protect their futures. I don't think it's soon to be a major motion picture."

"Where'd you get it?"

I stopped the tape. "I'll tell if you don't lecture me on ethics. In fact, I'll tell you everything about today if I can be spared the voice of the law."

"Stole it, didn't you?" He sighed, then smiled. "That wasn't a lecture, so tell me about your day."

I did, as much as I could remember in one gulp. He already knew whatever Sasha had said this morning, so I began with the business with the chambermaid, awaited applause, which I found rather stingily meted out, then grudgingly continued with Frankie's additions and the details of my expedition to Cherry Hill.

"I just wish I could have found out why he was in Atlantic City, if not to gamble," I said. "The fact that Norma Evans wouldn't say means it must be important. She's shielding him."

"Maybe she didn't say simply because she didn't know."

"You're kidding. The woman made it very clear— was very proud of the fact—that she organized every detail of his life and had done so for seventeen years."

"Maybe this one time he had no intention of lettin' her know, and she couldn't admit it. The woman's embarrassed."

"But she was there. She didn't say so, but Sasha mentioned somebody with a blue and purple leather pocketbook, and there was one like it under Norma Evans's desk."

"Don't women change purses?" Mackenzie asked with real curiosity.

"She isn't exactly a fashion plate. The bag, to tell the truth, was a lot spiffier than the rest of her. I bet it was a gift from Reese. For Secretary's Day or something."

"But don't hundreds of women own the same bag?"

Of course they did.

"Did you ask her where she was that night? Her whereabouts?"

I shook my head. "I was supposed to be writing about investments for seniors. Interrogation didn't exactly fit the role. Sorry."

"Well . . . good job, anyway," Mackenzie said. Rather grudging, just because it would have been illogical to ask the question he had in mind. I wondered if Mackenzie's competitive streak was as erratic and ineradicable as mine, and whether it bothered him that I'd detected something on my own.

I moved the topic slightly off the mined ground. "What happens when an investment advisor dies?" I asked, somewhat rhetorically, because there wasn't a business-oriented brain between us. "Who takes care of the money that's invested?"

Mackenzie slowly unwrapped one of several peppermint candies in a small glass bowl. "Probably just give it back and the folks have to choose somebody new." He didn't seem particularly worried about Jesse Reese's clients.

"Do you think one of his investors could have had it in for him?"

His voice was muffled around the candy, which bulged in his cheek and compounded his accent. Slowly, I deciphered each word. "Anything's possible," he said, "though I thought his clients tended toward senior citizenship. Could they overpower him? Bash him with that heavy lamp?"

There was that. "A surrogate?" I asked halfheartedly.

"I did find out some about Dunstan," he said when the candy was down to talking size. "At least where he lives. Lived. His place was locked up and his next-door neighbor told me he'd gone away for an indefinite period. Left early this mornin'. So I didn't find out much. He lived out a piece in one of those standard-issue condos. Fake Tudor half-timbering on a three-year-old cinder-block building, for whatever that says 'bout his character, taste, or means." He slouched in his chair, long legs straight out into the room.

I couldn't believe it, but I had forgotten to tell Mackenzie about my phone call to Wisconsin. "Well, I found out more than that. I found out that Dunstan Farmer died in some big city in the South when he was in high school." I thoroughly enjoyed the blue flash of interest that ignited Mackenzie's pale eyes. Gotcha. I know that my competitive attitude is unworthy of me and unhealthy for any relationship I might have, but it feels good not to squelch it all the time. Besides, if *that*'s what terminates C.K. and me, if we can ever whittle our problems down to one such issue, I'll be happy to work on it. And very surprised.

"The dead Dunstan wasn't foreign-born, was he?" Mackenzie asked.

I shook my head. "Dunstan Farmer's family goes way back in Wisconsin, where he, too, was born, although they moved to the South when he was in high school."

Mackenzie sat up straighter and rewarded me with a companionable grin. "Good goin'," he said, not at all grudgingly.

Brilliant going, I told myself.

"That's what I figured myself," he said, even more slowly than was normal.

"How?" I said. "Why?"

He shrugged. "Why not? Had lots of time to think today. Couldn't find his place—he's moved three times
recently. That ride was incredibly boring. How come
they call this the Garden State?"

Only God—or the advertising agency that had in-
vented the slogan—knew. And the garden's culmina-
tion, America's number one vacation destination, was
no more picturesque than the roads that led here. Driving back from Cherry Hill, I'd again been struck by the
depressing decay behind the boardwalk. Atlantic City
was a one-dimensional backlot facade, the only place I
know where the expression "The buck stops here" is lit-
eral and visual. The place where the bucks stop is one
block back from the boardwalk and as clearly marked
as a high-tide line.

But that was beside the point. Dunstan was the point.
Mackenzie's ability to have known my great revelation
in advance was the point. The itchy flare of that competitive annoyance was yet another point.

"You know," he said, "I should have mentioned
somethin' this mornin'. Maybe could have saved us
both time."

"Mentioned something like what?" It didn't matter
what Mackenzie would specifically say. The thing was,
he'd been ahead of me all the time. I was no more than
a dogsbody. The dummy Watson bringing home tidbits
to Holmes. "Something like what?" I repeated, trying
not to snivel. I hate not knowing things.

He stood up, making the room look even smaller, the
ceiling even lower. He's not gigantic, although he is tall,
but wherever he is, in some secret alchemy I have yet to
figure out, he dominates the space. He can stand unob-
trusively, his colors pastel—blue eyes, salt and pepper
hair, unflashy clothing—slouching mildly, and he will
nonetheless still be the focal point of the room, its chief
architectural adornment. Besides, this particular room
didn't have much space for pacing, but moving his long
legs seems to crank his brain, so I let him pick his way

in a half loop around the bed, then back. And again. "You told me this mornin' and it makes sense, long as we assume Sasha's tellin' the truth," he said. "An' why shouldn't we?"

That was kind of him. There were actually lots of reasons why we possibly shouldn't, given that she was charged with murder.

"An' anyway, I'd already been wonderin' what would have kept Dunstan from simply admittin' he was with her, except bein' afraid of the law. An' why would he be afraid, this photographer who's unknown to the local police, unknown far as we could check to anybody much, certainly not *wanted*? Why would he refuse to just plain say he was with Sasha?"

I twiddled with the cellophane wrapper of another peppermint. I could nearly hear him processing his thoughts, the squeak of ideas moving through neural pathways, each grabbing the next connector, whispering "Pass it on."

"I considered that maybe Dunstan was part of the witness protection program," he said, "afraid of havin' his picture in the papers. But hell, he's a photographer. Out at public functions all the time, an' the kind of functions where distant relatives and complete unknowns are likely to show. Weddings, bar mitzvahs, anniversary parties in the number one vacation destination of the entire country just doesn't seem a way to hide. Besides, he's obviously foreign-born, some English-speakin' country, so if he needed protection, why wouldn't we send him back home, wherever that is, but out of the USA, and safe?"

Mackenzie was remarkably calm about the idea of somebody's being an imposter. Was the world, then, full of Dunstans, people trying to be invisible? The landscape suddenly became one of those hidden pictures of flowers and butterflies that turn out to be people upside down and in fetal positions. How many convicts and escapees can you find in this drawing? I didn't like the idea one bit.

"So I figured his fear prob'ly wasn't based on what he'd done, but on what he *hadn't* done." Mackenzie stopped next to the night table and held up a hand, like a professor. "Or maybe," he added, "it was based on both. What he had and hadn't done." Then, having dramatized his cryptic point, he started pacing again, but at a speedier, corner-cutting tempo that didn't work. He bumped into the edge of the bed in his excitement, then bent to rub his shin. "So," he said, his voice muffled, "it seemed a matter of finding out what country and what he was running from and why he didn't become a citizen the normal way, with a green card, etcetera. Then you told me about that drunk who called Dunstan 'Egbert.'"

"Edgar." At least he'd slipped up somewhere, even if it was on an irrelevancy.

"So he ran away from Yorkshire and his wife, faked a drowning, and became Dunstan Farmer." Mackenzie straightened up, probably so that I could see how innocent, how truly superior, how devoid of smugness he managed to be.

"It's hard to think of Dunstan as an illegal alien," I muttered.

"Not quite the stereotype, is he? He's countin' on that. So do a lot of other Brits. Right color skin, an' even though he has an accent, it's our accent of choice, the one we've decided shows breedin' and class."

Mackenzie was a tad oversensitive on the subject of accents, but I shelved that issue for another time.

"What he's done is a good way of establishin' a whole new identity," Mackenzie said. "Take the name of a dead person who'd be near your age and whose birth record is in one part of the country and death certificate in another. The records aren't consolidated anywhere, an' anybody can get anybody's birth certificate. Then you're off and runnin'. You get a new Social Security number based on the certificate, ditto a driver's license. Get a passport with that piece of photo ID, and so forth. Build a person from scratch, each new piece of ID leadin' to more. Show the driver's license and get a charge at a department store. Show that and get a credit card. And so forth."

I forgave him for figuring out the essential points without my help. I even admired him for it. I didn't feel the need to tell him that, however. Instead, I simply said, "You can make yourself up, then. Make yourself over."

Mackenzie nodded. "And you can unmake a whole life that you didn't like. Egbert—"

"Edgar."

"Edgar of Yorkshire was uninvented, and I'll bet Dunstan Farmer is currently evaporating and somebody new is startin' even as we speak. We are never going to find the man. At least not in time for Sasha."

His words made me feel imprisoned along with my friend. I had to establish my own freedom, at least. "Let's get out of here," I said. "Let's take a walk."

Mackenzie, rubbing his injured shin again, agreed.

The rain that had hit me in Cherry Hill had not made it all the way to the ocean. The afternoon was cloudy, but dry. Georgette was no longer anywhere in sight, which I mentioned to Mackenzie.

"She's homeless, not immobilized," he said. "We tend to look at those people as if they're less than human, a different species. Don' patronize her or infantilize her."

"Is it my imagination, or have you mutated into a pompous, pontifical, pretentious, self-important, bombastic bore?"

"It's your imagination," he said.

The boardwalk was not exactly the fix I needed. After two blocks I felt terminally bombarded by blinking lights, blasts of music and electronic sound, the mixed aromas of grease and plastic, and the people. Nothing connected or made a whole. Not on the boards, not in real life. "Let's go on the beach," I said. "I love it when the shadows start getting long."

Holding our shoes in our hands, we walked down to the surf line, where tiny stalk-legged birds rushed for crabs each time a wave receded, then backtracked as a new wave came in. Talk about a lousy way to make a living.

Finally there was time to tell Mackenzie about the little boy, Lucky. I felt a residual flare of anger at the child's mother and at the hotel management. "I think it's criminal," I said.

"So does the law," Mackenzie said. "Leaving a kid unattended is neglect or abuse, and there are laws against it. And, in fact, it's also a crime to not report it when you've seen it."

"So why aren't all those parents being hauled off to prison? Because it's bad for business?"

"Maybe because the witnesses are troubled by the same issues that must be troubling you, or else why haven't you reported Lucky's mother to the police yet?" he asked in that infuriatingly noncombative tone of his.

"Because it seemed . . . because I don't want anything more to do with the local police right now?"

He turned toward me and raised one eyebrow.

"Okay, because I want a chance to warn her first. It isn't going to make Lucky's life better if his mother's in jail. That should be a last step."

Mackenzie nodded. "You could work on the business end of it, alleviate the problem by makin' a stink with the casinos for child care centers."

I hadn't even made a small peep, let alone the squawk I'd promised myself. I felt the full weight of my crimes of omission.

"But you're right to hold off on an all-out effort in that direction till after Sasha's out of jail."

He was a kind, face-saving man, I decided. And then

I thought about how many times a day I revised my opinion and description of him. I wondered what that meant.

Mackenzie told me that he'd spoken to Sasha again. The imminent arrival of her cousin the lawyer had elevated her spirits. "She says this is all a crock," he relayed, "and that she didn't do it, and that all she's letting herself worry about is whether the saltwater taffy people won't mind a short delay."

We talked more about the case. "I still can't figure out who in that bar did do it, though," I said. "None of them fit the witness's description."

"Except Sasha." Mackenzie spoke softly, watching me all the while.

"What?" I asked with a smile.

"You really, truly believe the killer was in that lounge?"

I nodded. "At least one of them. There were two, remember? Killers. Plural."

He brushed my small point away. "In the lounge, already festerin' about how to get rid of Jesse Reese—for reasons we cannot even begin to speculate on now, correct?"

I nodded twice for that one.

"An' this killer person, he says, 'How convenient. Just as soon as I finish this martini, here, I'll frame that big black-haired woman.' "

"Well," I said. "Well . . . *yes*."

He shook his head and said nothing, which is one of the single most annoying actions a person can make. Back and forth, back and forth, despairing of my logic, of my intelligence.

"Mandy." He finally spoke, thereby avoiding death by mischance at my hands by a fraction of a silent second. "Mandy." He made my name sound heavy, something he must bear. "That is just too . . . Sure, there could be a little coincidence in this world, and if you consider bad timin' a form of coincidence, then there's sure a lot of it in crime. But still, somebody who wants to kill Reese happens to be there, in the same cocktail lounge? What is he doin', trailin' him? And Reese wouldn't notice or react?"

"Yes. He was there, drugging him, too. Starting his plan. The bar was *full* of people who knew Reese. Frankie. His wife. A woman with rings on her toes." He was decent enough to refrain from once again pointing out that none of the aforementioned fit the witness's description. Only Sasha did.

I kept pushing my theory, ignoring its holes. "Even Lala's boyfriend Tommy pointed him out and knew who he was. Maybe Reese didn't know that the other person wanted to do him in, but that's not relevant. Why are you acting like this is all silly?"

Mackenzie shook his head again. "We don't *require* fancy theories like that—"

"*Requahr!* We don' *requahr?*"

He sighed rather histrionically. "That sure wasn't a professional assassin that did Reese in. It was somebody madder than hell at him. Right then. Doesn't require old secrets or a long history, either. A minute of fury, that's all it took." His voice dropped until it was barely audible above the soft hum of the sea. "Enough anger and a key to that room, that's all it took."

"Not a key—I *told* you." But that hadn't been his point. I lowered my voice. "You're not a hundred percent sure that it wasn't Sasha, are you? You've been really nice about this, and I thought you—but you aren't sure, are you?"

He didn't answer right away. "I'm a hundred percent sure I don't *want* it to be Sasha," he finally said.

"But what?"

"But nothin' else—nobody else—makes a bit of sense."

"*Sense!* How could it make sense to bludgeon a man you didn't even know? How could it make sense to think that my friend since childhood, that Sasha Berg could ever, *ever*—"

He was shaking his head back and forth again. I shut my eyes and resumed ranting blindly until I ran out of steam.

"The *witness*—" Mackenzie began.

I found a further supply of steam. "The so-called witness saw *two* people. A woman and a man. If you're so eager to lynch Sasha, tell me who the man was."

Return to head shaking. I was causing him either palsy or massive despair, and worse, it was giving me a bitter pleasure. He had to atone for his lack of faith, for his policeman-deep love of evidence. "That second-man business doesn't help Sasha's case, y'know." His voice was soft and menacing, as if a silencer had been put on it. "Or Dunstan's, either. Bein' party to a murder is a mighty good reason all by itself to not want to be found."

That's about when I stopped talking to him and started wondering how deep a hole I'd have to dig to bury a body Mackenzie's size in the sand and keep it hidden through the time, tides, and tourists of the summer season ahead.

Ten

"MAYBE," MACKENZIE SAID AS WE WALKED BACK ACROSS the soft sand, "we need a little perspective."

Our silences had grown incrementally along with the lengthening shadows of afternoon. "Everybody needs perspective on everything." I admit I was snappish. I also admit I didn't care. "What else is new?"

"Maybe we need a little distance, a little time apart."

I didn't know what to say to that. It's scary when men overuse adjectives, as in a *little* distance, a *little* perspective, a *little* time apart. Besides, Mackenzie and I already had our full measure of distance, only not in well-placed or meaningful spaces. That was part of the problem. Plus, *I* was supposed to be the one saying sentences like that. When I decided to say them.

"Ahm not much use here. The police are real competent, an' Ahm an outsider."

He sounded serene, devoid of emotions, but according to the *ahm*-slurs-per-second test, he was either upset or pissed with me. Sometimes, it's affection that's on the upswing, but I was pretty sure this was not one of those times.

We meandered toward the boardwalk. It looked chilly and dark in the recesses under it, but Georgette wasn't underneath. She was, however, crossing the sand toward us along with a shaggy, bearded man. Both were swathed in layers of shirts and socks, and both carried lumpy bundles.

"So now that you can get your things back," Mackenzie said, apropos of nothing.

It took me a second to grasp his meaning. "My things? The things up in the, ah, suite? They'll let me have them now?"

He nodded.

I felt a new surge of irritation. Why hadn't he told me sooner? My *feet* hurt. I wanted my other shoes.

"Hey! Where's the kid?" Georgette's voice was loud and hearty.

I could sense Mackenzie's muscles tense at the ready, so I spoke quickly. "Hi, Georgette, this is Mackenzie."

She nodded. "Didn't think anybody grew up that fast."

"Lucky's with his mother, or at least with the security guard."

She pointed one half-gloved finger at me. "He'll be out again before the sun's down. I see him and lots others all the time. I always watch. I see everything. And this here is Blinks."

He was aptly named. It was a twitch or an old injury or a tic, but his eyes moved up and down double time.

"Been hunting." Georgette lifted her bundle as proof. "Tuesday pickings are best, you know."

"Wednesday's trash day." Blinks was either ill or had a naturally hoarse voice. "Won't be much for the next few days." His unkempt beard and bleary eyes made him look old, but he was really only worn, the lines on his face unnatural, like scribbles defacing a photo. His hardscrabble life didn't allow people to live long enough to be as old as he looked like he was.

Georgette's age was equally unreadable. The etchings on her forehead and below her eyes were like scars, the result of external, not internal, processes. Her lips were chapped, she was missing teeth, and her wispy brown hair belonged on a person twice the age I was sure she must be.

She smiled now, cradling a bundle that was larger and more bulgy than her companion's, but less expertly tied. "Didn't I say this was my lucky day?" she asked with a low chuckle. The high heel of a shoe poked out of one of the bundle's openings, although I couldn't imagine her tottering on spikes across the sand. In another gap in the fabric, I glimpsed something metallic, and in still another break, a brown and hairy swatch I didn't want to think about. I just hoped it had never been alive. I could see, too, the edge of a bright red book. Not her *War and Peace*, then, but another paperback chucked by a tourist. Georgette was a literate pack rat.

"Didn't I say?" she repeated, looking right at me.

"You did, indeed." Seeing her clutching other people's trash and beaming her gap-toothed smile produced a dull ache at my center. What made a day lucky for her except that it hadn't rained or snowed and no one had hurt her?

Oh, yes, the zapping of her enemies, she'd said. Well, whatever her imagination seized upon as a source of joy, whatever provided her with a sense of justice, was fine with me. The woman had precious little to hang on to in her life.

"I thought Mr. Hoover would get him," she told Mackenzie.

"Who's that?" he asked mildly.

"J. Edgar. Our FBI in action."

"Yes, but I meant—who was the person he was going to get?"

"That no-good Reese."

"Jesse Reese?" His deceptively mild voice was a dead giveaway that he was suddenly and intensely interested.

Wisps of her fine hair floated as she nodded. "Hoover didn't care. President Reagan wrote me back, though.

Thanked me for my interest. Presidential seal on the paper and everything."

Mackenzie's interest level flagged. Georgette's combo platter of Ronald Reagan and the long-dead J. Edgar was a bit much for credibility. "So . . . you knew Jesse Reese," he said with minimal interest.

Georgette nodded. "Not like I know *you*. Not to *hang out* with, friendly like. But I knew him. So did my sister. He gave talks. Took money. I know lots of people. Everybody on the beach and on the boards. Everybody. Like The Donald, you know?"

My turn to nod.

"And Prince Charles? People think he's stuffy, but he's a very good singer. Lots of pep, poor, blind thing. Wouldn't think he was royalty."

"You mean Ray Charles, maybe?" I asked.

She waved the question away and peered at Mackenzie. "This your husband?"

I shook my head. I didn't look at my nonhusband because I didn't want to know how he had greeted this suggestion.

"Husbands don't last," Georgette said. "My Kurt died." She seemed still surprised by the loss. "Went like that." She tried to snap her fingers, but the cut-off gloves got in the way.

The Ancient Mariness was at it again, schlepping out her story at the slightest—or no—provocation. I remembered Kurt's name from this afternoon's portion, and now I knew he'd been her husband. She'd been married. She'd had a sister, a home with curtains on her windows, and a child. She'd had more ties and more stability, at least at one point, than I'd yet managed to obtain. And she'd wound up on the beach.

"No money then," she said. "No job. No more house." Her eyes misted up, then over. "Money thought I was dead."

Mackenzie's interest reignited. "Heap o' stir and no bisquits," he said.

"Hey!" Georgette smiled with delighted recognition.

Blinks and I stood watching. It was hard, though, with his incessant eye movements, to know whether he was as confused by the exchange as I was.

"Enjoyin' poor health," Mackenzie went on. "Life is short and full of blisters. Money thinks I'm dead."

"How'd you know that?" Georgette asked.

"Had an uncle sang it all the time," Mackenzie said. "Kind of the family theme song, to tell the truth."

"He's okay," Georgette said to me.

Blinks, still clutching his hobo pack, winged out an elbow and pushed at her. "Hurry up," he said. "You gab too much. Everybody we meet. Makes me crazy. Miss dinner you keep talking."

I thought she might slug him, but instead she smiled almost coquettishly. *"Men,"* she said, but she turned and followed him up the stairs and onto the boardwalk.

" 'Home is the place where, when you have to go there, they have to take you in,' " Mackenzie murmured after they were gone. "Do you think Frost was talking about a rescue mission?" We slowly walked toward the boardwalk. "What a life. Particularly in the shadow of those casinos. You know they give away seventy mil a year in complimentary food and drink and rooms like yours?" He appeared lost in his own dark thoughts. " 'And homeless near a thousand homes I stood / And near a thousand tables pined and wanted food.' "

"Who said that one?" It was embarrassing that a cop knew more poetry—or at least could quote more—than an English teacher, but that's how it was.

"Wordsworth, a hundred years ago. How did he know how it was going to be?"

"Sometimes," I said, "I think about the poorhouse scenes in Dickens, and how righteously superior to those times I used to feel. Now, I'm not sure. Maybe they were kinder back then. A poorhouse has to be better than no house at all, no place on earth that has to take you in."

"Or my grandma," Mackenzie said. "She used to talk about how her house was marked with a chalk that told hobos—a nicer word than *homeless*, don't you think?— she'd feed them. Somehow, back then, they were thought of as unlucky victims of the system. Now, we blame the victims instead. I know some of them made bad choices and crash-landed on the streets, but still . . ."

My urge, as always, was to do something about it, but this one was beyond even my most ambitious imagination. We walked along, kicking sand, sighing, lost in our separate thoughts. But by the top of the steps Mackenzie began talking again, and not about contemporary social problems. Georgette and Blinks had not been forgotten, but put in a mental pending file, to be retrieved only in proper sequence. Meanwhile, like a needle lifted from, then put back on the same track of a still-whirring record, to use an archaic image, he was right back where he'd been when we were interrupted.

"So you can get your things," he said, "then pack up. I have my car, too, a real shame, but if you want, we could both use mine, then come down on the train later this week or whenever, and both use yours and—"

"Wait a minute." I stopped just in front of the hotel doors and nearly caused a domino effect of falling pedestrians. But once inside, I'd have to be more polite to Mackenzie than I thought he warranted. Out of doors, almost anything goes.

"Can't wait a whole lot of minutes," he said. "I'm really tired from last night, and I'm due in early tomorrow. You know I'm here—officially—to check Nicky B.'s old haunts. How long can I pretend to inspect a city block that no longer exists?"

"But that has nothing to do with me. I'm not leaving. Not tonight, anyway."

He looked flabbergasted. "Why not? You can't be havin' a good time." People shoved their way around him, clearing their throats, trying to make him aware that he was blocking the door. He finally noticed and moved to the side, and I shifted over as well. "Your roomie's in jail, it's too cold for the beach, and you don't gamble," he said. "Why not?"

His argument contained several salient points, but it nonetheless missed the relevant one, which was Sasha. "I can't walk away and leave her here to rot!"

He rolled his eyes, seeking the compassion of the patron saint of those who deal with nincompoops. "You watch too many old movies. Sasha's not likely to rot. That jail's not even damp. Besides, her lawyer cousin's goin' to spring her."

"How do I know that? And won't she still need some kind of help, or attention? And even if the lawyer gets her bail, which isn't a for sure, will they let her leave the state? Go back to Philadelphia?"

"Depends," Mackenzie said. "Long as there's no threat she'd run, they probably will."

"But you don't know for sure and you don't really care." It was literally painful to say the words. "Not enough. Not about anything, except crime." Somewhere in the last twenty-four hours I had been pushed over my emotional boundary lines, into the swamp of sloppy sentiment. I was not only ready to cry about Mackenzie's callousness, I wanted to, I ached to do so. "You aren't really committed to—to *anything*!" A small and rational part of me knew that was unfair as well as untrue, but it *felt* right. And I was sick of facts. Facts didn't make sense. "*Nobody's* committed to anything!" I lamented. "The whole world's—"

"For Pete's sake!" he said.

A kid of about thirteen, in uniform—baseball hat turned backward, baggy droopy pants, cloaked expression—stopped about three feet from us and watched, warily. I couldn't decide if he wanted to prevent violence or witness it firsthand. I gave the kid my best teacherly scowl, meant to pierce and draw blood.

The kid shrugged a shoulder, said, "It's your funeral, lady," and meandered off.

"That's what I mean!" I said. "If he really thought something bad was going to happen, he should have stayed!"

"After you made it clear he should leave? Give him a break. Give ever'body a break."

I could hear the exhaustion in his voice, and that should have slowed me down, but it didn't. I don't know if anything could have. Accumulated frustration pressed at my back like the Furies. I felt the pressure of the long teaching year and my mother's reality-based nagging about my lack of financial security and my own ambivalence about my lack of emotional security, and—and—and— "Nobody cares *enough*. Not Reese, as far as his wedding vows, not Lucky's mother. And Dunstan's not even committed to being himself!" Everything I said felt urgent, as if I were carrying the single message that could save the planet. Paulette Revere waving her lantern and shouting, "Commit! Commit!" I couldn't have said to what he or I was supposed to commit—that was part of the problem—but I also couldn't bear for Mackenzie to be part of the great indifferent, to be like everybody else.

"I'm impressed, or depressed," he said, "by the scum and cads you've encountered, but it's nonetheless time I headed home."

"And what about Lala?"

"That a person or a pastime?"

"The woman who told me a man was harassing her so I'd make him jealous and get him to propose marriage to her. How's that for integrity?"

"Have you switched tirades? I thought you were doin' commitment, not integrity."

I heard him through an internal yapping chorus, each voice cataloguing offenses against my person. "I thought you were *committed* to helping Sasha!" He surely wasn't committed to *me*—and I still didn't know if I wanted him to be, but I knew I wanted him to want that—but I couldn't, wouldn't, say that. Yet. Talking—yelling—about Sasha and Mackenzie's relationship was much, much easier. "So now you want to shrug it off, return to business as usual, not try to prevent a horrible miscarriage of—"

"Whoah!" He took a step back and looked at me with a profoundly sorrowful expression. "Mandy," he said, his voice low, "what's this really about?" His eyes narrowed, upped their intensity. "Tell me this isn't that talk you've been sayin' we should have."

"Well, of course I wouldn't—this isn't the time or—"

"You sure?"

I stopped. The blithering emotional surge drained and I was riding on empty. "I don't know," I said, softly and honestly.

"This is an awesomely dumb time and place for it." He was almost whispering. We were retreating, voices first.

"I came here—to Atlantic City—in the first place, mostly to figure out—to think through—"

He took both my hands. "An' I didn't really come here to find out about Nicky B. But . . . stuff happens. Your friend got herself in big trouble."

"Framed. Got herself framed."

"An' you're rattled."

"Of course I am! I'm sane, I'm human. But under the rattles, I still have questions."

"Such is the nature of existence," he said. "It generates business for philosophers, theologians, and comedians."

Such was the nature of our current existence that two things were true: one, that wasn't at all the answer I'd wanted, and two, he didn't know that. I looked at him and felt wistful, a galloping case of the might-have-beens, and for what blighted outcome, I couldn't even say.

A bad blend, my granny would have cautioned me.

Two people trying to have street smarts above love, or whatever it was we'd have if we relaxed long enough to define it. Dummies, she'd have called us. But it was easier for Granny, who married her first love at sixteen with the optimism that only a person with zero experience can possibly have.

"A man died in your hotel room, Sasha's in jail, you've been meetin' slippery characters, an' you're probably hungry," Mackenzie said. "Look, it's gotten dark. So here's the plan."

I shook my head, refusing him the right to organize my thoughts or behavior, but he ignored me.

"I'm goin' back to my hotel. Give us tahm to ... think."

He meant to calm down. He meant me.

"I'll get my bag—I checked out earlier and left it in storage—"

So his leave-taking had been a fait accompli hours ago, not subject to discussion, and I could have skipped my Elegy on a Theme of Noncommitment.

"—then I'll pick you up and we'll go to dinner and, although Ah have never found it an aid to digestion—" He swallowed and took a deep breath while I translated his words, which were drenched and runny with emotion. There wasn't a consonant or hard end to one of them. He cleared his throat. "—we'll Talk. Like you mean. With a capital T."

I don't remember agreeing, but I must have, because I remember watching him walk down the boardwalk—his hotel was many blocks up and a few over—lit by the bulbs of the stores along his route, his salt and pepper curls jostling, and for one sudden burst, neon-pink.

And I remember thinking that for all my insistence, we really could skip the capital-T talk. It would only be a stopgap gesture. We were a wrong combination, a forced match. I was incredibly fond of him, but I couldn't handle the way he could segment his life, his attention, and his emotions. I couldn't handle some of what kept him sane—a rational detachment, an objectivity in the face of horror. His work had changed and hardened him, I thought. He was used to ugliness and violence, and charming though he was, he'd curled up inside himself and taken to hiding, and at this stage in my life, I couldn't handle it.

I couldn't cope with his job—his real life—and its intrusions and messiness. I couldn't deal with the uncertainty it produced.

They say a man's job is a tough mistress, but Mackenzie's was worse than another woman would be. It was his other self, a doppelgänger. And all for the sake of goodness and right, which made the struggle between us impossible.

Of course, he thought I created artificial barriers and hair splits. He thought this was all my problem, easily remedied by an attitude adjustment on my part.

We were both bullheaded and stubborn, unlikely to give up beloved convictions, so what was the point of discussing and analyzing and trying to effect change?

Look, I've read too many books not to recognize when a story is winding down, when logically, the next words have to be: The End.

Eleven

FOR A NANOSECOND MY EMOTIONAL TANK REGISTERED empty, but that vacuum, being abhorred by nature, was immediately replaced by a depression that barreled in with the force of a typhoon. I could barely drag myself through the enormous front doors of the hotel.

If I'd been asked to design the atmosphere I least desired, it would have been the one I was now in, the bustling, bemarbled commercial palace's. The building was much fancier than its mostly elderly tenants dressed in the nondescript pastel knits and cottons that are supposed to camouflage middle- and post-middle-aged indignities, but instead advertise that they're there.

There's a comic who claims that the average age of Atlantic City's visitors is dead. It always gets a big laugh.

And among the average-aged gamblers was Lala, straight ahead and waving to catch my attention. I refused to let it be caught. This was the worst possible time to hear her version of the war between the sexes. I simply couldn't.

My only available escape route was the casino, into which I hustled, sure that I could make a quick detour and lose her in its blinking, dazzling interior.

And I did. Until, that is, I decided to get on with my

life and reemerge, and there she was again. I turned and reentered the casino's inner recesses.

I watched a determined, jaw-set elderly man pull the handle of a machine edged in blue light. The machine twinkled a message: COLUMBUS TOOK CHANCES, TOO!

Columbus was a better gambler. He found a new world. The man I was watching lost a dollar, stared blankly, put more coins in and pulled again. GOOD LUCK, the machine responded with a flirty twinkle of lights.

I walked down the row. The opulent, almost hysterically exuberant surroundings were in depressing contrast to the players, most of whom looked as if they needed those quarters and nickels—an elderly and frail woman on a walker—a thin man in threadworn work clothes and floppy hat, a young woman who could be Lucky's mother. Their faces and movements had the grim resignation of people working on a factory line.

I moved to the craps table, where there was a little more life but even less sense. I had assumed that I could comprehend anything Nathan Detroit understood. Yet another wrong assumption. I tried to decipher the many meanings stenciled on the table, the source of the muted excitement of the people gathered around, but quickly gave it up. It would take too long to understand. Besides, I felt a certain urgency about getting my belongings from upstairs quickly, before they locked up for the night. But as I turned, there was Lala again. The woman was really good at dogging a person. She could have bailed herself out financially by becoming a P.I. instead of Tommy's wife.

I slipped out of her line of sight and found myself having another unasked-for reality check outside the baccarat salon. Somebody had told me that baccarat was the one card game that required absolutely no skill, and in fact couldn't utilize it, because it was based on pure chance. Which left it with only style, precious little of which was evident. The table, separated from the rest of the casino by a maroon velvet rope, was surrounded by Asian men in windbreakers. The *shoe* that held the cards was red plastic.

Baccarat. I yearned for tuxedos, Grace Kelly, Monte Carlo, the splash of the Mediterranean on the rocky coast outside, balconies and palaces, designer gowns, and croupiers with sexy accents and knowledge of old world evil.

"You all right, hon?" The accent was domestic, the voice metallic, and my clean escape a flop. Lala peered at me from beneath aquafrosted eyelids. "I've been calling and calling," she said. "You were a million miles away. I'm out of breath from trying to catch you."

I wondered if there were equally annoying people in Monte Carlo, and whether it would be my fate to attract them there as well.

She put her hand on my forearm. Her engagement ring sparkled. "I wanted to explain," she said. "About, well, you know."

"No need."

"You're young; you can't possibly understand."

I wondered why people always insist on telling you that you're not going to understand something they are going to insist upon telling you anyway.

"About how it is to be an older woman, alone and without money," she continued. "You know how many of the poor people in this country are women?"

"How many?"

Her mouth opened and closed a few times. Then she pursed her lips and spoke. "A *lot*, that's how many. Maybe *most*. Women just like *me*."

I moved in the direction of the lobby.

"I never worked," she said, hustling to keep up with me. "My husband wouldn't hear of it." She sounded as if she were hyperventilating, in some medical danger.

I slowed my pace, accepting my fate and not willing to be responsible for hers.

"I had no idea we were in debt, or that he didn't have enough insurance until after he died."

What was it I did that made people decide it was always story hour? "I'm sorry," I said, "but I have something I really have to do upstairs. Excuse me." That was true, but another truth was that I didn't want to hear about how easy it was to become frighteningly poor. I wanted to reclaim my possessions and pretend they were protection from becoming old and without resources.

"But I got a job then." She trotted behind me, as if my words had been no more than white sound. "I had to. Didn't have a cent. I worked in a discount luggage store. Three years, and then I was a recession cutback. My rent went up. My son's wife left him and their boy and he needed help, and money for help." Her voice dropped to dirge level. "A woman alone . . ."

Oh, goody. You could really try hard and things could still get worse. Things *would* get worse. First aid for the insufficiently depressed.

"He liked me," Lala said. "Tommy. But I could not get him to go one step further, to get off the stick, you understand?"

It's an interesting expression: *get off the stick.* Doesn't make any sense when you think about it, unless it meant get unstuck. But yes, I definitely understood what she meant.

"So I thought," she said, "if I made Tommy a little bit scared, less sure of himself . . . It always worked in the old movies."

We had reached the elevators. "Do you love him?" I asked.

Once again Lala put her hand on my arm. "Even in the dictionary, love means a lot of things, darling. But having nothing only means trouble."

I got onto the elevator. By the third floor I couldn't hear even her echo. By the top floor I had almost convinced myself that I had nothing in common with Lala, and that there were no similar sticks to get off of between C. K. Mackenzie and Tommy.

A drowsy security guard sat outside the suite. "Can't come in here, ma'am," he said. "This here area is not open to the public."

I told him my name and purpose. He checked a clipboard and looked disappointed that I had passed muster. "Thought you were another gaper. People act like this is a set for *Unsolved Mysteries*." His scowl made him look like a pink-skinned bulldog as he heaved himself out of his chair with a great sigh and turned the knob of the suite.

"Thanks." I stepped in. I expected many things, but not a curvacious bit of a woman dressed entirely in black—hat, gloves, shoes, stockings, slacks—except for the flashes of brass on every one of the above garments and the yellow-gold hair cascading over her shoulders. Even her cane had a brass head and rivets all the way down its shaft.

Rivets, I thought. The bolted Mrs. Reese. Jesse's widow. But something was wrong.

The widow Reese stood near the door in the suite's foyer, pursing her red-gold mouth, tilting her head and listening intently to a stocky patrolman in uniform. He interrupted himself and looked me over.

"She's the one," the hall monitor said.

"Oh, yeah?" He looked disgusted.

"The last to know," the woman in black said in a gravelly voice. She pressed one gloved hand to her ample bosom. "Like they always say. Isn't that so, Holly?"

A loud, commiserating *tsk* came from a blaze of hot color across the entryway, and then a slow "he was—such a—son of"—words rolling out in a deep female voice—"a bitch."

The widow sniffled into a black lacy handkerchief. I knew what was wrong. She'd bleached her hair overnight. From raven to brass. What a weird expression of grief. Or was it suspicious?

The patrolman looked at me with contempt. "What do you want?"

"My clothing and things."

"You?" The widow practically shouted it. "You're the one he was shacked up here with?"

I shook my head. "I'm here for my toothbrush and—"

"They let you *free*?" Her voice sounded stone-washed and bruised.

The deep voice of the other woman, the pink one, joined in. "You have some nerve showing your face. Don't you have any respect?"

"Listen, I'm not—this isn't—" I glared at the policeman.

"My poor sister. Bad enough that son of a bitch humiliates her with his bimbos!" I wondered how she'd define herself, bandaged as she was in hot-pink spandex that barely coexisted with her carotene hair. "But to have his playmate—his *murderer*—"

I was almost flattered at being called a bimbo. I felt haggard and shabby in my oversized borrowed sweater and yesterday's slacks, my too-tight loafers and my post-Mackenzie, post-Sasha, post-Georgette, post-Lala, post-Lucky funk.

"This here's the *other* one was staying here," the policeman said. "Needs her toothbrush and things."

"What did you have planned for up here? Something really kinky with both you girls?" the hot-pink woman demanded. Her ensemble was also outlined in rivets. The bolted look was a fashion development I didn't mind having missed.

"Didnja hear what he said? She isn't the one who was here," the widow told her sister. "I didn't mean to infer. Imply. Suggest. I'm rattled, you know?" She put out her gloved hand. "I'm Poppy Reese," she said solemnly. "That's my sister Holly."

I wondered if they had other botanically named siblings, if there were boy-children with plant names as well.

Then she turned to the patrolman. "We spent a lot of

time here together, you know. It brings back too
many . . ." She dabbed at her eyes, although there was
no moisture for her black lace hanky to catch.

"Sorry, ma'am. We thought maybe you'd see something out of place, or wrong. You know."

"My sister's upset," the woman in pink said. She
lounged against the silk-covered wall and tapped one
hot-pink shoe. "Her *husband*—her lying, cheating, no-
good husband who'd already wasted half *their* money—
was killed yesterday, in case you forgot. Her whole
entire world has just collapsed."

"We're out of here," Poppy Reese said.

The law nodded. "You'll be home, then? In Haddonfield?"

Poppy shook her head. "My *sister's* house. Holly
Booker, up at the end of the boardwalk, in Ventnor. I
gave you the address already."

"Why should my sister be in her big house all alone?
It's too far away and too full of memories, am I right,
Poppy?"

Poppy's nod was woe itself.

"This way, we can walk the boards, come in here for
a massage, a little workout. It'll be good for her. Physical activity, a little pampering—it's always good for a
person."

"She works here," Poppy said. "In the spa."

Holly worked here. And what was her relationship
with the deceased? Could Jesse have happened to be
around the bar because he was seeing Sis on the sly?

"Besides," Holly said, "we haven't seen each other
for a while. Ever since her car went into the shop, like
a year ago, she can't get here, and that no-good husband
of hers, you'd think he'd bring her? I picked her up this
morning. I said, 'You're staying with me.' "

"It's been in the shop two weeks," Poppy corrected
her. "Not a year. I drive a special car," she said to the
policeman. "Because of my . . ." She looked momentarily sad for real.

"Besides," Holly said again, "she has her businesses to look after. Especially now that—"

"Business?" the cop asked.

Wait, I thought. Wait. This was all wrong. Poppy was in Atlantic City last night. Why didn't she want her sister to know? Also, if she couldn't drive herself, then with whom had she come, if not her husband? The suspicion that she'd been spying on Jesse, perhaps because of her sister, grew.

I'd have to talk with Mackenzie about this—but when? We were supposed to for once and finally talk about *us*, and who knew what would happen after that?

"Businesses," Holly said. "My sister's very talented. You're looking at the next Liz Claiborne, so help me."

Holly wasn't behaving like my idea of a woman who'd been cheating with her sister's husband. Or someone whose lover had just been offed. Or maybe she was. Maybe she was being overly solicitous, overly obvious about her solicitousness.

Holly patted her sister's shoulder and winked at the cop, like a mother pushing her child forward for praise. Make the kid feel better, she seemed to be saying. "The store has three lines—Glitz for Gals, Studz—with a *z*—for Guys, Twinklz—with another *z*—for Tots. Three entire lines. Rivets are her personal fashion statement. You heard it first here."

"I'm sorry." The patrolman looked apologetic. "I don't know a whole lot about fashion, so . . ."

"Well," Holly said, "it isn't exactly open yet." She sounded a little testy, as if we were demeaning her sister by quibbling over inessentials—real store or figment, who cared?

"And now, look what happened. Talk about a setback," the widow said. I found it an interesting way to categorize—or dismiss—her husband's death. "You never know, do you?"

Poppy took a deep breath. "Still, life must go on." And then, followed by her pink sibling, she left.

The patrolman stared at her afterimage. "Did you know she was Miss Nebraska or Kansas—someplace like that—awhile back?" he asked me. "They're usually a lot taller. A real shame about her being lame now and all." He kept staring at the space she'd vacated until her lingering spell finally broke. Then he nodded me in the general direction of the bedroom.

Once again, and probably for the last time, I admired the elegant serenity of the Eastern Suite. Only its name troubled me. East for me would be England. A room filled with Hepplewhite would be an Eastern Suite. Why had we adopted England's egocentric and geographically backward labels, as if we were still their colony?

"Don't touch anything except what you have to," the cop said. I wondered why, at this point, it mattered. Everything must have been long since dusted, sprayed, photographed, documented, or removed. I decided he'd said it out of sheer spite. He wanted to make everything hard for me because he didn't like me as much as he'd liked the widow Poppy. But then, I'd never been Miss Anything except Pepper.

At the bedroom door I gasped and put both my hands up to my mouth. Perhaps I'd unconsciously assumed that once everything was measured and noted, the room would be freshened up by a special postmortem chambermaid, but the room looked as if the murder were happening now, but for the absence of the victim.

One of the two beds was pulled apart, the bedding dangling onto the floor, pulled half off the mattress, but that wasn't it.

It was the red-brown splat on the sheeting, the gory spread, the rusty mattress pad. *It* was where blood had arced and dripped in splatters across the once beautiful screen behind the bed, and onto the wall beyond it.

"Dear God." I turned my head away, nauseous and on the verge of tears.

The detective said nothing, but I felt his eyes on my

skin, studying me, as if my every word and action were important evidence.

I ducked my head, averted my eyes, and pulled my suitcase out of the closet.

"Make sure you only take your own things," he said. "Let me know if you notice anything out of the ordinary—you don't have to check the pockets or anything."

Because they already had. The idea made me even sicker. Had I left anything peculiar, unethical, or unworthy in my pockets? Was this like having an accident with ripped underwear?

Oh, God, my underwear. Surely they'd been through that, too, so it was *exactly* like that! I hoped nobody told my mother.

"But anything out of the ordinary," he repeated.

Such as what? A ten-million-dollar check from Publishers Clearing House stapled to the hem of my green blouse? A komodo dragon on my blazer lapel? My jeans' legs sewn together? What could possibly be out of the ordinary about my pathetic wardrobe, given that disarray and poor maintenance was the norm, and that they'd already examined every fiber of it, anyway?

I folded each piece carefully, wanting to impress the officer with my wholesome packing expertise. "Couldn't somebody from the hotel do this?" I finally asked. "Bring a rack and hang everything up?"

He nodded. "Except you'd still have to say which is yours and which is hers, you know. This is just as efficient."

Not for me. The process seemed voyeuristic and creepy. I tucked the sandals I'd optimistically packed for the beach into the edge of the suitcase, scooped up my underwear without checking it for imperfections or fingerprints, and retrieved my tennis shoes, remembering bitterly the peaceful solitary walks I'd also fantasized. "Is it all right if I change shoes?" I asked the detective. "These loafers are . . . my feet have been hurting since last night."

I wanted him to smile, to ease up, but he didn't oblige me. He shook his head, somehow conveying that I was yet another Cinderella wannabe, squeezing my feet into tiny sizes. Or was that my own crabbed conscience speaking? In any case, the man said my footwear didn't make any difference to him.

I didn't think I should muss the good bed, certainly didn't want to go near the gory bed and didn't want to ask Officer Smiles's permission to sit on any other surface, so I accomplished the great shoe switch on the floor. The back throb I'd felt earlier with Lucky upped its voltage. I switched positions along with shoes and convinced myself that I did not have anything as trite and boring as a back problem. What I did have were blisters on both my heels and, when I stood up, a very sharp and extremely painful pressure on a toe.

"You done, then?" the policeman asked.

"No. Sorry." I sat back down. "A pebble," I said by way of explanation as I pulled the shoe off and shook it. He yawned and turned away.

A former pebble, I should have said. Once upon a time, when it lodged itself in the belly of an oyster. Now, a pearl earring with a sharp post that had been drilling through my toe. I shook the shoe some more, to see if the clasp was in there as well, but it was not.

I bent over the earring on the carpet, afraid to touch it. Surely it had prints on it. I didn't know good pearls from paste, but this one had a nice sheen and a quietly elegant setting that suggested it had not been a K mart special.

I stood up straight and rubbed my back. I didn't own anything like that earring, and Sasha wouldn't. It was too understated, too unobtrusive. With her wild curly mane, she felt there was no point to earrings unless they were humungous enough to swing free and shine.

"Excuse me," I told the cop, whose back was to me

as he stared out the window. I was glad he didn't seem literate enough to read my mind and find me thinking of the expression pearls before swine.

"Yeah?" he asked, back still to me.

"I did."

He turned my way slowly, reluctantly. "You did what?"

"Find something out of the ordinary in my clothes."

Twelve

You'd THINK HE'D BE EXCITED—A GENUINE, HONEST-TO-God clue to the presence, in this room, of another woman besides Sasha. But his attitude suggested that I was fixating on a bit of flotsam simply to add to his workload and give him grief.

He lumbered over with all deliberate sloth, grunted as he bent and reached for the pearl with thick fingers.

"Wait!" I said. "I mean, of course you know what you're doing, but isn't it possible that—don't you think an earring might—probably would—have fingerprints on it? I mean, given how you'd—how I'd—put one in, you'd almost have to get your prints on it, wouldn't you? Do you think you—do you think we should touch it that way?" It was necessary to overstate the case because he failed to react normally. He hunched over the earring, watching it with the blank goggle eyes of a guppy.

I was proud of my tact and reserve. I had refrained from using the word *stupid* or any of its synonyms, which was better than he deserved. But virtue was rewarded because the patrolman slowly unbent and gave me a hooded, disdainful look, as if all on his own he'd decided against pawing the earring with his bare hands. "It's not like I don't know about prints," he said.

It was no mystery why, at nearly retirement age, he was still precariously balanced on a very low rung of the police ladder.

"But have it your way," he said in a standard-issue dismissive male tone that makes my viscera churn. He picked the earring up in a piece of tissue, looked at it and made a small *pfffut* exhalation. "Not much," he said. "What do you people see in pearls, anyway?"

"Us people?"

"Yeah. You people. Women. What do you see in pearls?"

"Normally, nothing. Right now, *evidence*."

"Not really. Lots of people use this room. Atlantic City's real popular, you know. Number one tourist destination in the U.S."

I wondered how many times a day that statistic was dragged out.

"You know," he continued, "some of the help nowadays, well, they're not necessarily the most perfect cleaners in the world. I could tell you stories—"

"I'll bet you could. But as I'm sure you realize, that particular earring couldn't have been left here by a previous tenant. No matter how sloppy the chambermaid was. Don't you agree?" I was really afraid that out of spite toward me, or life, or bad cleaning-women, the oaf was going to discount and thereby ruin this chance to prove Sasha's innocence. "I mean," I said in such a simpering tone I nearly made myself nauseous, "one need not be female to know that does not compute, isn't that so?"

"Well," he said with a shrug, "I guess I . . . what was that again about computers?" His face grew ruddy, as if slowly building up pressure.

"What I mean is, even if a person doesn't *wear* earrings, he can understand that a little leftover pearl earring cannot jump into a shoe. It's funny even to think of such a thing."

"Not so silly if you think about it a little longer, miss.

If you think about it *logically*, you'll realize that if, say, it gets itself stepped on the right way and ricochets . . ."

I cut to the chase and did not react to his emphasized *logically* and its sexist undertones. "Have you ever noticed that if the back of an earring comes off—as in a struggle of some kind—then the front part's unmoored and it can fly through the air like a little missile when the woman shakes her head. Want me to show you how?" I reached for my own earring.

He didn't want to see, which was lucky, since I was wearing a hoop that was all one piece, and I couldn't have demonstrated a thing. "Somebody wearing that earring was in this room last night," I said. "Somebody who is not my friend Sasha."

"Yeah? How can you prove this doesn't belong to your friend? Or even"—an actual idea had just now crept into his head—"it could belong to *you!*" His voice dripped with suspicion—of what, I couldn't have said.

Did the dimwit think I would have mentioned the earring if it belonged to one of us, or that I would have shown the thing to him if it were in any way self-incriminating? He should have been suspicious about whether I was planting false evidence to implicate somebody else. But I saw no need to direct his thinking or to instruct him. I was on vacation, after all.

"Maybe you brought it from Philly," he said.

"You mean accidentally? The way ships carry rats, or produce carries insects?"

"You probably packed it. It's pretty small, you know."

"I don't own pearl earrings." I had to grit my teeth to keep my temper. "So it wouldn't have been around my house, falling into my shoes. Besides, I wore those shoes yesterday. Here. I drove down here in them and kept on wearing them when I went on the beach. I didn't change my shoes until I was going out later on. There wasn't any earring inside of them. I would have felt it."

"Okay, fine. We're wasting time. I'll take care of it. You packed?"

I ran into the bathroom for my toiletries, which were in appalling disarray all over the counter.

"Looks like they scuffled in here, too," the patrolman said.

It wasn't a question, so I said nothing, just tossed shampoo and eyeliner into my travel pack. I was relieved that I'd screwed the top back on the toothpaste before I left last evening, and ashamed of myself for thinking about such an inanity.

He stood at the bathroom door, arms crossed over his chest, waiting for me to finish.

"Okay, that's it." I rushed back to the bedroom and tossed the last of my belongings into the suitcase. I was beyond caring what he thought of my packing expertise or how I handled toothpaste tubes. "I'm out of here, okay?"

He shook his head. I had to walk through the living room with him, slowly checking whether any other possessions of mine were in evidence. I retrieved my untouched books, hoping he'd noticed *War and Peace* or *Gift from the Sea* and not the sex and shopping tome, and solemnly assured him that there was now not a trace of me left in there because I hadn't had the time to further litter the premises.

"You know," he said, "the eyewitness ... what he saw was a tall dark-haired woman. You think much about that? Because you know, you're not exactly short yourself, are you? What do you have to say about that?"

All I said was goodbye.

I COULDN'T REMEMBER WHETHER MACKENZIE HAD MENtioned when he'd be back. Since the scheduled program for the evening was breaking up, perhaps I'd blocked the time frame specifics. I tried reading *War and Peace*, but like Georgette, I had trouble concentrating on their various names. I wondered if life was more interesting when everybody called you something different the way they did in old Russia. I wondered if that tradition had persisted right through Perestroika.

I wondered, too, whether Mackenzie, had he been born Russian, would have actual names, and lots of them—or would he simply be known by ever-shifting initials? C.K. for one social situation, T.K. for another, and so forth, à la russe.

I wondered where Mackenzie was.

Although I was staying in Atlantic City for only one more day, I completely unpacked, stacking undies tidily, making sure my toiletries were arranged with military precision. Nothing encourages good housekeeping as effectively as having your most personal objects pawed through by officials.

I waited for Mackenzie some more. I was no longer certain that the man was ever going to show up, although a silent disappearance was not his style.

"I was stood up for my break-up," I sang, plucking at an imaginary guitar. "Stood up 'fore my break-up. Breakin' up is harder to do if there's no one to break up with you." The next Nashville sensation. Words and life by Mandy Pepper.

Just as I got to wondering whether I could stand a life of eternal touring and whether female stars had groupies, the phone rang.

The man sounded anxious and official. "Miss Pepper?" he asked solemnly.

"Yes?"

"I'm calling from the Atlantic City Medical Center to notify you that we've admitted Mr. Mackenzie."

"*Mister* Mackenzie?" I pictured someone foreign, a gentleman in a bowler hat, a spy on *Masterpiece Theatre*.

Medical Center, he'd said. My pulse escalated and words popped up and down like frightening flashcards. Hospital. Injury. Accident. Emergency. Dead? "But how could he be in the hospital? He isn't even working!" I said.

"Am I speaking to the right person? Is this Amanda Pepper?"

"I . . . ah, *yes*."

"Because your name was in his wallet as someone to call in case of an emergency. The message on your answering machine in Philadelphia said you could be reached at—"

"He has my name in his wallet?" I was surprised at how profoundly that affected me. I had my mother's and sister's names in those slots, but Mackenzie had mine. I would never have dreamed. Besides, while I fixated on that, I avoided letting the word "emergency" fully register.

"—this hotel, so I—"

"Please," I finally dared. "What . . . what happened?" Everything slowed down—my breathing, time, the speed of light, and the course of my words, floating listlessly as dandelion fluff. Slowly—more slowly, please—toward the receiver, into the phone wires, down, through—everything slow except my brain, which was snapping and connecting double time and in no particular direction, so that between my question and his reply there was an epoch filled with theories and refutations.

First theory. Mackenzie's heart broke. Literally. Heartbroken suitor—with my name in his wallet—requiring hospitalization. Extremely romantic. A reunion at bedside, complete with violin background.

Second theory. Mackenzie was dead.

The man from the hospital cleared his throat, hiding in my time warp, afraid to break the news. They must rotate the chore, take turns, punish employees by forcing them to make these calls.

Food poisoning. Something he bought en route to the hotel. Some sleazy off-boardwalk stall food. My mother was right. You couldn't trust those food vendors.

I knew it wasn't that. Okay, then. What happened was: he gagged on the idea of our Talk with a capital T. Had to go to the hospital to have a Heimlich maneuver to get his heart out of his throat.

Appendicitis.

Jackpot. I'd found the acceptable emergency. I could imagine them wheeling him into surgery, no time to phone and cancel our last date.

"There was an accident, ma'am," the man said with excessive politeness and patience. "He's in surgery now."

It took me a moment to remember what *accident* and *surgery* meant. "A collision?" Why hadn't I thought of that? Of all the possibilities, the most logical, a car smash hadn't even crossed my— He had walked back to his hotel, so this must have happened later, while he was driving to see me, and—

"A gun, ma'am."

"A *gun*? He hit a gun?" An incredibly dumb response, but trust me, as soon as I'd heard this stranger say "Medical Center," I'd burned off half my IQ, and whatever was left was busy trying hard to not hear, not know, not get it.

"A gun hit *him*, ma'am," he said gravely, precisely, kindly, as if he weren't talking to an idiot. "Or rather, a bullet from a gun."

"You mean . . . you mean . . ." I knew what he meant. He'd been as clear and coherent as a person could be. But I couldn't believe it or accept it until I heard the actual words, one after the other, in an orderly, definitive sentence.

So he provided that sentence. "Yes'm," he said softly and gently. "I'm sorry, but your friend, Mr. Mackenzie, has been shot."

Thirteen

"YOU'LL DO ANYTHING, MACKENZIE, WON'T YOU? You'll even get yourself shot to get out of a capital-T talk."

He didn't seem to be registering what was in front of him, i.e., me. He blinked, proving that he was at least partially alive. Otherwise, no matter what the nurse had said, I'm not sure I'd have believed it. His skin was a close match for the gray sprinkles in his curly hair, his features expressionless, his body inert.

And then he blinked again, did a double take as comprehension flooded his eyes into such neon-bright intensity, I was surprised the bandages on his head didn't catch any of their blue light. For once, I knew precisely what it was to be a sight for sore eyes, and I knew how good it felt, too.

"Welcome back." I was proud of my composure and lack of sentimentality. Here I was in a hospital room, the perfect setting for a schmaltz-intensive scene, and I was having none of it. I spoke in an upbeat bedside voice. "Do you know you're in a hospital with a Frank Sinatra wing? And that you're a stone's throw away from Bally's Grand and Caesar's Palace?"

"Hey," he whispered. He looked like a fair-skinned

Sikh in his gauze turban. "You're here. You're really here."

And that was it for stoicism and ironic detachment. I burst into tears. Flying Chagall characters did a freefall through the room, their violin bows going a mile a minute. So much for aplomb.

Hours had gone by. Hours that took days to pass. Hours during his surgery and postop, during which I grappled with *War and Peace* until I realized that I had read a sentence about Prince Nikolay Andreivitch Bolkonsky's need for a regular schedule for seventeen minutes straight. Or perhaps it was seventeen hours straight. After that, I switched to a *Vegetarian Times* magazine that was sitting on a nearby table. After a few more decades, I retained only a headache and an impression that the rigid Prince Bolkonsky had eaten, at a set and specific moment each day, Easy Tofu Whip. And that the wait had been interminable.

The kindly woman whose function was, at least metaphorically, to hold relatives' and friends' hands, told me as much as she could find out about the shooting. It appeared that Mackenzie had attempted to stop an ordinary, garden-variety mugging. The woman's purse and person were saved and the would-be thief arrested, but C.K.'s right leg had been taken hostage. As a result, he was going to go through the rest of his life setting off metal detectors at airports, given the number of pins now holding a significant portion of his skeleton together. He had also fallen sideways from the force of the blast and done a minor number on his skull, which obviously wasn't nearly as thick as I'd assumed.

I couldn't stop blubbering. I wanted to be angry with him. Who did Mackenzie think he was, Superman saving Metropolis? But it was too much of a stretch, because I knew if I were being robbed by a street thug, I'd want a Mackenzie of my own. That particular thought sent me into further spasms.

"For our hero." In walked a pair of feet topped by a

gigantic vase of red roses. "From Mrs. Weinstein and her children and grandchildren." The nurse put the bouquet on his nightstand. The vase occupied so much space, there was no longer room enough for a pill bottle.

"So embarrassin'." Mackenzie spoke dreamily, as if the anesthesia hadn't completely worn off. "Didn't see the gun until . . . Feel like a fool. Wait till they hear about it. What was wrong with me? Where *was* I?"

I appropriated one of his tissues and blew my nose. "You know," I said, "they just stitched you up, so self-laceration seems pretty ungrateful." My voice wobbled and I sniffled some more.

"Huh?" He was still lost in the fog zone.

"Stop beating yourself up." I sat down beside the bed, blew my nose again, and took three deep breaths. "You saved that woman. You're a hero, and not only to Mrs. Weinstein."

"Shoulda seen her. Littlest lady I ever saw. Like in a fairy tale. Four-foot-something. Square little body. Old. And poor-lookin'. Old coat, old kerchief on her head. What kind of kid sees that and—" He winced and gasped. He had attempted to shake his head for emphasis.

He wasn't as thoroughly hardened as I sometimes made myself believe he was. He was still amazed and disgusted by what people did to one another. However, he was going to have to hold off on the body language for a while.

"You're a really good human being." I barely got the words out before I was sucked into another emotional wind tunnel.

He waited through my siege of snuffling, either through gallantry or druggy oblivion, I wouldn't know. "So," he finally said, very softly, "here I am. Captive audience. Don' want you thinkin' I forgot our capital-T talk. Shoot. Or is that a poor choice of expressions today?"

"Now? You want to talk *now*?"

"Don' ever want to have that kind of talk, so why not?"

"Did they check for brain injuries, C.K.?"

He grinned. "Lots of time for once. It's a good bet I'm not goin' to rush off for a sudden emergency."

"Is this a play for sympathy? You, wounded and lying there, looking like—"

"No?" he asked.

I shook my head.

"Good, then. Ah gave it my best shot. Why *do* we have so many gun images in our speech, do you think? Anyway, give me points for tryin'." He smiled crookedly and put out his hand. I took it in both of mine. "Feel like a fool, though. A laughingstock. A cop who didn't see a kid's gun. Barely saw the kid—or Mrs. Weinstein. I was lost in my head, a million miles away."

"I understand. It was that kind of time. I was thinking, too." We were having that capital-T talk after all.

"Walkin' back, it dawned on me that I hadn't been payin' real attention. Just goin' along the same old way, in the same old patterns."

"I'm also responsible," I murmured, meeting him halfway. They say compromise is the basis of good relationships, after all. "I didn't make myself clear enough." I squeezed his hand—gently—to show how touched I was with this new Mackenzie. Why had I thought he was one-track, unable to change? "When they called me and said you were hurt—" I hesitated, then decided to be completely honest, the way he was being. "I—"

"So there I was," he said, continuing his monologue, "walkin', tryin' to figure my way out of my rut, to really *listen*, I mean really *hear*, and—"

"—realized how much you mattered to me even if there are problems," I said. "Tonight's been a hard lesson in how much I care about—"

"—even if she's cracked—"

"She?" The word reverberated in my brain. *She? She?*

"Mandy? You okay?"

I shook my head, nodded, felt my chin dangle, my cheeks burn with humiliation. What had we been talking about? Not a tender, if cryptic, lovers' reconciliation, that was for sure. Mackenzie had been off in hyperspace, talking about somebody else—a female somebody else.

"Say somethin'. You sick? What is it?"

I wasn't uttering another word until I had some sense of the topic. Instead, in a mean-spirited urge for revenge, I turned his hand palm up. At least I'd find out one of his secrets—his first name.

The plastic hospital wristband said only *Mackenzie, C. K.* It didn't say *Gotcha!* but it might as well have.

"Livin' on the beach doesn't mean she doesn't know somethin'." Mackenzie continued on in his parallel dimension. "She did mention Jesse Reese by name, after all."

"Georgette?" It emerged a squeak.

He made a throaty noise of assent. "Georgette. I was tryin' to remember her name an' exactly what she said when Mrs. Weinstein and the kid came out of nowhere."

"Georgette?" There it was. And there Mackenzie was, still and always putting murder first. Except . . . my name had been in his wallet. I knew that now, and he knew that I knew it, too.

I gave up. There was simply too much feeling—good and bad, loving and infuriated, pro and con—to be ignored at this stage. We had flubbed breaking up. Done it wrong, thwarted our mutual escapes, thanks to fate in the squatty shape of Mrs. Weinstein.

"So do you think she knows somethin'? Could Reese maybe have robbed old women the way she said?"

I shrugged. "Perhaps you've forgotten that she also said Prince Charles was a good singer and had a lot of pep."

"He may."

"She said he was blind." I realized I was trying to discount Georgette, because Mackenzie had been thinking about her when he should have been thinking about me.

"Why Reese?" Mackenzie said in a slightly dreamy voice. His mind was fighting through the drugs and making it halfway. "She said J. Edgar Hoover, Prince Charles—"

"She meant Ray Charles."

"Donald Trump, George Bush, an' Jesse Reese. That's like one of those lists on a test—which one doesn't belong."

I wouldn't think he could have carried the woman's monologue through a trauma, but I seem to consistently underrate him.

"Hate things that don' make sense," he said softly. "Makes me mad to be stuck here, not knowin'." He closed his eyes, breathed deeply. "An' I . . . I think I need a little . . ."

"Sleep? Bedpan? Food? Quiet?"

He inhaled sharply. "Oh, boy," he said in an exhale. "Painkiller?"

He tried to nod, winced again and grunted. It was almost a relief to know he really, truly wasn't Superman.

I rang for the nurse and kissed him very lightly on the forehead. "So this is how it feels to know exactly where you are," I said. "And where you'll be. I thought it'd be more fun than this. See you tomorrow. Heal."

I was at the door when he said, in an almost inaudible murmur, "Tonight made me realize how much I care, too."

I was going to have to really get it that no matter how slow and out of it he might seem, even when drugged, Mackenzie heard and remembered. His brain had parallel tracks, and he could monitor them all, and make you think he was daydreaming the whole time. I was going to have to stop underestimating the man.

Although, of course, he hadn't said just what it was he so much cared about. Or even who. Or even whom.

THE NEXT DAY DAWNED SUNNY AND CALM, VERY CLOSE TO beach weather. Good thing I had no hopes of enjoying it, or I'd have been more upset when I swung my feet off the bed and my lower back clenched like a fist.

Hysterical ailment, I told myself. Jealous of the attention Mackenzie is getting. Garden-variety back pain, the first herald of middle age.

I walked around like a crone, trying, perhaps, to look like Mrs. Weinstein so that Mackenzie would come rescue me, too. Then I forced myself to stand straight. Later I would arrange for a massage in the health club. Until then I didn't want to think about it.

The *USA Today* shoved under my door didn't mention anything as mundane as a local murder. But downstairs the Atlantic City newspaper on the rack outside the coffee shop still featured the story. NO FURTHER CLUES IN BRUTAL SLAYING, the headline said. SUSPECT IN CUSTODY. And then it rehashed Sasha's long-ago association with the dead mobster. I read on with incredulous amazement.

"It's not that much of a surprise. Sasha Berg always played with fire," former high school classmate and current A.C. resident Candace Winter was quoted as saying.

Candace Winter? My former high school classmate as well, then, but the name . . . Then I realized who it had to be. Smarmy Candy Conroy, whose boyfriend had dropped her because of an infatuation with Sasha, who, for once, had done nothing to provoke trouble. Candy had screamed, "I'll never forgive you for this!" at Sasha—and at me, too, for remaining Sasha's friend. Who could have dreamed that she meant it?

But, incredibly, thirteen years later, Candy, married, settled down, was still angry enough to call the papers and have her revenge. People were perpetually amazing.

I took the paper to a table and settled in, marveling at Candy's ability to hate. For one happily crazed moment I decided that Candy Conroy Winter had murdered Jesse Reese and framed Sasha as final payment for the shame of losing Elliot "Rocky" Feinstock.

I'd thought that having breakfast in the coffee shop would be quicker than room service, and I expected it to be a quiet and meditative kickoff to the day's work. I was wrong on both counts because I hadn't factored in yet another encounter with Lala.

The woman was certainly making the most of her fiancé's largesse. She'd come to Atlantic City as a day-tripper, yet she never left, and furthermore, each time I'd seen her, she'd been in different ensembles.

This morning's was nautical. Her sailor collar was trimmed in gold braid, as were the cuffs of her slacks. She looked like an admiral in the AARP's navy.

"May I?" she asked even as she pulled out the chair across from me. I guess I could have said no, grabbed the chair, held her under the arms to stop her from sitting, but that required too much energy. "I had no idea Tommy was such a slugabed!" She shook her head, but the lacquer kept her buttercup curls immobile. "He'd like to sleep till noon and be up all night. What am I going to do?"

What she was going to do was have serious marital problems. Or perhaps no problems at all, because they'd never see each other.

"It's like I was telling my cousin Belle," Lala said. "Who, by the way, is down here. Arrived last night. You'll just love her, sweetheart. I told her all about you—well, not exactly about how we met, if you know what I mean. But I was saying to her that I'm a morning person. And Belle said—oh look, there she is now. Would you mind awfully if she joined us? She's dying to meet you."

Something about Lala's delivery convinced me that there were no random situations in her life because she scripted each encounter. The only reason I didn't react to her manipulations with more anger was that I also suspected that fear prompted her careful planning and avoidance of chance.

Lala was peroxide and morning-bright, and Belle was inky darkness—black hair streaked with gray, and a still darker expression in her deep brown eyes. The yin and yang of cousinhood.

"Meet Belle, honey," Lala said.

"Pleased to meet you," Belle said. "What's Honey short for? Honora?"

"Amanda," I said.

She sat down and switched topics. "I just this minute got off the phone," she said. "I can hardly believe what I heard. Oh, boy, could I tell you things. . . ."

She was a Pushmi-Pullyu conversationalist. "Ah, please, Belle," we were supposed to whine. "Tell us." Well, I, for one, didn't.

"Do you know what she's talking about?" Lala asked me.

I shook my head.

"We don't mean to be rude."

"Who wouldn't know?" Belle asked.

"What if a person down here for a good time was too busy yesterday to pick up a local paper!" Lala snapped.

"I heard it on the car radio on Tuesday," Belle muttered. "Just that I'm not so good about names, but faces—"

"So there," Lala said. "So somebody might not know. The hotel is certainly keeping mum about it. Listen, darling, I don't want to upset you, but a man was killed in this hotel Monday, night before last. In one of the rooms. Murdered."

"Oh, that. Yes. I heard."

"Of course!" Lala slapped the side of her head. "My own Tommy told you yesterday. I was there!"

I raised my eyebrows and looked pleadingly at the waitress who hovered nearby.

"No place is safe anymore. You come to a nice hotel, meet somebody, expect . . ." Lala shuddered. "It makes me mighty happy to be out of the dating game. You never know."

"You take your life in your hands. Literally," Belle agreed.

"A bagel," I told the waitress. "Toasted."

"And a smear?" she asked.

I nodded. "And coffee."

Lala and Belle paused from their death and doom lip-smacking long enough to order French toast and a "crew-sant" with a side of prunes, respectively.

Then Lala leaned over and patted my wrist. "I hope you find somebody like my Tommy, too, but until then, I hope you're always very careful."

"And not only with your body," Belle said, intimations of disaster hanging off every word. "They talk about safe sex, but what about safe money, I want to know."

"They already have that," Lala said. "You ever hear of banks?"

"My condominium has a social club," Belle said. "But at first, I didn't connect that to his face."

"She means she wasn't sure of who had died until she saw the dead man's photograph in the paper," Lala explained. I felt like Alice, perhaps, in the company of Tweedledum and Tweedledee.

Belle nodded. "Then I made the connection. He spoke to our group a year ago. I remember the face, even though I didn't invest with him. I have my pension, my Social Security, and some C.D.'s, but I went to hear what he had to say. About *protecting* yourself. Especially single women. Widows. Besides, it was a night out. A little entertainment. So yesterday, I called Myrna Myers. I said did you see in the paper? Jesse Reese, that man who talked to the social club, was murdered. And she started spluttering and carrying on like I couldn't believe!"

Lala leaned over the table and wagged her finger in front of her cousin. "Do you remember how angry Grandma would get with you? 'Get to the point!' she'd shout."

"Huh?" Belle said.

"What about Myrna Myers, Belle?"

Belle sat up straighter and spent a moment pouting, then got on with it. "She hadn't seen the item. It was only a little notice, a little photo, on the second page of the *Inquirer*. I was surprised, frankly. I thought he was such an important man. Maybe that's just what they tell social clubs, so we'll feel like our speakers are top quality."

Second page. Small photo. Perhaps the whole story was so inconspicuous as to be passed over by most people. Perhaps it wouldn't include any mention of Sasha or me. Perhaps not a single relative would see it or worry over it or think to share the concern long-distance with my parents.

"Honestly, Belle!" Lala snapped. "Get to the point!"

Belle slowly pulled off a greasy corner of her croissant and stalled before speaking again, reestablishing control of her tempo, delivery, and news. "So I told her what happened, and Myrna gets all crazy, saying he wouldn't give her the time of day for such a long time, and now, finally, when she thought it was settled, she'll never get her money. Makes no sense to me, and before she can explain, she says she's got to tell the others, has to tell everybody. A couple hours later she calls me back. You know how she is, she went knocking door to door, all the club members, the ones she remembered had gone to hear him speak, especially one or two."

"This better be good," Lala grumbled.

"See, at least ten people had invested with him. Some gave him everything they had." She sipped delicately at her tea.

"So what? That's what he did. Invest money."

"Maybe yes, maybe no."

Lala raised a warning finger, then shook her head. "You're impossible. These people who invested with him, did they make out all right? Yes or no."

"Well, they got dividends right away, so everything seemed fine unless you had an emergency and wanted your real money back. The capital, as they say. That's the problem. What happened to the big money is a mystery."

Being with Belle was as good as a session at the gym upstairs. My pulse had reached near-aerobic speed and I could almost hear my heart pound. She was talking about a motive, one of the best—money. A motive Sasha Berg did not possess.

"It turns out that three months ago, when Myrna's son had that auto accident," Belle continued, "there were things the insurance didn't cover, like baby-sitters, because his wife had to go back to work and he was in no shape to—they have twins, you know—"

"Get to the point!"

Belle folded her hands and glared. We'd reached an impasse.

But it was an old game between them, and only after Belle had punished Lala a sufficiently annoying length of time did she clear her throat and continue. "So she asked for the capital. To liquidate her account. I think it's a bad idea to give your son everything, even if he had an accident, especially a son that hadn't exactly been the most self-sufficient type, but—" She looked at her cousin. "Okay, okay. Like I said, that was three months ago. She still can't get her money back. They stalled, said she'd be losing money, said it was unwise, said that she'd wind up paying too many taxes. She kept saying she needed it. It's her right, you know. It's her money. But they did this and they did that—and in the meantime, another woman in the social club—she'd seen Myrna at the laundry—heard what was going on and she got nervous, too, and also asked for her money, and what do you think happened?"

"Nothing?" Lala whispered.

Belle nodded. "Exactly. One excuse after another about funds being tied up and Mr. Reese being unavailable. And Mr. Perrillo, too, he tried. His wife has the Alzheimer's now and he's not exactly too swift himself, and they convinced him that he had almost nothing in the account. He just gave up and said he must be confused. But even without him, by last week Myrna was boiling. Couldn't get a straight answer. Called the District Attorney's office and they said it would take time, did she have any evidence, Myrna's in Pennsylvania and Reese is in Jersey . . . you know the runaround. Let's be honest—who wants to help an old lady? Especially a poor one."

Lala nodded and twisted her new diamond ring. Her hand shook a bit as she did so, and I understood how tenuous her hold had been on security—at least until Tommy gave her some. I tried to be less judgmental about how she'd chosen to avert a poverty-stricken old age.

Meantime, Belle continued her agonizingly slow and convoluted trip through every trivial detail of the lives of everyone who'd come near her orbit. Her ideal audience would be an archeologist, used to patiently sifting through tons of detritus for one shard of value. I, however, practice a less patient profession.

I pulled a small piece off my bagel and dropped it on the plate, only to pull off another piece. What definite bits of information had I gotten from the woman's meandering conversational path? Mostly that Jesse Reese had taken old people's money and had possibly done something wrong with it, or at least wouldn't readily return it.

And during the months or weeks before he died, some people were aware of his shenanigans with the money, or were at least suspicious.

Belle had derailed and was now describing a gall-bladder operation, slowly reciting each symptom and stitch. For a moment there was some question of whether the patient had lived through it, then I realized we were still talking about Myrna. The operation had been a year ago.

How many people had been alerted to Jesse Reese's hanky-pank? I wondered. How effective were the condominium tom-toms? To how many people had Myrna directly expressed her confusion, irritation, and concern over the last three months—and to whom had those people spoken?

"The poor woman," Belle said. "She's finally over that, and now the whole business made her so upset, her angina started up. Almost every single cent she had saved in her whole life—twenty-four thousand six hundred and fifty dollars—was tied up with that man. As if she didn't have enough troubles with her son and his lazy wife and those twins, now. But then, finally, they tell her to come to the office on Wednesday. That there will be a check for all the money waiting, and Mr. Reese will explain everything. Sorry for the delay. Wednesday, so you understand why she was upset about his dying on Monday? I told her it will just take a little longer, that's all. She'll get her money. Maybe the check's already signed and waiting for her. It's like I always say. The squeaky wheel gets the worm."

I always said that, too. But right now I said, "I wonder if you'd be willing to make a few more phone calls, find out who Myrna talked to about Jesse Reese during the past few months, people at other condominiums, or people who go to churches that Jesse Reese addressed. Then try to reach those people and find out whether they talked to Jesse Reese themselves and what happened." I needed to know how much pressure had been on Jesse Reese these last few months.

"Why?" Lala asked. "Why do you care about old people?"

I tried to look indignant. "I'm hoping to be one someday. Besides, it's the right thing to do."

"A regular do-gooder," Belle said, but with admiration, not contempt.

"If we can find enough people with stories like Myrna's," I said, "then maybe they'd have a class action suit, get more respect from the D.A.'s office." I had no idea whether what I was saying made any sense postmortem. "Keep notes. I'll meet with you later today and we'll go over everything together."

Belle nodded. "So like I was saying, when Myrna's angina started, she called the doctor, and who does he turn out to be but Selma's son-in-law, you know—married to the daughter with the funny teeth?"

At this point I did not care for whom Belle told. I put my share of the breakfast costs on the table and stood up.

"Hon," Lala said as I said goodbye, "do you realize it's long-distance to Philadelphia? Tommy has a calling card, but—"

"Use it. You'll be reimbursed."

"Honey, it's peak hours, you understand?" Lala said.

"No matter." I nearly gagged getting that one out. One medical monologue of Belle's all on its own was beyond my financial capacity, but it was important to know what kinds of pressures, from where, had been on Jesse Reese in the last few weeks of his life.

"A lot of money," Lala murmured, but then she nodded, and seemed to trust me.

It was worth the risk. I'd find the money somewhere.

This was probably precisely the way the late Jesse Reese had thought, and look where it had gotten him.

Fourteen

I WALKED THROUGH THE LOBBY TICKING OFF THE DAY'S OB-
ligations and thinking as well about the data Lala and
Belle had provided. There was a new and interesting
light on everything.

I was consumed by the idea of a horde of angry and
frightened senior citizens, worried, possibly with cause,
that they'd been taken.

What had Reese really done, if anything, and what
was facing him, and how much did it matter to him?

There was, of course, the possibility that Belle and
her friends were on the wrong track. I didn't understand
finance, let alone its nuances, so perhaps there were real
reasons Reese couldn't or shouldn't liquidate the old
people's accounts. Maybe he'd been in the right, protecting their funds.

On the other hand, was it possible that the small man
seen by the witness was one of the elderly and enraged?
And if so—who was his Sasha-look-alike cohort? An
able-bodied child? A would-be heir avenging the evap-
oration of her inheritance?

But—in my hotel room? Why on earth?

It wasn't clear whether any legal action against him
had been begun, either. It would be nice to think it had,

that Reese was in immediate danger of exposure, but it would take Belle and Lala a while to find that out.

I sighed and thought about more tangible issues. Mackenzie's luggage still needed retrieving, and he and Sasha both needed revisiting. I'd never gotten to Reese's ex-partner Palford, and I wanted to talk with Poppy and/or Holly again, probe the inconsistencies in Poppy's story.

I did such a good job of ticking and thinking that I forgot to take the elevator down to the parking garage, and found myself, instead, standing at the boardwalk railing.

I breathed deeply of the beautiful June day surrounding me, and looked longingly toward the beach. It was not yet bikini weather, but it would have been a fine day to lie inert as a dead battery being recharged after a winter's worth of dimness.

If only it weren't for details like my best friend's being in prison and my whatchamacallit's being in the hospital. As the only ambulatory member of the trio, I had obligations. I stood at the railing, trying to savor and prolong the moment.

I looked out to sea while trying to organize my various errands geographically. Each of them would take me to a different part of the city. Picking up Mackenzie's suitcase at his hotel seemed a good first stop. Then down to the hospital, and back to the county jail and Sasha. Palford, then Poppy and Holly.

Maybe the police would give me more time with Sasha, even without Mackenzie's intervention. Maybe her cousin would be there. Maybe she'd even be released this morning.

I gasped, because just then, far down on the beach, I saw Sasha. She *had* been released and she was here, on the hard-packed sand near the water, the horrendously out-of-style brown hair that belonged on a country singer or a go-go girl an extravagant tangle, a tan cape swirling around her as she moved. I called her name, but the sounds floated away long before they reached her. I felt giddy with relief. Sasha was free! Case closed!

Unless, of course, I applied a modicum of logic, which against my will I began to do. It was June, and even if it wasn't setting heat records, it wasn't the frigid temperatures that called for Sasha's wool cape. Which wasn't tan, anyway. And which Sasha hadn't brought to the beach.

And which, therefore, she couldn't now be wearing.

The figure near the surf wasn't Sasha at all, but a creature of my wish-fulfillment. The woman on the sand turned toward the boardwalk and picked her way up. Not Sasha in the least, except for the hair. Another person with liberated locks, that was all.

Back to square one. I might as well get going to the dungeon to retrieve the car. I took one last sniff of salt air and turned.

"Hey! Where you going? I was coming up here to you, didn't you see?"

I swiveled back. The wild mass of curls had completely altered Georgette's appearance, subtracting years and creating a whole new persona.

"Didn't recognize you," I said as she approached. "You're looking very fancy."

Her missing teeth gave her laugh a melancholy note. "You like?" She patted her hair. "When I was a kid, I thought if I had curls, lots of thick hair, oh, then I'd be completely happy."

"Well, now you have them."

"A few problems left, though," she said with another smile. She seemed altogether buoyant today.

"Nonetheless, my compliments to your beautician."

"You mean the Dumpster on Pacific, behind Trump's. Got a pair of high heels there yesterday, can you imagine? Perfectly good shoes, and somebody throws them away." She patted her head again. "Just as good as the ones Zsa Zsa advertises. Or is it her sister? Where's the cute boyfriend?"

"He's—I never said he was my boyfriend."

"Well, if he isn't, you're the dumb one." She giggled and looked almost coy. "Unless he's no good, that is. Some are. Maybe most. So be careful." And like that, the merriment was gone. Her eyes deadened, her mouth curled downward. I wondered whether she was on medication, or should be.

"Wish my son . . . if I had curly hair and a house somewhere for my son . . . only wanted to be *ordinary*." She looked at me. "If wishes were horses, right?" And then she sat down on the steps up from the sand and cried, rubbing a hand across her eyes.

I walked down to where she was and sat beside her, hoping my presence would provide comfort, since I had no idea what to say.

"Kurt Junior. He . . ." She shook her head with its heavy brown curls. "Drunk one night after his father died, and drove away and crashed and . . ." She exhaled and shook her head again.

"And Big Kurt." She waved her arms at the empty air. "Out of work, no insurance, then he gets sick. Dies, but the money, the money, it thinks I'm dead, too. Except for my sister."

I patted her hand, gloveless today. The cape, its former life as a well-used tablecloth recognizable up close, slipped off her shoulders. She wore a reindeer-patterned cardigan over a blouse with a round collar, and two skirts that I could see.

"I worked, you know, when he got so sick. Waited tables, but I couldn't always . . . after my son . . . headaches all the time. Couldn't sleep. My sister said not to worry, just get well, and as long as she had a roof over her head . . . And even after. Happily ever after, like in stories." She breathed in raggedly and looked at me. "Who is your boyfriend, then, if Mack isn't?"

"I'm sorry about your son and your husband and your

sister. That's really hard." Everybody, I thought. Everybody gone and no safe harbor anywhere.

Her eyebrows arched in surprise, almost as if she'd forgotten that she'd just told me about her family. Then she looked down at her hands. "My sister worked so hard, her heart gave out. She'd be sorry, too, if she could see me now. She thought our old age was taken care of. It's not her fault. Can't trust anybody. Do you have a job?"

I nodded.

"Not waitressing, right?"

"Right."

"Good." She leaned to whisper something. Once again a mild whiff of alcohol accompanied her closeness. "Shelters are no good. Too scary."

"Well, maybe not all of them. Maybe we could find one that wasn't—"

She shook her head vigorously, curls flying, and waved my suggestion off with both hands rapidly crisscrossing in front of her face. "No shelters for me."

"Can't you get welfare money, then? Get your own place?"

She shook the curls again. "Need an address to get benefit checks."

"You mean you have to get off the streets before you can get the check that would get you off the streets?"

She flashed the gap-toothed grin again. "Something like that. I saw him once, right over back there." She pointed over her shoulder, back toward the boardwalk and its buildings. "Dressed all fancy. He gave me a quarter. I said 'Where's the rest? Where's the part you kept?' He looked at me like I was scum. I'da had my sister's apartment if he hadn't robbed her."

The scattered elements of her stories began to pull together like pieces of a puzzle, and the picture that began to emerge frightened me on her behalf. The robbery, the sister's safety net—investments?—gone, the newspaper story she considered lucky, even the chambermaids who let her into vacant hotel rooms so she could shower. Access. Motive? "Georgette," I said, "who was it that gave you the quarter?" Would she still say it was Reese? Or would it now be J. Edgar Hoover, or Michael Jackson?

"I thought he was cute."

"The man who robbed you?"

"Mack. That's the problem, isn't it? They're so cute. And where's Lucky? His mother watching him for once? People who have kids and don't even . . ." She looked at her hands again. One of her fingernails was black, as if something heavy had crashed onto it.

"The man who robbed your sister and you," I persisted. "What was his name?"

And with that, for her own unknowable reasons, I had crossed an invisible line, intruded, become a danger. She pulled away, emotionally and physically, moving to the edge of the stairs. "What's it to you?" she asked in a sullen tone.

I couldn't manage more than fish noises, semisilent bubbles of sound replacing words. "I—I didn't mean to pry," I finally stammered.

"Yes you did. You meant to."

"I—" My denial froze in my throat. What were the rules of etiquette to her? Why tell a polite lie to this woman while I was asking her for the truth? "Yes," I said. "I was prying and I meant to."

She rewarded me with a smile again. "Well, then it's okay." She sat forward and clasped her hands around her knees. "It's the lying that gets me. How about you?"

I nodded, somewhat shamefully, given my recent record.

"Does Mack lie?"

"He isn't like the man who robbed you and your sister." I hoped that put us back on course.

"He sure is a looker."

"Yes," I agreed. "More's the pity."

"My sister never married. Much older. Took care of me when our mother died. He told her the money was

safe. Her life's earnings. Wigs itch, you know that?
Ever wear one?"

I shook my head. "Did you try to get the money
back? Did you see a lawyer about it?"

"Oh . . . all those papers to get together, and the land-
lord when I didn't have the rent made me leave before
I finished, and where was I supposed to put everything
then, so I lost stuff and in the first place, I don't know
any lawyers, so . . ." She shrugged. "I don't know. . . ."

In Philadelphia there are always ads for people who,
for a fee, promise to organize your life, from your
kitchen cupboards to your time schedule. I wished
there'd have been one for Georgette, for all the Geor-
gettes. Somebody who'd have kept them from smothering in the minutiae of daily life and bureaucratic
rigamarole, someone who'd have held them tight before
they disconnected and drifted loose into the void.

"Wait here," she said, and with surprising speed and
agility she was up and onto the sand and under the
boardwalk to her private quarters.

I tried to estimate her height before she bent over to
enter her lair. She was on the tall side, a rangy woman
with big bones and wild hair. I, who surely knew more
about the original than an old man with failing eyesight
who was the only witness—I had mistaken her for
Sasha.

A minute or so later she was back, holding yesterday's rumpled newspaper with Jesse Reese's face on the
front. "Him," she said, putting the paper in my lap,
photo up. "Serves him right. Why should he have a nice
old age if my sister didn't?"

Her words were emphatic, but her voice was always
low, a bit flat, as if by now she lacked the psychic energy to shout or rail. I wished I were as convinced that
she lacked the energy required to murder. I did not want
this woman to have been the killer of Jesse Reese.
"When you read about it in the newspaper," I prompted,
"you must have been surprised."

"I always knew it was going to happen. He was a bad man and he had to pay. *You* might have been surprised, but not me. I saw him. He liked that casino over there. I watched and I waited for this to happen."

"The wig," I said, trying a new tack. "It's really quite beautiful. Has it always itched? Or did that just happen when it got old—or is it old? It looks brand-new."

She looked completely fuddled. "New to me," she said after due consideration.

"How long have you had it?"

She continued to look confused. A sense of time was most likely not her strong suit. "Blinks and me, we go out on Tuesdays," she said. "That's the best time, when the stuff is out there for pickup. Is that what you mean?"

I nodded. "Do you know which Tuesday it was? Yesterday was a Tuesday. Was it then?"

"You won't find one now," she said. "They took it all away this morning. They take everything away on Wednesdays." Her expression cleared. "But hey, you like the wig?" And she pulled it off and tossed it to me, like a dead animal. "You can have it." She overrode my protests. "Too itchy, anyway."

Now surely, if she'd committed the murder and read about it in the paper and noted mention of a brown-haired tall woman—surely not even Georgette would casually toss me criminal evidence. I didn't want to take away her thick brown hair, the source of her happiness, but I definitely wanted hard evidence. And I wanted the police lab to find out whether there was blood on it. Something. Perhaps evidence of someone else who had worn it. Someone who now had only one tiny pearl earring.

Georgette's head was slightly cocked, as if waiting for something.

"I'll borrow it," I said. "You'll get it back." I hoped that was true. If not, I'd find a way to buy her a thick-haired wig of her own.

"Aw," she said. "It's not like it's a pet you have to return to its owner. It's a wig, and I only had it for one day."

I remembered that yesterday she'd carried a roughly tied packet, the one with the high heels and the book. I'd thought she had a pelt in there, and I'd imagined dead animals, not a disguise chucked nearly at the scene of the murder. "So who cares about it, anyway?" she asked.

I grabbed one of her hands as I clutched the wig in the other. "I do," I said. "I really do!"

"Yeah?" She looked at me appraisingly, tightening her eyes like a merchant weighing produce. "How much?"

Georgette was no longer, if she'd ever been, a creature of sentiment. She couldn't afford to be one. "Let me rent it." I pulled out bills. "And you get yourself a room for the night, okay? Not in a shelter, a hotel."

She pushed the bills into the pocket of an underskirt, looking much more exposed and unprotected with her wispy hair, the skull showing through.

"You know, Georgette, you may have just saved somebody's life." I controlled the urge to dance, to shout, to carry on.

She showed no interest or curiosity. I couldn't blame her. When you're barely holding on yourself, you don't have hands left over for reaching out to save others.

But intentionally or not, she had provided the possible means to turn the searchlights off Sasha, and, waving the shank of hair like a talisman, giddy with hope, I descended into the bowels of the earth to find my trusty steed and charge off in defense of justice, truth, and horrific wigs.

When all of this was over, I was going to *insist* that Sasha get a decent haircut.

Fifteen

THE WIG FELT LIKE AN ALIEN BEING, THE SPIRIT OF THE non-Sasha who had murdered Jesse Reese. Forget Mackenzie's luggage. It could surely wait to be retrieved. Nobody was going to be able to use it for a while now. I turned my itinerary around and went directly to jail. "Do not pass Go," I muttered to myself as I drove past the Monopoly board streets. The buildings were not nearly as well preserved or tidy as the little green houses and big red hotels I remembered struggling to acquire. Real-life properties in the real-life game had a shorter shelf life than their plastic equivalents.

I entered the station like a scalper, toting my trophy.

The desk sergeant seemed to endure rather than hear me as I explained the hows and whys of the wig. "Her? Hell, I know crazy Georgette," he said when I'd finished my presentation. "Everybody does. Always some bug up her—" He cleared his throat. "I used to patrol that area, and every time she'd see me, there'd be another complaint about being robbed. A real one-trick pony, except she wouldn't fill out forms or do anything except complain. Doesn't trust anybody. Can barely get her into a shelter when it's zero out."

"But this is different," I reminded him, all the while feeling sorrier than ever for Georgette, who had only

166

half the idea and no ability to get her albatross off her back. "A separate issue. She found this in a trash can behind the casino, the day after Jesse Reese was murdered by somebody who had this kind of hair. When Georgette was wearing this wig, she almost looked like Sasha Berg, the woman you've arrested. Anybody tall would. This could be important evidence."

He poked a finger into his ear and shook his head, as if trying to scratch his brain.

If you want to push a woman toward hysteria, there is nothing quite as effective as confronting her with a truly impassive man, is there? My vocal cords twisted and strained, my decibel level rose to get through to the man—and I knew that if he dared to say "No need to get all upset about it," I'd kill him, right here, in the police station. "And there was a *pearl earring* yesterday," I said. "In my *shoe*! In the room *where it happened*! Do you know if they have the earring now? If they found out whose earring it was?"

"I'm not a homicide detective. Not on the case, ma'am." His face contorted as he attempted to swallow a yawn. Then he coughed and cleared his throat. "If you were told the earring would get to the proper authorities, it did. And so will the hairpiece." And before I could complete a request to see somebody who was directly involved in the case, the sergeant raised his hand like a traffic cop. "Person in charge isn't here."

"But you'll tell him where and how it—"

He nodded and tilted his head back, scratching his neck with his uniform collar. "You wanted to see your friend?" he asked.

"Sasha Berg. Yes."

"She's in there."

"Right, but you have my phone number in case he—"

"Better hurry, she doesn't have use of that room forever."

Dismissed. I gave the sergeant a vote of no confidence, and beseeched the gods of criminal justice to properly track the wig and the pearl earring.

Sasha needed to get out of this place, quickly. Even the small portion of the jail we now shared was the antithesis of welcoming, comfortable, or human. The walls looked painted with high-gloss fungus, the floor was dull black tile with an unsettling white squiggle, and the furnishings were equally inhospitable—a fake-wood Formica-topped table and chairs with slats that deliberately aimed for the aching small of my back.

And this was the nice part, the reception area. I could see a small reflection of what the cells must be like on Sasha. There is a thin and easily worn-away patina of confidence that separates winners from losers, and I already could see rusty patches in Sasha's armor. She shook her head at my suggestions of toiletries or fresh underwear or even a book, because she needed to believe she was getting out of here this afternoon. Her cousin the lawyer from New Jersey had said so.

"But in case it's not till tomorrow?" I quietly suggested. Her cousin had to file a motion. I had no idea whether that would move as quickly as filing his nails—or as slowly as filing her way out of the cell. Sasha grudgingly agreed to a short list.

"They probably won't let you take any of my things," she said in a flattened-out voice. "My underwear is evidence. I can't stand it." She put her head in her hands. I'd never seen her this way before.

"Then I'll buy something new, or you can have some of mine."

She looked up and raised her eyebrows. "Surely that exceeds the bounds of friendship, don't you think?" When I didn't answer, she sighed. "Okay, then. But if you bring a book, make it sleazy, all right?"

"I was going to loan you my personal copy of *War and Peace* along with the unmentionables."

She rolled her eyes. "If I thought I'd be here long

enough to read it, I'd hang myself with my bra as a noose."

It wasn't easy making conversation. This was not exactly a forum designed to encourage the exchange of ideas. Besides, most ideas would have been impolite, insensitive. One avoided, for kindness' sake, the topic of what was currently going on—as in being locked up; what had been going on—as in having been locked up and accused of murder; and what presumably would continue to go on—as in being locked up forever. There are precious few topics left when the past, present, and future are eliminated.

"So Dunstan's really gone," she said after I'd brought her up to date. "Or Edgar, as it were. He's kind of intriguing, though, don't you think?" That's the kind of thinking that ensures that she'll get herself in trouble again, given the chance.

"You need monitoring," I said. "A caretaker. You make spectacular mistakes of judgment."

"Find me a woman who's still dating at age thirty and who hasn't made spectacular mistakes of judgment, then we'll talk. Meanwhile, let's stay with this mistake. The one about putting me in jail for something I never did and never could have done. They'll find Dunstan, won't they? Whoever he's becoming. He's the one who knows where I was."

"I'm sure they're giving it their all." That was a gross distortion of the truth. First of all, everything that pointed away from Sasha—Dunstan, the wig, the earring—was irrelevant if a person was completely satisfied pointing at Sasha. Second of all, unless *America's Missing Persons* decided to feature Dunstan this very week, he could be gone a long, long time. He was a man who knew how to establish a new identity, so where and for whom did one begin to look?

Still, this did not seem a time for the absolute truth. I couldn't bear the idea of turning the screws, then leaving her alone to dwell on the terrifying possibilities ahead, so I changed the subject. "Mackenzie isn't going to find much except a bedpan for a while," I said. "He's in the hospital. He was shot."

Her eyes opened so wide, I could see white above the pupil. "Because of . . . did Dunstan do it?"

I shook my head. "Don't laugh, promise? I don't think I could handle it right now if you make fun of this."

She nodded.

"A kid did it. On the street. Mackenzie stopped him from mugging a little old lady."

"Shot," she said. "Jesus. What—shot where?"

"Atlantic Avenue, about—"

"For God's sake—I mean where is he wounded? What's hurt?"

"His leg and his ego. And he bumped his head, too."

She was quiet for a while. Her relationship with Mackenzie had been prickly for so long, I thought she might snicker, or cast aspersions on his expertise. Instead, she asked decent and appropriate questions about his prognosis and current condition. She expressed sympathy. "When Mackenzie came here Monday night—"

I was startled. She hadn't called him the flatfoot or the law or the narc or the pig or Eliott Ness or any of her other pet tags for him. She'd used his name—or the part of it we knew. That was a historic first.

"—I kind of started to realize he was probably . . . okay," she said.

All right, it wasn't an overwhelming endorsement, but it was close enough. I quietly rejoiced. Crime had accomplished what I never could. Sasha had mellowed toward C.K. "He *is* an okay sort," I agreed. "My life would be less complicated if he were not. But what made you change your mind about him?"

"I don't know. He came back again yesterday, before he went to look for Dunstan, and we talked. He said it was time for a truce so we could work together and get me out. Asked a lot about what I knew, which was pretty much nothing. And he showed me a photo of Jesse Reese. That was the first time I recognized him. The person I saw dead was so ... oh, it was horrible. But the photo—it was the man I talked to in the bar, before I went out with Dunstan. Anyway, Mackenzie promised to help any way he could, and to push on the police here, see who in Philly knew people on the force here. Things like that. I was impressed."

"Frankly," I said with a grin, "it worries me when you approve of somebody I'm seeing. You have such terrible taste in men."

She shrugged. "Didn't he tell you he was here again yesterday?"

He'd said something about talking with her, but I didn't remember discussion of a second visit. Maybe he hadn't had time to tell me, or maybe he'd forgotten, or maybe he truly believed charity should be anonymous. Or maybe he was such an okay sort, he took for granted such acts and didn't think they required explanation. I told her about the earring. "Did Jesse Reese by any chance wear small pearl buttons on his ears?" I asked. She nearly smiled. I told her about the glitzy and lame widow Reese and her sister-in-botany, Holly, about Georgette and the wig, and about Lala's cousin Belle and her friends. "There seem to be lots of people now who might have wanted the man gone."

"And probably every one of them knew who had that room." She sounded weary. "Frankie and his big mouth. He was proud of being able to comp me that room, so who knows who else he told? And whoever it was decided to become me by putting on a wig. That's all it takes. Can I tell you how awful that feels?" She twisted a somewhat spiritless tendril of hair around her index finger. "And I would *never* wear little pearl button earrings, so I'm doubly insulted."

"The witness was fairly senior. His eyes might not be the best for details. But even I, when I saw Georgette with the hair and the cape, for a minute, was sure it was you."

"What do you think it is, mass hysteria?" Sasha asked. "The miraculous vision of Sasha that opens locked doors? Can the room become a shrine?"

"Ah, but I know how the real killers got in." I explained about my experiment with the chambermaid. It was clever, Sasha agreed, but then her spirits sagged again. None of this answered the only important question, which was: Who was the make-believe Sasha? Until we found that out, the real Sasha remained framed.

"I didn't know anybody in the bar except you and Frankie." Sasha played with a loose button on her cuff, tapping it with a fingernail until it rolled off onto the table. She put it in her shirt pocket with a satisfied smile, as if she'd completed a difficult job. "Did you frame me?" she asked. "The more I think about it, the more likely it seems. In fact, it's the only logical explanation. Admit it: you committed the murder. It all makes sense, then, except why you did it, of course."

"Thanks, but it works out even more perfectly if *you* committed the murder, and it saves time, too, since they've already fingerprinted you."

"Why would I murder somebody like Reese? I couldn't have gotten sufficiently involved to feel the urge. He was salt of the earth. Solid citizen. Man of the year. Not my type at all."

"There's a good chance he may have been a lying, cheating creep," I said.

"But I didn't know that soon enough. Had I but known he was a rat-bastard, I would of course have fallen for him and have been an actual, logical suspect. Instead, here I am, an actual, illogical suspect, and I didn't even get to have fun with the man first."

"You'll be out of here in no time." I hoped I sounded more convinced of that than I felt.

"Anybody could have done it, you know." She

sounded morose. "A man, even, under the wig and a skirt."

"The kind of man you'd probably date," I said. It almost made her smile.

Still, by the time I left, not long after, I realized that the only impact my trip to the jailhouse was going to make was to ease Sasha's incarceration with clean undies and dirty reading material.

FROM THE IMMEDIATE LOOKS OF IT, MY VISIT WITH Mackenzie was going to be as unproductive as the one with Sasha had been. When I walked into his room, bearing his suitcase, he already had a visitor. So much for the quiet and private session I'd imagined.

"This is Pete," Mackenzie said. "He's on the force here, but he's got family in Louisiana an' he spent lots of time there. We're comparin' notes. Have a seat, let us bore you to tears."

The tears I shed were produced by yawns I couldn't prevent while the fellows reminisced about good times with their similarly enormous families on the bayou, and later, on the Atlantic City and Philadelphia forces respectively. Mackenzie's color was much better than it had been the day before, and his level of animation high. He was happy, having a great time.

This is who he is, I told myself. Adorable, fun, sexy, smart. But most of all, cop. You give yourself grief about it, dither over it, debate it, but the only thing you can really do about it is take it or leave it.

I left it, but only for a moment. I'm not proud of how I decided to improve the shining hour, but the truth is, I went to the nurse's station. "Could I see Mr. Mackenzie's medical record?" I asked.

"I'm not permitted to do that."

"I only want . . ."

She looked stern and intractable.

"Not the medical part."

"*Yes?*" She was not one of the more sensitive nurses

on the floor. I hoped she specialized in comatose patients.

"His name. Could you just tell me what his name is on the chart?"

She looked at me as if perhaps she should wrap me tight in a white, sleeveless jacket.

"What harm could it do?" I asked in my sweetest, most subservient voice. That produced absolutely no response. "Then only his first name? Please?"

Her brow furrowed. "I don't think so." She shook her head.

"Why not?"

"Well . . ." She grudgingly pulled the file. "C," she hissed. "Plain C." She smiled meanly, triumphantly. "*Now* are you satisfied?"

When Mackenzie was well enough to face charges, I would have him hauled in for failure to provide the hospital with full information about his name. Surely it was illegal, an insurance fraud or something.

Pete finally left, with promises to be back soon, and after the most cursory questions about health, comfort, plan of treatment, and the like, I continued the crime-oriented conversational theme, to keep up Mackenzie's level of enthusiasm.

We had catching up to do, all the way back to the flashy widow and her sister, then through the earring, the wig, the angry old folk, and, just because I was so proud of having figured it out, a reprise of the killer's method of entry into the hotel room.

Had even Scheherazade done a better job of producing engaging adventure stories? Mackenzie not only looked enchanted, he seemed impressed. For once, he didn't belittle my findings. "Interestin'," he kept murmuring. "All fits together."

I hated to end, but I had nothing left to pull out of my bag of clues. "That's about it so far," I said. "Except for a peculiar sense that the people here are too satisfied with the status quo and they aren't going to do a thing about changing it. I mean, are they searching for Dunstan, for example?"

He sighed, which I interpreted as a negative answer—nobody was overly interested in expending energy in a direction considered extraneous.

"How easy is it to get hold of a wig on a Monday night?" I asked.

"If, say, seized by a sudden inspiration to impersonate somebody else?" Mackenzie asked.

"Precisely. Is there a neighborhood Wigs Я Us? Would there be purchase records?"

Mackenzie was quiet for a while. "Lots of questions and directions," he finally said. "I will talk to Pete about them. Also was wonderin' where the man's car is. Thought maybe there'd be something in the trunk or the glove compartment that would shed light. It's an outside chance, but all the same—where is it? Pete says his car keys weren't on him and they haven't found a vehicle yet. Not at his house, either. Didn't seem the kind for a bus, and the train schedule was wrong for his timin'." Mackenzie shrugged. "Pete's a good guy, but I get the distinct sense they consider this thing solved and feel in need of no more than tidyin' up. So they maybe need help pointin' the way."

"Well, if you're going to be the helper, I hope you literally mean nothing more strenuous than pointing."

"That's precisely what I meant. But you're still mobile. Nobody took a potshot at you."

I pointed at my chest. Moi? He was suggesting that I sleuth? The one he called the overage Nancy Drew?

"There's a certain urgency in these things." He looked uncomfortable with the situation he had created. "Have to move quickly or ever'thin' goes cold. Think we could be a team?"

I nodded dumbly. A team. Following in the footsteps of Archie Goodwin and Nero Wolfe, Sherlock and the doc, Nick and Nora.

"I'll do the thinkin' here and you'll—"

"Yes?" I snapped. Maybe I even shrieked it. It was
definitely not a hospital-smooth sound. "What is it you
think I'll do as my part of the teamwork?"

"What do *you* think you'll do? What do you think I'd
think you'd do? You'll have to be out there thinkin' *an'*
walkin'." He grinned.

I wasn't sure if that's what he'd meant all along, or
whether he'd reversed direction and bamboozled me.

"Down to business now," he said. "I think maybe we
should know a little more about those investment plans
and how they work."

"That's out of my league, you know. Anything that
has to do with money."

"That partner of his. Ex-partner. He'd have an opinion on the man, don't you think? Could you freelance
another article? Or pretend to investigate on your parents' behalf? Whatever works."

"I was going there *anyway*," I said. "He was on my
list before I even got here."

Mackenzie rolled his eyes. "I don't remember Nora
telling Nick that she had the idea first. An' surely not
snarlin' it."

I didn't say I was sorry, but I did smile.

"Ah hereby deputize you," Mackenzie said.

It felt more like being knighted.

We were off and running, or at least one of us was.

Sixteen

RAY PALFORD'S OFFICES WERE IN A CONVERTED HOUSE IN
Margate. I climbed three broad wooden steps edged by
blue-purple hydrangea bushes onto a wide white-
painted porch filled with wicker furniture. For the first
time, I felt at the shore. The real shore, as it should be.

Inside, the office was much closer to my fantasies of
how a citadel of money should look than Jesse Reese's
had been. Every furnishing had started out in the best
circles and had since mellowed into understatement. At-
tractively aged Persian carpets, an inlaid wood coffee
table, and buttery leather couches softened the reception
area.

I wouldn't know from personal experience, but I assume that the harsh realities of profit and loss sound a
lot better in this muted environment.

His receptionist was considerably younger than Miss
Evans. A new generation, which was, perhaps, why I
never once heard her echo the older woman's "I'm
sorry." This time, when asked my business, I said something that was almost the truth. "I'm collecting information about the late Mr. Reese. Mr. Palford's former
partner. My name is . . . Harriet. Harriet Vane." Well,
part of it was the truth. Almost.

She nodded, rather curtly. Good thing so few people

177

read these days, although I had heard that mysteries were enjoying a renaissance. Not Dorothy Sayers, perhaps? In any case, the general illiteracy makes it easier for the basically unimaginative to come up with an alias.

The receptionist checked her watch and double-checked his appointment book, then pressed a button on her phone and explained. I heard squawks and clipped questions. "Yes, Mr. Palford, I remember." She replaced the receiver and flashed me a wide, insincere smile. "He can see you for a few minutes. Then he has to leave for his scheduled meeting."

I thanked her and was ushered into larger, still more upholstered and waxed quarters. Surely investment counseling involved computer programs, numbers and guesstimates and projections on a little screen, but there was no hint of electronics. The office would have felt homey and familiar to Mary, Queen of Scots.

Computations were being made offstage, possibly in a galley belowstairs, filled with chained and half-naked economist slaves punching keypads.

Ray Palford stood behind a massive expanse of polished mahogany and slipped papers into a briefcase that looked made of glove leather. He himself appeared stitched of the same material. Tall, fit, smooth-skinned, younger than his dead ex-partner. "What is it this time?" he asked by way of greeting.

"Excuse me?"

"Brooke said you were investigating Jesse Reese, not me, so if you're here, there must be yet another snafu. I was afraid of this." He stopped filling his briefcase and gave me a stern look. "And I assume you have notified my lawyer that you were questioning me directly. Well," he said, "out with it. What now?"

"Listen, Mr. Palford, you've got me confused with somebody else. I don't have an 'it' to bring out. I just want to know about your former partner."

"What's happened with the suit?"

"You've mixed me up with your tailor?"

He settled into an amused relief. "Have a seat, have a seat." He waved me into a wing chair with a petit point design of the hunt. "Who are you, then? What's this about?"

"Grandmother Vane—she's housebound, but she's adamant about this, hysterical almost, and it does horrible things to her blood pressure and her heart—but she wants to call the police because she thinks Jesse Reese took her money. I'm not sure she's exactly . . . all there, you know? And now, of course, to make things worse, he's dead, poor man. I mean, I don't think the police would be interested in a half-crazed old woman's . . . Anyway, I told her I'd consult another expert, and since you were once his partner, I thought maybe you could help explain things to her. We'd pay, of course, but I'm really at a loss. If we could make an appointment for you to talk with her, would you? I just had to find out—I promised her I'd find out today. She's panicking because of the news, you see."

He shook his head. "I'm sorry for your grandmother," he said. "If her suspicions are grounded in reality, of course. But as you may have inferred from my erroneous greeting to you, I am already embroiled in a lawsuit with the late Mr. Reese, and I feel that it would be improper for me to . . . well, I'm not exactly an impartial judge of Mr. Reese's fiduciary ethics."

"I don't know what to do," I said. "I tried talking to his assistant, but she—"

"Poor, pathetic Norma? You won't get anything except adoration from her. She'd faint if you suggested foul play. When they finally release Jesse's body, she'll probably commit suttee—immolate herself on his funeral pyre. She was Jesse's ideal woman, completely acquiescent. When I read the newspaper account of the manner of his death, about that big woman who killed him, I was surprised, in fact, that Jesse had taken up with a strong creature long enough for her to belt him.

A fatal experiment, a very wrong change of pace for him. He likes people he can dominate, intimidate. Of course, even little flowers turn into man-eating plants. Look at his widow, an example in point. She was once Miss Sweetness and Light."

"Off the record," I said. "I really need some help. This is out of my league completely."

"What's off the record? What are we talking about?"

"Anything you say. Is it possible that Grandma's not crazy? That the man did worse than make bad investment judgments?"

Ray Palford raised his eyebrows and almost nodded. He looked at his watch, a wafer of gold, and scowled. "Let us say that Jesse Reese's and my philosophies of business—in fact our philosophies of life—were incompatible. I choose to believe that in both arenas, my preferences are the civilized ones. Mr. Reese, of course, would have and indeed did consider them timid or unimaginative. Had we both lived to be centenarians, we would have come no closer to agreement."

I picked my way through his weedy sentences. Was he angry? Enough to have killed Reese? I pictured him in a wild brown wig. It wasn't much of a stretch. A dab of lipstick. He had an androgynous face, fine-featured and smooth-skinned. "I've been told he was a gambler," I said. "Which is worrisome. Is that what you meant when you said he thought you were too timid?"

"Not necessarily or exclusively. We definitely don't—didn't—agree about ethics: business, professional, personal. We didn't even like the same music. Which is not to say that gambling wasn't a dangerous component of our incompatibility. Markers, like pipers, must be paid. But Jesse wasn't one to agonize over the future or contingencies. Agonizing over anything was one job Jesse had no trouble delegating."

I wondered if he could speak this way—full and flowery sentences and no hesitations—on any subject, or whether Jesse Reese in all his permutations had been discussed until the subject was as polished as the man's carved desk. I pondered this while looking at the photo on the console behind Ray Palford's desk. No pageant contestants here. His was a silver-framed portrait of three polished children, a woman straight out of *Town and Country*, and a man who looked like him, except for the mustache. He noticed what I was looking at. "A lovely family," I murmured.

"Thank you. It is a great comfort to have managed one partnership that worked out." He fingered his smooth upper lip. "I still feel naked. My dog didn't recognize me." He chuckled. "Now, where were we again?"

I looked at his smooth face. The better to impersonate a woman, my dear? "So, ah, given your differences," I said, "can I ask how the two of you ever became partners?"

"Much in the same way people who later divorce get married. We noticed the things that turned out not to matter and failed to notice the things that did matter. I thought the sum would be better than its parts. I have the analytic skills and I'm good at following things through, paying attention to details. Jesse had an excellent intuitive mind plus a quick wit and an easy way with people. An appealing combination, in theory."

"But the things you failed to notice?"

He stood up. I was afraid my time was up, but he instead paced the rug. "The greed, the gambling, the womanizing—oh, especially the choice of Miss Bloodsucker as his wife, which escalated and intensified all of the above but still, I thought, belonged to his personal life and was no business of mine, but I was woefully innocent and therefore incorrect about that. The man's only ethical doctrine is to always pay his debts, a definite virtue, to be sure, but less so if and when accounts have to be churned in order to do so, or values compromised in order to make the money to pay the debts."

Apparently, when started, the man did not need to breathe. He spoke like a Teletype machine.

"We shared overhead and research fees and the like but had separate lists of clients. Which is why it took being presented with a lawsuit before I realized what was going on. He had been borrowing from the general fund, from our own retirement fund. He had clients whose tiny life savings he risked or squandered—"

"Oh, no!" I said. "So it is, really and truly, possible!"

He raised his eyebrows again. "Off the record, remember? Because when one of those clients sued us, I also filed suit and severed the partnership of Reese and Palford. You know what they were calling us? Fleece and Pilfer. Can you imagine how it feels to have your name and reputation tarnished so unfairly?"

"And the lawsuit continues?" I asked.

He shook his head and made a half shrug. "Not that one. That woman died, and then nobody could prove anything coherent about what assets she may have had. Her heir was a disoriented relative—a sister, as I recall—who didn't pursue the logical course of action. I, of course, did not insist. Still, you can understand why I wanted no further association with the man."

I felt ill. She had been telling the truth, telling everyone, telling the policeman on the beat, telling passersby, telling it for years, but in the same disorganized fashion that had kept her from successfully suing Reese. All Jesse's victims now had a face—Georgette's—seared and defeated.

But the lawsuit I had meant was the one he had filed against his erstwhile partner. The lawsuit that was still pending after three years. Palford seemed capable of carrying a long-term hate. And I wondered, too, whether it was more expedient to sue the estate than the living man.

He glanced at his watch again.

I stood up. "You've been generous with your time," I said. "I guess it's best to know the truth, awful as it is. It feels even worse to speak so ill of the dead, after what happened to him. I really didn't want it to be true."

"Well, somebody certainly did."

"I don't think it was that woman they have in jail," I said. "She said she didn't even know him."

He raised both his eyebrows and looked diabolically amused. "If I were the police, I'd cherchez la femme, but la other femme. I'd cherchez la iron maiden. A very angry, insulted iron maiden with a bad, bad temper and enormous, deluded ambitions, la femme whose husband flagrantly cheats and—to add insult to injury—commits the *real* sin, which is to lose their money."

"His *wife*?" I said, with much too much forced naiveté. I silently apologized to Harriet Vane, who would never have taken on this role of dummy. Was this a real case of using a name in vane?

Ray Palford shrugged. "Who knows? Ultimately, who cares? Trust me, my dear, his loss is nothing to grieve over. What I mind is that his death has once again linked my name with his in news stories. And that is all I will say on the subject, which means, therefore, this is the end of the interview."

En route to the jail, I stopped to buy Sasha prison panties. My affordable choices were divided between the garish, the pathetic, and the overly utilitarian. I picked through a pair with pitchfork-bearing devils stamped around the bikini line, a black and red pair with strategically placed hearts and flowers that didn't seem suited for solitary incarceration, and a cotton pair that might as well have had *Institutionalized* stamped on them. I finally decided that a pair saying *This is the day we wash our clothes* was the least likely to depress upon wearing or discarding. Even this purchase stretched my shaky budget. I had an ominous sense that I was heading for financial catastrophe. I was probably going to have to pay for my hotel room, plus Lala and

Belle's telephone calls, plus the gas back and forth today, plus who knew what else ahead. I'd change my name to Mandy Pauper. I got so depressed about my perpetually pathetic finances that I returned to the hotel and snagged the shampoo and soap offerings, rather than buy large varieties of those items. "Little bottles are more optimistic," I told Sasha a few minutes later.

"They'll set bail tomorrow." Her expression was dark.

"Tomorrow!" I was surprised and delighted. Nothing on the faces of the officials I'd encountered had led me to believe they would release her in their lifetimes. "Tomorrow!" I repeated.

"Keep sounding like Orphan Annie," Sasha said, "and I will actually commit murder." She exhaled and looked a bit relieved. "You know anything about bail?" she asked. "Do I have to pay interest for the loan? Oh, I must, or why would they give it to me? Geez, I was just getting ahead a little. Now I don't know if I'll get rehired by the saltwater taffy people and I'll have this miserable bail to pay for and how the hell did this happen? And you forgot my trashy book, too."

"Did not." I extracted the book. "From my own personal collection. Vacation reading from Philly Prep to you. Genuine, one hundred percent trash. Check it out. It has an all-verb blurb. Says it will make you shudder, throb, and pulsate."

"I've done enough of that for a while. It's expectations like those that got me in here in the first place. Tell me what I don't already know about."

I told her everything I knew—precious little, when I said it out loud—and what I didn't know for sure, but strongly suspected, which was that Reese's feeble ethics had disappeared altogether once Palford was out of the picture, until finally he was not only mismanaging but manipulating the old folk's funds.

"I don't know about money," she said, "but I know about scams. Remember Riley?"

"I've never been sure whether that was his first or last name," I said.

"That was his both. Riley No Middle Name Riley. His parents weren't famous for having great imaginations."

I did remember Riley was the scam artist, successful and dangerous because of his astounding charm.

"Riley taught me a lot about the less than legal." Sasha sighed and apparently lost her train of thought. She looked dreamy-eyed.

"Reality check. Riley took your grandmother's cameo," I reminded her.

She snapped back. "And didn't even hock or sell it, there's the real pain. He gave it to another woman. So where were we?"

"The less than legal."

"It sounds to me like the late Mr. Reese was working what Riley called a Ponzi scheme. It's a pyramid scheme. Basically, you give me money to invest, but instead of really investing it, I keep it. I pay you what seems like your interest, or dividends, or profits out of what the next person gives me, and so on and so forth. So you think everything's fine—but the real capital, the money you invested, is nowhere—except in my pockets."

"And Reese didn't expect a problem about paying back that money, ever, because most of his clients were old and would die. Their heirs would get the big surprise." The blatant cynicism of it made me furious.

"Listen, Mandy, that suite we were given, that one he usually was comped? They don't give that to little old ladies who play the nickel machines. Those perks are based on a percentage of how much they expect you to *lose*. A suite like the one we had? That's for a five-hundred to thousand-dollar-a-hand kind of player. Reese was a big, big loser, and that's probably where the money went."

The old folk would have been as well off putting

their savings directly on the craps table. They wound up in the casino's vaults, anyway.

And how had the gambler's wife felt about the drain of her capital? Was she the greedy demon Ray Palford had painted? Was Jesse's murder her personal savings plan? And if that little lame creature had, indeed, murdered or arranged for it—who had been her accomplice?

I needed to talk to the former Miss Whatever, find out how much her Glitz store—or stores—needed an infusion of funds, and where they'd gotten their earlier supplies, find out whatever I could.

Immediately after leaving Sasha, I used the public phone in the courthouse, dialing information for her sister's number. Holly Booker. It was an easy last name to remember. Like the English literary award, like "book her."

The voice that answered belonged to neither of the sisters. "Mrs. Booker, she is at the work," I was told. "And her sister with her, too. Exercise, dinner. They not be back until many late."

What kind of a grieving widow was she, anyway? First she bleaches her hair, and now mourning becomes a facial?

"Many late" meant I didn't have to hurry. Besides, business didn't always have to come before pleasure, not if the business was busy in a casino spa. I'd go see Mackenzie first, give him an update. This time it'd be pleasure before business.

I thought I could be creative and reverse the cliché, but there's a reason it's so ingrained in our speech. So in order to teach me that, life provided the off-duty teacher with another damned learning experience.

Seventeen

A HOSPITALIZED MAN NEEDED COMPANY. THAT WAS A given and reason enough for the visit. But I needed help as well. I had felt like a sea creature with aimlessly waving stalk eyes this morning.

I was sure that Mackenzie would have found USDA Prime clues in Ray Palford's office, surely something more than the fact that the man had shaved off his mustache. I wanted a cram course in Detecting 101. I needed to know how to notice the right things.

Besides, it wasn't ever the worst thing on earth to see Mackenzie. Particularly now. He was definitely on the mend. His coloring had returned. Although it embarrasses him—he thinks it's something little boys are supposed to outgrow—the man's cheeks—except when the rest of him's been recently shot at—are always burnished, as if he's just breezed in from a wintry wonderland. With his rosy cheeks, blue-blue eyes, and partly silver curls, he's very much like a human version of our own red, white, and blue. Very patriotic man.

I settled next to the bed on a molded plastic chair so uncomfortable, I could no longer ignore my backache. I suspected the chairs had been purchased by an entrepreneurial orthopedic surgeon elsewhere in the building. "I think there are two definite possibilities," I began.

"As suspects? You're sayin' two, so it can't be an idea I had of a team of angry oldsters, workin' together like the seven dwarves did when they dragged Snow White to safety. So tell me about the two you suspect, startin' with his ex-partner."

"Damn, Mackenzie. Can't you let me have my moment?"

"I made some calls. Nothin' else to do except watch godforsaken talk shows. The topic on one was children who murder their siblings: Could your kids do it, too? Good lord—it makes the soap operas—yeah, thought I'd find out what they are, too—makes them look *pristine*."

"There's the wife, too," I said.

"There was always the wife. There *is* always the wife, in any case. So tell me about the ex-partner. I love story hour." He leaned back and smiled.

I realized how little I actually had to say. Ray Palford hadn't added much more than his own rancor and clean-shaved face. "What if," I said, "Ray Palford wore an enormous brown wig . . . ?"

Mackenzie looked dubious, so when I heard the knock, having no more to add, I welcomed an interruption. But only at first, and only for a very brief increment, because the nurse who bounced in looked as if her various parts were spring activated even though she was carrying a bouquet roughly the size of Vermont.

"Hello, hello, Mr. Mackenzie!" she said. "Look what just this minute arrived! I said I'd bring it in since I was heading this way, anyway! So—how are we doing today?" She beamed at the fallen hero with much more intensity than his wounds warranted, and carefully placed the bouquet on the windowsill, after handing Mackenzie the card.

"The Weinstein family," he whispered. "Again."

"Yes, yes," Miss Pert said. "We're all so darn proud of you!" She clucked further admiration and sympathy and patted sheets and plumped pillows with unnecessary zeal. If you ask me.

"Need anything?" she asked him. "Anything at all?"

There is nothing more disgusting than enduring an adorable woman-child paying homage to a man with whom you are affiliated—particularly when you are not only older, nastier, and much less adorable and/or pneumatic than the aforesaid, but have failed in the only competition in which you had a chance—that of snagging significant information for the detective.

Nursie never once acknowledged my existence. I believe she mistook me for one of those life-sized replicas of people, something an earlier well-wisher had left behind as a prop for photo ops.

And despite our current crisis in health care, the city's finest did not object to his unfair share of hospital staff time, did not tell her to peddle the Florence Nightingale schtick to more needy patients who did not already have semisignificant others at their bedsides.

I ignored her as best as I could. I thought about the many questions still surrounding Jesse Reese's death. I pondered again why he was in Atlantic City with no intention of gambling. I wondered how much it had to do—if at all—with the old people at the condominiums. I wondered if anyone had found his car.

And meantime, although I was, of course, barely noticing Mackenzie's personal angel of mercy, it somehow came to my attention that she checked the room temperature, the condition of the water pitcher, the position of the window blinds, the chart at the foot of the bed, and the tilt of the quiet television set. Just when I thought she was going to offer to redecorate the room in any style he preferred and I was going to strangle her, she left.

"Where were we?" Mackenzie sounded dazed.

"You were lost in the swamp of hormones." It just ruins a man, treating him that way. "I, on the other hand, was figuring things out."

"Oh, yeah?" With Nursie no longer bobbling nearby, Mackenzie appeared to be regaining the ability to think. I didn't know whether to take that as good news or a personal insult.

"I don't think Reese was here for the salt air," I said. "He was a gambler. A man who didn't worry about contingencies or the future, according to his ex-partner."

"Not about other people's futures, maybe."

"Did they find his car?"

"No car, no car keys. Not here, not home, not anywhere near his office in Cherry Hill." Mackenzie sighed. "What if he was checkin' out?" he said mildly.

"Killing himself?"

"Not the type. I meant literally. Leavin'."

"Leaving what?"

"The whole shebang. The U.S. If we could subpoena his financial dealin's those last few days, I wonder how much cash left the country, or was converted into bearer bonds or—"

"Why? How are you managing this enormous leap?"

He blinked and looked slightly surprised, then spoke in a soft slur that should have to be declared a concealed weapon. "I'm basin' it on two things—one you noticed and one you heard."

"I hate when you do this."

"Yesterday, when you went to Reese's office? The photograph that wasn't on his desk. Why would it be missin'? The way you told me, Norma Evans didn't just shrug it off. She must have thought it was significant, too. If it'd have been of him, then I'd think she took it herself and was too embarrassed to say. But it was of Poppy. I think it was kind of a souvenir of his wife. She meant somethin' to him, or did when she was in the pageant."

"It could have been removed some other time."

"I think Norma Evans would have said so."

"And the other thing?" I asked. "The one I heard?"

"That he always paid his gamblin' debts. His one

point of honor. I think he came to Atlantic City to clear up what he owed—using, of course, other people's money."

"The Condominium Club."

"Other groups' funds, too, I'll bet. It's one thing to have powerless old people enraged with you. Very different thing to have a casino on your tail. And that's not maybe the kind of thing you'd tell your secretary unless you wanted her to be able to guess what was really goin' on, which you do not want to have happen. You do not want her knowin' you're about to skip an' put her out of a job to which she's dedicated her life. Ditto for the wife you aren't takin' along. An' you know what? I'll bet his wife—maybe in cahoots with the ex-partner—knew he was skippin'. Could you really keep a wife from spottin' clues here and there?"

"They say they're the last to know."

"That concerns a different kind of cheat."

"Anyway, Palford and Poppy as partners? He had nothing good to say about her."

"Maybe the gentleman doth protest too much this time." Mackenzie twisted his torso and awkwardly attempted to pour himself water, although with one leg trussed and plastered and hanging in a sling, body torque was not easy.

"Mind if I pour us both a drink?" I didn't want to suggest that he needed assistance. If the truth were told, dealing with the fragile male ego—unless you're wearing a nurse's uniform—is certainly the equivalent of coping with PMS, except that the male ego is needy every day of every month, forever. He shrugged. I poured.

And the detecto gods rewarded me for this small act of mercy with a gift of sudden insight. "Airport," I said.

"Huh?"

"He chartered a plane. That's why there's no car anywhere. It's near an airfield somewhere, or he gave it away. He flew in—and he was going to fly out. Fly away, isn't that what you said?"

"Checking out is what I said." Then he looked at me with all the approval he'd beamed onto Florence Nightingale earlier. Some of us just have to do it with our brains, I guess.

I beamed back. Felt pretty good, too. "Was there money in his briefcase?"

"No money. But a passport."

"His killer took it. The money, I mean." I pulled out my little map of Atlantic City and there it was, the private airport, Bader Field, not more than ten minutes away.

"Nice goin'," he said. No small print.

One small nonpneumatic step for womankind.

Eighteen

I LIKE HAVING AN AGENDA, A PLAN OF ACTION, A PURPOSE, even if I'm not at all sure how to implement it. But in this case, snooping around an airfield, even a private and presumably small one, was intimidatingly official. Even in my imagination, the web of regulations choked me. I felt silly saying words as innocent as *flight logs*, let alone attempting plane-person jargon.

The entrance to Bader Field was peculiar—tall redbrick pillars that belonged more at the approach to Tara than an airfield, but there they were. Once through them, the oddness continued with an actual field—the kind used for football—to the left of the gateway. The first airport with bleachers I'd ever heard of. I was sure there was a story there, but I certainly couldn't figure it out.

Beyond a nondescript building and an equally nondescript firehouse was a turkey-wire fence, and beyond it, finally, rows of small private planes parked on grass, near a runway that looked like a nice suburban street. I watched an elegantly attired middle-aged couple emerge from a red and white plane and stroll to a waiting limousine positioned in front of the firehouse.

Life was certainly sweet and easy for some.

I walked into the square, one-story office building,

into a deserted front room dominated by a snack machine and an empty glass display counter. Luckily, the vending machine was full, its peanut-butter crackers looking good. I bought a package of them along with a soda. On the wall, a clock told military time. It was now 1326.

I munched and sipped and cleared my throat, but that didn't catch the attention of the male voices I heard in a back room.

I read a framed clipping on the wall and learned that this idiosyncratic little strip was the first place in the world to be called an AIR PORT, right around 1920. I've been saving factoids like that for years, in the event I'm someday invited to an actual cocktail party where people exchange bon mots and amusing bits of information.

Somebody went by the window in a hot-looking long orange coat. I quickly swallowed my peanut-butter cracker, but the man didn't come in. The plane people debated and laughed in deep male voices in the back room. I read the only remaining print material, which was laminated onto the display case. It was a newspaper photograph of blurry-faced early fliers hanging out here at the World's First Air Port. They looked to be having a good time. The figures were identified as Eddie Rickenbacker, Charles Lindbergh, and Amelia Earhart. "Wow," I muttered. "Wow," hoping this wasn't some archaic forerunner of the Elvis sightings in today's tabloids.

Although a small sign told me there was an attendant on duty, nobody appeared. The laughter grew more raucous from the back room. I walked over and knocked on the open door.

Unreadable maps hung on nearly all the wall space. I looked at the one nearest to me, a map of air routes, climatological areas. Someone had been charting a path on it. A green chalkboard had pink airplane silhouettes in odd formations, with squiggly lines—maneuvers? spy information?—swirling around them. I felt as if I'd walked into the wizard's studio.

"Excuse me," I said, too softly. The three men remained huddled over a desk, intently studying something.

It was time for drastic action. Time for Ultra-Girl!

I silently apologized to Gloria Steinem, and walked toward the group in the style of Mackenzie's bubbly nurse, trying for her I'd-do-anything-to-please ambience. There must be something to it—some invisible rays it emits, amino acid production it stimulates—because without a word, the men slowly straightened up and turned toward me. "Hi!" I said with a Monroe wave, small and slightly incompetent. One man, quite tall and sunburned, wore a bowling shirt with BILL embroidered on its pocket flap. "Hi, Bill?" He smiled back at me. Actually, he looked delighted.

"I have this, um, business thing to discuss?" Nothing like making every sentence a question to establish yourself as a nonthreat. Or, of course, as a Valley Girl, but we were in New Jersey, after all.

"Business?" Bill looked sincerely disappointed. "Probably should talk to Jimmy, here," he said.

I would have voted Jimmy least likely to run an airport, unless by virtue of being too heavy to fly under any conditions, he handled the ground-based business by default.

"What for can I do you today, girlie?" He'd obviously had his head up a helicopter when advice was given about nonsexist behavior and vocabulary. However, I couldn't play Ultra-Girl and then protest being addressed as same.

"It's about, um, my uncle? He died?" I stalled, frantically searching for logical grounds on which to ask for information about flight records. The definition of foolish optimism was my stupid but persistent belief that last-minute inspiration will save the day.

"Sorry to hear that." Jimmy did not offer grief counseling. Instead, he looked wistfully down at the document they'd all been studying: *Sports Illustrated*'s swimwear issue. I had lost him to the ultimate ultragirls.

"See, well, he rented a plane from you right before he, um, you know, died?"

"This isn't Avis, babe. We don't rent planes." He rolled a toothpick from one side of his mouth to the other.

So much for my brilliant theory. I felt crushed, and my back, in sympathy, had another, more serious spasm.

"Maybe he owned his own plane," Bill offered.

I hadn't thought of that. But since nobody had ever mentioned flying in connection with Jesse Reese's interest or activities, I shook my head. "I don't think so. Maybe you'd call it chartering, not renting?"

Jimmy rolled his eyes. I was a trial to him. "We don't charter, lady. People here own their planes."

I'd hit the wall and dead-ended. "Well, but," I began, hoping my mouth would lead me to a new perspective, because my brain wasn't. "Could . . . could he have chartered a plane somewhere else and had it take him here, then pick him up here?"

"Well yeah, sure," Jimmy said, as if I should have thought of that obvious, low-level concept before I started talking. "What about it?"

"Well, he did that, for this past Monday evening? And see, he couldn't use the second half because, well, like I said. Do you have the record? His name's—his name was Jesse Reese?"

"Hey!" Bill said, his eyebrows rising. "Isn't that—didn't I say that was the guy? Remember how I told you? On the news? The guy who got offed at the casino? In the bedroom, Jimmy, remember?" Bill spoke now to both of us, Jimmy and me, explaining. "Remember that guy was here from Pomona? Royally pissed because he wound up wasting half the night? Even though the guy—your uncle—had paid in advance. A lot of money, too, all the way to the Baha-mas."

Gambling heaven. I should have guessed. To Nassau, to Nassau, with Grandma's money we go. And then, af-ter that, who knew to where?

"I told you it was the guy on the news," Bill said. "When I heard the name, I said how many men named Jesse could there be? Couldn't remember the last name, but aside from Jesse James, who else—"

"All right, all *right*! So I was wrong." Jimmy's eyes were now tight slits, but even so, I could see them flash with either interest or anger as they viewed me. He put both his hands up, palms out, making himself a breath-ing brick wall. No passage, no thoroughfare here. "No refunds," he said. "My condolences and all, but I can save you time and energy goin' after them. It's not like a round-trip ticket, it's a charter. That plane was rented for a certain amount of time, you know what I mean? And a rule's a rule."

I felt obliged to stay in character. "Not even for the gas that nobody used?"

"Wouldn't matter if your uncle was only going to Philly, doll. The price was the price. There's overhead, maintenance, rentals, and there's rules. You got your troubles and I got mine, and you can go all over the state, find the place where he chartered it—which sounds like it's Pomona—and for sure, that place'll have its own troubles."

"Well, then," I told the philosopher king, "at least make sure he's credited with his frequent flier miles." And I was out of there, but not before I heard Bill.

"Frequent flier miles?" he echoed with mild wonder before Jimmy brusquely shut him up.

SOMEDAY I'M BUYING ONE OF THOSE FAKE CAR PHONES SO I won't feel so conspicuous when I have to say my thoughts out loud, particularly in a convertible on a June day. For the time being, however, I accepted look-

ing like someone with serious problems as I nattered
on, alternately arguing and agreeing with myself and
my conclusions. Whenever I stopped for a light, I tried
to speak more softly, but I nonetheless generated funny
looks from people in adjoining lanes.

The emerging picture still had gaps, but if you fill in
enough background, the foreground has nowhere to go
but right in front of your eyes. So I muttered my story
to the visor, hoping people thought I was talking to a
speaker phone, wishing I didn't care what people
thought.

For years, I told my windshield, at least back to
Georgette's sister, probably before, Jesse Reese had
been preying on old people with failing memories and
increasing confusion, people who could be manipulated
out of their life savings.

But recently, with particularly bad timing, he found
himself squeezed between large gambling debts and the
dawning wrath of some of his victims in the geriatric
social clubs—all of whom had friends who were potential victims. The very connections that had supported
his endeavors and his lifestyle now threatened to strangle him. His methods and practices were within hours
of becoming public knowledge through a lawsuit, but
he couldn't repay the old people and get them off his
back, because he owed whatever he thought of as dis-
posable cash to the casino. Add this squeeze to the
problem of an expensive and enraged wife who had de-
lusions of becoming the next Queen of Seventh Avenue,
and a former partner who was determined to sue him to
death even if it took forever, and Jesse Reese was in a
serious pickle. So he decided to skip.

I stopped for a light. I loved how logically it all
worked out. To a point. But what then? *"But,"* I said,
angry with my own quibbles. "Why does there always
have to be a *but*? Why is there always a very *big but*?"

A chubby man in the next lane turned, his mouth a
belligerent pout.

"The *conjunction*," I shouted. "Not the noun!" My explanation was lost in his exhaust fumes, but maybe he wasn't great with parts of speech.

But. What had happened then?

"Here's what I think." I looked around guiltily, but the pickup now in the next lane blared apocalyptic hip-hop and couldn't have heard a nuclear explosion, so I talked on. "I think the ungrieving widow figured out that her no-good, cheating hubby was going to split. Maybe his travel kit was missing or the checking account was suddenly gone, or the Pomona pilot called to verify his flight time—but something clued her in and she decided to plug her leaking resources by terminating her husband."

Women and Money: The Saga Continues. Georgette lost and slept on the sand; Lala snared Tommy; Lucky's mother gambled; I taught summer school and Poppy murdered.

My vote for the tall accomplice was a man in drag, probably Dunstan, if he'd ever show up, although Ray Palford now seemed a potentially good bet.

Or else the cross-dressing part was last-minute inspiration, along with the site. Pure serendipity because Reese's customary room had been given to Sasha and me. Or else they had always meant to use the room, his favorite room, but not to dress like Sasha. Or else . . . or else, or else.

WHEN I REPORTED BACK TO MACKENZIE, I WAS GIVEN AN-other ego-boosting round of approval. However, my back was now clenched as tight as a fist, and I couldn't relax enough to gloat. I rubbed it while I was being complimented.

"By the way," he said, "I called the precinct here 'bout Poppy and Dunstan and Ray Palford, too. They were real interested, particularly in Poppy. Said they'd talk to her right away. An' my man says Sasha's cousin finally arrived. I think a strain of flakiness runs through the whole family."

"As long as it's just a personality defect and doesn't interfere with legal expertise," I murmured.

"I think this means you're retired, or at least on sabbatical for the rest of the day," Mackenzie said. "Whyn't you take care of that back? Doesn't your hotel have a spa?"

The thought of a massage shimmered just ahead like a mirage.

"Everybody's in place at the moment, so you're finally on vacation," Mackenzie said. "At least for an hour or so."

I MADE MY WAY ACROSS THE LOBBY OF THE HOTEL, AIMING my feet for the elevator bank.

"Sweetie pie! We were looking for you!" Lala and Belle advanced on me, talking all the while. "We made a million phone calls," they said in unison. "Going to cost a fortune!"

My back went crazy. "Don't worry about it, but right now, I am on my way up to the health—"

"Every apartment and church and synagogue and seniors' complex we could find in the book," Belle said with obvious pride.

"Incredible. Could we make a date for later? I have this thing in my back and I—"

"It's not really so incredible," Lala said. "We used a Philadelphia directory."

"We called Jesse Reese's office," Belle said.

It was easier to wait than keep protesting. Maybe they'd notice I looked like Quasimodo.

"I had such a good idea. I made up this whole speech. I'd say I was from the Greater Delaware Valley Seniors' Coalition—you like that? The GDVSC, I'd say, and then I'd explain. I said we wanted to put a notice in our bulletin about Jesse Reese's passing since so many of our people—I like that, don't you—our people—"

"Belle!"

"—and we thought it would be nice to mention some of his most recent appearances. So I found out his number and I dialed, but—"

"His office is closed," Lala said. "Permanently."

Belle sulked. "I was going to say that," she muttered.

"We have a few hundred names so far," Lala said. "People who gave him money. Some of them told us the amount. Twelve thousand, twenty-five, one gave him seventy-five thousand. Adds up."

"You're not kidding. I kept the tallies," Belle agreed. "I do it for our Thursday night consecutive rummy games. I'm good at it, I don't know why. It's kind of a gift."

Lala leaned near me. "Five and one-half million dollars we know of already."

I didn't have to pretend to be stunned. I thought their math must be wrong, despite Belle's expertise.

"After all," Belle said. "If two hundred and fifty people give him twelve thousand dollars each—and that is not exactly big money in this world, and most of the people gave him twice that, three times—that's three million dollars right there. The amount he gave back as dividends—peanuts. Besides, there's more people—we didn't even *try* New Jersey, but I thought you don't have all the money in the world, do you? Phone bills aren't cheap, and even with a card, the hotel adds on its—"

"One woman who answered," Lala said, "had just come back from the hospital. She told us that while she was sick, and her son was going through her accounts, trying to take care of things, he'd gone to see Jesse Reese twice. Last week and this Monday."

"Monday? The day he . . ."

Both women nodded. "She said that Reese was very rude. Her son went to the office in Cherry Hill—he had an appointment—but Reese said something had come up, he had to leave. So this man followed him here."

I wondered if he was tall, if he knew Poppy.

"Another man said his son was a stockbroker who tried to transfer funds, to invest some differently. He said that he tried to check out some of the investments and he couldn't find anything about them. Thinks they were made-up companies. Fakes. He had a word for it, his son did. Something like that movie star, from *Casablanca*."

"Ingrid?" She shook her head. "Bergman? Humphrey? Bogart? Sam?"

"That's it—Bogart."

"That's the name of a company?"

"No, no, all those investments were Bogarts."

I didn't correct her and say *bogus*. The image of tough investments with cigarettes hanging off their lips was too appealing.

"So the son, he got real worried and called his lawyer."

"When?" How much pressure was hitting Reese all at once?

Belle shook her head.

Lala seemed to stretch, to grow taller. "And my Tommy heard that Miglio's mother had turned over a nice amount to Reese last year, and about a month ago decided she wanted to surprise her children with a trip for everybody back to Italy, but Jesse Reese didn't know who he was messing with. Miglio has a very bad temper, particularly when mothers or money are concerned."

The woods were suddenly crawling with would-be Reese lawsuits or assassins, or at least serious irritants. No wonder the man was leaving the country. "You're incredible detectives," I said. "I salute you. If we could get that list together, I think the police might be interested."

"You're standing funny," Lala said.

"Yes. My back. I pulled something yesterday."

"So why aren't you upstairs with the masseuse? Honestly, young people don't know how to take care of themselves. You act as if there's no tomorrow. You have to take care of your body. When you're older, you'll understand. Go!"

I went. Next to the spa entrance was a glass-walled room in which Holly Booker led an aerobics class. Actually, it was more of a tutorial, with one apple-shaped and unenthusiastic participant. I have to hand it to Holly. She wasn't daunted by her class size or by vigorous exercise. She shouted encouragement and popped on and off the step and clapped her hands as if she were guiding the entire world through its paces. And she had been doing so in her glass cage for forty-five minutes already, according to the schedule on the wall.

"Quite amazing, is she not?" the statuesque blond woman behind the desk said. "She does that a few times every day."

I tried to squelch my guilt at still not getting around to a regular exercise program. Each day, I devise another plan. I'll walk to school and back, I'll jog there extra early and shower in the girl's gym, I'll go to the Y three times a week, and so forth. And each day, the plan that wins consists of sleeping that extra hour and promising to begin the next day.

Anyway, today my back hurt too much to climb that imaginary staircase. I expressed my need for a massage. Anytime at all, I said, but soon. "My back is killing me."

"Have you been under any tension lately?" she asked sympathetically. I nearly laughed, but it hurt my back. I thought about the last three days, and my ligaments twisted and double-knotted themselves. "I'm a schoolteacher," I said, instead of even trying to explain. "Finished the term last Friday."

"Ah." She stood up. "That explains everything. And you're in luck. I've been sitting out here for twenty minutes, waiting for my four o'clock. At this point, I consider her a cancellation, wouldn't you?"

It wasn't really a question, but I nodded agreement anyway, and probably, in my mean-spirited and selfish way, would have considered it a cancellation one minute after the hour.

"If you'll accept forty minutes instead of a full hour, I'll reduce the rate."

Her name was Greta, she told me as we walked down a door-lined hall. We passed several women having tune-ups—one in red stripes on the treadmill, one in a tropical print leotard on the StairMaster, one in gray sweats doing leg lifts. The wardrobe demands of exercising are an additional hurdle. Do I really need one more area in which to be poorly dressed?

We passed a cubicle in which a woman was having a pedicure. Then we were at the door that said MASSAGE. And all would be well, all would be well.

And all was, until we opened the door. Because the table was already occupied by someone—something—its head covered by a bloody towel. A free weight—not particularly large, probably ten pounds at most—was on the floor, along with a dark puddle.

Greta's four o'clock.

Greta screamed and screamed. She was so solid-looking, her hysteria came as a shock. The women in the other section stopped their machines and came over and then they, too, screamed. The pedicure woman walked in like a duck with cotton wads between her splayed toes. She screamed, too.

The body on the table was silent. Its small, bare feet poked out of the sheet covering the rest of its torso.

A large white hook on the wall held the clothing that had been discarded in anticipation of a massage. A pink sweat suit—unremarkable except for the square brass rivets that accented each leg and arm. A brass-topped pink cane lay on the floor.

Poppy's last fashion statement.

I, too, would definitely consider this a cancellation.

Nineteen

MY THOUGHTS PILED ONE ON TOP OF THE OTHER, CLASHING and competing. I needed an auxiliary head to hold the overflow.

Women crowded at the doorway, their numbers ever-increasing. I watched with remote horror as a green mudpack cracked and fissured with its wearer's screams. We surged and withdrew. The massage room was tiny to begin with, and we were all huddled as close to and as far from the table as possible, trying to be near, but to avoid even proximity with the corpse.

For what felt a very long while, I let my thoughts accumulate without trying to sort them. *But she . . .* echoed between my ears. *But she's the murderer.* I shook my head. She was the victim. *But that doesn't make any sense.* I couldn't fault that one.

Why was she dead? Who killed her? Her partner? How would he have gotten into or out of this all-female enclave?

Wigs. Sweats.

But the police had the wig.

Anybody can get a wig!

In that case . . . who?

For a second I felt too tired to even consider possibilities. I nearly wept. My back hurt. I wanted to lie down and have somebody press out the pain. I looked at the figure on the massage table almost enviously.

"Should I call an ambulance?" somebody behind me asked. "Has anybody called?" After a lot of consultation, it appeared we were all better at gaping than at doing something. The questioner was delegated to phone.

"The police!" I roused myself long enough to call after her. "Call them, too!" I stared at the remains of Poppy Reese again and tried to connect a few synapses.

Ray Palford's smooth, newly shaved face intruded.

Yes, I decided. He was the one. The accomplice who decided to use her and lose her. Or maybe Poppy had never been his accomplice. Maybe Ray Palford and a small buddy had killed one and then the other of the detested Reeses. With both of them gone and no children to challenge his claims against the estate, he'd most likely get what he wanted.

It made sense, if murder can ever be said to make sense.

Outside the room, across the hall, thumping music still pounded, encouraging imaginary women to work those muscles. It reminded me of the aerobics class near the entryway. Somebody had to tell Holly.

Greta suddenly advanced to the table and reached out, lifting a corner of the towel.

"No!" I said. "Don't touch anything until the police get here."

Greta's hand opened and the stained terry cloth once again camouflaged the victim. "How is this possible?" she screamed. "In *my* room! I was here with my last— minutes ago! I was just *here*! And I never saw her! The police, are they going to think that I did this?"

"No, of course not," I said, but I did notice that the rest of the group remained silent and became even wider of eye.

"I think I know who that is. . . ." The manicurist, small and curly-haired, had edged to the side of the clump of women. "I could be sure if I could see her fingers." She walked up to the table, bent over and studied one of the dangling hands. Then she straightened up, smoothed her pink smock and nodded. "Royal Raspberry. Acrylic refills. Just like I thought. My three o'clock."

"Holy God," another pink-smocked employee said. "I gave her a cleansing facial at two. She said she was having her nails done and then a massage." She backed up, her hand to her mouth.

Another pink smock spoke. "Her? The red crew cut?" Crew cut? Red?

The manicurist nodded. "No wig today. I think—I thought the crew cut was kinda kicky. She liked short hair with workout clothes. Always matched hair color and style to her ensemble, she told me. Part of her fashion philosophy." She blew her nose.

A crew cut. Then both her hairdos and colors had been wigs. The big dark hair Sasha described in the bar Monday night and the brassy 'do I'd thought a bleach job the next day. The big dark wig in the hotel room on Monday . . . But she was so short, never to be confused with Sasha.

"Ohmigod." One of the bright leotards had now made it to the front of the little crowd. "I thought maybe somebody had a heart attack, and I know CPR, but . . . ohmigod! What's that towel . . . ohmigod! It's all stained, and that dumbbell, there, it looks smeared with . . . *ohmigod*!"

The free weight's brushed aluminum surface was gory. It was relatively small and would normally be innocuous-looking, not that difficult to lift and very easy to swing. We didn't have to search for a Schwarzenegger.

I heard her from out in the hall. "That's crazy," Holly insisted in her deep voice. "I just saw her an hour ago." She sounded like a very untough child convincing herself that nothing lurked in the night closet. "Had her nails done and wanted me to see the color. She was perfectly—" Then Holly Booker pushed her way through the women and gasped.

"Are you sure?" I whispered. "Don't rush to any conclusions. It might not be . . ." After all, we only had a similar body size and wardrobe in front of us. Until the police arrived, the face and definite identity of the dead woman would remain speculation. Maybe Poppy's rivets were popular in these parts.

"Poppy!" Holly cried out when she spied the pink sweats on the wall. She walked over and turned them around. "Oh, Poppy! She just showed me this new design. Watermelon Workout, she called it." And, indeed, on this side there was a big green-edged slice of fruit with brass sequin studs for seeds. "It's a prototype," Holly whispered. "One of a kind." She ran out of steam and stared at her sister, then back at the floor. She pointed down and sobbed.

For the first time, I noticed a pair of pink gym shoes halfway under the table.

"See those socks? They match the sweats. She was a genius!" Holly's voice softened, became almost reverent and definitely heartbroken. "And there's a gym bag option that—that"—her voice cracked as she sobbed out— "looks like a gigantic watermelon slice!"

"Everybody stay where you are!" The voice was male and gruff. "Hotel security," he said. "Police on the way, meanwhile, what's the problem?"

Silently, everyone except Greta, who stood mourning the sanctity of her room and her table, stepped back and out, allowing security a free view of precisely what was wrong. I watched his head pivot from the inert form on the table to the bloody free weight, then back up. The gray-brown fabric of his shirt strained across his back as he took a deep breath. He was the man who'd been stationed outside the ill-fated Eastern Suite when I came to retrieve my clothing. I hoped his short-term memory was bleared and that he didn't remember me.

He cleared his throat and turned to face the gaggle of women. "Everybody here who was here?" he asked. "I mean, nobody left, correct?"

My eyes roved over the one who knew about the hair, then the manicurist and her client, toes still splayed around cotton. The duo in leotards, the candy cane and the jungle print. The green face and she who applied the gunk to her client. Holly and her aerobics student, both of whom appeared to be in shock. Greta the masseuse.

"Where's the one, you remember?" The candy-stripe leotard elbowed the other. "The one doing stretches."

"Stretches. Geez, I'll never get to that now, and I'm so tight. Geez." She patted her nonexistent stomach.

"Wasn't there somebody on the mat?"

"I was," a slightly rounded woman said. She wore gray sweats and I remembered having watched her lift her legs.

The second one nodded rather dubiously. "Yeah, but before you. Somebody else. I remember because I wanted to use it after her, so I was watching how long she took, but my time wasn't up on the treadmill, so you started. I think she left just before we heard the ruckus."

"What did she look like?" I asked.

Both leotard women's mouths opened slightly. "*Look* like?" the one in the red and white repeated, as if it were an incredible question.

I nodded. I knew they'd get the concept eventually.

"She needed work. More than leg lifts. I mean she wasn't gross, but still . . ."

"She had dark sweats, plain. Like guys wear, you know?" her friend said.

"How about age, or hair color, or height?" I suggested.

They looked surprised and challenged by the questions. "Faded blond, maybe?" candy-stripe said. "Maybe not, though. I don't know. She wasn't eye-catching. Not *feminine*. Nothing special."

Nothing special and gone. A depressing combination.

THE POLICE CAME, LOOKING PERTURBED. THEY HERDED US into the exercise room so that the forensics team could work on the crime scene. It was surprising how chilly the room felt in the absence of vigorous movement. Getting someone to raise the temperature was our first big challenge.

Controlling postmurder politics was another problem. Both Greta and Holly claimed stage front. "*I* found her. *My* room," and the like from the former, and, sadly, "*My* sister," from the latter. The manicurist and skin care specialist had their moments as well.

Since the crime appeared to be no more than twenty minutes old, we were all questioned, whether or not we had something to say. I waited my turn with the others. We all seemed to have a postdisaster need to discuss what little we knew of recent events.

"She was right on the brink of fame," Holly said. "So excited about the store. Signed the lease yesterday. Just this morning, she said, 'Everything's going to be all right from now on, Sis.' "

Since nobody else seemed to know that the deceased had been a recent widow—so recent that her husband had not yet been buried—nobody else appeared to find her optimistic outlook and time of lease-signing as inappropriate and suspicious as I did.

"Brave," Holly added. "Good things were going to happen to her, and she deserved it. She worked her whole life to get somewhere, and had so much bad luck. Her first husband was such a . . . and this second one . . ." She shook her head. Mere words could not convey what Jesse had been. "And the accident, too, of course. But now, everything was going to be different. She had a dream and it wouldn't quit. I ask you, how many people have a vision? A whole look that is theirs? This is given to very few."

The women murmured. Our group was taking on the tenor of a camp meeting, but before we canonized St. Poppy of the Rivets, her sister was summoned for her session with the detectives.

I wondered whether Sis had much to gain from the recent deaths. Somebody should check whether she was heir to the Reese money. I was warming to that when I suddenly stopped dead. There was no way to commit murder while leading an aerobics class in a fishbowl of a room.

I worried about my turn with the police, gnawed at what might happen, and thereby missed what was actually going on until the leotard twins cleared their throats. "—count you in?" the jungle-printed one asked me.

"For what?"

"For Holly's sister. I mean, we can't have been here and not do something, act like we don't know."

"Flowers?" her companion said. "From all of us?"

They looked eager and enthusiastic, so I obviously was the only one who found it somewhat bizarre. Greetings and consolation from the strangers who found your sister's corpse. "Sure," I said. Probably, in the face of such random cruelty, we all needed to do something, anything, to feel a bit more in control. Besides, perhaps any comfort, however bizarre, would be welcome.

"Holly's a gem," Greta said. "A treasure. And very close to her sister."

"A *large* bouquet," the candy-stripe leotard said.

I extracted my share from my ever-thinning wallet. And then it was my turn to be questioned.

I need not have worried. The police were only interested in one murder, even after I reminded them that the corpse's husband had been similarly bludgeoned two days earlier.

"Not with a dumbbell!" one who looked straight out of *Night of the Living Dead* exclaimed.

"All the same," I said, "they're connected, don't you think?"

"Whatever we think, we'll think. How about you let us do it—the thinking—and you help us do it by answering our questions. Where exactly were you?"

I kept trying and they kept putting me down, shushing and patronizing me.

So, finally they knew only what they wanted to know, which was pretty much nothing. "Don't leave the area yet," the older one said. "We might need more information."

What a laugh. I decided that the indoor plumbing was part of the area, and I made my way to the john. The security guard I'd seen earlier was stationed by the exit near the combination changing room, shower, and bathroom.

"I just figured out who you are," he said. "What's with you and your friend? Some kind of grudge against the Reeses? The police are going to be very interested. You'd better be careful, young woman. Watch your step."

"Thanks for your concern. I really appreciate it, but right now, I'd appreciate the ladies' room even more." Having further offended him, I left.

I was tossing the paper towel into the wire basket when I became fully aware of how large and excessively empty the tiled space was. It wasn't surprising, given the situation, but still, it felt unnatural and chilling, as if the absence of sound could also echo off the white tile walls. The facility was probably never crowded, even when the police hadn't rounded up the few attendees. People did not come to Atlantic City for a healthy getaway. The spas were entertainment centers for wives bored with their husbands' gambling. Still, the changing room wasn't meant to be a ghost hall. The showers were empty, the blow dryers still, the benches unoccupied, and the lockers closed.

It had the drained and unnatural silence of a school at

night. And the trash, too. The only sign that life had ever been in here was in the wicker container brimming over with used bath towels. It looked like the wastepaper baskets at Philly Prep each night, another phenomenon that confused me. Our students write so little and yet produce so much trash.

Maybe those kids grew up to be the people who don't exercise, but produce countless used towels.

I am not fond of things that do not make sense, mostly because when investigated, they do make sense, only not the way you wanted.

I poked a finger into the towels and stirred. A bit of black fabric appeared. I pulled off the top few towels, and then the overlarge pile made sense. It was boosted by a discarded and empty workout bag, plus a warm-up suit. Black, so the dirt didn't show. Basic sweats—was it what the exercise sisters outside had considered a masculine workout ensemble? Worn by the person who was not *feminine*?

I held up the pants. I could have worn them. Ditto for the top.

Not that I was thinking of taking them, you understand. Particularly not after I noticed the wet splat on the front, or after I'd touched it, to find out what it was, and found out that it was blood.

Fresh blood that I bet would test out to be Poppy's type. I dropped the sweats and took several deep breaths. I looked around, double-checking that my impression of emptiness was accurate. I tiptoed toward the bathroom stalls and checked the open portions at the bottom of each. And then stood sideways and looked through the slats for shadows crouching on toilets.

There were none. There was nobody in the showers. I was alone. I breathed slightly more easily.

A shower and dressing room is not often provided at the scene of a murder. How convenient this one was. And it was standard operating procedure to arrive with a change of clothes as well. He must have been in the exercise room, on the mat, the leotards had said, then gone into the massage room for murder, then into here until everyone was in a group elsewhere—until the police came in, passing the ladies' locker room—until it was safe to strip, wash, change, and leave. Which brought us up to just about now.

I knew I could rush in to the police and tell them about my find—and face a forever of questioning and then a jail cell for two.

I was too easy a suspect—in collusion, I was positive they'd say, with Sasha. I could be, with a stretch of the imagination and a shrink of my torso and hair, the still-missing shorter partner. Case closed.

I took deep breaths to quell a flurry of panic—and knew I wasn't going to offer myself to the police like an unsanctified sacrifice.

Besides, the unfeminine, sweat-suit-shucking, freshly washed Ray Palford was very possibly still in this building, but not for as long as it would take the police to question me.

I opted to run now, talk later, to hit his trail before he disappeared. Catch the culprit before the police caught me.

I opened the locker room door and looked right and left. The security guard was off telling the cops of my guilt by association. Very soon the law would be aimed my way, in search of half of a murderous duo. It was a theory they'd love. High-concept. All the makings of a movie of the week or an Oprah special. Girlfriends who kill. Could yours?

I was getting out of here not a second too soon.

Twenty

I REALLY MISSED SASHA. I PUSHED THE LOBBY BUTTON, breathing hard. I needed her nearby, saying, "Are you out of your mind? Get back in there and tell the police about the sweatpants. It's their job to find the person who wore them."

Sasha and I are a good balance because our forms of insanity differ. She's berserk when it comes to men, but is otherwise fairly rational. I tend to veer off track in matters civil, and at such times I need a monitor.

Speaking of which, I missed Mackenzie, too, even though when he monitored me, I found it oppressive and annoying. In any case, I had neither of my brakes on hand, and about when I realized that, I arrived at the lobby and there was too much to do to waste time wondering if I should do it.

The one thing I was sure the leotard women would have noticed—even on an otherwise completely forgettable person—was an ensemble that didn't fit properly. So despite the little man's description of the tall woman who'd killed Jesse Reese, if she'd actually been as tall as Sasha, those sweats would have looked like knickers and note would have been made. Unless, of course, we had a tall but anorexically thin murderer, on whose

216

frame fabric drooped, but that, too, the leotards would have noticed.

I didn't realize how much I wanted to discover Ray Palford trying to blend into the crowd, wending his no-fuss, nonnoticeable way to the exit with the kind of cool deliberation it had taken to murder, shower, and change—until I absolutely couldn't find him. Every time I saw a brown-haired man his size, I speeded up as much as my still-aching back allowed and scanned, but Palford must have been a common variety of man, because there were dozens of almosts, but no Ray.

I peered into the casino, where the light was dark and bright at the same time. Tricky. A great place to disappear, and I certainly couldn't find Ray Palford. Instead, I gaped at what appeared to be a seven-foot man with a tiny head bobbling above a row of slot machines.

"Don't stare," my mother had taught me. "It's rude." I tried not to—besides, I didn't have time for staring—but the man was so very odd. And then he really appeared—all of him this time, and I realized the figure, or at least its topping, was Lucky, my tough-talking, self-sufficient five-year-old former companion. At the moment, he'd dropped precocity and reverted to his rightful childhood. His face was puckered and fuchsia, and he was sobbing, "Mommy!" My former homeroom student, Eric, had the boy riding on his shoulders. I could see a rip in Lucky's jeans and what looked like a bad bruise.

How had they gotten in there? The casino was absolutely off-limits, and Eric was already skirting the law with his job permit.

"Lucky!" I called. "Eric!" But Eric was playing hero at the moment, carrying the wounded to safety, his step sure and forward-moving and not about to be deterred.

He moved with such confident stride that nobody stopped him. There was a message there for all of us.

Another message, just for me, was that I had lost my killer.

"Precious! Stop!"

I half turned and saw Lala and Belle, both waving broadly. "More news!" they cried out.

"No time!" I called. There was, alas, all the time in the world now, but it wasn't socially acceptable to say, "No patience!"

"It's important!" Lala had changed into a new ensemble, turquoise this time. Old Tommy had better have deep pockets, because Lala was diving into that pot of gold headfirst.

Belle, still in this morning's outfit, had relacquered against the humidity. Her hair sat on her head like a fibrous hat. "You wouldn't believe," she said.

"The *wig!*" I suddenly remembered. "What happened to the wig?"

Belle raised her hand to the top layer of her hair. "This is not a—I never wore a—Lala's the one who wears wigs."

Lala colored deeply. "You could have had the decency to say it looked funny." She blinked hard and for a moment dropped all the effort and muscular skill that kept her face in place, and turned into a seriously old woman.

"I didn't mean either of you," I said. "Your hair always looks beautiful. I meant . . . the killer's wig."

"Killer? Weren't we talking about a lawsuit?" Belle asked. "The missing money?"

If Ray Palford had been the one in the black workout suit, then surely he'd worn a wig—and where was it? Would he dump the suit and bag and carry incriminating evidence along with him in his briefcase? And what about the earring? Poppy wasn't the sort for pearl earrings—they didn't go with brass—but Palford was even less likely to have been wearing a pearl stud in the ear while killing. What was wrong with my brain?

"We have five more names," Belle said, "and one of them has a nephew who's a lawyer, and he's absolutely going to start a class action suit, to get the money from the estate."

"Great going," I said. "There's a woman named Georgette. She lives under the boardwalk. Add her name to the list."

"Under the boardwalk?" Lala's mouth hung slightly open. "Georgette?" All her worst nightmares were reflected on her face. All mine, too. Except for the ones about a killer in pearl earrings.

Pearl earrings. There was only one pearl-earring type out of all the characters I'd met lately. Her. Norma Evans, the barely visible woman. Perfect in pearls. Perfect all around, except for any apparent motive.

I'd worry about that later. Right now, I was thinking of Norma Evans in partnership with Poppy Reese. Tiny, wig-and slacks-wearing, cane-toting Poppy. Capable—when she took off her luxuriant brown wig and put it on Norma's head, and when she was seen by a passing elderly gentleman—of being mistaken for a small man herself. As was Norma capable of being mistaken for Sasha.

It was all perfect, except that by now Norma would have dissolved into the wallpaper and the floorboards, never to be found if she didn't want to be.

I couldn't imagine her running out of the hotel, so I tried to imagine, instead, where and how she would have proceeded once she left the spa.

Where would I go if I could go anywhere, because nobody ever noticed me?

I'd go anywhere I damned well pleased, I thought. And I also thought that if I'd just killed my second victim, my former partner in crime, and I'd done it with the cool aplomb that had me showering and changing at the scene of the crime—I'd want a drink. I'd maybe need a drink. And I'd have it. Why not? I certainly wouldn't rush outside, where, as far as she knew, the police might already be, waiting for someone who might fit the black and bloody workouts.

Belle was still talking. I heard her voice as if coming from a passing car, distant and unrelated to me. I walked toward the bar and looked in.

She was sitting almost where Jesse Reese had been two nights earlier. I wouldn't have recognized her, and I was sure Frankie didn't.

Norma Evans had cut her gray-brown hair and she was wearing dark red lipstick and tortoiseshell eyeglass frames. It was enough to give her an entirely new, albeit equally forgettable, persona.

She saw me and stood up, pushing so hard that her drink fell on the floor.

"You!" I said. I moved toward her. "It's you!"

"Hey!" Frankie shouted. "Mandy, isn't it? Have you heard any—"

And during the split-second automatic head turn at his *hey!* Norma Evans shot around and past me with amazing speed. I turned and ran after her through the lobby, limping and lurching with the hot spears of pain in my back.

"Baby doll!" Lala called out. "What are you—"

"Stop her!" I shouted. I looked for a guard, even as I realized how futile my request was, how much time and explanation it would require. Grab that incredibly respectable-looking woman? She was everyone's third grade teacher, favorite lingerie clerk. The aunt the family felt sorry for.

But she had done it, I was positive. Finally, all the jarring details quieted down and fit. She was the one who'd driven Poppy down here. The two of them had known Reese's escape plans and were following him— probably with murder in mind. And then they saw Sasha and heard, via Frankie's joke, what room she was in, and the coincidence of hair and place altered the details of their plans. It didn't take much.

And it didn't matter much because Norma Evans was gone. Sucked into the casino, a gray invisibility in the chronic glare.

I searched for her inconspicuous, well-tailored shoulders, her demure skirt, her low-heeled pumps.

"Have you gone crazy?" Lala screeched from behind me. "You'll give us heart attacks."

That angry voice on the answering machine in Jesse Reese's outer office—the voice that sounded like metal grating. Poppy had every right to call her husband's office—but so angrily? And Norma, who'd ignored an earlier caller, had leaped to silence that one.

One thing didn't yet make sense. Poppy's motives were easy enough—she'd be financially better off with a dead husband than one who fled the country with his fund, but I didn't understand what drove Norma Evans.

"Miss Pepper! Tell him I'm okay." Eric, with Lucky still on his shoulders, was being propelled toward the exit by a security guard, his hand on the young man's elbow. "This guy's like accusing me of kidnapping!"

"I never said kidnap," the guard insisted. "I said—"

"Abducted," Eric said. "Geez!"

"The little boy's mother's in here." I kept moving, searching for a sign of Norma. "Eric's trying to help." Norma Evans was gone, lost in the maze of money machines. Soon she'd be out the door and gone for real and forever.

And then I spotted her. I thought. "See that woman?" I said to the guard. "Get her. She murdered somebody."

"Miss Pepper!" Eric nearly dropped his grip on Lucky's legs.

The guard, on the other hand, didn't even pretend to look. "That's a cheap way of getting these kids off the hook," he said. "I'm a little too savvy for the old look-over-there game, anyway."

"What's going on?" Lala and Belle arrived together, puffing between words. "Honey," Lala panted, "if it's about the phone bill—if you're afraid we're dunning you, don't worry. We only—"

"Either of you these kids' mother?" the guard asked

the two women. His eyes weren't all that functional, unless he was flirting.

Lala shrieked with laughter. "My *grandchildren* are twice his age!"

"Poor tyke has a boo-boo." Belle's voice had gone high and singsongy. "Do you have an itsy boo-boo, little boy?"

Lucky stopped snuffling. "Who you calling a little boy?" he demanded.

Once again I thought I saw gray dim the neon-brights of a slot machine. I took a step away. "Help him find the little boy's mother, please," I said to Belle. "She's gambling in here somewhere. I can't. I have to—" Their voices faded as I moved toward where I thought I'd seen Norma, past the center row of poker and craps tables. The robotic voices of machines encouraged the players on. The background music softly pulsed out of the walls, and always, from everywhere, was the sound of silver going in and coming out of machines. Above the bank of tall slots an electronic machine tabulated total winnings, a number that escalated even as I glanced up at it.

But I wasn't a winner. I had lost Norma and the game was over. Doom was setting in with cement hardness. The very worst scenario—Sasha permanently accused—was becoming inevitable. I needed Norma Evans right now. I needed to be able to show her to the leotard girls and the masseuse and Holly while whatever memory they had was fresh. If she left, she would blend into her surroundings somewhere else. She could imitate her former boss's aborted plans and take the money and run. Take it right now.

In fact, she probably was doing just that.

I had to find her and keep her right now.

And even then I'd have no real proof. A pocketbook that kept reappearing, an overheard voice on an answering machine, and maybe a pearl earring. If I was unbelievably lucky, and she was much dumber than I thought, she'd have kept the earring's mate, hoping to find the lost one. Great.

If I was even luckier than that, her pocketbook would be full of incriminating money in one form or another.

I rounded one corner, scanned the row, saw only three ancient stone-faced women offering up coins to their machines, and a young girl with orange hair sipping a drink and giggling while her boyfriend—his hair butter-yellow and frizzy and even bigger than hers—popped coins.

I turned and scanned another row, then moved on toward the craps tables, chasing shadows. There were too many corners and possibilities. She could appear where she had not been the second after I left and this could go on forever, until she reached the exit.

I moved toward the door that led to the boardwalk, then backtracked—what if she exited via the casino lobby, instead?

I looked longingly up toward the ceiling where, I knew, everybody—or at least everybody's money—was being observed nonstop. I wondered what level of commotion it would create if I tried to get up there, to enlist their assistance, to signal from below.

I didn't have to wonder long, because at that moment I spotted Norma nearing the exit.

"Hey!" I shouted, running in her direction. "*Stop!* Somebody stop her!"

She stopped herself, looking completely innocuous. When I reached her, therefore, she was ready. Her right arm grabbed my shoulder in what must have looked the friendliest of poses, but which hurt. "Shut up, now. Don't move. There's a sharp cutting object between your third and fourth ribs," she said.

I was wearing a green linen blazer, white T-shirt, and tan slacks, none of which offered the protection of, say, a bulletproof vest, so I was immediately able to verify that she was telling the truth. Something pointed was about to do painful acupuncture on internal organs about which I'm sentimental and possessive.

"You're in big trouble," Miss Evans whispered.

I'm mortified to admit that my first response was more suitable for Scarlett O'Hara. My knees buckled, my head grew light. But Philadelphia never was a part of the Old South, so I shook myself back to consciousness. It was too late for a swoon.

It was, I feared, too late for everything.

Twenty-one

"SURPRISED?" NORMA EVANS SAID, PROPELLING ME along. "Blinded by preconceptions about women of a certain age? By your own stereotypes? Call yourself a feminist, I bet. Sisterhood is all—but you still underrate middle-aged sisters. My hair turns a little gray and I become invisible, a nonperson, ready to be victimized, right? I'm certainly not an actor, a doer, a person to notice. Who'da thought the old dame packed a knife? Can you pack a knife or only a gun?" She interrupted herself to giggle, which didn't seem much improvement or much endorsement of her mental health.

"Help!" I squawked.

"Stop sniveling! Act like a *woman*!" She managed to simultaneously clutch my arm tighter and press the knife in closer. I gasped—shallowly. A normal inhale would result in a puncture wound. I tried to contract all my muscles—but the one in my back that was already in a slipknot made any movement tricky.

" 'S killing me!" I croaked, conserving my air and rib cage.

A man at a computerized poker game looked my way. "This one's killing me, too." He returned to his game.

"No joke!" I pushed out words with the exhale, feeling my sides shrink in. "This woman's—" I was out of air.

Norma pushed the knife along my newly tightened sides. My skin gave way with the sharp hot rip of shredding nerve ends. My eyes teared.

"People in here don't *care* about us," Norma said. "They're too busy with their own good times. You know that a man once had a heart attack and died, right on the floor—literally, down on the floor, dead. And people walked over him to get to the machines? That I once saw the doctor administering CPR under the craps table—but the game went right on above them? The way those sick people felt is exactly how it feels to be *me*, all the time now. To be no longer valuable, over-the-hill."

Was this really the time for polemics? Still, I wondered whether I'd live long enough to experience mid-life devaluation firsthand.

And while I mused and winced and worried, she steered me toward the outer wall of the casino. Her grip on my upper arm was amazingly tight. I tried to shake loose but couldn't. I used my free hand to claw at hers—but she immediately scraped me with the knife in response. My side was on fire. Surface wound, I reminded myself. Surface.

"Another myth shot to hell," she said. "I'm strong. I work out. I lift weights. A woman alone has to be able to take care of herself. You aren't much of a reporter, are you, Hildy? Came to find out about me and you didn't learn the first thing."

"I didn't—I was trying to find out about *him*. Jesse. I never connected you with—"

"Nonsense," she said.

"Help!" I shouted.

"Testing me?" She gave the knife another jab. Once again I told myself that if she were wounding me seriously I wouldn't feel it this much, that superficial cuts hurt worse than deep ones because with the latter, the nerve was severed. Therefore, even as I felt the wet warmth of my own blood—therefore, I had to stifle my panic and understand that I had no more than a paper cut on my side. Several paper cuts. That's why I hurt like hell.

I glanced down, just to check that no vital organs were now on the outside. What I saw was a small but growing rusty stain wending its way between the green linen fibers of my blazer. My jacket's ruined, I thought inappropriately.

I controlled the urge to bawl.

I was less able to stifle a ridiculous flood of household hints that flashed onto my mental screen. Ought to get this into cold water. Pour baking soda on it—or was it club soda?

I was obviously losing my mind, worrying about laundry problems when I was being knifed.

And nobody turned to look, to wonder, to speculate on what my words—or the stain—meant.

Norma chuckled, a sound that made me shudder. But then, over the mildly insane laughter, I heard an Ethel Merman boom of a voice from somewhere behind me.

"How'm I supposed to find his mother, a woman I never saw?"

"Lala!" I shouted. "Help!" I could almost see my words absorbed by the noise of the machines, the clothing of the players, the distance.

But I had caught someone's attention. A man actually looked up from something called a Triple-Play. "Need help?" he asked. His eyes, however, were on Norma.

Nonetheless, I nodded, vigorously. "She has a kni—"

Norma pressed and spoke right over me. "It's all right." Her voice was soothing, telegraphing not to worry, all was well, as long as all was in her hands. "She's had these attacks since she was fifteen," she said. "Chronic hysteria. Takes time and fresh air."

The man looked from the great gray and solid woman to me.

"What kind of a mother leaves her little boy alone, anyway?" It was Lala again, somewhere close.

"Lala!" I screamed.

"Lala? Jesus." The man twirled his finger in a small circle next to his head, using the universal sign for insanity. He whistled softly, then nodded sympathetically at Norma. "I don't envy you," he said. Of course. Who was he going to believe? Stability itself or incoherent, screaming, tear-streaked, and disheveled me? Lala's parents chose a bizarre moniker—and it would cost me my life.

Norma jabbed me again. I was going to look like a scored piece of meat. I was going to *be* a scored piece of meat. "Absolutely no more screams." Norma's mouth was close to my ear. "Cut it out, or I will. Get it?" She laughed at her grisly pun. "You're not even smiling," she said. "But I myself find my wordplay *side-splitting*. Get it?" I felt mildly ill, couldn't bear thinking about my split side, my injuries, my bleeding, and what they might mean. Not to mention my back, which at this point, all on its own, was enough to paralyze me with pain. I nodded woozily. We must have looked like mildly drunk women, steering ourselves toward the exit.

"I was really surprised to see you—little Hildy Johnson, from McKeesport, Pennsylvania, and formerly of *His Girl Friday*—showing up in a bar in Atlantic City? What an incredible coincidence, and what a stroke of luck. I never thought I'd find you again, although I wanted to."

"I get around, so what? And why would you want to see me again?"

She pulled the outside door open and shoved me through it. "You stole a *tape*," she added, as if that act were the very heart of the problem.

I instinctively pulled back, to express amazement, but she had me in her grip too tightly. "It wasn't like it had state secrets on it," I said. "The whole world was supposed to see it."

We were outside now, on the boardwalk. I eyed the crowds. Nobody eyed me back with any real interest. I felt again how alone a person could be no matter the numbers around her. I knew that if I screamed and Norma remained calm, looking like somebody caring for me, passersby, who didn't want to be involved in the first place, would happily accept the idea that they weren't needed and would move on. And then Norma would kill me with her stiletto. It seemed wiser to stay alert and see what she had planned next. Surely she didn't intend to do away with me while this many witnesses were around. Since they weren't gambling at the moment, they'd pay attention to a capital crime happening in front of their eyes, wouldn't they?

She turned and stood in front of me now, as if in intense conversation, and the knife was rerouted to just below where I put my hand when I pledge allegiance to the flag. I tried to decide whether I could pull her off me with my one good arm and my very bad back faster than she could slice my heart.

"Let me go," I said in a reasonable voice. "You're outside now. You can leave."

"Did you make a copy of that tape?" she asked. "Tell me the truth."

"Are you telling me this is about pirating laws? I don't get it. I'm sorry, but it was boring. Why on earth would I copy . . . ?" But given that she was, as they say, in my face, almost literally, I thought about hers. That ignorable, forgettable face had been on the tape.

Somebody with the tape could identify her. Give the police five minutes of talking heads—her talking head. Otherwise, she was a woman no one would clearly remember, a woman who could disappear in a moment, and undoubtedly had planned to do just that. Maybe still did.

Her breath on my face was minty. "Jesse thought I'd

be perfect. People would identify with me, he said. He was right. I was perfect. A pathetically perfect target for him. So yes. That was me playing me, telling the entire world that I was a single, self-supporting fool who invested her savings—*all* her savings—in Jesse Reese's no-fail fund. That was his form of pension plan. He added to the amount twice a year, too. But who cares? He was leaving, skipping out, taking it all. Of course, when we filmed that, I had no idea he planned to rob me of everything."

Of course. It wasn't about pirating or love or power. How had I not realized that the same terror I felt and Lala felt and Lucky's mother probably felt was driving Norma Evans as well? None of us wanted to wind up penniless and alone. And of the two options, alone was by far the preferable one. That's all it was, and it was everything and all around me, like a message being shouted in Sensurround for days now—and I had missed it. I didn't exactly feel sorry for her, but I did *see* her for the first time, and understand at least a bit of her. "How did you find out about what Jesse was doing?" I asked her.

She looked in pain herself. "That was the worst part. He didn't even try to be subtle about it—as if he didn't *remember* that I'm the one who took care of his life. That I knew every one of his secrets—his other secrets. Suddenly, he acted like I was an idiot—*me!* Like I was the same as everybody else. As if I wouldn't notice that he was keeping his passport in his briefcase, or that he'd packed up his wife's photograph, or—this was the giveaway—that he agreed to appointments with threatening lawyers and a bunch of really angry old people who were suing. For seventeen years he'd made me tell people he was out of town or already busy or otherwise unavailable if it was going to be a sticky situation. I always had to force him to deal with reality. He made sure it was next to impossible to see him when he didn't want to be seen. Then suddenly, we had real problems—disaster looming—and he'd say sure, schedule them for next Tuesday, for June the tenth. Everything he wanted to avoid was scheduled—no problem—on June tenth or after, until I knew that he was going to disappear on June ninth."

She had one hand on my shoulder and the other, the knife hand, to my diaphragm, and she leaned in close, her face twisted with rage. To anyone passing by—to all the people passing us by in wide arcs—we looked like a local nuisance to be avoided.

I kept scanning them, however, looking for an expression of human concern. Human curiosity. Who is that woman being chewed out on the boardwalk, Mom? I thought I saw Eric Stotsle and a small dancing figure that could be Lucky up ahead. They'd been freed.

"But did Jesse Reese ever once say you must know what's going on, Norma, but don't worry—I've taken care of you, protected you? Did he say you won't wind up without a job, without a cent, living out of a shopping cart? Did he *care*! Like I was *invisible*—or didn't matter—he was going to rip me off along with everybody else! Or else he thought I was as dumb as his wife."

"So you called her. Became partners, a team."

"Why not? We had similar concerns. You don't have to be a rocket scientist to know that if your no-good husband skips the country with all the money anybody ever gave him—less the part he lost at the tables, of course—you're never going to have your precious store."

Those Reeses were really bad at picking partners.

"Besides," she said, "together we could take him. She was the one could doctor his drink, invite him up for a quickie, as he called it. I surely couldn't. But I'm strong. I could finish it. I made up some stupid pretext. Papers he forgot to sign. He didn't pay enough attention to me to care. She was fine until after, until she changed her mind about the fifty-fifty and wanted it all. She was the *wife*, she said. She was going to frame me and keep everything except for a *pittance*."

It was amazing how wonderfully this two-time murderer distinguished between transgressions. Taking lives was a necessity, but taking money was serious.

"Since her accident, Poppy had painkillers that could stun a mule. We were going to make it look like a mugging—until we saw your friend. The hair, the room—it was perfect. Destiny."

"You went in while the maid was turning down the beds, didn't you? And stayed till she left, and wedged the door so it wouldn't lock." Why did I have to ask that? Why did I care, unless I wanted a tombstone that said, "She figured some of it out."

Norma shrugged acknowledgment. Her mind was on the future, not the past. "Now," she said, "we're going around the corner."

I felt the knife point at what I thought was my breast bone, and I froze in place. I really, truly, didn't want to test out how penetrable or not that portion of my anatomy might be.

"Why?" I knew the answer. With great frugality, she was going to recycle her original mugging plan. Once off the boardwalk, Atlantic City's untended streets are great places to get rid of somebody, and this time Norma could handle the job all on her own. And no Mackenzie to the rescue.

I knew I should have paid more attention in geometry. If only theorems would have mentioned times like this—times when the issue of whether a knee raised to a forty-five-degree angle is on the proper trajectory, and whether the impact of said knee would push the hand of the kicked forward or backward—seemed of vital importance. Or was that physics?

Too late to find out, except by experiment. I took a deep breath, looked her in the eye, and raised my knee as hard as I could, as fast as I could.

It didn't have the same dramatic effect as it would

have with a man. All the same, it surprised her and threw her off balance, which was enough. Her grip on me loosened, and I pushed and kicked. Even better, her grip on the knife also loosened. It clattered to the boards as she staggered back.

"Lookit!" A ten-year-old boy in a T-shirt that reached his knees stared at the knife covetously.

"Get over here, Tyler!" a woman in yellow screamed. "Right now!"

I raced to the knife. No pain, no gain, I told my back as it screamed in protest. No pain, no life. I put my foot on the knife. The boy galloped away.

Now, people were paying a little more attention. They stood back warily and kept their distance. "Somebody call the police!" I shouted. "Stop that woman!"

The two women nearest me looked puzzled by my remark. "Stop *who*?" one of them finally said.

The other shook her head. "She's crazy," she said. "Leave her alone."

"Lucky?" A high-pitched voice called his name. "Lucky, where are you? It's Mommy!"

"You better find him," a familiar voice warned her. "It's not right for a mother to leave her kid—I should tell the cops about you— Look over there! It's her! Darling, it's you, oh, my God!"

"Lala—" I realized that the spectator's gallery thought I'd been the knife wielder, the one who'd dropped it. "And you," I said to Lucky's mother, "take care of your son or we'll have to—" But this wasn't the time. What I had to do was pay attention to Norma, who was backing her way into invisibility. *"Her!"* I shouted.

"Oh, hey!" Georgette had entered the circle. "Mandy. Where you been all day?"

People backed off from Georgette. I seized the moment and the knife and ran after Norma. The sight of me, knife in hand, triggered screaming, seething pandemonium. For the first time, somebody actually shouted for the police.

Meantime, I got to Norma, or at least to the gray collar of her blouse, and I tugged with my unarmed hand.

"It's Miss *Pepper*," I heard. "Miss Pepper in a cat-fight!"

"She has a *knife*!" somebody screamed.

That was true. I did. But I wasn't planning to cut anyone with it, not even Norma. I didn't even think to use it. My desires were simple—I wanted to make her stop killing people, including me.

We failed, however, to discuss our various agendas, and I'm afraid we couldn't have made them mesh in any case. As it was, while people screamed and Eric enthused and Lucky's mother called his name and Lala said, "Darling, you aren't that kind of a girl, you have to stop," and Georgette burst into tears, Norma twisted inside her blouse, just enough to give her a decent trajectory.

The patchwork pocketbook hit my head with much more force than I'd have predicted. It must be that geometry thing again. I don't know what all she carried inside that bag. Not cosmetics, surely. Perhaps all of Reese's money was in coins. Or she'd stolen Poppy's stash of brass rivets along with Reese's money. Most likely it was just another example of her skill and expertise at bonking—after all, she'd slammed Jesse with a lamp, and Poppy with a free weight. She was good at this.

But something hurt enough to make the clunk of impact the next sound I heard as I collapsed onto the boardwalk. It isn't true that you see stars. I didn't, at least. It was more like those damned casino lights—trails of them blinking and wound around with neon.

The last thing I heard was somebody saying, "Look at that drunk. Dead to the world."

I knew he wasn't right about the drunk part. I hoped he wasn't right about the rest.

Twenty-two

SOMETIMES IT TAKES A LOT—LIKE A SEMICONSCIOUS woman sprawled on the boardwalk—to demonstrate the basic humanity and decency of people, even at America's favorite vacation destination. The point is, they cared.

"You all right? Hey, lady, are you okay? She didn't hurt you too much, did she? Need a doctor? Need help?"

Don't tell me people have gotten callous, I thought. Despite the wind tunnel howling between my ears, I heard those lovely, considerate sentiments. They gave me heart, gave me reason to struggle to keep afloat, to fight the swirling dark that wanted to swamp me.

It took a half-dozen more solicitous questions for me to realize that not a one of them was directed down at me. All, all were for sweet graying, genteel Norma.

"Don't worry. I got her knife," a man said. "She can't hurt you anymore."

From then on, rage and indignation kept me from passing out. I wanted to tell them they were wrong, but I was in something like that paralytic nightmare state when danger is at your heels but you can't lift a foot to run, can't move.

And while I struggled for breath and an end to the

black dizziness gulping me down, I heard Norma play right back into their hands. She murmured something about "crazy young people and drugs," and I heard a knee-jerk ready assent, as if I were the very image of a junkie.

"If you'll keep her here, I'll call the police," Norma said.

"N-N—" I managed. The resourceful Miss Evans had just given herself an exit line. The odds against ever sighting her again escalated. My protests, however, became mush on my thick and cottony lips, and I could almost feel the boardwalk planks shake gently as she strode off with the crowd's blessings.

Their attention turned to me, their captive. Some had never seen a junkie mugger before, and several felt obliged to share the nuances of their astonishment at the sight of me. But they didn't quite know what to do next. The baddie was flat on her back. The goodie was off to get the sheriff. Wasn't this the happy ending? Or was there some important, possibly dangerous element they hadn't quite grasped?

There was a lot of speculation about what to do till the law arrived—tie me up, perhaps? One woman, for reasons that escaped me, gave me a long look, then screamed "Help! Help!" in a fake voice, like a bad movie extra. It certainly couldn't have been because she feared me. There I lay, as threatening and active as road kill. Maybe I offended her aesthetically.

I began to understand that I was neither dead, unconscious, nor likely to become either. I had just been seriously stunned. I was becoming unstunned.

"Miss Pepper's *down*! You see that, Lucky?" That was Eric, somewhere out of my line of vision—a line that for the moment only went straight up—behaving as if this were a sporting event. If I ever got him in my class, I was going to flunk him, based on today's performance.

"You know her?" a spectator asked.

"She's a *teacher*!" Eric said. "At Philly Prep, my school."

In fact, I would flunk him in subjects I didn't even teach.

"A teacher! My God, no wonder schools are in trouble. A teacher with a knife, did you ever hear such a thing?"

"Why do you think they have metal detectors in them nowadays?"

"Metal detectors in teachers?"

"You read that things have gotten tough in the schools, but really, this is—"

"You're hurt!" A familiar voice amidst the idiot din. Belle, telling me what I already knew. "That woman you were with is no good! She looked like such a nice person, but—"

"Stop 'er—" I began. "She—"

Lala bent over me.

"Don't get near her!" The speaker looked ready to stomp me.

"She's not contagious," Lala said. The skin of her concerned face sagged and pooched forward like a basset hound's. I forgave her all her manipulative sins and decided I was, in fact, in love with her. "We'll get her, cookie," she whispered for my ears only. "Tommy's here, too." And with a sigh and a creak of bones, she stood back up and the world's oldest posse was off and if not quite running, then at least huffing and puffing as quickly as it could.

"Lucky, you come down from that boy's shoulders," his mother said.

"You'd better keep an eye on him," I said to the sky above my face. But I had a real sense that the grandma patrol had successfully intimidated her.

"Isn't anybody going to do anything?" It was Eric again. I could see a long, tall two-headed body. Lucky was still riding Eric's shoulders. "The old lady bashed Miss Pepper!"

"No . . ." someone in the crowd said.

"She did! The old lady's crazy! And look—Miss Pepper's bleeding!"

"Young man . . ." But the objections were less emphatic, enough so that I thought perhaps Eric had actually planted a seed of doubt. Maybe I'd reconsider that grade.

"Somebody ought to stop her," Eric said. "I don't care if she's old."

"Eric, please—" I began, but he couldn't hear me. I was having a very bad day, and my back was having an even worse one. A splat on the boards is not a therapeutic alternative to a massage. I was probably paralyzed for life. And julienned. A very, very bad day.

"Where's that cop she called?" somebody asked.

"You know how they are when you need them."

They could await Norma's cop along with world peace, and both would arrive at about the same time. I therefore had a chance, a window of opportunity, if only I could open it. My energy pumped back in, fueled by the vision of Norma Evans in pursuit of her imaginary telephone, melting into the traffic, ignored and invisible.

This was no time to be on my back. I rolled over, slowly, and worked my way into an undignified crawl position. Halfway there, I saw a tidy flash of gray about a block away. "There!" I shouted. "She's—"

"She's trying to stand up," a woman explained to the others, as if I were some alien species. "Is that all right?"

Nobody bothered to answer. The little crowd was rapidly losing interest. We had lasted longer than a sound bite.

I closed my eyes, took a deep breath, and pushed myself up onto elbows and knees. Norma Evans had disappeared into the horizon. What was visible was Georgette, staring at me and sobbing, her skirts shaking with misery.

"No," I said. "I'm okay. Nothing bad happened." I

wasn't sure which layer of her woeful history she was revisiting through the sight of me. "I'll be fine." I said it emphatically, and decided that perhaps it was actually so. Or maybe it was the four-footed position. This was how humans were meant to get around, and we'd screwed everything up trying to balance the whole shebang on two legs. Maybe I'd stay this way, start a trend.

"That woman," I said to Georgette and anyone who'd listen, "that woman in the gray blouse—you can't let her get away. She isn't calling the police—she's escaping. She killed two people."

"Oh, really," the scowling woman near me said. "I've heard crazy things in my time, but this . . ."

"Who?" Georgette sniffled, looked around. "What woman?"

Where was Norma Evans? I pushed on my hands and unscrunched into a standing position. My back throbbed out an S.O.S., demanded bed rest and peace, remembered that this was supposed to be my vacation. My bloody side seconded the motion.

I thought of people with broken backs who lifted cars off their injured children, or ran for help on shattered tibias.

But my new Spartan bite-the-bullet determination didn't help me spot Norma. What I saw instead was a cluster of uncentered turbulence—Lala's turquoise suit, Belle's blue back, Tommy in spiffy whites, Eric with Lucky on his shoulders, and Georgette loping in their general direction, although she had a tendency to stop and talk en route.

They were all still moving, which meant Norma Evans was still uncaught but in their sight. I took an experimental step, winced, and clenching my teeth, made a second, slightly less painful move. I could do it. I would do it. I would get her.

"Here he is!" someone shouted. "The cop!"

Norma had actually called the police? I was stunned into immobility, and afraid, suddenly, that I'd made up everything about her. Good lord—maybe what she said was true and I *was* the criminal. I felt another attack of dizziness.

"Okay, who's been shouting for help here?" The policeman did not look pleased by the commotion. He was beefy and slow, moving as if his bunions ached. "What's the ruckus about? What's going on?" His eyes squinted in suspicion.

"It's like she told you when she called," a woman said.

"Who you talking about?"

"That *lady*," the woman insisted. "She was with this other lady, a younger one, who had a knife. I think she was mugged. The lady who called you."

The straggly crowd's attention had shifted to the patrolman, who had every right to be mystified about what was going on, since it was obvious to anyone who wasn't fixed on Norma's eternal innocence that she hadn't called him. I felt some relief.

A burly man who, if he had a single operational brain cell, could have been helping to catch a murderer, instead pointed at me. "It's her! She had a knife!" he shouted. "But I disarmed her."

Disarmed me? Picked the thing up off the boardwalk was more like it.

"You still talking about the lady who supposedly called me?" the cop asked.

I backed up, step by step.

The burly man held out the knife. "See? I took it from her." In a few days he'd probably receive the Mayor's Award for heroism and believe he'd earned it.

He deserved the booby prize. He brandished the knife, obliterating whatever fingerprints might have been left. Didn't he know anything? Watch TV or read books?

"Hey," the policeman said. "If that's evidence of some crime . . ."

I backed up more as the crowd moved in to see more

clearly, to watch the handing over of the knife to the patrolman.

It was my exit cue. While the patrolman took out a notepad and asked him to explain everything again, I headed for the wings and ran. Or, more accurately, hobbled and staggered, hunched over.

"Hey!" a woman said. "She's— Wasn't she out cold? I thought—"

"Stop her!" the knife man called. "She's the one!"

"The one what?" the policeman asked in his methodical voice.

"The *one*! The knife girl!"

It had a certain ring, that. Mandy the knife girl. As in, perhaps, knife girls finish last?

"She went after the old lady with a knife."

"Oh," the policeman said. "Stop!" He'd finally gotten it. "Stop!" he shouted, loudly enough for me to hear it a half block away. "Stop or I'll—"

But he couldn't shoot into a crowd of people. And meanwhile I was nearly at the second commotion, in front of a store with a green-and-white-striped awning.

"She was right here!" Lala said.

"Where?" I could see only my little band of stalwarts and a cluttered souvenir storefront window. And, of course, a lot of red streaks of pain.

"Stop!" the patrolman shouted.

"Maybe she went down the ramp," Belle said. "Toward Pacific Avenue." She and Lala and Tommy took off again. Georgette looked the wrong way, surveying the watery horizon. We were not the world's best posse.

"No! She's *there*!" Lucky shouted from atop Eric's shoulders. He was barely noticed by the rest of what I'd begun to think of as our gang. Being five and ignorable was the story of his life. I followed the trajectory of his index finger. It led behind us, through the window filled with pennants and plastic Miss America and Bert Parks dolls and miniature rolling chairs and inflatable money and shell-encrusted picture frames and a red and yellow plastic globe that said I HAD A BALL IN A.C.—and into the store. I wasn't seven feet up in the air the way Lucky was, so I couldn't see beyond the display, but the high wall of clutter made the store a perfect place to disappear. And it probably had a back door.

The patrolman approached. Talk about flatfoots. This man was not built for the chase. He waddled, side to side, in obvious foot pain. No wonder he was in such a testy mood. "Avoiding arrest is a serious offense, lady!" he shouted.

Being arrested seemed even more seriously offensive. I was too easy a scapegoat. Another bad girl from out of town, Sasha's sidekick, trying for a third kill.

"Nobody ever listens to me," Lucky whined.

"Lucky! Get down from there!" his mother shouted. "You could get hurt!"

"In a minute." He was beginning to sound like a normal kid, and she like a normal mother.

I reached for the store's door. It felt too heavy to move. My back pulsated.

"Stop!" It was the knife man taking vigilantism too seriously. "Gotcha!" But he hadn't got me. Not quite.

I pulled the door half open.

This time the man's hand made contact. Actually, two did. They felt thick and damp and final, one on each of my shoulders.

"Not *me!*" I shouted. "I didn't—" No use, no use. I could see through the half-open door that there, at the back of the store, was Norma in huddled conference with a salesperson. I guessed what she was asking, what safe exit she was requesting. And here we were, making a chaotic ruckus and justifying whatever paranoid story she'd tell.

Goodbye, Norma Evans. Hello, lockup.

Except that at precisely that instant there was the bellowing, cracked-voice, adolescent shout of "Go!"

And, almost simultaneously, a fearsome shriek—the long, banshee type that only young, young vocal cords can manage or find intriguing—and through the air, like a trapeze artist without any equipment, like Tarzan without vines, like a wild avenging bird or a cannonball with a five-year-old's features, flew Lucky.

People screamed and rushed forward to grab him, but he arced down, landing smack on the man grabbing me.

The man bellowed and let go. Lucky, his face radiantly triumphant, clung to his back, pulling on his hair like a baby monkey.

I had never seen anything like it in my life. I applauded.

"Run, Miss Pepper!" Eric shouted. "Get her!"

An A, Eric. An A plus. The kid was a genius. Reckless, maybe, but definitely a creative thinker. My running was not quite as graceful as Lucky's dive, but I raced into the store, inspired by both boys. If Lucky could ignore the laws of thermodynamics and fly, then I could move fast, ignore my twisted muscles and cuts.

"Stop!" I screamed because the saleswoman, a wrinkled and frightened creature, was pointing through a stack of cartons. That way to freedom, I was sure. The saleswoman relocated her pointing hand to her chest, crossed herself and mouthed a silent, urgent prayer.

Outside, there was a lot of audible scrambling. I could hear Lucky's piping voice and the deep grumble of the patrolman. I knew what was next. The law would amble in, grab me, and let Norma become history.

The saleswoman could pray all she liked. Norma, a foot or two beyond my reach, was no dummy. She bolted in the direction the finger had pointed.

I had no choice but to do a Lucky.

It gets harder all the time to have the imagination and heart to fly, particularly from a standing position and with a seriously hurting back and side, but I did my best. I visualized myself in the NFL, a quarterback or a tight end, or whoever it was that used his body as a javelin and hurtled. I imagined myself a five-year-old boy with a daredevil's heart. I even screeched, à la my mentor, and it indeed had a momentary opiate effect.

Just long enough for it to work. Not, perhaps, with grace and elegance. I managed more of a splat than a soar, but the thing is . . . I grounded her.

I grounded her and then, because I'd had a very long day and it definitely seemed time to relax, I sat on her. She was as comfortable as an ergonomic chair, and my back didn't feel half bad.

The saleswoman sobbed, even though at this point crying seemed redundant and unnecessary. Even the dunderhead policeman would surely be swayed when he saw the contents of Norma's pocketbook. I was sure she had been en route to her disappearance, and whatever she'd taken must be close to her person.

"Look, look!" the saleswoman cried. I had brought down more than Norma. We now sat and lay, respectively, amongst the porcelain shards of playing-card salt and pepper shakers and a music box, which had become excited by its plunge and played "By the Sea, By the Sea" in a tinny up-tempo while miniature bathers in 1890 suits twirled under a beach umbrella.

"MY HERO," MACKENZIE SAID LATER THAT EVENING, WHEN I was allowed to violate visiting hours partially by virtue of having become an emergency room patient myself. "Notice my nonsexist language," he added.

Half my side was bandaged and the other half was black and blue; my back felt as if it contained a large, electrically charged metal plate; my green blazer was ruined; and the saltwater people were not rehiring Sasha, which meant the two of us were stuck with the hotel bill.

"I have to be honest," I said. "You make a pretty shabby Nero Wolfe. I was supposed to do a little footwork, that was all, then we were supposed to gather all the suspects around this bed. And then you'd tell them who the guilty one was, and that guilty one would crumple."

"I must have forgotten." He looked almost sympathetic. His color was completely back, and his smile once again unfairly dazzling. "I would have helped you tomorrow, if you'd waited. They're releasing me."

"Sasha's getting out, too," I said. "It all worked quite tidily, don't you think? You're shot, she's imprisoned, and I'm embarking on a life of chronic pain. This qualifies as the world's worst vacation ever."

"If, that is, I can establish that I have somebody to, well, kind of . . ." It wasn't like Mackenzie to be coy or evasive. "Well, see," he said, "I can't move the leg for a while now, so I'm going to have some trouble takin' care of . . . of ever'thin'. Of me."

His eyes were back to their neon-blue and laugh lines—or perhaps slightly anxious lines—fanned out from them while he waited.

I spoke very softly. We were on thin and uncertain ground. "I assume that your medical coverage would handle a visiting nurse, wouldn't it?"

He nodded.

"So this isn't about saving money, as in C for cheap?"

He shook his head. "No, on both counts."

"Or about having an in-house slavey?"

He shook his head so vigorously his salt and pepper curls bounced. "You're a regionist. Unfair to the South and its people."

His accent escalated even though he appeared semiconscious on the surface. "As an experiment?" he asked softly.

I privately acknowledged that I had come to the beach to rest and to think the two of us through, and it was Mackenzie who'd wound up with both the time and the ability to do so. And he obviously had. Despite being a poetry lover, Mackenzie wasn't exactly quoting the Passionate Shepherd and saying "Come live with me and be my love"—but he was nonetheless saying "Let's get this moving forward."

And scaring me more than anything else had this week—or year.

Was it possible that *I* was the one who wasn't ready? That *I* counted on our never having the Big Talk or reaching crucial junctures? That I needed distance while Mackenzie needed partnership—the way the arcade computer had said?

"Well, hey," he said. "Don't panic. Since we both have time off now, I was thinkin' we could try this somewhere else, you know?"

He sounded like pure mush, farina with a few consonants, but he was giving me an out, a compromise solution.

"Mandy," he said. "I don' really need nursin' a-tall. Been trainin' on crutches and I did fine." The words drizzled out, consonants vaporized. His speech was in meltdown.

The man cared.

"You deserve a vacation," he said.

I laughed, even though it hurt. "Nobody deserves another vacation like the one I just had. Or, in fact, the one you just tried to have. Could we call it something else?"

"Agreed," he said softly. "So how 'bout we call it a start?"

The City of Brotherly Love is
sometimes the City of Maximum Hostility
in the newest crime-solving adventure of
English teacher Amanda Pepper!

IN THE DEAD
OF SUMMER

—

The new novel from award-winner
Gillian Roberts

Upon her return from a sojourn in Atlantic
City, Amanda Pepper is back in her native
Philadelphia teaching summer school at Philly
Prep. With a curriculum that includes hate
crimes, abductions, and drive-by shootings,
Amanda will need all of her wits about her to
survive this long, hot, and deadly summer.

Published by Ballantine Books.

Available in your local bookstore.

More adventures of English teacher/amateur sleuth
Amanda Pepper by award-winning author

GILLIAN ROBERTS

"Here's the Dorothy Parker of mystery writers...giving more wit per page than most writers give per book."

—NANCY PICKARD